KING JESUS

MAP
of
PALESTINE

ENGLISH MILES
0   5   10   15   20   25   30

SCALE: 1:660,000

KING JESUS

A NOVEL BY

ROBERT GRAVES

FARRAR · STRAUS · GIROUX

New York

CONTENTS

Part One

Part Two

Part Three

KING JESUS

When in *The Gospel according to the Egyptians*, Shelom asked the Lord: "How long shall death prevail?" He answered: "So long as you women bear children. . . ." And when she asked again: "I have done well then in not bearing children? He answered: "Eat every plant but that which is bitter. . . ." And when she inquired at what time the things concerning which she had questioned Him should be known, He answered: "When you women have trampled on the garment of shame and when the two become one, and when the male with the female is neither male nor female. . . ." And the Saviour said in the same Gospel: "I have come to destroy the works of the Female."

CLEMENT OF ALEXANDRIA
(*Stromata*, iii.).

. . . Commentators refer to Jeshu-ha-Notzri [i.e. Jesus] by mention of the wicked kingdom of Edom, since that was his nation. . . . He was hanged on a Passover Eve. . . . He was near to the Kingdom [i.e. in order of succession].

Balaam the Lame [i.e. Jesus] was 33 years old when Pintias the Robber [i.e. Pontius Pilate] killed him. . . . They say that his mother was descended from princes and rulers, but consorted with carpenters.

Lexicon Talmudicum, *sub* "Abanarbel"
and *Talmud Babli Sanhedrin* 106b, 43a, 51a.

Part One

CHAPTER ONE

SIMPLETONS

I, AGABUS the Decapolitan, began this work at Alexandria in the ninth year of the Emperor Domitian and completed it at Rome in the thirteenth year of the same.[1] It is the history of the wonder-worker Jesus, rightful heir-at-law to the dominions of Herod, King of the Jews, who in the fifteenth year of the Emperor Tiberius was sentenced to death by Pontius Pilate, the Governor-General of Judaea. Not the least wonderful of Jesus's many feats was that, though certified dead by his executioners after a regular crucifixion, and laid in a tomb, he returned two days later to his Galilean friends at Jerusalem and satisfied them that he was no ghost; then said farewell and disappeared in equally mysterious fashion. King Jesus (for he was entitled to be so addressed) is now worshipped as a god by a sect known as the Gentile Chrestians.

Chrestians is the commoner name for Christians, that is to say, "followers of the Anointed King". Chrestians means "followers of the Chrestos, or Good Man"—good in the sense of simple, wholesome, plain, auspicious—and is therefore a term less suspect to the authorities than "Christians"; for the word Christos suggests defiance of the Emperor, who has expressed his intention of stamping out Jewish nationalism once and for all. "Chrestos", of course, can also be used in the derogatory sense of "simpleton". "Chrestos ei"— "What a simple-minded fellow you are!"—were the very words which Pontius Pilate addressed in scorn to Jesus on the morning of crucifixion; and since the Christians glory in their simplicity, which the

[1] A.D. 89-93.

3

most sincere of them carry to extravagant lengths, and in receiving the same scorn from the world as King Jesus himself, they do not refuse the name of "The Simpletons".

Originally this faith was confined to Jews, who held a very different view of Jesus from that popularized by the Gentile Chrestians; then it gradually spread from the Jews of Palestine to those of the Dispersion, whose communities are to be found in Babylonia, Syria, Greece, Italy, Egypt, Asia Minor, Libya, Spain—in fact, in almost every country of the world—and has now become international, with Gentiles decidedly in the majority. For the visionary Paul of Tarsus, who led the Gentile schism and was himself only a half-Jew, welcomed to membership of his Church the very numerous Gentile converts to the Jewish faith, known as God-fearers, who had shrunk from circumcision and the ritual rigours of Judaism and were thus precluded from becoming honorary Sons of Abraham. Paul declared that circumcision was unnecessary to salvation and that Jesus had himself made light of Jewish ceremonial laws on the ground that moral virtue outweighs ritual scrupulousness in the eyes of Jehovah, the Jewish God. Paul also assured them that Jesus (whom he had never met) had posthumously ordained that a symbolic eating of his body and drinking of his blood was to be a permanent institution in the Chrestian Church. This rite, known as the Eucharist, provides a welcome bridge between Judaism and the Greek and Syrian mystery-cults—I mean those in which the sacred body of Tammuz is sacramentally eaten and the sacred blood of Dionysus is sacramentally drunk; and by this bridge thousands of converts have come over. The Judaic Chrestians, however, have rejected the Eucharist as idolatrous. They also have rejected as blasphemous the Gentile Chrestian view that Jesus stands in much the same relation to Jehovah as, for example, the God Dionysus does to Father Zeus, who begot him on the nymph Semele. A begotten God, the Jews say, must logically have a mother; and they deny that Jehovah has ever had any truck with either nymphs or goddesses.

The fact is that the Jews as a nation have persuaded themselves that they differ in one main particular from all others that live on the shores of the Mediterranean Sea: namely, that they never owed any duty either to the Great Triple Moon-goddess who is generally reputed to have mothered the Mediterranean races, or to any other goddess or nymph whatsoever. This claim is untenable, for their sacred books preserve clear traces of their former attachment, notably in the accounts that they give of their heroes Adam, Noah, Abraham, Jacob and Moses. Indeed, that the Jews are at the present day per-

4

haps the most miserable of all civilized nations—scattered, homeless, suspect—is ascribed by the superstitious to the Goddess's inèluctable vengeance: for the Jews have been prime leaders in the religious movement against her not only in their own country but in all the countries of the Dispersion. They have proclaimed Jehovah as the sole Ruler of the Universe and represented the Goddess as a mere demoness, witch, Queen of Harlots, succuba and prime mischief-maker.

Jehovah, it seems clear, was once regarded as a devoted son of the Great Goddess, who obeyed her in all things and by her favour swallowed up a number of variously named rival gods and godlings—the Terebinth-god, the Thunder-god, the Pomegranate-god, the Bull-god, the Goat-god, the Antelope-god, the Calf-god, the Porpoise-god, the Ram-god, the Ass-god, the Barley-god, the god of Healing, the Moon-god, the god of the Dog-star, the Sun-god. Later (if it is permitted to write in this style) he did exactly what his Roman counterpart, Capitoline Jove, has done: he formed a supernal Trinity in conjunction with two of the Goddess's three persons, namely, Anatha of the Lions and Ashima of the Doves, the counterparts of Juno and Minerva; the remaining person, a sort of Hecate named Sheol, retiring to rule the infernal regions. Most Jews hold that she still reigns there, for they say: "Jehovah has no part in Sheol", and quote the authority of the 115th Psalm: "The dead praise not Jehovah, neither do any that go down into silence." But Jove, whose wife and former mother, Juno, is still in sole charge of women's affairs and whose so-called daughter Minerva still presides over all intellectual activities, and who is himself bisexual, has never cared to do what Jehovah did just before his enforced captivity at Babylon: that is, to repudiate his two Goddess partners and in solitary splendour attempt to rule over men and women alike. Nor has Olympian Zeus dared to do this. He also, it is said, was once the devoted son of the Triple Goddess and later, after castrating her paramour Cronos, annulled her sovereignty: but he leaves the charge of women's affairs to his wife Hera, his sister Demeter, and his daughters Artemis, Aphrodite and Athene. Severity towards them he has certainly shown at times (if the mythographers are to be trusted), but he cannot rule satisfactorily without them. God without Goddess, the Romans and Greeks agree, is spiritual insufficiency; but this the Jews deny.

In a somewhat obscene passage in the Book of the Prophet Ezekiel is to be found Jehovah's bill of divorcement against his two partner-Goddesses, who are there named Aholah and Aholibah. Nevertheless, the Trinity continued undissolved in a Jewish Temple at Elephantine in Upper Egypt until five hundred years ago.

Nobody can understand the story of Jesus except in the light of this Jewish obsession of celestial patriarchy; for it must never be forgotten that, despite all appearances, despite even his apparent sponsorship of the Eucharistical rite, Jesus was true to Jehovah from his childhood onward without a single lapse in loyalty. He once told Shelom, the midwife who had brought him into the world, that he had "come to destroy the work of the female"; he accepted the title of "Son of David"—King David who had stabilized the Jewish monarchy and persuaded the priestesses of Anatha, until then the proud rulers of clans and tribes, to content themselves with membership of his royal harem. And as the Second Adam Jesus's self-imposed task was to undo the evil which, according to the patriarchal legend, the First Adam had caused by sinfully listening to the seductive plea of his wife Eve.

Whether patriarchy is a better solution to the eternal problem of the relations of men and women than matriarchy or than the various compromises which civilized nations have adopted, who shall decide? All that needs to be recorded here is that at a critical stage in their history the Jews decided to forbid the further participation of priestesses in their sacred rites. Women, they said, have an unsettling effect on religious life: they introduce the sexual element, which inevitably tends to confuse mystical ecstasy with eroticism. For this point of view there is much to be said, because the effect of sexual promiscuity in festival time is to loosen the ties of family life and disorder the social system. Besides, there was a political side to the Jewish theory: namely, that the only hope of survival for the nation, which was settled at the cross-roads of the world, lay in its keeping strictly to itself and avoiding the foreign entanglements in which amorous and luxury-loving queens and priestesses invariably involve their subjects. Yet the Jews, who are Orientals only in part, have never been able to keep their women in perfect subjection; and have never therefore succeeded in serving Jehovah with the purity that they profess. The Great Goddess, to whom the land of Palestine originally belonged, is always tripping them up and seducing them into folly. Belili, her earliest name, they spell Belial, meaning Utter Destruction. Their apostasy from the Goddess gave them qualms at first, and the poet Jeremiah who lived at this period quotes some of them as saying: "We will now again burn incense to the Queen of Heaven and pour libations to her as we once did, and our fathers, our kings and princes in the cities of Judaea and in the streets of

6

Jerusalem, for then we had food in plenty and health and prosperity. But since we ceased to burn incense and pour libations to her, we have been in distress, consumed by the sword and by famine." But the rest stood fast by their resolution.

The Goddess's venerable Temple at Hierapolis, on the Syrian bank of the Upper Euphrates, a region connected in Biblical legend with the patriarchs Abraham and Isaac, is well worth a visit. There, a Sun-god, a sort of Dionysus-Apollo-Zeus who rides a bull, is married to his mother the Moon-goddess who rides a lion and grasps a snake in her hand. The Trinity, which is ruled by the Mother, is completed by an ambiguous bisexual deity to whom the dove is sacred. The Temple, which is served by oracular women and eunuch priests, faces East; outside the portals are two enormous phallic pillars like those which stood outside King Solomon's Temple; inside, all is gold and gems and marble. The ritual is a complicated one and includes pre-marital prostitution for young women, self-castration for young men; for others, intercessions, comminations, hymns of praise, libations, purifications, incense-burning, sacrifices of sheep, goats and children; holocausts of live beasts hanged from terebinth-trees; and oracles taken from sacred fish and sweating statutes. The Temple is said to have been founded in honour of the Moon-goddess by Deucalion (whom the Jews call Noah) when the Deluge which had overwhelmed Asia at last subsided. In his honour a sacred ark of acacia-wood is exhibited and water is poured down the chasm through which, it is said, the waters of the Deluge were carried away.

The Canaanites, whom the Israelites conquered and enslaved under Joshua, were devotees of this Goddess. Their remnants still cling to the cult of the terebinth-tree, the dove and the snake; still bake barley-cakes in honour of the Goddess, and still maintain the right of every young woman to provide herself with a dowry by prostitution.

I grant the political expediency of keeping certain remarkable facts connected with Jesus's birth and parentage concealed from all but the inner circle of Chrestian initiates. I have discovered these by patient and discreet inquiry, and it is clear to me that if they were laid before the Emperor he could hardly be blamed for suspecting that the other-worldly religious communism of Chrestianity was a cloak for militant Jewish royalism. I also grant the expediency of Paul's decision to dissociate the new faith as far as possible from the faith from which it sprang, and though it is untrue to say that the Jews as a nation rejected Jesus, it is true enough that ever since the Fall of Jerusalem the poor remnants of the Jewish nationalists have detested not only the Gentile Chrestians but the Judaic sort as well.

These offended by what seemed at the time a cowardly and un-patriotic refusal to assist in the defence of the Holy City: quitting Judaea and settling at Pella across the Jordan.

The Judaic Chrestians had kept strictly to the letter of the Law under the original leadership of James (I mean the Bishop of Jerusalem, who was the half-brother of Jesus). They were no cowards, but merely considered it a sin to engage in war; since Jesus himself had foreseen the fate of Jerusalem and had shed tears for it, they could hardly have been expected to risk their eternal salvation by defending the walls. After its capture by Titus many of them were tempted to renounce Judaism because of the double disadvantage of being ill-treated as Jews by the Romans and despised by the Jews as traitors. But they would not renounce their allegiance to Jesus. Must they then modify their principles and enter the Gentile Chrestian Church originally controlled by the Apostle Philip but reorganized after Philip's death by their former enemy and persecutor Paul—the very man who had once thrown James down the steps of the Temple? That would mean consorting with uncircumcised and ceremonially unclean Chrestian converts of all classes and conditions —few of whom knew as many as five words of Hebrew and who all considered the Mosaic Law to be virtually abrogated.

It was a hard choice, and only a few chose the more heroic alternative of keeping true to the Law. The Gentile Chrestians were accommodating to those who compounded, for James was dead and Paul was dead and Peter was dead and they had instructions from Jesus himself to forgive their enemies. It was important that a religion of brotherly love should not be contradicted by indecent dissensions. Though there was no question of the circumcision problem being raised again, the breach was repaired with a doctrinal compromise; and what was more, the Gentiles, as they put it, heaped coals of fire on the heads of the Judaists by relieving their financial distresses. For Paul's quarrel with the original Church had been largely a money quarrel. He had counted on a large sum of money collected from converts in Asia Minor, and on an ecstatic vision of Heaven vouchsafed him in an epileptic trance, to win admission to the Apostleship. He was informed coldly that the gifts of the spirit could not be bought and that the vision was indecently ambitious.

This compromise had its disadvantages, as all compromises have: the greatest of which was the mass of petty contradictions in the official account of the life and teachings of Jesus which resulted from the fusion of rival traditions. The mediators between the two

8

societies were the Petrines, or followers of the Galilean apostle Peter, strangely enough a converted Zealot, or militant nationalist, who had been rejected by the followers of James for consorting with the followers of Paul, and by the followers of Paul for consorting with the followers of James. As Jesus had foreseen, it was on the Petrine rock that the Church was finally founded: Peter's name now stands on the diptychs before that of Paul.

Let nobody be misled by the libels against the Jews in general and the Pharisees in particular which, despite the nominal reconciliation of the Churches, are still circulated among the Chrestians of Rome. The Jews are accused by the Gentile libellists of having universally rejected Jesus. Let me repeat that the Jews did nothing of the sort. All his disciples were Jews. The Judaic Chrestians remained an honourable sect in Judaea and Galilee until the so-called "secession to Pella". Throughout the years intervening, they had taken part without question in Temple worship and in that of the synagogue; which is not surprising, seeing that Jesus himself had done the same and had explicitly told the woman of Samaritan Schechem: "Salvation comes from the Jews."

The Jews are also accused of having officially sentenced Jesus to death by crucifixion after a formal trial by the Beth Din, or religious High Court; they did nothing of the sort. Nobody with the least knowledge of Jewish legal procedure can possibly credit that the High Court condemned him to death, or doubt that it was the Roman soldiers who crucified him at Pilate's order.

As for the Pharisees, who are represented by the libellists as having been Jesus's greatest enemies: he never denounced this enlightened sect as a whole, but only individual members who failed in their high moral pretensions, or outsiders who falsely pretended to be Pharisees—especially those who, taking advantage of his dialectical method of teaching, tried to entrap him into revolutionary statements. For the Pharisees softened by their remarkable humanity the harsher provisions of the ancient Mosaic Law and both preached and practised those very virtues which Gentile Chrestians now pretend to be exclusively and originally Chrestian. Their moral code was first formulated shortly after the Exile by descendants of the original Aaronic priesthood which had been removed from high office in the reign of King Solomon by the usurping Zadokites, or Sadducees; as priests without stipend or distractive ecclesiastical duties they were able to refine spiritual values without the taint of politics. Jesus denouncing the Pharisees indeed! It is as though

9

Socrates were represented as having denounced philosophers in general because he had found flaws in the arguments of particular sophists.

The ecclesiastical Sadducees, who were necessarily politicians, had little sense of the peculiar spiritual mission with which the Jews as a whole considered themselves entrusted, and were always ready to meet foreigners half-way by a deliberate blurring of their national peculiarities. When the Pharisees, which means the Separated Ones —those who separate themselves from what is impure—had made their popular religious revolt under Maccabee leadership against the Hellenizing Seleucids, the Syrian heirs of King Alexander the Great, it was the Sadducees who undid their work by persuading the later Maccabees to backslide half-way to Hellenism again. The Pharisaic principle of taking arms only in defence of religious freedom was abandoned by the Sadducees, and the consequent enlargement of a small poor kingdom by wars of aggression against Edom and Samaria proved its eventual undoing.

Gentile Chrestians who quote Jesus as having made apparently damaging criticisms of the Mosaic Law are unaware that, as often as not, he was merely quoting with approval the critical remarks of Rabbi Hillel, the most revered of all Pharisaic doctors; and I would not have you ignorant that in certain remote Syrian villages where Judaic Chrestians and Jews still manage to live amicably side by side, the Chrestians are admitted to worship in the synagogues and are reckoned as a sub-sect of the Pharisees.

There were, I grant, degrees of Pharisaism in the time of Jesus; as he pointed out, material prosperity tends to weaken the spiritual sense, and many so-called Pharisees had forgotten the spirit of the Law and remembered only the letter; but in general the spirit triumphed over the letter, and in the monastic order of the Essenes, who were the most conservative sort of Pharisees, spirituality and loving-kindness were practised in a more orderly and humane style than in any Chrestian society of to-day which has not modelled its discipline closely upon theirs.

It will be asked: What reason have the libellists to circulate these statements if there is no truth in them? The answer is plain. Not only do the remaining Judaic Chrestians still refuse to deify Jesus, since for Jews there is only one God; but, the Gentile Chrestians being ignorant of Hebrew, Judaists naturally stand at a great advantage in expounding both the Messianic prophecies relating to Jesus and the collected corpus of his moral discourses and pronouncements. This has bred jealousy and resentment. Truths that to a Gentile brought up in the Olympian faith seem a wholly original illumination appear to the Judaists as a logical development of Pharisaism.

I once heard a Roman Chrestian cry out at a love-feast where I was a guest: "Listen, brothers and sisters in Christ, I bring glad tidings! Jesus rolled up the Ten Commandments given to Moses, by substituting two of his own: 'Thou shalt love the Lord thy God with all thy heart and with all thy soul and with all thy strength.' And 'Thou shalt love thy neighbour as thyself.'"

Great applause.

A former Judaist sitting next to me blinked a little and then said dryly: "Yes, brother, that was well said by the Christ! And now I hear that those rascally Jewish copyists have stolen his wisdom and interpolated the first of these two overriding Commandments into the sixth chapter of the Book of Deuteronomy, and the second into the nineteenth chapter of the Book of Leviticus!"

"May the Lord God pardon their thievish wickedness!" cried a pious matron from the other end of the table. "I am sure that the Pharisees are at the bottom of it!"

Not wishing to cause a tumult, I refrained from reminding her that Jesus had praised the Pharisees as "the righteous who need no repentance" and as "the able-bodied who have no need of a physician", and in his fable of the spendthrift runaway had made them the type of the honest son who stayed at home: "Son, you have always remained dutifully with me and all my goods are yours."

In Chrestian Churches, as among the Orphics and other religious societies, secret doctrine is taught largely in the form of drama. This, though an ancient and admirable way of conveying religious truth, has its disadvantages when the characters are historical rather than mythical; and when the worshippers accept as literally true what is merely dramatic invention. I have before me a copy of the Nativity Drama now used by the Egyptian Church, in which the principal speakers are the Angel Gabriel, Mary the Mother of Jesus, Mary's cousin Elizabeth, Elizabeth's husband Zacharias the Priest, Joseph, Mary's husband, three shepherds, three astrologers, the midwife Salome, King Herod, Anna the prophetess and Simeon the Priest. The play is simply but skilfully written, and I have no fault at all to find with it as devotional literature. Its purpose is to demonstrate that Jesus was the expected Jewish Messiah, and more than this, that he was the same Divine Child who had been foreshadowed in all the ancient mysteries—Greek, Egyptian, Celtic, Armenian and even Indian. The third scene, for instance, opens in the Bethlehem stable on a darkened stage.

The Cock (crowing): "Christ is born!"
The Bull (lowing): "Where?"
The Ass (braying): *"In Bethlehem!"*

These creatures, by the way, are not quaint characters borrowed from the Fables of Aesop: they are sacred animals. The cock is sacred to Hermes Conductor of Souls and to Aesculapius the Healer. It dispels the darkness of night, is the augur of the reborn Sun. You will recall that almost the last words spoken by Socrates before he drank the hemlock were a reminder to a friend that he had vowed a cock to Aesculapius: he was expressing, I suppose, his hope in resurrection. The cock likewise figures in the story of Jesus's last sufferings and is now interpreted as an augur of his resurrection; though I find this notion far-fetched. The bull and the ass are the symbolic beasts of the two promised Messiahs, the Messiah Son of Joseph and the Messiah Son of David, with both of whom the Chrestians identify Jesus. The "feet of the bull and the ass" mentioned in the thirty-second chapter of Isaiah are invariably explained by Jewish commentators as referring to the two Messiahs.

After this brief dialogue between the creatures, the day dawns, and the Holy Family are discovered together. Virgin Mother and Child in their ancient pose: the mother wearing a blue robe and a crown of silver stars, the child traditionally laid in the manger-basket which is used for the same purpose in both the Delphic and Eleusinian mysteries. Bearded Joseph leans on a staff a little way off, not crowned nor even clothed in purple—the type of all just men whose virtue has earned them a part in the divine illumination. Distant sounds of drum and pipe, gradually nearing. Enter three joyful shepherds, like those of Mount Ida who adored the infant Zeus. . . . Or (if it is permitted to disclose this) like the mystagogues dressed as shepherds who, at the ceremony of Advent which gives its name to the Eleusinian mysteries, introduce the virgin-born infant by torchlight and cry: "Rejoice, rejoice, we have found our King, son of the Daughter of the Sea, lying in this basket among the river reeds!"

Now, I do not question the tradition that the infant Jesus was laid in a manger-basket in a stable, nor that shepherds arrived to adore him, but the rest of the scene must not be read as literally true: it is rather what Aristotle in his *Poetics* terms "philosophically true". And I cannot, though my authorities are reliable, be sure that my own Nativity narrative is correct in every particular, but I will say this much. An expert in Greek sculpture or pottery can usually restore the lost details of a damaged work of art: take for example a black-figured vase, with a scene of the harrowing of Hell by Orpheus. If the Danaids are there with their sieves and, next to them, above a defaced patch, the expert notices part of a bunch of grapes and two fingers of a clutching hand and, beyond, a rough piece of rock, that is detail enough: he imaginatively sees Tantalus gasping for thirst, and his fellow-criminal Sisyphus pushing the outrageous boulder up the hill. My own problem of reconstruction is very much more difficult, because history, not myth, is in question. Yet the history of Jesus from his Nativity onwards keeps so close to what may be regarded as a pre-ordained mythical pattern, that I have in many instances been able to presume events which I afterwards proved by historical research to have taken place, and this has encouraged me to hope that where my account cannot be substantiated it is not altogether without truth. For instance, Jesus has so much in common with the hero Perseus, that the attempt made by King Acrisius to kill the infant Perseus seems relevant to the story of Jesus too; this Acrisius was the grandfather of Perseus.

I have also witnessed the performance of another religious drama, concerned with the final sufferings of Jesus. The Chrestian fear of offending the Romans makes this play a masterpiece of disingenuousness. Since only what was publicly said or done on that painful occasion is enacted on the stage, Pilate's infamous behaviour appears correct and even magnanimous and the entire blame for the judicial murder is, by implication, laid upon the Jews whose spokesman the High Priest claims to be.

But I must now warn you against accepting the Hebrew Scriptures at their face value. Only the rhapsodies of the Hebrew poets, the so-called "prophetic books", can be read without constant suspicion that the text has been tampered with by priestly editors, and these too are for the most part incorrectly dated and credited to authors who could not possibly have written them. These unscholarly practices the Jews justify with: "Whoever speaks a good thing in the name of the one who should have spoken it brings salvation to the world." The historical and legal books have become so corrupted in the course of time, partly by accident and partly by editing, that even the shrewdest scholars cannot hope to unravel all the tangles and restore the original text. Still, by comparison of Hebrew myths with the popular myths of Canaan, and of Jewish history with the history of neighbouring nations, a general working knowledge can be won of the ancient events and legal traditions most relevant to the secret story of Jesus, which is all that need concern us here.

What an extraordinary story it is, too! Slave to books though I am, I have never in all my reading come across its match. And, after all, if the Gentile Chrestians, despite the clear prohibitions of the Hebrew Law against idolatry, are moved to partake of Jesus's substance in their symbolic Eucharist and to worship him as a God, declaring: "None was ever like him before, nor will be again, until he returns to earth!"—who, except the devout Jew, can blame them? To be laid at birth in a manger-basket, to be crowned King, to suffer voluntarily on a cross, to conquer death, to become immortal: such was the destiny of this last and noblest scion of the most venerable royal line in the world.

CHAPTER TWO

CHILDREN OF RAHAB

ANNA, daughter of Phanuel of the tribe of Asher, had been widowed for sixty-five years; but the memory of her husband's benefactions to the Temple and her own remarkable devoutness which kept her in the Women's Court of the Temple night and day, had secured her at last an honourable office, that of guardian mother to the holy virgins. These were wards of the Temple, and were instructed by her in obedience and humility, in music and dancing, in spinning and embroidery, and in the management of a household. All were Daughters of Aaron, members of the ancient Levite nobility, and had for the most part been dedicated to the Temple by their parents as an insurance against an unworthy marriage. Pious, rich and well-born husbands could always be found for Temple virgins. Their initiation into the lore of their clan was in the hands of the guardian mother, who was tested by the High Priest's deputy for knowledge of Temple procedure and correct deportment but, being a woman, was not expected to have a perfect understanding of religious doctrine. Since their return from Babylonian captivity under Ezra, the Levites had denied the Daughters of Aaron their former function as priestesses, debarring them, with all other women, from any closer approach to the Sanctuary than the Women's Court, which was separated from it by a massive wall and the spacious Men's Court, or Court of Israel.

Anna whined and mumbled in a devout sing-song whenever she moved among priests and Temple servants, but when alone with her charges spoke to them in a voice of calm authority.

The eldest of the virgins was Miriam, whom the Chrestians call Mary, the only child of Joachim the Levite, one of the so-called Heirs of David, or Royal Heirs. She had been a Temple ward since the age of five and had been born on the very day that masons first began to work on King Herod's Temple. Year by year the glorious building was swallowing up the battered old Temple, called Zerubbabel's, which had risen from the ruins of King Solomon's Temple but had been several times seized by foreign armies and seemed to have lost a great deal of its virtue since its desecration by the Syrian king Antiochos Epiphanes. Thirteen years had now passed, and though the central Sanctuary—the House of Jehovah and the Court of the Priests—was completed, and the greater part of the two Inner Courts as well, it was to be nearly seventy more years before the masons ceased work on the Court of the Gentiles and the enclosing walls. The new Temple grounds were twice as large as the old ones, and it was necessary to build out vast substructures on the southern side of the hill-top to allow sufficient space for them.

Anna had been entrusted with dyed flax from Pelusium in Egypt, to be spun into thread for the annually renewed curtain of the sacred chamber called the Holy of Holies—a task which virgins were alone permitted to undertake. She cast lots in turn among her elder charges for the honour of spinning the purple, the scarlet, the violet and the white threads. The purple fell to Miriam, which excited the envy of the rest, who teasingly called her a "little queen" because purple is a royal colour. But Anna said: "Daughters, it is vain to dispute the lots, which are of Heaven. Consider, does anyone else among you bear the name Miriam? And did not Miriam, the royal sister of Moses, dance in triumph with her companions beside the purple sea?"

When she cast lots again and the royal scarlet also fell to Miriam, Anna said to forestall their jealousy: "Is it to be wondered at? Who else among you is of Cocheba?" For the village of Cocheba is named after the star of David, and the Heirs of David owned Cocheba.

Tamar, one of the virgins, asked: "But, Mother, is not the scarlet thread the sign of a harlot?"

"Does Tamar ask me this? Did not Tamar the wife of Er, Judah's first-born, play the harlot with her father-in-law? Did not the other

Tamar play the harlot with Amnon her brother, David's first-born? Does a third Tamar covet the scarlet thread because she wishes to do as they did?"

Tamar asked demurely: "Is it recorded, Mother, that either Tamar was punished for her sins by barrenness or by stoning?"

"These times are not those, child. Do not think that by emulating the first Tamar you will be enrolled among the glorious ancestors of another David."

Miriam said: "With your permission, Mother, Tamar shall help me spin the scarlet, for the sake of the scarlet thread that Tamar the wife of Er tied about the wrist of Zarah, twin to our common ancestor Pharez; they had quarrelled for precedence within her womb."

The violet and the white flax were allotted to two other virgins, and as the distractive noise of spinning might not be heard in the Temple, the four spinners were set to work in private houses. Miriam was entrusted to the care of her cousin Lysia, Joseph of Emmaus's daughter; Joseph's wife, now dead, had been the eldest sister of Miriam's mother. She had borne him four sons and two daughters, of whom the elder, Lysia, was married to a purple-seller of Jerusalem, another of the Heirs, and lived near the Temple, just across the Bridge. To Lysia's house Miriam went with Tamar every morning to spin; every evening they came back together across the Bridge and through the Beautiful Gate to the Virgins' College in the Women's Court.

This is the story of Miriam's birth. Her mother, Hannah, had been married ten years but continued childless, to her grief and shame, and found little comfort in the riches of her husband, Joachim. Every year at the appointed day he rode up to Jerusalem from Cocheba to offer a donation to the Temple. There, because of the nobility of his birth and the riches of his estate, he usually took first place in the line of gift-bringers, the elders of Israel dressed in long Babylonian robes embroidered with flowers. It was his custom to say, as he dropped his gold pieces through the slot of the chest: "Whatever I give of my earnings is for the whole people; and here I give it. But these other coins, which represent a diminution of my estate, are for the Lord—a plea for his forgiveness if I have done anything amiss or displeasing to his eye."

Joachim, a High Court judge, was a Pharisee—not one of the Shoulder Pharisees, as those are called who seem to wear on their shoulders a list of their own good actions; nor a Calculating Pharisee, who says: "My sins are more than counterbalanced by my virtues"; nor a Saving Pharisee, who says: "I will save a little from my fortune to perform a work of charity." He could well be reckoned one of the God-fearing Pharisees who, despite the sneers of Christians who hate to be in their spiritual debt, compose by far the larger part of that humane sect.

This year, the seventeenth of Herod's reign, as the elders of Israel stood waiting for the hour of donation, Reuben son of Abdiel, a Sadducee of the old school, stood next below Joachim. Reuben had recently gone to law with him about the possession of a well in the hills beyond Hebron, and lost his case. It irked him that Joachim should be devoutly offering to the Treasury, as his own gift, part of the value of the well, which would water a thousand sheep even in the height of summer.

Reuben cried aloud: "Neighbour Joachim, why do you thrust yourself to the head of this line? Why do you boast yourself above us all? Every one of us elders of Israel is blessed with children—with sons like sturdy plants, with daughters like the polished corners of a palace—everyone but only you, and you are childless. The Lord's displeasure must be heavy on your head, for in the last three years you have, to common knowledge, taken three lusty young concubines, yet still you remain a dried stock without green shoots. Humble your heart, Pharisee, and take a lower place."

Joachim answered: "Forgive me, Neighbour Reuben, if I have offended against you in the matter of the well, for I suppose that it is this memory, rather than some notorious offence of mine against the Law, that prompts you to reproach me. You surely cannot be gainsaying the verdict of the Court of Disputes?"

Reuben's brother, who had been a witness in the case and who stood further down the line, spoke up for Reuben: "Neighbour Joachim, it is ungenerous in you to triumph over my brother in the matter of the Well of the Jawbone, and unseemly not to answer him fairly in the matter of your childlessness."

Joachim replied meekly: "The Lord forbid that I should dispute with any man on this holy hill, or harbour evil thoughts." Then he turned to Reuben: "Tell me, Son of Abdiel, were there never found honourable men in Israel who remained childless to the last?"

"Find me the text that mitigates the force of the Lord God's commandment that we should increase and multiply, and you may keep your place with good courage. But I think that not even the ingenious Hillel will help you over this gate."

All who stood in the line were now listening. A low laugh went up and a soft hissing; then, for shame, Joachim lifted up his two bags of gold from the pavement and went down to the lowest place in the line.

The news of his discomfiture ran quickly through the Courts of the Temple. The Doctors, when asked for an opinion, gave it in the same words: "He did well to yield his place; there is no such text in the Scriptures, blessed be the name of the Lord!"

Joachim offered his donation with the accustomed words, and the Treasurer pronounced a blessing on him; but it seemed to him afterwards that the elders avoided his company as if he were a creature of ill-luck. He was about to return home with a sad heart when a Temple servant saluted him and said softly: "The word of a prophetess. Do not return to Cocheba, Benefactor, but remain here all night in prayer. In the morning ride out into the wilderness, towards Edom. Take only one servant, and as you travel abase yourself before the Lord at every holy place, eat only the locust-bean, drink only pure water, abstain from ointment, perfume and women, and continue southward until you are granted a sign from the Lord. On the last day of the Feast of Tabernacles, which will be forty days from the beginning of your journey, be back here at Jerusalem. It is likely that the Lord will have heard your prayer and shown his mercy to you."

"Who is this prophetess? I had thought that her race was extinct in Jerusalem."

"A Daughter of Asher, an aged and devout widow, who waits in prayer and fasting for the consolation of Israel."

Joachim sent his servants home, all but one, and spent the night on his knees in the Temple. At dawn he rode out towards the wilderness with only the one servant at his back: he took no food with him but a bag of locust-beans, and no drink but pure water in a goatskin bottle. On the morning of the fifth day, as he passed over the border into Edom, he fell in with a company of tented Rechabites, or Kenites, a Canaanite tribe with whom the Jews had been allied since the days of Moses. He saluted them civilly and was for passing on, but the tribal chieftain restrained him. "You will not reach water before nightfall, my lord," he said, "unless you ride throughout the heat of the day, which would be cruelty to your beasts, and this evening the Sabbath begins, when it will be unlawful for you to travel. Be the guest of Rahab's Children until the Sabbath has ended."

Joachim turned aside, and presently the Rechabites, who were of the smith-guild, pitched their tents in a valley where there was a little water. When the chieftain saw the face of his guest, which until then had been covered up against the heat and dust, he cried out: "Aha, well met! Is this not Joachim of Cocheba to whose corn-lands we come yearly in the winter with our lyres to sing praises to the Lord? Our young men and women tumble about on your rich plough-land together and offer up prayers that the grain may sprout sturdily and be heavy in the ear."

Joachim answered: "And is this not Kenah, Chieftain of the Children of Rahab? Well met! Your craftsmen repair the mattocks, sickles, pruning-hooks, cauldrons and kettles of my labourers, and your work is excellent. But the annual invitation to perform your rustic rites on my land comes from my bailiff, not from myself; he is a Canaanite, I am an Israelite."

Kenah laughed. "Since we Canaanites have the more ancient title to the land, it is only reasonable to suppose that we know best which rites will please the Deity of the land. You cannot complain of your harvest, surely?"

"The Lord has been most bountiful to me," said Joachim, "and if your intercession has carried any weight with him, I should be ungrateful not to acknowledge it. But how am I to know whether I stand in your debt or not?"

"Your bailiff has rewarded us well with sacks of corn from your bins, and though you may be unaware of your debt to us, we are well disposed towards you. By the same token, most noble Joachim, it was only three nights ago that I had a dream of your coming. I dreamed that you freely presented to my people the Well of the Jawbone, near Cushan, the same well that your neighbour Reüben grudges you: you gave it to us for a perpetual possession. And in my dream you called it a gift well bestowed, for your heart was dancing with gladness. You would have given us seven such wells had you possessed them, and all the sheep that watered there besides."

Joachim was not pleased. He replied: "Some dreams are from God, noble Kenah, but some from God's Adversary. How can I tell what reliance to lay upon your dream?"

"By waiting patiently."

"How many days must I be patient?"

"It still wants thirty-five of the appointed number, or so I was assured in my dream."

Here evidently, thought Joachim, was the promised sign. For how, except in a dream, could Kenah have learned of the forty days' journey ordained by the prophetess?

That night, in the black goat's-hair tent, Joachim had no need to excuse himself from wine-drinking, for the Rechabites themselves are forbidden either to own vineyards or, except once a year at their five-day festival, when they also shave their heads, to consume any part of the grape—juice, seed or skin. But when he refrained from the tender mutton prepared for him, and from the little honey-cakes enriched with pistachio, and from the scented junkets, Kenah asked him: "Alas, most noble Joachim, are you sick? Or are you used to daintier food than ours? Or have we unwittingly offended you in some way, that you refuse to eat with us?"

"No, but I have a vow. Give me locust-beans and I will eat greedily."

The servant fetched him locust-beans. As they sat in peace together after they had eaten, a young man, Kenah's sister's son, seized his lyre and sang to it in a loud voice. In his song he prophesied that Hannah, the wife of an Heir of David, would presently conceive and bear a child, a child famous for many ages. Hannah would be one with Sarai of the silver face who had been long barren and laughed to hear the angel's assurance to Father Abraham that she would presently bear him a child. Hannah would also be one with Rachel of the crisp curls, who likewise was barren at first, yet became the mother of the patriarchs Joseph and Benjamin, and through them the ancestress of countless thousands of the Lord God's Israelitish people.

The spirit of the lyre stirred in the singer and he seemed to swell before their eyes as in a changed voice he chanted of a certain mighty hunter, a red hairy king, whom three hundred and sixty-five valiant men followed into battle: how he/rode in his ass-chariot over that very border in the days gone by and drove out the usurping giants from the pleasant valley of Hebron and from the Oaks of Mamre, beloved of Rahab. His garments were stained red with wine, and panthers bounded by his side, sweet of breath. The shoes on his feet were of dolphin-skin, a fir wand was in his hand, and a fawn-skin mantle covered his shoulders. Nimrod he was called. And another of his names was Jerahmeel, the beloved of the Moon.

Then the Kenite sang over and over again: "Glory, glory, glory to the land of Edom, for the Hairy One shall come again, breaking the yoke to which his smooth brother, the supplanter, has subjected him!"

He ceased singing but continued to thrum the strings meditatively. Joachim asked: "This Nimrod whom you celebrate, he is surely not the same Nimrod of whom the Scriptures tell?"

"I sing only what the singing lyre puts into my mouth." He prophesied again: "Nimrod shall come once more. He shall soar aloft upon his eight gryphon wings, he shall make the mountains smoke with his fury—Nimrod, known to the three queens. Cry ha! for Nimrod, who is named Jerahmeel, and ha! for the three queens, each with her thrice forty maidens of honour! The first queen bore him and reared him; the second loved him and slew him; the third anointed him and laid him to rest in the House of Spirals. His soul was carried in her ark across the water to the first queen once again. It was five days' sail in the ark of acacia-wood across the water. It was five days' sail from the Land of the Unborn. To the City of Birth it was a five days' sail; five sea-beasts drew the ark along to the sound of music. There the queen bore him, and named him Jerahmeel, the Moon's beloved."

He was singing a parable of the Sun, who turns about in his sacred year through three Egyptian seasons of one hundred and twenty days apiece. At midsummer he burns with destructive passion, and at mid-winter, enfeebled by time, comes to the five days that are left over, crosses the gap, and turns about again; when he becomes a child, his own son Jerahmeel. Both Jerahmeel and Nimrod were titles of Kozi, the red hairy Sun-god of the Edomites, but a smooth-faced Israelitish Moon-god had long usurped his glory. This usurpation was justified in the myth of Jacob and Esau, and also plainly established in the calendar of the Jews—who now let their year turn with the Moon, not with the Sun as in ancient days.

Joachim said: "This child born to Hannah, will it be male or female? Prophesy again."

The Kenite, still radiant with the spirit of the lyre, answered: "Who can prophesy whether the Sun or the Moon was first created? But if the Sun, then let him be called the Sun's name, Jerahmeel; and if the Moon, then let her be called by the Moon's name, Miriam."

"Is the Moon named Miriam among you?"

"The Moon has many names among our poets. She is Lilith and Eve and Ashtaroth and Rahab and Tamar and Leah and Rachel and Michal and Anatha; but she is Miriam when her star rises in love from the salt sea at evening."

Joachim was seized with a doubt. He asked: "The lyre which you have in your hand is made from the branching horns of the clean oryx, but what of the strings and the pegs that secure them? What reliance is to be placed on your prophecy?"

"My lyre is of oryx-horn, made by the lame craftsman. The strings are fastened with the triangular teeth of the rock-badger, and are themselves the twisted guts of the wild-cat; both of which you call unclean beasts. But this lyre was so stringed and pegged when Miriam played on it in the days before the Levitical laws were uttered. It was clean then, and it is clean now, in the hands of the Children of Rahab."

Joachim asked no more, and when the young man laid down his lyre he cried: "Be witness, poet, that if the Lord blesses my wife's womb—for I am an Heir of David and her name is Hannah—and if a child is born to her, then I will make a free gift to your clan of the Well of the Jawbone, according to your uncle Kenah's dream, and as many sheep as my wife and I together have lived years, which is now ninety. But the child I vow to our God as a Temple ward, whether it be Jerahmeel or Miriam, and I shall call you to witness in that also."

Cries of acclamation and astonishment arose. Kenah presented the young man with a jewelled quiver. "You have brought us all delight with your sweet song," he said.

Kenah himself took the lyre. He played and sang the lament for Tubal Cain. "We are of Tubal, alas for Tubal Cain! He was hornsmith and carpenter; he was goldsmith and lapidary; he was silversmith and whitesmith. He ordered the calendar, he codified the laws. Alas for Tubal the mighty, of whose sons only a remnant is left! It has gone hard with us since the day that the hairy male Sun went down behind the hills and a smooth male Moon rose again without him. Yet still we honour Mother Rahab with scarlet, purple and white; all is not yet lost, nor are we the doomed folk that we seem. Is Caleb not of Tubal? In the likeness of a dog he minded the sheep of his uncle Jabal; in the form of a dog he discovered the purple-fish for his uncle Jubal. Caleb is the perfection of Tubal. He reigned, ceased, reigned again, and will reign once more. When the hour comes, when the Virgin of the Moon conceives, when the Sun Child is begotten again in Caleb, when Jerahmeel puts on cloth of Bozrah scarlet and all the valiant men of Edom shout together for joy, then we will be a great people again, as in ancient times."

Kenah's ecstatic words fell so wide of the Jewish Scriptures that Joachim piously stopped his ears against them; yet wagged his head out of courtesy. He continued with the Kenites in their slow wanderings northward until the appointed forty days were nearly done; then parted from them in friendship and hastened hopefully back to Jerusalem.

CHAPTER THREE

THE BIRTH OF MARY

MEANWHILE Joachim's servants had returned to Hannah at Cocheba, but without any message from him. They said: "Our lord ordered us to return home, all except the groom; our lord appeared to be resolved on a journey."

When she pressed them, they told her the Temple rumour of Joachim's humiliation at the gate of the Treasury. She grew heavy-hearted and said to Judith, her little maid: "Bring me my mourning garments."

"Oh, mistress, is one of your kinsfolk dead?"

"No, but I am mourning for the child that will never be born to me, and for the husband who has left me without a word and gone, I fear, to search for a likely concubine, or it may even be for another wife."

Judith tried to comfort her. "You are young yet and beautiful, and my lord is old. If he should presently fall sick and die, then it would be his brother's duty by the Levirate Law to marry you and raise up children in his memory. Your husband's brother is the younger by twenty years, and a hearty man with seven fine children of his own."

Hannah said: "The Lord forbid that I should ever look forward to the death of my husband, who has never stinted me in anything and is a just and devout man." She cut her hair close to her head and continued to mourn while four Sabbaths passed.

Judith came to Hannah early one morning. "Mistress, do you not hear the shouting and music in the streets? Do you not know that the Feast of Tabernacles is already upon us? Take off your mourning garments and let us ride up together to Jerusalem in the company of your neighbours to lodge with your sister there and celebrate the season of love."

Hannah said angrily: "Leave me to my grief!"

But Judith would not leave her. "Mistress," she cried, "your kinsfolk will be coming to the Feast from all the villages, and if you miss

23

their gossip you will grieve for a twelvemonth. Why heap misery upon misery?"

"Leave me to my grief," Hannah repeated, but in a gentler voice.

Judith stood there boldly, arms akimbo and legs straddled apart. "There was a woman," she said, "in the days of the Judges and she was childless like yourself, and of the same name. What did she do? She did not sit at home, mourning to herself like an old owl in a bush. She went up to the Lord's chief sanctuary, which was at Shiloh, to welcome in the New Year, and there she ate and drank, concealing her misery. Afterwards she caught hold of one of the pillars of the Shrine and prayed to the Lord for a child, silently and grimly like one who at the sheep-shearing wrestles for a prize. Eli the High Priest, my lord's ancestor, saw her lips moving and her body writhing. He took her for a drunkard; but she told him what was amiss, how she was childless and how her neighbours taunted her. At this, Eli assured her that all would be well if she came to the Shrine to worship early in the morning while it was still dark. She did so, and nine months later a fine child was born to her, and a fine child indeed, for it was Samuel the prophet.

"Fetch me clean clothes," said Hannah with sudden resolution. "Select some fitting for the occasion, for I will go to Jerusalem after all. And my bond-maid Judith shall come with me." As she spoke the high tenor voice of the priest rang down the village street: "Arise, let us go up to Zion, to the House of the Lord!"

They rode up together to Jerusalem the same day, in a carriage drawn by white asses. Joachim owned six pairs of white asses, and this was the finest pair of all. Presently they overtook the faithful of Cocheba who had started some hours before them: men, women and children in holiday dress trudging on foot with gifts of grapes and figs and pigeons carried in baskets on their shoulders; driving before them a fat bullock with gilded horns and a crown of olive for sacrifice; flute-players leading the procession. Every village of Judah was honouring Jehovah in the same style and the roads were clouded with dust. Outside the gates of Jerusalem the citizens lined the roads and shouted greetings.

The streets of the City resembled a forest. Green branches were fastened to the houses: arbours had been built at each of the City gates, in every square and on every house-top. In the markets, beasts and poultry were for sale in prodigious quantity, warranted suitable for sacrifice. There were stalls for fruit and sweetmeats, and wine-stalls; everywhere little boys ran about with armfuls of thyrsi for sale, and branches of quince. The thyrsi were for celebrants to carry in their right hands during their joyful procession around the altar of burned offering; the branches of quince were to be carried in their left hands at the same time.

Judith asked Hannah: "Mistress, is it true that this Feast was instituted to remind the Israelites of their desert wanderings with Moses, when they lived in arbours, not in stone houses? It is hard to believe that the desert provided sufficient leafy trees for the purpose."

"You are right, daughter. The Feast was celebrated on this mountain centuries before the birth of Moses, but do not quote me as having said so, for I shall deny it."

"Since it seems that you know more than the priests, Mistress, will you tell me why the branches of the thyrsus are tied together in threes—willow, palm and myrtle—the palm in the middle, the myrtle on the right hand, the willow on the left?"

"Though I do not know more than the priests, at least I am free to tell you what I do know. This is the Festival of Fruits, the Festival of Eve's Full Moon. Once when the moon shone full in Eden the Second Eve, our mother, plucked myrtle and smelt it, saying: 'A tree fit for an arbour of love', for she longed for Adam's kisses. She plucked a palm leaf and plaited it into a fan, saying: 'Here is a fan to warm up the fire', for at that time Adam loved her only as a sister. This fan she hid. She also plucked a palm branch, with the leaf still in its knob, saying: 'Here is a sceptre. I will give it to Adam, telling him: "Rule me, if you will, with this knobbed sceptre." ' Lastly she plucked willow—the willow that has red rind and lance-like foliage—saying: 'Here are branches suitable for a cradle.' For the new moon seemed like a cradle to her, and Eve longed for a child."

"Mistress, the quince boughs that I see—for what reason are they carried?"

"It is said that our mother Eve, by giving Adam quince to eat, forced him to love her as she required to be loved."

"But the star of the quince which childless women eat in the hope of quickening their wombs—"

"It has no virtue," Hannah interrupted. "I have eaten the thing with prayers every Feast for seven years."

"They say that the quinces of Corfu succeed where all others fail."

"Then they are wrong. Twice I have sent for Corfu quinces, once from the islet of Macris itself. It was money thrown away."

Judith clucked in commiseration.

"I have tried everything," sighed Hannah.

They drove on in silence for a while.

Judith began again: "I once heard a woman say—an old, old Jebusite woman—that it was the First Eve who planted the tree of the garden, and Adam who plucked the forbidden fruit, and the First Eve who expelled him for his fault."

Hannah flushed. "The old woman must have been drunken. You abuse my confidence. Let me never hear you repeat such dangerous tales again in my hearing."

Judith laughed silently, for she was herself a Jebusite. The Jebusites were the poor people of Jerusalem, descended from the original Canaanite inhabitants, whom because of their usefulness as slaves and menials the Jews forgave their many idolatrous superstitions. At this Feast they still secretly worshipped the Goddess Anatha, after whom the village of Bethany was named and whose sacred lioness had mothered the tribe of Judah; and at the Passover, or Feast of Unleavened Bread, they still mourned for Tammuz, her murdered son, the God of the Barley Sheaf.

Hannah's sister welcomed them to her house, where they sang hymns, told tales and gossiped in the roof-top arbour until midnight. On the next day the Feast began. The sacrifices on this first day were a he-goat for a sin-offering, two rams, thirteen bullocks with gilded horns, and fourteen lambs. The goat was for the past year; the rams for summer and winter; the bullocks for the thirteen new moons; the lambs for the first fourteen days of each month, when the moon is young. With each beast went a sacrifice of flour and oil, and salt to make the flames burn blue. Then followed the Night of the Women, when tall golden four-branched candlesticks were erected and lighted up in the Women's Court at the Temple, and the priests and Levites danced a torch-dance around them, with trumpet music and rhythmic shaking of the thyrsi to each of the four quarters of Heaven in turn, and aloft to the zenith. These gestures had once been made in honour of Anatha, marking out the five points of her pyramid of power; but now Jehovah claimed all the honour.

Towards evening Judith said to Hannah: "Mistress, let us go to the Women's Court and afterwards join the merry-makers in the streets."

"We will go to the Court, but afterwards we will return to this house. Since my husband has ridden off, I do not know where, it would be unseemly for me to go about the streets with you and seem to rejoice."

"Eve's moon shines only once a year. Here are the clothes fitting

26

for the occasion which you asked me to select from your cedar-wood coffer."

Hannah recognized the bridal dress which she had worn ten years before at her wedding. She looked steadily into Judith's eyes and asked: "What is this folly, daughter?"

Judith blushed. "We are commanded to rejoice to-night and to put on our richest clothes. These are your richest clothes, Mistress, and what woman rejoices more than one who wears her bridal dress?"

Hannah gently fingered the many-coloured embroidery and said after a long silence, but in the voice of one who wishes to be persuaded: "How can I go dressed as a bride, daughter, when I have been married for ten years?"

"If you wear your bridal dress nobody will know you for the wife of my lord Joachim; and you may rejoice in the streets to your heart's content."

"But the headband is missing. The moths fretted away the wool and I put it aside to mend."

"Here is a better headband, Mistress, than the one in which you were married. It is a gift from your bond-maid Judith, who loves you."

Hannah looked at the purple headband, braided with pearls and embroidered with gold and scarlet thread. She asked severely: "From whom is this beautiful thing stolen?"

"It is stolen from nobody. Before I came to you I was under bond to my lord's kinswoman Jemima, who inherited jewels and clothes from her stepmother. When I left her, she praised me for my dutifulness and gave me the headband. She said: 'Since you are now to serve in the house of Joachim of Cocheba, who is of the Heirs of David, this headband may win your mistress's favour or soften her heart if you displease her. I am not of royal blood and neither are you; we may not wear it.'"

Hannah's tears flowed afresh. She was sorely tempted to wear the dress and the headband; but dared not.

Judith asked: "How long will you continue to humble your heart, Mistress?"

"So long as my double grief continues. Is it a little thing to be childless? Is it a little thing to be suddenly forsaken by a noble husband?"

Judith laughed gaily. "Wash your face, paint your eyes with green copper paint from Sinai, rub spikenard between your breasts. Wear this royal headband and the bridal dress and come out with me quickly while the household is busily feasting in the arbour."

27

"Begone from my presence," Hannah cried angrily. "I have never sinned against my husband all these years and it would be folly to begin now. Someone has lent you this headband in the hope that it will lure me out merry-making to my shame; it is some bold lover of your own who wishes me to become an accomplice in your wantonness."

"The headband was given me by a devout woman, as I call the Lord to witness! Are you inviting me to answer your anger with curses? I should do so indeed if I thought that any curse of mine would sting you into wisdom. But it would be presumptuous in me to say more when the Lord himself has cursed you by shutting up your womb and making you the butt of your fertile sisters." With that she ran away.

Hannah took up the purple headband, of which the chief ornament was a silver crescent-moon, curved around a six-pointed Star of David stitched in gold and scarlet: the golden pyramid of Anatha, interlocked with the scarlet *vau* triangle, her wedge. On either side of the star were embroidered myrtle-twigs, bells, cedar-trees, scallop-shells and pomegranates, the tokens of queenship. She considered the headband and tied it across her brow, but it looked out of place on her cropped head. Then she noticed that Judith had set a large round basket beside the bed; and in it lay an Egyptian wig with crimped golden hair. She tried it on and it fitted her. She bound the headband across her brow again, then picked up her copper mirror and looked at herself. "Judith is right," she thought. "I am still young, still beautiful." Her image smiled back at her. She washed her face, painted her eyes, rubbed spikenard between her breasts, perfumed her bridal dress with myrrh and put it on. Then she clapped her hands for Judith, who came running in, dressed in gaily coloured clothes. They went out together quickly, shrouded in dark cloaks, without a word to anyone; and no one saw them go.

When they came to the end of the street, Hannah said: "I hear the sound of trumpets. My heart fails me. I am ashamed to go up to the Women's Court; if I do, someone in the crowd will surely recognize me."

"Where then shall we go?"

"Let the Lord guide our feet."

Judith led her this way and that through the narrow streets of the Old Quarter in the direction of the Fish Gate. This was the Jebusite quarter.

It seemed like a dream to Hannah. Her shoes seemed scarcely to touch the pavement, she skimmed like a swallow. No man molested them as they went, though the City was filled with drunkards that night and twice they avoided a skirmish between screaming partisans who used the festal thyrsus for a club. At last Judith led Hannah down a narrow lane and, without pausing, pushed at a great gate which stood at the end of it. It swung open on well-oiled hinges and they found themselves in a deserted court; on the left hand were stables, on the right an ancient wall with an ornamental door standing ajar.

They passed through the door into a garden. It was dusk and the noise of the festival came thinly through the boughs of the fruit-trees, so that as she paused for a moment with pounding heart Hannah could hear the plash of a fountain from the further end of the garden, where coloured lights were burning. She went eagerly towards the lights, while Judith remained standing at the garden door. They were lanterns, with coloured panes, hung outside a spacious arbour, at the back of which wax candles were burning steadily in a tall eight-branched candlestick. In the middle grew a laurel-tree, and fastened to it was a nest of silver filigree work containing golden sparrow fledgelings, with wide-open mouths; the hen-bird perched on the edge of the nest, a jewelled butterfly in her bill.

"Come here, Judith!" called Hannah. "Come quickly, my child, and see this pretty nest."

There was no answer, and when Hannah went back to the door she found it bolted and Judith gone away. Yet she was not a prisoner, for the bolts were shot from inside. She returned wonderingly to the arbour. In a dark corner she saw a couch, spread with a purple cloth, which had escaped her notice when she first went in. She lay down upon it, with her head on a soft pillow, and sighed for pleasure, smiling up at the nest of sparrows.

Presently she closed her eyes and began to pray, silently and grimly, as her namesake had once prayed at Shiloh; and when she opened them again, a grave bearded man was bending over her, so splendidly dressed that he seemed to be an envoy of some god. On a blue cord about his neck he wore an egg-shaped jewel set with twelve bright gems of different colours which winked in the candle-light. He took her by the wrist of the right hand and said in a deep voice: "Your prayer has been heard, Hannah. Take this cup and drink it, in honour of the Lord of this Feast."

She asked: "Sir, who are you?"

"I am the servant of One of whom it is written: 'He scorneth the multitude of the City.'"

She asked again: "Sir, what is the egg-shaped jewel that you wear about your neck?"

"When the childless Shulamite heiress asked the prophet Elisha this very question, he answered: 'Beloved of the Lord, consult the silver moon of your headband.' Now drink as the Shulamite woman also drank."

He put a goblet into her hand. She raised it to her lips and drank obediently. It was sweet wine, with an aromatic scent and a bitter after-taste. It seemed to her that the arbour was filled with music though she saw no musicians. Then the candles were suddenly extinguished and the air grew bright with torches whirled in a figure-of-eight. He set the seed of a lotus between her lips, saying: "Swallow this seed whole, Daughter of Michal: do not mar it with your teeth, for it is a human soul."

She swallowed the seed, and presently her limbs grew numb and her senses began to fail her. There was a roaring in her ears, like a tempest at sea, and it seemed to her that the round earth was wrenched from its socket and the stars danced in ecstasy; the Moon and the Sun rushed together with a shout. She was caught up in a whirlwind to heaven; and knew no more.

When she awoke, she was lying in her own bed at her sister's house and it was the evening of the second day of the Feast. She clapped her hands for Judith, who hastened to her bedside and wept for joy. "Oh, Mistress," she said, "I had thought you dead, you lay in so deep a swoon. You have slept now for a whole night and day."

Hannah, still drowsy, asked: "How did I come here, daughter?"

Judith opened her eyes wide. "How did you come here indeed! I do not know what my mistress means."

"How? Did I find my way home from the garden of the laurel-tree without your guidance?"

"Mistress, you have lain here without stirring for a whole night and day since you took this mirror to look into it."

Hannah found that she was not wearing her bridal dress as she had thought, but the one in which she had come to Jerusalem, and that she had no wig on her head nor any headband about it. She sighed and said: "Why, then it is the Lord's mercy. I was tempted to a great sin, and might perhaps have enticed your feet into the snare as well, had you come out with me."

"The Lord forbid! I do not know what my mistress means."

"Instead," Hannah continued, "I have been rewarded with a wonderful dream. I dreamed that I went out in my bridal dress wearing a royal headband that you had offered me, and a head of golden curls, and presently came into an arbour of laurels where I saw a golden candlestick lighted, and a silver nest filled with golden sparrows. There I prayed fervently, reclining on a couch until an angel of the Lord appeared. He called me by my name and said that my prayer had been heard. In my dream he gave me scented wine to drink and a lotus-seed to swallow whole, and my soul was caught up in a whirlwind to the third heaven."

"Oh, Mistress, what a dream of dreams! May it prove prophetic of good!"

They both offered up praise together. Hannah said: "I charge you to tell nobody of my dream."

"I am a discreet woman."

"You have been a kind and faithful servant to me, Judith, and I will reward you well. I will buy you three ells of fine cloth and a new cloak before we return to Cocheba."

"Give, Mistress, and I will be grateful, but I am already well recompensed for any service that I may have done you."

"For your modest answer I will make it six ells of cloth and a pair of shoes besides the cloak."

Yet Judith spoke the truth. She had already taken back the royal headband and the wig to Anna, the guardian mother of the Temple virgins. She had said: "Here are the things, Holy One, that you entrusted to me. Praise me, if you please, and say that I have obeyed your orders well."

Anna had answered: "I praise you, daughter, and twenty pieces of gold will to-day be paid to your mother to buy you a worthy husband; but if you let anyone know, by sign or word, what you have done to-night you shall die miserably, you and all your household."

"I am a discreet woman."

The Feast of Tabernacles was over. Hannah one morning came to Joachim, to whisper in his ear: "Husband, I think that I am with child."

He looked strangely at her. After a while he said: "Tell me again, woman, when you are sure of the matter. 'I think' is nothing."

A month later, as he returned from a visit to Jericho, Hannah came to meet him, and this time she said: "Husband, I know that I am with child." She clasped his neck and wept for joy.

Joachim was astonished and yet not astonished. He presently summoned his bailiff and ordered him to choose unblemished lambs and calves for sacrifice—twelve lambs and ten calves, and a score of kids as well. These he took next day in a wagon to Jerusalem and presented them at the Temple for a sacrifice of prosperity, but without explaining in what his prosperity consisted.

He still doubted in his heart as he approached the steps of the Priests' Court, though in conformity with Temple ritual he mounted them with as much show of alacrity as if he were assaulting a city. He thought: "If the Lord is indeed reconciled to me and has granted my prayer, doubtless the golden plate on the High Priest's mitre above his brow will make this plain to me."

For as it happened, the High Priest himself was officiating that day; it was a feast of the New Moon. As he approached the High Priest, who stood by the Altar of Sacrifice, and asked permission to make his offerings, Joachim gazed earnestly at the golden plate, to see whether it were bright or cloudy. It shone bright as flame, and he said to himself: "Now I know that my sins are forgiven me and my prayers heard, and the prayers of my wife Hannah."

The High Priest readily gave him permission, addressing him by name and asking whether Peace were with him.

A subordinate priest took Joachim's beasts from the hands of the Temple servants. They kicked and struggled and the priest commented on their fine condition; then, turning their heads to the north, one after the other, with a short prayer of dedication, he cut their throats and, catching the blood in a silver vessel, poured it on the earth around the altar. He next entrusted the carcases to the team of Levite butchers, who, working dexterously on their marble slabs, drew out the entrails, which were at once washed in the fountain of the court, and cut out the joint of oblation—the thigh piece— from each carcase, together with the breast and right shoulder, which were the Levite's perquisites. Next, each oblation was wrapped around with a length of entrails and enclosed in a double layer of fat. The priest laid it on a golden plate, sprinkled it with sacred incense and salt, and finally, ascending the ramp of the altar barefooted, cast it with a short prayer on the sacrificial fire, which blazed up fiercely. The smoke rose straight upwards instead of eddying sickeningly around the Court, as often happened in wintry weather; and Joachim read this as another propitious sign.

The priest instructed him to send his servants to fetch what remained of the carcases, but he waived the privilege. "No, no, let them be given to the Temple servants, for this is truly an offering of prosperity." He went down from the Temple with a serene mind, and meeting by chance with his neighbour Reuben saluted him with surprising kindness, but told him nothing; not wishing to speak prematurely, lest his wife might miscarry or the child be born crooked.

RITUAL SLAYING OF KING-GOD
(From "The Origins of Early Semitic Ritual" by S. H. Hooke,
British Academy, Oxford University Press, 1938)

"YAHU" AS A SOLAR ZEUS
(From "The Religion of Ancient Palestine in the Light of Archaeology,"
by S. A. Cook, British Academy, Oxford University Press, 1930)

KADESH WITH MIN AND RESHEPH
(From "The Religion of Ancient Palestine in the Light of Archaeology,"
by S A. Cook, British Academy, Oxford University Press, 1930)

The months went by, and in the height of summer Hannah was brought to bed and delivered of a daughter. When she held the child in her arms and found it perfect in all its limbs, she cried: "The widow is no longer a widow and the childless woman is a mother. Who will run to my scornful neighbour, Reuben's wife, and tell her that I have borne a fine child?"

Joachim said: "Let no one go; for the child is young yet and may not live." But he was a scrupulous man and immediately sent out two servants to fetch Kenah the Rechabite. When he came, the Well of the Jawbone would be made over to him and his people by a deed of gift, and ninety-two sheep besides.

Kenah rode down from Carmel a week later, accompanied by witnesses. The gift was made and registered, and the young man, Kenah's nephew, prophesied sweetly as he played on the lyre. Kenah swore an oath of friendship with Joachim, saying: "If you or your wife or the child should ever stand in need of our help, these tents are your tents, come what may, and this people is your people." When he had returned to his pastures, he sent a woman secretly to Anna the guardian mother of the Temple virgins, to give her a set of carved Egyptian jewels for the casting of lots and for divination; with this gift went a casting-cup of Edomite sard and a white linen napkin to receive the lots.

Everyone was well satisfied: those who lived in houses as well as those who lived in tents.

CHAPTER FOUR

A CERTAIN MAN

JOACHIM and his garrulous brother-in-law Cleopas were talking together in low tones by the well under the mulberry-tree at Cocheba. They did not refer to King Herod by name. It was always "He" or "That Man" or "A Certain Man", except that once or twice Joachim called him "The Edomite". There was no danger whatever of their remarks being overheard by one of Herod's numerous spies, but talking in this guarded way had become habitual with them. They knew that Herod himself would sometimes darken his hair with charcoal, disguise his features, put on common clothes and go out among the people as his own chief spy.

"For one of so wild and petulant a nature," said Cleopas, "a Certain Man has shown surprising patience in the development of his plans. How many years is it now since he first was set in authority over us?"

"It must be more than twenty-five years."

"It seems longer. Almost I could admire him for his political skill and the energy of his rule, which has brought peace and a sort of prosperity to Israel, did I not hate him so sincerely as a secret enemy of our God."

"Prosperity?" cried Joachim. "The shadow of prosperity, not the substance: the palace enriched at the expense of the hut, the robes of State dyed in the life-blood of the peasant. Peace? A Roman peace, imposed on the remnant who survive the slaughter."

Cleopas agreed. "To be sure, we must never forget his impious assault on the Holy City, how the madmen under his command (though he made a pretence of restraining their fury) reddened their swords in the narrow streets on the aged, on children, even on women. We must never forget the principal men whom he murdered for remaining loyal to King Antigonus the Maccabee, and whose confiscated treasures filled his coffers. Forty-five of them he murdered, among them my own uncle Phineas. The passage of time cannot wipe out the blood. But is it not strange that though in our hearts we know the Edomite to be an enemy of our God, there are so few open breaches of the Law with which we can reproach him? The Alexandrian Doctors whom he employs to justify his actions are more cunning than foxes or serpents."

"I hear that he has won another legal victory, in the matter of the edict about house-breakers."

"He has indeed."

"Tell me about it, my dear Cleopas. It has come to me only as vague gossip, brought in by the servants."

"There were, as you know, numerous cases of daylight house-breaking reported in Jerusalem during Passover week, all the work of a single powerful gang, and then more at Purim. The thieves made some wonderful hauls while the householders and their families were away at the Temple, usually having left only some old crippled servant to guard the house. In festival times, of course, there are so many strangers in the streets that detection is almost impossible once the thieves have left the house with their spoil. The victims of these robberies, as it happened, were all either Edomites, Greeks or Egyptian Jews of That Man's party. Naturally this discrimination vexed him: last week he issued an edict ordering convicted house-breakers to be stripped of all their goods and permanently banished from his dominions. The Presidents of the High Court were shocked. They sent delegates to protest that this was dead contrary to the Law of Moses."

"They were right. The punishment for theft is that the convicted person must, with certain exceptions, restore fourfold what he has taken; and if he cannot do so, then he may be sold into slavery for no longer than six years, but sold to a Jew, not a foreigner, so that he may continue as a member of the congregation."

"The delegates," continued Cleopas, "pointed out that to banish the offender from this kingdom is to cut him off from the congregation and to prevent his return even in festival time, when it is his duty to join in public devotions."

"Exactly."

"And 'Exactly,' said That Man too. 'Exactly,' he said. 'The robberies are all committed on holy days, which is the very time that thieves must be forbidden the City. My edict is directed against the Sons of Belial who instead of religiously joining in public devotions break irreligiously into the houses of those who do.' 'But,' the delegates further protest, 'to banish the offender from the kingdom without a penny is equivalent to selling him into foreign slavery, which is dead contrary to the Law.' 'Not so,' says he. 'In the time of Moses there were no Israelitish communities outside the boundaries of the desert camp. But now there are as many of the Lord's people resident outside my dominions as inside, or more; if any one of them is forbidden to worship the Lord in his ancestral manner that is no fault of mine. I have intervened often and successfully on their behalf. Let the thieves go to your kinsfolk of Alexandria or Damascus or Babylon or Pontus or wherever they please, but I will not tolerate them in the kingdom.' The delegates exclaim: 'Well did David say that he would rather be a janitor of the Lord's House than dwell comfortably in the tents of the heathen!' Herod answers: 'And what honest man would not? But the Eighth Commandment is positive: "Thou shalt not steal." And theft is there listed with Sabbath-breaking, adultery, murder, idolatry, blasphemy, witchcraft, false-witness—all sins that are punished with death. Learned men, do you not think it an anomaly that the Eighth Commandment should be the only one of the ten which may be broken without fear of death or disgrace?' Then the delegates bow so low as nearly to knock their heads on the floor and ask humbly: 'Who are we to question the wisdom of the Law?' Herod says: 'Menelaus, fetch me the ancient roll of the Law! Find me the passage about thieving.' "

"You imitate him to the life."

"And that greasy cemetery-hog Menelaus waddles to the book-case and fumbles about among the brittle papyrus-rolls and presently in his snuffling voice reads out a text from the twenty-second chapter of Exodus which none of us have ever heard before, to the effect that any man who breaks into a neighbour's house on a Feast day shall surely die, for he dishonours the Lord besides wronging his neighbour. Herod then dismisses the delegates, saying: 'You have heard the words. And is not my roll of the Law of greater authority than yours, learned men? Read the title. Does it not date from the reign of King Hezekiah? Was it not brought to Egypt by Onias the High Priest, from whose lineal successor I had it as a precious gift? I fear that your rolls have become defective by rough handling and careless copying from a tattered original.' So his edict stands. Nobody dares accuse the King of forgery, or publicly plead on behalf of the house-breakers that the spoiling of Egyptians is no crime, and that over Edom the Lord has cast his shoe to enslave it."

Joachim said warmly: "Brother, it is as well that such puerile pleas are not raised. Our learned teacher Hillel has warned us to distinguish between particular and general commandments of our God. A particular commandment was given to our ancestors for the despoliation of those who had robbed and enslaved them; but to interpret it as a general licence to cheat and steal from Egyptians to-day, is that not monstrous? The text about Edom is also quoted shamefully out of context; that the anger of the Lord was kindled against Edom centuries ago does not license house-breakers nowadays to carry off the goods of individual Edomites. Well, as for the edict, we shall see whether it has the deterrent effect that its author hopes. But I dislike the innovation. I should even prefer to see the rascals stoned to death for a breach of the Sabbath—to force one's way into a locked house is undoubtedly work, just as fighting is, and fighting on a holy day is forbidden. That they should be banished for theft is intolerable."

"But why, Brother Joachim, do you call him the Edomite? You must know as well as I do that, though born in Edom, he is no more descended from Esau than I am."

"I call him an Edomite to avoid the necessity of using a more honourable name. Yes, I am aware that his grandfather was captured as a child by Edomite brigands in their sack of Philistine Ascalon—

the son of a priest of the abominable local Sun-god, and that the priest was unable to pay the immense ransom demanded so that the child was brought up as an Edomite. But if a mere Philistine slave, why was his ransom set at so high a figure? Why was he given high rank by the Edomites and afterwards courted by King Alexander Jannaeus the Maccabee? The child's father was a Slave of the God, which in Philistia usually means a member of a captured, or refugee, priesthood. Can you positively declare that he was a Philistine? Nicolaus of Damascus writes that the ancestors of That Man returned from Babylon with Ezra, being Calebites of Bethlehem."

"Nicolaus of Damascus is a liar!"

"Nicolaus as an eminent barrister has no conscience in his handling of a brief, but I have never known him to tamper with historical facts. And is it impossible that a Certain Man is indeed a Calebite of Bethlehem and that his fathers served idols of the Abominable One in the days of our disgrace? And that during the Maccabean Wars the priesthood fled with their idols to Philistia, where they were welcomed by their co-religionists?"

Cleopas grunted doubtfully. "Be that as it may, it was an evil hour in which King Alexander Jannaeus befriended the grandfather of That Man, who has cut off the last male remnants of the House of Maccabee, one by one."

They pondered the matter in silence. After a while Cleopas said again, recalling the death of Herod's Maccabean wife Mariamne: "I was present at the execution of a Certain Man's lovely wife. Oh, who can describe her beauty, the last brilliant flower of a heroic race? The Rose of Sharon was a weed compared with her. Yet a worm lay in the bloom. Her own mother, condemned on the same occasion, heaped reproaches on her for having involved both of them in ruin by her wantonness. And though it was thought by some that Alexandra spoke as she did in hope of saving her own life at the expense of her daughter's honour, alas, in my ears the words rang true! Mariamne walked too scornfully for innocence. Oh, Joachim, adultery is a sin that cannot be either palliated or pardoned. Granted that Mariamne's husband had been responsible for the death of her father, her brother, her uncle and her venerable maimed grandfather, and that he had twice given provisional orders, when setting out on a dangerous mission, that she should be despatched if he failed to return: yet let us be just to him. He never raised his voice or hand against her, and her duty was clearly towards him as her husband and the father of her sons. A woman must obey her husband and be faithful to his bed, whatever the provocation. For she is only a woman, though the best of women; and he is at least a man, though the worst of men."

"It is a severe law and lays a great burden of responsibility on a father in the choice of a son-in-law. I am glad to be quit of the burden in the case of my daughter Miriam: Simon the High Priest is to choose a husband for her."

"Simon, for all his faults, has a good conscience towards the Lord and men, and you may be sure that you will not be disgraced in your son-in-law. But we were speaking of Mariamne's infidelities."

"Some declare that the Edomite loved her so dearly that he could not bear to think of her lying in the arms of another even when he was himself dead, and that this was why he gave the provisional order for her despatch. They recall the extravagant signs of grief that he showed after her death, and there is even an obscene story current that he preserved her corpse in myrrh with necrophilous intention. Yet they forget that he appeared no less afflicted and distraught after her brother had been drowned in the Bath at Jericho, as if by accident, but, as we know, at his express order. Such grief is feigned as much to placate the dead person's ghost as to distract public inquiry. He never loved her. He married her to benefit from the popular esteem in which the Maccabees had for so long been held in Israel. Yet one by one he rooted them out, and finally he destroyed her too, without pity—as, mark my words, he will destroy the handsome sons whom she bore him and to whom he pretends such fatherly affection."

"I will mark your words," said Cleopas, "but I cannot believe that he is such a wild beast that he would kill his own sons merely because their mother was a Maccabee. Besides, if he did not love her passionately, why did he trouble to order her despatch in the event of his death?"

"He feared, I suppose, that she would marry some enemy of his and found a new dynasty upon the issue of the marriage. He could not bear to think that the heirs of his body would not reign over Israel for as many generations at least as David's did."

"Why then do you suppose that he is intent on killing Mariamne's sons? Does he doubt their paternity? They certainly resemble him closely."

"They are nothing to him. He hates to think that we say secretly of them: 'They are well-born on one side at least.' But he has other sons. Do not overlook his eldest, Antipater, who is marked out as the future king. It was for his benefit that Mariamne was to die, and later did die; it will be for his benefit that Mariamne's son; will die in their turn. Let no one underrate Antipater's claims. Herod may even make him co-ruler with himself one day, in the Egyptian style."

"I had forgotten his very existence. What sort of a man is he, kinsman?"

"Though I have inquired closely, I cannot pretend that I have yet heard one evil word spoken against him by those who know him well. He is reputedly studious and generous, without ambition or malice, punctual in payment, scrupulous in his observance of the Law, besides being a wonderful huntsman of the desert ostrich, the antelope and the wild-ox. Nevertheless, even if this account is true, such good qualities are wasted on his father's son; and for all I know he may be as false a dissembler as ever wore sandals. But I will not reveal my worst fears to you until That Man's plots have matured. When you hear news that the sons of Mariamne are dead, come to my house again, and I will sing you a further prophecy. Meanwhile, I will give you a clue to my fears. Do you recollect the story of the golden fetish of Dora?"

Cleopas smiled. This trophy had been taken from the Edomites by King Alexander Jannaeus in the wars, the hollow head of an onager, or wild-ass, made of pure gold, with red jewels for eyes and teeth of ivory: it was thought to be of ancient Egyptian workmanship. Alexander Jannaeus had captured it from the Edomites of Dora or Adoraim, a city close to Hebron, for while the Jews were in Captivity, the Edomites had reconquered their ancient territories in Southern Judaea. They set great store by this fetish, which they called the Mask of Nimrod. When it was brought back in triumph to Jerusalem, an Edomite named Zabidus who pretended to be a traitor to his country had come before Alexander Jannaeus and said: "Do you not know your good fortune? By means of this mask you can utterly defeat Kozi, who is called Nimrod, the Abominable God of Dora, and expel him from the whole region."

Alexander, who was High Priest as well as King, asked: "How can that be?"

Zabidus replied: "The Evil One can be enticed to this mountain by conjuration."

"That is forbidden by the Law."

"I will perform the elicitation without offence to the Law."

Alexander gave his consent when Zabidus undertook to utter the necessary spells outside the Temple precincts in the Valley of the Jebusites, also called the Cheesemongers' Valley.

Zabidus took down the mask from the Beautiful Gate where it was fastened, wrapped it in a dark blanket and set the bundle high on a cornice of the wall. He warned those who watched him: "If you value your lives, keep away from this accursed trophy."

Then, dressed all in white, he descended into the valley and stood alone in the level place at the bottom. On his head he set a round wooden frame in which fifteen lighted candles were arranged at intervals, ensconced in stained-glass lamps, besides five flaming torches fixed in an inner ring of the frame. He then danced slowly about in geometrical figures, blessing the name of Jehovah and calling upon the God of Dora to come up in haste to Jerusalem and there make obeisance to his rightful Lord, the God of Israel. A multitude of Jews watched from the City walls and the sides of the valley, being forbidden to approach anywhere near him or to utter any sound that might break the spell. The night was moonless and the whirling and twinkling of the tiny lamps below as Zabidus moved, now in a spiral, now in an ellipse, now in a figure-of-eight, fascinated them. Suddenly he uttered a great cry, as of despair and terror, the lights went out and a horrific wailing noise was heard.

No one knew what had happened. Some believed that Zabidus, failing in his project, had been struck dead by Jehovah for his presumption. Others, that all was well, that they had heard the death-cry of the Abomination of Dora. But none ventured into the valley to discover the truth until dawn broke. Then they found the frame with the lamps, and the white robes which Zabidus had worn, neatly folded, but nothing else. When a servant of the King opened the bundle on the wall, intending to restore the mask to the Beautiful Gate, it was found to contain only a lump of red clay, which is the sign-manual of the Edomite. The mask was never recovered.

"He was a bold rogue," said Cleopas. "But I cannot grieve greatly for the loss long ago of a golden ass's head from the Temple trophies."

"It is my conviction," said Joachim slowly, "that the Edomite has obtained the relic from the family of Zabidus by marriage with Doris, whose home is at Dora, and intends to make mischief with it in the name of Nimrod. You are mistaken in calling it an ass's head; for though a man may pile burdens on an ass and beat it to his heart's content, he would be either a fool or a Samson who dared to do the same with an onager. Onagers are man-killers, as is often proved in the Circus when prisoners of war are set to hunt wild beasts. They are swift as swallows, cunning as ichneumons, murderous as Arabian bandits."

"But who or what is Nimrod? The Nimrod of whom I have read was a son of Cush, dead these two thousand years."

"I should soil my mouth if I told you who and what the Edomites believe him to be. But you may be sure that he is a power to be reckoned with. You will remember at least that Nimrod, the lord of three hundred and sixty-five warriors, persecuted Abraham because he would not fall down and worship false gods? I fear that a Certain Man will persecute Israel for the same reason in the name of Nimrod."

"The Lord God forbid!" cried Cleopas in alarm.

Herod took his sons by Mariamne to Rome, where they were given a suite of rooms in the Palace of the Emperor Augustus. He supplied them with an over-generous allowance of money, and the Jewish tutors in whose charge he left them, though of upright soul and orthodox views, were chosen by him principally for their lack of courage and authority. It seems that his secret intention was that the boys should learn to love the profligate habits of the Roman youth and ruin themselves by a scornful disregard of the Law of Israel; for when after a few years he had assured himself that they were perfect Romans he called them home and at Jerusalem subjected them to a strict religious discipline. He married one of them to his niece, the daughter of his sister Salome, and the other to a daughter of Archelaus, the petty king of Cappadocia. Neither was satisfied with his marriage, and both chafed at their enforced studies of the Hebrew Scriptures, at the grave and tedious devotions, the irritating formalities required of them, the Law's restrictions on their eating, drinking and vicious pursuits, and at the monotony of Sabbath-day observance. Cunning Herod also arranged that they should hear Palace gossip about events which until then had been kept secret from them, so that they should learn to hate him as the murderer of their mother and relatives. Alexander, the elder, was told that the beautiful dresses and jewels worn by their father's latest wives were really his own property, having been part of his mother's wardrobe. Aristobulus, the younger, was taught to think himself disgraced by marriage to the daughter of Salome, whose accusations had brought his mother to execution. But for a long while Herod played the indulgent father and turned a blind eye and a deaf ear to their rebellious ways, until they dared to go further and hint at their intention of avenging their mother's murder.

About this time Herod left Jerusalem for Asia Minor, where his old friend Agrippa, the victor of Actium, and next to Augustus himself the most influential man in the Empire, was about to relinquish his command of the Armies of the East. Herod begged Agrippa to restore the Jewish merchants settled in certain Ionian cities to the ancient privileges which the Greek civic authorities had denied them, especially freedom to worship in their ancestral manner, the right to send gifts to the Temple, and exemption from military service. Agrippa thanked Herod heartily for calling the abuses to his attention; he confirmed the privileges of the merchants and sent an unfavourable report to Rome on the insolence and malice of the Greeks. When Herod returned to Jerusalem with this good news, and celebrated the occasion by remitting a quarter of the year's taxes, the leading Jews wished him all manner of happiness; and for once meant it.

During his absence Aristobulus and Alexander had become more resentful of him than ever. They had spoken openly of going to Rome and charging him before the Emperor with having brought false witnesses to destroy their innocent mother, and mentioned Archelaus of Cappadocia as the man who would intervene and secure justice for them. Their indiscretions were so notorious that Herod could not be easily reproached for his next action, that of restoring his eldest son Antipater to favour, as a warning to them that if they did not behave themselves better they might find themselves disinherited. Antipater had hitherto been forbidden to visit Jerusalem except for the festivals which every Jew who lived within a week's travel from the City was expected to attend. Now his arrival at the Palace excited the bitterest anger in the two princes, who continually insulted and abused him; but he bore their insults with good-humour and by assuming indifference earned Herod's public approval for his forbearance. Antipater was a grown man, of settled habits and unimpeachable character, but, since he had been educated in the Jewish colony of Alexandria, his Greek was not the purest Attic and his Latin was barbarous. When one day Alexander taunted him at a banquet for his provincialism and ignorance of the ways of the world, Herod good-humouredly undertook to repair these failings: he would send Antipater off at once to complete his education at Rome. Perhaps, when he returned, Alexander would think more highly of him.

Antipater was sent to Rome under the protection of Agrippa, and there he made as favourable an impression on the Imperial family as his two brothers had made an unfavourable one. Since Herod's father had been granted the Roman citizenship, Antipater was a citizen of the third generation, and Augustus gave him command of a regiment of allied cavalry. This appointment was no sinecure and Antipater soon distinguished himself as an energetic and capable officer. When news of his success reached Jerusalem, jealousy provoked Alexander to a passionate outburst of anger in the presence of his mother-in-law Salome, who repeated his words to Herod. Herod sternly cautioned Alexander, declaring that he was thoroughly displeased with his way of life and that of Aristobulus, that he had shown great forbearance towards them on account of their maternal ancestors, but that unless he observed an immediate improvement in both he would be forced to alter his Will in favour of their eldest brother.

Thereupon Alexander bought poison, intending, it is supposed, to destroy Herod before he had time to alter his Will, though this is not certain. Watchful spies seized the poison, and Herod immediately brought both sons to Rome, with witnesses, to accuse them before Augustus of a plot against his life.

The case against the princes looked black, and Augustus, who was under a long-standing obligation to Herod for his loyal maintenance of peace in the Near East, might well have condemned them to death, had not his sister Octavia, Mark Antony's widow, who had befriended them during their stay in Rome, pleaded for their lives; and had not certain influential senators, to whom Archelaus of Cappadocia had written letters, supported her plea.

Augustus decided that the evidence was not conclusive. He summed up: "Poisoners work in secret. They do not, my dear Herod, advertise their intentions beforehand as your sons are said to have done. Alexander and Aristobulus have in my opinion behaved like naughty children, not like mature criminals. They are jealous of the honours that their elder brother has earned by his prudence and modesty. And, by the by, it is only fair now to let them know that he has joined with my dear sister Octavia in a plea for clemency. He is their true friend, as an elder brother should be, and I trust that their unworthy jealousy of him will give place to gratitude and admiration. I cannot find it in my heart to condemn them, having suffered so many domestic misfortunes myself, and having seen so many vicious young men repent and reform in later life."

When the princes had recovered from their fright they were galled to think that their humiliation had been witnessed by Antipater, and exasperated by Antipater's congratulations on their acquittal. The truth was that he had too generous a heart to wish for the throne at the expense of his brothers' lives; but they judged him by their own standards of conduct to be a hypocrite and decided that his plea for clemency had been made solely to clear himself of the suspicion of having been concerned in their deaths.

They all sailed back to Judaea, where Herod called the leading Jews together at his Palace and informed them of what had happened. To the embarrassment of Antipater, who was present, he then said: "The Emperor has graciously permitted me to appoint my successor. I should dearly have loved to name Alexander and Aristobulus, my sons by the ill-fated Mariamne, as co-heirs in my dominions, for they are of the royal Maccabee blood, descendants of the glorious heroes who won for Israel the freedom which by the Lord's grace I have been able to preserve for you and your children through years of the greatest danger. Alas, they have not yet proved worthy to rule in Israel, and were my soul to be required of me to-night, with my former Will still remaining in force, I should die miserably, expecting that all my work would be undone within a few months. These princes do not yet understand the necessity of obeying the Law faithfully, and what is reprehensible in a private person is fifty times more so in a king to whom a vast multitude looks for guidance. I have decided to appoint my generous and pious son Antipater to succeed me, with the succession, however, to revert to Alexander and Aristobulus, jointly, after his death, though he may have sons surviving, if in your opinion they are then worthy to rule. If any of you, however, has cause to complain of this decision, I hope that he will speak up boldly at once before I record and seal it in a new Will."

No one dared to complain. Unquestionably Antipater was by far the most suitable man of the three to inherit the throne, and was moreover Herod's eldest son.

Antipater rose and briefly thanked his father for the good opinion he had of him, which he would try never to forfeit; but hoped, he said, that no new king would be crowned at Jerusalem for very many years to come. He ended: "And should it happen, Father, that my brothers please you better by their behaviour before long—and I am convinced that they are nobler men at heart than their rash tongues acknowledge them to be—I would not take it ill if you then decided them to be, after all, worthy of the throne of their maternal ancestors. On the contrary, I would be happy in their happiness, for we are all sons of one father and are bound together by natural obligations of love. I have only one modest request to make of you, for which nobody here can dare to blame me since I am commanded by our God to honour my mother as well as my father. It is this, that you will restore my mother Doris to your favour, seeing that you put her away for no fault of hers when you married Mariamne. She has remained faithful to you these many years, separated from your protection and care, without a word of complaint."

Herod cheerfully granted this request, restoring Doris to her former rights by an edict which he signed on the spot.

Alexander and Aristobulus presently found an unexpected ally in their Aunt Salome, who had fallen in love with an Arabian petty king named Sylleus but had been forbidden by Herod to marry him unless he consented to be circumcised. Sylleus explained that if he were circumcised his people would stone him to death, and therefore begged to be excused the rite, but Herod could not give his sister to an uncircumcised infidel without weakening his position with the Jews; he preferred to risk the enmity of both Salome and Sylleus. Salome was mad with rage. The intricacies of the subsequent Palace plots and counter-plots, in which most of Herod's wives became involved, are hardly worth unravelling, but at last she succeeded in stirring up trouble for Herod at Rome with the help of her lover Sylleus and of the influential Ionian Greeks whom Herod had offended in the matter of the Jewish merchants.

Now, Herod had been provoked into sending a small punitive expedition into Arabia, where Sylleus, who owed him a great deal of money, was harbouring robber bands and assisting them, with arms and remounts, to raid Herod's frontier villages. The expedition was successful; the robbers were caught and the debt recovered. About twenty-five Arabians were killed. Sylleus fled to Rome and complained to Augustus that Herod was seeking to dominate all Arabia, which he had invaded at the head of an enormous army. "He has already destroyed two thousand five hundred of our principal citizens," Sylleus lamented, "and carried off untold wealth."

Augustus was somehow persuaded to believe this nonsense and wrote sharply to Herod: "You must now regard yourself as my subject, no longer my friend." For no petty king was allowed to wage an offensive war without Imperial permission. The contents of the letter became known and it was generally considered that Herod's throne was tottering. With Salome's help, Alexander and Aristobulus then bribed two of his bodyguard to murder him while he was hunting in the desert, but in such a way that it would seem to be an accident. They also secured a verbal promise from the leaders of the Sadducee party to assist their claims to the throne should Herod die suddenly, and arranged with the commander of the fortress of Alexandrium to give them temporary refuge as soon as the accident should be reported. But Herod was informed of the plot in good time by the repentant Salome, who suddenly realized that she had behaved rashly and that Sylleus had no real love for her. She assured Herod that she had been acting in his interests all the time, by tempting his enemies to show their hand prematurely, and that if he went to Rome he would have no difficulty in regaining the Emperor's confidence: she knew, she said, that he had been careful to obtain the consent of the nearest Imperial authorities before sending his men against Sylleus.

Herod sailed to Rome at once and soon made Augustus see reason. Augustus apologized handsomely for having doubted him, and ordered Sylleus to be put on trial for his life on the charges of disturbing the peace, plotting the death of Herod, and perjury. Herod's lawyers pleaded for a postponement of the trial until Sylleus had been sent under escort to Antioch, headquarters of Saturninus the Governor-General of Syria who would decide whether or not the money seized in Arabia was a full and equitable settlement of the debt owed to Herod. The postponement was granted, and Sylleus was sent to Antioch at once.

Herod then reported the new plot against his life by Alexander and Aristobulus, whom he accused of having engineered the whole Arabian conspiracy. Augustus readily gave him permission to put them to death as parricides.

Presently Cleopas visited Joachim again at Cocheba. He found him in the harvest-field, supervising the carting of the sheaves. "I have come here at your invitation, brother Joachim," said Cleopas.

"You are welcome; but I sent you no invitation."

"You invited me to come to your house again when That Man's two sons were dead. They were strangled three days ago at Samaria. The game is played. Nicolaus of Damascus was their accuser, and Antipater was called to give evidence in the matter of the two murderous guards, whose confessions he had secured. Sing me your prophecy!"

"This is bad news."

"They were evil men, and news of their death is good news."

"It is bad news, I say, for last night in my dream I saw the lamps of Zabidus lighted again and heard his idolatrous spells chanted within the very Courts of the Temple. I saw Sacrilege, Blasphemy and Idolatry, three loathsome hags, at a merry-making in the blessed

Sanctuary, so that the whole congregation of Israel was defiled—may the Lord God defend his servant Israel from all those that seek to do him harm."

"You foresaw the deaths of Alexander and Aristobulus and the succession of Antipater. What do you foresee now?"

"Answer me this one question and you shall have your reply—and it is no grand baffling riddle, such as those that Solomon and Hiram of Tyre exchanged in ancient times, but a simple question. Why has Herod shown such great kindness to the people of Rhodes, rebuilding the temple of Apollo, their abominable Sun-god; and to the people of Cos, another place sacred of Apollo's; and to the Phoenicians of Beyrout and Tyre and Sidon; and to the Spartans and Lycians and Samians and Mysians, all of whom worship the same abomination under one name or another? Why did he, by great presents to the Elians, persuade them to make him Perpetual President of the Olympic Games?"

"I cannot explain why these things have been done," said Cleopas. "I can only condemn. It is written: 'Thou shalt have no other Gods but me.'"

CHAPTER FIVE

THE HEIRESS OF MICHAL

KING HEROD'S first choice of a High Priest after the destruction of his predecessor, King Antigonus the Maccabee, had been an obscure Babylonian Jew of the House of Zadok, named Ananel. He soon deposed him in favour of Mariamne's brother, the Maccabean heir, who was only seventeen years old; but the ill-timed enthusiasm of the mob when the boy officiated at the Feast of Tabernacles was a warrant for his execution. He was drowned one evening in the public Bath at Jericho, after a merry ducking match between two teams of Herod's courtiers in which he had incautiously joined. Ananel was restored to the High Priesthood, but not for long. The office had changed hands several times more before Simon son of Boethus was appointed, when Herod considered it to be in safe hands at last.

Simon was an Alexandrian Jew and, though a Levite, not of High-Priestly family: a small, shrewd, diffident man, the soundest scholar in Alexandria, idealistic, upright and apparently without prejudice in religious matters. Herod had employed him to check the genealogy of a certain candidate for the priesthood whose family had been settled in Armenia for some generations; and Simon in his adverse report had frankly revealed the flaws in the pedigrees of several members of the Sanhedrin who happened to be related to the man. Among them were one or two active critics of Herod's own pedigree, which Simon obligingly undertook to prove more illustrious by far than he had himself supposed. Herod decided that Simon was wasted at Alexandria. He pretended to be so passionately in love with Simon's daughter that he could not live without her; yet how could he decently marry the girl—he asked his brother Pheroras—except by raising her father to a position of such dignity that she would not be despised by his other wives? He deposed Jeshua the Zadokite, who was then High Priest, and appointed Simon in his place. Simon's daughter happened to be sufficiently good-looking for the world to believe that he owed his office to her royal marriage, rather than the other way about.

Simon, bound to Herod by the strongest ties of gratitude, for Herod treated him with respect and generosity, became his faithful servant. His family, the Cantheres, were named after the scarab-beetle, the Egyptian emblem of immortality, and were Pharisees of a sort, but had become so soaked in Greek philosophy that they regarded the original Hebrew Scriptures as the quaint relics of a barbarous age. They kept the Law scrupulously, but only because they wished to remind the unilluminated mass of the people that "the fear of the Lord is the beginning of wisdom"—by which they meant that conformity even in a barbarous religion is preferable to atheistic anarchy or the clash of competitive cults. They privately regretted the conservative Jewish view of Jehovah as a solitary who would have no dealings with any other gods and whose people were unique —a view that excited scorn or jealousy in foreigners according as the national fortunes declined or prospered.

To the Cantheres, Jehovah was merely an anomalous local variant of Olympian Zeus, and they heartily wished that the differences which distinguished him from Zeus, and from the corresponding gods of Rome, Egypt, Syria, Persia and India, could be smoothed out for the sake of international peace. Their own conception of the Deity was so grandiose and abstract that Jehovah seemed a mere tribal demon by comparison. The Jews, they held, must somehow come to terms with the Greeks who were their neighbours. Ah, if only the Greeks were not so childish, laughter-loving and irreverent even when they had arrived at mature age, and if only the Jews were not so grave and old-mannish and devout even while they were still children, how happy everyone would be! Young people should be allowed to enjoy life to the full and think of gods and goddesses, in the popular way, as tall, shining-faced men and women gifted with supernatural powers, though of gross human passions, who plagued the race of men and one another by their headstrong fancies. As they grew to maturity, they should gradually be initiated into the moral and historical meaning of the ancient myths, until they knew at last, in their old age, that gods and goddesses were merely figures of speech, and that God was what transcended physical nature—immortal wisdom, the answer to all questions that could ever be asked.

They followed Hillel, one of the two joint-Presidents of the High Court and the most revered theologian of the day, in treating the Scriptures as oracular in their phrasing: with hardly any text meaning precisely what it seemed to mean. For example, Hillel generously laid down that the old law "an eye for an eye and a tooth for a tooth" did not mean what it means in barbarous codes—that if a man blinds his neighbour even accidentally he must himself be blinded; if he knocks out his neighbour's teeth he must suffer the same inconvenience. Hillel said: "The loss of one man's eye or tooth is not repaired by the loss of another man's. The Lord in his wisdom ordained, rather, that the compensation in money or goods or land, paid to the injured man, should be equivalent to the loss suffered."

Simon was no typical member of his family. He agreed with them that, in theory, the works of Homer and Hesiod, regarded as inspired religious texts, would serve as well as those of Moses; for a true philosopher can hang his grey cloak on a peg of any timber. But he also held that in practice the Jewish Scriptures, the prophetic books especially, had one overwhelming advantage: he found them alive with a faith in the future, a steady belief in the perfectibility of mankind. Of what other national literature could the same be said? And even the solitariness of Jehovah was commendable: he could be regarded as a type of the original Singleness of Truth everywhere confused by contradictory local truths. Again, the Jews were indeed unique in one sense: they were the only people in the world who carried the thought of God continually in their hearts.

Herod was neither philosopher nor poet. He made fun of Simon's divided devotion to Plato and Ezekiel the prophet. He put his faith in the crude exercise of power—in power won by the capture of a national oracle, power then extended by compelling neighbouring nations to serve the god whom, as king, he had made the instrument of his own greatness; but he also secretly held the mystical belief that by a splendid propitiation of Jehovah he would one day renew his youth and achieve a sort of immortality. He was not a man to shrink from any deed, however desperate or unnatural, that would make his name as glorious as those of Hercules, Osiris, Alexànder and other mortal rulers who had become gods by the greatness of their feats.

Simon did not know the full extent of Herod's ambitions but was aware at times of a presumptuous spirit in him, which, when he allowed his mind to dwell on it, troubled him as grossly irreligious; however, he was never troubled to the extent of offering his resignation. What was the need? Did Herod perhaps fancy himself as the promised Messiah? But the military strength of the Roman Empire was sufficient guarantee against his undertaking any rash war of religious conquest; and though he might overbear the Temple lawyers in many cases where the Law admitted of more than one interpretation, there was no question of his defying the Law as a whole. And however oppressive he might feel the constriction of his royal spirit, he must remain all his days a humble servant of the many times conquered Jehovah; and at the same time acknowledge himself a mere petty king, a client of the Roman Empire; and must eventually die like any other man. Surely Herod did not consider that his virtues entitled him to be caught up alive into Heaven like an Enoch or an Elijah? Yes, between the power of the Roman legions and the authority of the Mosaic Law, the field for the exercise of Herod's ambitions was a narrow one.

With Antipater, as soon as he was preferred to Mariamne's sons, Simon formed a close friendship. Antipater had studied at Alexandria under a relative of Simon's. He took the Law more literally than the Cantheres, and though prepared to accept Hillel's liberal interpretations of its harsher articles, was averse to Greek philosophy, in which he saw a danger to the authority of the Scriptures. He had been married by his father to the daughter of King Antigonus, but she was now dead. There were two children by the marriage, a boy and a girl. The boy, Antipater the Younger, was being educated in Egypt with the Cantheres family; he was quiet and studious. The girl, Cypros, was betrothed to the son of Aristobulus who afterwards became famous as King Herod Agrippa, but was still a child. Antipater himself was betrothed to Aristobulus's infant daughter, but had no wife. He felt lonely without one. His father hinted that he had some other match in view for him and that meanwhile he should amuse himself with mistresses; but to keep a mistress went against Antipater's conscience. He took the Pharisaic view that to lie with a woman except with the intention of progeny was displeasing to the Lord, as was exemplified in the history of Onan. Yet he did not wish to beget children on a Jewess or an Edomite woman, for as bastards they would be cut off from the congregation of Israel; and the Law forbade him any sexual traffic with Greek or Phoenician women or other foreigners.

One early spring morning, a few months before his brothers' execution, Antipater visited Simon in his luxurious Temple apartments overlooking the Court of Israel.

"You are troubled, Prince," said Simon, as soon as they were alone. "You seldom seem to be untroubled nowadays. Your frown grieves me."

Antipater barely wetted his lips with the wine which Simon offered him. He took up a handful of milky new almonds and began absent-mindedly breaking them into pieces which he arranged on the broad edge of a golden salver in geometrical patterns. "Yes, Simon, I am troubled," he said with a sigh. "For a man to be King in Israel, or the King's son and deputy, is a poor thing when all his subjects despise him as an upstart. The orders which I give in my father's name are obeyed, but without alacrity except by the baser sort of people, and by the governing classes with studied surliness. Just now, as I crossed the Court, the ironical salutations with which I was greeted by the grandees were like whips across my face. I knew what they were thinking: 'What title has his father to the throne except that granted him by our enemies, the heathen Romans? And he himself is not even half Maccabee. He is the son of a heathenish Edomite woman, a grandniece of the accursed Zabidus.' If I am stern with them, they hate me as an oppressor; if indulgent, they despise me as a weakling. I know in my bones and blood that I am of their own race, and Jerusalem to me is home and the most wonderful city in the world. What I have come to ask you is this: how can I ever hope to earn the love and confidence of my people?"

Simon might have been expecting the question, so readily came his answer: "I will tell you, Prince. Royalty lies in a consciousness of royalty, as liberty lies in a consciousness of liberty. Know yourself royal, and royalty blazes golden from your forehead. Believe yourself an upstart, and you defeat yourself with that leaden belief."

"Cold comfort," said Antipater. "I cannot alter my condition by wishing that my mother at least had been a Hasmonean Maccabee."

52

Simon laughed dryly. "Prince, who are these royal Maccabees? Their ancestors were village joiners of Modin not more than a hundred and fifty years ago; Maccabee, as you know, means 'mallet' and was the nickname of Judas, son of Matathias, who led the rebellion. His brothers were all similarly nicknamed by their father after tools in his joiner's chest—for example, Eleazer was called 'Avaran', the awl. The Maccabee pedigree, if one searches back two or three generations beyond Matathias the joiner, is as full of holes as a sieve. It is not even established that he was a Levite. Certainly he was not of the House of Aaron."

"Nevertheless," said Antipater, "by their courage and virtue the Maccabees advanced themselves to royal dignity."

"Your father has done the same."

"Yet the Temple grandees sneeringly call him 'Herod of Ascalon', and 'Edomite Slave', rejecting him as a foreigner and usurper. 'The Maccabees,' they say, 'freed us from a foreign yoke. The man of Ascalon has fastened another yoke securely across our shoulders.' "

"Has your father never told you, Prince, that you are a thousand times better born than any Maccabee? That you stand in a direct line of succession from Caleb son of Jephunneh, who conquered Hebron in the days of Joshua?"

"He has hinted that we are Calebites, but I took this for one of his fancies. When he has dined well his mind teems with strange fancies."

"It is the truth, and he had it from me. Your great-grandfather's grandfather was a Calebite of Bethlehem who took refuge at Ascalon; as a child your great-grandfather was stolen from Ascalon by the Edomites, who honoured him as their prince."

"You did not tell my father this merely to please him?"

"Prince, I would even rather displease the King than forfeit my reputation as a scholar among my fellow-scholars."

"I did not accuse you of lying. I wondered whether you were perhaps retailing an old legend without troubling to test it historically."

"That is not my habit."

"Forgive me!"

"I forgive you. But, before you can follow my argument, you must disabuse your mind of the notion that your ancestor Caleb was a Judaean—a great-grandson of Judah himself through the bastard Pharez. Caleb was a Kenite of Hebron, and Hebron in ancient times was the hearthstone of Edom. The genealogical table that is given in the Book of Chronicles, the second chapter, is an interpolation of recent times. The more reliable myth, which we have

53

preserved in Egypt, is that Hur son of Caleb, who was the son of Hezron the Kenizzite, married Miriam the sister of Aaron, though she was 'neither fair nor healthy' and died in the desert soon afterwards; Hur assisted Moses in the Battle of Rephidim. Caleb was one of the ten champions sent to spy out Canaan before Joshua's invasion; passing through Hebron, then occupied by the Anakin, he visited Machpelah, the tomb of his ancestor Abraham, where he received encouragement from the priestess who interpreted the utterances of Abraham's oracular jawbone. When the invasion began he conquered Hebron, drove out the Giants and married Azubah Jerioth, 'the deserted woman of the tent-curtains'. Later he also married Ephrath of Bethlehem."

"How do you read this account?" asked Antipater.

"I read it as meaning that the Calebites were Kenites of Edom—the Kenizzites are a branch of the Kenites—who originally possessed Hebron but when driven out by an invading tribe of tall Northerners took refuge with the Midianites of Hezron, at the border of the Sinai desert, who like themselves worshipped the Goddess Miriam. Miriam, also known as Rahab, was the Goddess of the Sea, whose sign is the scarlet thread. On the arrival of the Children of Israel from Egypt under Moses, the Calebites became their allies and later joined with them in the invasion of Canaan; but the Midianites would not share in the adventure and the alliance with them was dissolved. After reconnoitring the ground, the Calebites reconquered Hebron, and once more intermarried with the priestesses of Abraham's oracle, whom the Giants deserted in their wild flight. Eventually they extended their rule a few miles northward to Ephrath, which is the region about Bethlehem. I hardly think that you will dispute the common sense of this explanation?"

Antipater looked troubled.

Simon continued: "But just as the Calebites of Ephrath were later swallowed up by their allies the Benjamites, so were those of Hebron by their allies the Judaeans; and a century or two after Hebron had been incorporated in the Jewish Kingdom by David the Calebite—for David traced his descent from Hur—the tribal genealogy was adjusted to make Caleb a descendant of Judah, and by a further interpolation Kenaz, the eponymous ancestor of the Kenizzites, was absurdly reckoned a son of Caleb. The Calebites, however, still obstinately regarded themselves as Kenizzites, and Children of Edom. The unfavourable Judaic view of this tribe's history is expressed by the Chronicler in the names of the children begotten by Caleb on Azubah Jerioth: namely, 'Upright', 'Backsliding' and 'Destruction'. It is clear that they resisted all attempts to make them conform with changes in the Jewish faith, and being still a tented people they avoided the Babylonian Captivity by escaping in a body to Edom, whence they soon afterwards returned with an armed following of Edomites. Moreover, one of their clans, that of Salma, went on to reoccupy Ephrath. The Salma chieftain married the priestess of Bethlehem, and you, Prince, are lineally descended in the elder line from this chieftain."

Antipater took another handful of almonds and began arranging them in five-pointed stars. He said slowly: "I cannot disprove your argument, but I am loth indeed to think that there are interpolations in the Scriptures."

"Is it not better to believe that interpolations have crept in than to accept an historical untruth? Well, I have told the King this much and proved his pedigree by research at Ascalon, Dora, Hebron and Bethlehem, and confirmed my findings with genealogical material submitted to me by my colleagues at Babylon, Petra and Damascus; but I cannot persuade the Pharisee Doctors to accept it, their prejudices against Herod being so strong. Yet there is another point of great historical importance which I have never raised with him, and which I do not propose to raise."

"You mean that you will, however, raise it with me?"

"Only under a pledge of secrecy: you must not divulge the information to a soul while your father lives."

"You whet my curiosity. But why are you willing to tell me what you conceal from my father?"

"Because your father seems perfectly content with his title to the throne, whereas if he knew what I know he might become restless and be tempted into dangerous action."

"I doubt whether I should listen to you. Am I less likely to ruin myself by this knowledge than he?"

"As you will. But you can never have ease in your mind until you acquire this knowledge, which concerns your title to the throne."

Antipater flushed: "Simon," he said, "as my father's friend you have no right to put me into this dilemma. I do not wish to be told State secrets which I must conceal from my father." He took his leave abruptly.

Simon returned to the citron-wood table and studied the dish decorated with the interlaced triangles and stars of Antipater's almonds. He hurriedly disarranged them with his hands lest one of his servants should mistake them for a magical spell. "Alas, if he should go to the King and report what I have said!" he muttered.

"But, please God, he will not. The hook is in his lip, of that I am sure. Please God, my line will hold!"

Two days later Antipater returned, fretful and pale. "I have come to take the oath of secrecy of which you spoke, Simon. Your words have preyed on my mind and prevented me from sleeping."

Simon said: "Prince, I was greatly at fault; I should have restrained the impulse to speak. No, I require no oath. Your bare word is sufficient pledge."

Then he confided to Antipater a most unorthodox historical theory: that in Israel every ancient chieftain or king had ruled by woman-right: namely by marriage with the hereditary owner of the soil. Adam by marriage with Eve; Abraham by marriage with Sarah, Hagar and Keturah; Isaac by marriage with Rebeccah; Jacob by marriage with Leah, Rachel, Bilhah and Zilpah; Joseph by marriage with Asenath; Caleb by marriage with Ephrath and Azubah; Hur by marriage with Miriam; David by marriage with Abigail of Carmel and Michal of Hebron; and every subsequent king of the line of David by marriage with a matrilineal descendant of Michal. He also told Antipater that at the extinction of the monarchy the female line of Michal was engrossed by the House of Eli, the senior line of priests descended from Aaron, who were on that account styled the Heirs of David, or the Royal Heirs.

He ended solemnly: "Prince, what I have not told your father Herod is this, that no king has a true title to rule in Israel unless he is not only a Calebite but also married to the Heiress of Michal; and that the heiress inherits by ultimogeniture and not by primogeniture —that is to say, she is always the youngest daughter of the line, not the eldest."

Antipater was incredulous at first. He objected: "There is no word about this theory either in the Scriptures or the Commentary."

"Except for those who can read between the lines."

"It seems a strange and unlikely notion to me."

"You are aware that in Egypt, for example, the Pharaoh always marries his sister."

"Yes; but I have never troubled to ask why."

"That is because the ownership of the land properly goes from mother to daughter. It was the same once in Crete and Cyprus and Greece. It was the same at Rome under the Kings."

"I know nothing of Crete or Cyprus or ancient Greece, but it was certainly not so at Rome, according to the school histories."

"The object of all school histories everywhere is to enhance the glory of existing institutions and efface the memory of superseded ones. Well, I will show you what I mean. Do you remember the story of the expulsion of the Tarquin dynasty and the inauguration of the Roman Republic by Lucius Brutus? Probably you were asked to compose a set speech on the subject for your tutor while you were studying Latin oratory?"

"Yes, every student is given the task. Let me see! Tarquin the First was succeeded, was he not, by a certain Tullius who had married one of his two daughters, although Tarquin had a grown son, Tarquin the Proud . . ."

"Well, why did Tarquin the Proud not immediately succeed Tarquin the First? Why had no single early King of Rome ever succeeded his father? Simply because the title was carried through the female, not the male, line. The king was the man who married his predecessor's younger daughter; and since marriage with a sister, though permitted in Egypt, was considered incestuous at Rome, the king's son customarily married a foreign princess and said goodbye to his native land. The case of Tarquin the Proud was unusual. He eventually succeeded to the throne in virtue of his marriage to Tullius's daughter Tullia."

"The historians say that Tarquin the Proud regarded Tullius as an usurper."

"That is natural. And that Tarquin the Proud killed Tullius with Tullia's assistance was nothing remarkable either. On the contrary, every king of this antique sort expected to be killed by his son-in-law when his term of office expired. But by an unlucky accident Tullia was defiled by her father's blood and obliged to retire into private life. Thus Tarquin lost his title to the throne, which could only be renewed by marriage with the next heiress-at-law, namely Lucretia, the wife of his cousin Collatinus, who was descended from a sister of King Numa's wife. It was not Lucretia's beauty but her title that attracted Tarquin; except for his sister Tarquinia, who was the mother of Lucius Brutus and who was now past child-bearing, and Tullia, who was defiled, Lucretia was the only surviving heiress of the ancient royal House of Carmenta. Tarquin carried Lucretia off and forced her to become his wife; but she committed suicide to spite him. So both Collatinus and Tarquin were now without a title to the throne and the monarchy became extinct, for Tarquin had no daughters, and neither Brutus nor Collatinus had sisters. Tarquin was then driven out by his enraged people, and Brutus and Collatinus became co-rulers of Rome—Brutus as the son of Tarquinia, and Collatinus as the son of Egeria, a descendant of King Numa's sister of the same name. But they could not call themselves Kings because they lacked the necessary marriage title; instead, they called themselves Consuls, or Consultants. Lucretia had killed more than a woman when she committed suicide: she had killed Carmenta."

"Carmenta?"

"An Arcadian goddess whom King Evander had brought to Italy in the generation before the Trojan War. She had migrated to Arcadia from Byblos in Phoenicia. By 'goddess' I mean, of course, a line of priestesses in whom a divinity is held to be incarnate, as Miriam (or Rahab) is incarnate in the Michal line."

"I understand the theory," said Antipater. "But before I examine its relevance to Jewish history I must protest that according to the First Book of Chronicles the House of Eli has no claim to be regarded as the senior line of Aaron's family. And does it not lie under a divine curse since Eli's day?"

"That curse is an unhistorical interpolation of the time of King Josiah, who reigned some six centuries ago. Eli's son Abiathar, King David's faithful High Priest, remained loyal after the King's death to Adonijah the heir to the throne, whom Solomon supplanted with the help of his chaplain Zadok. With Solomon's help Zadok similarly supplanted Abiathar, who was forced into retirement, and the Zadokites have regarded themselves as the only legitimate High Priests ever since."

"But surely it was Zadok who was descended from Eleazer the elder son of Aaron, and Abiathar who was descended from Eleazer's younger brother Ithamar? I was reading the First Book of Chronicles only yesterday."

"No, Prince, that is another interpolation of the same date. In the First Book of Samuel it is stated that Eli, Abiathar's ancestor, was of the original priestly House; and it is also stated in the Second Book of Kings that Zadok was not of this House. In other words, Zadok, like Solomon, was a usurper and his descendants tampered with the genealogies. A plausible reason had to be found for Abiathar's supersession in the High Priesthood. It was given in the form of a fable about some man of God or other who prophesied that the High Priesthood would leave the House of Eli as a punishment for Eli's indulgence of his wicked sons, and that the House would be reduced to beggary. But the Zadokites were clumsy. They should have stuck to a single story: either that Zadok was of the elder line and Abiathar of the younger, or else that Abiathar was of the elder line but lost his ancient privileges because the curse of Eli happened to fall on him. They cannot have it both ways: that Abiathar was of the younger line and also that he lost the ancient privileges which

58

he enjoyed as a member of the elder line. As I say, the texts were tampered with by King Josiah, nearly four hundred years after the time of King Solomon, when with the help of the Zadokites he expelled the descendants of Abiathar from the priesthood altogether."

"Loth as I am to believe that there are unhistorical interpolations in the Scriptures, I am still more loth to believe that it contains forgeries."

"Is it not better to believe even this than to weaken your intellect by accepting logical absurdities?"

Antipater was not easily convinced. "You may be right about the law of succession in Rome and other western cities and islands, but you have yet to prove to me from the Scriptures that matrilineal descent was of any regard even as early as the time of Abraham, let alone that of Saul and David."

"I can do so easily," said Simon. "You will find the relevant text in the twelfth chapter of Genesis: Abraham when he visited Egypt gave his wife Sarah in marriage to the Pharaoh, whom I take, however, to be the Pelasgian King of Pharos; whom the Greeks call Proteus. But Sarah, though the daughter of Abraham's father Terah, did not rank as Abraham's sister because she was the daughter of a different mother. In other words, descent in Abraham's time was traced in Aegean style through the mother, not the father; and women were polyandrous. Isaac's wife Rebeccah similarly married a King of Gerar in Isaac's lifetime. And since you doubt what I have told you about the swallowing up of Caleb by Judah, you will find the event obscurely recorded in the account of Judah's rape of his daughter-in-law Tamar after the death of his wicked son Er (which means the Calebites); for Tamar, the palm-tree, is another title of the ancient Goddess of Hebron. The identification of Tamar with Rahab is made in the same chapter of Genesis, the thirty-fourth, where she plays the harlot, bears twins to Judah and ties the scarlet thread of Rahab about the wrist of Zarah, who is supplanted by his brother Pharez—the bastard whom the Judahites have unkindly made Caleb's great-grandfather, as if to prove the Calebites dishonourable upstarts. But Zarah is an Edomite, ancestor of a clan renowned for their wisdom; therefore his twin Pharez is also of Edom. Moreover, that David ruled over Israel in virtue of his marriage with the heiresses of the twelve tribes—Levi excepted—is distinctly stated in the story of Barzillai. The northern tribes complained that, instead of making a royal progress from one tribal shrine to another, he favoured the tribe of Judah above all others and lingered at Jerusalem. His defiant answer was to refuse marital intercourse to the ten northern heiresses, reserving his favours for the heiress of Judah, presumably Eglah, the youngest daughter of Michal."

Antipater sighed. After a pause he said: "Well, let me be sure that I have understood you clearly. My father is, you say, descended from Caleb the Kenite, a sort of Edomite, whose sons were reckoned to Judah and one of whom, Salma, eventually became the lord of Bethlehem. After some centuries the head of this House was expelled from Bethlehem by the Maccabees, presumably because he was an idolator, and fled to Ascalon, where he became a priest of the god Hercules-Melkarth. The Edomites raided Ascalon and carried off his grandson, my great-grandfather, because of his Calebite blood, and made him their prince. To this House of Salma, since David's royal line became extinct, reverts the title to the throne of Israel. You have told my father so much, but not that his title can be traditionally perfected only by marriage to the heiress of the still extant Michal line, who is the daughter of a Levite of the House of Eli."

Simon nodded slowly, without a word.

"But why do you not tell my father about the Michal heiress?"

"For several reasons. The first, because the House of Eli hate your father, and would never tolerate the marriage. The second, because they would refuse their consent on the ground of his being a foreigner; which would incense him to such a degree that lopped heads would soon go bowling down the steep streets of this city. The third, because if he succeeded in marrying the heiress in spite of all, your mother and my daughter, who are at present the King's two senior wives, would lose their ascendancy at Court. The fourth, because the King would insist on elevating the girl's father to the High Priesthood and I should be obliged to step down, which I should not enjoy. The fifth, because if an heir were born of the marriage, he would be preferred in the succession both to you and to my grandson, who I hope will one day become your junior colleague in the Kingdom. The sixth, because the King is happy in his ignorance. The seventh, because the girl has been committed by her father to my own tutelage, and to give her in marriage to the King, while knowing how much trouble must grow out of such a union, would go against my conscience."

"I understand your reasons for not wishing my father to marry the girl, but I cannot understand why you have confided in me. Do you wish me to marry her myself? Surely, if the House of Eli would not tolerate my father's marrying her, they would not tolerate my marrying her either."

"True, but in your case the marriage could be kept secret, whereas your father—"

"Such a marriage would be indecent: it would give me a truer title to the throne than my father."

"Only to the spiritual throne; the political sovereignty conferred on him by the Romans would remain his, and you would continue to be his junior colleague. Besides, he would not be aware of your title. Nobody would be aware of it except yourself and myself and one or two others who are perfectly to be trusted."

"This is absurd! And tell me, how would the title benefit me?"

"It would benefit you by a sense of royalty which would strengthen you and abash your enemies. They would be aware that they stood in the presence of their rightful King. They might even learn to love and honour your father for your sake."

"Who is this girl?"

"She is a Temple ward and therefore under my tutelage. Her mother is Hannah, wife of Joachim the Levite."

"This is a strange way of saying that Joachim is her father."

"He is her father according to the Law, but the girl was born under the old dispensation. If you do not understand me, read again the story of the rich Shulamite, or rather Shunemite, woman and her son; and of Hannah, mother of Samuel. She is, in a sense, a daughter of the Lord. In any case, it is her maternal ancestry that conveys the title: to mention Hannah's marriage to Joachim is, genealogically speaking, irrelevant."

"Tell me more of Hannah's daughter," Antipater said.

"She is young, beautiful, good-natured, high-spirited, truthful. She carries herself with royal dignity."

"Her name?"

"Miriam."

"Simon, what is your intention? How could I marry this girl secretly? Within two days the whole world would hear of it."

"I have considered the problem carefully. Let her pass as the wife of another until you can acknowledge her as your queen. Neither she nor anyone else need be injured by the ruse. Leave everything to me!"

"The notion of marrying a wife whom I dare not acknowledge displeases me."

"It will not be long before you can acknowledge her."

"Why do you say this?"

"Your father, I fear, has not long to live. This grievous news was recently given me in confidence by Machaon of Cos, his physician."

"My father sick?" The news surprised and shocked Antipater. "Can it really be so? His seventy years lie more lightly on him than fifty on most other men. Oh, the unfortunate man! May the Lord postpone his end for many years! Has Machaon told him the worst?"

"Machaon has wisely told him nothing. But there is a cancerous lump in the King's bowels which he recognizes as a certain messenger of death within the next two years at the most. The end will be very painful. It was in this knowledge that I dared speak to you about your marriage."

"If my father is to die so soon I prefer to postpone this marriage."

"The girl is already nubile. I cannot long delay her betrothal."

"You are forcing my hand."

"Not I, but Time. However, at present she is spinning flax for the Sacred Curtain, and I can keep her at the task for some months yet."

Antipater asked after a pause: "You believe that I can undertake this marriage with a clear conscience towards the Lord and my father?"

"I do. You are free to marry without your father's consent, as is proved in the classical case of Esau. Though Esau grieved his parents by a foreign marriage they could not forbid him to take what wives he pleased or force him to put them away. And no law compels you to make a detailed report to your father of all your domestic affairs."

"But to pass off one's bride as the wife of another!"

"Abraham—if you care to read the story literally—not only concealed his marriage with Sarah but allowed her to marry the Pharaoh of Egypt; Isaac not only concealed his marriage with Rebeccah but allowed her to marry Abimelech of Gerar. I do not propose that you should go as far in your deception as these patriarchs are said to have gone: the supposed husband will be denied sexual access to her, as Pharaoh and Abimelech, according to the story, were not."

"I scorn ruses and stratagems of whatever sort, and all who employ them."

"Come, Prince, that is too downright a declaration. It is to express contempt not only for Abraham and Isaac but for Jacob too, whose whole life was a network of ruses, and who did not hesitate to trick his old blind father in order to obtain the blessing destined for Esau. Yet Jacob became Israel, and you would be a hardy man if you dared to confess a scorn for Israel. After all, you are the King's eldest son. The succession to the throne is yours by birthright, according both to Jewish and Roman law, and your father has already bestowed his blessing on you and made you his colleague. Why be so squeamish? Esau vexed his father by a foreign marriage; but the marriage which I am counselling you to make is with a virgin of your own tribe, and it is the only marriage by which you can become the authentic King of Israel."

"Simon, your words are sober enough, but the suppressed vehemence of your tones does not escape me. Confess, you have some other motive for urging me to this dangerous course than a desire to see me happy?"

Simon did not reply at first. He took a sip of wine and twisted his fingers in his little beard.

"Simon, now your eyes are shining as I have never before seen them shine. Your hands are trembling as you play with your beard. Tell me honestly what is in your mind. You are a philosopher and conduct your life according to strict philosophic principles. You keep hope and joy on the curb like unruly stallions, but they are champing and rearing and the white froth flies from their mouths."

"Prince," said Simon at last in an uneven voice, "it is this. Jerusalem is at the meeting-place of continents, it is the fortress commanding the cross-roads through which all nations have marched and counter-marched since history began. Jerusalem lies midway between India and Spain, between the frozen White Sea of the North where the were-wolf Finns are found, and the insufferably hot deserts beyond Punt to the Southward, where the ape-men beat devilishly upon their hairy chests and East and West are confounded. Jerusalem is the centre of the known Universe; here we are centrally situated in Space. And what of Time? The Egyptians reckon the life of a nation at eight thousand years, and in two years' time, by our reckoning, Adam will have been born four thousand years ago."

"I have heard otherwise: I have heard that the fourth millennium ended a century and a half ago in the days of Judas the Maccabee."

"Judas misreckoned. We are at the meridian of Adam's day. The fourth millennium draws swiftly to a close, and the close of each millennium has always been marked by some great event. At the close of the first millennium Enoch the Perfect One, Keeper of Books, was caught up alive into Heaven. At the close of the second, the Lord swore his covenant with Abraham. At the close of the third, King Solomon with great magnificence celebrated the dedication of the First Temple, at which time the All-Merciful granted him a visible sign of favour. Ah, Prince, does not your heart beat

63

with pride and hope to think what the Lord in his bounty may hold in store for us at this four-thousandth year, this half-way house of destiny? Adam was true-born; Enoch, Keeper of Books, was without sin; Abraham obeyed the Lord with superb faith; Solomon, when asked by the Lord in a dream what gift he most desired, chose wisdom. All these men are counted as patriarchs of our nation, and are reckoned in a single genealogical line. What if this latest millennium should close with the appearance of a King who combines all the qualities of his predecessors: true-born like Adam, sinless like Enoch, faithful like Abraham, wise like Solomon?"

A puzzled smile played over Antipater's face. He said: "I never expected to hear you speak in this rapt millennial strain, Son of Boethus. And I do not know how to answer you, except by asking: 'What of Moses?' For Moses is not reckoned in the same line of descent with the other patriarchs, yet nobody can deny him equal dignity with them; and neither his birth nor his death nor any other event of his life coincides with the close of any of the millennia of which you speak. And what of the patriarch Noah, with whom a new age certainly began?"

Simon answered very gravely: "Spoken like a sage! Indeed, were it not for Noah and Moses you might well dismiss my argument as inconclusive; but their cases make it irresistible. The fact is, that the close of this fourth millennium coincides with a Phoenix year. As you know, the residue of hours of the solar year that exceed three hundred and sixty-five days add up every 1460 years to an entire year, which in Egypt is called the Phoenix year or Sothic Great Year: for then the Celestial Bird is consumed upon his palm-tree pyre at On-Heliopolis and from his ashes rises the new Phoenix. Moses worshipped the Almighty in Heliopolis, and when he removed from that city with his fellow-priests the Phoenix age ended which had begun with the patriarch Noah—with Noah who, like Enoch, was judged worthy to walk with the Lord. A new Phoenix age was then inaugurated on Sinai with the institution of the Mosaic Law; this age in turn is all but completed—the old Phoenix must die and a new Phoenix be born. Here, then, we stand at the crossroads of Space, but also at the cross-roads of Time: not only at the meridian of Adam's day but at the precise point where the Phoenix line intersects with the Millennary line. Is it any wonder that I should wish the eldest son of my King to undertake a fortunate marriage, a marriage which promises a shower of the greatest possible blessings for Israel and all mankind?"

"Nevertheless, I am an Edomite, and Esau sold his birthright to

Jacob for a bowl of red-lentil-porridge, and forfeited his blessing too."

"Esau was famished and would have died but for that meal. Jacob did evil in making Esau pay for the hospitality which was his guest-right. The blessing, too, was stolen by Jacob; and it is written that a thief must restore fourfold. That neither the blessing nor the birthright was permanently forfeited in the judgment of their father Isaac is made clear in the twenty-seventh chapter of Genesis where Isaac says:

Your brother came with subtlety and took away your blessing. Nevertheless, though you serve your brother at the first, the time will come when you shall have the dominion over him, and break his yoke from about your neck.

And Isaiah enlarges on this prophecy in the sixty-third chapter of his book, the Vision of the Messiah, when he writes: 'Who is this that comes from Edom with dyed garments from Bozrah, glorious in his apparel, travelling in the greatness of his strength?' Back comes the answer: 'It is I—I who speak in righteousness, mighty to save.' Isaiah asks again: 'Why are you red in your apparel, like one who tramples in the vine-vat?' The answer comes again: 'I trod the vine-vat alone'—that is to say, without my brother Jacob—'for the year of my redeemed has come.'"

"Who is the redeemed?"

"Edom is to be redeemed. The meaning is that the Edomites, not the Israelites, are the original people of Jehovah. When Jacob supplanted Esau, Jehovah adopted the Israelites as his children and showed them wonderful kindness; but they rebelled against.him. Now the Edomites call themselves to his remembrance and cry to him through the mouth of Isaiah: 'We are yours. You never were their God. They were not at first called by your name. They trod down your sanctuary.'"

"Then is the promised Messiah to be an Edomite?" cried Antipater in astonishment.

"How else can he be the Second Adam? For Edom and Adam are the same person, the Red Man of Hebron. Or how else can he be the Second David? But his mother is to be of the tribe of Levi, a daughter of Aaron. Thus since Caleb, the royal part of Edom, is now reckoned to Judah, it is foretold in the Testament of the Twelve Patriarchs that 'the Messiah shall be raised up from the Tribe of Levi as High Priest and from the Tribe of Judah as King: in person sacrosanct'."

65

His breast heaved for emotion and he began to declaim from the Testament of Levi:

> *Then shall the Lord God raise up a new priest*
> *To whom his very words revealed shall be:*
> *Judgement of righteousness to execute*
> *Upon this earth for multitudes of days.*
>
> *His star shall rise in Heaven like to a King,*
> *Lighting up knowledge as the Sun the day.*
> *He on this wide earth shall be magnified,*
> *And like the shining Sun darkness dispel.*
>
> *Peace universal shall attend his days,*
> *Heaven shall exult and all the earth be glad.*
> *Glory of the Most High shall speak for him,*
> *Wisdom and holiness on him shall rest.*
>
> *He shall present the Lord God's majesty*
> *Unto his sons in truth for evermore.*
> *None shall succeed him of the race of man.*
> *His priesthood shall instruct all men on earth*
> *And that enlightenment through grace begin,*
> *The end whereof shall be the end of sin.*

CHAPTER SIX

THE APPARITION

ANTIPATER was in the Court of Israel, praying. It was his custom to go across the valley to the Temple every day at dawn for his devotions. As he prayed, in Jewish fashion, on his knees he became suddenly aware from the confused noises behind him that some terrible event had occurred. He turned and saw grave elders hurrying up dressed in sackcloth, wailing aloud, with their heads sprinkled with ashes; they whispered their news to those already present, who

66

gaped with horror and began to rip the seams of their beautiful garments. Soon the wailing arose on all sides.

Antipater hurried to the nearest of his acquaintances, Reuben, Joachim's adversary, whom he found in earnest conversation with Zacharias the Zadokite. He asked: "Son of Abdiel, what is amiss? What disastrous blow has descended upon us?"

Reuben did not reply. He turned away and began to wail with the rest, calling loudly upon Jehovah to be avenged on his sacrilegious foes. Zacharias followed his example.

Antipater left them and went out into the Court of Women, where the same bad news was current. Everyone avoided his glance and he began to have the disagreeable sense that the wailing and the imprecations which accompanied it were in some degree aimed at himself.

"Should I mourn too?" he wondered. "No, not until I know what has happened."

In the Court of the Gentiles he found Carmi the Captain of the Temple, who had arrived with the Levite Guard to keep order. He spoke sharply: "Carmi, what is the meaning of this uproar? I can persuade nobody to answer me. I hear the words 'desecration' and 'abomination' shouted, but they mean nothing to me. These good people seem to be accusing me of participating in some act of sacrilege, and I resent it. My conscience is clear both towards the Lord and towards men. If I have offended unwittingly in anything, may the Lord pardon me!"

Carmi saluted with punctilio. It was seldom that this tall, lean priest, notorious as one of Herod's creatures, looked anxious, but he looked so now. "Majesty, a nonsensical rumour is running round the city that thieves have broken into the tombs of King David and King Solomon. Some of these shameless dogs even dare to accuse your royal father of having headed the party."

He spoke in a loud voice so that everyone present should hear him.

Antipater was shocked. "The Lord grant that the tombs remain unviolated!"

A shrivelled hag came hobbling up and caught hold of Antipater's sleeve. "Oho," she squeaked, "you are altogether innocent, are you? This is the first news you have had of it, is it not? Very well, let me tell you that last night a certain Edomite slave, the author of an unholy edict against house-breakers, led a pack of uncircumcised Greek dogs into the royal tombs. A line of mule-wagons was waiting at the entrance, and a thousand talents' weight of silver ingots was presently loaded into them and driven back to the Palace. What other treasures were taken off is not known, for they were stowed in sacks. It is said that among them were sixty shields of gold and seven bronze basins; but the silver ingots at least were seen and counted. Confess, what is your share in the loot to be, Son of the Slave?"

She was marched away under arrest, laughing discordantly and crying:

"The old goat has despoiled the living, now he despoils the dead. But the Lord will assuredly judge him according to his own unholy edict, and fling him head over heels from this kingdom into the bottomless abyss!"

When he reached the Palace again, Antipater discovered to his surprise and chagrin that nobody at the Palace troubled to deny the report, though it was generally agreed that the King had not broken the seals of the burial-chambers: he had merely stripped the adjoining treasure-rooms. Herod himself made light of the matter. He said to the deputation of Zadokites who came to him to protest: "O you hypocrites. Am I the first who has borrowed silver from the treasure-house of David and Solomon? Answer me that!"

Zacharias, the spokesman of the deputation, answered frankly: "No, Majesty. The same was done before when this City was besieged by Antiochus the Syrian. King Hyrcanus the Maccabee bought him off with three thousand silver talents taken from the tomb of King David. But that was done at a time of national distress, and done publicly."

"I wonder at your insolence, priest. Hyrcanus took three thousand silver talents from the tomb to buy off an invader, instead of trusting to the might of his God and to the strong hearts of his men, and you applaud it as a righteous action! I borrow less than one-third that sum from the tomb to pay the workmen who are rebuilding the Lord's Temple and you howl at me as if I were a pickpocket. Since when, Zacharias, have you become a Pharisee?"

"The Lord forbid that I should ever become such a thing."

"You do not, then, believe in the resurrection?"

"I am a Sadducee and the son of a Sadducee."

"But if David and Solomon are not to rise again, what use have they of silver ingots and shields of gold and bronze basins? Everything that I have taken from the tomb is for the use of the Ever-Living God. Did not David himself confess in his psalm that naked he came from his mother's womb and naked he should return to the earth? The rich furnishings of his tomb are clean against Scripture. I removed the treasures privately in order to cause no offence. If I had done so publicly you would have complained all the louder of my shamelessness. Be off now, stiff-necks, and trouble me no further."

Seeing that the Pharisees present were smiling at his discomfiture, Zacharias asked: "Majesty, had I been a Pharisee and believed in the resurrection, how would you have answered my protest?"

Herod flushed angrily, and Menelaus the fat librarian stepped forward to reprove Zacharias. "Is this an honest way for a subject to address his King? But let me speak on the King's behalf, to such of you as are Pharisees. At the last day, when King David and Solomon his son arise together in glory, they will claim credit with Enoch the book-keeper, pointing with their fingers at the Temple and saying: 'These massive walls, these fair courts—do you know how the cost of their building was defrayed? Was it not with money which we lent without usury to our son who reigned after us, and who piously completed the work which we began?' "

Zacharias asked: "Can dead men lend money?"

"The money that a man owns he can lend," Menelaus, replied. "And if dead men cannot own, then King Herod has done David and Solomon no injury in removing treasure from their tombs."

The Pharisees could not resist a murmur of satisfaction; and once a religious problem could be reduced to a dispute between Pharisee and Sadducee, Herod had no reason to fear a general revolt.

It became known that two of the men who had gone with Herod into the tombs had not returned. Some Jews said that in trying to open the stone chest containing the bones of Solomon they had been killed by a sudden dart of fire. Others said that Herod had killed them himself because they had seen what they should never have seen. However, both men were Celts and the death of Celts did not grieve the Jews. What caused both surprise and scandal was the white stone monument which Herod set up at the entrance to the tomb; it bore no inscription but was cut in the conical shape of the altars erected in honour of the Great Goddess. But the Greeks and Syrians whispered to one another: "Wisely done! It is to the Great Goddess, to Hecate, that the souls of dead men return. The treasure that accompanies dead kings to their grave is an offering made to her, and any man who robs Hecate of a thousand silver talents will be wise to pay her a high fee in compensation: doubtless the King killed those Celtic soldiers to placate the Dog-headed One. Very wisely done!"

The Jebusites of the Fish Gate were in a fever of excitement. Had Herod rifled the tombs merely because he was in need of money?

It was rumoured that no bullion had been found in the tomb—Hyrcanus had removed it all—and that the supposed ingots in the carts were nothing more valuable than large stones put there to deceive. Had Herod's intention been to seize the golden sceptre from the coffin of David and the golden dog from the coffin of Solomon? And had he succeeded? They said nothing to their Jewish neighbours, and it was not for a year or two that prodigies began to be reported in the streets of Jerusalem with which they naturally connected the despoliation of the royal tombs.

Most of these prodigies took place at night—men in white armour and mounted on white horses galloping in pairs at break-neck speed through the streets and disappearing as suddenly as they came; prophetic cries and knockings from under the Courts of the Temple itself; unexplained outbreaks of fire on the roof of the Royal Palace which made the whole building seem ablaze. Similar prodigies were reported from Bethlehem, Hebron, Samaria and elsewhere. Swords were seen at night glittering in the sky among the western stars; desert rocks dripped with blood; and a young crocodile with a jewelled necklet was caught on the banks of the Jordan near the Dead Sea, though crocodiles had hitherto been supposed peculiar to the Nile.

The people grew nervous. Strange dreams were dreamed and visions seen, the most persistent of which were battles fought in the clouds between phantom armies. There was a sense of impending wonders with which the name of the Messiah was freely connected; yet the kingdom was at peace, the harvests were abundant, the seasons equable, no remarkable news came from Italy, Egypt or the East.

It was announced that Prince Antipater would shortly sail to Rome, taking his father's Will with him for the Emperor's approval. His principal business would be to prosecute the case against Sylleus, who had by now been sent back to Rome from Antioch to be tried for his life. The prodigies, which had ceased for a while, began suddenly to increase both in number and strangeness: headless spectres, sudden fanfares blown from massed trumpets in the dead of night, a tall veiled woman seen walking along the Jericho road hand-in-hand with an ape.

The culmination of these wonders came one evening in the very Sanctuary of the Temple.

Zacharias, of the House of Zadok, was related to Joachim by marriage, his wife Elizabeth being the eldest of Hannah's four sisters, two of whom had married outside the clan of Royal Heirs for lack of suitable husbands within it. Zacharias was the most conservative of all the elder priests in the Temple service, and one of the few men in Jerusalem who refused to be perturbed by the hauntings. "Either they are hallucinations," he said, "or else some mischievous person is playing tricks on us. These things are not of the Lord, who declares his will openly and frankly; a true believer has neither eyes nor ears for such apparitions."

It was Zacharias's day of ministration at the Altar of Incense. His was the eighth course of priests, the Course of Abijah, whose turn for duty came round every second year in the eighth month, the month of the wheat harvest. Fasting, ceremonially clean, correctly robed, he entered the Sanctuary at sundown to dress the seven lamps of the golden Candlestick and offer sweet incense on the Altar, and remained there alone while the congregation stood outside in prayer. With delicate and practised gestures he trimmed the wicks with snuffers and filled the bowls with sacred oil to the brim. Then he fetched the cones of incense from a shelf of the ambry and laid them in a golden bowl; prostrated himself and prayed; raised himself up and with tongs set the cones on the glowing coals of the Altar; sprinkled them with salt; prostrated himself again, and again prayed, while the overpowering scent of the incense began to fill the Sanctuary.

The fumes spread to the waiting congregation outside and Zacharias heard the collect of blessing being sung by the choir of Asaph:

Truly thou art the Lord our God, the God also of our fathers; our King, the King also of our fathers; our Redeemer, the Redeemer also of our fathers; our Maker, the Maker also of our fathers; our Rescuer and Deliverer. Thy name is from everlasting, there is no God but thou. The redeemed sang a new song to thy name by the sea-shore. Together they praised and owned thee as their King and said: "The Lord shall reign, the Saviour of his people Israel." . . .

The singing ceased and Zacharias knew that the evening lamb had been sacrificed and that its pieces were being burned on the Altar in the fore-court. Presently he must return there, pronounce the priestly blessing and accept the meat and drink offerings.

As he waited, calm and at ease, the perfect stillness of the Sanctuary was broken by a voice: a small voice, between a whisper and a pipe, like the voice of a sinner's conscience.

"Zacharias!" it said.

Zacharias was aware that the voice proceeded from the Holy of Holies itself, which no man might enter but only the High Priest once a year; the empty chamber where the God of Israel himself dwelt.

His heart gave a leap and he answered: "Here am I, Lord! Speak, for thy servant heareth!"—the archaic words in which, many generations before at Shiloh, the infant Samuel had replied when similarly summoned.

The small voice questioned him: "Zacharias, what things are these that are burning on my altar?"

Zacharias replied, muttering: "The sweet incense, Lord, according to the Law that thou gavest thy servant Moses."

The voice asked severely: "Is the Sun of Holiness a harlot or a catamite? Do my nostrils smell storax, hinge of scallop, frankincense, narthex, all smouldering together on coals of cedar-wood? Would you make a sweat-bath for the Sun of Holiness?"

Now, the holy incense was compounded according to a very ancient recipe. It had been the custom of the priestesses of the Love-goddess Rahab, on the eve of the May love-orgy, to burn this incense in a hole under the floor of the Goddess's sanctuary. Each woman in turn would crouch for a while over the aperture in a close tent of seal-skin, until her skin sweated and drank in the scent and she became irresistible to her lovers. The ingredients were all of aphrodisiac virtue. Storax is the gum of a white-flowered tree resembling a plane, sacred to the Goddess Isis: the name is derived from the Greek word meaning "causing to lust". Scallop is sacred to the Cyprian and Phoenician Love-goddess Aphrodite, who is represented in the myths as sailing across the sea in a great scallop-shell drawn by dolphins. Great quantities of scallops are eaten at Ascalon and Paphos at her love-feasts, and the hinge of the shell is a symbol of the sexual bond. Frankincense, which is brought from Southern Arabia and the African coast lying opposite, is a fragrant milky resin from the libanus-shrub—white tears mixed with red—and its fumes are credited with the power of inducing amatory eloquence; moreover, the Phoenix is said to burn at Heliopolis on a pyre of frankincense twigs. Narthex is the giant fennel, the wand of office carried by Silenus, the goatish master of the Dionysian revels; and in the pith of its stalk Prometheus is said to have hidden the fire that he stole from Heaven. The gum it exudes is of only a faint odour; but in the holy incense the gums of the storax and frankincense compensated for this deficiency and also drowned the disagreeable stench of the scallop hinge.

Zacharias could make no reply, but knocked seven times with his forehead on the ground, not daring to raise his eyes. He heard sounds of the Curtain being drawn, and the ring of majestic steps approaching over the marble floor. There was a pause, and then a sudden hiss and splutter from the Altar. The steps retreated and Zacharias fainted away.

When he came to himself a few minutes later, he could not for a while recall where he was or what had happened. The lamps were still burning with a steady flame, but the fire on the Altar had been quenched. The hem of his robe was damp with the water that had trickled from the Altar-top. Fear surged back to his mind. He groaned and raised his eyes slowly towards the Sacred Curtain as if to reassure himself that his God did not hate him.

Worse was yet to come. Between the Curtain and the wall stood a tremendous figure clothed in robes shimmering like moonlight on a troubled pool. O horror! The head was that of a wild-ass with glaring red eye-balls and ivory-white teeth, and it was with gold-shod hooves that the figure hugged to its breast the sceptre and dog of monarchy.

From the mouth of the beast came the piping voice. "Be not afraid, Zacharias! Go out now and tell my people truthfully what you have heard and seen!"

Zacharias, half-dead with fear, shrouded his face in his robe. Then he knocked seven times on the floor with his forehead and went stumbling out to the fore-court, where everyone was wondering anxiously at his delay.

He shut the door behind him and stood panting. The cold air revived him. He stared wildly at the placid faces of his kinsmen and the musicians of Asaph. He took a deep breath, and the terrible words that rose in his heart were: "O Men of Israel, hear me! All these generations we have unknowingly worshipped not the true God, but a Golden Ass!"

His lips moved, but no sound came from them. He had been struck dumb.

His kinsmen led him gently away to his own house, but one of them, Reuben, son of Abdiel, whose duty it was to take his place if he fell suddenly ill or became accidentally defiled, pronounced the blessing, accepted the meat and drink offerings and gave the signal for the evening psalm to be sung by the Sons of Asaph.

When the service was over and the priests and musicians had dispersed, Reuben entered the Sanctuary to see whether all were in order. Finding the fire extinguished and dirty water splashed around the Altar, he was astonished and alarmed. Had his staid kinsman Zacharias been overtaken by a sudden frenzy? His first thought was for the Course, which must not be disgraced. No one must know that the fire had been extinguished. With a silent prayer that what he was about to do might not be done amiss, Reuben hastily removed the wet cinders from the Altar, wrapped them in his cloak, relaid and rekindled the fire, and offered more incense with the customary rites.

As he was wiping the floor of the Sanctuary with a napkin the same horror seized him as had seized Zacharias, and the skin of his scalp began to crawl. For he suddenly noticed a wet track of hooves leading towards the Holy of Holies. He stared long at them. There could be no mistake. They were the hoof-tracks of a mule or ass. His mind was in a whirl. All that he could think was that Zacharias had been engaged in black magic and had summoned an ass-demon, one of the Lilim, who had put out the fire on the Altar. A demon of sorts it must have been, for where was the water-jar that had been used for quenching the fire? Zacharias had brought none out with him into the fore-court.

"Alas, alas!" Reuben cried. Casting himself on the floor he prayed aloud: "O Lord of Hosts, protect your servant! Seal the mouths of those that would question him. For I will never publish the disgrace of my House, unless I am required to do so on oath before the High Court."

In the morning Zacharias was questioned kindly by the High Priest at an informal session of the High Court. Writing-tablets were set before him, but he put them aside, shaking his head. When asked whether he had seen a vision he nodded, and a look of such terror came into his face that the High Priest refrained from questioning him further. The Council recommended that he should leave Jerusalem and retire to his country seat at Ain-Rimmon, a prosperous village lying nine miles north of Beersheba. The inquiry was adjourned *sine die*, to Reuben's great relief.

Extravagant rumours about what Zacharias had seen began to fly round the country, and the priests of the Course of Abijah consulted together to decide on an answer to the persistent questions that were being asked. Reuben did not attend the meeting, and in his absence the Sons of Abijah decided that what Zacharias had seen must have been an angel who had given him surprising domestic news. For it had so happened that Zacharias on his return home to Ain-Rimmon was greeted with the news that his wife Elizabeth, who had been childless for more than twenty years, was about to become a mother at last. What was even more remarkable, when Zacharias had left Ain-Rimmon six weeks before, to attend the Passover Week at Jerusalem, he and Elizabeth had both been bound by a local obligation of marital continence, and during the previous thirty days had exchanged only chaste kisses. Her fidelity being beyond question, he could not conceal his astonishment, but took refuge in his dumbness and abstained from written comment. His kinsmen concluded that the vision which he had seen in the Temple was of an angel prophesying that the child which Elizabeth was to bear in her old age would be one of remarkable holiness; and this was the story which they circulated in Jerusalem.

Elizabeth was embarrassed by the interest that her kinsfolk showed in her condition and retired to an inner room of the house whenever visitors called. The manor of Ain-Rimmon was a large, rich house with extensive orchards and vineyards watered by a spring formerly sacred to Rimmon, the Pomegranate-god. The worship of Rimmon had been swallowed up by that of Jehovah, who had taken over his titles and emblems, as might be understood from the little golden pomegranates, alternating with bells shaped like the opening pomegranate blossom, sewn on the vestments of the High Priest, and the large ones carved in marble on the columns of the Temple. But the country people remembered Rimmon; they still celebrated a love-festival in his honour at the time of the spring budding of his beautiful scarlet blossom, when the Pomegranate King, his face coloured scarlet with the dye extracted from the shell and crown of the fruit, held a mock Court with the Queen of Flowers. This same festival, at which the celebrants wear masks and fanciful disguises, is observed to this day in the remoter parts of Galilee. The festival chants are collected in the Canticles ascribed to Solomon. One of them runs:

> *Let us go up to the vineyards,*
> *Let us see whether the vines flourish,*
> *Whether the tender grape appear*
> *And the pomegranate bud forth.*
> *There I will give thee my love.*

The Greek mythographers relate that it was from the blood of the slain Dionysus that the pomegranate-tree first sprang; for this reason the women of Athens abstain from eating the seeds of the pomegranate fruit at the festival of the Thesmophoria. In Cyprus, Dionysus is Adonis; in Syria, Tammuz. By what title King Saul addressed the god of the sacred pomegranate grove at Benjamite Gibeah is not recorded; but it is likely to have been Rimmon. For Rimmon is clearly the Canaanitish Dionysus, the lusty god of the year, incarnate in the Sacred King of the year. He presides in glory at the budding of his scarlet blossoms, he is doomed to death by the ripening of his crimson fruit. After the Exile his name was purposely confused by the priesthood of Jerusalem with "Ramman", the Thunder-god, a title of Jehovah. They absurdly interpreted the pomegranates sewn on the hem of the High Priest's vestment as symbolizing lightning, and the bells with which they alternated as symbolizing thunder. But both were put there in honour of the God Rimmon and clashed merrily together as a charm against evil spirits.

It was whispered by Elizabeth's servants that the mystery of the approaching birth was bound up with the love-festival of Rimmon; for the seasons corresponded. They expected great things of the child.

CHAPTER SEVEN

MARY AT AIN-RIMMON

ONE evening a maid-servant knocked softly at the door of Elizabeth's boudoir where she sat at her needlework.

"A young woman, a stranger, desires the honour of greeting your ladyship."

"I am not receiving guests to-day."

"Your servants told the young woman so, but she persists in her request."

"Who is this importunate person?"

"She will not reveal her name or family."

"Who brought her here?"

"She came under escort of a party of tented Rechabites who rode off at once on their asses in a cloud of dust."

"Rechabites, did you say? What were her words as she entered our gate?"

"She said: 'In the name of the Mother.'"

76

Elizabeth grew angry. "You granddaughter of a camel, why did you not tell me so at once? Has the lady eaten? Have you washed her feet? Oh, you wretches! Bring water and a basin at once, bring soap and a linen towel. Bring food, the best in the house. Bring sweet wine. Make no delay." Elizabeth threw down her tambour-frame and hurried out.

Soon she returned, leading a young woman by the hand, to whom she said solemnly, as she shut the door: "In the name of the Mother, this house is your house and these servants are your servants, whoever you may be, and whatever your business."

For reply, the young woman unveiled with a rapid movement of her arm, kissed Elizabeth on both cheeks and began to weep silently.

Elizabeth cried in astonishment: "Can it be? Can it truly be? It is the face of my sister Hannah when she was a child. The same sea-green eyes, straight nose, courageous chin. Child, you are Hannah's daughter?"

Mary nodded, dashing away the tears with her fingers.

"Why do you weep?"

"For joy to be safely under your roof."

Elizabeth clapped her hands. "Hurry, sluts, hurry, as if wolves were at your heels!"

They came running in helter-skelter, one with warm water in a silver ewer; another with a silver basin embossed with an interlace of fish, perfumed soap and an embroidered towel; another with a great brass tray covered with little platters of relishes—sweet pickles, olives, herbbenjamin, cucumber—arranged around a brace of cold roast pigeons stuffed with savoury herbs and garnished with Cos lettuce. Elizabeth sliced the fine wheat loaf for Mary and spread it with conserve of quince. She asked her servants over her shoulder: "Where are the Jericho dates? And the honey-figs soaked in Cyprus wine?"

"They are coming, Mistress! Here they are, coming behind us. And a flagon of sweet wine of Lebanon!"

"Now, begone, children! I will wash this lady's feet myself."

They stared and retired in silence.

Elizabeth put her hand affectionately under Mary's chin and tilted her face to look at it more closely.

"You look faint with hunger, daughter," she said. "Here is water for your hands. Eat and drink, why do you hesitate? I will be washing your feet meanwhile."

Mary smiled as she answered: "Soap is unknown in the black tents of the Rechabites. A kindly folk, but filthy in their habits. Before

77

I eat, give me leave to enjoy the luxury of dabbling my fingers a while in this basin of soft warm water."

"Your dear mother was the same: she would not be hurried."

Mary ate and drank well. When she had done she washed her hands again, wiped her mouth, gave thanks to the Lord, and sat silent.

Elizabeth waited for her to speak.

Mary said at last politely, noticing Elizabeth's condition: "The Lord's blessing on the fruit of your womb!"

Elizabeth answered: "When you kissed me, the babe inside me leaped for joy."

"Is all well with my uncle, the lord Zacharias?"

"All is well, except that he has been struck dumb, as you doubtless have heard. Yet dumbness is no great fault in a husband, and it keeps him from continually disputing vexatious points of the Law with his cronies—a habit that I have never learned to love. Zacharias knows the Law backwards and forwards and upside down and never fails to win the argument, though it is not always that he succeeds in convincing his opponent. Is all well with your dear mother and the learned Joachim?"

"All was well at our last meeting. Three times a year they have always visited me, when they come up for the grand festivals."

"Every year I plan to make the journey to Jerusalem, but somehow I never go. I cannot bear crowds. Tell me, when do they intend to redeem you and find you a husband? It is time enough now, and the redemption fee for a girl under the age of twenty is fixed at a mere ten shekels."

"It was as a gift, not as a loan, that they offered me to the Lord; which gave the High Priest the authority to bestow me in marriage. And so I was married."

"Married! To whom? When? Why was I not invited to the wedding?"

Mary was troubled. "The High Priest decided to betroth me to Joseph of Emmaus, who married your sister Abigail." She added hurriedly: "I have been staying at Lysia's house—your niece, I mean. Lysia has been very kind to me, kindness itself."

"Joseph of Emmaus! What an extraordinary choice! He must be nearly seventy and has six grown children. Joseph, indeed! He is not rich. Nor learned. Nor influential. I remember that we girls all grimaced when he was chosen for Abigail; but of course Abigail had a club foot and was not presentable in other respects."

"He is a good man, so they say!"

"Oh yes, too good in a sense. Generous and pious to the point of simple-mindedness. Does he treat you well?"

"I have never seen him."

"But you said that you were married to him."

"No, I did not say that."

"But if you and he are betrothed, why does he not take you to his house? Why have you come running here like a fugitive?"

Mary whispered: "Forgive me, Aunt, but I cannot tell you that."

"Does 'cannot' mean that you are forbidden to tell me, or that you do not know?"

Mary began to weep again. "Do not press me to answer, dear Aunt Elizabeth. Give me refuge and peace. Let nobody know that I am here. Nobody at all."

Elizabeth was greatly puzzled. "Who sent you here to me under escort of the Sons of Rahab?"

"Is was Anna daughter of Phanuel, our guardian mother."

"A shrewd old lady. Tell me, does old Joseph know that you have come?"

"I am not sure. And I do not think that he would greatly care if he did know."

"Not care what has become of his betrothed wife?" Elizabeth's tone was indignant.

"I beg you not to question me," cried Mary in alarm. "I will be your devoted servant, Aunt. I will lie on straw and eat husks, if need be, and serve you foot and hand, but I beg you not to question me. Already I have said too much."

Elizabeth laughed. "I will restrain my curiosity, my dear, though upon my word yours is a very extraordinary visit. But this I demand to know—are you in trouble? Are you running away from Jerusalem because you have committed some crime? At least you can tell me that."

"As the Lord lives, I am not guilty of any crime!"

"Good. I asked only to know where I stand; I should not have liked to compromise my poor Zacharias by harbouring a criminal without his knowledge, though of course a guest is a guest. And there are degrees of criminality. Every girl is liable to make a fool of herself, especially with men, and I should not have been harsh to you if you had done so. Well, that is all I needed to know. I am delighted to have you here as a companion during my confinement; your presence, I hope, will keep me from losing my temper with the maids. Besides, I love your mother. She was my darling from the day that she was born until the day that marriage parted us. For her sake I will cosset you as tenderly as childless Roman matrons cosset their Indian marmosets."

Mary smiled faintly. "But what will you tell my Uncle Zacharias?"

"Nothing at all. What female companions I have with me in my inner apartments are no business of his. After all, I redeemed this estate from mortgage with my marriage gift. He would have lost all but for me. Do you play draughts? Are you skilled at embroidery? Do you play the lyre?"

Mary answered modestly: "Our Temple education was thorough."

"Good again! Tell me, daughter: what is the latest news from Jerusalem? What is happening at the Palace? Is Queen Doris still in favour? I know Doris well. Dora, which is her family seat, lies not far from here, and she was in residence there during her long exile from Court. Has Prince Antipater sailed for Rome yet?"

Mary began to say something, but stopped and sat silent again.

"Why, come now, these are not close secrets too, are they?"

Mary answered, as off-handedly as she could: "I know nothing about Queen Doris. Her son sailed from Caesarea a month ago." She added in a rush: "But he is King Antipater now, co-ruler of the Jews with his father, not merely a prince."

Elizabeth looked incredulous. "What? Are you sure?"

"Am I sure of what? That he has sailed?"

"That he has been made a colleague of his father's."

"Yes indeed. I was present when it was publicly announced in the Court of the Gentiles. The Levites blew a great many trumpets and everyone shouted 'God save the King!' "

Elizabeth rose from the floor where they had been sitting cross-legged and began to walk about restlessly. "Now what in the world is the meaning of this new move on the board?" she cried. "Are they anxious or alarmed about it at Jerusalem?"

"Alarmed? Why should they be alarmed?"

"You know King Herod's reputation?"

"I have heard many things spoken about him, both good and bad."

"Fewer good than bad?"

"Fewer by far, I grant you."

"Does it not surprise everyone that Herod should have raised his son to this dignity? Is it thought consistent with his jealous and tyrannical disposition?"

"I have not heard surprise expressed. King Antipater has never offended against his father in the least degree. Even those who have good excuse for hating the House of Herod confess that Antipater has given proof of a pious and noble nature. Besides, King Herod is growing old. I know little about these matters, but is it not natural that after his disappointment in the matter of the princes Alexander and Aristobulus he should lean on Antipater as on a staff that will never break and pierce his hands?"

"You champion Antipater with pleasant warmth. It is lucky that your Uncle Zacharias is not with us to hear you. How he detests the Herodians!"

"But why should the people of Jerusalem be alarmed when Antipater is awarded a diadem?"

"Because Herod in a generous mood is Herod in a dangerous mood. Your learned father Joachim made this remark to my husband and myself some years ago. Often since then we have verified its truth. By the by, have there been any more hauntings lately in the City?"

"People still tell ridiculous stories of what has been seen or heard or dreamed. I pay no attention to them."

"I take them seriously. Hauntings, whether real or imaginary, are usually the prelude to deeds of blood."

"May the Lord avert them by his mercy!"

Elizabeth was puzzled. As she lay sleepless that night she went over the evening's conversation in her mind. Mary had said that she was betrothed to Joseph, while admitting that Joseph possibly did not know and probably did not care where she might be. Surely Mary had not been lying? Her mother Hannah had never lied: evaded a question, yes, but never lied. And surely that absurdly upright old Joseph was not a man to treat Joachim's daughter with scorn or disrespect? He was courteous to a fault: there was a story that he once sent a servant in pursuit of a guest who had robbed him of a silver flagon, to present him with the stopper, saying: "Sir, this also was part of my master's gift to you." Yet Joseph was a very odd choice for a husband. Old Joachim was exceedingly rich. Mary was his only child and would inherit everything.

Elizabeth began to wonder: had Mary been seduced by someone who either could not or would not marry her? Had the High Priest tried to fob her off in a hurry on old Joseph? Had Joseph, after paying the bride-money, become aware of the deception and, not wishing to father another man's child, returned her quietly to the Temple? Had Anna then, to avoid a scandal, sent her down here, with the High Priest's connivance, under escort of the Rechabites? Mary, however, had sworn that she was innocent of any sin. Had she perhaps been violated?

Suddenly Elizabeth remembered that Mary had said at first that she was married. Not merely betrothed, but married! And afterwards she had distinguished the marriage from the betrothal. But a woman once married could not be betrothed unless the marriage had first been dissolved. Was this what she had meant? It did not seem likely. And had she said in so many words that she had been betrothed to Joseph? No, only that the High Priest had decided on the betrothal.

Elizabeth could not solve the problem but decided to let it cost her no more sleep. Perhaps Mary would give away the secret one day by a chance indiscretion.

Two pleasant months went by, and then Shelom of Rehoboth, a former confidential maid of Elizabeth's, came to Ain-Rimmon from Jerusalem with her husband. Elizabeth had sent for her because of her skill as a midwife. A woman who first conceives at the age of thirty-six must be prepared for a difficult confinement.

Shelom was married to the son of a former steward of the estate. She brought a budget of news about troubles in Herod's palace. "Yes, my lady, the whole City is disturbed, I am sorry to say. Nobody seems to know how it all began or how it is likely to end. My sister-in-law was saying, the day that we came away: 'It is indecent. We might be living among the barbarous Parthians, not in God-fearing Jerusalem.' She is an excitable woman, is my sister-in-law, but there are many like her in our quarter. It is the yells and screams from the Palace at night that disturb her. The eunuchs are worse than the women, the way they scream under torture: they have no pride of sex, I suppose."

"It must be most unsettling, my dear Shelom. But you have yet to tell me what has happened?"

"I know nothing for certain and fear to earn Solomon's reproof of babblers and tale-bearers. However, I will tell you what is said. The story begins with Jochebed, the wife of the King's brother Pheroras. She comes from Bethany, you know; her father was a travelling tree-grafter. I cannot speak from any personal knowledge, but my husband's family call her the cunningest schemer in all Israel. 'How Prince Pheroras ever came to marry a woman of such low birth,' my husband says, 'I do not know; he must have been bewitched.' However that may be, she formed a close league with the Pharisee nationalists. You remember how heavily King Herod fined them when they refused to take the oath of allegiance to the Emperor, and how obligingly Jochebed paid the fine? Well, some of them began prophesying, to please her, that the sceptre of Herod would pass to Pheroras and herself. Herod's spies soon reported this prophecy to him and he ordered Pheroras to divorce her, but Pheroras refused to do so, saying that he would rather die. What made things worse was that Queen Doris is Jochebed's closest friend, and King Antipater himself is intimate with Prince Pheroras, who was a generous uncle to him while he was a private citizen. Then Salome, King Herod's sister, took a hand in the game. Herod had been living on good terms with her since he married her off to his friend Alexas, the rich Philistine, who is reputedly one of the Lady Livia's agents. She managed to prove to his satisfaction that the prophecy was bound up with some wild talk of a Messiah, and that behind the prophecy lay a plot against his life in which the royal Chamberlain Bagoas was implicated. So he arrested everyone whom she named."

"Was Pheroras perhaps to be the Messiah?"

"Oh no, my lady, not Prince Pheroras but a son who was to be born to him and his wife; and Bagoas's son was to be this Messiah's principal minister. So of course the King—who, if I may put it that way, will tolerate no Messiahs but himself—immediately disproved the prophecy. . . ."

Elizabeth interrupted the story with a burst of loud laughter. "How very comical, my dear Shelom! Either you have misheard the name or else it is another Bagoas. Bagoas the Chamberlain has been a eunuch from childhood!"

"Comical or sad, my lady, it is nevertheless the truth. According to the prophecy, the infant Messiah would miraculously restore Bagoas to virility and enable him to beget children. So, as I was telling your ladyship, King Herod immediately disproved the prophecy by having Bagoas strangled. He also made an example of nine of the leading nationalists. Being Pharisees, of course, they believed in bodily resurrection, but he cheated them of their hopes by burning them alive. Twenty-three other men were executed and four women strangled. Oh, and he also impaled his pretty little catamite Gratus, the one who always used to tuck him up in bed and kiss him good-night. But he did not choose to do anything to Pheroras or Jochebed at the time—I suppose because there was no evidence to connect them with the plot—and Pheroras was indignant to be suspected of high treason and vowed that he would return at once to his principality across Jordan and not visit Jerusalem again until the King were dead."

"Boldly spoken. I suppose that Herod has done away with the poor fellow by now?"

"Yes, my lady, he died very soon afterwards, and the King brought his body back to Jerusalem just to prove him a liar, and gave him one of those costly funerals which he reserves for members of his family whom he has helped out of this world, and wept tears by the jarful."

"What has happened to Jochebed? If I know the Herodian way, she was at once accused of poisoning Pheroras."

"You know the King's way well, my lady, but his scheme was a somewhat more complex one than you perhaps have in mind. He gave out that she had administered what she thought to be a love-philtre but which proved to be a poison; and that the drug had been provided by Queen Doris, for whom it was procured some months ago by Sylleus the Arabian. He put the ladies and maid-servants of Pheroras's Court to the torture, and by asking them leading questions tried to persuade them to incriminate the Queen. They did not at first understand what they were being asked to confess, but at last one of them was shrewd enough to cry out from the rack: 'May the God who governs this earth and the heavens above punish Queen Doris, the sole cause of my anguish!' The screws were immediately slackened and she swore to the required story, and then other women who had been waiting their turn for the rack corroborated it with the necessary detail. So now Queen Doris has been stripped of all her costly robes and jewels and sent packing."

"My poor friend Doris! But what a queer story! Was any charge against King Antipater included in these confessions?"

"King Antipater's name is not mentioned in the official account of the trial."

"No, that was not to be expected. But he is in great danger, none the less."

"Do you think so, indeed? The plot, if it was a real plot, implied the removal of Herod and the usurpation of the throne by Prince Pheroras, so that Antipater cannot be reasonably accused of complicity. People are saying that the King used the occasion as an excuse for removing Doris, who had vexed him by treating his junior wives a little severely—she was a great stickler for Court etiquette, I suppose from having been so long exiled from Court—but that when Antipater returns from Rome she will be restored to favour. They say that the news will grieve Antipater, but cannot alarm him for his own safety, and that if there is one element in this obscure affair of which they can be sure, it is that King Antipater is the most wilfully loyal son a wicked father ever had."

"They are right in saying that King Antipater will not be alarmed:

his wilful loyalty will blind him to the danger. But that the danger is real and deadly I am certain."

"Why do you think, my lady, that the King should desire Antipater's death?"

"I have not the least idea. I only know this, that Herod would never have made him a king had he not intended to destroy him soon afterwards. Now that Doris has left the Palace for good, Antipater has no better chance of life than a little child playing with a horned viper."

Mary had been sitting apart with her needlework. She suddenly gave a cry and turned pale.

"Why, daughter, what is amiss? You look like a phantom."

"I have pricked my finger; look, it bleeds!"

"So good a needle-woman as yourself should be accustomed to pricks by now. Are you terrified at the sight of a little blood?"

"It was a sharp prick. It seemed to stab me to the very heart."

"Quick, Shelom," said Elizabeth. "Fetch a cordial. The kerm is best. You know the shelf. Why, upon my living soul, the child has fainted! Is that not strange?"

"I was watching her. She pricked herself because she felt faint; she did not faint because she pricked herself. But oh, my lady, you cannot hide the truth from me. When I first came to your father's house your sister Hannah was the same age, or a little younger, and this girl is my lady Hannah all over again. The Lord shower blessings on her pretty face! Here is the kerm. Give me leave to put it to her lips. Remember, my lady, that you sent me as midwife to your sister Hannah when she was to be delivered of a child; this is the very child that I brought into the world."

"Shelom, not another word! You are as impudent as ever!"

"Yes, my lady, and you will forgive me once more, out of old habit."

Mary revived and continued quietly with her needlework as if nothing had happened to disturb her tranquillity, but soon afterwards excused herself and went to bed.

A few days later Shelom was sitting in the walled garden with Elizabeth. Between them on the flagstones lay a sackful of the lopped heads of roses, and they were plucking off the petals to make perfume. Shelom said: "My lady, a certain young woman who is your companion, about whom I am forbidden to know anything—have you observed her colour?"

"No, what do you mean?"

"I mean that in a few months' time, when you have been safely delivered of your child, I shall have another confinement on hand. I judge from the unevenness of colour in her cheeks."

"Oh, Shelom, you are not teasing? You are so fond of teasing. Is it really true?"

"It is true. Why do you stare at me, my lady? I have heard about the child's marriage, though why she has been sent here who can tell?"

"How much do you know, Shelom?"

"My husband's brother happens to be the Temple scribe who drafted the marriage contract between this child and your brother-in-law Joseph of Emmaus, of the House of David. He mentioned it to my husband because he remembered that I had been in the service of the child's mother."

"But when was this marriage celebrated?"

"That I cannot tell you. Soon afterwards, one would suppose, to judge from the child's condition."

"Shelom, upon my word I am in a very uneasy situation, and the worst of it is that I know as little as you do."

"You fear that the child who is to be born may not be Joseph's?"

"I cannot permit myself to fear anything of the sort, and I forbid you to suggest it."

"I am under your orders, my lady."

"Shelom, you are a good creature. You must stand by us both."

"Yes, my lady. For my lady Hannah's sake and for yours, and for the girl's. But why should she have fainted? Were we discussing anything of concern to herself?"

"No, you were telling me about Prince Pheroras and his wife, and about King Antipater. Perhaps she was not listening but pursuing her own thoughts, and suddenly was overcome by anxiety for herself and her child. The last words that I had spoken were about a child playing with a horned viper. They frightened her, I suppose."

"It is likely enough, my lady. I wonder whether she is aware of her condition?"

"Perhaps not. But soon she will be, and then she must say something to me about it. Meanwhile, I propose to say nothing to her, and I beg that you will do the same."

That same evening Mary came to Shelom. "The lady Elizabeth assures me that you are a discreet woman."

"The lady Elizabeth is not given to bestowing idle praise, and I thank her for her good opinion."

"Shelom, there is something which I cannot ask your mistress to do for me. Perhaps you will help me. It is of the greatest importance.

There is someone in Italy to whom I wish to send a message. You say that your husband has dealings with the merchants of Caesarea—could he arrange to have the message secretly delivered? I have a little gold with me: you shall have it all if you can arrange the matter quietly. And look, here is a Babylonian gold pin. You shall have this too, though it was a gift to me from my own dear mother."

Shelom replied in the calmest of voices: "Keep your pin, child. The message has already been sent."

Mary stared at her. "But I have not yet told you the message."

"You told it to me when you pricked your finger."

"I do not understand you."

"The message was sent off on the day that I left Jerusalem."

"This is absurd. To whom was it sent?"

"To the man whom you have in mind. A message of warning about his father's intentions. I did not let the lady Elizabeth know that I had already foreseen the danger which threatens your friend."

"Have you a familiar spirit?"

"No, but I love you. And I have sent off another message since I came here, to the same man. My husband rode off with it a week ago; he will give it to his agent at Jamnia."

"What message did you send?"

"I told him how it was with you."

"In what words?"

"In these words." Shelom bent down and wrote in the dust these antique Hebrew letters:

> TETH-KAPH-DALETH-HE
> HE-YODH-ALEPH-YODH
> LAMEDH-BETH-TETH-VAV

"That is a novel way of writing," said Mary. "Do the letters stand for numbers? It looks like a charm."

"A charm that will cheer him."

"Why do you not tell me more?"

"I have told you far more than you have told me."

Mary eyed Shelom steadily, and Shelom returned her gaze with the air of a servant who has done her duty well.

"You are a strange woman," Mary said at last.

"You will come to understand me in time, Daughter of the Lotus!"

At Jerusalem, Cleopas was saying to Joachim as they went up the steep road together towards the Temple: "But it is not true, surely?"

"Why should it not be true? Simon the High Priest had the right to bestow her in marriage on whatever man he pleased. And Joseph of Emmaus is of honourable family."

"Though not a Levite."

"Nevertheless he married the sister of your wife, and of mine."

"The club-footed one. When that marriage was arranged he was a prosperous merchant of middle age. Now he is old and bald and has already divided the greater part of his property between his four sons."

"He still has property at Emmaus."

Cleopas said impetuously: "Something is being concealed from you, honest Joachim. I believe that the High Priest betrothed her to Joseph because nobody else could be found to marry her."

Joachim stopped dead. "You mean?"

"Perhaps she acted foolishly," said Cleopas, trying to speak in a light tone.

"You mean my daughter?" asked Joachim, narrowing his eyes and speaking softly. "Brother, put a bridle on your tongue, lest you offend me." His fingers tightened on his almond-wood staff.

Cleopas blustered. "I meant nothing, nothing whatever. Girls often behave thoughtlessly, especially in festival time: become compromised—innocently, very often. Why, my own sister . . ."

"Yes, Cleopas, your sister perhaps, but not my daughter!" He turned his back on Cleopas and slowly went down the hill again; he did not wish to enter the Temple with furious passions surging in his heart.

Cleopas was irritated with himself for having blundered so stupidly. He had been trying to find out from Joachim the truth of the rumour that Joseph, having agreed to marry the girl, had come to the High Priest's house with the redemption fee of ten shekels as bride-money, but that for some unexplained reason the contract had not been signed. If only he had refrained from that unfortunate remark! Now he had mortally offended Joachim, one of his dearest friends, and he would have to suffer the reproaches of his wife, whose sister Hannah was Joachim's wife. He stood for a while where Joachim had left him, then turned and hurried down the hill.

He soon overtook Joachim, plucked him by the sleeve and said: "Brother Joachim, forgive me my folly! It is written: 'Even a fool when he holds his peace is accounted wise.' But I, being worse than a fool, have forfeited that consolation."

Joachim answered: "And it is written in the same book: 'A soft answer turns away wrath', and again: 'It is an honour in a man to cease from strife.' Come, let us go up again to praise the Lord together in the Temple." But as they neared the top he said quietly: "Cleopas, I did wrong to boast in your presence that I had rid myself of the burdensome responsibility of providing a husband for my daughter. Since you have proved yourself a wise man by the confession of your folly, I will confide to you my sorrow, which is too much for one heart to bear. The High Priest was directed in a dream to betroth my child to Joseph of Emmaus, in the house of whose married daughter Lysia she had spun the purple flax for the Holy Curtain. He sent to Joseph asking him whether he were willing to consider the marriage and whether, if so, he would ride up from Emmaus on a certain day with the bride-money. Joseph was willing enough; but he came a day too late. Early on the previous morning as my poor child was walking with a companion from the College of Virgins to Lysia's house they were both seized upon by bandits in a narrow lane and carried of. They set the other virgin free outside the City gates and she returned unharmed—none of her golden ornaments had been taken from her—but not my child. The High Priest would not raise a hue-and-cry in the City for fear of damaging her reputation; he hoped that in good time the bandits would state the price of her ransom, which he would pay quietly. But not a word has been heard of her since. I am distracted with anxiety."

"Brother Joachim, I do not wish to add another faggot to the burden of your sorrow, but I suspect the hand of a Certain Man in this. If ransom had been the object of the abduction, why did the bandits release your daughter's companion? Or why did they not at least rob her? It may be that at a time like this, when Messianic prophecies are flying from mouth to mouth, a Certain Man might not be pleased with a marriage between an elder of the House of David and a daughter of the Royal Heirs. It may be that he has ordered one of his Levite creatures to debauch her. You know the Law. Since the contract was not signed at the time of the abduction she was still a virgin, and the man who enticed her need now only offer her guardian the bride-money in quittance; he is then free to marry her at his leisure."

"If, as you suppose, the Man of Sodom has stolen my ewe lamb he will never escape my rage. I am an old man, but my hands are strong to strangle."

Cleopas frowned. Lifting his hand in warning he said: "Be silent, fool! Is it not written: 'Vengeance is mine, saith the Lord, I will repay'?"

Joachim's lips writhed as he struggled with himself, but at last he had the mastery. "And it is written also: 'He who hearkens to reproof gets understanding.' I thank you, brother Cleopas!"

They passed on and entered the Temple at peace with the Lord and with each other.

CHAPTER   EIGHT

THE TRIAL OF KING ANTIPATER

IT WAS some months before King Antipater, who headed Herod's embassy at Rome, finally persuaded the President of the Senatorial Court to pronounce sentence of death against Sylleus the Arabian.

This cost him twenty silver talents, for the President had been bribed by the other side to reserve judgement until the embassy had returned to Judaea—it was hoped that if none of them were present in Rome to remind the Emperor of the seriousness of the case he might be persuaded to grant a reprieve. All Antipater's other business was finished, including that of submitting his father's Will to the Emperor's approval. The Emperor had expressed his satisfaction with it and entrusted it to the safe-keeping of the Vestal Virgins. But Antipater still could not sail home until he had secured an undertaking from the Commander of the Praetorian Guards that he would not postpone the date of Sylleus's execution. This would probably cost another three or four talents.

Ten days later, while he was still negotiating with the Commander, Antipater was angered rather than alarmed by an anonymous letter, dated four months previously, which reached him from Jerusalem. He found it folded in his napkin at breakfast. It contained circumstantial news of the nationalist plot, the subsequent death of his uncle Pheroras, the torture of the Court ladies, and the criminal charges brought against his mother, Queen Doris; but he could not believe that any of these events had taken place, because there had been no mention or hint of them in despatches of later date which had regularly reached him from his father.

He showed the letter to two reliable members of his staff, expecting them to echo his disgust of anonymous libels. To his surprise, they did nothing of the sort. They confessed that the letter substantiated hints and rumours which had reached them from trustworthy sources in Jerusalem, but with which they had not cared to trouble him at the time. Antipater could read in their faces that the letter contained nothing that they had not already heard. They begged him to remain at Rome under the Emperor's protection until he knew whether his father suspected him of complicity in the nationalists' plot or the murder of Pheroras.

Antipater reproved them for their credulity; he said that a clear conscience was the best possible armour against lies and malice, as his father himself had recently proved when he came to Rome unsummoned to answer Sylleus's baseless charges. He would therefore return to Jerusalem as soon as Sylleus had been safely despatched. He wrote immediately to his father to say that he hoped to sail in ten days' time and meanwhile gave him an itemized list of his expenses at Rome, regretting that the legal expenses in the Sylleus case had been so heavy. They amounted to nearly two hundred silver talents, sixty of which had gone in bribes to judges and court officials.

Augustus expressed sincere sorrow when Antipater came to take his leave. He gave him costly presents as well as a letter of commendation for delivery to Herod. In this he characteristically punned on Antipater's name: "A son so dutiful should not be called Antipater, but Philopater—one who cherishes his father, not one who opposes him. I envy you, dear Herod, in having a Philopater as your royal colleague whom you can trust to take from your shoulders some of the burdensome weight of public business. His zeal on your behalf has been remarkable." Augustus knew, of course, that Antipater does not really mean "one who opposes a father", but, in the other sense of the preposition *Anti*, "one who acts as deputy of a father". It was a hereditary forename of the House of Herod, and originally, I suppose, signified "Priest of Hercules-Melkarth".

He then condoled with Antipater on the death of his uncle Pheroras, the news of which had reached him officially from Antioch in a recent quarterly despatch.

"Oh, then it is true!" cried Antipater, and could not restrain his tears.

"A word to the wise," said Augustus kindly. "Unofficial reports have also reached me that Queen Doris, your mother, is in disgrace.

I advise you not to champion her cause blindly, as a son of your generous nature might be tempted to do. Your father is easily vexed; assume her guilty until you have clear proof of her innocence."

Antipater asked: "Of what is my mother accused, Caesar?"

But Augustus would divulge no more. "The report was unofficial," he said, with a smile of dismissal.

Sylleus was executed on the Ides of September, and on the next day Antipater and his staff sailed for home in a fast galley, the *Fortune*. In the Ionian Sea they ran into foul weather, and again in the Cretan; but the weather was calm when they sighted the coast of Cilicia and were hailed by a packet-vessel from Caesarea. Among the mail which they took aboard was a letter from Herod addressed to Antipater at Rome, begging him to return at once, whether the Sylleus case were concluded or not, since his long absence from public business was being felt more keenly each succeeding day. Herod, who wrote in most affectionate terms, referred only incidentally to the death of Pheroras, which led Antipater to conclude that a previous despatch had gone astray; and also touched on a "slight difficulty" with Queen Doris, who after showing "a somewhat stepmotherly severity" towards his younger wives had not accepted his rebukes in as good a spirit as he had a right to expect. "Doubtless all will be well, Royal Son, when you return as a visible pledge of the love between your mother and myself; and for this reason, as well as for the others upon which I have already enlarged, pray make no delay, but spread your sails wide to catch the West Wind."

Antipater, a great weight lifted from his heart, showed this letter to the same two members of his staff. "Read for yourselves," he said. "The mysterious letter of warning came from enemies trying to foment trouble between my loving father and myself. No wonder it was anonymous. How glad I am that I rejected your advice!"

"May you continue so, Majesty! Pray forget what it was that we advised you to do."

Antipater had noticed a mysterious group of Hebrew letters, evidently numerals, written small on the back of the letter. He had puzzled over a similar group on a letter which had reached him from Jerusalem some weeks previously. He now unpacked the files and searched for the earlier letter, which, he remembered, was a report from the steward of his Jamnian estates. He found it without trouble and compared the figures. This was the earlier group, reading from right to left in Oriental style:

1.	19.	17.
18.	18.	8.
12.	3.	27.

The latter group was:

5.	24.	9.
10.	11.	5.
6.	15.	32.

The handwriting was identical, but what could the figures mean? Were these cipher messages? Then they could not be addressed to himself, since he had made no arrangements to correspond in cipher with anyone. Perhaps they were intended for some member of his staff? Or were they merely registration numbers used by the packet-service?

He copied out both groups on a small scrap of parchment and studied them with the absorbed intentness that travellers often bestow on trifles during an uneventful voyage in calm weather; but could make nothing of them. What puzzled him most was that they were written in the antique characters used in the earliest Scriptural texts, not in the modern Square script.

The ship sailed up the Orontes to Antioch, where Antipater went ashore to pay his respects to Quinctilius Varus, the newly appointed Governor-General of Syria, with whom he had long been on friendly terms. Varus welcomed him with a quizzical look, and invited him to a private audience, but when, instead of making some tearful confession or passionate appeal for help, Antipater spoke cheerfully about current affairs and mutual acquaintances, he grew impatient and at last asked him point-blank whether the death of Pheroras had not greatly complicated his affairs.

"No, Excellency: none of my business was in his hands. This is not to deny that the news was a sudden and bitter blow. I loved Pheroras well. He was more like a father than an uncle to me in the days when I was in exile, and I confess that I wept when I heard that he was dead; indeed, I fasted in sackcloth and ashes for a whole day, as our custom is."

"Majesty, why do you hesitate to confide in me? I am your friend!"

"What have I to confide?"

"Your well-founded apprehensions."

"I do not understand Your Excellency."

"Nor I Your Majesty. Well, I can be as silent as yourself if I please, but I have this at least to say. Your father has invited me to Jerusalem on legal business—which he does not specify but at the nature of which I can guess—and I propose to travel there in a few days' time by way of Damascus, where I have been asked to adjudicate in a boundary dispute. I shall be most happy if you will ride in my coach with me. Reason tells me that you will be assured a more honourable welcome as my friend than either as your mother's son or as your father's colleague and heir-at-law. Have I made myself plain?"

"Your Excellency is most kind, but if my royal father has any suspicions of my loyalty, as you seem to hint, I should be unwise to increase them by placing myself under your protection, as if I knew myself guilty of some crime. Besides, he has begged me to make haste, and I cannot disobey him. I shall continue my journey by sea, and unless the wind changes I should be home in four days' time."

"You have a noble soul, Majesty, but this is not an age in which nobility of soul is often rewarded. Remain with me, and I will take full responsibility for the delay, and help you to the utmost of my powers should your father bring any charges against you. For hand washes hand, and when you are sole sovereign, you will doubtless remember your debt to me. Refuse my offer, and you may find yourself without a friend in the world to support you in trouble."

"Your Excellency must forgive me. My duty to my father comes first."

Varus lost his temper. "They say, Majesty, that nobody can persuade a fool that the rainbow is not his foot-bridge. I leave you to your own devices. When the bridge melts under your feet and you fall into the water, do not call on me for an oar or keg to buoy you up. Your father has other sons who may be more anxious than you are to secure my favour and friendship."

"I do not fear drowning. As your admired Pindar writes:

> If Heaven designs to save you, safe you are
> Though wallowing in mid-ocean in a sieve."

So they parted, and the *Fortune*, in which Antipater had re-embarked, stood out to sea again: but as she put in at Sidon she fouled a sunken wreck and sprang a leak. This delayed her for several days, and when she sailed once more she was caught by a violent North-easter, dismasted and driven to within a few miles of Alexandria. She had to battle back slowly, under oars, with many men injured and provisions running short.

It was the last day of October before she made Caesarea. The fine double harbour of Caesarea, carved by Herod at huge expense out of a featureless coast and dominated by a colossal statue of Augustus visible from miles away at sea, is as commodious as that of the Peiraeus. The long mole which breaks the force of the waves and encloses the outer harbour measures not less than two hundred feet across, and the capacious wharves of the inner harbour are protected by strong forts. The city is magnificent, with temples, baths, market-places, gymnasia and an amphitheatre in the best Greek style.

The *Fortune* sailed into the outer harbour, the entrance of which is to the north, and her captain hailed the harbour-master: "Ahoy there! We are the *Fortune* galley, Firmicus Sidonius captain, two hundred tons, homeward bound from Rome. We have His Majesty King Antipater aboard and a consignment of copper ingots from Sidon. Clear of fever. A surgeon is needed for ten men injured in the recent gale. We propose to berth at the Royal Pavilion abaft Fort Drusus."

After a pause the answer was trumpeted back by the harbour-master's loud-voiced slave. "Your instructions are: tie up at the copper-wharf on the west quay and discharge cargo."

The captain repeated: "Ahoy there! I repeat that we have His Majesty King Antipater aboard. We propose to berth at the Royal Pavilion."

The reply came back: "Instructions repeated. You are to tie up at the copper-wharf and discharge cargo there. A surgeon will be sent to you."

The captain apologized to Antipater. "Majesty, the harbour-master is a mad little tyrant and I dare not disobey him without your sanction. What am I to do?"

"Perhaps the Royal berth is fouled by a wreck. Make for the copper-wharf as he orders. I will enjoy the walk along the quay to the city. My legs long for dry land."

The *Fortune* drew in at the copper-wharf and immediately slaves ran aboard to help unbatten the hatches. "Back, dogs!" shouted the master, cracking his whip at them. "Let His Majesty disembark first before you tread filth into my decks!"

The gang-plank was put down and made fast to a bollard. Antipater's aides covered it with a purple cloth, ran across and stood waiting officiously on the wharf to welcome him ashore.

One of them whispered to another: "This is a strange home-coming. Do you remember with what pomp we were sent off to Rome?"

"Why is the Commander of Fort Drusus not here to salute the King? Is everyone crazy in Caesarea?"

"See that the injured men are put ashore first," said Antipater, "and find someone to buy them fresh fruit, poor fellows."

When this had been done and the surgeon arrived, Antipater went ashore himself. A sergeant of Herod's bodyguard with a file of soldiers at his back now sauntered out from behind a building. He saluted Antipater and said: "Majesty, King Herod requires your presence in Jerusalem immediately; you are to take the post-chaise without delay."

The aides were astonished. Only a sergeant! One of them asked him: "Where is your commander? Why has he not come in person to welcome the King?"

The sergeant answered: "My instructions, which are directly from the King, are to answer no questions and permit no delays. The post-chaise is ready for His Majesty yonder by the weighing-shed, and I am to accompany him to Jerusalem. I am also instructed to disarm His Majesty."

"I carry no arms," said Antipater.

"I am to search Your Majesty, nevertheless."

"What of my staff?"

"I have no instructions about your staff: they may please themselves whether they escort you on hired horses or whether they remain here."

"Is my father the King in good health?"

"Your Majesty will pardon me, but I am not permitted to answer questions of any sort."

"First show me your warrant."

The warrant was in order and Antipater permitted himself to be searched. Then he climbed into the chaise, and the cobs set off at a trot along the quay. The staff stood gaping after him, but presently the more loyal members set off on foot for the city, hired horses and rode in pursuit. Jerusalem lay twenty-five miles away inland.

Antipater arrived at the Palace unescorted except by the sergeant; for Herod's guards posted at the City gate had detained the members of his staff who had overtaken him. The sergeant handed him over to the head-porter, who admitted him with surly looks, saying nothing and giving him a most perfunctory salute. No one came forward to welcome him, and a young officer to whom he had once shown favour shrank away hurriedly at his approach and concealed himself behind a pillar.

With head erect, Antipater entered the tessellated Judgement Hall, where he was expected, the news of his arrival at Caesarea having been conveyed by smoke-signal some hours before. Herod, looking pale and thin, sat upon his throne, propped with cushions; Varus in an ivory curule chair at his right hand. They had been settling a dispute about the grazing rights in Transjordania of certain Syrian nomads.

Antipater greeted them both with punctilio. A sudden silence fell as he walked the length of the hall, mounted the steps of the throne and made to embrace Herod.

Herod repelled him violently, turned his head away and cried: "The Lord confound you, you vile wretch, do not dare to touch me! Oh, Varus, is this not the perfect parricide? He treacherously plots my death, and then slobbers over me with kisses. Out of my sight, sirrah, and prepare your defence in the few hours that remain to you! You shall be tried to-morrow for your life, and the excellent Quinctilius Varus, who by a fortunate accident has arrived here to-day, is to be your judge."

Antipater stood stupefied. He turned appealingly towards Varus, who answered him with a wooden look, then again towards his father, who would not meet his eye but shouted: "Begone, begone, I say!"

Antipater made him a deep reverence, and then addressed Varus: "Your Excellency, I have not yet been acquainted with the charges against me; how shall I prepare a defence?"

"Doubtless the charge will be put in writing and handed to you within the hour."

Herod bellowed: "No, Varus, no! By Hercules, no! If I acquaint him with the charges he will use his interest with the warders to secure false witnesses for his trial, and have time to concoct his devilish excuses."

Varus answered mildly: "It is usual in criminal cases to give the accused sufficient time to prepare his defence."

"This is no usual case. This is plain parricide." Then he shouted at Antipater: "Why did you not make haste to return as I ordered? Where have you been all this long while since you left Antioch? You set off ten days before Varus yet arrive four days after him. Have you been visiting your fellow-criminal Antiphilus in Egypt? No, no, do not reply, pray! Save your lies until to-morrow!"

Antipater spent the night under guard in the Palace prison and was forbidden to communicate with anybody. He presently called for the Scriptures, hoping to calm his mind by reading, and they brought him a tattered set of scrolls. The Book of Genesis happened to be rolled back to the chapter which concerns the destruction of

Sodom. He began reading at random and the first text that caught his eye was this:

Escape for your life, look not behind you nor stay in the plain. Escape to the mountain lest you be consumed.

He sighed and thought: "The First Book of Moses, the nineteenth chapter and the seventeenth verse: 'Escape for your life, look not behind you, lest you be consumed!' The warning comes too late." Suddenly a light shóne through his mind and he remembered the groups of figures written on the back of his letters. They had begun with that very same series, 1. 19. 17. He remembered them all without difficulty from having studied them so intently; and now with trembling hands began to search the Scriptures and look up the remaining two quotations of the first series. The eighteenth book in the Jerusalem Canon was Job.

18. 18. 8. The eighteenth chapter of Job, the eighth verse. He found it:

He is cast into a net, he walks upon a snare.

12. 3. 27. The third chapter of the Second Book of Kings, the twenty-seventh verse. He found it:

Then he took his eldest son that should have reigned and offered him for a burned offering upon the wall.

The three texts comprised a warning not to walk into the snare that his father had set for him, but to escape for his life; for his father intended to destroy him as pitilessly as the King of Moab had destroyed his eldest son. A warning that had come too late. He supposed the other message to be of the same drift. But it was altogether different: it conveyed news.

Deuteronomy 24. 9:

Remember what the Lord your God did to Miriam by the way, after you were come forth out of Egypt.

II Samuel 11. 5:

And the woman conceived and sent and told David: "I am with child."

Joshua 15. 32:

And Lebaoth and Shilhim and Ain and Rimmon.

98

Then Antipater began to weep, caught between joy and apprehension. Mary was with child and safe with her kinsfolk at Ain-Rimmon; or was she still safe? Was it possible that Herod's anger had been provoked by the discovery of their secret marriage? Had Mary's secret perhaps been betrayed by one of the tented Rechabites who had carried her off? Had Herod arrested her and put her to the torture?

He prayed silently to his God that, whatever happened to himself, Mary might escape from the malice of his enemies and bear her child in safety. His love for her was like none other that he had ever experienced. He seemed at once her father, her child and her lover. No sooner had he joined hands with her at their marriage, and tasted the fragment of quince which, she placed between his lips, than he felt suddenly enroyalled—enroyalled in the very sense that Simon had proposed. It was as though he had died to his old faded world and been instantly reborn to her new, glorious one. Her image, as he had seen her for the first time, remained fixed in his mind; motionless and calm like the statue of a goddess. Her bridal robe was of white linen banded with blue, her mantle was cloth of gold edged with scarlet, her girdle of golden scallop-shells. Her silver shoes were curved like crescent moons; a jewelled serpent was grasped in her hand. Her diadem twinkled with twelve clusters of diamonds above her calm sea-green eyes; above her brow was the royal headband of Michal. Holiness emanated from her, and when she addressed him in the antique formula: "I am the Mother of Adam, I am the Mother of Salma, I have chosen you Caleb, Caleb of Mamre, to be my love", he had trembled as with an ague.

Now he trembled again to think of her. Only the one meeting, the first and last, and before dawn of the same night she had returned to Lysia's house; and he had ridden off to Caesarea to take ship for Rome. He would barter a year of his life for a sight of her, or a word with her. A year of his life? Had he even a week of life left to enjoy?

And the child?

All that night, stretched on the stone floor in his purple cloak, he brooded on the child. Would it be a son? His heart told him so. When he fell asleep he had wonderful dreams, the glory of which still illuminated his cell when the gaoler entered, an hour after dawn, bringing his breakfast: water in an earthenware jug and a crust of stale barley-bread.

"What have you there?" asked Antipater, still half asleep.

"Bread of affliction and water of affliction until I come again."

"Words of good omen! The prisoner to whom those words were first addressed was set free."

"Was he so? Then I dare undertake that his crimes were less odious than yours." He clanged the cell-door after him.

Antipater gave thanks to the Lord for a new day, washed his hands and began to eat. The spell of the dreams continued to hold him so that the water tasted like snow-cooled Lemnian wine, the bread like honey-cracknels. He spent the rest of the morning reading the Scriptures with a composed mind; especially, the chapter in Genesis which concerns the delivery of Isaac from his father Abraham's sacrificial knife gave him hope and comfort.

About noon he was again summoned to the Judgement Hall, known to the Jews as Gabbatha, or The Pavement. He found Varus and his father once more seated side by side, saluted them respectfully and abased himself as a suppliant at some distance from them, waiting to hear the charges read.

Herod stood up, waved a paper at him and cried: "It is absurd to go through the motions of a formal trial when I have evidence like this in my hand—a letter sent you by your accursed dam Doris, whom I have now divorced and banished. It was despatched a month after you sailed, but my faithful servants in the police service intercepted it. She writes: 'Remain in Rome, dear son. All is discovered. Throw yourself on Caesar's protection.'"

He handed the letter to Varus, who observed dryly: "Queen Doris when she wrote this letter must have been suffering from some painful rheumatic complaint. It has the shakiness that is characteristic of confessions extorted by torture."

Herod glared at Varus and bawled out between fits of wheezing: "It is the writing of a guilty woman who can hardly hold the pen for trembling. I trust, Excellency, that you will regard this evidence as conclusive and pronounce your verdict at once."

"Your son is a Roman citizen, Majesty, and I fear that we cannot curtail proceedings in the way that you suggest—unless, of course, he cares to plead guilty to the charges against him—without grave offence to the Emperor."

Antipater rose to his knees. "Father, I cannot plead guilty to charges that I have not heard. And I beg that you will not condemn me without a hearing. That my mother may have written to tell me 'all is discovered' should not be regarded as a proof either of my guilt or of her own. She may have temporarily lost her reason, which would account for the shakiness of her usually steady hand.

It is even possible that the letter has been forged by someone who wishes to discredit us both."

Herod interrupted him with cries of rage and lamentation, declaring that never had a kind father been so ill-used by his children, and that the worst ingrate of all was his eldest son Antipater. What care and love, honour and treasure he had lavished on him! And now this same Antipater vilely plotted to murder him in his old age, not content to wait until the dry knuckle-end of life that remained to him had been picked clean by the kites of Time. "And oh, the prodigious hypocrisy of the last years! How egregiously well he has pretended to watch over me, to proffer me sage advice, to dismiss unfaithful servants, to lighten my burden of business—all this only to strike me down in the end!" Then he laid the whole responsibility for the deaths of Alexander and Aristobulus on Antipater's shoulders, accusing him of forging evidence, suborning witnesses and having been the power behind the prosecution. He now believed, he said—wiping his eyes and groaning—that the poor fellows had been innocent after all; but he himself was not their murderer, it was Antipater. His false son Antipater, whose whole life might be summed up in the phrase "a mystery of evil".

He buried his head on his hands and pretended to sob. At this, Nicolaus of Damascus, who had been counsel for the prosecution at the trial of Alexander and Aristobulus, and also at that of Sylleus, came forward and read out the charges. He was a small dry man with a twisted neck and sneering lips.

The first charge: that Antipater had complained to his mother Queen Doris, on such and such a date, that his father King Herod had lived too long and grew younger every day—that he himself would be grey-bearded before he succeeded him, too old to take pleasure in the sole possession of the kingdom.

The second: that in conversation with his uncle Pheroras, on approximately such and such a date, Antipater had called his father the King a "wild beast and murderer" and said "if we have but courage and the hands of men we shall be free to live our lives without fear".

The third: that Antipater had sent to On-Heliopolis in Egypt for a deadly and subtle poison, which was brought back by one Antiphilus, a member of his staff, and secretly handed to his uncle Pheroras: and that this poison would have been administered to Herod by Pheroras—Antipater, having been sent to Rome by his father on urgent business, would have evaded suspicion—had he not hung back and destroyed all the poison but one small dose, which would be produced in Court.

The fourth: that Bathyllus, the freedman whom Antipater had sent back from Rome with despatches to the King shortly after his arrival there, brought a new pottle of poison with him from Antipater to deliver to Pheroras, in case the other proved ineffective; which poison had been seized and would also be produced in Court.

Nicolaus then offered written evidence of Antipater's guilt under each of these four counts in the form of depositions extracted by torture from Queen Doris, from ten Court-ladies in the employment of Pheroras, from Jochebed the wife of Pheroras and from her sister Naomi, also from Antiphilus, Bathyllus and others. These depositions he rapidly read out and then laid before Varus.

Varus, scrutinizing them with interest, remarked that Queen Doris's handwriting after torture was indistinguishable from her handwriting when she was merely oppressed with guilt, and that she used the same cheap quality of paper and the same muddy ink on both occasions—which he considered strange.

"Why strange, Excellency?" asked Nicolaus.

"My good Nicolaus, do you ask 'why'? Why—because it is the same paper on which all the witnesses have recorded their depositions: typical prison paper, and prison ink too. I make no pretence at being an expert criminologist, but, by the body of Bacchus, I have not been thirty years a magistrate for nothing. I have learned to cultivate elementary common sense. What stationery do queens use? The very best smooth-laid paper, at fifty drachmae a short roll, and they scent it with musk or roses. But this tattered, stained, corrugated stuff, full of lumps and thin patches—it is unthinkable that it ever reposed in the boudoir of a queen as elegant as Doris. If I had not King Herod's assurance to the contrary, I should suppose that the Queen's private letter to King Antipater at Rome had been written on the same occasion as the confession, which was admittedly extracted by torture."

Nicolaus was taken aback by this answer, and Varus continued: "In the ten depositions made by the Court-ladies of Pheroras, who tell their story in almost identical words, King Antipater is alleged to have informed his mother in their presence that he was going to Rome 'to get as far away as possible from that wild beast, my father'. This does not square with the statement in the third charge, according to which King Antipater was sent to Rome by his father on urgent business, or with a letter sent to me by King Herod some months ago to the same effect. King Antipater is also credited with accusing his father of 'cruelty in so wording his Will that my son will never reign after me. He is passed over in favour of my brother, Prince Herod Philip.' This accusation I cannot credit. King Antipater and Queen Doris both knew the contents of the Will—the Will, I mean, that has now been cancelled—and he could therefore never have said anything of the sort: for the Will, as I was officially informed at the time that it was drafted, made Prince Herod Philip heir to the throne only if King Antipater should be the first to die; and even in that event, the succession was to revert to Antipater's children upon Prince Heroa Philip's decease or abdication. But if King Antipater were to survive and succeed his father, Prince Herod Philip's claim would lapse, and King Antipater, with the Emperor's consent, might then appoint his son as the sole heir if he pleased. This discrepancy shakes my faith in the evidence as a whole."

In the silence that followed, Antipater was emboldened to make his defence, which he did briefly and simply. "Father, His Excellency Quinctilius Varus encourages me to suggest to you that these depositions are not reliable because extracted by torture, every one of them; and that the letter from my mother to me was also, though of course without your knowledge, extracted from her by torture. I undertake further to prove not only that my mother's letters to me are invariably written on the best Alexandrian paper but also that they are written in the Edomite dialect and the Hebrew script, not in Greek. My mother talks Greek ungrammatically and cannot write it except with the greatest difficulty. Moreover, as you know yourself, I was ordered to Rome by you, greatly against my inclination: I did not go there of my own free will to avoid you. And I am grateful to you, Father, for your admission that I have been a loyal and dutiful son to you ever since you lifted me out of private life and showed the world what a father's love can do. But that you can believe me not only a hypocrite, a fratricide and a parricide but demented as well, is hard to bear. I have lived forty years of my life, free from any accusation of crime, and could have had no expectations whatever from your murder except a tortured spirit and eventual damnation. Consider: my yearly income of fifty talents, over and above your gifts to me and the perquisites of my various offices, is far more than I ever spend; I enjoy the title and power of King; you have recommended me to the protection of the noblest men in the Empire. What is still more to the point, I have never received an unkind word from you in all my life nor had any occasion to complain of your treatment of me, which has been consistently generous and just. There is no one in the whole world, from your meanest subject to our great benefactor the Emperor Augustus Caesar himself, who can honestly deny the truth of what I say. That I should now turn and savage you, as sometimes a Molossian shepherd dog suddenly turns on his master, could be explained only as a fit of insanity; yet if I were insane the sickness would surely appear in my other actions as well. Do you perhaps believe that I am possessed of an evil spirit? Then cast it out, I beseech you, in the name of the Holy One of Israel, blessed be he."

Herod ground his teeth and tore at his small tufted beard. "I will cast this evil spirit out, but not in the Lord's name," he said. "I will cast it out in the Emperor's name with the rack, the brazier and the thumb-screw."

"I am ready to submit to the torture, Father, since it seems that my case is pre-judged."

Varus objected: "No, no, King Antipater, you are a Roman citizen and therefore exempt from torture. The Emperor would never approve of torture practised under Roman Law on a high officer of the Imperial forces. Would you care, by the by, to submit an evidence of the affection and confidence which you boasted just now that the Emperor reposes in you?"

"Here are two letters—the one from the Emperor himself, the other from his wife the Lady Livia. They are addressed to my father, but are open for all to read."

"They may be read later," said Herod, snatching the letters and stuffing them behind the cushions of his throne. "Nicolaus, proceed with the prosecution!"

Nicolaus realized that the case was going badly. The sympathy of almost everyone present except Herod himself and his sons Archelaus and Philip, who had designs on the throne, had swung about in Antipater's favour. The evidence that had at first sight seemed conclusive was now shown to be forged at least in part, and Antipater's demeanour had been that of an innocent and deeply injured man. Nicolaus therefore drew on rich resources of the forensic art when he rose to attack Antipater: reviling him as a cockatrice, a filthy ibis, a black Psyllian snake, a parricide of a unique kind. He denounced him as the betrayer and murderer of his innocent brothers and alleged him to have been Jochebed's seducer and the seducer of Jochebed's sister Naomi, and regularly to have played the part of the demon Azazel in a witches' frolic of lust and blasphemy, leaping about naked under the full moon in a circle of twelve naked women. "By your own confession, detestable he-goat, you had no motive for *your* crime of patricide but sheer devilry—the ambition, I suppose, to commit a crime unparalleled in history or legend, to poison the father from whom you yourself admit never to have heard an unkind word or experienced the least injustice, and to involve your mother and your father's last surviving brother in your own execrable guilt." Then he turned to Varus and urged him to "destroy this ravening wolf, this hyaena! Are you not aware that a parricide is a universal evil, the existence of which outrages Nature and spreads ill-luck wherever his infected feet may tread, and that the judge who fails to punish such a monster must himself face the frown of Divine Justice?"

When he had done with his raving, Varus asked Antipater in a matter-of-fact voice what reply he had to make.

"Nicolaus has brought against me a random accusation of witchcraft and blasphemy, which he makes no attempt to substantiate, and which he cannot substantiate, and which forms no part of the charges read out at the beginning of the trial. Beyond calling me evil names, he has added nothing new to the case and I am content to refrain from a reply: for I am no fishmonger and disdain to bandy foul language with any man. Instead, I call the God of my fathers to witness that I am entirely innocent of any of the crimes charged against me."

Nicolaus then urged Varus to examine the poison remaining in the pottle alleged to have been brought out of Egypt by Antiphilus. He suggested that a condemned criminal should be instructed to taste it, to prove whether it were deadly or not.

Varus agreed.

A Galilean bandit, who had been held in readiness for this demonstration, was led in and offered a free pardon on condition that he swallowed a little of the powder, mixed with honey. He agreed, swallowed, and very soon fell writhing on the floor, clutching his throat and belly and shrieking horribly. He was taken outside to die.

Varus laughed. "This is no subtle drug," he said. "This is arsenic, one of the crudest and most violent of all poisons. The symptoms of arsenical poisoning are well known and unmistakable, and Pheroras would never have risked detection by its use unless perhaps he had been the victim of the same unaccountable madness of which Antipater is accused. If this bandit, after swallowing the mixture, had grinned and thanked his God that he had escaped from harm, and had then left the Palace rejoicing, I should have suspended judgement and waited to see whether it were a drug of slow action. But now I cannot believe in the testimony, extracted by torture from Jochebed the wife of Pheroras, that this was the subtle poison allegedly brought by Antiphilus out of Egypt. My experience of Egyptian poisoners has taught me to rate their ingenuity far more highly than this. King Herod, may I have a word with you in private?"

The Court was adjourned, and what Varus said to King Herod was not disclosed; but there at least the proceedings ended and on the next day Varus courteously took his leave and returned to Antioch without delivering judgement.

A week later Herod reopened the case, on the ground that new evidence had been discovered. His agents, he said, had seized a letter, written by Antiphilus in Egypt, from the slave who was conveying it to Antipater at Jerusalem. It ran as follows:

"I have sent you Acme's letter at the risk of my life from two reigning houses. Success to your affairs!"

Herod instructed his agents that the other letter must be found at all costs, and suggested that they should search the slave. Sewn in the lining of his coat, sure enough, was the letter, supposedly from Acme, who was a Jewess in Livia's service, and addressed to Antipater:

"I have written to your father in the exact words you dictated to me, and have followed this up by handing a letter to my Lady Livia, also in your exact words as if sent by your Aunt Salome. This should result in Salome's well-merited death, for King Herod will naturally believe that she has been plotting against him."

Herod then produced still another letter, which he said had just arrived by courier from Rome. It was supposedly the letter written to him by Acme at Antipater's dictation and ran:

"As a true daughter of Israel I have been watching your interests here. I have just made an accurate copy of a letter written to my Lady Livia by your sister Salome. As you will see, it accuses you of treason and perjury; doubtless it was prompted by the old grudge that you had prevented her from marrying that heathen rascal Sylleus. Please destroy this when you have read it, because it is written at the hazard of my life." An alleged copy of a scurrilous letter signed "Salome" was appended.

Antipater was hauled out of prison in the middle of the night and confronted with these documents. He denied having had any communication with Acme and suggested that the letters had been forged by Antiphilus.

"That is for the Emperor to decide," Herod answered. "I shall send you to Rome to stand your trial there."

"Do so, Father. The Emperor is just and not easily imposed upon. He will be able to determine whether the letters signed 'Acme' are really written by Acme or are forgeries by some enemy of mine."

However, Herod did not venture to send him to Rome. Nicolaus and Archelaus went instead with a digest of the evidence quoted at the first hearing of Antipater's case, copies of the letters (though not the originals) produced at the second hearing, and an urgent request for permission to execute the parricide at once. Herod armed these envoys with rich gifts for Livia and the Emperor's legal secretary, and at the same time sent plate to the value of twenty talents to Varus at Antioch.

CHAPTER NINE

THE BLOOD OF ZACHARIAS

ELIZABETH was safely delivered of a sturdy boy. When the women of her household gathered around to admire him and affectionately called him "little Zacharias" she cried out: "Do not praise the child! It is unlucky! And, pray, do not call him little Zacharias. His name is to be John."

"Oh," they cried, "you are surely mistaken, my lady! Your husband would never name him John. It is not a family name. Naturally, he would not give the child the same name as himself: that would breed confusion. But what about 'Zephaniah'? It is a similar name, yet different, and comes close to Zacharias in the Canon of the Prophets. Or he might perhaps call him Abijah or Samuel, or perhaps Hezron—all these are family names, but John—oh never!"

"I am naming this child myself, because my husband is dumb, and John is the name that I have chosen. For the rubric of the circumcision service says explicitly: 'The father shall speak and say the child's name; or the father's nearest kinsman, if he be dead.' But my husband cannot speak, yet is not dead."

They protested: "A woman cannot name her son. It is indecent."

"Women, to what tribe are you reckoned?"

"To Judah."

"And both my lord your master and myself are reckoned to Levi. Search the Scriptures and you will find that our mother Leah named both Judah and Levi without troubling to consult her husband Jacob."

On the eighth day, the day after Elizabeth had ceased to be ceremonially unclean, the town rabbi rode up from Beersheba to circumcise the child. He took it from Shelom's arms and said: "His name is to be Zephaniah, the porter tells me."

"No, no," said Shelom. "John is his name. The lady Elizabeth has made that clear enough."

"I will not circumcise him in that name," the rabbi cried, "without his father's permission in writing."

Zacharias was called from his study, where he was preparing a concordance of Messianic prophecies with a commentary, a work on which he had been engaged for several years. The rabbi handed him a writing-tablet and asked: "What is his name to be?"

Elizabeth bustled out from her bedroom and stood between the rabbi and Zacharias. She said indignantly: "Husband, I am naming this child John and my impudent household wish to name him Zephaniah. Tell them that they have no right to interfere with my choice!"

Zacharias wrote: "His name is John."

"John? What is John?" cried the testy old rabbi. "My lord of Ain-Rimmon, I should be ashamed to address a Son of Aaron by so new-fangled a name as John. There were no Johns in Israel until the day before yesterday!"

Zacharias grew angry. He shouted: "Fool, fool, mule, creature of stubbornness! His name is JOHN, I say!"

Everyone was astounded to hear Zacharias speak. He was astounded himself. He fell on his face and gave thanks to the Lord for loosening the strings of his tongue.

The circumcision ceremony was then carried out in the customary manner, and the rabbi prayed: "Our God and God of our fathers! Preserve this child to his father and mother, and let his name be called, in Israel, John the son of Zacharias. Let the father rejoice in him that came forth from his loins and let the mother be glad in the fruit of her womb." It was not until the rabbi had taken his leave and the screams of the child had been somewhat hushed that Zacharias began to consider with apprehension what the effects would be of his restoration to speech, and heartily wished himself dumb again: he recollected the horror of his vision in the Sanctuary and knew that he must now testify before the High Court. He said sadly to the child: "Alas, little John, I fear that I shall never live to see you walk and talk!"

Elizabeth protested in astonishment: "Why, husband, have you no better blessing for my child than this, that he will be orphaned within the year?"

Zacharias felt the justice of the reproach. He answered: "Give me leave to return to my study, wife, for I have not the art of extempore speech, but before nightfall, by the grace of the Lord, I shall have composed the blessing that you ask."

Now, when he had been called suddenly from his study to answer the rabbi, two strips of parchment, which were texts from his concordance, had been carried across the table by the draught from the door and lay close to his pen and sand-caster. He picked them up and read them. The first was the well-known passage from the fortieth chapter of Isaiah beginning:

> The voice of one who cries in the desert: "Clear the way for the Lord, build a straight highway for our God through this desert."

And the other was the equally well-known passage from the Psalms beginning:

> The Lord has sworn a firm oath to David. . . .

The verse that caught his eye was:

> There I will cause the horn of David to bud: I have ordained a lamp for my Messiah.

The accident provided him with what the poets of the Negeb term "a kindling": as it were a sudden tongue of flame that seizes upon the poetic sacrifice and consumes it. He muttered: "It is said that every man who loves the Lord and his neighbour will find one poem at least written on his heart, if he searches closely. May he give me the skill and patience to transcribe mine!"

With trembling hands he set to work, writing, cancelling and rewriting until his goose-feather quill grew blunt and blotched the letters. Too busied with his thoughts to trim it, he threw it over his shoulder and seized another. And hardly half an hour had passed before he came running out from his study, parchment in hand, stood over the sleeping child and chanted:

> The God of Israël, blessèd be he,
> Who visited his sons in majesty
> And bought them from Egyptian slavery.
>
> Will he not cause a tender horn to bud
> Above a brow of David's princely blood
> For the renascence of our nationhood?
>
> The same is told by every poet's tongue
> Who truth has uttered since the world was young
> And in his Name prophetically has sung:
>
> Promise of rescue from our foes, of peace
> To serve him righteously, with huge increase,
> Holy and fearless, until life shall cease.
>
> Now is renewed the oath which once before
> To our great father Abraham he swore
> That Canaan should be ours for evermore.
>
> And of you, Child, the wondering world shall say:
> "Look, the King's outrider who clears the way
> Preaching salvation and the longed-for day,
>
> Who like the dawn scatters the doubts of night
> With largesse of pure gold, in sin's despite
> Leading our feet to mercy by his light."

When the infant John was one month old, Elizabeth vowed to dedicate him to Jehovah as a life-long Nazirite, according to the regulations set out in the sixth chapter of the Book of Numbers: his hair was never to be shaved and he was never to eat grapes or drink wine. And in emulation of Zacharias's poem she composed a lullaby for him which is still current at Ain-Rimmon, where I myself heard it sung by a village woman to her fretful child:

> Down in the garden as I walked
>   One lovely day of spring
> A tall pomegranate-tree I spied,
>   Of every tree the king.

More green his leaf than beryl stone
Caught in a blaze of sun;
His scarlet flowers that budded out
More sweet than cinnamon.

With trembling hand a flower I plucked
Between my breasts to lie—
Fruit of the tall pomegranate-tree,
Sleep well and lullaby!

The news that Zacharias had suddenly been cured of his dumbness soon reached Jerusalem. Summoned to appear before the High Priest, he locked his unfinished concordance in a cedar box, signed and sealed his Will, kissed Elizabeth and the infant John goodbye and rode off alone towards the City, his heart heavy with foreboding.

When on the following afternoon he reported his arrival at Simon's house in the Old Quarter he was instructed to wait in an ante-chamber, where refreshments would be brought him. Then Simon summoned the Great Sanhedrin, or Council; they were to meet as soon as possible at his house, not at the House of Hewn Stone, as they usually did, "for the purpose of investigating the nature and circumstances of the priest Zacharias's recent experience in the Sanctuary, in so far as it raises any question of political importance". He requested them to keep secret the time, place and business.

The Great Sanhedrin must not be confused with the other Sanhedrin, called the Beth Din, or High Court. Originally there had been only one Sanhedrin, but when Queen Alexandra, widow of King Alexander Jannaeus the backsliding Maccabee, was forbidden by the dominant Pharisee party to give his body decent burial she had persuaded them to change their attitude by promising that the Sanhedrin should thereafter consist only of Pharisees, to the exclusion of the Sadducees who had been Alexander's chief supporters and who had assisted him in the massacre of eight hundred Pharisees. The Sadducees had then formed a rival Sanhedrin, to which Herod's father, when Julius Caesar made him Governor-General of Judaea, gave official recognition. The original Sanhedrin, the High Court, remained exclusively Pharisee, and dealt with religious questions only; but the political Sanhedrin, which called itself the Great Sanhedrin and dealt with lay questions, was prominently Sadducee, though the Pharisees were represented in it. Ideally, there was no distinction between religious and lay questions among the Jews, because the Law of Moses governed all social and economic life; yet the Great Sanhedrin was a political convenience, since it could take realistic cognizance of foreign institutions within the Judaean state which for the Pharisees had no existence. For this reason the High Court insisted that the *Mezuzah*, which was fixed on the door-post of every building not sacred in itself, should be displayed at the House of Hewn Stone when the Great Sanhedrin met there; yet when the High Court met there it became a sacred building and the *Mezuzah* was temporarily removed. (The *Mezuzah* is a piece of parchment inscribed on one side with the "Hear, O Israel" text from Deuteronomy and on the other with the divine Name SHADDAI; it is rolled up in a container of horn or wood with the Name showing through an aperture.)

Simon had decided to call Zacharias's case before the Great Sanhedrin, although the matter seemed to lie wholly in the jurisdiction of the High Court, because if Zacharias should be proved guilty of any ceremonial irregularity, the Leader of the Course of Abijah would be able to persuade his broad-minded Sadducee colleagues to quash the matter with a discreetly worded report and an adjournment *sine die*. He acted quickly and secretly in order to forestall a claim by the joint-Presidents of the High Court that the inquiry should be conducted by themselves. The members of the Great Sanhedrin were all men of wide juridical experience, and since they were required to understand foreign languages and the humane sciences, besides being word-perfect in the Canonical Scriptures, would be sufficiently men of the world, Simon trusted, to settle the affair without scandal.

By the time that his messengers had gone the rounds and a full Court of Inquiry had assembled under Simon's Presidency, it was an hour after nightfall; but Zacharias was not brought before them at once. Simon preferred to begin his investigation by questioning Reuben the son of Abdiel, who was asked to explain why, on the night that Zacharias had been struck dumb, just before dawn, he had secretly removed from the Sanctuary some wet object wrapped in his cloak.

When Reuben looked around him—at the grave elders, priests and doctors, full members of the Court, seated in a semicircle about the President's chair, with three rows of associate members ranked behind them, all fully qualified magistrates, at the two clerks with pens poised and paper ready to record the proceedings—he was seized with sudden alarm. He decided to reveal the whole truth, rather than continue to shield Zacharias.

He deposed on oath that when he had entered the Sanctuary on the evening in question he had found the sacrificial fire quenched on the Altar of Incense, though the seven lamps of the Sacred Candlestick were still burning brightly. Then, to preserve the honour of the Course of Abijah, he had taken the wet cinders from the Altar, relaid and rekindled the fire and duly burned incense; it was these wet cinders that he had removed from the Sanctuary in his cloak at first cock-crow, when he went off duty, hoping that the Watcher of the Curtain who had come to relieve him would not notice anything amiss.

Simon commented: "In my opinion you did well, Son of Abdiel, though you would doubtless have done better still had you immediately reported the occurrence either to myself or to the venerable Leader of your Course." Here he bowed to the aged priest, who nodded gravely. Then he added: "Brothers and Sons, does any of you wish to question the learned Reuben further?"

A curly-bearded, youthful associate member sprang up and cried impetuously: "Holy Father, ask him this: 'By what evil hand do you suppose that the fire was quenched?'"

There was a murmur of agreement, mixed with exclamations of disgust. The white-bearded elders of the front row craned around to glare their disapproval of this unseemly interruption. It was held that associates of the back row should be always seen but seldom heard. Moreover, the rules of the Court forbade them to speak for the prosecution, and though no charge was being preferred against either Reuben or Zacharias, so that the distinction between prosecution and defence could not yet be drawn, it was clear that this associate wished Zacharias no good.

Simon reluctantly asked the question.

Reuben answered: "Holy Son of Boethus, if I tell you how I think that the fire was quenched this honourable Court will be angry with me. I shall therefore refrain from an opinion. I am bound to disclose facts, but I am ignorant of any rule that compels me to disclose the innermost thoughts of my heart."

"I undertake," said Simon, "that your opinion will not be censured by this Court, whatever its nature."

Then Reuben said: "Notables of the Sanhedrin, none of you is admitted as a member of this famous tribunal who is so little experienced in the magical arts that he cannot expose and punish magic when it is practised by the enemies of our religion. Seventy-one of you, a full Court, are assembled in this hall, and only one chair is empty, the chair reserved for the great prophet Elijah, who has not yet suffered death. I call this same Elijah to witness, if he is within hearing, as he may invisibly be, that what I say is the whole truth, with nothing added or omitted. It was thus. When I entered the Sanctuary that evening as deputy for my kinsman Zacharias, I noticed at once that the air was noxious and that wet marks sullied the clean marble floor. The smell may have been merely the stale odour of quenched incense and embers, but I fancied that my nostrils distinguished something else: the subtle but pervasive odour of evil. And when I stooped to wipe the marks away with the broidered napkin, in horror I recoiled. O learned Elders of Israel, refrain from anger against me—for alas, as the Lord our God lives, the marks that I saw were the clear imprints not of a man's feet but, horrible to relate, of hooves—the narrow hooves of an unshod ass!

Without pausing to observe the effect on the Court of the dreadful declaration, Reuben continued: "I am asked my opinion on how the fire at the Altar of Incense was quenched. I will give it. My opinion is that by blasphemous and abominable charms, there in the very Sanctuary of our God, my kinsman Zacharias had conjured up one of the fiendish ass-haunched Lilim and compelled him to his service. But why? Was it to persuade the demon to quicken the womb of his wife Elizabeth who had been barren twenty years? For demons are credited with such powers. Or was the demon summoned to reveal the whereabouts of buried treasure? Or to do a cruel injury to some man whom Zacharias hated? These are questions that I cannot resolve, but my studied opinion is that a fiend was summoned and that, pricked by diabolic spite, this fiend quenched the coals with a spurt of foul water from his mouth. And why do I believe this unlikely thing? Because, though I looked carefully about me, I could find no vessel of any sort in the Sanctuary by means of which the fire could have been extinguished. And if I am asked why I consider that Zacharias was struck dumb, this is my reply: in my opinion Zacharias was struck dumb by an angel of the Lord so that he might utter no further blasphemies, charms or abominable incantations."

Simon asked again: "Brothers and Sons, does any of you wish to question the learned Reuben further?"

All sat silent, awed and scandalized, each hoping that his neighbour would speak before him. At last the same curly-bearded associate arose, but this time looked modestly about him and coughed inquiringly as if seeking permission to ask another question.

Encouraged by a low murmur, he said: "Holy Father, pray ask him this: 'Were the tracks that you saw like those of an ass walking on all fours, or like those of an ass walking on his hind legs?'"

Simon asked the question.

"On his hind legs," answered Reuben, shuddering. He persisted in his story without contradicting himself, though Simon attempted to shake his evidence by ridicule.

Simon then requested the associates to retire while he consulted with the full members: the question was, whether the case should at this point be referred to the High Court, since it had taken so painful and embarrassing a turn. But jealousy triumphed over embarrassment. A vote was taken and it was decided to continue with the inquiry.

The associates were recalled, and when the clerks had read out Reuben's deposition Zacharias was summoned to appear. He came in blinking, for he had fallen asleep from weariness.

Simon began mildly: "Son of Barachias, this Court wishes to know how it happened that the fire was extinguished on the Altar of Incense during the evening of your ministry, when you were struck dumb. Let me warn you, before you answer: you have been accused of sorcery."

Zacharias stood silent for a while. Then he asked bitterly: "Shall I tell you the truth, which will outrage you, or shall I tell you a comfortable lie?" He added with a groan: "Would to God that I were dumb again!"

"You are to tell the truth, Brother, as you desire justice."

"You will kill me if I tell you the truth; yet my soul will have no peace if I lie to you or withhold the truth. Will you not mercifully leave me in peace? Will you not dismiss the Court?"

"I cannot dismiss this Court, which is a Court of Inquiry. I may only adjourn it. Do you pray for an adjournment?"

Zacharias considered. After a while he said: "An adjournment would mean only increased misery of soul. No; so be it! I will tell you the truth to-night, but you shall swear by the living God that if I must die because I have told it, you will take no vengeance on my family, and that you will kill me cleanly, for the truth's sake. Do you hear me? You shall swear by the Holy Name that I shall not die by hanging or strangulation or fire: that you will grant my body decent burial at least. For to die is hateful; but to die accursed is to wander houseless among lizards and jackals, an unquiet phantom perpetually seeking rest."

Simon answered gently: "There is no need for the swearing of

oaths. Tell the whole truth and trust to the mercy of the Lord."
He then read Reuben's deposition and asked Zacharias whether it
were true.

"That Reuben saw what he deposes that he saw," said Zacharias,
"I do not doubt, nor that in the uncharitableness of his heart he
thought, and thinks, that I am capable of abominable crime. His
anger has been hot against me ever since I testified before the Court
of Disputes sixteen years ago in the matter of the Well of the Jawbone, the property of my brother-in-law Joachim, whom I see yonder:
for Reuben's heart is a nest of grudges. May the Lord cleanse it
with a sudden scare-fire!" He fell silent again, but at last, by fits and
starts, nervously fumbling with the phylactery on his arm, he told
his story.

"I was offering incense on the Altar, clean in body and clean in
dress, having fasted all day. The Watcher of the Curtain had left
the Sanctuary upon my arrival, as the custom is. And as I was
finishing the rite, suddenly I heard the sound of a still, small voice.
It proceeded from behind the Holy Curtain and it called me by my
name: 'Zacharias!' I answered: 'Here I am, Lord! Speak, for thy
servant heareth.' The voice said: 'What things are these that you
are burning at my altar?' And I answered: 'The sweet incense,
Lord, according to the command that thou gavest to thy servant
Moses.' Then the voice asked: 'Is the Sun of Holiness a harlot or a
catamite? Do my nostrils snuff storax, hinge of scallop, frankincense, narthex, pounded together and smoking on coals of cedar-
wood? Would you make a sweat-bath for the Sun of Holiness?' I
could make no reply. Then, as I abased myself, I heard the Curtain
drawn and majestic steps approaching. And I heard a hissing and a
spluttering as the fire was suddenly extinguished on the Altar. My
senses left me."

The Sanhedrin listened in a fearful silence. Not a man dared
look his neighbour in the face to read what was written there.

At last Simon spoke in a faint voice: "Once to John Hyrcanus the
High Priest, when he was offering incense at the same altar and at
the very hour, came a divine voice informing him of the victory of
his sons over the evil King Antiochus. But a voice only was heard:
no sound of footsteps. Proceed with your evidence!"

"Have I not told you enough?"

"You have more to tell. Proceed!"

"Then, when I came to myself I saw—and I saw, when at last I
came to myself, and when I raised my head to look, I saw—"

"What did you see?"

"I saw—O merciful God, return to me my dumbness!"

"What did·you see?"

"Holy Son of Boethus, pity me that I have to declare the nature of my vision! I saw a Power clothed in robes of light that resembled the same sacred robes which you yourself wear at the grand festivals. And this Power hugged to its breast a triple-headed golden dog and a golden sceptre in the form of a budding palm branch; and, as the Lord our God lives, this Power stood in a gap between the Curtain and the wall on the right hand; and this Power was of more than human stature; and this Power spoke in the same still, small voice that I had heard before, saying: 'Be not afraid, Zacharias! Go out now and tell my people truthfully what you have both heard and seen!' But I could not, for I was struck dumb."

Beads of sweat started on Zacharias's brow and rolled down into his beard, where they hung shining in the light of the pine-torches that blazed beside him in an iron cresset. He opened his mouth to say more, but closed it again convulsively.

Simon's heart ached for Zacharias. He told the Court: "I have done with my questions. Need we question the son of Barachias further? These are words of frenzy or of a sick imagination. To record them in the minutes of this meeting would be injudicious in the extreme."

An old Doctor named Matthias son of Margalothus rose resolutely. "Holy Son of Boethus," he said, "if Zacharias alone had testified to the apparition, I should support your kindly proposal to stop our ears to his raving. But what of Reuben's testimony? Reuben saw tracks. Am I permitted to cross-examine the son of Barachias?"

"You are permitted," said Simon.

Matthias said: "Zacharias, answer me with care. Did this Power who spoke in the Name of the Holy One reveal his countenance to you?"

Zacharias answered with trembling lips: "Son of Margalothus, I am commanded to tell the truth. The countenance was revealed."

"Listen to his blasphemies, elders and sons of Israel! What need have we of further evidence? Is it not written that the Lord instructed his servant Moses: 'But for my face, thou canst not see it; for there shall no man see it and live'?"

Zacharias stood like an antelope-ox at bay. He shouted out: "The Lord God has given me ears to hear, eyes to see, a mouth to speak. Why should I deny these holy gifts? Hear me, all you Elders and Sons of Israel, hear me well! What did I see? I say that I saw the face of the Power, and the face shone, though not unmercifully

bright, and the likeness of the face"—his voice rose to a scream—
"and the likeness of the face was that of a Wild Ass!"

Then a sigh arose and a murmur, like the sigh and murmur that
precedes a thunder-storm. A subdued cry arose here and there:
"Alas! Blasphemy, blasphemy!"

Every man in the hall stood up and began to tear his garments.
These were stolid men, men of the world, and refrained from the
wild rending and ripping practised by Jewish village folk when a
blasphemous word is spoken. They were content to pull open the
short blasphemy-seams of their coat-lapels, and exclaim: "Woe to
the mouth that utters these things!"

Reuben raised his voice above the clamour. "Simon son of
Boethus, I declare this man, though he is my kinsman, to be a
sorcerer and by sorcery to have defiled the Sanctuary! I demand
that this declaration be converted into a charge, that Zacharias be
instructed to answer it immediately, and that, if he cannot do so, a
vote be taken and counted for a summary death verdict."

Simon replied sternly: "Not so, Son of Abdiel! Summoned before
us as a witness, do you set yourself up as an accuser? And must I
remind you that we have met here as a Court of Inquiry, not as a
Court of Justice? Even as a Court of Justice qualified to try this
case we could not condemn the son of Barachias at once. For the
rule runs: 'If a verdict is for acquittal it may be spoken to-day; if for
death, it cannot be pronounced until to-morrow.' And are you
ignorant of the Law itself, which forbids a man to be tried, as you
would have him tried, without at least two witnesses called against
him?"

Simon was in anguish of mind. Though he knew in his heart
that Zacharias was innocent of sorcery, he could not put it to the
Court that the vision might perhaps have been a divine or angelic
one. Still less could he publish his own suspicions, which if they
had been accepted would have plunged the nation headlong into
civil war. Yet these suspicions were so strong that he would have
been prepared to announce them as fact. Only one explanation of
the vision was possible, now that he connected it with an incident
reported to him on the following day by the priest of the Temple
Watch. The Temple Watch was a standing patrol of one priest and
seven Levites: they marched around the Temple all night and all
day at regular intervals to see that the various priestly sentries were
vigilant and that all was in order. One sentry was posted at the
Chamber of the Hearth, another at the Chamber of the Flame, a
third in the Attic. The Priest of the First Watch had reported to

his superior officer, the Captain of the Temple: "As I passed with the Watch into the Attic, shortly after my relief of the Third Watch, I found the sentry Zichri son of Shammai asleep. I set light to his sleeve with my torch, as my orders are, but even then he did not wake. Almost he seemed drugged or drunken, for the flesh of his arm was well scorched before he awoke." The Captain of the Temple, passing on the report, had pleaded: "Pray, Holy Father, do not bring the matter before the High Court, for this Zichri is brother to my own wife, and has already suffered for his folly. Besides, let me tell you frankly, the last refreshment that he took was at my own table."

Simon could picture the whole scene as vividly as if he had witnessed it from the steps of the Altar. The clue to the apparition lay in the secret underground passage which ran from the Tower of Antonia to the Inner Court; Herod's excuse for building it had been that if a sudden riot in the Temple endangered the sacred instruments of worship they might be quickly borne away to the security of the Tower. Near the outlet of the passage a narrow stairway led to the store-rooms above the Sanctuary, and thence to the empty chamber immediately above the Holy of Holies—the Attic where the sentry stood guard. And in the floor of this empty chamber was a trap-door through which, very rarely, after a propitiatory sacrifice and a warning tinkle of bells, seven times repeated, Telmenite workmen were lowered to perform necessary repairs to the fabric of the Holy of Holies itself; for to descend from above into this awful place, in case of need, was to evade the curse of entrance. Moreover, the robes and regalia peculiar to the High Priest, which the Power was said to have worn, were now laid up in the Tower of Antonia under the charge of the Captain of the Temple, who had been appointed by Herod himself. The golden onager's head of Dora, the golden dog of Solomon, the golden sceptre of David— Simon recognized all three by Zacharias's description.

Who was the Power? Simon knew. He had read the *Histories* of the Egyptian Manetho. Manetho recorded that the City of Jerusalem was first founded by the Shepherd Kings of Egypt when they were expelled from their great city of Pelusium, the City of the Sun, by the Pharaohs of the Eighteenth Dynasty. The Israelites had been vassals of the Shepherds. When, a generation or two later, they themselves fled from Egypt under Moses, and—after a long stay in the wilderness—returned to Canaan, they there renewed their homage to the God of the Shepherds, and to his bride, the Moon-goddess Anatha. With the homage went a mass-offering of foreskins; for during their wanderings the Israelites had abandoned the Egyptian custom of circumcision.

The God of the Shepherds was the Egyptian Sun-god Sutekh, or Set, who appears in Genesis as Seth son of Adam, and when King David captured Jerusalem from the Jebusites, the descendants of the Shepherds, Set became the god of all Israel under the title of Jehovah. The Menorah, the sacred seven-branched Candlestick of the Sanctuary, was a reminder of his history. It was constructed to represent the Sun, the Moon and the five planets Mars, Mercury, Jupiter, Venus and Saturn; and according to the Doctors of the Law it illustrated the text in Genesis where on the fourth day of Creation Jehovah said: "Let there be lights." The Menorah faced west-south-west, a quarter of the heavens not obviously connected with the Sun, except as he approaches his decline; so that when the Jewish Solar religion was reformed under King Josiah the ancient tradition, "In that direction the Lord God has his habitation", was not either altered or suppressed. Yet draw a map of Judaea and Egypt and make Jerusalem the centre of a twelve-pointed compass and follow along the ray running west-south-west. The eye travels over wild hills and desert places until it strikes the Nile at the head of the Delta, and there on the eastern bank stands On-Heliopolis, the oldest and holiest city in all Egypt, the city of the Sun-god Ra, whose titles, when he grew senile and dribbled, Set won by conquest: On-Heliopolis, where the sacred persea-tree grows from whose branches the Sun-god is said to arise each morning; On-Heliopolis, where the sacred bull Mnevis is stabled and gives oracular responses; On-Heliopolis, where the long-lived Phoenix dies and in a nest of frankincense is renewed; On-Heliopolis, where Moses was a priest; On-Heliopolis, near to where in the days of Ptolemy Philometor the fugitive Jewish High Priest Onias built a rival Temple to that of Jerusalem, justifying his action by the nineteenth chapter of Isaiah:

> In that day shall five cities in the land of Egypt speak the language of Canaan and swear allegiance to the Lord of Hosts.
> One of these shall be the City of the Sun.
> And in that day an altar shall be raised to the Lord in the middle of the land of Egypt, and a pillar to the Lord at its border.

For On-Heliopolis lies both in the middle of Egypt and at its border.

Who, then, was the Power? The Power could only be Herod himself, impersonating the Deity. He had crowned half a lifetime of premeditation by this outrageously daring act—a pretended theophany of the Lord God of Israel in his archaic character of Set, whom the Egyptians worship in the likeness of an onager, or wild-ass!

"Oh, the mad fool!" thought Simon. To suppose that he could turn the shadow back on the sun-dial, to suppose that the elders of Israel who had now for centuries worshipped a transcendent God, a Being so unique and so remote that neither his nature nor his appearance could be comprehended, but a God of mercy and justice and loving-kindness for all that, could be tricked into bowing the knee to this barbarous beast-headed deity! To the infamous Set, who had torn his brother Osiris in pieces and sent scorpions to sting the Child Horus to death; to Set, the fire-breathing sirocco-demon, hated by the gods, whom the Greeks also call Typhon; to Set, the great oppressor of mankind, in whose odious name victims were still yearly tossed to the beast of the reeds, the musky yellow-fanged crocodile of Pelusium!

Simon knew that Zacharias was in peril of death. The very walls of the Chamber seemed to cry out against him. He should never have been deceived: he should have distinguished instantly between the voice of the Lord which speaks inwardly, and the voice of man which strikes through the gross outward ear; between the majesty of the Lord which glows in the heart and mind, and the pomp of man which flatters the gross outward eye; between the timber of the grove, as poets call it, and Divine Wisdom who had hewn out the choicest timber for her holy temple.

Simon called for silence while he summed up the case. "If the son of Barachias, by conjuration, summoned an evil demon to defile the Sanctuary, as Reuben son of Abdiel charges without the warrant of this Court, then the wrath of the Lord will assuredly overtake him. For it is written: 'Against him that turns after familiar spirits and after wizards, I will set my face and cut him off from among his people.' And that no false demon, but the Lord God himself, has appeared to Zacharias is manifestly impossible, since Zacharias is yet alive, whereas it is established that all who look upon the Lord's face must instantly die; Moses saw the Holy One's hinder parts only. Moreover, Zacharias, even if he did not conjure up this demon himself but accidentally encountered him in the Sanctuary, yet by his own admission addressed him reverently as though he were the Lord himself. Has he not therefore broken the First Commandment, which runs: 'Thou shalt have no other gods but me'? For my part, I cannot conceive Zacharias to be guiltless of a grave fault; yet I doubt whether this honourable Court, even if convened as a Court of Justice, is empowered to try the case. It seems to me that we have no choice but to refer it to the High Court, where charges of this unusual sort are tried."

Reuben interrupted indignantly: "But we have heard his blasphemies with our own ears! For those alone he deserves death by stoning."

"Son of Abdiel, do not insult us by your continued pretence of ignorance. Death by stoning is meted out to a blasphemer only if he joins the Holy Name with a curse or an obscenity; blasphemy of the Lord God's attributes earns no more than a severe flogging. And it is my duty to warn you that if you are found to have borne false witness against your kinsman in a capital case you yourself will fall under the shadow of death." Simon then dismissed the Court with a decisive gesture, after thanking them for their correctness in painful circumstances and requesting the twelve senior members to remain behind and advise him what precise charge, or charges, if any, should be preferred against Zacharias, and in which Court.

Zacharias himself was now free to return to his own house, for in Jewish law an accused person is regarded as wholly innocent until sentence has been passed, and is subject to no bodily restraint. But he remained brooding in his chair until Simon desired him to leave. After a formal reverence he walked slowly out into the lobby crowded with members and associates whispering excitedly to one another in groups. His distraught looks persuaded some of them that he had devils nestling in the lap of his robe and they shrank away from his shadow as if it were a leper's.

Reuben pointed with his finger and cried: "This clemency is not to be borne. He must die tonight, else all Israel will be shamed. The sorcerer must not be permitted to look upon another sun!"

Joachim, Mary's father, who had been sitting as a full member, reproved him: "Son of Abdiel, this is contempt of court. You take too much upon yourself." But the words served only to rouse still angrier passions in Reuben's heart.

Outside a noisy crowd was assembled. A junior club-meeting of the Sons of Zadok had just broken up after a festive banquet near by, and about a hundred young men, flushed with wine, were gathered at the door of the High Priest's house, drawn by a rumour that something extraordinary was happening there. Some of them had already ventured into the lobby, where Reuben gave them a hurried and inaccurate summary of the proceedings and was now inciting them to take the law into their own hands. He advised them: "Do nothing to this sorcerer yet, my sons—do nothing in the sight or hearing of the people. But do not flinch from the deed. This touches the honour of our own House."

Zacharias went out into the street, and Reuben with the club-members followed after him in silence. As he crossed the court-yard between the house and the gate Reuben ostentatiously prised up a cobble-stone and dropped it into the lap of his robe. The Sons of Zadok followed his example. From what Reuben had told them they expected that Zacharias would go out through the Southern Gate into the wilderness, making for the cliff of Beth Hadudo where he would claim the protection of the demon Azazel to whom the scape-goat is yearly sacrificed on the Day of Atonement. Fortified with wine, they did not fear the wiles of this fiend. But instead, he led them uphill, hurrying towards the Temple. The few passers-by were unaware that anything of importance was happening: if the Sons of Zadok had dispersed after their club-meeting and the more zealous of them were now going up to the Temple for prayer, what was that?

The moon was full, and shone so brightly that the colours of Zacharias's embroidered cloak showed almost as truly as by day, but the shadows in the clefts of the Cheesemongers' Valley, as they passed over the Bridge, were as black as tar. He reached the Temple and glided like a sleep-walker across the Courts. The Zadokite clubmen, in a pack, pressed hard on his heels; behind them in a ragged procession panted the members and associates of the Great Sanhedrin, most of them anxious to restrain Reuben from an act of violence, a few, however, secretly hoping that justice would be done in the antique manner.

Zacharias entered the Sanctuary. At this, the associate with the curly beard, who had been among those most deeply moved to anger by the confession of Zacharias, drew a cobble-stone from the lap of his robe and laid it down on the pavement. He cried out loudly: "Stay, brothers, for the son of Barachias goes to be judged by the Lord God himself! Is it not written: 'Vengeance is mine, saith the Lord, I will repay'?" With these words he restrained the clubmen who were near him, and they in turn restrained those that followed. But about twenty others had by this time followed Zacharias into the Sanctuary.

Zacharias took his stand by the Altar of Incense and flung out his hands in despair. He cried: "Men of Israel, in what way have I sinned? In this Holy Place I call the Lord God to witness that I have used neither conjuration nor other forbidden sorcery; that I love him only and detest the princes of evil; and that I have told only the truth!"

Reuben replied passionately: "Have you not heard the decision of the High Priest? You have defiled this Holy Place, Son of Barachias, and only your hot life-blood can cleanse it."

He took the cobble-stone from his robe and let fly. It struck Zacharias full in the mouth. "Ha! Ha!" Reuben cried. " 'He breaketh the teeth of the ungodly!' "

Zacharias chanted in a quavering voice:

> *The God of Israel, blessèd be he,*
> *Who visited his sons in majesty*
> *And bought them from Egyptian slavery!*

Ten of Reuben's companions were abashed and fled hastily. But those who remained took courage from him and pelted Zacharias until he fell dead with a great cry to the Lord for vengeance. His blood was spattered on the Altar and even on the lilies of the Candlestick.

Simon came stumbling in when all was over, accompanied by the Temple Watch. He was horrified by the bloody scene. "Alas, brothers!" he cried. "If you could but have waited until morning!" Reuben and his companions stood triumphant, for according to ancient tradition the crime of sorcery could be expiated only by the shedding of the sorcerer's life-blood, and where could this expiation be more fittingly made than at the Altar which he had defiled?

Reuben answered him boldly: "Son of Boethus, do not reprove our zeal! You are provoking the Lord to anger. Come, give us instructions for expelling the demons who may still be lurking in some corner of this holy place!"

Again, Simon was faced by a painful decision. Either he must approve the act as a just one inspired by righteous zeal and transcending juridical forms or else he must condemn it as a sacrilegious murder by a drunken gang of young patricians. To approve was to sanction contempt of court and so to weaken the authority of the Great Sanhedrin, of which he was President. Yet the young men had not acted maliciously or impiously; it was Reuben who had misled them. And to have them condemned to death for their folly would cause endless trouble and distress: nearly every one of them was nearly related to some member of the Great Sanhedrin. Nor would their deaths recall Zacharias to life.

Simon chose the lesser of the two evils: he signified his approval, though without heartiness. Then to satisfy Reuben he ordered the heart and liver of a letos-fish to be burned on a pan over a fire, as the Angel Raphael had once advised Tobit the Babylonian to do as a charm for the expulsion of the demon Asmodeus. Evil spirits, it is said, loathe the stench of burning fish, but none more than Asmodeus, who shares with the Demoness Lilith, the First Eve, the dominion of all the Lilim, or Children of Lilith, and is believed to live in the burning deserts of Upper Egypt.

When the heart and liver had been duly burned, the work of purification continued with sulphur and brimstone, after which came washings with pure water—seven times seven washings of every stone and piece of furniture in the Sanctuary—and prayers and litanies and sin-offerings and fastings.

All concerned in these events were sworn to silence, but the news of Zacharias's death had already been brought to Herod by the Captain of the Temple. He was greatly angered, yet not dismayed. If the Great Sanhedrin had unanimously rejected the theophany— though not one of them, it seemed, had suspected an imposture or doubted that the vision was supernatural—then, the stiff-necked bigots, they had lost the chance which he had offered them of assisting in his religious revolution; they had condemned themselves to destruction. A fine sort of Jehovah they now worshipped! An impotent Moon-thing from Babylon! A dead-alive god of reason and legality who had ousted the god of life, love and death. A monomaniac recluse who brooded all the year round in his Sanctuary on the three paltry articles of furniture with which his worshippers saw fit to supply him: a yardstick, a liquid measure and a set of standard weights! Yet inconsistent in this boast of mathematical perfection, still daily swilling the hot blood of sheep and goats, still demanding the music of trumpets, and dressed in the stolen garments of the Great Goddess Anatha, absurdly perfumed in her scent! Well, he would wait patiently another few months and then stage a second and final theophany. This time the ruling priesthood would not be given the chance to reject their ancestral God—the ageless God in whose honour all the lesser gods of Egypt wield the ass-headed sceptre—he would sweep them away, forged Scriptures and all, and the whole indecent cult would be abolished for ever.

There remained one well-organized body of Israelites true to the Sun of Holiness; and these he would reward for their faithfulness by establishing them as the priests of the Most High God on the Sacred Hill from which they had been so long banished. He had not yet told them what he had in store for them, because they were quietists and might well shrink from becoming accessories to a massacre; nevertheless, once the deed was done, how could they refuse? They were four thousand men, none of whom had bowed his knees faithlessly to the Usurper of the Sanctuary; they served the true God in desert communities apart, singing their morning-hymn to him at sunrise, and celebrating a love-feast on the first day of every week— the day sacred to the Sun.

Meanwhile he kept silence, pretending complete ignorance of what had occurred; but his anger fell upon Simon because of his ritual burning of the heart and liver of the letos-fish, sacred to Set's murdered brother Osiris; for this is the very charm which the Egyptians use against the blowing of the hot desert wind, called the Breath of Set. He charged Simon and the Queen, his daughter, with having been criminally aware of Antipater's plot against him. He removed Simon from the High Priesthood, divorced the Queen, and blotted from his Will her mild and studious son Prince Herod Philip, who stood next in succession to Antipater.

C H A P T E R   T E N

THE NATIVITY

EARLY one morning at Ain-Rimmon, Shelom awakened Mary and said: "My lady, I have news for you. It is heavy news, sent you by Anna daughter of Phanuel. The Rechabite has brought it and awaits your reply."

Mary bowed her head. She said: "These five days I have known that evil news is on the way. My soul has followed it from stage to stage, and from well to well. I am prepared to receive your evil news."

"It is a whip with three lashes. But you are royal-hearted and will not flinch from it."

"I bare my shoulders."

"First, Simon the High Priest has been deposed by the King on a false charge of conspiracy. You can no longer count on his protection, and therefore stand in great danger of your life. What if King Herod should have learned of a certain royal marriage? It would be folly to remain here with your Aunt Elizabeth, when already his soldiers may be on your trail. You are advised to set off at once—"

"Lay on the second lash; the advice can wait. The first lash stings!"

"Second, my lord Zàcharias has been stoned to death. His enemy Reuben the son of Abdiel brought against him the monstrous charge of traffic with the demon Asmodeus. His blood cries for vengeance; it was spilt in the very Sanctuary of the Temple."

Mary said, in a voice that trembled: "Zacharias was a God-fearing man, and very kind to me. I will teach my child to honour his name always, though others may still revile and curse it. Oh, the anguish and disgrace that has fallen on this pleasant house! The lady Elizabeth reviled as the widow of a renegade priest, little John shunned as the son of a condemned sorcerer! That lash breaks the flesh and draws blood. Nevertheless, lay on once more!"

"Third, a certain king, home at last from Italy after narrowly escaping shipwreck, has been tried and sentenced to death in a Roman Court on the false charge of attempting his father's life. Never, I swear, since kings were first crowned in this land was·a loving son so outrageously served! Though the old King must still wait for permission from the Emperor to execute him, count him as already dead."

A long silence followed. Then Mary raised her head and said: "The third lash cuts me to the bone, the third lash cuts me to the heart. Yet still I live, for my child must live."

"My daughter, my Queen!"

They spoke together quietly for an hour or more, Mary trying to catch at straws to buoy her drowning hopes. The Emperor might perhaps refuse his assent; Herod might die, or repent; the indignant people of Jerusalem might break open the prison and release the innocent captive. But always Shelom told her the same thing: "Count him as already dead," and at last persuaded her to realize the danger of her position and the need for immediate flight. Mary asked wearily: "But where can I go when I leave Ain-Rimmon? I may not now return to the College of Virgins. I dare not return to my father's house at Cocheba."

"You must go to Emmaus. And I will accompany you, come what may."

"What? To Joseph of Emmaus who should have married me?"

"To Joseph. Only by returning to the son of Heli can you and your child be safe."

"But, Shelom, I cannot be his wife."

"No, but you must pass as his wife."

"Does he know the truth?"

"He knows nothing."

"How can I pass as his wife, how can he accept me as his wife even in name only—when I am already with child?"

"Throw yourself on his mercy and he will not reject you. He has the warmest heart in all Judaea."

"It is very hard."

"But the only way."

Then again in grief and pain Mary cried out bitterly: "Why is my King condemned? Oh, how can such things be?"

"I tell you, it is because his father is possessed by an evil spirit."

"Can nobody save him? Oh, Shelom, I charge you not to refuse me a last hope!"

"The Lord alone can save him," said Shelom.

"May he extend a strong arm!"

"And a mighty hand!"

"Leave me now, gentle Shelom. I will presently give Kenah his answer."

Joseph was a retired timber-merchant. He had begun life as a carpenter, his family having been ruined in the Civil Wars, but had grown fairly prosperous and raised a large family. His small estate at the village of Emmaus, which lay some twenty miles to the north-west of Jerusalem, consisted of two or three acres of vineyard and orchard. There was an adjoining timber-yard which Jose his eldest son managed for him, with James the youngest acting as his apprentice, and which, with half the value of the estate, was bequeathed to these two in his Will. The other two sons, Simeon and Judah, were in the Galilean timber trade. Their share of the estate at Joseph's death would be some forest-land on the eastern shore of the Lake of Galilee and the remaining half-value of the Emmaus estate. Jose, Simeon and Judah were industrious close-fisted honest men, with industrious close-fisted honest wives; they were leagued in a firm resolve not to let Joseph fall a prey to schemers and spongers and so reduce the value of the estate still further by his absurd generosity. But they could not persuade him to change his ways.

James the youngest had an altogether different character. He was useless as an apprentice, for all his thoughts were on holiness and salvation and he spent half his days in prayer on his knees.

One evening Joseph, returning from a visit to a neighbour, had just laid his hand on the latch of his gate when he heard his name called from behind. Kenah the Rechabite ran up to salute him.

"I have a word for your private ear, Son of Heli."

Joseph bowed and replied: "It is pleasant under my fig-tree. You are welcome to enter, Kenah, lord of the desert. Eat and drink of the best that this house has to offer."

But as they went towards the fig-tree Kenah said: "Forgive me, my lord, if I give you my news with discourteous haste, for, upon my word, it will not wait."

"Say on, by all means!"

"It is this: I have brought you back one who went astray. It is Miriam your bride. She took refuge in our black tents because she knew of the love that we have borne her father Joachim ever since he gave us the Well of the Jawbone for a perpetual possession."

Joseph concealed his astonishment. He asked: "Is all well with the lady Miriam?"

"All is well, and she can have little cause to hate us."

"How may I requite your kindness?"

"By loving her well, for the sake of her father, my benefactor."

"That is no hard request, for I honour Joachim the Heir, and I thank you heartily. Pray, bring her to me at once!"

Kenah uttered a shrill cry, and presently Mary came riding in at the gate on a fine white ass. She alighted and abased herself as a suppliant at Joseph's feet. He lifted her up, set her on the bench under the fig-tree, and hurried away to call his servants. But by the time that he had found one of them, ordered water, towels and refreshments to be brought instantly, and had returned to the bench, Kenah was gone. The sound of the hooves of his galloping ass gradually died away in the distance. Joseph and Mary were left alone.

Mary spoke first: "My lord Joseph, you are reported to be a just and merciful man."

"Daughter, only One is just and merciful."

She paused, not knowing how to continue, but at last said with a sigh: "My lord, you see how it is with your hand-maid."

Joseph answered in commiseration: "Daughter, I see."

"The contract is signed for our marriage?"

"Drafted and signed, but not yet implemented by a payment of bride-money to your guardian, the High Priest."

"My lord, say—will you be merciful to me? Will you save me and my unborn child from death?"

"From death? How from death? You talk wildly, daughter. What would you have me do?"

"I would have you give the bride-money, all but a single half-shekel, to Simon the High Priest. He will pay the whole sum into the Treasury, but make an entry in the account that the half-shekel is still owed to himself."

"Who has planned this ruse and why should it be necessary?"

"Anna daughter of Phanuel, who was my guardian mother—she planned it. It is necessary because—because it is necessary."

"But, daughter, you are not what I contracted to marry. You are with child by another."

"I do not ask you to marry me. I do not wish to live with you as your wife; but I wish it to be thought that we are married and that my child is your child. The Treasury will thus be the richer by the bride-money; yet the contract will not be fully implemented. If you refuse me this request you are condemning two souls to a cruel death!"

"Who is the father of your child?"

"You will be the father in the eyes of the world."

"Kenah calls you the strayed one. Who enticed you to sin, daughter?"

"I am free of sin. I strayed as a lamb strays."

"How can that be?"

"I will tell you as much as is permitted. A richly dressed messenger came to me seven months ago while I was still at your daughter Lysia's house. He saluted me and I asked him his name. He answered: 'This day is Monday; therefore call me Gabriel, who is Monday's angel.' Then he said: 'Lady, I salute you, highly favoured one! The Lord be with you, most blessed of women.' I was troubled by this, and asked him his business. He replied: 'Fear not, Lady, for you have found favour with a glorious King, and if the Lord be willing, you shall conceive and bear a son to him, who shall be the great one, the promised one, the Son of the Highest; and the Lord God shall bestow on him the throne of David.' But I asked him: 'How can this be? I know no glorious King. And I am contracted in marriage to Joseph Emmaus.' He answered: 'The contract with Joseph is signed, but not yet implemented. You are Miriam, the youngest daughter of the line of Michal, and the holy Power of

Michal has therefore descended upon you, and you shall be joined in love with the glorious one whose paranymph I am; and the holy thing that is born of you shall be called the Child of God.' Then Simon the High Priest came out from behind the door where he was hidden, and he said: 'Child, this is a messenger of truth. You must believe his words.' So I answered: 'I am your hand-maid. Let it be as you say.'"

"And then?"

"I may tell no more, and what I have already told you must not be revealed."

"Last week Simon was deposed by the King and must return in ignominy to Egypt before the month is out."

"I am grieved on his account. Yet Anna assures me that he will conclude this business of the contract before he goes away."

"You are asking much of me."

"I am asking you more than you know. I am asking you to risk your life for me."

Joseph pondered a while. "If I give you my protection, what shall I tell my neighbours?"

"Let us ask my woman Shelom; she is in my confidence and has more wit by far than I have."

"Where is this ingenious woman to be found?"

"Sitting under the plane-tree by your gate." She clapped her hands.

When Shelom appeared, Joseph asked her directly: "Woman, what am I to tell my neighbours when they inquire about your mistress?"

"Why, you need tell them nothing. When I am questioned by your men-servants and maid-servants I will lead them to believe by hints, not by lies, that you married my mistress secretly and brought her to Jerusalem, to your little house in the wall, where you go for the Feasts; and that you then left her for a while under the charge of your daughter Lysia, in whose house she had spun the holy flax. And that you did all this because you feared to be mocked by your neighbours for marrying a young girl when already an old man; but that as soon as you learned that my mistress was with child you sent for her and had her secretly conveyed here. Then they will laugh good-humouredly and praise you for your modesty and prudence, and congratulate you on your manhood; and your son Jose will confirm that you rode up to Jerusalem on such and such a day with money for the marriage."

"It is well. Let them believe that if they please." Joseph turned to Mary, took her by the hand and said: "I am an old man, indeed, and the Lord has greatly blessed my life. I read the truth in your eyes, and I can refuse you nothing. Be called my wife, be called the mistress of this house. And though you sleep beside me in my bedchamber, you need not fear for your chastity. And when your child is born and learns to speak, let him call me 'Father' and I shall answer 'My son'."

Mary cried: "May the Lord God who is in Heaven bless you, Joseph, for the love you have shown him to-day!"

Presently she said: "My lord, I have a further request to make. The messenger Gabriel assured me that my child will be born at Bethlehem. Will you therefore ride with me to Bethlehem when my time is near, under colour of visiting the home of your ancestor David?"

"We will surely visit Bethlehem together when you give me the word. And meanwhile, daughter, I have a request to make of you in return. It is that when you are set in authority over my sons' wives and over my two widowed nieces you will treat them gently, showing them the respect due to their age. Rule them, but let them believe that they are ruling you. They will not be pleased at first to hear that I have spent money on a new wife, and that she is already with child by me."

"They will learn to love me, I trust, for your sake."

In his palace at Rome the Emperor Augustus was saying to his wife, the Lady Livia: "This request from our friend Herod the Idumaean is preposterous. I cannot possibly give my consent."

"And why not?"

"Because Antipater's trial was fraudulent from start to finish—Varus's private memorandum makes that clear—and this new portfolio of evidence is not supported by any original documents. I suppose that you *did* receive the letter from Salome which Herod quotes?"

"I have just found one posted in the Judaean secret file, but it has been placed there very recently and without my knowledge. My woman Acme did not have access to the file at any time. She could not possibly have taken a copy of the letter. You see, she has been on a visit to her parents in Cyrene for the last four months. Herod's intelligence system is faulty."

"You mean that the new evidence is fraudulent too?"

"Of course: it reeks!"

"Then why in the world, my dear, should I consent to Antipater's execution?"

"Because you owe more to Herod than you owe to Antipater. Besides, old Herod is no fool. He must have some very solid reason for wishing to eliminate Antipater. After the mistake that you made in the Syllaeus case—against my advice, remember—you cannot afford to offend him again."

"What sort of reason do you mean?"

"To be frank, I have no idea. I suspect a religious reason. These Jews are very queer people; their cousins the Idumaeans are queerer still. Old Athenodorus would probably know. He comes from that part of the world and is something of an authority on Hebrew superstitions. My point is, that with Antipater and Herod Philip removed, Prince Archelaus becomes Herod's successor, and if I know that stupid young man he will soon set the Jews by the ears. Embassies will arrive from Jerusalem, and counter-embassies, and there will be riots and breaches of the peace, and presently we shall have the satisfaction of deposing him and proclaiming Judaea a province under our direct control. With Antipater as king we could not hope for anything of the sort—he is as prudent as he is energetic—yet the longer the country retains its independence the more difficult it will be to secure its eventual conformation to the Imperial system. I have nothing against the Jews as a nation, but the Jews as a fanatic sect who make converts among Greeks and Syrians and Orientals and enrol them as spiritual sons of their ancestor Abraham are extraordinarily dangerous. I wonder whether you realize that not only are three million Jews settled within Herod's Palestinian territories, but nearly four million more of this energetic and thrifty race are dispersed throughout the rest of your dominions, and that of these Dispersed Jews only a million or so are of Palestinian ancestry: the rest are converts. If the sect continues to grow at the present rate it will soon swallow up all the ancient religious cults of Greece and Italy; for to make a convert is esteemed a highly meritorious act in a Jew, and to become a convert is to benefit from the highly organized system of mutual assistance which Judaism offers. And the Jews are clever: they make converts only of the more intelligent and industrious type of foreigner. It is quite an honour to be enrolled as a Jew. There are no two ways about it: one day we shall have to smash the power of the Jerusalem Temple which focuses the loyalties and ambitions of all Jews everywhere. Meanwhile, shall I send for Athenodorus?"

"Do so!"

Athenodorus of Tarsus was called from the Library. He sauntered in, smiling cheerfully, stroking his long white beard. He was one of the few people in the world who were never disconcerted by a sudden summons to the Imperial presence. He knew well who was the real ruler of the Empire and therefore saluted Livia a trifle more formally than he saluted Augustus, which pleased both of them.

"You have another literary or historical problem for me to sharpen my wits upon?" he asked.

"Precisely, my good Athenodorus," said Livia. "We wish you to adjudicate in a slight dispute between us."

"Madam, let me assure you at once: you are right!"

Livia laughed. "As usual?"

"As usual; but doubtless the Emperor needs convincing."

"Athenodorus, the case is this. A petty-king ruling within a few hundred miles of your beloved city has a son. He loves him, cherishes him, raises him to co-sovereignty with himself, then suddenly condemns him to death on a palpably false charge and asks our permission to execute him in whatever way he pleases. Now, why? Why?"

Athenodorus rubbed his hooked nose. "You have withheld one or two important elements in the case. May I presume the prince in question to be an eldest or perhaps an only son?"

"You may."

"And the father is one of your subject allies, with an honorary Roman citizenship?"

"He is."

"In that case, I suppose that either the Emperor or yourself believes that the King is a homicidal maniac?"

"Yes, I must confess that this is what I believe," said Augustus. "Unless perhaps he has good cause for putting his son to death, but has not ventured to try him on the real evidence for fear of incriminating some person whom he either wishes to shield or hesitates to offend."

Athenodorus continued: "But you, my Lady Livia, with feminine intuition, suspect that the reason is to be found in some barbarous Eastern superstition?"

Livia clapped her hands. "Athenodorus, what an intelligent man you are! I will give you that Hecataeus manuscript of mine that you have so long coveted."

Athenodorus beamed. "Yes, Caesar, the Lady Livia is likely, as usual, to be right. As you know, Father Zeus himself once—according to the mystics at least—invested his son Dionysus with full power and glory for a short season, seating him upon his Olympian throne and putting thunderbolts in his hands, but then pitilessly destroyed him. The legend of Apollo and his son Phaethon is analogous; and so is that of the Pelasgian Sun-god Daedalus and his son Icarus. For though the deaths of these two young men, both of whom were temporarily invested with royalty, are ascribed by the mythographers to their imprudence, it is difficult to exculpate the divine fathers, each of whom, as the Sun, was the direct cause of the accident. Hercules, too, as an archaic Sun-god, repeatedly killed his eldest son; the mythographers pretend that he had fits of insanity. Not to be tedious, the royal investiture of an eldest or only son, followed by his sacrifice and incineration, is common form in the whole group of near-Eastern nations that claim Agenor, or his brother Belus, as their ancestor. I came across a reference to the same practice in the Jewish Scriptures the other day: an ancient King of Moab offered up his eldest son in this way to Belus. It is their way of propitiating the Sun-god during a religious crisis, either when the country as a whole is in danger or when the king has personally incurred the god's displeasure. The history of Tarsus contains several instances. Well, then, this unnamed king happens to be an ally of yours and therefore cannot risk your displeasure by killing his son, who is a Roman citizen by birth, without sufficient cause. So he forges evidence of high treason and asks your permission to carry out the sentence in whatever way be pleases. Yet the killing of the eldest son is as stern a religious duty among this group of nations, which includes the Egyptians of the Delta, as circumcision and the avoidance of pork; and this is a matter of plain religious logic."

Augustus, a trifle vexed at the ease with which Athenodorus had solved the riddle, said: "Come now, learned one, you surely do not pretend that there is any logical connexion between the three religious aberrations you have just mentioned?"

"I do, Caesar," said Athenodorus. "The Egyptian god Set in the form of a wild boar tears his brother Osiris into pieces. Syrian Apollo does the same with Adonis. They are both Sun-gods. The boar is their sacred beast and must therefore not be eaten except on very special occasions. In Palestine and Syria generally, foreskins were formerly taken as trophies of battle and dedicated to the Sun-god, that is to say, the Sacred King, on the occasion of his marriage with the Moon-goddess, the Sacred Queen. And if the King fell sick his eldest son was circumcised by the Queen with a flint knife, to turn away the anger of Heaven—as we read in the story of Moses the Hebrew and his son Gershom—from which derives the custom of circumcising all male infants on the eighth day after birth. This propitiary rite is connected with the now happily abandoned one of butchering all first-born males, both animal and human, on that day. The number eight, as you know, expresses increase. Moreover, the foreskin—"

"We love you well," said Livia graciously. "You have judged the case with admirable precision. But pray, no more antiquarian discussion of a topic which is hardly suitable for a lady's ears."

Athenodorus with an apologetic smile saluted and sauntered out again, hand to beard. .

"So you see—" said Livia.

"My dear, it is very well, but we cannot allow an innocent man, and a capable cavalry officer too, with the makings of a first-class petty king, to die in this barbarous manner."

"No?" said Livia coolly. "What has become of your famous principle never on any occasion to interfere with the religious abnormalities of your subject allies so long as they cause no breach of the peace?"

"It is odious to destroy one's own child."

"To do so for the good of the nation is a very praiseworthy act. Early Roman history bristles with examples of noble fathers who put their sons to death."

"Their wicked sons."

"How do we know that they were wicked? Perhaps the evidence was forged. In any case, my advice is: do not refuse Herod's request unless you wish to find yourself with an awkward war on your hands. You can hardly afford a war, with the Treasury in its present state. I am sorry for Antipater, but what can we do? It is his fate. And I am sorry for Acme; she will have to be executed in token of your goodwill towards Herod. Not that she will be much of a loss, the slut."

So Livia had her way, as usual. But Augustus sighed and said: "A religious duty like circumcision or the avoidance of pork! By Hercules, it were better to be Herod's pig than his eldest son!"

King Herod was sick. Becoming aware of a congestion in his bowels he consulted his physician Machaon, who confessed that he could do nothing but palliate the pain that it caused him, and that his end would not be an easy one.

Herod asked: "Have I a full year of life left to me?"

Machaon answered: "I can promise you a full year if you submit to my tedious regimen, but I cannot promise more."

"It is enough," said Herod. That day he sent for craftsmen out of Egypt, who made him a great golden eagle of the sort called a griffon-vulture, sacred to the Sun. He had it fixed high above the East Gate of the Temple, where he dedicated it to Jehovah. Underneath he wrote the divine words spoken to Moses:

I bare you on eagle-wings and brought you unto myself.

It was calculated to stir up trouble, for though this was not the only text in the Pentateuch which identified Jehovah with an eagle, the god was never depicted in bird form, and the Roman military standards had made the eagle symbolical of foreign oppression; besides, the Law of Moses forbade the making of any graven image whatsoever.

Herod's son Prince Archelaus, now the heir-apparent, wished to secure the goodwill of the Sanhedrin. When the new High Priest came to him in tears and implored him to persuade his father to remove the eagle, he promised to do his best. He went to Herod in company with his brother Prince Philip—who is not to be confused with the studious Prince Herod Philip, grandson of Simon the High Priest—but they had hardly begun their plea when Herod stormed and raged at them, heaved himself from his chair, spat in their faces and buffeted them. They counted themselves lucky to escape with their lives. That same day Herod announced that he had again altered his Will. The names of Archelaus and Philip were blotted out, and Herod Antipas, his youngest son, was named as his successor.

When the High Priest informed the Sanhedrin that Herod would not remove the eagle, Judas son of Sepphorus, Matthias son of Margalothus and other patriotic Pharisees incited their disciples to remove it for him. The young men went to work with great boldness. Some of them climbed to the top of the gate in broad daylight and let themselves down with cords until they were on a level with the eagle, at which they hacked with axes and pruning-hooks. The rest, and with them the same party of young Zadokites that had stoned Zacharias, stood below with swords in their hands to prevent any attempt at interference with the work; but just as the eagle came crashing down, Carmi the Captain of the Temple Guard came running up with a full company of Levites, reinforced by Celtic javelin-men from Herod's Palace, and arrested the entire band, forty in all. Carmi brought them before Herod, who sat growling to himself like an old lion in his den. In a terrible voice he asked who had ordered them to cut down the eagle.

They answered humbly: "The Lord God, if it pleases your Majesty, through the mouth of his servant Moses."

"You have committed a horrid sacrilege, and must all die instantly!"

A young Pharisee answered: "What is that to us? The soul is immortal, and for obeying the Law we shall be suitably rewarded after our bodies are laid in the grave."

Herod roared: "Not so, for your carrion bodies will not be buried. They shall be burned—burned, do you hear?—and your ashes shall be scattered in an abominable place, from which there is neither resurrection nor hope of resurrection!"

Then Herod went up in his litter to the Court of the Gentiles, where he addressed a passionate speech to the mixed assembly, accusing the High Priest of instigating a rebellion; it was expected that he would massacre the entire, Sanhedrin without further delay. However, the High Priest came down from the Sanctuary dressed in mourning garments and abased himself before Herod, pleading for mercy, and undertook to hand over to his vengeance every one of the elders who had prompted their disciples to this outrageous act.

Herod pretended to relent. He ordered the men who had merely stood guard to be stoned to death, and allowed their bodies to be decently buried; only those who had cut down the eagle, together with the two Pharisee elders who had prompted the deed, and Reuben son of Abdiel as the instigator of the young Zadokites, he burned alive in the court of his Palace and dedicated their bodies to the God of his fathers. Thus Zacharias was avenged. And on that very night, which was the thirteenth night of March, occurred an eclipse of the Moon, which both amazed and delighted Herod by its appositeness.

On the next day Prince Archelaus sent the King a message: "Father, you hate me, yet I love you and I have news for you of great importance. You will see that my heart yearns to be restored to your love."

Herod sent for him.

Archelaus, weeping tears of pretended joy to see his father again, asked for a private audience.

Herod dismissed all but his deaf mutes and ordered him to speak briefly and to the point.

"Father, it happened at Bethlehem between two or three months ago. Everyone there is talking about it. In Bethlehem of Ephrath, I mean, not the Galilean Bethlehem."

"*What* happened, rambler in words?"

"A child was born, in the cave—in the cave called the Grotto of Tammuz. The people of Bethlehem say that it is the Child who has been prophesied."

Herod leaned forward intently in his chair. "Are the parents known?" he asked.

"Nobody can tell me their names, though it is agreed that they were members of the House of David come on a visit to Bethlehem. The woman, who was young and beautiful, was overcome by the pains of childbirth at some distance from the town. She was taken to the Grotto and delivered there. Her servant, who acted as midwife, called out to some Kenite shepherds who have grazing rights thereabouts to fetch her water for the childbirth washings. The shepherds were superstitiously excited that a child had been born in the Grotto, and on a day too which is locally called 'The Day of Peace'. They came crowding up and found the child cradled in a harvest-basket of the sort used in the Tammuz cult; but what excited them most of all was that the midwife testified that she had found the woman's maidenhead intact, which recalled the prophecy of Isaiah, that 'A virgin shall conceive and bear a son'. This is, of course, against the laws of nature, but I report what I heard. The parents remained in the cave for three days and then rode off again by night with the child; meanwhile Kenites and peasants had streamed in from fifteen miles around to adore and serenade him. The father, it is said, was elderly and mild-mannered and appeared to be a man of substance."

"You can tell me nothing more?"

"It is said that as the old man and his young wife were walking along the road before they came to the Grotto, he said to her: 'Woman, why are you laughing and weeping alternately in this strange manner?' And that she answered: 'It is because in my mind's eye I see two peoples—those on my left hand weeping and lamenting, and those on my right hand laughing and exulting.' And there is another nonsensicality. The shepherds claim that about noon on that day, just before the news reached them from the Grotto, they became aware of a sudden suspension of time. One of them was seated at the stream-side washing his hands after dinner when he saw a heron flap across the valley. Suddenly it seemed to stand still in the sky as if arrested in flight by an invisible hand. He looked towards his companions, who had not yet finished their dinner; they were seated around a dish of mutton boiled in barley and pulling pieces out with their hands in shepherd fashion. But those who had their hands in the dish kept them there; those who were conveying food to their mouths sat frozen with their hands raised half-way; those who were chewing ceased to chew. A shepherd was watering his flocks a little way upstream; the sheep had their mouths in the water but ceased to drink. The illusion persisted for as long as it would have taken him to count up to fifty, and then slowly all things moved onward again on their course, while a burst of music sounded from the grove on the hill-top—the grove sacred to Tammuz—and a voice cried out: 'The Virgin has brought forth. The Light is waking.' "

Herod said slowly: "It is an extraordinary story, my son, and I thank you heartily for bringing it to me. Even the account of the suspension of time is useful since it confirms the day of the child's birth. The nomad Kenites pretend that when the Sun stands still in midwinter, having reached the day on which he rallies his failing strength, all Nature does the same, which accounts for the name 'The Day of Peace'. The superstition has indeed become absurdly incorporated in the story of Joshua's victory over the five Amorite kings, from a misunderstanding of the ancient poem: 'Sun, upon Gibeon stand thou still!' which celebrates the birth of the Sun-god at that season. Nor can I reject the story of the virgin birth as necessarily false, for a child may be conceived without breach of maidenhead; there are several attested cases. Now, Archelaus, my son, I would have you prove your wisdom. The child, if he lives, is bound to cause immense trouble to our country because of the coincidence of his birth with popular Messianic prophecy, unless I intervene decisively before the mischief ripens. What do you advise?"

Archelaus answered after reflexion: "Father, my advice is this. Issue an edict, endorsed by the High Priest, that according to many complaints that have reached you of late certain persons are fraudulently claiming to be members of the famous House of David; and that you have therefore decided to compile an accurate register of the entire House. Henceforth nobody who cannot produce a certificate proving that he has been registered as a Davidite will be accepted in the quality that he professes. Order the registration to be held at Bethlehem in three weeks' time, when all Davidite heads of houses must appear in person and bring with them such of their sons as have been born since the last registration—which was, I believe, fifteen years ago. The parents of the child are bound to attend, and their arrival will attract the same popular excitement as before. Supply me with soldiers and I will soon settle the matter for you."

"And if they fail to attend?"

"Then their names and the child's name will not appear on the register, and the child will forfeit his claim to be called a Son of David."

"Three weeks' time? Short notice for the Davidites of Babylonia, Asia Minor and Greece!"

"A later registration date can be arranged for them in their own countries."

Herod slapped his knee and cried: "Admirably argued. You are to-day restored to your rank and place, my dear Archelaus. And if you succeed in this business I shall appoint you my colleague; you are a man after my own heart."

It was not until Archelaus's return to the Palace that Herod's sickness took a turn for the worse. The symptoms were a low fever and an intolerable itching all over his body, constant diarrhoea, a foul breath, inflammation of the belly, swollen feet, and a throat so dry that he could hardly breathe. When the palliatives prescribed by Machaon and his other physicians ceased to have any effect on him, he dismissed them with ignominy, flinging them out of the Palace barefoot and naked. He was his own physician for a while but then, his health growing steadily worse, he sent for others. At last he decided to put himself under the care of the Essenes of Callirrhoë, where the chief physician prescribed draughts of the hot medicinal spring which flows into the Dead Sea; and a bath in a great jar of sanctified olive oil. But he vomited up the water, and he fainted in the jar and when they pulled him out the whites of his eyes turned up and he seemed to be dying. But still he fought death off.

The edict about the coming registration of the Sons of David reached Joseph at Emmaus and put him in a quandary. He could not leave Mary's child behind, since to do so would amount to a public disavowal of paternity; yet to take him might be dangerous. He consulted Mary, who answered at once: "Take us with you, Joseph, and put your trust in the Lord."

"But I cannot write the child down as a member of the House of David!"

"Do not let that trouble you yet. There are still ten days before we need travel to Bethlehem. Much may happen in those ten days."

Much did happen. Herod returned in melancholy to Jerusalem and found despatches waiting there from Augustus. He tore them open and uttered a shout of triumph. Augustus commiserated with him on the disaffection of yet another of his sons, and one who had hitherto shown no signs of disloyalty; the evidence of treachery, he wrote, seemed conclusive and Antipater might be executed as soon as his father pleased, and in whatever manner he pleased, though the Lady Livia and himself counselled the more merciful punishment of perpetual exile.

In whatever manner he pleased! There was only one manner of sacrifice acceptable to Set, the true Jehovah, and only one place where the sacrifice might properly be made. The text was to be found in Genesis: "Take now thy son, thine only son Isaac whom thou lovest, and get thee into the land of Moriah and offer him there upon one of the mountains which I will tell thee of." It was the very mountain-top on which the Temple stood, and the present Altar of Burned Offering was the very stone to which the unsuspecting Isaac had been bound. This offering of his first-born, the son whom he secretly cherished and pitied, would alone satisfy Jehovah and persuade him to renew the covenant sworn with Abraham. Jehovah, whether or not he again chose to substitute ram for man, would thereupon heal him of all his bodily distresses and renew his youth, as Abraham's youth had been renewed, and grant him victory over his multitudinous enemies. But even this supreme sacrifice would be insufficient unless the Temple Hill were first purged of its rabble of false priests; they must be hewn in pieces as the resolute Elijah had hewn in pieces the priests of Baal. Set must sail back to glory over billows of blood.

Herod called his officers together and gave them great presents of money to secure their further loyal service, with a donation of fifty drachmae, besides, to every soldier in the ranks. He told them: "Children, I shall have work for you soon." These soldiers were all foreigners: the bodyguard were Edomites mixed with Nabataeans from Petra—Herod's mother had been a Nabataean—and with the permission of Augustus he had also recruited a regiment of Belgian Celts, another of Thracians, and another of Galatian Gauls—all of them devotees of the same variously named Sun-god. Edomites called this god Kozi or Nimrod; the Nabataeans, Ouri-tal Dusares; the Thracians, Dionysus; the Galatians, Esu; and the Celts, Lugos.

CHAPTER ELEVEN

THE FLIGHT INTO EGYPT

THROUGHOUT his long life Herod had studied the stars intently and directed his policy according to their guidance. His birth had been heralded by a close conjunction of the great planets Jupiter and Saturn, and in his fifty-eighth year a recurrence of the same rare event had assured him that the years of patient preparation were over: the period of bold action was to begin. In the three ensuing years he had put into execution the preliminary plans which culminated in the theophany witnessed by Zacharias and in the condemnation of his son Antipater. Now the dawn of the fifth millennium, and of the third Phoenix Age, was breaking, and the hour of deliverance long ago promised by the patriarch Isaac to his son Esau, which is to say Edom, had been sounded as it were with trumpets: the celestial sign had been a total eclipse of the Moon. His grand plan could at last be put into execution—must be put into execution before it was too late. His aches and itchings had grown almost past bearing and drove him into fits of uncontrollable rage, so that even the valets were terrified to enter his presence. His sense of urgency was heightened by a private letter from the Emperor's Oriental Secretary warning him that the princes Archelaus and Philip were building up a secret army in Samaria (their mother was a Samaritan) and intended to seize the throne as soon as Antipater had been executed. The letter was inspired by Livia, who could not refrain from further confusing the situation at Jerusalem: the Roman Imperial system is founded on a policy of *divide et impera*—"Cause divisions in your neighbour's kingdom and profit from them by assuming the sovereignty yourself." Herod did not believe the accusation, but the letter caused him anxiety nevertheless.

He issued an edict summoning the whole ruling priesthood of Jerusalem, and every Levitical Doctor of the Law from all over the kingdom, to assemble in his Palace grounds at Jericho on the following Sunday, under pain of death. Some fifteen thousand men obeyed, not without fear, but trusting that there would be safety in numbers.

Towards the evening of this day, when all were assembled on the immense parade-ground in front of the Palace, crowded together in no order, Herod appeared on a balcony and laughed silently at them, but could not speak because of the dryness of his throat. He handed a paper to Ptolemy, his chamberlain, which Ptolemy read as follows, shouting the words through his trumpeted hands:

"The words of your August Sovereign, Herod, King of the Jews:

"Priests and Doctors of Israel! You are assembled here on the opening day of a new week, of a great week, of a week that will be remembered by your children and your children's children for ever. Raphael the archangel is the warden of this day, which is called the Day of the Sun. Those of you who are skilled in angelology will bear me out when I declare that it is this archangel who is destined at last to heal Ephraim—which is customarily understood to signify the ten tribes of the North—by converting them all at once from their prolonged iniquity. Yet let Raphael first practise his curative art upon you who boast yourselves Sons of Levi—a tribe which for its bloody-mindedness, in ancient days, was granted no single stretch of territory but dispersed instead in mischievous pockets and enclaves throughout the land of Israel; let Raphael, I say, heal you by the rays of the fiery Being to whose service he is dedicated.

"I have summoned you here, rebellious ones, to recall to your memory a psalm composed by David son of Jesse, my predecessor in this troublesome kingdom. In it he extols the Creator in the familiar stanzas beginning:

> Far in the East a stable for the Sun
>   The Lord our God has set, whence with a shout
>   Titan springs rutilant out,
>   Like a bridegroom
>   From his anointing room,
> Rejoicing across Heaven his wheelèd race to run.

Your pious ancestors once kept white horses stabled on the Temple Hill and every morning harnessed them to golden chariots which were driven out splendidly to meet the rising Sun. Who commanded you to turn your backs to the Sun when you worship? Who led you astray? Did you dredge up this impious custom from the stinking canals of Babylon?

"Deaf adders, blind moles! I have built a beautiful hippodrome below the Temple of Jerusalem, a marble hippodrome with gilded bronze gates and barriers, capacious benches and an exquisitely adorned spina—by which is meant the middle space enclosed by the track—such as would not disgrace any of the richest and greatest cities of the Greeks. But to what purpose? You never frequent that admirable place, because of your superstitious obstinacy. You close your eyes to its very existence; on festival days you fastidiously stop your ears against the shouts of joy which flow in great waves from the benches, when in rivalry around the elliptical track gallop teams of beautiful horses, urging along chariots decorated with red, white, blue and green. The teams run sun-wise, in honour of the supreme luminary for which the Lord God, as David testifies, has provided a hippodrome in Heaven and rosy stables in the East. Their chariot colours are those of the four prime seasons, and upright stands each resolute charioteer.

"Come, stiff-necks, dunces, abecedarians, off with you now to the hippodrome, to the other wonderful hippodrome which I have built here at Jericho. Off with you now, like little scampering children who are taken to see their first negro, or their first captive lion, or their first view of the wide shining sea. I desire you to meditate throughout the coming night on the stanza of the psalm which I have quoted to you; for to-morrow your new illumination must begin. This is not to say that to-morrow chariot teams will compete for your entertainment; but that since the hippodrome is roofless and un-provided with awnings you will at last, willy-nilly, become aware of the fiery Titan whom all the civilized world delights to honour, yourselves alone excepted: to-morrow you will have nothing else to do all day but dutifully to mark the stages of his course from sunrise to noon, from noon to sunset, and the same simple task will be yours the next day, and the next, until you shall have thoroughly learned your lesson.

"In honour of the Sun, King Solomon set up those pillars and groves which in the littleness of your hearts and the darkness of your intellect you condemn as idolatrous—Solomon the son of David, I say, whom you name the wisest of men, notwithstanding! How is it, renegades from your ancient faith, that you adore our God in the character of the thievish Moon, that you blow trumpets every month to greet that absurd silver shred which gives neither warmth nor light to man? The prophet Jonah—how did he name Jerusalem? Was it as Beth Sin, the abode of the aberrant Moon-god Sin, hated by all good-hearted men throughout the world, or as Nineveh, the abode of Nimrod, resplendent Lord of the Solar Year?

"Be off now, hurry, go, I say, moon-struck fools, for my soldiery are the warders who will escort you to the curative building of which I have spoken!"

Troops had been posted all about the Palace grounds with drawn swords and javelins at the ready, and the great crowd, puzzled, helpless and without a leader, began to move down the slope towards the hippodrome, the soldiers guarding every path of escape and encouraging laggards with kicks and blows.

As soon as the officers were able to report to Herod that the entire priesthood, except those who were officiating at the Temple, had been herded into the empty hippodrome and that the gates had been locked, he issued a new edict deposing Matthias the High Priest and appointing to the office Matthias's brother-in-law, who was absent in Cyprus. At Jerusalem, on the same day, Carmi had summoned all the priests in the Temple, except the three or four without whom the rites would have come to a sudden standstill, to a brief conference in the Court of the Gentiles. There they were arrested and sent down to Jericho under escort to join their comrades in the hippodrome. The stage was cleared for the performance, next day, of a terrible sacrifice at the Altar of Burned Offering.

That same night, three Damascene Jews of the tribe of Issachar arrived at the Jericho Palace and demanded an audience with the King. They announced themselves as astrologers and Herod consented to see them. They proved to be Covenanters, a sect who claimed to have made a new covenant with God through the mediation of a spirit named "The Coming One" or "The Star", whom they expected shortly to become incarnate in human form. They seemed eager, simple-minded men, and their leader told Herod: "Your name shall be glorious for ever, Majesty, for the stars tell us that the Prince of Righteousness has been born at last under your benignant sway, to be your heir and to rule over all Israel for a thousand years. We know that you are sensible of this great honour bestowed on you by the Lord God, for we have handled the coins struck at your Royal Mint, where a six-pointed star is shown shining upon the sacred mountain-top."

Herod smiled encouragingly. "To whom, learned Damascenes, do you suppose this Prince to have been born?"

They bowed and replied: "We are ignorant men, but since it is known that he is to be the King of the Jews, we presume him to be either your son or your grandson. We are not believers in the direct descent of the Coming One from David, for as one of our teachers

146

has said: 'He will be called David even if he is not of David's blood.' Well, now he is born at last. The stars do not lie."

"No, they do not lie, but often they mislead. When do you suppose this child to have been born?"

"By our calculations he was born at this last winter solstice."

"And where?"

"We do not know, but we presume at Bethlehem of Ephrath. As your Majesty knows, the prophet Micah wrote distinctly: 'And you, Bethlehem in the land of Judah, are not the least of the Princes of Judah, for out of you shall come one who shall rule my people Israel.'"

"Would you recognize the child if you were to see him?"

"Certainly! He would have marks of royalty on him."

"You have my permission to go to Bethlehem to search for him, good men. If you find him let me know and I shall come and worship him. But in this at least you are mistaken: he is no son or grandson of mine."

"May Your Majesty live for ever! We will set out at once."

Herod was astonished by the coincidence; for the House of David were to be registered at Bethlehem on the following day.

When the Damascenes had gone, Herod began to doubt first whether Archelaus could be trusted to destroy the child and then whether the tale of the birth in the Grotto were true. Had it perhaps been ingeniously fabricated by him as a means of getting command of troops with which to raise a revolt? Were the Damascenes his accomplices? Was the standard of revolt to be raised at Bethlehem? Thus from a single doubt his mind raced through a whole circuit of doubts. He even felt uncertain of the loyalty of his cousin-german the Edomite Achiabus, the only man whom he had taken wholly into his confidence about the grand plan—Achiabus who had accompanied him into the tombs of Solomon and David, and who was to become High Priest of the reformed religion. He began to groan and complained once more of the pain in his bowels and presently in a piteous voice asked Achiabus, who was sitting with him, for an apple to cool his parched throat and a knife with which to pare the apple. When Achiabus fetched them, Herod pretended that his pains had suddenly become so violent that he could not bear to live even an hour longer, and made as if to stab himself with the knife. Would Achiabus try to restrain him, or would he allow him to die without hindrance? That was a fair test of his love.

Achiabus wrenched the knife away and cried: "Help! Help!" The servants came in at a run, and seeing the two men struggling for the knife concluded that Achiabus was a secret assassin. A great outcry and commotion followed; the word ran through the Palace "The Lion is dead". His name was so feared that a huge wailing arose from far and near to frighten the ghost away from the scene of his horrid crimes.

The frightful noise and the rumour of Herod's death reached the Royal prison, where Antipater was now confined. A quick-witted young warder hurried into his cell, knocked off his gyves and fetters and led him tottering towards the gate. But the gate was barred and the porter surly; before he could be persuaded to open it, the prison governor, to whom Archelaus had made large presents, intercepted Antipater and marched him back to his cell. The governor sent a hurried message to Archelaus informing him of what had happened, and begging to be the first to congratulate him on his accession to the Throne. But the other warders crowded around, shouting: "Release King Antipater, release him! He is innocent! He is our own true King. He will reward us all with wonderful gifts."

The governor made a quick decision: he sent two of his men into Antipater's cell, who struck him suddenly from behind as he knelt in prayer and killed him outright.

Thus by too great cunning Herod had over-reached himself, and the antique God of Jerusalem was cheated of his burned offering.

The news reached Emmaus on the following night. When Mary heard that Antipater was dead she could not weep openly nor unburden her heart even to the faithful Shelom. But she whispered in the ear of her infant son, whom she called Jesus: "O my son, he is dead! O little son, do you hear, he is dead!" The child wailed. He was all the world to her now: her first child, and her last. She began to rock him and soothe him, telling him of the journey that lay ahead of them. "You and I are going on a journey in the morning. We are going to the place where you were born. We are going to Bethlehem. I will take good care of you, and do you take good care of me, and the Lord will take good care of us both, and good old Joseph will travel with us." At this the child smiled, which was the first smile she had ever had from him. She kissed him tenderly and said: "Sleep now, Son Jesus, for soon we go on a long, long journey." But she little guessed how long and weary a journey it would be.

They were delayed on the road by the lameness of one of their asses and did not reach Bethlehem until after midnight. Then it was too late to knock up a merchant of the town with whom Joseph had once dealt in business; but he led the lame ass to the backside of the merchant's house and tied it up in the stable with the other beasts. Then they continued up the hill to the village inn, Mary riding, Joseph walking beside her with his hand on the bridle. They found the inn filled to overflowing with members of the House of David who had come for the registration. Men were sleeping huddled in blankets in the doorway and under the porch, so close together that Joseph could not have entered without treading on one of them. The night was cold, with rain drizzling down. He looked for shelter in the barn; but the barn was also crowded, and as he tried to thrust his way in someone banged the door and barred it from inside.

The inn-keeper, who came up at that moment with a lantern, said to Joseph: "Sir, I do not know your name, but I see that you are an old man and that your wife has a young child with her. I cannot refuse you what poor hospitality it still remains in my power to offer. Just over the brow of the hill in a clearing of the wood stands a shed where one of my sons keeps his beasts; I will accompany you to it. It is a small, foul-smelling place, but warm and dry at least."

They thanked him and he led them through the mire to the shed, and wished them goodnight, promising to come again in the morning to salute them. They settled down in the straw and slept until daylight.

The next morning, while Mary cooked breakfast in the earthenware pots that she found in a corner of the shed, Joseph walked down to the village to see to the needs of his lame ass; he said: "It is written that a merciful man is merciful also to his beast." As he went he was trying to recall a frightful dream that had disturbed his night but had vanished at dawn, leaving a vague sense of fear and uneasiness. His merchant friend was not at home, so Joseph took the ass in search of a surgeon. As he stood doubtfully at the cross-roads, he heard three rich Jews, Damascenes by their dress, in earnest conversation with a Kenite tribesman. The man was saying: "As the Lord lives, eminent merchants, I do not lie. The bird came sailing across the valley with lazy flappings of her wings, but when she reached the point in the sky directly above the cave where the child was being born, she was arrested in flight and stood poised there like a buzzard. Indeed, my lords, as I watched I was aware that my heart had stopped beating, and I believed myself a dead man. Only my eyes still had motion in them, and when I turned them towards the Grotto it seemed to me that a great glory shone above it—"

Joseph hastily moved on, for he recognized the Kenite's face and did not wish to be recognized himself. But the man cried out: "Hist! If this is not the very person! I am not an ass-surgeon for nothing. I know him again by his she-ass. I treated her hock—it was the hock of the off-foreleg—and now she has gone lame in the off-hindleg."

He ran after Joseph and said: "Sir, leave the she-ass in my care. In three weeks' time, please the Lord, she will be running races."

"Sir, I thank you. But I cannot wait for three weeks."

"Take my ass in exchange, and keep her for your own."

"What sort of a man are you to offer me a fine young white ass in exchange for my old lame red beast? Upon my word, you do not drive a very hard bargain."

"Did not your lady and the child ride that ass on their journey to Bethlehem three months ago? I will sell the braided hairs of that ass's tail to my kinsmen as charms of good luck; they will pay five shekels a braid and think the money well spent. The ass I will keep for myself."

"Take the old ass, then, and give me the new, for my foreboding is that I shall need a reliable beast before the day is out; and may the Lord go with you! Yet I charge you not to tell a soul that I am here in Bethlehem until the registration of our House is completed and I have returned home."

Joseph began to unsaddle the ass, but the Kenite protested: "No, no, the saddle goes with each ass. Is mine not handsome enough? Its silver bells and green tassels will please your lady and her child. But I require your own saddle for the sake of the precious burden that it has supported: it will be a glorious legacy for my children and my children's children."

The three Damascenes stood listening in silence. When Joseph rode off, they followed him hastily and watched from a distance where he went. Then they returned to their camp for the sacred gifts they had brought, washed and perfumed themselves and put on their richest ceremonial robes so that they appeared like kings.

Mary was giving suck to her child when they appeared at the door of the shed. She looked up in alarm. But they made the sign of peace to Joseph and prostrating themselves on the floor of rammed earth, which Mary had swept well, did silent homage to the child. One of them laid at his feet a twelve-pointed golden crown, with a different jewel for each point, according to the jewels of the twelve tribes, and whispered:

"In token of thy sovereignty, Great One!"

The next set an alabaster pot of myrrh to the left of the crown and said:

"In token, Great One, of thy love!"

The third set an ivory casket of frankincense drops to the right of the crown and said:

"In token, Great One, of thy immortality!"

Mary, her eyes wet with tears, said gravely: "My lords, I thank you on behalf of my son. Your gifts are rightly bestowed. Go, with the blessing of the Lord!"

They went off singing a psalm, the words of which could not have been more apposite:

> In Ephrath, lo, the truth we understood,
> And found it in a clearing of the wood.
> Into his arbour, brothers, let us go,
> At his foot-stool abase ourselves full low . . .
> Arise, Lord. . . .

Joseph pretended to have heard and seen nothing and left the gifts where they lay until Mary put them into a place of safety. Breakfast was eaten in silence, and presently Joseph went over to the inn to inquire at what hour the registration was to begin. He wished to finish the business and get home as soon as possible. But as he turned the corner by the barn he heard a cry: "Soldiers are coming! Look, a troop—a whole squadron—of the King's soldiers!"

He suddenly remembered his dream, which had begun with that very cry, and his head swam with the terror of it. He turned at once and hurried back to the shed. He whispered hoarsely: "Quick, do not waste a moment. There is death in the air. Pack up everything while I saddle the asses!"

Mary said calmly: "We are in the Lord's hands. By your leave, I shall first wash and dress my little child."

"Only make haste!"

Prince Archelaus rode into Bethlehem at the head of a Thracian squadron and gave orders to his officers. A dozen troopers were to guard each road and lane leading out of the place and let nobody pass; the remainder to round up all the Sons of David, together with their families. "Let all be done quietly and without violence. When you have separated the Davidites from the natives of the place, the slaughter can begin. Mind you, only male infants are to die. No grown persons unless they offer resistance. No female infants or elder children. The creature of ill-luck which we are instructed to destroy is not four months old yet, and still at the breast; but for safety's sake we are to kill all male infants of two years old and under. These are the orders of King Herod."

The ass-surgeon and his Kenite kinsmen were waiting for Joseph at the fringe of the wood. They urged him: "Quick, my lord! Death has ridden into Bethlehem—take off your gay merchant's cloak and put on this old and ragged one. You and your lady and the little one must pass for Children of Rahab."

Joseph did as he was told, and then all together rode down to the pasture, where the tribesmen rounded up their scattered sheep and drove them along the road towards the Jordan. A party of Thracians were posted at the toll-house, but their sergeant let the nomads pass without question; and they travelled slowly on until presently down the wind came a terrifying sound of confused shouting, screams and cries. The ass-surgeon said: "Leave us now, my lord and my lady. Strike across the hills to the oak-wood yonder under the jagged cliff, the one with the fringe of pines. Friends are there who will conduct you to a place of safety. It is dangerous to remain with us. Be of good courage; and may the Lord protect his own!"

In the oak-wood Joseph found a shepherd seated by a fire, a glum, murderous-looking man, with three long knives in his girdle, and stood at a loss, not knowing how to address him. But Mary spoke up readily: "Generous son of the Tent Curtains, I charge you in the name of our mother Rahab, leave these flocks under the care of the lad and convey us with all haste to your lord Kenah!"

They found Kenah encamped at Beth-Zur, ten miles away to the south-west. He greeted Mary and the child with lively joy, and for their sakes showed respect to Joseph.

After three days in the nomad camp they were ready to set out again. When Kenah asked Joseph where he was bound, he answered: "To Egypt, to pay a debt to Simon son of Boethus who was lately High Priest."

"Is it a great sum? The road to Egypt is not safe for rich men travelling unescorted."

"No, it is no great sum, but a mere half-shekel, which is two Alexandrian drachmae; a debt of honour, notwithstanding."

"My sister's son will ride with you and make music by the way. You need fear nothing in his company."

They rode towards Egypt accompanied by Kenah's nephew. When they reached Hebron news overtook them of Herod's death and the release of the Jews awaiting destruction in the hippodrome. The messenger said that Herod, feeling death suddenly stealing over him, had given orders that every one of them should be killed; but that his sister Salome had prevented the massacre.

At this, Kenah's nephew began to weep and improvised a song of lost hopes, how Jacob had triumphed once more and Esau was thrown back into darkness. Filled with poetic insight, he fixed his eyes upon a green plant growing from a sandy patch and cried: "May the Lord God curse you, wicked plant, for the mischief that you have done!"

Joseph asked: "Friend, why do you curse that plant?"

"I curse the wild cucumber. Do you not know the wild cucumber?"

Joseph remembered the story of Elisha and the soup-kettle: how once an ignorant townsman shredded wild cucumber into the soup, mistaking it for the garden kind, and how one of his fellows, spoon to mouth, cried in agony: "O Man of God, there is death in the pot!", and how Elisha saved them all from death by a miracle. He asked: "Into whose pot has death now been shredded?"

"The King suffered from a tumour, but he did not die of it. I am the physician of my clan, and I know the virtues and qualities of every herb in the desert. Only the wild cucumber could have caused the dry throat, the stinking breath, the itching, the perpetual flux. A curse on this unprofitable plant for postponing the day of settlement!"

"Yet Esau forgave his brother Jacob when he might have destroyed him on the way to Succoth; and his magnanimity is not forgotten by us Israelites. No reckoning was ever settled by the sword, noble nephew of Kenah. Sing your song rather in praise of the wild cucumber that has saved the lives of fifteen thousand men."

Mary added: "And it may well be that the wild cucumber has saved the life of a child upon whom both Esau and Jacob, clasping hands, may fix their hopes of peace."

They turned aside to Ain-Rimmon, where Mary and Elizabeth met again and each sorrowfully but proudly showed the other her fatherless child. Thence they continued to Beersheba, where they heard further news of events in Jerusalem: how civil war between Herod's sons had been avoided by an unexpected agreement between them. It was reported that Prince Philip had gone into hiding when the false news of Herod's death was announced, and that when the true news came he had hastened to Jerusalem and seized the Palace with the help of the Belgian Celts whom he had attached to his interest. There Archelaus had joined him with the Thracians, and Antipas had sent a message of peace to them both from Sepphoris in Galilee, where he had collected the garrisons of all the cities for fifty miles around. The three princes then met in the presence of their Aunt Salome, who acted as peacemaker, and agreed to divide the kingdom between them into three tetrarchies, if the Emperor gave his consent. With the help of Ptolemy the Chamberlain, to whom Herod had entrusted his signet, they forged the draft of a new Will confirming the arrangement. They did not, however, alter the bequests to the Emperor and the Lady Livia, or the bequest of half a million silver drachmae to their Aunt Salome. The kingship of Judaea with Edom and Samaria was awarded to Archelaus; Galilee and Lower Transjordania to Antipas; Philip received Upper Transjordania as far as Mount Hermon; and Salome, in recognition of her services, a little queendom in what had once been Philistia. Prince Herod Philip received nothing in the Will, but in return for a sworn renunciation of his claims to any part of Herod's dominions, Archelaus, Philip and Antipas together allotted him a yearly pension. As for Antipater the Younger, Prince Philip's agents murdered him in Alexandria and threw his body into the sea; or so a merchant reported who had just come from that city.

There was nothing in this news which could alter Joseph's decision to travel to Egypt, for he had divined Mary's secret. It was plain to him that Herod's original Will, which Augustus had approved, was the only binding one. By this instrument the succession to the Throne had been awarded first to Antipater; then to Herod Philip, if Antipater predeceased him; lastly to Antipater's heirs. Now, since Herod Philip had renounced his claim, and since Antipater the Younger was dead, the heir-at-law was Jesus, the child born of Antipater's secret marriage. Augustus might approve the arrangement entered upon by Herod's sons, but the original Will stood; hence the princes' murder of Antipater the Younger and their arrangement with Herod Philip. For Mary's sake, therefore, Joseph decided that he could not return to Emmaus while Archelaus was king, for if the secret of Jesus's identity leaked out, as well it might, assassins would be sent to despatch him.

From Rehoboth, Joseph sent a message to his sons that he was well but had gone on a long journey; and that they might enter now on their inheritance without waiting for news of his death.

He told Mary: "This journey gives me a new hold upon life. I was growing old and idle. In Alexandria I will return to my former trade: I was once well known for the making of ox-yokes and the coulters of wooden ploughs. The work is not exacting; it is a matter of knack, not strength. I will soon build up a trade again, please God, and one day your boy shall be my apprentice."

At the ancient city of On-Heliopolis, Kenah's nephew left them; and there in the stream by the gate Mary washed her child's swaddling-clothes and laid them to dry in the sun while she rested under the shade of an ancient olive-tree. The next day they went to the city of Leontopolis, named after Bast the Lioness, which lies a few miles to the northwest. There Joseph sold the white ass and the decorated saddle, and with part of the price that they fetched bought a bag of carpenter's tools from an Egyptian who was retiring from trade. He found lodgings not far from the Jewish Temple which had been founded by Onias the High Priest nearly two generations previously; and there presently he entered with Mary and gave thanks to the Lord for their escape.

The debt to Simon was soon paid, and Mary became Joseph's wife; and because trade was bad and Joseph's earnings small, she sold vegetables in the market for a market-gardener of their acquaintance, while the child played in the dust by her side.

Part Two

C H A P T E R   T W E L V E

AT LEONTOPOLIS

˙HEROD'S catafalque was followed by his numerous relatives, friends, freedmen and slaves, all weeping vigorously; also by sorrowful representatives of the many Greek and Syrian communities which he had befriended, by hundreds of Edomites and Nabataeans, besides a great team of professional mourners, and by the men of his private army who were attached to him by long years of loyal service. But the word went round among the pious Jews of Jerusalem that every man should abstain from demonstrations of grief that day, even if he had suffered a bereavement in his own family; and when the funeral was over a great rival procession of mourners went up to the Temple to bewail the young men who had been burned alive, with their rabbis, for cutting down the golden eagle from the East Gate. The noise that they raised was terrible and continued day after day and night after night until Archelaus lost his patience and sent the general officer commanding the Jerusalem garrison to find Carmi the Captain of the Temple Guard and request him peremptorily to abate the nuisance. Carmi was recognized on his way into the Temple and forced to retreat by a shower of stones. The wailing continued with even greater fury.

By this time, the usual flood of pious Jews was entering Jerusalem for the Passover, and their arrival was made the occasion for a mass meeting in the three Courts to demand the deposition of the absentee High Priest nominated by Herod just before his death—a notorious evil-liver—and the expulsion of all foreigners resident within the City walls. This second demand was not an expression of national xenophobia, for the people of Judaea were hospitably inclined to foreign residents and were enjoined by their Law never to forget the time when they themselves were guests of the Egyptians. It was a protest against the further employment of the Celtic and Galatian troops who had behaved with such brutality in the hippodrome affair and of the Thracians who had carried out the Bethlehem massacre; and against the presence in the Palace of Archelaus's mother Malthace the Samaritan, who was thought to have been Herod's evil genius in his last days. For the Samaritans, though they follow the Laws of Moses with praiseworthy exactitude, are regarded by the Jews as more foreign than any other foreigners. They are the descendants of Assyrian—or, as they themselves claim, Cypriot—colonists settled in Shechem many centuries ago, after the Ephraimite townsmen had been carried away into Assyrian captivity; those colonists adopted the Israelite religion in placation of the God whose city and shrine they had occupied, because at the time they were greatly troubled by the depredations of lions. A bitter feud has separated the Jews and the Samaritans ever since the Samaritan priesthood unsuccessfully opposed Nehemiah's rebuilding of the Temple at Jerusalem: their contention was that the centralizing of worship at Jerusalem, which was not authorized in the Pentateuch, would give the Jews a political power over Samaria which they had not earned and which they would certainly abuse. The Jews resented their interference, and when the revived Temple worship began to attract the Ephraimite peasantry with gifts to Jerusalem, the Samaritan priesthood built a rival Temple on Mount Gerizim, which eventually John Hyrcanus the Maccabee destroyed as idolatrous: for the Samaritans were continuing to worship Jehovah's divorced partner Ashima the Dove-goddess side by side with Jehovah. Samaritans were now still forbidden entrance into the Jerusalem Temple, even into the Court of the Gentiles, and the proverb current among the orthodox was: "Eat Samaritan bread, eat swine's flesh."

Archelaus, instead of either ignoring the protests of the people or reminding them of the duty that they owed to their foreign guests, sent his Celts to break up the meeting, and in the ensuing disturbances some three thousand people were slaughtered or trampled to death in a stampede. When, therefore, he sailed to Rome a few days later, accompanied by a large suite, to persuade the Emperor to approve the division of the kingdom into tetrarchies, an embassy of fifty members of the High Court sailed in another ship to plead for its conversion, instead, into a single Imperial province. They undertook that if such a province were administered by a High Priest of their own choice, supported by the High Court and the Great San-hedrin and a council of delegates from the Greek cities, the "Jewish problem", as Augustus had designated it in a recent speech to the Senate, would cease to exist. The embassy reached Rome on the same day as the Herodians, and on the following morning when both parties went to the Palace to pay their respects to the Emperor, three or four thousand Jewish merchants and clerks, their wives and children too, turned out to greet the ambassadors with shouts of en-couragement and at the same time to revile and hiss Archelaus.

Prince Philip had remained at Jerusalem as temporary adminis-trator of the kingdom, under the energetic protection of Varus the Governor-General of Syria; but both Antipas and Salome had ac-companied Archelaus to Rome, and, when they saw what an un-friendly reception he was given by the Jews, began to regret their agreement with him. Naturally, almost any political compromise was preferable to the plan put forward by the ambassadors of the High Court, but they were vexed that Archelaus had made matters so difficult for them all. Antipas managed to secure a private audi-ence with the Emperor before the hour appointed for the public audience and at once went behind his brothers' backs in a plea for the ratification of the latest Will that Herod had signed, the one drawn at the time that Archelaus and Philip were under his dis-pleasure. He showed Augustus a certified copy and pretended that he had been ignorant of the existence of this Will, in which he had been nominated sole heir to the kingdom; he would never otherwise have assented to the partition of a patrimony which was rightfully his.

Livia was present, and on her advice Augustus reminded Antipas of the impropriety of repudiating a sworn agreement however ig-norantly entered upon; and declared firmly that the only Will which had any legal validity was the original one deposited with the Vestals. Indeed, it was on the strength of this Will, Augustus said, that he proposed to approve the supplementary bequests made to the Lady Livia, himself and other members of his family in the latest, unsigned Will which had just been placed upon his table; for the Will that Antipas now produced had been so hurriedly drawn that certain of these bequests had been omitted, and he could not venture to pro-nounce valid in law an instrument which suggested that the testator was not in perfect command of his faculties at the time of signature. However, since the principal beneficiaries under the terms of the original Will, namely, the late King Antipater, Prince Herod Philip and their heirs, either were now dead or had resigned their claims to the estate, and since no provisions were to be found in the Will for the disposal of the estate in such a complex of events, the draft Will must perforce be taken as a good and sufficient indication of Herod's intentions at the time of his death.

He added: "In only one matter will I meet you. In default of any heir to Antipater—and by the by I heartily deplore the mysterious assassination of Antipater the Younger—the Crown may rest in abeyance: that is to say, I shall spare you any feeling of resentment by not bestowing on your brother Archelaus the title of King. He must content himself with that of Ethnarch." Ethnarch was a title of little honour; the commoner who presided over Jewish affairs in Alexandria was also called the Ethnarch.

It is said that Livia's main reason for pressing this settlement on Augustus was that Salome had urged her to do so. Only in the draft Will was Salome awarded her little Philistine queendom, or toparchy, which she now promised to bequeath to Livia in her Will if she might be allowed to enjoy its usufruct for the year or two of life that remained to her; she was in failing health.

Augustus next admitted Archelaus and Antipas to the public audience, at which he repeated his decisions, but thought it only just to tell Archelaus afterwards in private: "I will give you the title of King in ten years' time if you have earned it by then."

He called for the envoys of the High Court, who were loud in their complaints against Archelaus, and their arguments for the provincializing of Herod's kingdom and its administration by a representative assembly were so cogent that they nearly persuaded him to go back on his engagement to Archelaus and Antipas. He readily admitted that Archelaus's action in Passover week had been precipitate and regrettable, but said in conclusion: "Learned Jews, I cannot grant your plea. Frankly, my chief reason is the many thousands of your co-religionists now thronging the approaches to my palace who have intervened in a matter which does not in the least concern them. You plead that I should demand from the Senate the political autonomy of Palestine—"

"Within the Empire, Caesar!" interposed the leading ambassador.

"Yes, that goes without saying. But these demonstrators are not natives of Palestine, or very few of them, and their appearance in the streets to-day serves as a warning to me against strengthening the power of your High Priest by extending his temporal, and therefore his religious, power. How do I know that if I granted your plea Jerusalem would not become the focus of a world-conspiracy by the Jews against our Roman hegemony? There are Jews everywhere, all prosperous men and as thick as thieves in their business dealings."

"Alas, Caesar, it is a great mistake to generalize about either the prosperity or the unanimity of the Jews from your experience of the Jewish merchant colonies in Italy, Asia Minor and Egypt. There are hundreds of thousands of very poor Jews in the world, and in Palestine at least our religion is torn by numerous schisms. As for a world-wide conspiracy, rest assured that we of Jerusalem are peaceable people and have no desire whatsoever to extend the bounds of our religious influence. Already we regret the forcible conversion of the Edomites to Judaism by the Maccabee kings and the more recent voluntary conversion of great numbers of Greeks who have come over to us for reasons of trade rather than from religious conviction. The Jews of the Dispersal are, in general, as peaceable as ourselves and none follows the profession of arms."

"Nicolaus of Damascus tells a different story. He informs me that you have a Conquering Messiah promised you by your sacred poets and daily expected, whose destiny it is to overthrow us. I admit that the Jews of this city are for the most part merchants or accountants, not soldiers, but what of that? Rich men do not need to go into battle themselves nowadays when they can hire mercenary troops."

"You have been frank, Caesar, and we will be frank in return. There are indeed prophecies current among us of a king who is destined to free us from foreign oppression, as a certain King David delivered our ancestors from the Philistines some three hundred years before Rome was founded; but they do not refer to any particular date and some theologians even believe them to have been fulfilled fifty years before the foundation of the Roman Republic in the person of King Cyrus the Persian who delivered us from the oppression of King Darius the Mede. If you grant our present plea, the coming of this hypothetic king will no longer be looked for, if only because there will be no foreign oppression from which to expect deliverance. It is perfectly consonant with our national honour to remain a client nation of Rome—just as we were clients in ancient times of Assyria, Persia and Egypt—so long as you Romans permit us to live in peace and retain our ancestral institutions; if you grant our plea we will richly recompense you for the military and naval protection that you afford us."

But Augustus feared to offend Livia by listening to the ambassadors any longer and therefore dismissed them, saying politely: "Learned men, I hope one day to find time to study your sacred literature, though I am told that it cannot be readily mastered."

Joachim, the father of Mary, who was one of the leading ambassa-

161

dors, answered: "I have been studying the Scriptures for sixty-five years, Caesar, but many religious questions of the utmost importance still cheat my understanding."

Joachim might have instanced the questions concerned with the Messiah's eventual appearance; and unless the term "Messiah" is carefully defined here, the story of Jesus's life will lose something of its clear beauty.

The word Messiah signifies "the Christ" or "the Anointed One", and is therefore applicable only to an anointed king, not to a commoner however greatly distinguished by spiritual gifts or military achievements. The studious Zacharias, Joachim's brother-in-law, in his unfinished concordance of Messianic prophecy had distinguished five distinct Messiahs, namely, the Son of David, the Son of Joseph, the Son of Man, the Great Priest and the Suffering Servant. His concern, like that of most intelligent theologians of his day, was to discover whether all these distinctions were true ones: whether there were perhaps only four Messiahs, or three, or two, or even perhaps only one to whom all the titles and attributes of the other four could be reasonably attributed.

The Son of David was the most popular concept of the five. This Messiah was to be a monarch in the ordinary temporal sense, ruling the same territory over which David had once ruled. He was the pastoral king foretold by the prophet Ezekiel, by the author of the seventeenth and eighteenth Psalms, by the prophets Zechariah and Malachi, by the author of the second part of the Book of Isaiah, by the Sibyl of the *Oracles*, by the author of the *Psalter of Solomon*, by Esdras and by many others. He was to be born of a virgin mother in Judaean Bethlehem—Bethlehem of Ephrath—after a period crowded with wars, famines and natural calamities, the so-called Pangs of the Messiah, when the Jews were floundering in a slough of misery. He was to be called from an obscure home and anointed King by the ever-young prophet Elijah, of whom Ben-Sira the Preacher had written: "You who are ready for the Time, as it is prophesied, to still men's anger before the fierce anger of the Lord, to turn the hearts of the fathers to the children and to restore the tribes of Israel." Elijah was to prepare the way for the Messiah, who would thereupon enter Jerusalem riding in triumph on a young ass. This would be the signal for a bloody war against Jerusalem by the oppressors of Israel, in the course of which the City would be taken and two-thirds of the inhabitants be massacred. The Messiah, however, encouraged by divine portents, would rally the faithful survivors on the Mount of Olives and lead them to final victory. He would then reunite the scattered tribes and reign peacefully for four hundred or, some said, a thousand years, with the rulers of Egypt and Assyria and all the rest of the world doing homage to his throne in the newly sanctified City of Jerusalem. This Kingdom of Heaven would be an era of unexampled prosperity, a new Golden Age.

The Son of Joseph, or the Son of Ephraim, was another warlike Messiah, whose reign was similarly to be crowned with universal peace. His birthplace, too, was to be Judaean Bethlehem, the seat of his ancestress Rachel, but he was to reign principally over the ten tribes of the North which had seceded from Rehoboam, the last King of all Israel. Since Shechem had been defiled by the Samaritans, it was expected by some that he would reveal himself on Mount Tabor, the holy mountain of Galilee, but others expected that he would return to Shechem and cleanse it for his own uses. The Son of Joseph was, in fact, a rival concept to the Son of David whose cult was centralized at Jerusalem: for the Northerners considered that the blessing conferred by Jacob on his sons, according to the Book of Genesis, did not justify Judah, after whom the Jews are called, in claiming the perpetual leadership of Israel. The prophecy ran, somewhat ambiguously, as follows:

The sceptre shall not depart from Judah, nor the commander's baton from between his feet, until he approaches the man to whom they belong—him for whom the people wait.

When this happened, the Northerners held, the royal sceptre and the commander's baton would be made over by Judah to the Messiah —who must necessarily be a Josephite, for the patriarch Jacob had prophesied that from Joseph would proceed the Shepherd, the Rock of Israel, and that blessings were in store for him "to the utmost bounds of the everlasting hills". With this warrior Son of Joseph was associated a preacher of penitence, who might be Elijah.

But what did "Joseph" signify? Did it not perhaps signify the whole holy nation of Israel which had been led out of Egypt by Moses, rather than the two tribes of Ephraim and Manasseh with whom the name later became identified, and all but the poor remnants of whom had been carried away into Assyrian captivity seven hundred years previously, never to return? In that case, the Son of David might also be the Son of Joseph, and the meaning of the blessing of Judah might be that Judah should keep his tribal sovereignty until the time came to extend it to all Israel.

A puzzling particular about the warrior Messiah—whether the Son of David or the Son of Joseph was intended could not be agreed —was that according to Isaiah he would come marching out of Edom, which in Isaiah's day lay outside Jewish territory, in dyed garments from Bozrah. If Bozrah was given its obvious connotation, namely the Edomite capital city, this made him an Edomite prince. But perhaps, critics suggested, the other Bozrah on the Persian Gulf was intended, where a purple-dying industry had been established for centuries.

The third Messiah was the Son of Man, but this Messiahship was a doubtful tradition deduced from the seventh chapter of the apocalyptic Book of Daniel, where Daniel sees a certain Son of Man being given everlasting dominion by the white-headed Ancient of Days over all peoples, nations and languages. The Son of Man was not a human king, and would enter Jerusalem, so Daniel said, riding not on an ass but on a storm-cloud. He might, however, be regarded as the spirit or emanation of either of the first two Messiahs, performing in the Heavens what was simultaneously being performed on earth.

The fourth Messiah was to be a priest-king, with a Judaean general serving under him. The best text for studying his claims was the beautiful, if uncanonical, Testament of Levi. As a priest this Messiah must necessarily proceed from the tribe of Levi, not from either Judah or Joseph. He was to sanctify the conquests of his general, institute universal peace, reform the calendar, revise the Scriptural Canon, and cleanse the people from their sins. It was a concept difficult to reconcile with the others; yet Zacharias as a loyal Son of Zadok could not reject it out of hand, as he rejected, however, the Pharisaic theory of a universal resurrection at the close of the thousand years, and a Last Judgement by Jehovah of all souls who had ever lived.

Last in the list came the Suffering Servant, whose claims to be the true Messiah were studied by a small pessimistic group of Pharisees. His justificatory text was found in Isaiah, the fifty-third chapter, and he would be no glorious conqueror like the Son of David or the Son of Joseph, but a marred, uncomely, despised man, the scape-goat of the people, reckoned as a sinner, sentenced to dishonourable death, dumb before his accusers and hurried by them to the grave; yet somehow after death to be rewarded with the spoils of victory. There was also a reference to his death in the twelfth chapter of Zechariah: "They shall look upon him whom they have pierced and mourn for him as one mourns for his only son. They shall weep bitterly, as one weeps for his first-born." Zacharias, who took the Suffering Servant to be a type of rejected prophet, could not regard him as in any true sense a Messiah, for his kingdom was to be posthumous, and a posthumous kingdom seemed a contradiction in terms. Yet, for the sake of completeness, he had felt obliged to include in his concordance the texts referring to the Suffering Servant, together with the relevant commentaries, in some of which it was suggested that as the prophet Elijah had revived the widow's dead son at Sarepta or the prophet Elisha had revived the dead son of the Shunemite woman, so this Messiah was to suffer death but be raised from the dead by a special fiat of Jehovah.

The condition that the Messiah should be a royal heir, called suddenly from an obscure home and anointed by a prophet, was a remarkable one; for, generally speaking, a royal heir is either housed in a splendid palace and accorded the respect due to his station or else he is confined by a usurping rival to the dungeon of his strongest fortress, where no prophet is able to visit him with the traditional acclamation and the horn of sacred anointing oil. In the case of Jesus, however, this condition of obscurity was strictly fulfilled. His existence was unknown to all but a very few people, and of these none but his mother, her husband Joseph, and Simon son of Boethus, the former High Priest, knew his whereabouts. He himself, though aware from an early age that he was possessed of powers denied to other children of his acquaintance, and though subject to sudden visionary trances during which clear intimations of his fate came to him, remained in ignorance of his true identity until Mary confided it to him in his early manhood, and thereafter kept the secret even from his intimates until his thirtieth year.

At the age of seven he was the leader of a group of little boys, sons of the Jewish market women, who used to play in and out of the booths of the market-place at Leontopolis. He was small for his age, but hardy and broad-shouldered and had a pale face with large deep-sunken luminous eyes and reddish-black hair. The games that these boys played were for the most part dramatic versions of ancient Jewish history and were carefully planned and precisely carried out, for Jesus exacted obedience from his playmates by an exercise of authority which both awed and delighted them. As Moses, he led them out of Egypt into the wilderness laden with booty; as Gideon, he laid an ambush for the Midianites and pursued them across the Jordan for two hundred miles; as David, he fled from the Court of King Saul, the homicidal maniac, and communed in secret with Saul's son, his blood-brother Jonathan. Always he gave them the illusion that they were taking part in the real events, for he would describe with a wealth of circumstance each scene through which he conducted them, until it rose up plainly before their inward eyes.

One day he was reproached by the little sister of one of his playmates because he would not play weddings or funerals or any of the other usual games of the market-place: "We have piped for you and you have not danced. We have mourned for you and you have not pretended to weep with us." It was a reproach for which he could find no answer, except: "My games are better." Presently he was sorry and said to the child: "Come now, Dorcas, at what game do you wish me to play?"

"Let us play at Noah's Ark and the dove that flew out in search of land."

He sat down and made an ark with mud and little pieces of reed, and then animals of mud which went seven by seven, and two by two, into the ark.

Dorcas complained: "No, I did not mean a toy ark: I meant a real ark into which we can step ourselves."

"Patience, first let me finish my birds and beasts." His fingers worked quickly and she sat watching until he had done. Then he stood up, bowed to her gravely and said: "The rain is about to fall, Dorcas. Come into the ark with me. I am Noah and you are my wife; and our sons and their wives are following behind with the animals. Come inside with me."

She took his hand and they pretended to enter the ark. With her fingers tightly clasped in his, she seemed indeed to be stepping into a real ark with three storeys, like the one mentioned in Genesis, and above the loud noise of rain drumming on the roof she heard the lowing, roaring, braying, screaming, bleating noises of the animals. At last the rain ceased, and she watched the mud-pigeon in Jesus's other hand put on feathers and preen itself and fly whirring up through the skylight in the roof. She cried out for fear and he released her fingers, so that the illusion was broken. The ark was once more a toy ark made of Nile mud, and the toy pigeon lay broken-winged on the ground.

"Dorcas, Dorcas," he said, "could you not have waited for the olive leaf?"

Jesus was also possessed of a natural prophetic insight. When one day an Egyptian boy, playing at "camel broken loose", came running at Jesus with his shoulder so that both fell together, Jesus picked himself up and said: "Alas, that camel will never finish his course." This proved true, for the young Egyptian, resuming his play, ran bleating among the picketed market beasts; they stampeded, and a mule kicked him to death.

On another occasion he was playing "Spies in Jericho" on the roof of his father's lodging. He and a boy named Zeno were Caleb and his companion hiding in the stalks of flax on the roof of Rahab's house, and the girl acting as Rahab was about to lower them to the ground by a cord. But Zeno's foot slipped before he had firm hold of the cord; he fell sprawling off the roof and struck his head on a mounting-block twenty feet below. The other boys, who were representing the men of Jericho, cried out: "He is dead! He is dead!" and ran away. Jesus remained on the roof with his feet dangling over the edge, lost in thought. The mother and father of the injured boy ran shrieking out from the opposite house, and began mourning him for dead. A crowd of neighbours gathered and the mother pointed upward to Jesus on the roof, crying: "Look, neighbours, look! There sits my son's murderer, the Carpenter's son. He pushed my innocent child from the roof. This is his second victim. The first was the Egyptian boy on whom he laid a curse for knocking him down."

At this Jesus sprang from the roof in indignation and landed feet foremost on a heap of dust. "Woman," he said, "I did not push down your son, nor did I curse the Egyptian boy!"

He thrust his way through the crowd, stood over his playmate, whose face had gone chalky white, and taking him by the hand, cried: "Zeno, Zeno, answer me, I did not push you, did I?"

Zeno replied at once: "No, my lord Caleb, it was my foot that slipped. Quick, let us go up to hide in the mountain and after three days we shall return to our lord Joshua!" He leaped up unhurt, the colour flooding back into his cheeks.

About this time Joseph sent Jesus to school at the house of the nearest rabbi, not knowing that he had already learned to read Hebrew and Greek, the two languages of the market-place, at the booth of a professional letter-writer for whom he sometimes ran errands. Jesus was a child prodigy of a sort not rare among Jews: what he had once heard or read, he never forgot.

He arrived early at the school, before the other scholars, and the rabbi patted him on the head and said: "It is written:

I, wisdom, dwell with prudence, and find out knowledge of witty inventions. By me kings reign and princes decree justice. I love them that love me, and those that seek me early shall find me.

You have come early indeed." Then he prayed:

> Blessed art thou, God our Lord, King of the World, who hast commanded us to occupy ourselves with the word of the Law.

To which Jesus made the response that Joseph had taught him:

> And let the beauty of the Lord our God be upon us; and establish thou the work of our hands for us.

Then the rabbi asked: "To what witty inventions, child, do you suppose Solomon to refer?"

"First, I suppose, to the alphabet."

The rabbi was delighted. "Let us make haste to begin our studies together. I will teach you all about the alphabet."

He took a wooden stencil from his alphabet box and stamped a letter on a clay tablet. "This is *Aleph*, child, the first letter: say *Aleph*."

Jesus repeated obediently: "*Aleph*".

"Examine the character closely. It is *Aleph*; repeat the word."

Jesus repeated: "*Aleph*".

"And once again for good measure."

"*Aleph*."

"Excellent. Now we can proceed to the next letter, which is *Beth*."

"But, rabbi," cried Jesus in disappointment, "you have not yet taught me *Aleph*. What is the meaning of the character? The letter-writer told me that you would know."

The schoolmaster was surprised. "*Aleph* means *Aleph*, which is to say, an ox."

"Yes, rabbi. I know that *Aleph* means an ox, but why is the character shaped as it is shaped? It is like an ox's head with a yoke on its neck, but why is it tilted at such a strange angle?"

The rabbi smiled and said: "Patience, my son. First learn to recognize the letters and then, if you will, speculate on their shape. Yet I will tell you this much about *Aleph*. It is recorded that in the beginning of time there was a quarrel between the letters of the alphabet, each boastfully demanding precedence of the others. They pleaded their causes before the Lord at great length. Only the *Aleph* said nothing and made no claim. The Lord was pleased with *Aleph* and promised that he would begin the Ten Commandments with it; and so he did with ANOKHI ADONAI—'I am the Lord'. It is a lesson, child, in modesty and silence. Come. now, this is the letter *Beth*. Repeat: *Beth*."

"Since you order me to say *Beth*, I say it: *Beth*. But already I know the twenty-six letters and can write them out in their proper order both in the old style and the new. Will you not answer my question about *Aleph*? For surely every character of the alphabet, if it is indeed a witty invention, must represent some truth concerned with that letter? Is the ox tossing his head with impatience? Or has he fallen dead in his tracks?"

The rabbi sighed and said determinedly: "Return home in peace to your father, little Jesus, before the other scholars arrive, and tell him from me that he must send you to a more learned schoolmaster than myself."

Jesus went sadly back to Joseph with the message. Joseph asked: But why in the world has the rabbi sent you back so soon?"

"Because I asked him why the letter *Aleph* was shaped as it is shaped, and he did not know."

Joseph consulted with Mary and decided to send Jesus to another rabbi with a great reputation for learning, who taught at the further end of the town.

Next day Jesus went to the second schoolmaster, to whom, as it happened, the first had meanwhile mentioned his experience with Jesus; he resolved not to let the boy disturb the routine of the school by asking impertinent questions, as he called them.

"It is as clear as day," said the second schoolmaster. "The child was playing a trick on you. That scoundrelly letter-writer must have put him up to it."

"You may be right, but he seems to be an ingenuous child and I can hardly credit him with such naughtiness."

When Jesus entered the new class-room and saluted his master reverently and joined in the response to the blessing, and then sat down on the carpet cross-legged with the other boys, he was sharply ordered to stand up.

He stood up

"You have come to learn from me?" the master asked.

"Yes, rabbi."

"I hear from your former teacher, the learned rabbi Hoshea, that you already know your alphabet."

"It is true, rabbi."

"A learned child indeed you are! Perhaps you are already an exponent of sacred literature?"

"By the grace of our God I have made a beginning, rabbi."

"How a beginning?"

"I have begun with the letter *Aleph*."

"Wonderful, wonderful! Doubtless you have found out why the character is shaped as it is?"

"I pondered on the question all night with prayer, rabbi, and in the morning the answer was given to me."

"Deign to enlighten us with your marvellous illumination."

Jesus thoughtfully knitted his brows and then said: "It is this. *Aleph* is the first of letters, and *Aleph* is the ox which is the mainstay of man, the first and most honourable of his four-hoofed possessions."

"Justify that statement. Why is not the ass the most honourable?"

"The ox is mentioned before the ass in the commandment against the use of the evil eye."

"Impudence! And why not the sheep? Have you considered the sheep?"

"I have considered the sheep, though it is not mentioned in the commandment; and clearly the ox is the more honourable, as is shown in the allegory of Jacob's two marriages: for first he married Leah, which is to say the cow, and then Rachel, which is to say the ewe."

The schoolmaster bottled up his growing rage and said: "Proceed, Hiram of Tyre!"

"*Aleph*, as I understand the character, is an ox lying sacrificed, the yoke still on his neck; which signifies that the study of literature must begin with sacrifice. We must dedicate to the Lord our first and most precious possession, which is emblemized by the yoked ox, namely, our obedient labour until we drop dead. This was the answer given me."

"Tell me, have you come to this school as a pupil or as a Doctor of the Law?" cried the schoolmaster, speaking the slow ironic drawl which his pupils had learned to fear more than his roar of passion.

Jesus replied simply: "I have heard it said: 'Scatter where you gather, gather where you scatter.' You asked me why the first letter of the alphabet is shaped as it is shaped, and I gave you the explanation that came in answer to my prayer. This was my scattering. As for my gathering, I should like to know, if you will scatter in return, why the last letter of the alphabet is so shaped?"

The master grasped his rod of storax-wood and advanced towards Jesus with menacing grunts. He asked, his face pale with anger: "The last letter of the alphabet! Do you mean the letter *Tav*, Rabbi Jesus?"

"I am not the rabbi, you are the rabbi; and it is *Tav* that I mean."

"*Tav* is the last letter, and the reason for its shape is not far to seek.

For *Tav* is shaped like a cross, and the shameful cross is the destined end of shameless scholars who presume to chop logic with their teacher. Jesus son of the Carpenter, beware, for its shadow already falls across your path!"

Jesus faltered: "If I have offended, rabbi, I am truly sorry. I shall ask my father to send me to another school."

"Not before I have dealt faithfully with you, spawn of folly. For it is written: 'Folly is found in the heart of a child, but the rod of correction shall drive it far from him.' With the foolish and presumptuous child I have no patience at all; and the wise child stands in awe of my rod."

Boldly Jesus answered: "Rabbi, consider well what you are telling us. Do you not know the judgement of the learned Hillel: 'A passionate master cannot teach, nor a timid child learn'?"

This was more than the master could bear. He brought the rod down with all his might on Jesus's head, where it flew into pieces.

Jesus did not flinch or defend himself, but stood gazing fixedly at the angry man, who presently returned to his chair and tried to resume his teaching. But suddenly he clutched at his heart and fell forward dead.

So for a while ended the schooling of Jesus, for no other rabbi in Leontopolis would accept him as a pupil. For months afterwards passers-by in the street would point at him, shaking their heads and muttering: "The boy who killed his master by asking shameless questions! Yet they say that the learned man answered him witheringly before he died and prophesied that he would hang on a felon's cross."

CHAPTER THIRTEEN

THE RETURN FROM EGYPT

ONE of Joseph's customers, a retired schoolmaster from Alexandria, took a liking to Jesus and volunteered to undertake his education. Simeon was a learned, lonely old scholar who, though no longer capable of managing a class of boys, was ready, he said, to give his undivided attention to one of more than usual promise. He lived a few miles away from Leontopolis at Matarieh, a pleasant village, renowned for its figs.

Joseph was pleased and decided to move his business to Matarieh, where there was a small synagogue; and hearing that Simeon's wife had recently died invited him to share their house. So it was arranged. Jesus studied with Simeon every morning from dawn until two hours before midday; the rest of his day he spent in the workshop with Joseph, except for an hour of leisure in the cool of the evening. From Simeon, Jesus learned in three years as much as few children learn in ten years of ordinary schooling; for in a large class it always happens that the dull boys delay the intelligent, and that the schoolmaster cannot unbend lest the bad-hearted take advantage of a kindness suitable only for the good-hearted. Moreover, unless he treats every child with equal attention and equal severity, jealous parents will abuse him and charge him with favouritism. But in a class consisting of a single eager pupil, anything is possible.

Simeon's method was not to say: "Such-and-such is the meaning of this text", but "This text the Sadducees interpret in such-and-such a sense, whereas the Pharisees of the school of Rabbi Shammai interpret it in this other sense; and those of Rabbi Hillel's school, again, in this. The Essenes interpret it in still another sense, as follows. . . ."

Since Joseph was growing feeble and slow, Jesus was obliged gradually to take over a large part of the carpentry business from him, but never worked at his bench except with a chapter of the Scriptures close at hand for memorization or study. His work was sound and graceful, and he left to Joseph's spoke-shave and emery file only the subtler curves of yoke and plough, curves which no craftsman can master until he has spent a dozen years at the bench.

Those were happy years for Mary; she would have been content to live in their small neat house with Joseph and Jesus and Simeon for the rest of her life, had that been possible. Though she felt troubled at being the cause of Joseph's sudden departure and continued absence from his elder family and constantly told herself that he must somehow contrive to see them all again before he died, he appeared not to miss them greatly and assured her more than once that these last years of his life had been the sweetest of all. But Jesus: his was an altogether different case. Jesus, she knew, had a royal destiny to fulfil. He was preparing himself for it: one day it must lead him out of Egypt and back to the City which to her was the centre of the world. He had been there only once, as an infant, when she had brought him to the Temple to make the customary thank-offerings for her 'safe delivery, and had shown him to Anna the daughter of Phanuel.

One afternoon Simeon said to her, out of Jesus's hearing: "Your son is a good boy, a very good boy. He is modest, pious, courageous, prodigiously industrious and intelligent; yet he has one grave fault."

Mary asked in surprise: "Why, Simeon, what fault can that be?" In her heart she thought him perfect.

"That his extreme generosity of heart always draws him where his spirit suffers the most hurt."

"And is that a fault?"

"Do you know where he goes in the evenings between the end of his work and our supper?"

"What is he hiding from his mother and father?" she cried anxiously.

"Every evening he goes out to the Shame of Israel, as it is.called, or the Camp of Lost Souls."

"I cannot believe it!" Mary had heard of this camp, which was a group of filthy hovels on the fringe of the desert, inhabited by the outcasts of the Jewish congregation of Leontopolis and the villages near by. Thieves, beggars, maniacs, worn-out prostitutes, men and women entirely lost to shame, most of them suffering from loathsome diseases, eaters of crows, rats and lizards, people whose very existence offended the soul: for when Jews fall into the mire, they plunge down deeper than members of any other race—I suppose from having been stationed higher at first.

"It is true; I followed him there last night."

"Oh, Simeon, tell me, what takes him to that loathsome place?"

"He goes there to persuade the lost souls that they can still be found by the Lord's mercy. In one hand he holds a roll of the Scriptures, in the other a baton: he preaches to them from a hummock of sand and they listen, though the Lord alone knows what they hear when they listen. Last night I ventured out there to watch him and hid behind a ruined wall. The ragged and stinking crew squatted around him in a half-circle while he read to them from the Book of Job. This was a Jesus whom I had not hitherto known. For all his generous mind he spoke no soft words of comfort to them but boldly accused them in the words of Elihu the Jebusite of having hard and stubborn hearts, and ordered them to turn again with tears to their Creator before it was too late. They squinted up at him with eyes of rage and fear, snarling threats and blasphemies or irrelevantly whining for alms; but held there by some power which he possesses, the nature of which I do not altogether understand. As I watched, a madman made a rush at him but he drove him off with the baton and beat him over the head; at which the madman brayed horribly and went dancing away. The boy wept, but continued with his preaching. I came quietly away."

"I fear for the child. I know that I have no cause, but the fear steals over me in spite of myself."

"I do not blame you. He is far too young to undertake spiritual burdens as great as these."

"Have you told him that the Camp of Lost Souls is no place for him?"

"When I told him so this morning, he asked me: 'What of Job with his boils and blasphemies? Was Elihu the Jebusite at fault when he reasoned with Job?' I replied: 'Elihu was a grown man; you are a child. You are not yet of lawful age to read family prayers in your father's absence, and do you undertake to preach to those wolves and hyaenas?' He said: 'If I have sinned from presumption, may I be pardoned. Yet unless you forbid me, I will continue at the task that I have set myself, since it is one that no other Jew of Leontopolis is impelled to undertake.' I could not forbid him to go there again and, indeed, I felt his words as a deserved reproach; for, may the Lord forgive me, preaching to the Shame of Israel is a task from which my own soul shrinks."

When Jesus was twelve years old, Joseph awoke from sleep one morning and said: "Once at Emmaus, just before we set out on our journey to Bethlehem, I dreamed that I was reading in the Book of Genesis: 'Arise and get you into the land of Egypt!', but the remainder of the verse was hidden by the finger of the priest who held open the scroll. To-night in my dream I have read the same verse of the same chapter, but this time the priest's finger moved and covered up the first part of the verse, so that it read: 'For those who sought your life are dead.' Soon I expect to hear news."

They waited for a few days, and then news came, not of the death, but of the deposition, of Archelaus—for dreams are not always accurate—and of the conversion of Judaea, with Samaria, into a Roman Imperial province. In the division of his father's kingdom Archelaus had chosen unwisely. He should have been content with the tetrarchy that he had bestowed on his brother Philip: for in Upper Transjordania Philip had no political problems to handle comparable with those of Judaea, where three times a year the passage through the countryside of foreign pilgrims including bands of wild, proud Edomites, excitable tribesmen from Lower Transjordania and Galileans with knives concealed in their long sleeves, made the country seethe with unrest and spill over like an untended cooking-pot. In Philip's tetrarchy Jews were greatly outnumbered by Greeks and Syrians: he could even dare to strike copper coins with his own head on them.

Everything had gone wrong for Archelaus from the very start: first came the Passover disorders, next the poisoning of his Samaritan mother, and then, while he was still at Rome purchasing the good-will of leading Senators, Imperial secretaries and Livia's maids-of-honour, and showing the utmost obsequiousness to Livia herself, rioting had broken out all over the country. The immediate cause was the return of the High Court embassy with the news that their plea had been rejected by Augustus. Varus, foreseeing trouble, had moved a regular regiment down into Judaea from Antioch, but un-fortunately its regimental commander decided to overawe the civil population by the violent methods sanctioned in other provinces under direct Roman rule; and in a few weeks piled up a very large fortune by the loot of public buildings. At the Feast of Weeks, or Pentecost, which falls fifty days after Passover, the Roman garrison at Jerusalem was suddenly attacked by three large bodies of armed men, recruited from the pilgrims that had come up from the prov-inces, who besieged them in the Tower of Phasaël, the fortress ad-joining Herod's palace. The people of Jerusalem took little part in this revolt, having more cause than the pilgrims to fear reprisals, but the Romans made no distinction between metropolitan and pro-vincial Jews and killed a great many innocent people during sorties from the Tower. They also plundered the Temple Treasury of an enormous sum, a thousand talents or more, which was robbery of Jehovah and incited the insurgents to greater fury than ever. The beautiful gilded cloisters which enclosed the outer Courts of the Temple were burned to the ground and a great number of Jews per-ished in the flames.

Herod's private army went over to the Romans, three thousand of them standing a siege in the Royal Palace, and this action so divided the insurgents' forces that both the Romans and the Herodians were able to hold out until Varus, marching down from Antioch with two regular regiments and a large force of irregulars, raised the siege. He had paused on his way to crush a simultaneous revolt centred at Sepphoris in Galilee, which was destroyed in the course of the fight-ing, and another in the Judaean hills to the west of Jerusalem, and when his leading patrols reached the City, the insurgents broke camp and fled. His cavalry pursued and captured a great many of them, of whom he crucified some two thousand. His troops, for the most part Syrian Greeks from Beyrout and Arabs from the eastern desert, behaved with a savagery and indiscipline that disgusted Varus, who disbanded them as soon as possible: they had sacked and burned villages and farms by the score.

When Archelaus returned to his ethnarchy, he found everything in disorder: the Romans had plundered not only the Temple Treasury but several of the Herodian ones—for Herod had divided his great wealth into many packets disposed among his various fortresses. By the time that the legacies to Augustus, Livia, Salome and others had been paid from what moneys remained, Archelaus's purse was lean indeed. Besides, his royal residences had all been either destroyed or damaged, his private army was in revolt, he had quarrelled with his half-brother Antipas, the Jews hated him, and almost every mountain village in Judaea was occupied by bandits, some of them commanding considerable forces. Among the most troublesome insurgents was a Transjordanian Jew named Simon, a member of Herod's bodyguard, who had the boldness to crown himself King of the Jews; it was some months before he was surprised and killed by a flying column of Romans. A Judaean named Athronges, who lived near Modin the home of the Maccabees, also crowned himself King; he was more dangerous, because he set himself up as the Messiah, the Son of David, and happened to be a shepherd. His claim to be of the House of David could not be disproved, because during the massacre of Bethlehem Archelaus had seized the Davidic register and all the family records brought there by the heads of houses and made a bonfire of them in the courtyard of the inn—an act which he now heartily regretted. Athronges and his brothers were for three or four years in full possession of a wide region of hills west of Jerusalem, took toll of all merchandise that came through, and massacred all foreigners. They were victorious in several skirmishes with the Romans, and if they had only been men of education and piety might well have united the nation under one banner, as the four Maccabee brothers had once succeeded in doing. But they were bandits at heart and the problem that they set Archelaus was a military rather than a religious one.

The only alleviation of Archelaus's distresses was that the Samaritans had kept quiet all this time, and that Augustus generously made over to him the greater part of the enormous legacy left him by Herod; the remainder went to Antipas and Philip. He instituted military law throughout Judaea and managed to govern in some sort of a way for more than nine years; then he unwisely quarrelled with the High Court. They had upheld a decision of the Captain of the

Guard to refuse him entry into the Temple on the ground of ceremonial uncleanness: Archelaus had married his brother Alexander's widow Glaphyra. This marriage would have been his Levirate duty had Alexander died childless, but Glaphyra had borne him children; which made the new marriage technically incestuous. Archelaus's refusal to put her away had the surprising effect of uniting the Jews and the Samaritans in a temporary alliance against him, and it was the arrival at Rome of their joint embassy which persuaded Augustus to banish him: for when Samaritans and Jews made common cause, Livia reminded him, the Jewish problem had become critical.

However, even with Archelaus banished to Vienne in Gaul, Joseph did not think it safe to return to Judaea; and when he made inquiries from refugees he learned that his farm at Emmaus had become the headquarters of a bandit company, and that the Romans when they captured it had not only burned the buildings to the ground but also felled the orchards and rooted out the vines, broken the cisterns and blocked the wells. His two sons, he gathered, had escaped. Probably they had migrated to Galilee to become guests of their two other brothers. If he went to Galilean Cana, where the family sawmill was, he might find them all safe and well.

He invited Simeon to come with him to Galilee, but Simeon regretfully declined: he was too old for so lively a climate, and new wine should not be bottled in old skins. "Without you, dear friends, I shall be lonely, but I shall go to the Essene College at Callirrhoë by the Dead Sea, where the Overseer is an old acquaintance of mine. I shall become a member of that God-loving sect and find comradeship there, and friends to close my eyes when I die."

Joseph's business was sold to advantage and the family said goodbye to their friends and neighbours; but when Jesus went his last rounds of the village, collecting and paying small outstanding debts, he was told the same thing at each house: "Perhaps we shall meet again. Drink of the Nile once, drink of it twice!" Indeed, Egypt is a queen whose beauty exercises a powerful pull on the heart: as the Israelites in the Wilderness learned when they sighed for her green gardens, the leeks, the cucumbers and the garlic, forgetting the cruelty of their Ramasid task-masters.

They glided down by boat to Alexandria, where they chartered passages in a packet-galley bound for Tyre: she would sail in a week's time with mail for all intervening seaports. Joseph had decided that the sea-journey would be less fatiguing and not more expensive; also, they could bring their tools with them, and their clothes, and their books and household utensils, which it would be a pity to sell at a loss; and, he would prefer to enter Antipas's tetrarchy as an Egyptian Jewish immigrant, not as a Judaean exile. This was a courageous decision, since the Jews, like the Egyptians, have an innate horror of the sea. Most of them would rather travel overland for five hundred miles through sandstorms or thick forest than travel fifty by sea in the calmest weather. They regard the sea as their lifelong enemy, and seafaring for them is almost the most despised trade of any; but this is because they associate the sea with the Great Goddess in her erotic character of Rahab the Harlot —the Fish-tailed Aphrodite, in fact, of Joppa and Beyrout and Ascalon.

But to Jesus the sea, which he now visited for the first time, was the most beautiful sight that he had ever seen. It filled him with greater amazement than all the wonders of Alexandria, at that time the first city of the world after Rome, though he visited the docks and the Royal Library and the colonnades of the philosophers, and watched the enormous, mad crowd pouring out of the hippodrome and instantly engaging in bitter faction fights, blue against leek-green, with stones and clubs. An old business-acquaintance of Joseph's, met by chance, won him admission to the lighthouse on Pharos Island, where the famous steam-engine of Ctesibius was displayed, though no longer put to practical use; and he was allowed to ascend to the lantern-house to wonder at the optic device which enabled ships to be distinctly viewed at no less than twenty miles' distance. But the sea and the salty smell of the sea, and the sunset over the waters glowing with more royal colours (it seemed to him) than the desert sunset, and the sudden land-breeze as the stars came out, and the planet Venus brilliant in the west: these stirred his spirit in an extraordinary manner.

The roar of the city came confusedly down the wind, like moans and groans, the small waves frothed white along the reefs, and as the glory faded from the sky and the moon rose he repeated softly the words of the Psalm in which David praises God for the creation of the great, wide sea with innumerable fish concealed in it, besides the ships and the whales that proudly drive along its surface. He silently stretched out his hand to Mary and each had a perfect understanding of what was in the other's mind: "The sea is our mother. From the sea the dry land was delivered at the Creation as a child is delivered from the womb. How beautiful is our mother's face!" But old Joseph wrapped his cloak more tightly about him and shivered at the waste of waters.

They embarked the next morning in cloudless weather. Joseph

said: "We shall have a view of the Promised Land from a distance, like that granted to Moses from Pisgah." But first they rowed along the coast of the Delta through seas already discoloured by the Nile mud, for the floods had begun, and counted the seven principal mouths of the Nile; the Canopic first, and then, in order, the Bolbitinic, the Sebennytic, the Pineptimic, the Mendesic, the Tanitic and the Pelusiac—and anchored that night at Pelusium, formerly named Avaris, the gateway out of Egypt and the city from which the Israelites under Moses had begun their flight to the promised land. The next day, after taking bales of raw linen aboard, they coasted past the narrow spit of sand dividing the Lake of the Reeds from the sea. There the Egyptians in pursuit of Moses had been checked when a sudden north-east wind swamped the track. Numbers of them were swallowed up in the quicksands still prevalent there.

The ship laboured under oars along a low sandy coast, made dangerous by shoals, with Mount Seir, the great mountain of Edom, showing far away to the south-east through gaps in the white sandhills; and they presently could make out, directly ahead of them, the long bluish range of the Judaean hills. That night they anchored off Rhinocolura, at the mouth of the Torrent of Egypt which is the desert boundary between Canaan and Egypt; but the torrent flows only in the winter and spring. Jesus asked permission to swim ashore and set foot for the first time in his life on the soil of his forefathers: for in the fifteenth chapter of the Book of Joshua this river is mentioned at the southern boundary of the territory of Judah. The master consented, and he swam ashore and offered up a prayer from dry land; then plucked a sprig of rosemary from a hedge and swam back again, and gave the sprig to his mother.

The next day mail was put ashore for Gaza, but the town of Gaza, where Samson took the gates off their hinges and walked away with them, was hidden from the sea. Ain-Rimmon and Beersheba lay a day's journey inland. They coasted along the fertile plain of Philistia and some ten miles inland the hills rose in gentle slopes, dotted with villages. Soon they came to Ascalon, the former seat of the Herods, a beautiful city in the Greek style built in the shape of a theatre facing the sea, with the two horns of the semicircle abutting on bold cliffs, and by the sea a magnificent temple of the Goddess Aphrodite and another of Hercules-Melkarth, where Herod's great-grandfather had been a priest. On the next day they came to Joppa, on its well-walled conical hill, another seat of the worship of Aphrodite and Hercules; from here Jonah had, in the allegory, sailed on his famous voyage to Tarsus, the end of which was that he found himself in the

179

belly of a whale. Joppa was the nearest port to Jerusalem, and the peak of Mount Mizpeh, four miles to the north of Jerusalem, could be clearly distinguished from the ship. The anchorage here was very uncomfortable because of the swell. Then on they went past the red cliffs which bordered the Plain of Sharon, with the hills of Ephraim behind; and Joseph pointed out Mounts Ebal and Gerizim and said: "Shechem lies between them."

The colossal statue of a man now appeared on the coast to the northward with white buildings at its feet. Mary began to weep silently when she learned that this was Caesarea, where King Antipater had been arrested on his return from Rome. They rowed by the ancient tribal territory of Manasseh, and ahead of them loomed the great table-ridge of Mount Carmel. Joseph pointed out the peak to the south-east, saying: "The peak of Elijah, where he put the prophets of Baal to confusion." Soon they anchored in the port of Sycaminum where the River Kishon flows into the sea. Joseph paid the passage-money, they went ashore, bought an ass-cart and an ass, heaped their possessions on it and drove off eastward through the fruitful pomegranate groves.

Upper Galilee is a broad mountain-ridge jutting south from the Lebanon. The inhabitants distinguish it from Lower Galilee, a continuation of the same ridge, by its ability to produce sycomore figs, and by the greater excellence of its olives. But the olive is a tree that grows rank and yields little oil in rich and stoneless soil, and sycomore figs are not to be compared in flavour with true figs; and these are Upper Galilee's only two claims to superiority, except for an extraordinary richness in wild game. Old Herod loved Upper Galilee for the sport that the rugged hills and deep glens of its eastern districts afforded him. Panthers, leopards, bears, wolves, jackals, hyaenas, wild boars and gazelles—all fell to his lance and arrow. The summit of the ridge is undulating table-land, a former possession of the Kenites, who a thousand years ago were robbed of its rich pasture by the tribe of Naphtali; to the west the olive-land of Asher slopes down to a plain, called the Plain of Acre, through which Joseph now led his family towards Lower Galilee.

The hills of Lower Galilee, covered with evergreen oak, slope gently; the valleys, famous for their wheat, spread wide. In Egypt Jesus had seen no eminence higher than the pyramids, and it was some time before he could accustom his eye to recognize the mountains that towered in the distance as solid masses of earth and rock;

they seemed like clouds. The forests also astonished him: he had never before seen trees that were not planted by man, and found it difficult to believe Joseph's assurance that these dense forests were sown by the hand of God alone.

They took the crowded road to the large city of Sepphoris, twenty miles away, which was being rebuilt as handsomely as ever after its destruction by Varus. Here the land flowed with wine and milk. Fat cattle browsed in the valley meadows of the Kishon, the slopes were terraced for vines, mile after mile. They came upon a train of wagons, laden with timber, halted at the roadside. The merchant in charge was able to give them the information they needed. He said that Joseph's sons Judah and Simon had sold the Cana sawmill; two other brothers, refugees from Emmaus, were then living on their charity. When he had last seen them, six months before, they were settled on the further side of the Lake at Gergesa in Philip's tetrarchy.

Presently the road, which was the main highway from Egypt to Damascus, passed through a gap in the hills commanded by the ancient fortress of Hattin. There Mary and Jesus had their first view of the Sea of Galilee, the great freshwater lake through which the Jordan flows. Its western slopes are as populous as the Bay of Naples and even more marvellously fertile. City jostles city; and even some of the villages are as big as the capital towns of less prosperous provinces. They call this district "The Garden of Galilee", and it is never without fruit: in the only two months that are figless the pomegranate is ripe. There is a saying: "An acre of land in Judaea will support a child; an acre of land in Galilee will support a regiment."

They took the northern road around the Lake, through the towns of Capernaum and Chorazin, and crossed the Jordan into Philip's tetrarchy by a ford, where there was a customs station. On the eastern side of the Lake the mountains rise steeply and villages are not numerous. Joseph found Judah and Simon at Gergesa. They were surprised to see him still alive, since he had not written to them for twelve years and had gone away without bestowing the customary blessing on them. They were poorer than he had expected, having lately suffered severe losses from a fire in their principal timber-yard. Their greeting was respectful rather than cordial, and Joseph guessed that they did not welcome the notion of having to house and feed Mary, Jesus and himself, especially since Mary as their stepmother would now become the ruler of the kitchen. Perhaps they also resented the appearance of Jesus as a claimant to a

fifth share in the inheritance that had already been divided among them. But they said no more than that they had recently been put to great expense in setting up their brothers Jose and James in business at Bethlehem—the little-known Bethlehem of Galilee—which lies a few miles to the south of the Sepphoris highway.

Joseph said peaceably that his visit to Gergesa would be only a short one: he would go to Bethlehem and try to find a house there. Their brother Jesus was a good workman, and the two of them could set up their trade together again as in Egypt. As for the inheritance, he would leave to Jesus only the little that had been earned since it had been divided, and when he was gathered to his fathers the support of Mary could safely be entrusted to her son.

When Jesus had seen the principal sights of the Garden, which is inhabited by a motley race of Jews, Greeks, Phoenicians, Arabians, Syrians, Persians and Babylonians, the three of them returned westward and came to Bethlehem. "In Bethlehem," it is said, "only the dead live in stone houses." This is true, for all the houses there are of timber lined with wattle and daub and thatched with reeds; but on the hill facing west stand a few ancient tombs, among them that of Ibzan, a celebrated Judge, whose innovation it was to settle the family inheritance on the sons rather than the daughters. Joseph found his sons Jose and James living in a small clearing in the middle of an oak-wood: their trade was to fell timber, shape it roughly into logs and sell them to the building contractors of Sepphoris. Though they welcomed him more kindly than the other two, Joseph decided not to trespass on their filial affection, for they were miserably poor. They told him of a house for sale in the hamlet of Nazareth, five miles to the east, with a cave at the back providing convenient cellars and store-houses. Joseph bought the house cheaply, and within a fortnight he and Jesus were back at their carpentering.

This is how Jesus came to be called a native of Nazareth. Quirinus, the new Governor-General of Syria, had ordered a census to be taken that year and Jesus was registered soon after his arrival as "resident at Nazareth, in the district of Bethlehem of Galilee; son of Joseph, a carpenter of the same hamlet; born at Bethlehem, now aged twelve years". The census officials naturally supposed that the two Bethlehems were identical and he was listed as a Galilean, not a Judaean. This census was memorable for its disorders. The Galilean peasantry opposed it vigorously, not so much because it implemented a small poll-tax as because, according to an ancient Jewish superstition, a census of Jews, unless ordered by Jehovah himself, is considered unlucky; it is recorded that when King David, provoked by God's

Adversary, ordered the unwilling Joab to number the twelve tribes, Jehovah was incensed and destroyed seventy thousand men with a pestilence. The synagogue officials of Nazareth visited Joseph and asked him to refuse the summons of the census official, as they themselves proposed to do. He replied that had the census been designed to number all the Jews in the world, and none but Jews, he might have considered it his duty to absent himself; but since it was merely a census of the inhabitants of Syria, with Jews and Gentiles mixed, and did not apply to Jews living outside the Roman Empire, in Babylon and elsewhere, he could see no harm in it. Though his argument vexed them they could not deny its logic, and therefore contented themselves with confusing and misleading the census official instead of putting up armed resistance.

From the spring at the limestone summit of Nazareth hill, where Jesus would climb every morning with his pitcher to draw drinking-water, a most extraordinarily wide view could be seen. To the south the great plain of Esdraelon, backed by the hills of Samaria; six miles to the east the tremendous bulk of the holy mountain Tabor; to the north the white houses and temples of Sepphoris, and behind them, in the remote distance, the snowy peaks of Hermon. He began at last to understand parts of the Scriptures which had been unintelligible at Leontopolis; for Egypt was the level land of origin and of death, but this the hilly land of life and love. Here one could not shuffle along flat-footed in the level sand; one must always either ascend or descend. Soon the muscles of his legs ceased to ache, and before the year was out he could run confidently downhill, leaping from rock to rock like a wild goat.

He read the Scriptures as assiduously as ever, but in a new light, and the neighbouring countryside provided, as it were, a supplementary text. He visited the site of the battle-field of Harosheth where Sisera's chariots had been bogged in the Kishon valley and swept away by a sudden flood; and Gilboa, where King Saul fell in battle with the Philistines; and Jezreel (or Esdraelon) where Ahab's palace had been, and Naboth's vineyard which Ahab coveted, and where the usurper Jehu had encountered Jezebel, Ahab's bedizened widow

He proposed also to make the ascent of Tabor, which the Greeks call Atabyrion, but his mother would not allow him to go, even in the company of his elder brothers.

"It is a dangerous place," she said, "for those who are not afraid of wild beasts as well as for those who are."

"What is at the top?"

"A town to be avoided, bare rocks, evil spirits and a moving rock which they call the Heel Stone."

"Why do they call it the Heel Stone?"

"The story is not for children!"

CHAPTER FOURTEEN

THE DOCTORS

IN THE spring that followed his arrival in Galilee, Jesus went up with his parents and brothers to Jerusalem for the Passover. The journey was a pleasant one, across the plain rich in tall green corn to Shunem and Jezreel and thence by the mountain road which runs through Samaria, into Judaea; and every halting-place was a chapter of the Scriptures, or several chapters. Shunem, a village famous for its beautiful gardens and orchards, lies on the south-western slopes of Little Hermon; it is also famous for its women. Abishag, the loveliest girl in Israel, was chosen from Shunem to warm David's old bones through the cold Judaean winter—this was the Abishag on account of whom David's eldest son Adonijah was debarred from the succession. In Shunem, too, lived the "great woman" who entertained Elisha; and from Shunem came the beauty to whom Solomon is said to have addressed his famous love-songs. The mountain road begins at the frontier town of En-Gannim, which is to say "a fountain of gardens". This is a village of the same sort as Shunem, rich in pomegranates, figs and quinces, through which rushes a torrent, diverted into a hundred rivulets; Solomon compared the Shunemite to this place. Here Joseph and his family rested for the night.

The next morning they entered the region of Samaria, and by evening had passed between Mounts Ebal and Gerizim and watered their asses at Jacob's well, outside the holy city of Shechem, now inhabited by the Samaritans. Thence they continued a mile or two to Gilgal, where they passed the next night. This was the site of the first camp built by the Israelites after they had crossed the Jordan under Joshua, and the first place in Canaan where they celebrated the Passover. But the stone-circle which gave the place its name had been removed centuries before, during the reforms of Good King Josiah, because of the rites which were performed there in honour of the Goddess Ashima. Josiah had for the same reason hewn down the ancient terebinth grove of Moreh, where Abraham and Jacob had both worshipped; it had been one of the most famous shrines of Ephraim, but nothing of it survived now but the name.

The next day they came to Bethel, a former sanctuary of which the prophet Amos had written ironically: "Come to Bethel and transgress, and at Gilgal multiply your transgressions!" Here the patriarch Jacob was recorded to have dreamed of the ladder with angels ascending and descending and to have raised an altar to Jehovah; but good King Josiah had visited this place too and broken down the altar, and cut down the ancient terebinth-oak under which the priestess Deborah had judged Israel. What had once been a royal city, beautified by King Jeroboam, who set up the golden calves there, and a rival sanctuary to Jerusalem itself, was now a dirty village with not even a market-place: as poor as any other in the unfertile territory of Benjamin. Jesus saw cornfields here bearing the poorest crops he had ever seen, and asked Joseph why the peasants troubled to plant the grain. He answered: "To provide the seed-corn of the following year. It suffices for that in a good season." Jesus's brothers had brought a sheaf of Bethlehem wheat with them for a thank-offering, every ear of which contained a hundred plump grains.

By rough roads thronged with people in holiday dress they came to Ramah, which lies four miles north of Jerusalem. There the grave of Rachel was shown them and the inhabitants pretended not to have heard of the other grave of Rachel at Bethlehem of Judaea; and scornfully denied its authenticity. However, the truth was that Rachel had been a Canaanite goddess, not a mortal woman, and what was now called her sepulchral pillar had been her altar, of which she owned several in different regions.

So they came to Jerusalem, which was now the only place where the Passover sacrifice of a lamb might legitimately be slaughtered and eaten. Joseph and his family crowded into the house of his daughter Lysia, and there, as the custom was, hastily ate the feast, as if on a journey. With the lamb, which had to be roasted and left unjointed, went endives and unleavened cakes dipped in a sweet sauce, and the meal began with a cup of sweet wine blessed by Joseph.

It fell to Jesus, as the youngest son, to ask Joseph the meaning of the feast. He received the traditional answer: "It is the sacrifice of the Lord's Passover. For he passed over the houses of the Children of Israel in Egypt, when he smote the first-born of the Egyptians and delivered our houses." Then Joseph read—or pretended to read, for he knew it by heart—the account in the Book of Exodus of the institution of the feast. Next they sang the two Psalms of David: *Praise ye the Lord* and *When Israel went out of Egypt*, and drank the second cup, with which the meal ended; and what little meat had not been eaten was put aside to be burned. But after grace came a third cup, and a fourth, while they sang four more Psalms of David: *Not unto us, O Lord, not unto us, O Lord, but unto thy name give glory*, and *I love the Lord*, and *Praise the Lord, all ye nations*, and *O give thanks unto the Lord, for he is good*. It was wonderful to Jesus to have left Egypt, "the house of bondage", and to be performing this ceremony at Jerusalem, the goal of the Israelites' hopes. Soon he began to brood over details of the ceremony, and to ask his brothers difficult questions about them; but Jose roughly told him that the wine had gone to his head and that he had better keep silent. Undeterred, he asked Joseph whether he might presently be taken to hear one of the public debates in the Temple.

Joseph answered: "You are too young."

"And when will I be old enough?"

"When you are a man. You are not yet a man, though you do a man's work in the shop, and you will not be a man by the next Passover either. It would be unseemly to attend a public debate at your age, even if you could secure permission to attend."

A year went by, and another year, and one day when Joseph was lying sick with a swollen throat and could speak only with difficulty, Jesus was permitted to read the daily prayers for their small household; so that he could now reckon himself a man and wear the prayer-garment which is the Jewish equivalent to the "virile toga" of the Romans. It is a strange moment in a mother's life when she ceases to be responsible to her husband for the safety and good behaviour of her child—who suddenly becomes responsible to his father for hers. Yet the Jews do not signalize this change by a public ceremony as other nations do. It was sufficient that Jesus should kneel down before his parents and receive the blessings of both, and a kiss from each on his brow. Joseph then asked him whether he wished to make a "sacrifice of prosperity" at the Temple—a goat perhaps?

Jesus answered that his tutor Simeon had discouraged him from offering sacrifices not particularly demanded by the Law, and quoted the fiftieth Psalm:

> If I were hungry I would not tell you, for the world is mine with all its fullness.
> Will I eat the flesh of bulls or drink the blood of goats?
> Instead, offer thanksgiving and vows, and call upon me in the day of trouble.

That year, when they went up to the Passover, he remained behind in Jerusalem after the seven days of the Feast, and was not missed by Joseph and Mary until, on reaching the end of their first day's journey, they found that he was not in the company of his elder brothers, who had set off before them. They turned back and searched Jerusalem for him, but he was neither at Lysia's house nor at that of Lydia, his other sister, and nobody could give them news of him.

Meanwhile Jesus had obtained admission to a series of public debates in the Temple precincts, conducted by well-known Doctors of the Law for the enlightenment of provincial students. The porter at the barrier was amused to find so young a seeker after knowledge, but after testing him with a few questions to see whether he were worthy to enter, pushed him in with a friendly shove, saying: "May the Lord increase your wisdom!"

During the first two days he did not once open his mouth, but listened attentively, and his heart leaped whenever a Doctor said: "Ay, the learned Shammai said thus and thus, but what has the just and generous Hillel taught on the same subject?" Often he would mutter under his breath Hillel's pronouncement which he had learned from Simeon; for Hillel seemed to Jesus always to have been in the right. Hillel was still living, but Jesus never achieved his desire of conversing with him; he had for years been too old and frail to leave his room at the Academy.

On the third day it happened that he was attending a debate between two famous Doctors, on the shady side of the Women's Court. It was so well attended that he could not see the Doctors or their chairs because of the broad backs of the listeners in between. They were disputing a nice point of the Law: why the Paschal lamb must be chosen on the tenth day of the month and reserved until the evening of the fourteenth.

The First Doctor said: "It is clear as the sun shining on the Temple Court: ten is the number of completeness. No man in this world, unless he be a Philistine monster like the one mentioned in the Wars of David, has more than ten fingers and ten toes; or fewer than ten, unless he has suffered an accident. Ten men form a congregation. Ten persons are a sufficient household to eat a Paschal lamb. The ten-stringed harp is the completeness of music. With ten plagues the Lord visited the fullness of his wrath on the Egyptians. Between Adam and Noah, between Noah and Abraham, ten generations intervene. More than this: with ten utterances the Lord created the world. And in the evening twilight of the first Friday, the last day of Creation, he created the ten excellent things which, as you know, included the rainbow, the pen, the tongs and the two Tables of the Law—"

As he paused, one of his disciples asked leave to quote the song *Ten Measures of Wisdom* in proof of the traditional completeness of ten. The Doctor welcomed the interlude and the disciple began to sing mournfully:

> *Ten measures of wisdom were given the world—*

Another took up the refrain:

> *Israel took nine—*

and the whole company mournfully finished:

> *The rest took one.*

So it went on:

> *Ten measures of wealth were given the world.*
> *Rome took nine,*
> *The rest took one.*
>
> *Ten measures of poverty were given the world.*
> *Babylon took nine,*
> *The rest took one.*
>
> *Ten measures of pride were given the world.*
> *Elam took nine,*
> *The rest took one.*
>
> *Ten measures of courage were given the world.*
> *Persia took nine,*
> *The rest took one.*

> *Ten measures of magic were given the world.*
> *Egypt took nine,*
> *The rest took one.*
>
> *Ten measures of lechery were given the world.*
> *Arabia took nine,*
> *The rest took one.*
>
> *Ten measures of folly were given the world.*
> *Greece took nine,*
> *The rest took one.*
>
> *Ten measures of drunkenness were given the world.*
> *Ethiopia took nine,*
> *The rest took one.*
>
> *Ten measures of lousiness were given the world.*
> *Media took nine,*
> *The rest took one.*

The First Doctor continued: "But especially, as I read the Holy Book, the lamb is chosen on that tenth day in honour of the Ten Commandments. On each day of the ten the pious man reads and ponders one of the Commandments, and on the tenth his heart is ready and aware of his duty towards God and his neighbour; and he is sanctified, so that he may choose the unblemished lamb with a pure heart and eye. This is the practice in my house and we do not consider the Passover properly performed otherwise. Let any man dispute my words who has the hardihood!"

There was silence for a while and then, though the challenge was only a rhetorical one, Jesus could no longer restrain himself, but cried out: "Learned man: is your roll of the Law arranged in the same chapters as the roll which is fixed in the Chamber of Copyists?"

Everyone looked round in surprise, and when it was seen that the interrupter was a mere boy, the surprise was greater still.

The Doctor frowned and asked: "What impudent voice asked me that question? Let the speaker come forward and show himself boldly. Then I will answer him."

Jesus slipped through the crowd and stood before him in the front rank.

The Doctor said: "Little red-locked creature with the pale face, tell me why you have asked me this shameless question and then you shall have your answer. Though we are instructed not to turn away those that wish to hear, we are also instructed to correct folly and lay the rod to the fool's back."

"Learned teacher," Jesus answered, "I do not wish to be impudent, but being a stranger in Jerusalem I thought it possible that your roll of the Law differs from those that I have studied elsewhere. For I have read that the Passover was celebrated before the Ten Commandments were given. The Ten Commandments may be said to have existed from the sixth day of Creation, having been immanent in the mind of the Almighty—if it is true that he then created the Alphabet and the Two Tables—but they were not committed to the Tables or delivered to Moses until after he had brought the Children of Israel out of Egypt into Sinai. Until that time, as I read the Scriptures, no commandments had been given to man of a general nature, but only particular ones, such as the commandment not to eat from the tree of the knowledge of good and evil, or the commandment to build and stock an ark, or that which is now in question, which is the commandment for the eating of the Passover. For that this commandment was to eat a particular feast, rather than to inaugurate a sacrificial festival, the prophet Jeremiah plainly affirms. He prophesies in the name of the Lord: 'In the day that I brought your fathers out of Egypt I spoke not to them, nor commanded them, concerning burned offerings and sacrifices.' "

The Second Doctor, who did not wish his colleague to be confounded by so young a child, interposed: "You do not understand these matters. If the learned Doctor chooses to think that the ten days were appointed by the Lord in anticipation of the Ten Commandments, what is that to you?"

Jesus said: "It troubles me that he considers the first Passover feast to have been improperly conducted: for how could the Children of Israel while in Egypt have read and pondered commandments that had not been committed to writing and existed only in the mind of the Lord?"

He would have said more, but the Second Doctor broke in again: "In my opinion, the tenth day is chosen because the tithe, the tenth part, is sacred to the Lord, not because of the completeness of the number ten, for it goes without saying that seven is a number of greater completeness than ten. The world may have been created by ten commandments but the Lord hallowed the seventh day when he had done. That the Sacred Candlestick has seven branches, that seven clean beasts went into the ark, that seven times seven days separate the Passover from the Feast of Weeks, that seven times seven years make the Year of Jubilee—all these examples may be instanced, yet where is Perfection, where is Completeness, but in the Holy One? And there are seven elements to his Unspeakable Name. Tithes were instituted before Moses saw the light. Our Father Abraham gave tithes to Melchizedek King of Salem, as priest of the Most High God; our Father Jacob imitated the piety of his grandfather when he vowed to the Lord a tithe of all the substance that he should acquire in Mesopotamia; and later Moses ordained the tithing of all the fruits of this land. Let any man dispute this who has the hardihood!"

Jesus spoke up again: "Learned Doctor, though to give tithes is good, how is the Paschal lamb a tithe? If a man has ten lambs let him choose out one as a sacrifice to the Lord; but what if he has five, or twenty? And where is it written that tithes should be gathered on the tenth day of the month?"

Everyone present was astonished at the boldness and fluency of Jesus's argument, and the Second Doctor said to the First: "Brother, what shall we do with this child? Shall we turn him away?"

The First Doctor said gruffly: "Not until you have answered his argument, which indeed was on the lips of every man in the company; and I think it not unfitting that a mere child should have advanced it."

The Second Doctor vented his wrath on Jesus. "Are you of the bandits of Galilee who cut a man's throat and leave him wallowing in his blood? Are you of the Galilean bandits who tear down but never build up again?"

"No, though I live with my parents in Galilee I was born in Judaea, and if you have cut your own throat with a word indiscreetly spoken I beg that you will not charge me with murder. As for building up: if you ask me why the lamb was chosen on the tenth day, I will answer that the Children of Israel were preparing to depart on the fourteenth day when the moon is at its fullest, so that they could put as much distance between themselves and the armies of Pharaoh as possible. They chose the lamb and set it apart from the others as if for fattening; and this was to deceive the Egyptians. For when lambs are set apart to be fattened, a process which takes a month or more, nobody will expect them to be suddenly slaughtered and eaten unhung four nights later. But the ten days which are in question have not necessarily any greater significance than this, that ten days was a measure of time of frequent use among the Israelites during their bondage: for ten days made an Egyptian week then, as now. Ten days were allowed them by Moses for settling their affairs, and with the choosing of the lamb they made final preparation for their flight. The feast was in the evening, and by the time that it was finished the Egyptians were asleep, and away they stole, well fed and heartened with wine, by the narrow unguarded track which skirts the Lake of Reeds; thus avoiding the well-guarded highway to Philistia. Indeed, an Egyptian week of ten days, an *asor*, is still of repute in Israel. Is not the Day of Atonement celebrated on the last day of an *asor*? And for a less awful instance, did not Daniel and his three companions choose ten days as a testing period during which they were to subsist only on pulse and water?"

The Second Doctor smiled in quiet triumph: "You build your house on quicksand, Little Doctor," he said. "Our Israelitish month may, by a figure of speech, be described as divided into decades; but these decades have no reality in themselves, for, as you are not yet scholar enough to know, *asor* does not mean the decade itself. It means the tenth day of a decade. And so I come to the confounding of your previous argument. The month is tithed of its days, each tenth day having a certain sanctity—not equal to that of the seventh day, but still a sanctity—to remind us of our duty in tithing everything of use to our Lord."

"True, Great Doctor, the word *asor* means the tenth day, but it also means a decade. For the brother and mother of Rebeccah in the four-and-twentieth chapter of Genesis said to our father Isaac: 'Let the damsel abide with us for an *asor* at least', which is to say a week of ten days."

At this a little gasp of wonder arose among the Galilean visitors who sat together at one side. It was like the scene in a fencing-school when a novice by dexterous play not only parries every blow aimed at him by the master of fence, but with a quick turn of the wrist sends his sword spinning across the gymnasium so that the master stands disarmed and glaring foolishly. How the bystanders applaud! So now, forgetful of good manners, the Galileans clapped their hands for joy and began to laugh aloud, and someone cried out rudely: "A second David who has killed his lion and his bear!"

Affronted by this unseemly noise, the two Doctors rose as one man. They offered up the prayer that brought the debate to a close, and walked coldly away, dismissing their disciples.

The First Doctor said to the Second: "That boy is extraordinarily impudent. How has he not learned to hold his tongue and listen to his betters? I wonder who he is? I am convinced that he is a bastard. You can tell bastards by their shambling gait and by their reluctance to salute their elders."

"Surely that cannot be? For a boy so well grounded in the Law would know that no man born in bastardy is admitted into this Court, not until the tenth generation. Besides, he saluted us respectfully as we came away, and since you have not seen him walking, how can you know that he shambles?"

"It may be that he is not yet aware of his bastardy, but I am convinced that a bastard he is for all that."

"I deny it. If he were a bastard, though the fact might be hidden from him out of kindness, his teachers would know of it and he would not be so well instructed in the Scriptures: for what profit would it be to teach a bastard what only a member of the congregation can profitably learn?"

"Let us go back and discover his name, and then we can make inquiries."

When they returned to the place of the lecture, they found that it was occupied by another group of debaters who had moved there from the hot centre of the Court. They could not see Jesus anywhere but stayed to listen to what proved to be less a debate than a meeting of protest by certain Pharisees against what they took to be a clear breach of the Law by the High Priest. The question was, whether the High Priest had done right to accept a present for the Temple Treasury from a Jewish prostitute. She had repented of her ways and made a sin-offering to the Lord of all the money that she had earned by her profession. The Pharisees were arguing that the money should not have been handled by any priest at all, let alone the High Priest, and should have been distributed to the poor, not added to the Treasury funds. For in the twenty-third chapter of the Book of Deuteronomy it is distinctly laid down:

Thou shalt not bring the hire of a whore into the house of thy God.

This prohibition, by the way, though ascribed to Jehovah's servant Moses, is said to date only from the time of King Josiah. For he put an end to the ancient Jebusite custom by which the girls of Jerusalem prostituted themselves to strangers at the City gates and laid their earnings at the feet of Anatha, Jehovah's consort.

Each speaker vied with his fellows in denouncing the impropriety of the High Priest's action, and when all had said their say, the President of the debate asked: "Is any son of Israel hardy enough to dare speak on the other side of the question?"

Jesus rose and begged the President's permission to ask a question. ("Ah, there he is again!" said the First Doctor.)

"Ask on, hardy boy!"

"I have heard talk in the City about this gift. Was it not devoted by the High Priest to a particular object—namely, the building of a house of easement to the retiring chamber where he is required to pass the last week before the Day of Atonement?"

"It was so devoted, and the retiring chamber is, beyond doubt, a part of this Temple."

"Nevertheless, I hold that the money was well spent."

"How? What is that? What is this child of Belial saying?" every one cried.

"Is it not written by the prophet Micah in the first chapter and the seventh verse of his book: 'Of the hire of a harlot has she gathered them, and unto the hire of a harlot shall they return'? This text the learned Hillel has expounded in the sense that as clean things naturally consort with clean, so unclean consort with unclean. Would any man cry aloud with horror if he saw a swine-herd fondling his swine? No, but only if he saw the swine-herd fondling the child of a pious Israelite, or this child fondling a swine. Let like mate with like. A house of easement is an unclean place. It is an enclave of uncleanness in a clean Temple; it is not in the Temple, nor of it. If the woman has repented, all Israel should rejoice and the High Priest should not refuse her gift, which is of repentance. The house of easement, though unclean, is a necessity: let it therefore be bought not with clean money but with unclean."

The Doctor asked scornfully: "And is harlotry also a necessity if, as you say, like must mate with like?"

"A harlot sins for necessity, for no woman of Israel would make a harlot of herself for choice and be lost to her family and friends. Hunger and misery drive her to the trade. Every harlot in Israel, as my teacher the learned Simeon of Alexandria told me, is a virgin seduced and cast off by her house. From which I judge that so long as deceitful men must seduce virgins, and fools must company with harlots, harlotry is a necessity; equally, so long as High Priests do not fast in preparation for the Day of Atonement, a house of easement is a necessity."

No one had a reply to this argument, which followed the soundest Pharisaic principles: it was generous, practical and based on a sound text. "Good, good!" murmured the Second Doctor, and quoted to his companion: " 'Regard not the bottle, but what is in it. Some new bottles are full of old wine, and contrariwise.' "

Jesus added boldly: "Let any man dispute this who dare!"

There came an unexpected interruption from the fringe of the crowd. A voice cried out: "At last, at last! My son! We had thought you lost!"

Jesus slipped through the crowd and saluted Mary and Joseph reverently. Mary continued: "We have all been distraught with anxiety these last three days. Why did you not tell us that you were remaining behind at Jerusalem? Had you no thought for your mother?"

"I am no longer accountable to a mother for my goings and comings; I am engaged on the Father's business. Nevertheless, forgive me for the grief I have caused you. I told my cousin Palti to let you know where I was; the message has gone astray."

The First Doctor nudged the Second, drew him aside and said in a whisper: "You will see that I am right. Had that man been the boy's father, he could not have allowed the woman to do the talking. You will remember the judgement of Solomon: it is in moments of danger that parentage is proved."

"Oddly enough," said the Second Doctor, "I recognize the man, though he has aged greatly since we last met and his beard is cut in a different style, and his garments are poorer. He is one Joseph, son of Heli, of the House of David. Everyone supposed that he had been killed in the Bethlehem massacre, but he turned up again in Galilee last year."

"Joseph—Joseph of Emmaus? The Joseph who used to be in the timber business?"

"That is the man."

"I remember some talk, about ten years ago, or it may have been longer, of his marriage to a daughter of old Joachim the Heir, who died so miserably when Athronges made his last stand at Cocheba. I forget the exact circumstances of the marriage, but they were most unusual. I know that he arrived with the bride-money and found that the girl had been kidnapped by bandits. But what I cannot recall is whether she was restored to him. I was out of Jerusalem at the time, but I will wager you my old cloak against your new one that the girl was seduced by the kidnappers and that old Joseph made an honest woman of her. I know him to be a man of the greatest humanity."

"I will accept your wager. It cannot be so. Joseph would never allow the boy to enter the Temple if he knew him to be a bastard."

"No? Then perhaps that is why he let the boy's mother do the talking: he was scandalized to find him here."

"Well, we shall see."

"How? It is no use trying to consult the family records of the

House of David. The Wicked One and his son destroyed them all."

"The boy's mother, if my theory holds—if, that is to say, she was the girl whom the bandits kidnapped—was a Temple virgin, and the payment of the bride-money will have been recorded in the Temple Accounts. My son is a chief accountant. Let us go to him at once!"

An account of Jesus's intervention in the debate about the prostitute's gift was brought to Hillel on his sick-bed by his disciples. He approved it in this judgement, one of the last that he gave the world: "The generous heart will always find a door to open for those who seek the Lord; the niggard will always find a bolt to bar them out." The judgement was later reported to Jesus, who treasured it as proudly as a Roman soldier treasures his Civic Crown of gallantry.

That winter Hillel died, and never was a private citizen so widely mourned in the history of the Jewish nation. In every hamlet of Judaea and Galilee, in every synagogue of the Dispersion from Cadiz to Samarkand, from the outflow of the River Don to the Cataracts of the Nile, eyes were wet, heads were shrouded, shoulders heaved with sobs, mouths abstained from food and drink. "Hillel is dead, Hillel is dead!" the people mourned, "Hillel the sage, who first taught Israel to love." It was indeed Hillel who had first used the noun "creatures" in conjunction with the verb "to love". Such was the greatness of his heart that he preached love not merely to his fellow-Israelites, not merely to all Sons of Adam, that is to say his fellow-men in general, but to all living creatures of whatever sort, clean and unclean; justifying this apparent absurdity by the injunction given in the psalm to all things with breath in them—including whales, beasts, birds and creeping things—that they should praise the Lord. Even among the Sadducees of the Temple the sage's loss was felt keenly. "His word was always on the side of peace," they said.

At Nazareth, Mary wept and said to Jesus: "My son, when you come to die, may you be permitted to leave behind you something of the same fragrance that will ever cling to the name of Hillel."

"May I always be permitted to find the door of which he spoke, Mother, and wrench it open!"

CHAPTER FIFTEEN

THE SLUR

JESUS came to Jerusalem again with his parents for the next Passover. This time Joseph permitted him to remain behind, after the Feast, to attend the public debates and lectures.

After saying goodbye to his family outside the City walls, he went up to the Temple. A rheumy-eyed man squatting inside the East Gate·recognized him and said with an ingratiating smile: "Well met, learned Jesus of Nazareth! I expected to see you come walking in to-day. I have an invitation for you: to arbitrate impartially on a nice point of the Law which is being disputed between two patrons of mine. Each protests that he is right, and they have a wager on the matter."

"To make the Law the subject of a wager is unseemly. Besides, I am no Doctor of the Law."

"There is nothing unseemly in the argument itself; and you are well on the road to your Doctorate."

"By the favour of the Lord," said Jesus hastily. "Who are the disputants?"

"Teachers in an Academy."

"Then let them choose as arbiter the head of their Academy."

"I was to wait at the Gate until you came in; my patrons insist that you are the only one who can decide the point."

Jesus resisted the impulse to tell the old man to go about his business; there was something evil in his manner. But he remembered what patience the learned Hillel had always shown when asked to settle trivial questions—and on one occasion at least a wager had been concerned. "I will do as you ask," he said reluctantly.

He was led to a gloomy room overlooking the Court of the Gentiles. The old man said to a tall stupid-looking Levite who was gazing out of the window: "Detain this boy for a short time, friend, while I fetch the two persons of whom I spoke."

Jesus asked indignantly: "Did I not give you my word that I would arbitrate in the dispute?"

But the old man had already gone.

He said to the Levite: "By your dress, Sir, I take you to be a Levite of the Temple Watch. Can this be the guard-room?"

The Levite nodded without speaking.

"A strange place for a debate."

The Levite nodded sagely and then said after a long pause: "Very strange!" and after a still longer pause: "You must tell the truth, you know. It will be better for you to make a full confession and restore what you took. The Captain of the Watch does not lay on very hard. He deals with boys himself, you know."

"I do not understand. Who was that smiling old man who brought me here?"

"He? He is Hophni the Toad. He never forgets a face. You are the boy who was nearly caught at the Feast of Tabernacles, are you not? The one who robbed Meleager the money-changer, but managed to dodge out through the Gate and hide in the crowd?"

Jesus laughed. "I was not in Jerusalem for the Feast of Tabernacles."

"So you say! Well, then, what is your crime?"

"I am not accused of any crime. This is some witty fellow's jest at my expense. Let me go now!"

"I am instructed to detain you."

The Watch returned at that moment from their morning's round. The Captain asked: "Who is this boy?"

"Hophni brought him in, Reverend Sir."

The Captain frowned. He asked Jesus: "Are you by any chance the son of Joseph of Emmaus?"

"My father once lived at Emmaus. His name is Joseph son of Heli. He is now registered as of Nazareth in Galilee."

"Yes, that is the man. Then I am sorry to say that you must consider yourself under arrest."

"Sir, here comes Hophni with the witnesses," said the Levite.

The First and Second Doctors entered, followed by a younger man with an ink-horn and pen-case dangling from his belt. The First Doctor slipped four drachmae into the hand of Hophni who went back, chuckling, to his post at the Gate.

The Second Doctor, who looked ill at ease, said: "You understand, Captain, that we do not wish this matter to be made public—there must be no scandal. May we withdraw into your private room?"

"It is at your disposal, learned Doctor."

When Jesus was brought into the private room the Captain said gently to him: "You are no longer a child. Do you already understand something of the Law?"

Jesus bowed.

"You are styled Jesus the son of Joseph of Nazareth, formerly of Emmaus, and of his wife Miriam?"

"I am."

"You have always lived with them?"

"From birth. I was born at Bethlehem of Ephrath."

"How did you come to be born there?"

"My father took my mother to Bethlehem when she was nearing her account. Being of the House of David, he wished me to be born on family ground. That was the year in which King Herod died—about four months before his death."

"Who were your mother's parents?"

"She was a daughter of Joachim of Cocheba, one of the Heirs, since deceased in poverty; but a Temple ward."

"You can read fluently?"

"By the help of him who made me."

"Read this!"

It was a page detached from the Temple Treasury account book, recording a marriage contract between Joseph son of Heli, of the House of David and the tribe of Judah, a native of Emmaus, and Simon son of Boethus, High Priest, guardian of the Temple ward Miriam, daughter of Joachim the Heir, a native of Cocheba, and his wife Hannah. The instrument was dated ten months before the birth of Jesus, but the receipt for ten shekels was not recorded until four months later, and to the receipt was added in very small, very faint letters: "There is wanting one half-shekel."

The accountant said: "The words written small are in the hand of the then High Priest. It is a most unusual case. I have searched the records and found a receipt for the payment of the missing half-shekel; it was sent from Alexandria by the High Priest after his deposition by King Herod and has been glued to a later page. This receipt is dated a month after the King's death."

Jesus, very white now, asked: "You mean that my father Joseph did not marry my mother until after she was with child by him?"

"Either by him or by another," said the Captain of the Watch. "I have been making private inquiries, and I hear a rumour that your mother was carried off by bandits immediately after the drafting of the contract and held by them for some three months. This may well explain why Joseph was unwilling at first to put down the last half-shekel of his contract. Well, my boy, I do not wish to distress you, but I must explain the legal position. There is a rule which Moses, not I, made and which I am ordered to enforce: it is that nobody born out of wedlock is permitted to enter the sanctified Courts of this Temple. The penalty for a breach of this rule is death. You acted in ignorance—I can see that you acted in ignorance —and therefore I shall make no report in writing on the matter, in order not to bring scandal on your House, though I am obliged to inform the High Priest Annas of the action that I have taken. But unless you can satisfy me that you are mistaken as to the date of your birth and that you were born in legitimate wedlock, I have no alternative but to forbid you to enter. Mind you, I do not call you a bastard, and indeed cannot do so because I have no clear evi- · dence as to the date of your birth."

"Though I condemn myself from my own mouth," said Jesus, "I know that I was born four months before the death of King Herod; on the day of the winter solstice. My mother has often told me so."

The Second Doctor said passionately to the First, who was smiling triumphantly: "Take my new embroidered cloak, for you have won your wager. Grin like a dog and run about the city in it. Yet I would rather freeze to death than accept yours in exchange, for you have done a worse day's work than you know, and if I never see your face again it will not greatly grieve me.—Come with me, boy, to my house and be my guest until you return to your parents in Galilee. For you are a good boy, and was it not the learned Hillel (his memory be blessed) who justly said: 'A wise bastard is better than an ignorant High Priest'?"

But Jesus had toppled and fallen to the ground with his limbs rigid and his features distorted with pain. A terrible cry rang through the building.

The next day Jesus said faintly to the Second Doctor, who was tending him with remorseful care: "Learned man, it would be a kindness if you were to send one of your servants to fetch me a block of olive-wood, a chisel and a mallet."

"For what purpose, boy?"

"To see whether my hands have forgotten the trade upon which they must now depend for a livelihood; for a Doctor of the Law, it seems, I can never be. Yesterday a great white mist rose up over my mind and I find now that I cannot remember simple Scriptural texts that I thought were burned deep in my memory. A chisel, a mallet. a block of wood."

They were brought him, and finding that he could still manage his tools in workmanlike fashion, he gave thanks to his God. Then he said: "Add to your kindness, learned man, and send one of your servants with me a part of the way home, for I am not sure whether I can remember the road."

"He shall go the whole way with you, if you will."

Jesus returned to Galilee and parted from the Doctor's servant when within sight of his home. He said nothing to his mother or father about what had happened. He could not bring himself to do so. Nor did he need to absent himself from the synagogue on account of his bastardy, for the generous rule was that no man should be debarred from religious communion with his neighbours on account of some fault of his ancestors or parents. The chief sign that he gave of his spiritual disquiet was that he ceased to read more of the Scriptures than the ordained daily texts and would no longer discuss them with anyone at all. He worked all the more diligently at his trade and was more punctilious than ever in his behaviour towards his elders. Everyone noticed the change in him. On the whole, the people of Nazareth and Bethlehem agreed, it was a relief that he had ceased to be a boy prodigy and become an ordinary carpenter's apprentice. He had frightened them by his learning, his independence and the critical acuteness of his mind. "We have seen this before," the elders said. "The change comes with puberty. The visiting spirit flies off, never to return. There was a boy at Cana in our grandfathers' day, an Issacharite, who confounded by his knowledge all the Greek professors of astronomy and mathematics at Gadara University. Figures, figures, figures—they served him like a witch's familiars! But with puberty, off the spirit flew, and the boy, overcome by melancholy, disgraced his father's house by taking his own life."

Four years went by, and each year when the Passover or the Feast of Tabernacles came round again, Jesus told Jose and James: "No, brothers, go up yourselves to Jerusalem, and the Spirit of the Lord be with you! I am the youngest of us all—this time I will stay at home and mind the beasts. Next year, perhaps, I will go." It was at the Passover of the second year that a party of Samaritans broke into the Temple one night and, entering the Court of Priests, strewed it with human bones to make it unclean; for which the Samaritan nation was publicly cursed in the synagogues and forbidden entry for ever into the Court of the Gentiles.

In the fifth year old Joseph died. Jesus's grief was great and he

fasted for three full days. Afterwards, Mary took him aside and said: "While he lived, I could not tell you a secret about your parentage which you have a right to know. I feared that you might look on him with different eyes. Even now I shrink from hurting you."

"Mother, you could not hurt me now, even if grief for the dead did not so numb my senses that I can hardly tell hot from cold. For I was struck to the heart five years ago when I read the Temple records of a certain marriage contract, and the knife is still plunged in the wound. You are my mother, and I am commanded to honour you, and I do honour you. Yet I honour you the less for knowing that the man whom I called father was not my father according to the flesh; as I honour his memory the more on that account, having been treated by him as a well-beloved son. Mother, what have you to say? At Jerusalem I am written down as a bastard and you are accused of having wronged my father between the day that he undertook to marry you and the day that he came to fetch you away to his house. Why did you not tell me in good time of the flaw in my citizenship? You feed me with hopes, you send me to a learned rabbi, you persuade my father to introduce me into the synagogue of Nazareth; thinking, I suppose, that the truth will never come out. Did you even dare to take me to the Temple to be circumcised? Were you making me a partner at eight days old to a wicked breach of the Law? And how did Joseph find it in his conscience to humour you in this? Yet I dare not reproach the beloved dead."

Mary asked softly: "Jesus, little son, am I a woman who would sin, do you think? Do my eyes meet yours steadily? Do my cheeks show the guilty flush of shame?"

"Since the day that I was shown the Temple records by the Captain of the Watch, and warned never again to enter the Inner Courts until I could prove my legitimacy, a cloud has overhung my mind. Questions which once I had the power of solving quickly have become enigmas. Especially, your look of innocence and the written record of your shame stand in contradiction; I cannot reconcile them. If I could, perhaps the cloud might lift, for night and day this question tears like an eagle at my soul. I love the Lord still with all my heart, but among the torn shreds of my former learning a saying of the gloomy Shammai flaunts like an ensign. The same is true of every man alive: "It would be better for him that he had never been born."' This view Hillel attempted to confute, but Shammai for once won the debate. Every man, he said, is necessarily born into error; and error leads into sin; and sin to divine displeasure; and when a man displeases his Maker, it would be better that he had never been born. As heirs of Adam we pay for the sin of Adam. In my childhood, Mother, I could see myself a Doctor, a prophet, a king—surely it is this failure in humility which our God has now punished in me."

"It is written: 'Whom he loves, he chastens.' My son, listen to me. I swear to you, as our God lives, that I have never in my life sinned with any man, either willingly or unwillingly; I swear that you are no bastard, but born in royal wedlock. I did not marry the generous Joseph until my husband the King was dead, and then it was a marriage in appearance only, the one means by which your life could be preserved from your enemies."

Having said so much, Mary waited calmly for Jesus to speak, watching his face attentively.

At last in bewilderment, he asked: "Who am I, then, Mother?"

"You are the uncrowned King of the Jews, the secret heir to the throne which has stood empty since the days of King Herod!"

He gazed at her horror-stricken and incredulous. "Do you mean?" he began.

"Do I mean what, little son?"

"Almost I should have preferred bastardy to this," he said, groaning. "You mean, Mother, that you were the secret bride of King Herod the Wicked?"

"The Lord forbid!" she cried. "Your father was the noblest and gentlest and most unfortunate prince in the history of our race."

Slowly the mist drew off, the sun shone out. As Mary told Jesus the story of his birth, he felt the lost powers of his mind flooding back, with nothing lost or impaired; on the contrary, he knew himself capable of thought hitherto beyond his scope. He had not wept before, but now the tears flowed and he cried: "Oh, Mother, if only you had spoken before! If Joseph were alive, and I could fall at his feet and thank him for his great love!"

"You were the best of sons to him," she reassured him.

Then she told him of his adoration by the three astrologers, and of the massacre at Bethlehem, and how Kenah's nephew had conveyed Joseph and herself safely across the desert to On-Heliopolis. She ended: "And the learned Simeon who taught you at Matarieh: he was not the old schoolmaster that he pretended to be. He was Simon the son of Boethus, your father's friend, who was High Priest. Two months after his deposition he took Nazirite vows for a year and went out into the Arabian desert as a hermit. When he returned, gaunt and burned and unrecognizable, it was not to his luxurious home at Alexandria but to Matarieh and the mean lodgings where Joseph sought him out. As your spiritual guardian, he felt it his duty to watch over you in those days of hardship and danger, and educate you in a manner worthy of your destiny."

"How did he know that we were at Leontopolis?"

"Joseph and I took you to Alexandria with us soon after our arrival in Egypt, before he left for Arabia. We went there to pay the half-shekel which completed our interrupted marriage contract. But Joseph feared to show himself in the Jewish quarter because of Herod's agents, who were now active in the service of your uncle Archelaus the ethnarch of Judaea. So it was I who carried the money to Simon and told him how we were situated. I said nothing to Joseph and he never guessed Simeon's identity. The High Priest Simon was supposed to have died in the desert."

"Is he dead now?"

"He is still with the Essenes at Callirrhoë. I have news of him once a year."

"And what became of the gold crown that the three astrologers brought for me to the stable at Bethlehem?"

"It is at Ain-Rinon in the care of my Aunt Elizabeth. One day you shall claim it—one day you shall wear it."

"I wear it? The Emperor has abolished the Jewish monarchy."

"He has not abolished it. He has only withheld the royal title from unworthy and murderous claimants to it. The throne is yours by Roman Law, as your father's only surviving heir. King Herod's Will, by which it was conveyed to you, is laid up with the Vestal Virgins and cannot therefore be either overturned at law or set aside."

"I would scorn to wear a crown by favour of the Romans and be hated by the Sons of Israel for comforting their prime enemies."

"Your noble father wore a Roman crown."

"He was royal in his own right and would have been more greatly blessed if he had put it off his head."

"What other crown would you accept?"

"A crown bestowed on me by my own people."

"What? In defiance of the Romans? Would you lead your people to war?"

"No, to repentance and love. I accept your words as prophetic, Daughter of Rahab. One day, by the grace of the Lord, I will wear that crown."

"May it bring you happiness and peace, and freedom to your people!"

They talked together far into the night. In the morning Jesus made a decision: to go off with Mary's blessing, when the mourning for Joseph was over, and prepare himself for kingship under the guidance of Simon son of Boethus. He made over to her all the property bequeathed him by Joseph and all his own savings; and she remained at Nazareth. Old Shelom of Rehoboth, now widowed, came as her companion in the house.

Jesus took his toolbag on his shoulder and provisions of parched corn, dried fruit and a bottle of water, and set out for the nearest ford over the Jordan. He crossed it and travelled southward through Lower Transjordania until he came to the Dead Sea, continuing along its shores to the town of Callirrhoë. The Essene colony lived at some distance from the town. Their round wooden huts were arranged in circles within a large irregular compound enclosed by earthworks topped by thorn hedges and faced with stone. When he knocked at the gate of the compound and asked for admittance he saw Simeon himself coming towards him across the sandy ground. They kissed affectionately.

Simeon was dressed in a white robe and a white apron. Around his middle was a leather girdle—as a charm against the Adversary—through which a wooden trowel was thrust. All the Essenes carried a trowel in perpetuation of a custom followed by the Israelites during their residence in the wilderness of Zin. He told the porter: "Send for Father Manahem!"

The porter fetched another Essene, who was tall and gaunt with a fiery eye. He took Jesus by the right hand and then, to the surprise of Simeon, the porter and Jesus himself, gave him two smart cuffs on his head, saying: "Not in anger, not in reproof, but to remind you of Father Manahem!" Then he embraced him and led him to the Overseer.

The Overseer, who was very aged and had charge of this community of four hundred and fifty brothers and novices, rose to his feet when Jesus came in.

"A postulant for the novitiate!"

"A postulant."

"Who?"

Simeon answered for him: "Joshua son of Abiathar"—which was to say "Jesus son of Antipater", no Greek names being in use among the Essenes.

"Legitimate?"

"Legitimate."

"Of what tribe?"

"Of Judah."

"Of good disposition?"

"Of the best."

"Trade?"

"As you see."

"Instructed in the Law?"

"By myself."

"Let him take the vows."

Father Manahem told Jesus: "The vows are required for one year of service. If after one year you prove worthy of further progress in the Order, you will be made a partaker of the waters of purification and, as a novice, required to take further vows. If at the end of two years you are desirous of becoming a full member and no fault is found in you, you will be made a partaker of the Holy One and required to take lifelong vows."

"I did not come here as a postulant but to greet my teacher and renew my studies. If this is not permitted unless I become a postulant, I am content to do so. Father Manahem sees one in me, Father Simeon sees the same, and I will not dispute their judgement. What vows do you require of me?"

"Do you vow by the living God to show unhesitating obedience to the Overseer of this Order, and to whatever confessors and tutors he may set over you, and to keep all the rules of this Order as they are taught you? Do you vow to exercise piety towards the Lord and justice towards men; to aid the righteous and hate the wicked; to harm no one; to reprove liars; to waste no words; to utter no rash judgements; to refrain from women, perfumes, ointments, uncleanness, eggs and beans; to shed no blood of man, bird or beast; to love truth and to keep the Ten Commandments; to communicate to no one any mystery peculiar to this Order; to withhold no secret from your confessors; to take no other oath or vows while these remain in force?"

"I except the vow of secrecy. I cannot reveal to my confessors secrets that have been entrusted to me by others."

"Secrets that are not your own may be withheld from your confessor."

"Then I will take the vows."

They gave him a lotus-blue garment, a white apron, a girdle of calf-leather and a wooden trowel. The Overseer said to Simeon: "Father Simeon, instruct the boy in the use of the trowel. Father Manahem, remain behind."

When the door was shut the Overseer said to Manahem: "From my window I saw the cuffs dealt!"

"Rightfully bestowed."

"As by your predecessor's predecessor upon Herod the Edomite?"

"The boy has the marks of royalty."

"How do you read his destiny?"

"Glorious; miserable in the extreme; in the extreme again glorious!"

"Tend him well but impartially!"

Their meaning was this. When old Herod had been a child at Bozrah, where the Essene community had previously been settled, the Father who had the title "Manahem" had seen him pass by the gate of the compound on his way to school and beckoned him to come near. When Herod reached the gate Manahem dealt him two smart cuffs, saying: "Not in anger, not in reproof, but to remind you of Father Manahem!" Herod flushed red with passion but Manahem said: "When you are King of the Jews remember Father Manahem of Bozrah who cuffed you as a she-bear cuffs her young, wishing them well." Herod answered: "You mistake me for another. I am no Jew but an Edomite." Manahem said: "Nevertheless, it shall be as I say. You shall be a glorious king, and your dominions shall be wider than those of King Solomon; but though your intentions will be pious, your crimes will be terrible!" Herod never forgot Manahem, and towards the Essenes he was kindness itself throughout his life. He named a Gate of Jerusalem "the Gate of the Essenes" in their honour, though they never came up to worship in the Temple.

The first rule of the Order that Jesus learned was a prohibition against spitting in company; instead, he must retire apart and spit to the left hand, which was the side of evil and unclean things, not to the right hand, which was the side of good and clean things, and should cover over the spittle with sand thrown from the trowel. The next rule that he learned was that when he performed his necessities he must do it in a place apart, first digging a small pit with his trowel and then covering himself about with his garments, so that the eye of the Sun should not be affronted, and must then use his trowel again, as a lion its paws, to fill in the pit. The third rule that he learned was that he must rise before dawn every morning and speak no single word to anyone until he had offered up certain ancient prayers to Jehovah in supplication of the Sun's rising. The Essenes do not indeed venerate the Sun as a god, but they venerate Jehovah who made the Sun; and while the Temple was still standing they refrained from worship there. This was partly because, like the prophet Amos, they abhorred blood-sacrifices, but mainly because the priesthood prevented them from observing the custom of their forefathers: that of standing by the Eastern Gate at sunrise and worshipping towards the East, instead of turning towards the Sanctuary as the other Jews did. It was therefore to the Essenes that Herod had intended to commit the charge of the Temple, after he had purged it, under the High Priesthood of his cousin Achiabus, who was highly respected by them and had himself been educated at Callirrhoë.

The Law of Moses rules their lives, and anyone who blasphemes Moses is punished with death as if he had blasphemed Jehovah. This rule is unintelligible to other Jews, except to the Ebionite and Therapeutic sects which are allied to theirs, for the secret of the Essenes is that they give the name of Moses to the temporal aspect of Jehovah. Jehovah, that is to say, is the divine principle of life and light and truth; Moses is this principle translated into flesh. Those of you who have been partakers of certain Greek mysteries will understand what I mean, by a comparison of the Moses myth with those expounded to you by the mystagogues. According to the oral tradition of the Essenes, which differs in many respects from the account given in Exodus, Moses was the son of Pharaoh's daughter, not begotten but born from an almond secretly brought her at On-Heliopolis by an angel of Jehovah the God of Israel. Pharaoh sent assassins to kill the infant, whose real name was Osarsiph, but his Israelitish midwife hid him in a harvest-basket and committed him to the waters of the Nile. Jochebed, wife to Amram, a shepherd of Goshen, found him among the reeds, called him Moses, which means "drawn out", and brought him home to rear. As a young man Moses returned to On-Heliopolis and by a wonderful display of strength and intelligence attracted the attention of his grandfather Pharaoh, who was unaware of his identity. Moses then fought a successful war for Pharaoh against the Ethiopians, but when the crowds acclaimed him, Pharaoh grew jealous and sought to kill him. At Jehovah's order he then brought ten plagues on Egypt by the use of his magical staff of almond-wood and rescued Jehovah's chosen people from their cruel servitude at Pelusium. Pharaoh, rushing in pursuit, was swallowed up with his army in the quicksands of the Lake of Reeds. Moses became the Law-giver of the Israelites during their wanderings in Sinai, but, when already within sight of the Promised Land, was stung in the heel by a scorpion sent by God's Adversary. He gathered and cleft wood, built a pyre and was consumed upon it. His ashes were buried in a secret tomb; his soul mounted to Heaven in the form of an eagle, but his spirit journeyed to the sea at Hezron where three spectral queens approached in a boat, lamenting. They bore his spirit away with them to an island valley beyond the ocean, in the extreme west, the Island of Apple-trees, where there are no snows or intense heats or thunderstorms but the gentle west wind perpetually blows off the ocean.

Thus the life and death of Moses has for the Essenes the same double meaning as the life and death of Dionysus or Osiris or Hercules has for the mystagogues: Moses is regarded by them both as an ancient king and law-giver and as a symbol of the recurrent birth, fullness and decay of the year. They believe in the resurrection of the soul, which, they say, is united to the body as to a prison, and which when free from the bonds of the flesh mounts upwards shining and joins the cluster of shining souls which give the Sun its wonderful brightness; but the spirit, which they distinguish from the soul, and which has the form and likeness of the man's body, is conducted by Elijah or some other angel to the Paradise presided over by Moses. There the spirits live happily together in a glass castle at the doors of which fiery wheels of light perpetually turn. It is a doctrine that they received from the Pythagoreans, and the Pythagoreans had it from Abaris the Hyperborean; but the Essenes claim that the Hyperborean priesthood originally had it from Moses himself. However that may be, the Essene philosophy is also over-laid with much doctrine borrowed from the Persians and Chaldaeans.

Many of them are physicians and do remarkable cures by laying on of hands, and by use of herbal decoctions, spring water, sanctified oil, sacred songs, precious gems of different sorts, and spittle mixed with clay. They also heal possessed persons by invocation of Raphael and other angelic powers, whose names they keep secret, and of the demigod Moses under his twenty seasonal titles, particularly that of Jeshua, or Jesus. Others of them are skilled in the inter-pretation of dreams and in astrological prediction. Whenever an Essene wishes to withdraw himself for meditation, he shrouds his head and takes up his station fasting within a circle marked with certain letters or figures in intercession of God's favour; and will sit there motionless for days. Sometimes they occupy their circles in order to achieve mastery of evil spirits that have vexed them; or in placation of God's wrath. The most famous of all these Essene holy men was one Honi the Circle-drawer, celebrated also for his acute and lucid judgements on the Law, who lived in the time of the later Maccabees. He is popularly credited with the breaking of a great drought by fasting inside a circle until God pitied him and sent rain. It is said that he avoided death for seventy years by remaining fast in another circle, until released by some accidentally spoken word, about the time that Archelaus was banished; and that then, finding that all his friends and associates were dead, he implored God to take away his life too. But this is a fable only. He was stoned to death by the soldiers of Hyrcanus the Maccabee for refusing to curse the Temple priesthood when Jerusalem was being besieged.

No women, even old ones, are permitted into the compounds of the Essenes, and no children either. They are forbidden either to bear arms or make them, and consider laughter disgraceful except the laughter of joy in the bounty of their God. Some of the elder initiates go about chuckling continuously, but the younger ones are for the most part morose in the extreme. Besides the three main communities grouped around the Dead Sea there are also laxer ones in various parts of Judaea, where marriage is permitted, though only for the sake of procreation; the initiates, not being cloistered in a compound, are known as "Free Essenes". One of these communities, now no longer in existence, was at the village of Bethany close to Jerusalem.

CHAPTER SIXTEEN

ARROW AND TILE

AT CALLIRRHOE Jesus spent the first seven months of his postulancy in studying the Scriptures under the Master of Postulants, who set him to memorize the Books of Moses, and in plying his trade under the Chief Carpenter, who set him to make coffins. His cell-mate was his cousin John of Ain-Rimmon, whom he now met for the first time. When the Master of Postulants was satisfied that both of them were word-perfect in the Books of Moses, he ordered them to memorize the prophecies of Ezekiel, the reputed founder of their Order. This they did, and agreed that each in turn should repeat a chapter to the other, to see whether he were word-perfect. But when John had recited the first chapter without a fault, Jesus asked him: "How do you read this chapter, Cousin?"

"I learned it by heart, without considering the meaning."

"Is this not to dishonour Ezekiel?"

"I obey my tutor Gershon, who warned me that it is dangerous to ponder the meaning: he said that a Doctor to whom the meaning is known—and it is not every Doctor who is so favoured—may reveal it to a single chosen pupil only."

"From my tutor Simeon I have received no such warning; and since I have been granted understanding of the chapter, I shall expound it to you if you will listen. Are we commanded to burden our memory with texts that have no meaning?"

"As you will, Cousin, but beware of rash judgements," said John.

"Here at Callirrhoë we make our orisons not to the Sun but to One whom we worship in the figure of the Sun; as we use our trowel out of respect not for the Sun but for One whom we worship in the figure of the Sun. Listen again!"

He recited the verses:

And I looked, and, behold, a whirlwind came out of the north, a great cloud, and a fire infolding itself, and a brightness was about it, and out of the midst thereof as the colour of amber, out of the midst of the fire.

Also out of the midst thereof came the likeness of four living creatures. And this was their appearance; they had the likeness of a man.

And every one had four faces, and every one had four wings.

And their feet were straight feet; and the sole of their feet was like the sole of a calf's foot: and they sparkled like the colour of burnished brass.

And they had the hands of a man under their wings on their four sides; and they four had their faces and their wings.

Their wings were joined one to another; they turned not when they went; they went every one straight forward.

As for the likeness of their faces, they four had the face of a man, and the face of a lion, on the right side: and they four had the face of an ox on the left side; they four also had the face of an eagle.

Thus were their faces: and their wings were stretched upward; two wings of every one were joined one to another, and two covered their bodies.

And they went every one straight forward: whither the spirit was to go, they went; and they turned not when they went.

As for the likeness of the living creatures, their appearance was like burning coals of fire, and like the appearance of lamps: it went up and down among the living creatures; and the fire was bright, and out of the fire went forth lightning.

And the living creatures ran and returned as the appearance of a flash of lightning.

Now as I beheld the living creatures, behold one wheel upon the earth by the living creatures, with his four faces.

The appearance of the wheels and their work was like unto the colour of a beryl: and they four had one likeness: and their appearance and their work was as it were a wheel in the middle of a wheel.

When they went, they went upon their four sides: and they turned not when they went.

As for their rings, they were so high that they were dreadful; and their rings were full of eyes round about them four.

And when the living creatures went, the wheels went by them: and when the living creatures were lifted up from the earth, the wheels were lifted up.

Whithersoever the spirit was to go, they went, thither was their spirit to go; and the wheels were lifted up over against them: for the spirit of the living creature was in the wheels.

When those went, these went; and when those stood, these stood; and when those were lifted up from the earth, the wheels were lifted up over against them: for the spirit of the living creature was in the wheels.

And the likeness of the firmament upon the heads of the living creature was as the colour of the terrible crystal, stretched forth over their heads above.

And under the firmament were their wings straight, the one toward the other: every one had two, which covered on this side, and every one had two, which covered on that side, their bodies.

And when they went, I heard the noise of their wings, like the noise of great waters, as the voice of the Almighty, the voice of speech, as the noise of an host: when they stood, they let down their wings.

And there was a voice from the firmament that was over their heads, when they stood, and had let down their wings.

And above the firmament that was over their heads was the

likeness of a throne, as the appearance of a sapphire stone: and upon the likeness of the throne was the likeness as the appearance of a man above upon it.

And I saw as the colour of amber, as the appearance of fire round about within it, from the appearance of his loins even upward, and from the appearance of his loins even downward, I saw as it were the appearance of fire, and it had brightness round about.

As the appearance of the bow that is in the cloud in the day of rain, so was the appearance of the brightness round about. This was the appearance of the likeness of the glory of the Lord. And when I saw it, I fell upon my face, and I heard a voice of one that spake.

Then he expounded them as follows: "It is agreed that there are four New Years in a twelvemonth; at the autumnal equinox, at the vernal, at midwinter, at midsummer. As I read this vision of Ezekiel, each Cherub is a wheel of four spokes, with each New Year a spoke of the wheel. Each spoke has a face, part of the hub, that distinguishes its New Year: the Ox of seven combats for the new-born Sun of winter, and for the planet Ninib; the Lion for the young Sun in Spring and for the planet Marduk; the Eagle for the Sun in his prime and for the planet Nergal; the Man for the experienced Sun of autumn and for the planet Nabu. But each spoke is planted in the felloe of its wheel with a single golden calf's foot, so that each wheel is a four-legged calf. Each Cherub, then, is a wheeling year of four seasons, and each year is a wheel in a four-wheeled chariot, and rolls straight forward without deflection; and each of the many eyes upon the wheels is a day, for the Sun is called the eye of the day. Each wheel, also, turns within a wheel of four years (and so the Greeks reckon time by Olympiads), running from the beginning of things to the end of things. The Enthroned Man is an emanation of our God, but not our God himself. There are no beasts in the shafts of the Chariot, since the wheels themselves are the beasts, each wheel running, as I have said, upon the four feet of a golden calf. These wheels were the fiery steeds of the chariot in which the prophets Enoch and Elijah were carried up to Heaven. Yet Ezekiel hides a part of his vision from us: for the beast of midsummer is, in truth, an eagle-winged goat. Moreover, the beast of autumn is, in truth, a man-faced seraph, or fiery serpent. Thus each calf is in turn four beasts: it is lion, goat, seraph, and ox—the seraph when it is fully grown—and also it is a man, and an eagle. For this reason the Greeks and Cretans, who have drunk from the same well as ourselves, say: 'The Calf has many changes.' "

"Cousin, beware of rash judgements!" John repeated.

Jesus continued: "The golden calf is not an idol, unless it be worshipped as a god. Those who worshipped the golden calves by Mount Horeb said: 'These brought us out of Egypt!' They lied: it was by the power of our God alone that they were brought out. Now, the whirlwind and fire, as I read Ezekiel's vision, are an allegory of God's presence; for whirlwind and fire were the allegory of his presence on Mount Carmel when an inner voice spoke to Elijah. Yet an allegory only, for it is written: 'And yet the Lord was not in the whirlwind. And yet the Lord was not in the fire.' The whirlwind came from the North, the quarter from which the Sun never shines: from this we learn that our God transcends even the Sun, having no limitations to his power. (So when beasts are sacrificed in the Temple at Jerusalem the priest turns their heads to the North.) God is a spirit and his ministers are a flaming fire; the fire that Moses saw in the bush, that burned and was not consumed, was not God: it was the brightness of his ministers. The lightnings of Horeb were the same—not God but his ministers. And Ezekiel saw the rainbow about the throne of the Most High; for though the lightning leaps from the thundercloud for vengeance, the rainbow shines for mercy. Yet he hides another part of his vision from us. What of the other three Celestial Powers—the Sun, the Moon and the Planet of Love? Did he not see this fiery Trinity circling about the Throne? Listen again, and I will expound the Golden Calf whom the initiates name Moses."

"Have a care how you blaspheme, Cousin!"

"May my mouth be kept clean of offence! You know the names of the circles of huts in the compound?"

"I do. Those of the outer ring are: Babel, Lot, Ephron, Salma, Ne-Esthan (which was the seraph that Moses made his standard in the wilderness); Hur, David, Telmen, Kohath, Caleb; Moriah, Gath, Gomer, Jethro, Reu. Those of the inner ring are: Jacob, Jose, Jerah, Jeshua, Jachin."

"Why are these names chosen?"

"It is a prime secret known only to the Elders of this Order."

"Yet it has been revealed to me. The names of the outer ring spell out the calendar-story of the golden calf who becomes a bull and of whose torn flesh the Elders secretly partake at their initiation. Here are the words in Aeolic Greek; the founders of this Order learned them, I suppose, from the Greeks of Canopus and concealed their secret by transforming them into the names, nearest to them in form, which are found in our Scriptures:

> BOIBALION LOTO-PHORAMENON SALOÖMAI NEO-STHENARON.
> OURIOS DAFIZO, TLAMON KAIOMAI, KALYPTOMAI.
> MOIRAO, GATHEO GNORIMOS, IDRYOMAI, RHEO.

Which is to say:

> I, the bull-calf ferried on the blue lotus, rock to and fro, new-strengthened.
> I, the benignant one, cleave wood; in suffering am consumed by fire; am hidden away.
> I, the famous one, distribute, rejoice, establish, am borne off by water.

Each name stands for a period of three ogdoads; making in all three hundred and sixty days. And the other words are the five sacred days that remain to the year: ACHAIFA, OSSA (which gives its name to the lowest of the three degrees of initiation in this Order), OURANIA, HESUCHIA, IACHEMA—namely: The Spinner, Fame, the Queen of Heaven, Repose, Wailing. The Nabataeans of Arabia call the bull-calf 'Ouri-Tal', the Benignant Sufferer, and worship him with abominable rites as the son of the Goddess Lat; the Phoenicians call him Hercules-Melkarth and glorify his lechery; at Samaria he was worshipped as Egli-yahu, 'the Lord is a Calf', until the jealous hand of our God broke the city into pieces."

"Who then is the bull-calf if he is neither Ouri-tal nor Hercules nor Egli-yahu, and names the huts of this holy compound?"

"An acceptable emblem of the life of the solar year, and of the life of man since the Fall. To worship this bull-calf is idolatry, for the power of the Only God, who is timeless, is thereby denied. It is to honour the Female, whose five midwinter days (which are also five equal seasons of the year) epitomize the fate of fallen man, and of the year."

"And the two higher degrees of initiation?"

"The Samsonians are so called in honour of Samson, whose life they make an allegory of the solar year. The Helicaeans are instructed in the mystical lore of the Helix, that is to say, of the Cosmic Wheel."

"Tell me more of the Female."

"She is the threefold demoness who is Mother, Bride and Layer-Out to fallen man. On the first day of the five she spins the thread of his life; on the second she flatters him with hope of fame; on the third she corrupts him with her whoredoms; on the fourth she lulls him to deathly sleep; on the fifth she bewails his corpse. The Greeks worship her in trinity as the Three Fates—namely, the Spinner, the Distributor, the Cutter-off."

"But why is the bull-calf called Moses by the elders of our Order?"

"The name Moses signifies that in the spring of every year life is *drawn out* of the flood-water, as our Law-giver Moses was in infancy drawn out of the Nile; and that every child, until he is born, swims in water. The bull-calf, which is an emblem, cannot properly be blasphemed; nor can Moses the Law-giver be blasphemed, since he was man, not God. He was born, married, begot children, did bloody deeds, died and was buried. Yet he deserves our everlasting honour, because the Lord God committed the Law to him and because, when the sinful people worshipped the golden bull-calf at Horeb, he ground the idol into dust and forced them to drink it mixed with water. And as the sage Aristeas writes: 'Moses taught that God is One, that his power is manifested through all things, every place being filled with his sovereignty, and that nothing which is done in secret by men on earth is hidden from our God: for he knows all that is done, and all that is destined to be done.' And elsewhere Aristeas shows that our nation alone worships one God, not a multiplicity of gods; and for that we have Moses to thank, because he delivered the Law to us."

"Yet if Moses was but a man and cannot therefore be blasphemed, why do the Elders of our Order forbid us to blaspheme him?"

"That is not yet given me to understand, for I cannot believe these pious men to be idolaters."

"Who is the Enthroned Man of Ezekiel's vision, since he is neither the bull-calf nor God himself?"

"The same Son of Man of whom the prophet Daniel was granted a vision. He shall appear to all men on the day that the Female is defeated at last. He is neither God nor man: he is the image of God in which man was first made and which shall then be renewed in pure love of God for man, of man for God."

"May the Chariot roll us swiftly to that Day!"

At this, voices were heard outside and the Overseer hastened in, followed by Manahem and Simeon. The Overseer cried: "The whole compound is ablaze, yet nothing is consumed, and the wild-fire is leaping up from the roof of this hut. Joshua ben Abiathar, Johanan ben Zacharias, confess: are you studying the *Ma'aseh Merkabah* [which is to say, the Work of the Chariot], a mystery forbidden to anyone to study who is of less rank than Head of an Academy?"

"I was not forbidden by you or by my tutor to study the mystery. And who shall prevent me from understanding what I am ordered to memorize? And how shall I refrain from expounding what I understand, when I have vowed in your presence not to keep anything secret?"

"Have a care! A boy of Kadesh Barnea, in my father's days, who recognized the meaning of a single verse of the chapter was consumed by fire!"

"Yet I am not consumed! And I have heard it said: 'When fire descends from Heaven that burns but does not consume, then is the time to sing the Hymn of Praise.'"

"Are you instructing your Overseer?"

"As he wills."

"Have you never heard it said that he who speaks foolishly of the things which are before, behind, above and below—which is to say the *Merkabah*—it were better he had never been born?"

"I have heard that judgement, and I have also heard it said that Ezekiel will come again and unlock for Israel the chambers of the *Merkabah*. And what if Ezekiel has so come and unlocked them to-day?"

Then the Overseer said: "Joshua ben Abiathar! This place will not hold you: you will wrench the bars apart. Take your bag of tools again and go in peace through the same gate by which you entered. Yet be warned by me. It is recorded that Elijah, whose duty in the Land of the Blessed is to guide the spirits to their due stations—that Elijah, granted a holiday upon earth, visited an academy of Jerusalem. He heard the Doctors discussing the fiery steeds of the chariot that caught him up to Heaven. Finding that they were puzzled and at a loss, he intervened to put them right, and on his return was severely reprimanded by him who sees all."

"Who spitefully revealed to you Elijah's discomfiture? Was it perhaps God's Adversary? For now that you have released me from my vows of obedience and I can address you as man to man, I will tell you this. You flee from the world, yet no solemnly sworn vows of purity will preserve a timid man from sin; neither will the locked gate to this compound, nor the earthwork about it, nor the thorn-hedge that tops the earthwork, nor your prophylactic girdles of calf-skin, nor all the thousand and one jealous rules of this Order, serve to keep out God's Adversary when you spread so rich a table of temptation to entice him."

"May the Lord cleanse our hearts from their secret fault; for in him only is our strength! Go in peace now, bold son, and remember us kindly when you enter your kingdom."

A month later, walking in the market-place of On-Heliopolis, Jesus pondered the fate of Jerusalem. The words that Jehovah once spoke to the prophet Ezekiel came into his mind: "Son of man, take a tile and pourtray upon it the city of Jerusalem." His foot struck in the dust against a red tile. He picked it up, and sitting down on a stone, began to draw on it with a piece of charcoal. He pourtrayed the city in the archaic style, showing only the front of the Temple, with a wall about it, an ox and a lion within the wall, and a star shining above. Then he gazed steadfastly at the tile and his heart asked the question: "What is the judgement upon Jerusalem? Is she permitted to stand? Is she doomed to fall?"

Before his eyes rose a vision of a tottering balance, and an inner voice spoke to him: "A little more in this pan, a little more in that. The judgement is not yet." He laid the tile down.

To a man who was watching him from behind he said in Greek, without looking round: "If you are able to instruct me, do so; if unable, pass on."

The man came forward and asked: "Are you the Hebrew of whom I have come in search?"

"You know that I am, else you would not ask me."

The man was tall, with a pale face, blue eyes and long corn-coloured hair. He carried a golden-shafted arrow in his hand and was dressed in a white linen robe, white linen breeches and a cloak of six colours fastened with a great gold brooch. "Then let me sharpen my arrow on your tile," he said.

"You will need oil for that."

"I carry oil with me in a spiral flask."

"Is it clean oil for my tile? Are you one of the uncircumcised, an eater of the pig and the hare?"

"I am a Gadelian from the extreme West. My people observe the same divine ordinances as yours. We are of the posterity of Japhet, and I am a physician and a smith."

"Do your people not worship the Queen of Heaven?"

"No longer. As we tell the story, our God (who was first the God of the Hebrews) killed with a golden arrow the greatest she-bear in the Universe. Pray, expound the lion."

"Willingly. It names the city."

"Of Leontopolis?"

"No, of Ariel; the name which King David bestowed on Jerusalem."

"You have set palm-trees on the roof of the Temple."

"Solomon, son of King David, set palm-trees adorned with golden chains on the roof of his Temple. The ceiling was fir, overlaid with fine gold."

"I have heard of this King Solomon: how he fetched all the secrets of Asia from Byblos."

"We name the place Gebal. It is written in our Book of Kings that the men of Gebal assisted Solomon in the building of his Temple."

"On your showing, he knew the language of trees: for in our sacred tree-alphabet, which we also fetched from Byblos, the fir, there sacred to Adonis, is called *Aleph* and the palm *Double Aleph*; and *Aleph of Aleph* is a title of the Great God whom we delight to honour. It signifies the Ancient of Days."

"Teach me that alphabet."

"In good time. Why have you set an ox beside the lion?"

"The ox typifies the King who is to come, the Son of Joseph. The star foretells his coming."

"How do you say 'ox' in Hebrew?"

"We say *Aleph*."

Both laughed for pleasure and the Gadelian said: "I whet my arrow upon your tile. Is it recorded what were the dimensions of this Temple?"

"It is recorded."

"Tell me first, did Solomon place two great pillars before it, a green and a gold?"

"Two pillars; but their colours are not recorded in our books."

"What were the names of the pillars?"

"They were called Jachin and Boaz, but their true names are forgotten. No more is known than that Boaz is to Jachin as Mount Gerizim is to Mount Ebal, its twin across the vale of Shechem: as blessing is to cursing."

"Expound."

"It is written: 'A blessing upon Gerizim to those who obey the Lord God, a curse upon Ebal to those who turn away.'"

"I can restore their true names; also the name of the lintel. Tell me the height of these pillars."

"Tell me, first, the true name of Boaz: for I also have an arrow to whet."

"It is called Abolloneus."

"Why so?"

"Because of the consonants of the same tree-alphabet which run in this order: B.L.N.F.S. We set vowels between them."

"Should not the third letter be in the fifth place?"

"It is so in the Canopic alphabet of the Bull-calf and Lotus. The Acherusian tree-alphabet, which is the earlier, runs as I have told you."

Then Jesus said: "The height of the two pillars was thirty-five cubits."

"How do you read thirty-five?"

"They make seven lustra, half the years of a man's life."

"The pillar called Boaz ascends, the pillar called Jachin descends," said the Gadelian.

"The green pillar of growth and the sere pillar of decay."

"That is well said. Yet the most fortunate among you live to one hundred and ten, I surmise."

"You are right. The patriarch Joseph who first brought my people into Egypt lived to that age; completing the full circumference of his circle."

"You are indeed the Hebrew in search of whom I have come. Your God has a sacred ark?"

"It was hidden in a cave eighteen generations ago by the prophet Jeremiah; the whereabouts are secret."

"And the dimensions of this ark?"

"They are recorded: one and a half cubits, by one and a half, by two and a half."

"That is to say, one-eighth of forty-five square cubits—which is the contents of a chest measuring five cubits by three, by three."

"Your reckoning is correct, and these are the exact dimensions of the coffins that I have been making of late for the Essenes. How do you read them?"

"It is a calendar mystery," said the Gadelian. "The Great Ark measured five cubits in length by three in width because there are fifteen seasons in the Holy Year, and the depth is three cubits because each season is divided into three weeks of eight days apiece. The Great Ark contains forty-five square cubits; the Little Ark is one-eighth the size; because eight is the number of the year's increase from infancy to prime."

"You have ploughed the same furrows as I have ploughed. Forty-five was, also, the number of pillars in Solomon's House of Lebanon, which were set in three rows of fifteen pillars. Each was a week of eight days. Thus five days were left over when the three hundred and sixty days had been reckoned, and were set apart as holy days. How does the tree-alphabet run after its first flight?"

"SS.H.D.T.C.—and again CC.M.G.NG.R."

"Why are the S and the C doubled?"

"To make fifteen out of luckless thirteen."

"So the consonants are months, each of four weeks."

"How did you divine that?"

"Easily answered. Ezekiel the poet saw in a vision what trees grow on either side of the River of Healing, which flows eastward from the House of God in the Heavenly Kingdom. Their sustaining fruit and medicinal leaves do not corrupt, and their virtues are reckoned according to the month of the year. The thirteen tribes of Israel shall inherit the land watered by the river, to every tribe a strip running from east to west, from the Mountain of the South to the Mountain of the North. To every tribe a month, to every month a tree. What of the vowels in this tree-alphabet?"

"They are A.O.U.E.I."

"You are hiding two letters from me," said Jesus reproachfully, "a doubled *Iod* and the doubled *Aleph* of which you have already spoken. For there must be twenty-two letters in this alphabet, of which seven are vowels."

"I perceive that we can keep no secrets from each other, even the Prime Secret. You have a Typhonic, or harvest-red, beard, you write left-handedly, your nose is hooked like an eagle's beak, your face is pale, your eyes are sea-green and luminous, the veins in your forehead branch in a blue *Upsilon*. But the seventh sign of royalty?"

Jesus answered: "Under this garment my right shoulder is white as ivory."

"We have a saying:

> *Three royal things:*
> *Poets, groves, kings.*

I am a master-poet; you are a king, and by 'grove' is meant seven holy trees which are called the harbourage of the white hind of wisdom."

"One of our Hebrew poets has said: 'Wisdom has built her habitation with seven pillars.'"

"It is well said. What tree of the seven is best beloved of men?"

"The wild apple-tree of immortality."

"In agreement with us. The letter of the apple-tree is doubled C— C is the nut-tree of wisdom—which the Latins write as Q and the Greeks as Koppa. And doubled S is Z; S is the pitiless willow and Z the cruel white-thorn—trees of ill-luck."

"With us the nut is also the tree of wisdom. Our sacred Candle-stick, symbol of Divine Wisdom, is made in the form of the High Priest Aaron's almond-rod that put forth seven buds; each bud is a light and typifies one of the seven celestial powers. The shaft of the Candlestick is the rod itself."

"The fourth and central light, then, typifies the Planet Nabu, the power of wisdom?"

"On the fourth day our God said: 'Let there be Lights', and created these celestial powers."

"As in our tradition. Their seven letters in the tree-alphabet are B.S.T.C.D.CC.F."

"What do they spell out? They are the initial letters of the prayer that the Essenes use at dawn."

"The Gadelian you would not understand, but the Latin, which may be known to you, runs:

Benignissime Solo Tibi Cordis Devotionem Quotidianam Facio.

'Most Blessed One, to Thee alone I render the daily sacrifice of my heart.'"

"It is the very prayer."

They continued with question and counter-question and each was well pleased with the other. To the uninstructed what has been recorded here of their conversation will read strangely; but I write for the instructed. They will understand how Jesus had deduced from the Gadelian's mention of the number 110 that the alphabet concealed an ancient mathematical secret; the proportion of a circle's diameter to its circumference, which is as seven *lustra* to twenty-two. They will also understand that the Gadelian's reticence about the two doubled letters, A and I, drew Jesus's attention to them: he saw then that the seven vowels, read sun-wise, formed a sacred name. It was II.I.E.U.O.A.AA., which, when written in Latin letters, is JIEVOAĀ.

Here was a wonderful illumination. Jesus recognized at once that this name of seven letters, the prime secret to which the Gadelian referred, is that of the God of the Ark, who is worshipped by a great number of nations allied by blood. The Hebrews, who are conceded to be his chosen people, the spiritual mentors of all Sons of Adam, call him Jehovah, a purposely misleading form of the name; but their sacred rams' horns musically blare out the true name at high festivals. It was at that blared name, it is said, that the walls of

Jericho fell flat when Joshua besieged it. The ancient Phrygians knew the name, and knotted the letters on the ox-yoke at Gordium; but the insensate sword of Alexander struck the knot apart. The Gadelians still preserve it, but divulge it only to master-poets. Jesus could never have learned the Name among his own people, since no Israelite was taught it except the High Priest and his chosen successor; nor might it be written down or pronounced by human lips except once a year by the High Priest, when he entered the Holy of Holies and whispered it under his breath. It was communicated to him not by word of mouth, but by a display of seven sacred objects arranged in a set order, the initials of which spelt out the name. A name of proved power; by the use of it, the Jews say, Moses brought the plagues upon Egypt, and Elijah and Elisha raised men from the dead.

Jesus said to the Gadelian: "Without the first and seventh letters of the Name, the bull-calf (which is Man) has no escape from the Cosmic wheel which the Female turns: he has no beginning and no end. But the doubled *Iod* and the doubled *Aleph* will together give him immortality; as David says in a Psalm: 'Praise him in his Name JAH.' When the five days of the Female are lengthened to a week, then on the first day he celebrates his true origin and on the seventh he makes a perfect end: he is at one with the God whose name has been linked with his in the sacred wheel. Surely this is the hope of the Essenes who celebrate both the first day of the week and the last, and forbid the bull-calf, whom they call 'Moses', to be blasphemed."

"But who will make the bull-calf at one with God?"

"The suffering Servant of God, the destined Messiah, whose emblem is *Aleph*: he shall conquer death."

"How can death be conquered?"

"By denial of false beginnings and false endings."

"But who first brought this falsity upon earth?"

"God's Adversary, whom the Greeks call the Cosmocrator, the lord of the illusive material universe, when he seduced woman and through her estranged man from the God who created him: it is against this fiend that the Essenes wear their prophylactic girdles of calf-skin."

With the new knowledge that he had gained, Jesus was able also to understand the secret of the jewels in the sacred breastplate of the High Priest, and those formerly worn in the breastplate of the King of Tyre, both of them used for divination. The jewels were set in a golden plate and behind them was a wheel which spun round, and on the wheel was a patch of phosphorus which shone in the darkness of the room where the divination was made, lighting up whatever hollow-cut jewel it happened to rest behind. Each jewel was of a different colour, and by the turning of the wheel words were spelt out, though without vowels, for each jewel stood for a consonant of the Acherusian tree-alphabet. Each jewel was also inscribed with the name of one of the original tribes of Israel, Joseph being two tribes. The series began with the red Edomite sard for Reuben and, running sunwise from left to right, ended with amber for Benjamin; for Reuben the first-born of Israel means "See the Son", and Benjamin the last-born of Israel means "The Son of my Right Hand".

Jesus and the Gadelian engaged to take lodgings together and work at the same trade, for the Gadelian was a smith and could forge locks and hinges for the fine cabinets which Jesus was now making. The Gadelian urged Jesus to travel with him to Gordium in Galatia where the Knot was cut; to Asian Ephesus; to Gades and the country of the Turditanians in Spain; to the Acherusian headland of Bithynia; to Olbia in Scythia; to Hieropytna in Crete and to Lusi in Arcadia—places where the ancient wells of knowledge were sunk. But Jesus said: "On is a millstone" [which is the meaning of the word], "and here all the grist of knowledge is brought to grind: here you and I met in common search of learning. Wait patiently and all the learning that we need will come to us."

He was proved right. Every year they met some person of importance to them who had come on a pilgrimage to On-Heliopolis, the most ancient city of Egypt, in search of learning: a Persian, a Ligurian, a Galatian, a Phoenician, an Indian, a Caspian, a Greek, an Armenian, a Spaniard, or a Scythian. Thus they increased their knowledge of the state of the world, but were always met by the same sick longing for immortality and by the same complaint: "The nations are scattered and disunited. When will the word of salvation be spoken that will bind all together? We come as pilgrims to On in search of light and fullness; we find only a dark void."

Jesus would comfort them in these words: "Immortality is the reward of wisdom; wisdom the reward of seeking and suffering. To seek and suffer is to love God; and there is but One God, the God of Israel. Turn to him and the word of salvation will be spoken."

"And what of woman?" a Sidonian asked him.

"No man can at the same time love God as he demands to be loved and woman as she demands to be loved. He must choose between the Eternal Father and the fish-tailed Queen of Heaven."

He later enlarged on this saying to the midwife Shelom. She asked him: "Lord, how long will death prevail?"

"So long as women continue to bear children."

She answered: "I have done well, then, in bearing none."

"Since your barrenness was not of your own choosing, you have avoided one bitter herb only to eat of another. But I will tell you this: until the two sexes shall be as one, the male with the female neither male nor female, God's Adversary will still walk abroad."

"What of yourself? Are you not a true man?"

"I have come to destroy the works of the Female!"

"Would you destroy the work of your own mother?"

"I acknowledge as my mother only the Holy Spirit of God that moved upon the face of the waters before the Creation. The Female is Lust, the First Eve, who delays the hour of perfection."

"And are you proof against her beauty? Are you sterner of heart than our father Adam?"

"May it be granted me to dispel the curse of which the Preacher, the Son of Sira, writes:

An heavy yoke was ordained for the sons of Adam from the day they go out of their mother's womb till the day that they return to the mother of all things, from him who is clothed in blue silk and wears a crown even to him who wears simple linen —wrath, envy, trouble and unquietness, rigour, strife and fear of death in the time of rest.

For the First Eve, or Acco, or Lilith, or the Spinner, whom Solomon styles the Horse Leech, and whom the Preacher styles our universal mother, has two daughters: the Womb and the Grave. 'Give, give,' she cries. In the hour of perfection she shall be denied at last."

One morning in the last year of the five that the Gadelian and Jesus continued in partnership they found a man lying naked and wounded in an alley close to their lodging. They took him in, though he seemed to be dying, tended him, bound up his wounds, gave him food, and clothed him. When he had recovered his strength, he asked them: "My lords, how may I recompense you?"

Jesus answered: "We are well recompensed by seeing you live."

"But you, Sir, are a Jew, and according to your Law I am unclean, being an eater of rats and lizards!"

"All life is precious."

"Lord, I am sunk deep in your debt."

"Here is my hand; go in peace."

"I am ashamed to be thought so far lacking in generosity that when my life is saved I give nothing in return."

"Give us what you will to ease your heart: but, friend, your possessions are not great."

"I have a word to give."

"We gladly accept a word, if it is a good word."

"It is a word of power over venomous serpents: for I am a Psyllian from the Great Syrtis."

"The name of a demon of Libya? Then refrain: we may not use it."

"No, Lord. It is a master-word in use amongst serpents by which they recognize one another and abstain from offence: its meaning is Love. By use of it you will have the power to handle all serpents without fear."

"The word Love, spoken in love, is beautiful in any language."

The Gadelian cried: "Can any man but a Psyllian or a black Indian speak lovingly to a venomous serpent? The serpent would not be deceived, and the man would die."

"Let us make trial," said the Psyllian.

He went out with them about a mile into the desert, where he crouched down and began to sing in a strange croaking fashion. Presently the black snakes and asps came rustling through the sand towards him. He stooped, picked them up, one after the other, crooned over them and said to Jesus, who stood unafraid beside him: "Look, is this one not beautiful, and this, and this? Their sharp white fangs, their bright eyes, the pattern of their scales, their lissomness! Lord, now I will speak the word of Love; repeat it after me." He breathed the word gently and the snakes curled peacefully into whorls in the lap of his garment.

Jesus repeated the word after him, reached out his hand to an asp, took it up and made much of it.

"Let it coil about your neck, Lord!"

Jesus did so.

The Psyllian instructed the asp: "Brother, be off and tell your fellows that they have found a new friend, a Hebrew!"

The asp slipped away into the desert, and ever afterwards Jesus had mastery of serpents; he communicated the Psyllian's word to his disciples not long before he was crucified.

But the Gadelian refrained from following Jesus's example. He said: "I have little need of the word. There are no serpents in my country since my ancestor Gadelos expelled them with his wand."

When Jesus and the Gadelian parted, they exchanged tokens of love. The Gadelian went travelling into Africa, and Jesus returned to Nazareth to his carpentering, to meditate on all that he had learned. They had agreed that if either were at any time driven from his own land he would take refuge in the other's.

CHAPTER SEVENTEEN

FOUR BEASTS OF HOREB

AT NAZARETH Jesus found his mother in good health and lodged in her house for a while. She asked him no questions and he told her little of what had happened to him in Egypt. He learned from her that his brother Jose was prospering in trade at near-by Bethlehem; but that James, grown more and more pious, had taken vows and gone to join an ascetic society in Lower Transjordania, called Ebionites or "the poor men". The Ebionites were an off-shoot of the Essenes, from whom they differed chiefly in their abstention from the study of astrology, in never cutting their hair or drinking wine, and in not cloistering themselves in a compound. Their self-imposed task was calling the people to repentance and praying for them. They abominated blood-sacrifices and kept the Passover in the old style, as a festival of the barley-harvest, rejecting as spurious the passage in the Book of Exodus which orders the Paschal lamb to be ritually eaten at Jerusalem every year by all pious Jewish households. This was only one of many passages in the Books of Moses which they rejected: they accepted, for example, only a few verses of Deuteronomy, the book first published in the reign of Good King Josiah, which gave a pretended antiquity and divine sanction to current Temple practices. They lived on alms, which they did not, however, solicit; and the Transjordanians considered it meritorious to support such holy men, whose knees were as calloused as their bare feet, by constant prayer.

Jesus now went into partnership with one Judas, a carpenter from Capernaum, who resembled him in size, build and the colour of his hair. The sight of Jesus and Judas rhythmically sawing down a tree together with a two-handled saw gave Judas the nickname "the Twin" or, in the Aramaic, "Thomas"; for every third man in Nazareth was a Judas and all had distinguishing nicknames. Jesus attended the synagogue regularly and took his turn as the attendant who presented the sacred scrolls for reading by the synagogue elders, afterwards returning them to the sacred coffer. He also sometimes led the prayers, but refrained from expounding the Law, or from making use of the great powers that he had acquired in Egypt. He was patiently awaiting a sign. He waited for another seven years, lodging now in Thomas's house and giving most of his earnings to the poor; for he took to heart the text from Tobit: "Alms deliver a man from death."

The sign came at last during a visit from his brothers Judah and Simeon, who were now settled at Cana again. Almost the first words that Judah addressed to him were: "Brother Jesus, will you come with us down to Beth Arabah to be cleansed of your sins?"

Taken aback, he answered: "I am grateful to you for your solicitude, brother. But of what sins do I need to be cleansed? Evidently you are offended in me."

"What man is free of sin? And do you not commit a sin of presumption in asking me: 'Of what sins do I need to be cleansed?'"

"If I have offended, may the Lord forgive me! Have you also invited our brother Jose?"

"We have not. He is vexed with us over a small matter of a broken harness."

"Because a harness breaks, should the bond of brotherhood break with it? But tell me, brothers, who is to cleanse me of my sins? The power to wash away sins is given only to certain Great Ones."

"Why, brother Jesus, have you not heard of the wonders that are being done by our cousin John of Ain-Rimmon? He is assuredly a Great One! With a mouth like the vent of a furnace he preaches repentance to the four quarters of the world, and he dips into the swift stream of Jordan all sinners who come to seek him out. When they emerge they are like new men."

"Tell me more about this baptist, and if your account pleases me I will come with you, perhaps."

"He spent seven years at Callirrhoë with the godly Essenes, but has since been granted a dispensation to travel. He baptized at Ain-Rimmon first, but since at Beth Arabah. He is tall and gaunt. His food is carobs and wild honey; his drink, water. He wears a broad leather girdle and a white coat of camel's hair."

228

"Camel's hair? The Essenes hold that whoever wears camel's hair is either a fool, a sinner or Elijah himself!"

"How so?"

"The very first prohibition in the Law against eating the flesh of unclean beasts is against eating that of the camel. The camel is no less unclean than the hare or the hog. Though our father Abraham accepted camels as a present from Pharaoh, it is not recorded that he touched or mounted them. We read that Laban, Jacob's father-in-law, owned a camel, or at least the saddle of a camel; but Laban was not of the seed of Abraham. Though King David possessed camels, they were put in the care of an Ishmaelite, not of a Jew, and were pack-beasts, used for trade with Damascus and Babylon. The Land of Uz, where Job lived, is not within the boundaries of Israel and doubtless Uzzites tended his camels. Brothers, a camel is a dangerous possession, since a hair from its hide may blow into a man's food and defile him; and how can he avoid defilement if he wears a coat of camel's hair?"

"Camel's hair is not camel's flesh!"

"If you found a hog's bristle in your broth, would you not turn faint and pour away the bowlful? Then if John is neither a fool nor a sinner yet dares to wear camel's hair, trusting that the angels will guard his mouth from hairs, he must be a man among men."

"At least we can tell you this: Doctors from the High Court at Jerusalem have questioned him and he denies that he is Elijah. He claims to be the prophet foretold in Isaiah: the outrider who clears the way for the King, preaching repentance."

"That same repentance which every prophet has preached since prophecy began?"

"He declares that it is not enough for us Jews to boast: 'We are sons of Abraham'; for our God can transform desert stones into sons of Abraham, if he so pleases. He also declares that the days of trial are upon us, that the axe is already laid at the root of every unprofitable tree. And now that the path of the Phoenix has crossed the path of the Dove (but this is a dark saying), he is preparing the way for one greater than himself."

Here was the sign at last: the Phoenix and the Dove! Jesus asked in the calmest tones that he could muster: "For another greater even than this Great One? For the Messiah, Son of David?"

"We suppose, rather, that he means the Son of Man foretold by the prophet Daniel, who is to ride up to Jerusalem seated on a storm-cloud. He says: 'His winnowing fan is in his hand and he will blow away the chaff from the threshing floor and burn it in unquenchable fire; but the grain he will save.' "

"Your account pleases me. I am ready to come with you to see whether our cousin is a prophet, a madman or such a pretender as Athronges was. But first, pray, make your peace with Jose."

"We will not be the first to speak; the fault was his."

"He declares that it was yours."

"He lies."

"I will come with you as mediator and cast the fault upon God's Adversary."

The three of them went to Jose's timber-yard at Bethlehem. All agreed to cast the fault of the quarrel upon God's Adversary. They kissed and were reconciled; but it was left to Jesus to replace the broken harness with a new one, for they were proud men.

Jose also consented to be baptized, and all four brothers set off together on the next day for Beth Arabah, which lies in the gorge of the Lower Jordan, close to where it enters the Dead Sea: a gloomy and desolate place, overhung by tremendous rocks. They found a crowd of people waiting to be baptized, women as well as men; some had even brought their children with them. John stood straddle-legged in midstream, as if at a sheep-shearing, and dipped under the water all who came to him. If they struggled, he held them by force until their breath rose in great bubbles, and prayed loud and earnestly over them. When they had regained the bank, choking and spluttering, they presently began to laugh, shout and dance, glorifying the Lord for the new vistas of holiness that opened for them.

As Jesus and his brothers watched, John cried out suddenly: "I baptize with water, but after me comes one who will baptize with fire. What sins I have not washed away, he will burn away. He will burn them, I say, to white ash and clinker!"

Jose, Judah and Simeon entered the water with a rush, not waiting their turns, shouldering men aside zealously. John baptized them, and coming out glorified, they began to dance and shout on the river-bank with the rest, though they had the reputation of being staid men. They cried to Jesus, who sat on a tree-stump apart from the crowd: "Go in now, laggard, and be cleansed! Oh, what a joyful thing it is to feel the burden fallen from the back! Go in now, brother, and be freed of your black crusted sins! Why do you dawdle there?"

"I await my turn."

"Well, well, as you please. But we are busy men and must return at once. The joy of sinlessness wings our heels." So off they went.

Jesus waited until everyone had been baptized and had turned for home. Then he advanced towards John, who, hurrying out of the water, embraced him and cried: "At last, at last!"

"My brothers urged me to accept your baptism, Cousin," said Jesus.

"Let it wait until it may serve as a lustration when I anoint you King."

"Who put the word 'King' into your mouth?"

"The Watchman of the Mountain, who is your former tutor Simeon."

"Of Mount Horeb, the navel of this earth?"

"The same."

They forded the Jordan and skirted the eastern shores of the Dead Sea, passing by Callirrhoë and the fortress of Machaerus, counted next to Jerusalem in strength, and crossing the River Arnon into Moab. Then they turned towards the south-west, past the sites of the ancient cities of Sodom and Gomorrah, and began to ascend the foothills of the mountain-wilderness of Seir. A weary journey took them to the Ascent of Akrabbim, the winding path linking Petra with Hebron, and there above them towered the splendid limestone peak of Madara, which, under the names of Mount Horeb, "the Mountain of the Glowing Sun", and of Mount Hor, appears in the Book of Exodus as the sacred seat of Jehovah. The Zadokites denied that Madara was Horeb, resenting that it should lie in Edomite rather than Israelitish territory; and, concluding that Moses led his people out of Egypt by way of the Red Sea rather than the Sea of Reeds—the lagoon that lies eastward from Pelusium—they attached the name of "Horeb" to Mount Sinai, which rises colossally above Cape Poseidon, between the two arms of the Red Sea. However, the Essenes have preserved the true tradition. Kadesh Barnea, the tribal centre of the Israelites during their later wanderings in the wilderness, lies a day's travel to the westward of Horeb; there Jehovah first appeared to Moses.

When they had crossed the pass, John said: "Rest here under this tree of wild broom and sleep well, for you will need a store of sleep to draw upon in the days and nights that lie ahead."

Jesus slept, and when he awoke in the morning he found a pitcher of water and a batch of freshly baked ember-loaves at his side. He heard John's voice from behind him: "Eat and drink well, then sleep again, Lord, for you will need a store of food and drink to draw upon in the days and nights that lie ahead."

Jesus ate and drank and afterwards slept again. When he awoke in the evening, he found more ember-loaves ready baked, and water in the same pitcher. John told him: "Eat and drink, sleep another few hours yet; the trial will be too hard for you otherwise."

Once more he ate and drank, and once more slept.

While Jesus lay asleep, John climbed in moonlight up the white crags of Horeb until he came to a watch-tower which the Essenes had built there for the Watchman.

Simon son of Boethus, now very aged, greeted John tremulously, asking him: "Is it good news?"

"It is good."

"He is come?"

"He lies asleep under the tree of Elijah and will present himself for trial to-morrow."

"Many years I have waited for this day!"

In the morning John brought Jesus before Simon. They kissed and Simon asked: "Lord, are you instructed in the figure?"

"I am instructed."

Simon said to the single disciple whom he had with him, Judas of Kerioth: "Conduct my Lord to his station!"

Judas led Jesus to a level platform under a thorn-bush, close to the peak of the mountain, and there left him.

It was noon; and with his forefinger Jesus drew a circle in the dust about himself, revolving sunwise three times. Then he divided the circle into four by means of a cross of equal arms, and seated himself in the southern quarter, facing towards the Red Sea and the desert lands of Arabia.

Ten days and ten nights he waited there patiently under the thorn-bush, unsleeping, his pulse and respiration slow, eating nothing and drinking nothing, preoccupied with his vigil. On the morning of the tenth day, as the sun rose from the direction of Elam, a loud roaring sounded in his ears and it seemed to him that out of the eye of the sun a huge tawny lion with bloody jaws sprang into the circle to devour him. He addressed the lion: "Enter in peace, God's creature! There is room for both of us in this circle." He remembered the allegory in which Jehovah sent an angel to stop the lions' mouths that would otherwise have devoured the prophet Daniel. The lion roared and ramped for anger, lashing its tufted tail; but could do Jesus no harm, being confined by the cross within the eastern quarter of the circle.

232

Ten more days and nights passed. On the twentieth day at noon, it seemed that a wild he-goat with a single horn capered into the circle from the rear; and as the lion was Anger, so the goat was Lust. Jesus turned and said: "Enter in peace, God's creature! There is room for the three of us in this circle." The goat, which was of immense size, danced lecherously, rolling its eyes and tossing its horn; the smell of its rut was as pervasive as that of ambergris. Jesus remembered another allegory of the prophet Daniel, where it is written: "The he-goat waxed very great, but when he was strong, his great horn was broken." The goat could do Jesus no harm, being confined within the northern quarter of the circle. So lion and goat continued with him ten more days.

Then, at sunset, on the last day of his vigil, from the western side of the circle came a still more terrible beast: it was a seraph, a fiery serpent with fangs, hissing and rattling its brazen scales; and as the power of the lion was Anger, and that of the goat was Lust, so the seraph's power was Fear. Jesus said: "Enter in peace, God's creature! There is room for the four of us in this circle." But though he spoke the word of Love that he had learned from the Psyllian, the seraph hissed and darted its head towards him from sunset to midnight; and this was the hardest trial of all. But he remembered how good King Hezekiah had broken in pieces the seraph whom the men of Jerusalem held in awe, crying: "It is a mere piece of brass." The seraph could do Jesus no harm, being confined within the western quarter of the circle.

Then, at dawn, it seemed that the three creatures were joined together into one, with lion's head, goat's body and legs, seraph's tail. He recognized the Chimaera of the Carians, which is an emblem of their three seasons—for, like the Etruscans, they do not reckon the dead season of winter in their sacred year. The lion was the springtime aspect of the waxing sun; the goat the midsummer aspect of the sun in glory; the seraph the autumn aspect of the waning sun. "And I am child to the white bull of winter." Turning, he was suddenly aware that a great white bull had all the while shared the southern quarter of the circle with him, stretched out at his left side. But as soon as he attempted to study its power, it vanished. He said: "This beast has shared the southern quarter with me. Is it my secret fault? May our God protect me from its power!"

At noon the month of thirty days and nights was over, and out of the circle Jesus stepped; the lion, goat and seraph, discrete again, following subserviently at his heels. Thereafter he had authority over these three Powers: over Anger, Lust and Fear. But the thought of the white bull troubled him exceedingly.

Simon, as Master of the Trials, came up to greet him. He said: "Lord, you have endured your vigil well. The three beasts follow at your heel. Now is the time to break your fast. Here is bread freshly baked and fresh spring water fetched from the source of the Madara brook."

"Do not deceive me! You know that ten days and nights remain to be endured. Forty days were required of Moses and of Elijah on this very mountain—neither of whom ate bread or drank water during all that time."

"Moses was a prophet, Elijah was a prophet. But are you not more than a prophet? How are you bound by such trifles as a count of days?"

The smell of the water and of the freshly baked bread was delicious, yet Jesus took the bread, broke it, scattered it for the birds to eat and poured the water over his hands lest any fragment of bread should have clung to them.

Simon said: "Lord, that was honestly done. But why do you not change these stones into loaves and this sand into water: then though you eat stones, not bread, and drink sand, not water, your pangs will be eased."

"It is written that man shall not live by bread alone, but by the word of our God. My soul has eaten bread of Bethlehem for thirty days, and drunk water of Bethlehem." At these words, it seemed to Simon, a wild boar sprang up from where the bread was cast and followed obediently behind Jesus with the other three beasts; which was the power of Greed.

Simon said: "Lord, that was honestly done. Now you shall see your reward."

He led him up to a pinnacle of the mountain, and desired him to look east and west and north and south.

"Here," he said, "a fine prospect extends, does it not? To the west, the Mediterranean Sea and ancient Egypt; to the east, Moab and Elam; to the south, Arabia; to the north—ah, to the north the Holy Land of Israel stretches as far as Hermon, whose snowy peak glitters at us invitingly. Yet the regions that you view are in extent as nothing to those that will presently be yours. Beyond Arabia lie Ethiopia and Ophir and the Land of Frankincense; beyond Egypt lie Libya and Mauretania; beyond Elam lies India; beyond Israel lie Syria, Asia and the Black Sea; beyond the Mediterranean Sea lie Greece, Italy, Gaul, Spain, and the Land of the Hyperboreans. At the point of the lance you will drive the Romans out from every land that they have overrun; you will also break the Kings of the South and East; you will establish the Empire of our God over all the one hundred and fifty-three nations, to become the King of Kings, the greatest who ever reigned. Alexander beside you will seem a mere robber-chieftain!"

"It is recorded that the great Caesar killed a million men; Pompey the Great two million; Alexander the Great three million. Must your servant destroy ten million or more to earn the title of 'Greatest'? How may this be? Is your servant a warrior? Is it his destiny to spill blood and rule by the sword? And is it not written: 'Thou shalt not kill'?"

"Your ancestor David had never put on armour, yet the Spirit of the Lord came upon him in the valley of Elah and in the sight of two armies he destroyed Goliath the champion of the Philistines, whose height was six cubits and a span, and rescued his nation from oppression. Do you shrink from battle? Is it not prophesied that the Son of David shall rescue his people by a mighty hand, that he shall be victorious in a bloody battle, and shall restore peace to Israel for a thousand years?"

"Let others choose the path of conquest and petulantly sever with the sword the master-knot of mystery as did Alexander at Gordium. Let it rather be granted to me to weave the same sacred knot again, with golden wire, fastening it to the canopy bar above my throne. Have you not heard the judgement of the wise Hillel, how he said to the skull floating in the lake: 'Because you drowned, you are drowned; but in the end those who drowned you shall also drown'? So I say: 'The sword makes no decision, but only confusion; and he who lives by the sword, by the sword must perish.' The battle to be fought is on another field."

"Lord, that was honestly spoken. •Let the battlefield be of whatever kind you please: only rule your people and deliver them. You shall master the Empire of the Romans in the name of the Lord of this Mountain, whose image is the golden calf which was set up in this very place when the tribes first came out of Egypt. Look yonder, where his apparition stands gleaming. He is the gracious bull-calf of the Cow Leah (which is to say Libnah, the White One), the universal Mother whom the Greeks call Io and the Egyptians Isis or Hathor. Adore him now as he deserves, and the whole world through which his raging mother wandered, stung by the breese, is yours!"

"Would you have me adore a golden calf?"

235

"What else did Solomon worship, who was the wisest of men?"

"Behind me, God's Adversary! Is it not written: 'Thou shalt worship the Lord thy God, and him only shalt thou serve'?"

At these words it seemed to Simon that an elephant with a gilt tower on its back lurched from behind a rock and followed obediently behind Jesus with the other four beasts; which was the power of Pride.

Simon cried: "That was honestly spoken. I had feared that you might make the same choice that your grandfather Herod made at Dora—Herod whose mother was the heiress of Nabataean Lat and who married Doris, the heiress of Edomite Dora. Offered a kingdom greater than that of Solomon, with all the honours and trappings of royalty, if only he would bow his knee to the Baal of Dora, he swallowed the bait. Thus Herod was proved unworthy of the greater kingdom that you have chosen: the greater kingdom that carries with it the greater curse. He chose the lesser curse, which is a long, happy life with disaster at the close; but you will be shipwrecked before your prime."

"It is no news to me that Herod bowed to the Golden Onager. Tell me, rather, of his eldest son, enroyalled by birth from Caleb and by marriage with the Heiress of Michal."

"He reigned, but only as his father's son. Because he shrank from taking arms against his father his end was inglorious."

"No, but glorious; in a dream I have seen him sitting under a silver-blossomed apple-tree in an orchard of apples, the Western Paradise."

The fortieth night rolled away. At noon Jesus broke his fast with a little barley-porridge and smelt at an apple which John fetched him.

Then Simon broke into a song of praise which is still chanted among Chrestians, though its context is unknown except to a few initiates: "Lord, now let your servant depart in peace according to your word. For his eyes have seen your salvation, which is prepared before the face of all nations: to be a light to illumine the Gentiles and to glorify your people Israel."

He died there, on the very peak where Aaron the first High Priest had died, his life's work ended.

CHAPTER EIGHTEEN

THE TEREBINTH FAIR

SIMON was buried on Horeb in a cleft of the rock and John returned to Beth Arabah. Under the care of Judas of Kerioth, Jesus slowly regained his strength. After ten days he left the mountain and made for Hebron, fifty miles distant to the north, by way of the tortuous Ascent of Akrabbim.

Judas of Kerioth (a village not far from Hebron) accompanied him as his disciple. He was a prudent, generous-souled and learned man, formerly in partnership with his uncle, a merchant in the salt-fish trade, and had become an Ebionite from disgust with the world, after being wrongfully accused of incest with his uncle's young wife, who had thereupon hanged herself. He was to prove of great service to Jesus, for ten years of business had taught him to understand the ways of the Romans with their Greek and Syrian hangers-on, and how to address magistrates, synagogue officials, town-clerks and the like with dignified urbanity; seven years with the Ebionites had also taught him to understand the ways of the poor and the outcast.

At a narrow place in the pass the two overtook the rear-guard of a great company of men travelling together for safety through this desolate, bandit-ridden country. They seemed for the most part to be Edomites, and Arabians from Sinai, but among them were a party of Phoenician merchants, and two Greeks dressed in the grey cloaks of philosophers.

Judas saluted the captain of the rear-guard, an Arabian, and asked him courteously why the whole party wore mourning garments: had any public calamity occurred of which news had not reached him?

"We are pilgrims going to Hebron to mourn for our ancestor Abraham and sacrifice to his shade. Are you ignorant that on the day after to-morrow the Terebinth Fair begins? Our train of two hundred asses and camels is carrying valuable merchandise there."

"Graciously permit my master and myself to join your caravan. We also are Sons of Abraham."

"Of what nation?"

"We are Jews. My master is a holy man; I am his disciple."

That night, over a camp-fire of thorns, a group of learned pilgrims were discussing the antiquities of Hebron. Now, according to the Book of Genesis, it was in this fertile, cool and sheltered valley, which lies four thousand feet above the level of the Mediterranean Sea, that Abraham planted a sacred grove known as the Oaks of Mamre in honour of Jehovah, and dug a well. He was buried not far off in the cave of Machpelah, which he recorded to have bought from Ephron, one of the Children of Heth, as a burial-place for his sister Sarah, who was also his wife. The patriarchs Isaac and Jacob, with their wives Rebeccah and Leah, are recorded to have been buried in the same cave. But a merchant from Petra declared this account to be erroneous. "What the Jews call the Oaks of Mamre, we Petraeans call the Oaks of Miriam. According to our tradition, Miriam, sister of the demi-god Moses, was the goddess of those Calebites who came up from the south with the Jews and seized Hebron from the Anakim. The Jews, who have an aversion to all goddesses, conceal the truth by a transliteration and pretend that the place is named after a certain Mamre, an Amorite, brother to Eshcol. But you will see Miriam's effigy displayed in the sacred grove; she is a Love-goddess with a fish-tail like the Aphrodite of Joppa. The people of Hebron pretend that the effigy represents Sarah, wife of Abraham."

At this the elder Greek philosopher, a Spartan, who was making a tour of the world with his son in search of geographical knowledge, exclaimed: "Miriam is her name? She must be the ancient Phrygian Sea-goddess Myrine, who gave her name to the chief city of·Lemnos, and who according to Homer was the ancestress of the Dardanians of Troy. Scholiasts equate her with the Aegean Sea-goddess Thetis, or Tethys, whose name is linked by the mythographers with that of the hero Peleus. What if the Children of Heth were Aegeans, the Children of Thetis, and Machpelah was at one time an oracular shrine of *magus Peleus,* or Peleus the sooth-sayer?"

"You are suggesting, Father," asked his son, "that the Jews and Calebites whose ancestor was Abraham expelled Thetis from the shrine in favour of their goddess Sarah?"

"No, but rather that the clan of Caleb supplanted the clan of Ephron in the favour of Thetis, whom they renamed Sarah. Can any man here speak on the subject of this Sarah?"

The merchant from Petra answered: "Little is recorded of her except that she laughed at an angel who assured Abraham that her descendants were to outnumber the sands of the seashore."

"Good," said the elder Greek. "Then you may depend upon it that she is entitled to her fish-tail, and that Heth, Miriam and Sarah are a single deity. The mention of the seashore is sufficient indication, even if it were not for the laugh. Sea-goddesses, who are invariably also goddesses of Love, are famous for their laughter. I would have you know, Sirs, that this question is of more than academic interest to my son and myself. Our two Jewish fellow-travellers will bear me out when I maintain that we Spartans, being Dorians, are also Sons of Abraham."

Jesus kept silence, for he caught a mocking intonation in the Greek's voice, but Judas answered politely: "It is so. The historian of the First Book of Maccabees quotes a letter sent by your King Areus to Onias the High Priest of Jerusalem, shortly after the death of Alexander the Great. He claimed a cousinship of the two nations in virtue of a common descent from Abraham. A further letter was sent to the Spartans by Simon the Maccabee a century and a half later, confirming this cousinship. Yet I cannot think that you Dorians are Abraham's sons by Sarah; I suppose rather by his wife Keturah or by Hagar."

The Greek smiled indulgently. "Well, it is possible that Areus was right, and possible also that he was confusing Abraham with Hercules; both heroes are renowned for their readiness to destroy their sons. But as a lifelong student of myths I am prepared, rather, to believe that certain of our ancestors, in common with yours, once worshipped the same Sea-goddess at the Oaks of Mamre. Mind you, the legends of Hebron are so confused that I cannot commit myself outright to the theory that Heth was Thetis; she may perhaps have been Hathor, the Lady of the Turquoise, whose name means 'The abode of the Sun-god', that is to say 'The Sea'. So also Pelah may well have been the eponymous ancestor of the Pulesati, or Philistines."

"Who or what, then, do you suppose Abraham to have been, learned Greek?"

"The clue lies in his name, which, according to your tradition, was changed from 'Abram' on his arrival at Hebron. Some of your Doctors whom I have questioned say confidently that it means 'God Loves'. Others are less confident; and I have been convinced by a famous scholar of Alexandria who holds that the original change was from Aburamu, 'the Father is the High One', to Abrahab, meaning the 'Son of Rahab' or 'Rahab's chosen one'. Rahab is the common title of the Sea-goddess whom the Jews picture as a devouring sea-dragon, and a poetic name for Egypt in so far as Israel was swallowed by her but belched up again like Jason or Job. He holds that the

239

'Rahab' in Abraham's name was subsequently altered to 'Raham', the name of a so-called grandson of the hero Hebron, to break Abraham's dependence upon her. Therefore when you ask me: 'Who or what was Abraham?' I reply: 'A title of the kings of Hebron after the capture of the shrine by the Aramaeans.' "

Judas objected: "Learned Greek, you are right in making Abraham an Aramaean, for the formula at the first-fruits ceremony runs: 'A wandering Aramaean was my father.' But if you say that Abraham is a title of the former kings of Hebron, on the strength of Abraham's tomb, you might as well say the same of Abner. For the tomb of Abner son of Ner lies not far from that of Abraham. Though you may dispute the meaning of Abraham, beyond all doubt Abner means 'God is my Lamp', and a lamp has from the time of Moses been used in the cult of our God."

"Remind me of Abner. How did he die?"

"He was the chieftain from whom King David demanded Michal of Hebron in marriage, and was killed there by David's servants. David was his chief mourner."

"Then he must have been the king of Hebron whom David dispossessed. But Abner may equally mean, 'the chosen of Nereis'—another title of the same Sea-goddess, which gives the Nereids their name. Caleb must also be a royal title here. What is the meaning of Caleb? I am no Hebraist."

"It means Dog," answered the merchant of Petra. "I hardly think that 'Dog' would be a royal title."

"And why not?" chattered the Greek. "Why should not the Calebites have been Sons of the Dog-star? And unless the oracular cave of Machpelah differs from all other ancient oracular caves that my son and I have visited in our travels, the Great Goddess who inspires the oracles is also a dog. She is a dog both because of her promiscuity in love and because she is an eater of corpses; in her honour as lovely Isis, or Astarte, her initiates wear dog-masks, and in her honour as deathly Hecate, or Brimo, dogs are sacrificed where three roads meet. The Dog-star shines in the most pestilent season of the year. And dogs have always guarded the land of the dead for the Great Goddess. Witness Cerberus, and Egyptian Anubis, guardian of the Western Paradise. And is there no connexion between Caleb and the Goddess Calypso, queen of the Paradisal Island of Ogygia, whom the poets describe as a daughter of Oceanus and Tethys, or of Nereus, or of Atlas Telamon? And is not 'The Power of the Dog' a poetic synonym for Death in Hebrew poetry? I have read David's Psalms in Greek translation."

240

"Oracles are no longer given in the cave," said Judas, "since Good King Josiah blocked up the entrance to the innermost of the three chambers, the one in which the oracle of Adam was delivered to Caleb in the time of Moses. Only two chambers are now accessible, the inner one containing the tombs of the three patriarchs and their wives."

"An oracle of Adam? Not of Abraham? I had taken Adam for a primitive Chaldean hero."

"According to our Ebionite tradition he was both created and buried at Hebron. The Angel Michael formed him from dust within a mystic circle, scraping it together from east, west, south and north. When he and the Second Eve, his wife, were tricked by God's Adversary into disobeying the divine orders, he remained in Hebron (after a long penitential immersion up to the neck in Jordan), but outside the Garden, the entrances to which were guarded by seraphs; after many years he died at Hebron and was buried in the cave of Machpelah."

The merchant from Petra cried: "Michael? I think you are mistaken. Was not Adam the parthenogenous son of the Nymph Michal, otherwise called Miriam? And I will take you up on another point, Ebionite! The oracle is not silent, as you say. It is still to be consulted. The pythoness who controls the oracle is called Mary the Hairdresser."

The Greek asked: "In whose name does this woman speak oracles?"

"In the name of the Mother, using the oracular jawbone of Adam."

Judas interposed: "How can that be? It is recorded that when, after some seven years' residence at Hebron, King David moved his capital to Jerusalem, and there set up the Ark on the threshing-floor previously sacred to Araunah, he carried Adam's skull away with him and buried it as a protective charm at a cross-roads outside the City. Jerusalem thus became a colony of Hebron: as the prophet Ezekiel writes: 'Thy father was an Amorite'—I suppose that Mamre is intended—'thy mother á Daughter of Heth'."

"Yet David left the jawbone and the remainder of the skeleton. No, no, it is as I say! My own brother, now dead, has consulted the pythoness; by his account this Mary is a woman greatly to be feared."

The talk ran on, but Jesus took no part in it. The elder Greek said: "It interests me that this Fair coincides with the mourning season kept at Athens and Rome: the May season of purification, when sin-puppets of rushes are thrown into running water, and sexual intercourse is forbidden even between husband and wife, and temples are swept out and the sacred images washed and scrubbed,

241

and torches and lamps drive evil spirits from the fruit-trees, and everyone goes about without laughter in dirty clothes. I am told that almost precisely the same customs are observed at the Oaks of Mamre, but that the Festival has no sequel. Mourning and a religious ban on sexual intercourse normally imply that when the ban is lifted a sexual orgy ensues, with pent-up passions surging to joyful madness; but here, they say, nothing at all happens of that sort."

The Arabian captain laughed. "Hebron is no longer what it was when Absalom, the rebellious son of David, companied promiscuously on the palace roof in the sight of all the people with twenty or more princesses of his father's harem. But 'nothing at all' is an under-statement. Why do you suppose that we Arabians bring our barren wives to Hebron if not to be made fertile by the Kerm-king? But those rites, and the rite of equitation in which the Jebusite girls are deflowered by him, take place over the hill, outside the town limits, when the Fair is over."

"Now, who in the world is the Kerm-king?" asked the younger Greek.

"The murderer of the Terebinth-king for whom we mourn at this festival; and the principal mourner himself."

"Then Father Abraham is the Terebinth-king?"

The merchant of Petra explained: "The sacred grove consists of two sorts of oaks: the kerm-oak and the terebinth-oak. The Terebinth and Kerm-kings are twins and rivals, like Aleyn, the Osiris of Sinai, and his brother Mot. They share the year, and the favours of the Queen, equally between them. The son of the murdered Terebinth-king enjoys his revenge at the September New Year, when he murders the Kerm-king his uncle, and becomes his principal mourner, and succeeds to the Kingdom."

"Yes," said the Arabian, "we call the Terebinth-king Abraham, but the Jews are not pleased with us for doing so, for you will soon see what sort of a patriarch this Abraham is, and what a beauty is his fish-tailed wife."

It should here be explained that the terebinth, or pistachio-oak, is highly valued in Palestine because of its sweet nut and the valuable oil it yields, and because of the thick shade it affords in summer. It is the equivalent there of the royal oak, sacred to Mercury or Zeus in Greece, to Jupiter in Italy and to the Celtic Hercules in Gaul. As timber of the royal oak is almost invariably used in making statutes of these Western gods, so is that of terebinth-oak for the corresponding rustic gods of Palestine: indeed, "terebinth" and "statute" are synonymous terms in Hebrew.

The kerm-oak, or holly-oak, or scarlet oak, as it is variously called, is the evergreen tree that produces the kerm-berry, from which is extracted the sacred scarlet dye for which Hebron is famous. Some authorities deny that the kerm-berry is a fruit, on the ground that the tree also yields acorns: they take it for a sluggish female insect, since a peculiar fly, perhaps the male, is often found hovering near it. But in appearance, at least, it is a juicy berry and is credited with strong aphrodisiac virtue.

"Upon my word," said the Greek, "I am slowly beginning to understand the complex mythology of Hebron. Here, perhaps, you have a clue to the origin of the Aeolian double kingdom, as at Sparta, Argos, and Corinth; and also an explanation of the myths of Hercules and his twin Iphiclus, of Romulus and his twin Remus, of Idas and Lynceus, of Calaïs and Zetes, Pelias and Neleus, Proeteus and Acrisius who quarrelled for precedence within their mother's womb, and the numerous other pairs of royal twins that stud Apollodorus's mythological dictionary. But if Adam and Abraham and Abner are one, what of the dead heroes Isaac and Jacob who are also supposedly interred at Hebron?"

"They were Abraham's son and grandson," said Judas. "Isaac son of Sarah, whom we Ebionites call the Son of Laughter, lived at Beer-Lahai-Roi near Kadesh—the well of the antelope-ox's jawbone. It lies some fifty miles from here, to the southward."

"Good. Then the *boubalos,* or antelope-ox, must have been his sacred beast, and the well must have been an oracular one. And since laughing Sarah was his mother, laughing Isaac must have been one of the kings of Hebron. And Jacob?"

Judas was distressed at the freedom of the conversation, but the merchant of Petra replied: "At Petra we style him Jah Akeb, the demi-god of the sacred heel. He dislocated his right thigh in the wrestling ring so that his foot went into spasm and his heel was raised from the ground. By this means it was protected against scorpion, asp or the bristle of the boar maliciously laid in his path by his enemies; and for this reason it is held unlucky to mock at a cripple."

"Our Western gods Hephaestus and Vulcan are similarly lame," said the elder Greek, nodding sagely, "and so is Egyptian Ptah."

The younger Greek said: "Not only those three, Father. The Sicilians explain the name Dionysus as meaning not 'Zeus of Nysa' but 'Zeus the Lame'. Did the buskins on which he is depicted as swaggering originally compensate for an injury to his thigh, like those gold shoes of Hephaestus which Homer mentions? He is called Merotraphes, which may well mean 'One who takes good care of his thigh'. And now that you have mentioned the King of Argos, I recall that one King of Argos at least was lame and wore buskins: Nauplius the Argonaut. If the King of Hebron was either chosen king because of his lameness or ceremonially lamed when chosen, surely Jacob is also a dynastic title, not the name of a historical character?"

The elder Greek praised his son's acuteness.

"I know nothing and care nothing about your Greek gods," said the merchant, "but I can tell you something else about Jacob, which is that he dislocated his thigh at the marriage games at Penuel when he took the name of his wife Rachel and became Ish-rachel, or Israel. This sanctified his thigh, and from that day to this Jews do not eat the thigh-flesh of sacrificed beasts. And when he bound his son Joseph to an oath, he required him to place his hand under his sacred thigh; and nobody else in the Scriptures is recorded to have bound anyone by this form of oath, except Abraham."

"And what does the name Rachel mean?" asked the elder Greek.

"It means 'The Ewe'."

"That clinches the matter. For the Dove-goddess of Cyprus, who, as we learn from the myths of Cinyras and Adonis, had a Palestinian counterpart, is also a Ewe-goddess. Jacob's marriage was doubtless with the Queen of Hebron."

However, except for Jesus, nobody present could follow the ramblings of their argument, and he uttered no word either of approval or dissent.

At last the caravan reached Hebron, which was packed with pilgrims. The Fair was being held about a mile outside the town towards Jerusalem. The route lay along a fine flagged road through the extensive vineyards of Eshcol from which Joshua and Caleb, acting as spies for Moses, cut enormous bunches of grapes as samples of the prosperity of Canaan. On their left rose a hill terraced for olives and crowned with two very large standing-stones. The elder Greek said: "I wonder that one of your reforming kings did not remove those two sacred baetyls and convert them into rollers of a royal olive-mill."

"You are mistaken, Sir," Judas answered. "Those are not baetyls. They are the posts of the ancient town gates of Gaza which the hero Samson is recorded in the Book of Judges to have carried away, bar and all, from his Philistine enemies and planted there in scorn."

"Well," said the Greek, "to me they are plain baetyls raised in honour of the variously named goddess of this place. For it is clear that this shrine has had as many divine claimants as that of Delphi, which began as an oracle of the Python-priestess of Brimo and the Furies and was later captured by Apollo on behalf of his Hyperborean mother Latona of the palm-tree. Some say that the Bee-goddess Cybele also held the shrine for a while. But Apollo, who contains within himself the shades of numerous gods and demons, is now the sole master of Delphi. All secluded hill shrines with vents crannying down to Hades are the natural location of mysteries presided over by Sibyls: tribes destroy one another to gain possession of them and add the bones of their own oracular heroes to those already there. That the Sea-goddess should have become established here at Hebron is strange at first sight: one would not have expected to find her perched up on a high mountain so far from her native element. But Hebron is on a height between three seas—the Dead Sea, the Red Sea and the Mediterranean. And we must, of course, be careful to distinguish the Sea-goddess, who is a goddess of Love, from her sister-selves, the goddess of Birth, and the goddess of Death."

He went up with his son to examine the stones, and both came back delighted with the immensely wide prospect which opened to the west: a great part of the hill country of Judaea and a long stretch of what had once been Philistia. For this was the highest point of the Negeb range, and they could look across the rugged intervening ridges to the coastal plain, and forty miles or more away, to the row of famous cities: Gaza, Ascalon, Ashdod and Jamnia, and the broad sea stretching beyond. "If your Samson carried those posts up from Gaza," they pronounced, "he was a man who could have stuffed our Hercules into his wallet as a shepherd stuffs a strayed lamb."

They came to the Oaks of Mamre and Abraham's well lying close by, where a tent-village housing thousands of people had sprung up around a few ancient stone houses. The Sons of Abraham, all dressed in their oldest clothes—though the women by contrast wore holiday finery—were a motley, jabbering assemblage of Arabians, Edomites, Ishmaelites, Midianites, Jews, Galileans, Phoenicians, Dorites and Transjordanians. In the middle of the camp stood a stone altar held to mark the spot where Abraham heard the angel announce the approaching birth of his son Isaac. The place was shaded by the largest terebinth in existence, said to be coeval with the world, and by fifteen other trees of lesser size and age, embellished with votive garments tied around the trunks and, as the evening drew on, twinkling with numerous lanterns hung from the branches. The altar, of undressed stone, was red with the blood of sacrificed beasts and birds—chiefly cocks, rams and bulls—that flowed off into troughs and was subsequently used for sprinkling the fruit-trees and vines of the district to promote their fertility.

Loud and ceaseless mourning was made for Abraham's recumbent ithyphallic effigy, a sort of Osiris, which lay in state beside the altar waiting to be carried in procession to the well and there washed. This was done shortly after Jesus and his travelling companions arrived, and then, amid frightful howling, the image, which was golden-faced and ram-horned, with blue turquoise eyes, was liberally anointed with terebinth oil and laid in a coffin, while frankincense was burned to ward off evil spirits, and libations of wine poured on the earth to satisfy the thirsty dead. After this, the coffin was taken in procession to Machpelah, which lies nearer the town, and laid in the inner cave for safe keeping until the Autumn New Year.

The chief mourner was, as the Arabian had said, the murderous Kerm-king, a goat-headed, scarlet-faced, agate-eyed, phallic idol, borne upright. The two Greeks pronounced this King of Mamre to be indistinguishable from the Mamurius idols of the remote Latin villages and from the Hermes idols of Arcadia. His queen was a big-buttocked, spikenard-scented, scarlet-cloaked goddess with enormous breasts and a fish's tail, her face painted green with copper malachite as a Love-goddess's face should be, and necklaces of jewels and sea-shells about her neck. In one hand was a porpoise, in the other a dove. The elder Greek recalled an exactly similar festival at a terebinth grove sacred to the Sea-goddess of Cyprus; the grove, he said, is called Treminthus, which is the Cypriot word for terebinth.

The Jews and Edomites who attended the Fair for business purposes were careful to avoid looking at the royal images, or contaminating themselves with any idolatrous practice and, though they wailed with the rest, said that they did so to deplore the sacrifices offered to an obscene block of wood, not for any other reason. The Temple authorities at Jerusalem had long since forbidden the public orgies which formerly concluded the festival, but had refrained from removing the idols for fear of cutting off the valuable trade which the Fair attracted. The booths were arranged in circles and stocked with a wonderful variety of goods—gums, spices and perfumes were the chief foreign products offered—and the sanctity of the Fair was such that nobody carried arms or feared for his safety. For religious reasons, the pilgrims were forbidden to drink the well-water during the days of mourning, but were allowed to drop presents of silver and gold into it.

Jesus, though accustomed from his Egyptian childhood to the sight of idolatry, was grieved that it should be flourishing in a spot so sacred as this. He did not consider it his duty to interrupt or denounce the religious practices of strangers, but, being determined to measure and subdue the power of the Female, he searched out the merchant of Petra and asked him where Mary the Hairdresser was to be found.

The amused merchant answered: "Ask any of the harlots who have come here to catch the trade of the Fair. You will find them in an olive orchard beyond the hill waiting to welcome those Sons of Abraham who are less scrupulous in their mourning than others. Mary is their queen. A jill-of-all-trades is Mary. She dresses their hair for them, with embellishment of tresses stolen from the dead, receives their stolen jewels, regulates their prices, provides them with the necessary charms and philtres, and lays them out when they come to die. Though too old to continue in the profession, she rules them absolutely and they stand in mortal dread of her."

"Of what nation is she?"

"Mary is a Kenite, and so are most of her women. But let me advise you: it is best not to meddle with the Hairdresser. She will take the flesh of the ox, as they say, and leave you with the hide, bones and umbles."

Jesus thanked the merchant and, dismissing Judas for a while, went over the hill to the olive orchard. It was evening and the moon had just risen. He found the prostitutes dancing in a circle of admirers to tambourine and flute music. A party of young Arabians raised loud laughter when they saw him. "Oho! Oho! A Jew, here comes a Jew, and a holy one at that, by the cut of his beard!" Jesus observed that most of the women's customers were Arabians; it is true that of the ten measures of lechery given to the world, Arabia has taken nine.

Two or three Kenite girls who stood aside from the dance ran up to him. He addressed them cheerfully: "Daughters, I have not come to buy from you. I am under vows. But where is your queen to be found?"

At this they laughed more loudly even than the men and caused such a commotion that the flute-players laid down their flutes and turned round to see what was happening. The dance stopped. Soon a crowd of idle and inquisitive people clustered about him.

"What do you want with Mary, handsome fellow?" the women asked him. "A love-philtre? No? Then an oracle perhaps? Not an oracle? An injurious charm to bury in the sand under your neighbour's gate? A little quillful of poison to end the whining of a sick wife?"

"I am not buying to-night, busy daughters," Jesus answered.

"Then you are selling?" asked the leader of the dance, a Galilean by her dress and accent, tinkling her ankle-bells provokingly at him as she pranced up and down. "Aha, I have guessed your secret. Taper fingers, thieves' fingers! You are the clever fellow who tricked the watch and filched the fingers and nose of the bandit Obadas whom the Romans crucified by the pools of Bethlehem last week. But clever as you may be, Child, avoid the Hairdresser's company until the morning! A wise man will have no dealings with her unless he goes escorted by a trustworthy friend and in broad daylight. An incautious customer went to a rendezvous with her by moonlight three years ago, under Samson's pillars, hoping to sell her a hand-of-glory. She took the fellow by the wrist, pulled him between the pillars, slowly waved her hands before his face like weeds in a brook, and ordered him to lie down and sleep. When he awoke, she was gone; and so was the hand-of-glory. But the jest was, that when next he sneezed, he sneezed off his nose! It was a wax one that she had thoughtfully given him to replace the flesh and gristle she had taken off him."

"I am not selling to-night, daughter of Israel."

"I cannot guess your business then, Child. For nobody but a fool would seek out the Hairdresser, even by day, except to buy or sell."

"I am not revealing my business."

"Give me a blessing, with nothing in it said backwards, and I will take you to the place where she is to be found. But she will not greet you kindly; this is the night of her vigil in the willow."

"Do you indeed wish for a blessing?"

"Which of us does not? Blessings from holy men are hard to come by."

"Then may the Lord bless you with a sign of his mercy: a sudden splitting of the drum of your tambourine!"

She thrust out her tongue, returned to the dance and began beating her tambourine; but he followed her with his eyes and no sooner had she begun the movement called the Horse Leech than the drum suddenly split across. She stumbled, stopped, fell down and screamed. They carried her away and soused her with water; she stopped screaming, but did not dance again that night.

A Kenite girl said: "I will willingly conduct you to Mary the Hairdresser, holy spoilsport, and tell her of the broken tambourine."

"Do so, and earn my thanks."

She led him back over the hill and into the town. They came to the fish-pool of Hebron where the sacred fish had once been kept,

248

and she climbed over the wall of the enclosure and beckoned him to follow. But when they stood at the pool-side together, by a huge willow that leaned across a bed of reeds, she suddenly grew frightened. She left him there in the moonlight, saying as she ran off: "Knock at the door if you dare; she is within."

Jesus disdained to knock. He said in a voice of authority: "Willow-tree of Hebron, tree of death: for the sakes of Salmon and Salmah, and of Samson the strong who burst your green bonds apart, give up the witch who is hiding in your hollow trunk."

Mary the Hairdresser (who in Christian books is named Mary of Magdala) stepped out very angrily. She was a tall blue-eyed hag, her nose crooked like a falcon's beak. "Who disturbs my vigil?"

"Look!"

"I can see nothing."

"Your eyes are shut. Open them and you will see."

"Who gives me orders?"

"Unstop your ears, deaf adder, and you will hear."

"Master, what do you want of me?" she asked, taken aback.

"Your help against God's Adversary!"

"Against the champion of my Mistress?"

"Himself!"

"Follow me to my Mistress's house, madman, and dare repeat your request there!"

"I will come gladly."

CHAPTER NINETEEN

KING ADAM

MARY THE HAIRDRESSER led Jesus out through the gate of the enclosure, and past the entrance of the cave of Machpelah to a rocky place not far away where offal was flung. The pack of pariah dogs that had been nosing there among bones and rotten flesh howled a welcome to her, sitting in a row on their haunches. She ordered them to be silent; they ceased howling and whimpered softly. She picked her way through the filth to the rock-face and there uttered a prayer of placation in a language strange to Jesus, though he knew well who it was whom she invoked. Mary stood with her ear close to the rock as if waiting for an answer. Presently she pressed with her shoulder against a part of the rock that projected, and a great stone door rolled back in its socket. The moon shone full into a small square chamber from which a curved flight of steps descended into darkness.

They entered together and the stone clashed-to behind them. Mary pulled a lighted lamp from under her cloak and beckoned for Jesus to follow her. The air was sweet, and the shallow well-cut steps led them after a long spiral descent to another blank wall. She uttered the same prayer of placation and, after listening again and waiting and repeating the prayer, pressed against the stone, which rolled back in its socket.

They stood in a cave constructed in beehive shape with great unhewn slabs of limestone, painted in red and yellow ochre with spirals, double spirals, fylfots, reversed fylfots and forked lightning. In the middle rose a phallus-shaped pillar beside which lay a pair of crouched skeletons, one of them lacking its skull, and between them the gilded horns of an antelope-ox. Of the three recesses in the cave, the right-hand one was empty; in the left-hand recess stood two striped sacrificial basins, an ivory tripod, and the mask of a pale bearded man with sunken cheeks; in the central recess stood a small chest, with rings for two carrying poles, plated with gold and surmounted by golden cherubim. Opposite, a long narrow tunnel led away into darkness. Propped against the wall near its entrance were two narrow stone tablets, one of red Edomite sard and one of golden Numidian marble, carved on both sides with numerous small pictures.

Black blood coated the bottom of each of the striped basins. Jesus said to Mary in accusation: "It is bull's blood."

She asked him mockingly: "Have you not read how Moses raised a circle of twelve pillars and a thirteenth in the middle for an altar, and sacrificed bulls, and how he caught the gushing blood in these very basins?"

"I have read what I have read. But this blood is not that. You come here to lap bull's blood from the basins and to prophesy through the mouth of the death-mask in which Adam's jawbone is set."

"Whatever I do is done in obedience to my Mistress."

"I defy her in her own house!"

"Beware of gangrene in the thigh and leprosy in the lip!"

"Your Mistress has no power over me. I have never companied with any daughter of hers, nor ever called on her name. Therefore again I ask your help against her paramour."

"I refuse it, rebel. Why do you not abase yourself before the Cherubim? Do you not recognize the Holy Ark of the Covenant which the prophet Jeremiah restored to my Mistress for safe-keeping before he fled to Egypt?"

"The prophet Jeremiah did well to remove the thing from the sight of the congregation. Holy as it once was, the daughters of Aaron had defiled it with their abominations. It had become a thing of death, and he did well to lay it up in the house of death."

"Take my lamp and read the pictures on the two tablets, the golden and the red. They were laid up in the Ark together with the round black thunder-stone which your forefathers rolled about in it as a rain charm. Look, there the stone lies, at the foot of the Ark. It is the ancient dripping rock of Miriam, which (as is said) rolled and went along with Israel, and for striking which Moses forfeited his life."

He took the lamp and studied the tablets as if with indifference. "What are these to me, witch? Have I not read the Scriptures? Here, pictured in a confused order, are the annals of kings and princes and prophets of Israel."

"In your own heart lies the confusion. Here is one story and one story only. It runs bustrophedon—as one ploughs alternately from right to left and from left to right. When the golden tablet is done, the red begins. It is the story of the ancient covenant from which the Ark takes its name: the covenant sworn between my Mistress and the twin Kings of Hebron; that she will share her love and her anger equally between them both so long as they obey her will. Here it begins." She took the lamp from him and pointed with her finger.

A great contest ensued between Mary and Jesus over the interpretation of the pictures, and neither was ever at a loss for the word of contradiction.

Mary said: "*See where my Mistress, the First Eve, is seated on her birth-stool under the palm-tree. The people are awaiting a great event, for the pangs are upon her.*"

Swiftly Jesus answered her: "No, witch, that is not the First Eve: that is Deborah judging the Israelites under the palm-tree of Deborah. For so it is written."

"*Not so: for here my Mistress is delivered of twins, begotten of different fathers, namely Adam son of the Terebinth, and Azazel son of the Kerm-oak. She ties a red thread about the wrist of Azazel to distinguish him from his brother Adam."*

"No, but Tamar, Judah's daughter-in-law, is delivered of her bastards Zarah and Pharez and ties the thread about the wrist of Zarah. For so it is written."

"Not so: for here the infant Azazel is shown to his father the King, and here Adam is laid in the ark of osiers and sedge and committed to the waters of the Brook Eshcol, lest the King should destroy him."

"No, but the infant Samuel is presented to Eli at the tabernacle of Shiloh, and the infant Moses is committed to the waters of the Nile. For so it is written."

"Not so: for here the shepherd's wife takes and suckles Adam, while my Mistress, the First Eve, stands apart, watching."

"No, but Pharaoh's daughter finds Moses among the bulrushes and consigns him to the care of Jochebed, his own mother. For so it is written."

"Not so: for here my Mistress, the First Eve, restores her virginity by bathing in the fish-pool of Hebron and becomes the King's daughter, my Mistress, the Second Eve."

"No, but King David from the roof of his palace at Jerusalem sees the wife of Uriah the Hittite bathing and lusts after her. For so it is written."

"Not so: for here the tale of Adam continues. Adam, now a youth, destroys a lion and a bear which come among his flock, and here he is taken before his uncle the King, who is ignorant of his parentage."

"No, but the youth is David son of Jesse, and the King is Saul. For so it is written."

"Not so: for at the King's desire Adam also strangles a fearful serpent which has destroyed thousands of the King's people with its fiery breath, and displays it to the people."

"No, but Moses raises the brazen seraph in the wilderness to stay the pestilence. For so it is written."

"Not so: for here the King has taken Adam into his household; he and his brother Azazel are for a while united in loving comradeship."

"No, but David and Jonathan, Saul's son, become blood-brothers. For so it is written."

"Not so: for here Adam takes up an ox-goad and falls without warning upon the King's bodyguard."

"No, but Shamgar the son of Anath wields the goad against the Philistines. For so it is written."

"*Not so: for here Adam slays his uncle the King, and strikes off his head with his own sword.*"

"No, but David slays Goliath the Philistine. For so it is written."

"*Not so: for here Adam mourns for his uncle at the Oaks of Mamre.*"

"No, but David mourns there for his enemy Abner. For so it is written."

"*Not so: for here Adam is preparing for royalty. See, where he rests under a tree of royal broom to prepare for his vigil.*"

"No, but Elijah rests there. For so it is written."

"*Not so: for here Adam at his vigil tames the wild beasts that come against him.*"

"No, but Adam names them in Eden. For so it is written."

"*Not so: for here Adam is anointed King of Hebron.*"

"No, but Samuel anoints David King over Israel. For so it is written."

"*Not so: for here preparations are made for Adam's marriage feast to my Mistress, the Second Eve.*"

"No, but provisions of wheat and barley and flour and beans and honey and butter and mutton and cheese and beef, together with beds, basins and pots, are brought as a gift to David at Mahanaim. For so it is written."

"*Not so: for here other provisions that were lacking are brought to Adam's marriage feast.*"

"No, but Ziba the servant of Mephibosheth brings David bread and raisins and summer fruit and wine. For so it is written."

"*Not so: for here the marriage contest is depicted. Adam wrestles all night with his enemies until he is lamed, and at dawn halts upon the right thigh and becomes bull-footed.*"

"No, but our Father Jacob wrestles all night with an angel at Penuel and suffers that injury. For so it is written."

"*Not so: for here at Beth-Hoglah, the marriage-arbour of the Hobbler, bull-voiced mimes call upon the bridegroom Adam to come rushing with his bull-foot.*"

"No, but Baal's priests upon Carmel dance their hobbling *pesach* and cut themselves with knives and vainly invoke Baal. For so it is written."

"*No so: for here Adam comes rushing to his bride, my Mistress, the Second Eve, who dances by the reeded fish-pool with her fifty daughters.*"

"No, but Miriam and her maidens dance in triumph by the Sea of Reeds after the army of Pharaoh has been engulfed; and Aaron, her brother, joins in the dance. For so it is written."

"*Not so: for here the marriage feast of Adam has begun and here he sits at table, his bull-foot resting on a footstool.*"

"No, but lame Mephibosheth is invited to feast at the table of King David. For so it is written."

"*Not so: for when the feast is done Adam companies in public with my Mistress, the Second Eve, and with the fifty daughters of my Mistress.*"

"No, but the rebel Absalom companies in public with Abigail of Carmel and with the other wives and concubines of his father David. For so it is written."

"*The golden tablet is done, and the golden King has triumphed. Here begins the red tablet and the triumph of the red King. See, where Adam, inventor of the lyre, plays melodies and sings in his own honour. His twin, Azazel, son of the murdered King, glowers at him, javelin in hand, plotting revenge.*"

"No, but David plays and sings psalms to ease Saul's melancholy. For so it is written."

"*Not so: for here Azazel dances naked before the Ark of the Covenant, imploring my Mistress to keep faith with him. Wearing her horned moon headdress she smiles at him favourably.*"

"No, but David dances before the Ark and his wife Michal, otherwise named Eglah, 'the heifer', laughs scornfully at him from a lattice. For so it is written."

"*Not so: for here my Mistress, the Second Eve, true to her covenant, invites Azazel to her bed.*"

"No, but Amnon forces his sister Tamar. For so it is written."

"*Not so: for here my Mistress ties Adam's hair to his bedpost for Azazel to shear.*"

"No, but the deceitful Delilah ties the hair of her husband Samson to a weaver's beam. For so it is written."

"*Not so: for here Azazel comes by night into Adam's chamber with scissors to shear his sacred hair.*"

"No, but David finding King Saul asleep in a cave spares his life, and cuts off only the hem of his robe. For so it is written."

"*Not so: for here Adam's hair is cut off, and the sacred hem of his robe with its five blue tassels. And here Azazel with his companions pelt and revile him as he goes up the hill to his death.*"

"No, but Shimei and his fellows revile and pelt David at Bahurim. For so it is written."

"Not so: for here Adam is blinded by Azazel."

"No, but Samson is blinded by the Philistines at Gaza. For so it is written."

"Not so: for here Adam, with green bonds cut from the willow of Hebron, is tied by Azazel to the terebinth of Hebron and there unmanned."

"No, but the King of Ai is hanged on a tree by Joshua at Ai. For so it is written."

"Not so: for here Azazel raises a circle of twelve pillars, with an altar for a thirteenth. He will sacrifice Adam in honour of my Mistress, the Second Eve, and here are the striped basins for the blood."

"No, but Moses raises the twelve pillars at the foot of Sinai—which is Horeb—one for each tribe of Israel, and the basins are to catch the blood of slaughtered bullocks. For so it is written."

"Not so: here comes maimed Adam limping into the circle; and here he is hacked in pieces."

"No, but King Agag walks delicately into the Circle of Gilgal, where the prophet Samuel hacks him in pieces. For so it is written."

"Not so: for here twelve men of Hebron feast upon Adam's flesh, but Adam's shoulder-joint is reserved for Azazel's eating."

"No, but the shoulder-joint of the ox is reserved for King Saul by Samuel at the feast of Mizpeh. For so it is written."

"Not so: for here a messenger comes to my Mistress, the Second Eve, to tell her: 'It is done.' She shrouds herself and becomes the Third Eve with dog, owl and camel."

"No, but Rebeccah dismounts from her camel and veils herself when she sees our father Isaac approach to claim her in marriage. For so it is written."

"Not so: for here the people of Hebron mourn for Adam. Fool, do you not know where you stand? This is the innermost chamber of the cave of Machpelah. Josiah, that evil king, stopped up its entrance; but we Kenites have guarded the secret of its other door. See, where my Mistress, the Third Eve, carries away the stripped bones of Adam to this very cave to lay them in a burial ark."

"No, but the Children of Israel mourn for Moses at Pisgah; and the Lord God, who is veiled lest any man should see his face and die, buries him secretly in a valley of Moab. For so it is written."

"Not so: for here you cannot refute me. Here at last you see my Mistress in Trinity. My Mistress, the First Eve, white as leprosy; my Mistress, the Second Eve, black as the tents of my people; my Mistress, the Third Eve, her death's-head mercifully shrouded. See,

255

*where the spirit of Adam prostrates himself before my Triple Mistress
and holds her to her covenant, while Azazel looks on aghast."*

"No, but I refute you! Here Moses complains to the Lord against
Miriam his sister and Aaron his brother who have mocked his
Ethiopian wife. Aaron prostrates himself before the Lord, who
punishes Miriam with leprosy. For so it is written."

*"Not so: your prevarications will not serve you. For see, where my
Mistress has granted Adam his plea. His spirit rises from the dry
bones of the burial ark and, uttering threats to Azazel, returns once
more to the wheel of life. He will be born again to my Mistress,
the First Eve, as his own son and twin to the son of Azazel."*

"No, but I refute you. Here King Saul consults the witch of
Endor, who raises the spirit of Samuel from the dry bones of Samuel.
For so it is written."

*"Not so: have done, in the Mother's name! Here the red tablet
ends, and the golden tablet takes up the story again, with my Mistress, the First Eve, in pangs beneath her palm-tree."*

"You have had my answers. What need to give them again?"

"They are not acceptable to my Triple Mistress."

"The Living God in whom I trust is immeasurably stronger than
your Mistress. He can create what-is from what-is-not. He can
make what-was as though it had never been. Her ancient tables
record a covenant of death which the Lord God overturned and set
aside at the Well of Kadesh when he swore a new covenant of life
with his servant Moses. The Books of Moses record that covenant;
they are stored in the holy ark of every synagogue throughout Jewry
and written on the tablets of every loyal heart."

"Strong as he may be, how can your Living God rescue you from
this House of Death which lies in the Valley of Death? No man
ever defied my Mistress in her own house and escaped alive. Fool,
this place is the end of all venturesome fools. The stopped tunnel
is choked with their bones."

"It is written: 'Though I walk through the valley of the Shadow
of Death I shall fear no evil, for thou, Lord, art with me.' Therefore my fate will be as the Father ordains, not as your Mistress ordains. I am released from the jurisdiction of the Female; I have come
to destroy her works."

Mary the Hairdresser began to comb her long white hair with an
ivory comb and, as she combed, invoked the ancient powers of evil
one by one to rise against Jesus and overthrow him. She called upon
the scaly-footed Shedim and the snouted Ruhim and on the Mazzi-
kim, the harmers, and on the goat-like Seirim of the crags, and on

the ass-haunched Lilim of the sandy wastes, and on Shabiri the demon of blindness who haunts uncovered pools of water, and on Ruah Zelachta the demon of catalepsy, and on Ben Nefilim the demon of epilepsy, and on Ruah Kezarit the demon of nightmare, and on Ruah Tegazit the demon of delirium, and on Ruah Karde-yako the demon of melancholy, and on Shibbeta the demon of cramps, and on Ruah Zenunim the demon of sexual madness, and on Deber the demon of pestilence, and lastly on Pura the insidious demon of sloth and forgetfulness of whom God-fearing Jews stand in the greatest dread.

All these powers came flocking about him with fury and terror and whirrings, trying to tear the holy fringes from his garment, and the phylacteries from his arm and forehead. He remained quiet and undismayed, and his lips unfalteringly repeated the "Hear, O Israel" —three times against the First Eve, three times against the Second Eve, and three times against the Third Eve. When he had done, he said: "In the name of the Holy One of Israel—blessed be he—depart, creatures of night and death, to the desolate places assigned to you by the Disposer of All!"

They vanished, gibbering, one by one.

Mary suddenly screamed out: "I know you, Adversary of my Mistress! Are you come here at last, Son of David, apostate Adam?"

He commanded her to silence, but she stopped her ears and screamed again: "The apostate was driven from the paradise of Eden, which is Hebron. He was driven as a wanderer over the face of the earth, but it is prophesied that he shall return to Hebron at last to make his reckoning with the Great Goddess. The apostate may deny his mother, the First Eve; and his bride, the Second Eve, he may reject; yet the Third Eve, his grandam, will inexorably claim him for her own."

"If the First Eve be denied for the love of the Living God, and the Second Eve be rejected for the love of the Living God, will the Third Eve find bones to bury?"

Mary tore at the flesh of her forearm with her dog-teeth and greedily sucked the blood. Then, seizing the death-mask of the Old Adam from its peg in the recess and thrusting it on her head, she began to prophesy in rough hexameters, her voice piping and querulous:

ADAM, *son of the terebinth,* ADAM *only begotten,*
Born at the death of the year from green-eyed Miriam's birth-stool,
Rapt from Azazel's fury by wandering shepherds of Hebron:

Your first feats astonishment spread in a region of wonders.
None could divine your secret, you sucked all Solomon's wisdom.
ADAM, son of the terebinth, well you endured your vigil,
Two-score days upon Horeb defying bestial powers.
Now shall the ever-young prophet return once more to anoint you.
You shall be lord of the land, shall enter Miriam's chamber.
ADAM's path shall you tread, nor fail these covenant tables
Till at the last you hang, by friends and kindred forsaken,
Bound to the terebinth tree with strong green branches of willow,
Suffering there as is right, distressed with odious torments.
Twelve bold shepherds shall drink of your blood, shall eat of your
*   body.*
Eve, our mother, shall laugh; in dreams her pythoness bidding
ADAM's bones to recover, where ADAM's skull lies buried.

As she croaked the final spondees the flame of the lamp sputtered and shook. A clammy drop fell from the dome of the chamber on Jesus's foot, and after a minute's pause, another.

He spoke: "What have I to do with the Old Adam who speaks low out of the dust? A New Adam comes in the name of the Most High to make an end, to bind the Female with her own long hair, to fetter God's Adversary in chains of adamant. In the Old Adam all die; in the New all shall live."

"Beware! The beasts that entered the circle which you drew under the thorn-bush of Horeb were four in number. Three you tamed, but did not the fourth paw the ground apart?"

Trembling, Jesus prayed: "Lord, who can understand his errors? Oh, cleanse me from my secret fault!"

She laid the mask aside, laughed and blasphemed against Jehovah. Jesus seized her by the hair, though she struggled like a hyaena. "In the name of him who is Lord of the heights and depths, come out of her!" he cried.

One by one the unclean familiars issued reluctantly from her mouth. He named them each in turn and forbade them ever again to enter into her; the first, Alukah the horse-leech; the second, Zebub the blue-bottle; the third, Akbar the mouse; the fourth, Atalef the bat; the fifth, Tinshemet the lizard; the sixth, Arnebet the hare; and the seventh and last, Shaphan the coney. At each expulsion her struggles became the less violent, and at the end she stood trembling, lost, and without power, her mouth gaping.

He released her and spoke the word of peace. "Come, Mary! Let us return to the land of life. Have done now with your villainies."

She opened the door for him and went before him up the staircase, dizzily swaying from side to side. She opened the second door, the night wind blew out her lamp, and together they stepped out into star-light; for the moon was obscured by a bank of cloud.

Mary came a little of the way with Jesus on the road to Jerusalem; then fell and sat weeping great tears by the roadside. In a small voice she cried after him: "Nevertheless, Lord, the end is not yet, and when the Mother summons me to my duty, I will not fail her."

"The end is as the Living God wills!"

It was a few days before midsummer. Jesus had come to a ford of the Upper Jordan, where the stream runs broad between high crags. He waited meekly on the eastern bank. John, in a white linen garment girded up to his waist, stood in midstream, and nine witnesses were gathered on the other side of the ford.

"Come, Lord!" cried John, "for it is written: 'The Spirit of the Lord shall descend upon you, and you shall be changed to another man.'"

Naked, Jesus entered the water. John filled two pitchers from the flowing stream, one of gold, the other of white clay moulded in spiral form. He poured the double stream over Jesus's head and body and chanted the antique formula preserved, almost unaltered, in the second Psalm:

I will declare the decree that the Lord has put in my mouth, saying:
Son, I have set you upon my holy citadel in the Wilderness of Zin,
My beloved Son you are, this day have I begotten you.
Ask now of me and I shall give you all nations for your inheritance and the utmost parts of the earth for your possession,
To rule them with a rod of iron, dashing them into pieces like pots of clay.

Then he roared in ecstasy: "Look up, Lord, for your Ka descends upon you in the form of a dove!"

Jesus looked up. At that moment the sun surmounted the eastern crag and shone brilliantly down on the water. The Ka is the weird, or double, of a king, and at the coronation of an Egyptian pharaoh is pictured as descending upon him in the form of a hawk; but Jesus did not derive his royal title from the Hawk-goddess.

He passed glorified across to the other bank. John, following after, took a phial of terebinth oil and emptied it upon his head. "In the name of the Lord God of Israel, I anoint you King of all Israel!"

Some of the witnesses blew trumpets, others cried: "God save the King!" and shouted for joy.

Then Judas of Kerioth came forward with a seamless linen garment, of the sort reserved for High Priests, saying: "My former master, before he died, instructed me to put this on you at your anointing." He clothed Jesus in it.

John set Jesus in a covered litter and the nine witnesses carried him northward into Galilee, taking turns at the staves. On the second day they came to the steep slopes of Mount Tabor. John strode ahead through the thickets of kerm-oak, terebinth, myrtle, carob and mountain-olive, the wild beasts fleeing startled away from his path, until he reached the rocky platform at the top. There stands the small town of Atabyrium, formerly the market-place and common sanctuary of the three tribes Issachar, Zebulon and Naphtali.

It was at Atabyrium, in the days of the Judges, that these three tribes rallied under Barak and the priestess Deborah before charging down against Sisera's chariotry in the valley of the Kishon; and there in later times the golden calves—"snares to catch the deluded", as the prophet Hosea called them—were dedicated to Atabyrius, the god of the mountain. The men of Tabor identify Atabyrius with Jehovah; the Greek mythographers describe him as one of the Telchines, that is to say, as a god of the Pelasgians; and for the Essenes Atabyrius is a title of their demi-god Moses. Another mountain sanctuary of the same god is Atabyris in the island of Rhodes, where a pair of brazen bulls are said to roar aloud whenever anything extraordinary is about to happen. Atabyrius is credited with the power of transforming himself into any shape he pleases, like Dionysus, or like Pelasgian Proteus, or like the God of Horeb who appeared to Moses in the acacia bush of Kadesh and gave his name as "I am whatever I choose to be".

In ancient times Tabor was not his only sanctuary in Israel: the Terebinth of Atabyrius on Mount Ephraim was a station through which King Saul passed on his coronation journey. A yearly fair is still held on Tabor, and in the time of Jesus patriotic Galileans would refer to Jehovah as "the Lord of Zebulon", saying: "Nothing prevented that the Holy City should have been built on Tabor, but that it pleased the Lord to rule otherwise." "Nothing" was an exaggeration. There is no spring-water on Tabor and the inhabitants are dependent on rain-water for all purposes.

John went to the house of the Essene Watchman of Tabor, whose name was Nikki, that is Nicanor, and roused him from sleep. "The King is coming, Watchman, do you hear? The King is coming; the only son of Michal, his father a King!"

Nicanor, dizzied with sleep, cried: "Away, man, you speak wildly."

"I am John of Ain-Rimmon, the prophet who anointed him King, and I declare him to be true-born. As an infant he escaped from the sword of Archelaus at Bethlehem of Judaea, being carried to safety in Egypt by the Sons of Rahab."

"Are the signs of royalty upon him?"

"It remains to add the eighth. Already he has endured his vigil and tamed the wild beasts of Horeb. Already the new heiress of Michal has been summoned to the Heel Stone. The contract between the King and her guardian, Lazarus of Bethany, is sealed and witnessed."

"Where is this King?"

"He follows behind."

"Conduct him to the sacred grove, and we shall see how he comports himself."

As dawn was breaking, John guided the litter-bearers to the sacred grove, in a clearing of the forest, where Nicanor was awaiting Jesus. The litter was set down and Jesus stepped out.

Seven trees stood in a circular plot strewn with sea-sand; they were the broom, the willow, the kern-oak, the almond, the terebinth, the love-apple, the pomegranate. Jesus circumambulated the grove, blessing each tree in turn while Nicanor watched him intently. Jesus chanted:

Blessed in the Creator's Name be the Sun, and the first day of the week, which is the angel Raphael's. Blessed in his Name be the royal broom, beneath which the prophet Elijah took his rest and was fed.

Blessed in the Creator's Name be the Moon, and the second day of the week, which is the angel Gabriel's. Blessed in his Name be the willow, whose water-loving boughs deck the Great Altar on the Day of Willows.

Blessed in the Creator's Name be the planet Nergal, and the third day of the week, which is the angel Sammael's. Blessed in his Name be the kerm-oak, whose scarlet dyes the garments of the anointed king, a charm against the Female, the Leprous One.

Blessed in the Creator's Name be the planet Nabu, and the middle day of the week, which is the angel Michael's. Blessed in his Name be the almond-tree, whose rod budded for Aaron the wise, whose fruit cups each lamp of the seven-branched candlestick.

Blessed in the Creator's Name be the planet Marduk, and the fifth day of the week, which is the angel Izidkiel's. Blessed in his Name be the terebinth, under whose shade Abraham and Sarah his wife were promised increase as the sands on the seashore.

Blessed in the Creator's Name be the planet Ishtar and the sixth day of the week, which is the angel Hanael's. Blessed in his Name be the quince-tree, whose goodly fruit sweetens the Feast of Tabernacles.

Blessed in the Creator's Name be the planet Ninib and the seventh day of the week, which is the angel Kepharel's. Blessed in his Name be the pomegranate-tree, on whose bough the Paschal lamb is impaled, whose fruit alone may be fetched into the presence of the Living God.

Blessed above all be the Creator of all things, who is the candlestick to these seven lamps, cupping them with his wisdom, who planted the seven-branched tree of life.

To the Sun be granted the power either to warm or to scorch.

To the Moon be granted the power either to foster or to blight.

To the planet Nergal be granted the power either to strengthen or to make weak.

To the planet Nabu be granted the power either to make wise or to make foolish.

To the planet Marduk be granted the power either to make fruitful or to make barren.

To the planet Ishtar be granted the power either to grant or to withhold the heart's desire.

To the planet Ninib be granted the power either to make holy or to make accursed.

Blessed be the Disposer of powers, the Lord of the Sabbath. Him only I adore.

Nicanor looked to see under which of the seven trees Jesus would seat himself, and wondered that he abstained from the tree of royalty, the tree of magic, the tree of might, the tree of wisdom, the tree of prosperity, the tree of holiness, but rested submissively on his knees under the tree of love.

Jesus, reading his thoughts, asked: "Was it not of this tree that Solomon the wise prophesied in his allegory of God's love for Israel:

'I sat down under his shadow with great delight, for his banner over me was love'?"

Nicanor bowed before Jesus reverently and asked: "Lord, are you prepared to suffer the things that are necessary to royalty? Are you prepared for the marring?"

"I am prepared. It is written: 'Behold the Servant of the Lord shall prosper. He shall be exalted and praised and lifted high. Many were astonished, Lord, at your doing: for his face was marred more than any man's, and his body likewise. Thus marred, shall he sprinkle many nations with his lustral branch. Kings shall be dumb before him. They shall see what has not been told them, and learn what they have not before heard.'"

On the third day, just before dawn, they led him by torchlight to the Heel Stone, formerly the eastern altar of a gilgal, or stone circle, long since vanished. Mary of Bethany, the daughter of Jose styled Cleopas, a beautiful kinswoman of Mary the mother of Jesus, stood at one side of the stone; Mary herself stood next to her, and presently another woman came out of the darkness of the wood, her face shrouded in a shawl, and made a third with them, but said nothing.

Nicanor bound the ceremonial dove-wings to the shoulders of Jesus. "Have no fear, great Lord, for our God will give his angels charge of you, lest you dash your sacred foot against a rock."

As dawn was breaking, Jesus mounted upon the stone and Mary the daughter of Cleopas cried: "Fly, Dove of Doves, fly!"

At that signal the Kenites began to pelt him with stones and sticks and filth until his face was wounded and disfigured and he toppled forward from the stone, as the winged Icarus falls from Heaven in the famous picture by Zeuxis. But seven notables of Tabor, named after the archangels Raphael, Gabriel, Sammael, Michael, Izidkiel, Hanael and Kepharel, stood below the stone and caught him before his feet touched the ground.

Now, I have read that the Great King of Babylon himself would submit during his coronation to be buffeted in the face by a priest, and that King Herod when crowned King of the Jews underwent the same indignity, which was the occasion of his remembering the prophetic buffets that Father Manahem had dealt him at Bozrah. But the ritual assault upon King Jesus by the seven notables of Tabor was a more ancient and cruel one by far, performed again after more than a thousand years in fulfilment of prophecy.

They wrestled with him, seven against one, until they had forced him to kneel with thighs divaricated. Then the tallest and boldest of them climbed on the stone and leapt down on him, and by that act of violence the marring was completed. Jesus's left thigh was put out of joint, the head of the bone being displaced and lodged in the muscles of the thigh; and his left leg stretched out in spasm and twisted, so that thereafter he limped with what is called the sacred lameness. The eighth sign of royalty had been added and he had uttered no cry or word of complaint. Mary the elder and Mary the younger wept for pity. But the tall old woman standing beside them suddenly drew back her veil, kissed the younger Mary on both cheeks, laughed terribly and fled back into the wood.

The Kenites took Jesus up tenderly and implored his pardon. They washed his face, put salve on his wounds, and towards evening carried him in a litter to a spacious arbour of cedar and fir branches which had been erected in Nicanor's garden. As he entered, the whole assembly, who had been sworn to sacred silence, rose to their feet.

A throne hung with purple was prepared at the western end of the arbour. Mary the daughter of Cleopas was already seated on it, dressed like a queen in a robe of gold tissue; a necklace of amber and scallops about her neck and a diadem of stars on her head. The seven notables came forward and ministered to Jesus. Kepharel drew upon his feet the royal scarlet buskins with gold heels of tragical height; the four angels next in the hierarchy invested him with sacred garments; Raphael crowned him with his golden crown; Gabriel presented him with a sceptre of canna-reed.

When he was ready, the Queen smiled graciously at him, descended slowly from the throne and gave him her hand. Painfully he took three steps up the ramp and sat down beside her; for the meaning of coronation is marriage to the heiress of the land.

Rams' horns blew, the company shouted acclamations and the wedding feast began. An unblemished white ox had been slaughtered in honour of the King and Queen, and now the company, hungry for roast flesh after a night and a day of fasting, waited for him to inaugurate the banquet by partaking of the sacred shoulder reserved for him.

He set the shoulder aside, saying: "Those who love me will refrain with me. This custom is ended."

None dared eat, and the carcase of the ox was taken out for burial. However, he accepted a cup of red wine from Nazareth, the ancient House of Wine attached to the shrine of Tabor, and shared it with his queen. Even the Kenites now drank wine, dispensed from their Nazirite prohibition. He also accepted a loaf of bread from Bethlehem of Galilee, the ancient House of Bread, and shared it with his queen to the last crumb.

Then to music of pipe and drum the Kenites antiphonically sang Rachel's Blessing upon Israel. This is their mystic song of the Sacred Year and contains the names of the original fourteen tribes, Dinah among them, beginning with Reuben and ending with Benjamin:

> *See the Son, on the water tossed,*
> *In might and excellency of power,*
> *Resting at ease between two feats—*
> *He has paid the shipman all his hire—*
> *Dwelling secure in the hollow ship*
> *Until by winds he is wafted home.*
> *Hark, how he roars like a lion's whelp!*
> *Hark, how his brothers praise his name!*
> *For his eyes are red with Eshcol wine*
> *And his teeth are white with milk.*
>
> *Happy is he; his bread is fat,*
> *Royal dainties are on his plate.*
> *Though a troop of raiders cast him down,*
> *He will cast them down in his own good time.*
> *He is set apart from all his brothers*
> *And joined in marriage to Canaan's queen.*
> *His word is sharp, his anger fierce;*
> *The whole world listens to his commands.*
> *He makes fruitful by his right deeds,*
> *And the people swarm like fish.*
>
> *So his seed shall become a multitude.*
> *He bestows forgetfulness of pain;*
> *He is wise as a serpent, undeceived,*
> *His judgements bite like an adder's fangs.*
> *None dares murmur before the throne*
> *When he sits in judgement beside his queen.*
> *Wise-mouth wrestles against his foe,*
> *Who flees at dawn like a hind let loose—*
> *See the Son of my Right Hand,*
> *Divider of nightly spoil.*

Then the notables, who were the bridesmen, sang the first half of the forty-fifth Psalm, King David's royal marriage hymn, in which the King is invited to gird his sword on his thigh and ride forward in majesty to battle, seeing that God has established his throne for ever and has put a right sceptre in his hand, and has anointed him with the oil of gladness.

Mary's kinswomen, headed by her sister Martha, who were the bridesmaids, sang the second part of the psalm in which occur the verses:

> Kings' daughters were among thy honourable women: upon thy right hand did stand the queen in gold of Ophir.
>
> Hearken, O daughter, and consider, and incline thine ear; forget also thine own people, and thy father's house;
>
> So shall the king greatly desire thy beauty: for he is thy Lord; and worship thou him.
>
> The king's daughter is all glorious within: her clothing is of wrought gold.
>
> She shall be brought unto the king in raiment of needlework: the virgins her companions that follow her shall be brought unto thee.

The maskers came tumbling in, disguised as birds and beasts; they danced and made merry until it was time for Jesus and Mary to retire to the bridal chamber behind the curtain. But he turned to his queen and his words were far more terrible to the company even than his refusal of the reserved shoulder. He said in a clear voice: "I am your King, and I have come not to renew but to make an end. Beloved, let us not do the act of darkness, which is the act of death. You are my sister! You are my sister! You are my sister!"

By these words he chastely denied her the consummation of marriage. A silence as if of death fell on the astonished assembly; while Mary the Queen first flushed and then blanched.

Mary the mother of Jesus was the first to speak. She stood up and asked sternly: "My son, is this how you deal with your virgin bride? What if the King your father had shamefully done the same?"

He answered: "Woman, the Power of Michal has left you and lighted upon your kinswoman. The reckoning is now between herself and myself only."

Lazarus the Essene, the Queen's brother who had been her guardian since the death of their father Jose Cleopas, comforted her. "The King your husband has done wisely in trampling upon the garment of shame. Only by this road can we all walk together in pure love.

Dry your tears, Mary. Dry your tears, for the love of the Living God."

She answered: "Is my lord the King wiser than King Solomon, whose sister was also his spouse? For Solomon lay, dove-eyed, all night between her breasts, on a green bed in their spacious arbour; and like a dove he sought out the clefts of the rock. Yet who am I to be a judge in this matter? I unveil my face for the King, and his word is my law."

Part Three

CHAPTER TWENTY

THE HEALER

RELIGIOUS mysteries are largely concerned with astronomical prediction. The Chrestian mysteries are no exception. Jesus had been
born at the winter solstice, the birthday of the Sun when it attains
the southernmost, or right-hand, point of its course; but his baptism
and anointing were a ceremony of rebirth performed on the ninth
day of the month Ab, the date of the heliacal rising of the Dog-star.
According to Jewish apocalyptic writers, the ninth of Ab was also the
destined birthday of the Messiah, because the Messianic star of
Isaiah's prophecy was the Dog-star, the Calebite badge of the House
of David; moreover, the rising of the Dog-star determined the true
beginning and ending of the Phoenix (or Sothic) Year of 1460 ordinary years, and the Messiah Son of David had been mystically described as the new Phoenix. It is also noteworthy, by the by, that
in having two birthdays Jesus resembled the god Dionysus, "the
Child of the Double Door", born first of his mother Semele and then
of Father Zeus; and so initiates of the Alexandrian Church are
taught by the mystagogues when they pass into the Third Degree of
Recognition.

On the last evening of his marriage feast, which lasted for a week,
Jesus informed his courtiers that as soon as his injury permitted he
would go out to view his kingdom, and that if what he saw pleased
him, he would summon them again and issue his royal commands.
Meanwhile, let them all return to their homes, there to watch and
pray assiduously.

He told his queen: "I cannot take you to my house, Beloved,
though your bridesmaids promised you that I would; for I have no

house. Until I may occupy a palace I shall need no settled home. I will sleep under the stars or accept whatever poor shelter friends or strangers may offer me. However, if you wish to accompany me in my wanderings, I cannot turn you away."

"My lord, do you address me as 'Beloved' and say "if you wish to accompany me'? I am told that you once had a house and other possessions, but that you made them over to your mother and have since given away all your earnings. When you own a house again, call me to it; I do not ask for a palace. How could I have guessed when I put on these robes and this crown that I was to become the bride of a wandering beggar? My lord, either desire your servant to accompany you and she will obey, or allow her to return to Bethany and remain there patiently until the coming of better times."

"Return to Bethany in peace with your brother Lazarus and await me there."

"As my lord desires."

Mary was sick at heart. Against her will she had fallen in love with Jesus and would gladly have followed him to the ends of the earth in the hope that her devotion might at last persuade him to relent towards her in love; for, as she knew, there is a way out of every rash vow. Yet her woman's pride—or, one might say, the Power of Michal—forced her to feign indifference, and her sister Martha commended this discretion. "Your beauty will draw him, and he will presently ask as a favour what is no more than his right."

When Jesus was able to walk, though with great pain, he sent for John. John returned at once to Tabor and found him settled in the sacred grove. "Master of the vintage," he asked, "do you pluck the big grapes first, or the little ones, or do you pluck whichever comes to hand?"

"First the little ones; they have most need of me."

"The big grapes are better worth the plucking."

"Yet the whole vintage must be gathered in. Heads of Academies and rulers of the Sanhedrin may wait until the last; the poor and the outcast cannot wait."

"Your face is not turned towards Jerusalem. Tell me for what northern city you are bound, and I will prepare your way."

"I have seen it written: 'Behold upon the mountains the feet of the messenger of good tidings who publishes peace.'"

"What to do in that place?"

"To choose our pillars for my gilgal. One well-shaped pillar you have given me already."

"Do you need hewn pillars, or rough-hewn or unhewn?"

"Rough-hewn. The polishing is best done by my own hand."

So John ran ahead to prepare the way for Jesus, who followed riding on an ass, with Judas on foot by his side. He made for the town of Capernaum, aware that it takes its name from the tomb of the prophet Nahum, the author of the prophetic verse which Jesus had quoted. Capernaum is a small frontier town at the northern end of the Lake of Galilee and on the main road from Egypt to Damascus; it has a customs house, a fish-curing industry and famous wheat-lands.

When he reached the market-square John sat down in the dust beside a potter's booth and began to scan closely the faces of passers-by. Since none pleased him, he arose and went down to the port. There he saw two fishermen preparing to hoist their sails and follow a shoal of fish which had been sighted at some distance off-shore. He recognized them, having baptized them at Beth Arabah not many weeks before. "Come at once!" he called.

At the sight of his white camel's-hair garment they sprang overboard and swam ashore. Both were tall, rugged, excitable men, neither well read in the Law nor scrupulous in its observance, but members at least of a respectable synagogue. John cried: "Sons, look yonder! Here comes the Lamb of the Passover, born of a white Ewe, crowned with gold, a sceptre in his hand. I charge you to follow him and attend him in his palace!" He pointed along the road towards Jesus, who came riding up as he spoke.

The fishermen were perplexed by these wild words, but John was a prophet, and prophetic meanings, they knew, are not readily discerned. They went forward and bowed low to Jesus, who asked them: "Friends, what do you want of me?"

They answered in confusion: "Lord, where is your palace? We have been sent to attend you in your palace."

"Are you disciples of John?"

They looked around for John to prompt them, but he had disappeared. One answered impulsively: "Lord, I am now your disciple. I am Simon the son of Jonah; the Greeks in our fleet nickname me Peter, the Rock. This is my brother Netzer whom they nickname Andrew, the Bold Fellow."

"The Rock will serve as a sturdy pillar for my gilgal. So Simon comes. But you, Bold Fellow?"

Andrew stood, twitching his fingers. "John commanded us both to go with you."

"It is well. I will show you my palace."

271

He led them out of the town towards a terebinth-tree growing on a rocky mound by the Lake-side. There he dismounted, with difficulty, told Judas to tie up the ass, and said: "Here is my palace, and you are my honoured guests. Look, my lords, together we pass up the broad flights of marble stairs to the great oaken gates. We stand and knock; they open. We enter with heads erect, across the polished floors of serpentine and malachite, passing through a vast throng of my courtiers and servants. All are dressed in rich robes and are bowing low to us." He called to Judas over his shoulder: "Bring perfumed water, Chamberlain! Bring a golden ewer and two silver basins for my guests' feet! Is the banquet served? Where are the wreaths for their heads, and the ointment?"

Peter began to laugh. Andrew said: "Lord, with my right eye I see a green tree on a rocky knoll, with my left I see the regal glories that you describe."

"It is well, keep the two visions apart, the present from the future. Were you going out in pursuit of fish?"

"Yes, lord, but the fish are patient and will excuse us."

"I will instruct you in the art of catching men, not fish."

"With a hook and line?"

"Sometimes one at a time with hook and line; sometimes by the hundred with a net."

"Your hook is in our mouths. You may land us now with your gaff."

They remained talking all day under the tree and at evening returned to the port; but they did not yet know who he was, except that his name was Jesus of Nazareth and that he had studied with the Essenes.

In a boat moored to the quayside, mending their nets, he saw two men of his acquaintance: James and John, the shy, suspicious, bold sons of Zebedee the fisherman. They had once transported timber across the Lake for his brothers. He sent Andrew to fetch them to him. Andrew, who knew James and John well, ran to them and cried: "Come quickly, brothers! I have found him."

"Whom have you found?"

"The man who can answer every question!"

They recognized Jesus and leaped ashore to greet him. Some simple words that he had spoken on the occasion of their former meeting had burned in their hearts ever since, though at the time they had not willingly accepted them as true. He had said: "The learned Hillel—his memory be blessed—made a shrewd judgement: 'No man who is busied with trade can become wise.' I would say more: No man who is busied with trade can love God."

Now his words were: "James and John, I have need of you. Will you come with me?"

They did not understand at first what he was asking of them, but before nightfall they had become his disciples and were ready to go with him wherever he led. The Alexandrian Chrestians, in an attempt to identify James and John with the Greek heroes Castor and Pollux, pretend that he renamed them "The Sons of Thunder"; but the truth is that his name for them was *Benireem*, "The Sons of the Antelope-ox". This referred partly to a text in Job, according to which the shy, suspicious, bold antelope-ox is tamed only with the greatest difficulty, or not at all; but partly also to a verse in the Blessing of Moses, where Ephraim and Manasseh, the sons of Joseph, figure as the two horns of the antelope-ox—for Jesus later called each of his twelve disciples after one of the tribes of Israel.

His first appearance at a public assembly after his coronation was on the following Saturday, in conformity with the tradition that the Messiah Son of David would first show himself on a Sabbath day. No trumpets or shouts heralded his approach; and to Judas, the only man present who knew that Jesus was a king, the occasion appeared trivial and unworthy, though as a loyal disciple he abstained from comment. At the instance of James and John, who described him as "one most learned in the Law and the Prophets", Jesus had been invited to read the Second Lession in the smallest of the three Capernaum synagogues. He entered with the congregation, took his seat inconspicuously on a bench halfway down the aisle and joined in the prayers.

The passage that fell to him for reading consisted of the opening verses of the fifty-eighth chapter of the Book of Isaiah, in which Jehovah speaks to his prophet as follows:

Cry aloud insistently; raise your voice like a trumpet and show my people Jacob their transgressions and sins.

Indeed, they seek me daily and delight to learn my ways, as righteous people should who have not forsaken the commandments of their God. They beseech me to rule them with justice; they delight in approaching me.

Yet they say: "We have fasted and you did not regard our fast. We have afflicted our souls and you paid no heed. How is this, Lord?"

It is because when you fast you find no pleasure except in things which grieve your fellow-men.

You fast for the sake of strife and controversy, and in fasting you use your fists in wickedness. If you wish your voices to be heard in Heaven, a different spirit must rule you.

Is yours the sort of fast that I have ordered? Have I ordered a day on which to afflict the soul, to droop the head like a tufted reed and to sit in sackcloth and ashes? Can you regard this as a fast acceptable to me?

Is not my fast one on which to unbind the bonds of wickedness, to untie the heavy burden, to release the oppressed and free the slave?

A day on which to deal bread to the hungry, to invite the homeless poor to your house, and to clothe the naked—rather than a day for closeting yourselves away from your fellow-men?

After reading the eight verses aloud in their barely intelligible ancient Hebrew, Jesus began to expound them. The God of Israel, he declared, had ordained fasts, but not, as was generally supposed, in order to cause his people distress and misery. Fasting was instituted for three purposes: to purge the body of gross humours due to gluttony and over-drinking, to remind the faster of the nature of hunger, and to enable him to give the food that he would otherwise have eaten to those who needed it more than himself. The God of Israel was a merciful God, and to hold that he had ordained fasting as a proof of his severity or as a mortification of the excellent bodies that he had given to men was both erroneous and ungrateful.

Jesus preached without tedious references to what this rabbi or that had said, and on what occasion; and made no parade of literary knowledge. He spoke simply and authoritatively, in a manner rarely heard in the synagogue. Almost every man and woman present—for in country synagogues men and women sit together indiscriminately—felt drawn up as if by a sharp hook and strong line and resolved to lead a more righteous life than before. A deep sigh of repentance was heard.

At last Jesus said: "A rich man fasts at Capernaum. The fast vexes him. His belly cries within him for venison-pasty and date-wine of Jericho; his throat is dry, his mouth waters. In comes his Canaanite slave: 'My lord, guests are here from Chorazin. What food shall I set before them?' He spits in the slave's face, and says: 'What is that to me, dog? Tell them that I am fasting. They must wait until nightfall!' His brother reproaches him: 'Brother, that was not well done. To turn away a guest is to dishonour God.' The controversy grows bitter, and at last the rich man calls the brother a fool and turns his back on him. He has kept his fast until night-

274

fall, but at what a cost! Tell me—of what worth is such a fast in the eyes of our God?"

At this a rich corn-factor, one of the synagogue officers, rose up, beside himself with anger, pointed with a finger at Jesus, and bawled: "Let us alone, Sir! What concern is it to you how we at Capernaum live, and how we fast? It is said: 'No good comes out of Nazareth!' and from Nazareth you come. Go back to Nazareth; preach to the sinners there!"

Jesus answered at once, addressing not the man himself, but the evil spirit that possessed him: "Be silent, devil! Come out of that man!"

The corn-factor changed colour and began to whine in a changed voice, as it were the voice of the evil spirit. "Alas, I see who you are now—yes, I see who you are. You are the Holy One of God. You read our secret thoughts. You overhear our private talk. Are you come to destroy us?"

"Come out of him, I say!"

The man uttered a long howl like a wolf's and fell in a fit. Those who stood by caught hold of his arms to restrain him from self-injury, but he threw them off and beat his head against the solid benches.

"Come out, and never return to torment this man!"

He ceased to struggle, his limbs relaxed and presently he recovered his own voice. While the service continued, Jesus led him outside and spoke privately to him. He proved to be a man who had fallen into a despair that his sins would never be forgiven him. When Jesus confidently assured him of God's pardon, a great burden was lifted from his heart. The sudden change in the aspect and gait of this morose merchant on his return to the synagogue astonished the congregation.

When the last prayers had been said, Jesus went for his midday meal to Peter and Andrew's boat-house, which was also their dwelling-house. Here he found Peter's mother-in-law lying on a pile of sails in a dark corner under the stern of the boat, groaning miserably. Peter apologized for this inconvenience, explaining that the old woman had a bout of fever; but Jesus went over to her, took her by the hand and whispered in her ear. Then he lifted her to her feet, saying in a loud voice: "Woman, your fever has gone!"

He had instantly divined the truth. Peter's wife was disturbed that Peter and Andrew had not fished that week, and had begun to fret: what would become of the household if they did not soon return to their trade? She dared not reproach Peter herself, knowing his violent temper and seeing how whole-heartedly he had given himself to his new master: so her mother had made the quarrel her own. Jesus understood from her interruptive groans that she was vexed not only with Peter but with himself as the cause of Peter's idleness, and also with her daughter, who had humoured Peter by preparing a rich meal in honour of the occasion. She had decided to spoil the meal by taking to her bed and shamming a high fever. His whispered words were: "Mother, if you wish for salvation, forgive your son, honour your guest, spare your daughter shame!"

Peter and Andrew were astonished at the seeming miracle, and the old woman, now eating and drinking heartily, did not undeceive them. Her hostility to Jesus vanished when she found that he treated her with greater gentleness and respect than she had ever had from her son-in-law.

The news of these two spectacular cures spread quickly, and in the cool of the evening, when the Sabbath officially ended, a large number of sick people were brought to the boat-house for Jesus to heal. He was disconcerted by this turn of events, protesting that he had not come to Capernaum as a physician. But though he dismissed the sick people, they refused to go and insisted that he could cure them if he would. Some were incurable, and to them he could only speak words of solace; others he encouraged by a promise of recovery if they did nothing to aggravate their condition—for he found it easy to diagnose sicknesses caused by physical excess; on two or three of them he performed immediate cures. These last were cases in which the physical disability was caused by some disturbance of the spirit; and included one of long-standing paralysis in the leg. He allayed the disturbances, informed the sufferers that they were cured, and sent them away healed.

The most remarkable cure that he performed in the Capernaum district was on a leper—not a true leper but one who suffered from a vitiliginous face. The man came and knelt before him, saying: "Heal me, Lord. I know that your mother's son has the power."

Jesus touched the ravaged face, muttering a word of power, and then said aloud: "Be clean!"

As the five disciples watched, the white patches began to vanish from the leper's cheeks and forehead. "In the fourteenth chapter of Leviticus you will find the regulations for your cleansing," Jesus told him. "You must show your body to the priest of this town, and obey his orders strictly. When you see him taking twigs of marjoram, kerm-oak and cedar, and sprinkling the live bird with the blood of the bird killed over running water, remember this: your leprosy came in warning of your sin, the adulterous love you had for your brother's wife. At first it was low on the ground like marjoram; then it grew tall as a kerm-oak; then it overspread the sky like a cedar."

"Lord, the cedar is felled and I see the sapphire of the sky."

"It is the throne of our Father. Now go in peace; and tell no one but the priest what has been done."

The man promised and ran off happily, but the priest spread the report of the cure, and Jesus was presently beset by lepers begging to be healed, some of them with their faces eaten away by true leprosy. He spoke kindly to them but would not undertake to cure them. His position had become difficult: if he attended to all the sick who came to him he would not have time to eat, sleep, pray or meditate. His disciples grew weary of turning people away from the boat-house, and of saying: "Our master cannot attend to you." Some even came knocking after midnight.

One evening Jesus stood preaching behind bolted doors in the synagogue where he had healed the corn-factor. The mob shouted and whined and murmured outside, and suddenly his privacy was invaded from above. Someone began ripping the roof off, and down in the middle of the circle, lowered by cords, came a mattress-bed on which lay a paralytic. Everyone but Jesus was astonished and angry. Jesus smiled. He said to the paralytic: "My son, your sins are forgiven!"

The Doctors of the Law who were present gasped.

Jesus knew that they were thinking: "Only the Lord God and the Messiah are empowered to forgive sins." He asked: "Would you have me say merely: 'Roll up your bedding and take it away, Shameless One?' Would he be able to do so? He is paralysed, and his paralysis is caused by a sense of guilt. Until he knows that his sins are forgiven he must lie there rigid and you must remove him on your own shoulders. I did not say: 'I forgive you your sins.' None but our God can forgive sins. I told him only what he knows is true: that God has forgiven his sins, having now chastened him sufficiently. For 'Pain cleanses sin', as our fathers tell us. Come, Sir, roll up your bedding at once and take it away! This is no place for you to be lying sick."

The man climbed out of bed, rolled up his bedding and carried it out. Jesus continued unconcernedly to preach, though the congregation were so astonished by what they had seen that they lost the thread of his discourse.

He left Capernaum before daylight and went to pray in a lonely place some miles from the town; but he was followed by a company

277

of sick people who interrupted his devotions. He did for them what he could, and then, making a wide circuit, crossed the Jordan and entered the town of Old Bethsaida, where he had been invited to preach at the synagogue.

His fame had preceded him there, and he found so large a crowd waiting for him at the door of the synagogue that he hurried into an alley, which led him to the house of the president of the synagogue. The hue-and-cry was soon raised again, and the mob began to besiege the house, battering on the doors and windows to demand admittance. Trampling noises were heard from above and the president grew alarmed: "They will tear off the roof if you do not prevent them, and lepers will come leaping down by the score to defile us."

Jesus went to an upper window and addressed the crowd. "Open a lane for me to come out; and who touches me does so at his peril." They obeyed him. He came out, walked down to the quay, climbed into a small boat and pushed off. From the boat he preached to the crowd for some hours.

At night he told his disciple John: "The devil that possessed the man in the synagogue challenged me to return to Nazareth. It is a trial that I cannot evade. Let us go there to-morrow."

They rowed down the Lake, disembarked at a deserted spot, and set off for Nazareth. Nobody in the towns through which they passed recognized them, and they reached Nazareth unmolested; there Jesus rested in Mary's house.

He found his fellow-carpenter Thomas still working at the bench and invited him to become his sixth disciple. Thomas accepted the invitation with the words: "Certainly I will go with you. It is my trade to go with you. Where are you bound now?"

"This Son of Adam must make a journey up the hills and down into the valleys and through the waters and across the plains, a journey that will last until the Passover of next year."

"And where will he be then?"

"Where Adam's journey ended."

The news of Jesus's extraordinary progress through the Garden of Galilee had reached Nazareth. His neighbours were astonished, and one said: "It surely cannot be the same Jesus, Joseph the carpenter's son, the one whom we used to call the Egyptian?"

Another said: "Who knows? There was always something strange about the fellow. He could handle poisonous snakes with impunity, and wild birds used sometimes to fly down and perch on his shoulder."

278

And a third: "He has brought great credit on our village. If he can perform cures in Capernaum, why not here? For my part, I have hopes of ridding my shoulder of the rheumatism that wears me down every winter."

And the first one again: "If it comes to that, I suffer from constant biliousness after food, and if Jesus can cure it for me I do not greatly care how he does it, though they do say that his charms are not strictly in accordance with the Law."

Then scandal started. "They say that he learned his magic in Egypt when he was studying there, and managed to bring out the secret charm, written on a scrap of parchment, from the magicians' college."

"How did he do that?"

"They say that before he entered the college he made an incision in his scalp and kept a little pocket open there, and slipped the parchment in. He managed to take it out between the golden dogs at the entrance."

"It sounds a likely story. Of the ten measures of magic, Egypt took nine."

"On the other hand, it may be pure fiction. After all, he was invited to expound the prophet Isaiah in the fishermen's synagogue at Capernaum and acquitted himself creditably. We should be unwise not to ask him to do the same. If the man has an evil spirit in him, it is unlikely that he would have ventured to handle the sacred scrolls."

After long consultation a messenger was sent to Jesus, informing him that he had been honoured with the invitation to read and expound the Second Lesson on the coming Saturday. Peter, as porter, told the messenger to wait while he consulted the Master, who was resting; and presently returned to announce: "The Master will be pleased to do as you ask."

When the Sabbath day came, Jesus entered the synagogue with his six disciples. His mother remained behind; she was still vexed with him for his treatment of Mary Cleopas. The people of Nazareth were astonished to see their former village carpenter limp in painfully, with the muscles of one leg bunched at the hip, his face thin from fasting, drawn with pain, and more pallid than ever. A murmur and a titter rose about him. Jesus said nothing but joined in the opening prayers and listened while seven elders in turn read the portions of the Law of Moses and while the *Meturgaman*, or interpreter, translated them into vernacular Aramaic. Then came the time for the Second Lesson. Jesus called for the scroll of Isaiah, turned to the sixty-first chapter, which was the set passage, and began to read aloud the first three verses:

The Spirit of the Lord is upon me, because the Lord has anointed me to preach good tidings to the meek. He has sent me to bind up broken hearts, to give liberty to the captives and open the prison doors for them;

To proclaim the year acceptable to the Lord, and the time of his vengeance, and to comfort those who mourn;

To give those who mourn in Zion the gracious oil of joy instead of mourning ashes, the festal garment instead of the spirit of heaviness; so that they may be called "Trees of Righteousness" planted by the Lord for his own glory.

Then first he spoke of the trees of righteousness, the seven trees from which Wisdom has built her temple. He named them in order and described their several qualities, and also named the seven guardian archangels, explaining that each day of the week has a tree proper to it, from the first day, the day of the broom, to the seventh, the day of the pomegranate.

He asked: "Where is wisdom to be found?" and answered: "Where but under the love-apple, that is to say in God-loving meditation." And he said: "Feed on these apples in your heart. For one has been sent from the grove to preach good tidings to those of you who are meek, to bind up your broken hearts, to set free those of you who are prisoners and captives. Not captives bound with visible bonds, men incarcerated in jails of stone—to these other messengers are sent —but men and women bound by the chains of their own guilt and imprisoned in their own hardness of heart. Under the love-apple their sins shall be forgiven them: they shall rejoice in light and freedom."

He paused and a murmur arose, a murmur of impatience, but nobody dared to speak what was in the hearts of all.

He laid down the scroll. "This prophecy of Isaiah is fulfilled to-day. What more do you ask of me? I know well what is in your hearts. Two days ago I heard you discussing me in this very room, though the doors were locked. I heard what every man said. What? Do I need Egyptian magic to do works in Galilee? Egyptian magic is potent only in the Land of Egypt. In the Land of Israel the power of the Lord alone avails. Nor have I come here to set up as a village physician; you already have one in Nazareth. Have I come back here to steal his trade? Pay him well and he will prepare you medicines to ease your aching shoulders and bilious bellies—though not your broken hearts. As for myself: I was strange to you once. I am still stranger to you now. You despised me when I was one of you; now that I have gone from you, you hate me. You look at my twisted leg, and 'Physician, heal yourself!' you sneer. Shameless ones, is this not a taunt against our great ancestor Jacob who, in wrestling with the Adversary, suffered the same injury at Penuel? Is it not also a taunt against Moses, who, in Jacob's honour, ordained that the flesh of the thigh should be a sacred portion, as it is to this day? You ask: 'Why does he not perform in Nazareth what he performed in Capernaum?' Because in Capernaum he found belief, and not only among Jews. A Sidonian captain of police asked this Son of Adam: 'Pray, heal my servant Stephen, for he is a good man, a Jew of Jerusalem, and too sick to come to you himself.' This Son of Adam answered: 'If I went to heal the sick in every house of Capernaum, when would I be done? I have come to the whole, as well as to the sick!' He answered: 'Only speak the word and my servant will be healed, though you speak it at a distance of a mile.' So Stephen was released from his sins and healed."

Then, breaking off, he cried aloud: "Kinsmen and friends! No prophet is accepted by his own people until their jealousy is abated by his death and turned into a boast. Therefore I will tell you this: that in the days of Elijah, when famine oppressed all Israel for three years and a half, many starving widows were found in Israel. Yet Elijah was sent to none of them with his inexhaustible cruse of oil and his inexhaustible barrel of meal; he was sent only to the widow of Sidonian Sarepta. And of many Israelitish lepers in the days of Elisha not one was healed by him; he healed only Naaman the Syrian."

The officers of the synagogue were raging at these words and the six disciples began to fear for Jesus, Nazareth being notorious for its rough justice. In Jerusalem or the large cities of the Garden a man might inquisitively speculate on the nature of God, might interpret the Law of Moses in so free a way that only the shadow of it remained, might give himself out to be this Great One or that, and for his boldness earn no more than a reprimand or, at the worst, a beating. But in Nazareth, as in many of the hill villages of Upper Galilee, the old ways were still followed. They called a cliff above the village the "Cliff of the Meddlers", and the tradition was that any person who preached dangerous new doctrine, meddled with magic, or claimed to be what he was not, must be toppled from it to his death.

As soon as the service ended and Jesus came out of the synagogue he was seized upon by the villagers and hustled up the hill. He calmly ordered his disciples: "Return to the house, my sons. Inform my mother that I will be with her presently."

He did not struggle with his captors, but walked unconcernedly forward with them. Presently they released their hold of his arms because they found their fingers growing rigid with cramp. Jesus began to talk to them quietly about indifferent matters—the fruit crop, the high price lately paid for a certain field through which they passed, the habits of the lapwing. Everyone fell silent as he talked, his voice growing louder and louder until it rose to a shout which rang in their ears and made the drums tingle, but then gradually died down to conversational tones again. They soon ceased to have any sense of what he was saying. Each man caught hold of his neighbour for support, and arm was linked in arm. His voice came to them in broken waves, like distant singing down the wind, as they continued drowsily up the hill. Nearer and nearer to the cliff they stumbled, every man asleep on his feet like an old mule in the shafts of a market cart.

Suddenly a loud cry rang through their ears: "Halt! Halt, Meddlers of Nazareth, or you are all dead men!"

They obeyed and stood in a long row, stupidly gazing down over the steep cliff-face. Another three steps and they would have perished. From a thicket on their right hand came the voice of Jesus again, ordering them to return in peace to their homes.

They turned and fled away in terror as if the Shedim were in pursuit.

CHAPTER TWENTY-ONE

THE POET AND SAGE

THE Acts and Sayings of Jesus originally written in Aramaic but circulated in Greek translation among the Gentile Churches, should not be read without careful critical reserve. Several variants exist. The editing is often ignorant, sometimes disingenuous and occasionally fraudulent, yet it is a handbook which serves conveniently both to attract converts and to disarm the suspicions of those civil authorities for whom Chrestian is merely another name for Jew. Being no more than a skeleton of the full story of Jesus, it is supplemented by a secret oral tradition communicated stage by stage to initiates as they are judged worthy of the revelation.

It was by chance that I first became an authority on Chrestianity. An old sick Ebionite bishop who took refuge in my house at Alexandria during the persecutions volunteered to make me the repository of what he claimed was the only pure Chrestian tradition.

"Why do you propose to honour me with your confidence?" I asked. "I am not a Chrestian."

"Because, though no Chrestian, you have shown me Chrestian loving-kindness; because you have studied our Law and Prophets more closely than many Jews; and because to-day, like the prophet Elijah, I can justly complain to our God: 'I only am left, and they seek to take my life also.'"

"What do you mean by Chrestian loving-kindness?"

"You risked denunciation and looked for no reward."

"May I prove worthy of your trust," I told the poor fellow.

Yet I could see that he had fearful qualms about revealing the secret tradition to me, and would never have done so had he not feared that it would otherwise be lost for ever. He cried bitterly: "The traitors of Rome and Syria defile the holy truth and make a monster of him whose memory I honour above all others and whom I would have the whole world likewise honour."

I could not agree to this condemnation of the Gentile Chrestians as a whole, and the investigations that I have since undertaken prove that the present members of the Church, being unaware on what insecure historical ground their doctrine rests, cannot fairly be characterized as traitors. They have, moreover, shown remarkable fortitude under Imperial persecution, and when it is considered from what dregs of society many of them are recruited—here at Alexandria few of them would be eligible for initiation into the Greek Mysteries and not all of them could even qualify for membership of an ordinary drinking-club—it is wonderful what a reputation for decency and fair dealing they have built up. Yet clearly the trend and end and scope of Jesus's preaching cannot be properly understood except in the light of the authority by which he preached; and clearly, too, the founders of the Gentile Churches so strangely misunderstood his mission that they have made him the central figure of a new cult which, were he alive now, he could regard only with detestation and horror. They present him as a Jew of doubtful parentage, a renegade who abrogated the Mosaic Law and, throwing in his lot with the Greek Gnostics, pretended to a sort of Apollonian divinity, and this too on credentials which must be accepted on blind faith—I suppose because no reasonable person could possibly accept them otherwise. But, as has already been shown, Jesus was in fact not only royally born but as scrupulous in his observance of the Mosaic Law as any Jew who ever lived, and spent his entire life in trying to persuade his fellow-countrymen that there never had been, was not, and never could be, any other true god but the God of Israel. He once even refused the title "good master", addressed to him by a courteous stranger, on the ground that only God is good.

As a sacred King, the last legitimate ruler of an immensely ancient dynasty, his avowed intention was to fulfil all the ancient prophecies that concerned himself and bring the history of his House to a real and unexceptionable conclusion. He intended by an immense exercise of power and perfect trust in God the Father to annul the boastful tradition of royal pomp—dependent on armies, battles, taxes, mercantile adventures, marriages with foreign princesses, Court luxury and popular oppression—which King Solomon had initiated at Jerusalem; and at the same time to break the lamentable cycle of birth, procreation, death and rebirth in which both he and his subjects had been involved since Adam's day. Merely to resign his claim to temporal power was not enough. His resolute hope was to defeat Death itself by enduring with his people the so-called Pangs of the Messiah, the cataclysmic events which were the expected prelude to the coming of the Kingdom of God; and his justification of this hope was the prophecy in the twenty-fifth chapter of Isaiah: "He shall destroy Death for ever." In the Kingdom, which would be miraculously fertile and perfectly pacific, all Israelites would be his subjects who acknowledged him in his threefold capacity as king, prophet and healer, and under his benignant rule would live wholly free from error, want, sickness or fear of death for no less than a thousand years.

The Kingdom, it seems, was to consist of various estates, comprising various degrees of initiates. He himself was the destined Sovereign, personally answerable to God the Father and in direct authority over the tribe of Judah. Under him would serve twelve rulers, his twelve gilgal-pillars, each set in authority over one of the remaining twelve tribes. They would consist of the six disciples already named—Judas, Peter, James, John, Andrew, Thomas—and six more whom he chose in the Garden of Galilee after his Nazareth visit—

Philip, Bartholomew, Simon of Cana, James the Less, Matthew and Thaddaeus. These twelve, together with three hidden disciples— Nicanor the Essene; Nicodemon son of Gorion, a member of the Sanhedrin; and his own half-brother James the Ebionite—were to form his Inner Council, divided into three groups of five, namely, the healers, the prophets and the law-givers. Jesus designated Peter, James, John, Andrew and Thomas as the chosen healers; Judas, Philip, Bartholomew, Simon of Cana, James the Less as the chosen prophets; and Matthew, Thaddaeus, Nicanor, Nicodemon and James the Ebionite as the chosen law-givers. All these were Israelites, and they were to be assisted by a Grand Council of seventy-two, also Israelites. Five district synods, representative of the synagogues, would be obedient to this central body of spiritual government.

Women would have no part in government, yet they would be honoured citizens of the Kingdom and permitted to form sacred choirs, as among the Essene Therapeutics of Egypt, and even to prophesy, for according to Pharisaic tradition: "The man is not to be without the woman, nor the woman without the man, nor are both together to be without the Glory of the Lord." Other nations would be given the status of either allies or subject allies in a world empire dominated by the Kingdom of Israel; but the function of the Israelites was to be not arrogant overlords of the rest but the world's moral exemplars, and they would therefore be bound by the strictest observance of the Law. The allies would be bound by a general moral law and the acknowledgement of God's supreme sovereignty; and the same demands for holiness would not be immediately made from those whose closest link with the Israelites was a common descent from Noah—among them the Armenians, the Cypriots, the Ionians, the Assyrians and the Cimmerians of Northern Britain—as from those who, like the Arabians, Edomites and Dorians, could claim to be descended from Abraham. But before the thousand years were over, even the savage Moors and cannibalistic Finns would adopt circumcision and the Law and become true Children of Light.

Many men whom Jesus summoned to be his disciples excused themselves on one ground or another. To one who said: "I will come when my old father dies," he replied: "Let the dead bury their dead, as in the Egyptian fable." "Not yet, not yet!"

He was convinced that the Kingdom of God was close at hand, though the hour and day of its coming were known only to God himself, and that multitudes of those to whom he preached would survive the dreadful terrors that were to announce it, and would therefore never experience death. At the end of the thousand years, the physical world would come to an end, and a general Resurrection and Day of Judgement ensue: then the Kingdom of God would merge in the Kingdom of Heaven, a purely spiritual existence in which the souls of righteous men would become radiant elements of God's glory. In this firm belief he set out to refine religious faith and practice, choosing the best doctrinal elements from all the different sects of Jewry—including the Sadducees, Essenes, Zealots and Anavim, or Messianic mystics—and correlating these with the generous, yet scrupulous, Pharisaic system. He would travel the Holy Land from end to end, like a shepherd who rounds up his strayed sheep; even visiting Samaria, where the peasants belonged to the old Israelite stock, though the priesthood and aristocracy were foreigners who had originally embraced Judaism as a convenience.

In a version of the Acts and Sayings of Jesus current in the Roman Church, an incident of Jesus's audacious visit to the Samaritans is characteristically presented as having occurred at Jerusalem. And how clumsy the forgery is! Jesus is recorded as saving the life of a woman whom the Pharisees are about to stone for adultery by the simple ruse of saying: "Let the man among you who is sinless cast the first stone!" But for the past hundred years the law for the stoning of a Jewish adulteress had been a dead letter: she must be brought to Jerusalem for trial, even if taken in the act elsewhere. She needed only to plead ignorance of the Law before the Pharisaic High Court and she was acquitted, though liable to be divorced and warned before two witnesses never to meet her paramour again. She did not even lose her rights under the marriage contract. Where adultery was only suspected, not proved, she was given "bitter water" to drink in proof of her innocence; then if she died she was proved guilty, but since the bitter water was merely a strong purge, she was invariably proved innocent. It was only in Samaria that the penalty against adulteresses and their paramours was exacted with primitive fury.

In the same volume occurs another absurdity. According to the original Aramaic version, Jesus, in dispute with a Sadducee, tells the story of a Samaritan who goes from Jerusalem to Jericho and on the way is robbed, wounded and stripped by bandits. A priest passes by on the other side of the road, so does a Levite, but a simple God-loving Israelite takes him up, dresses his wounds, sets him on his own ass, and conveys him to an inn where he will be cared for. The moral of the story is that the common people of Israel—the common people educated in the Pharisaic synagogues—are more religious-minded than the Temple priesthood, and that when the Kingdom of

God is established it will contain very few of the natural religious leaders of Israel: "The first shall be the last; the last shall be the first." The Sadducees had, indeed, for centuries refused the Samaritans entry into the Inner Courts of the Temple and regarded them as unclean; which explains the reluctance of the priest and the Levite to aid the wounded man. Jesus, though aware of the Samaritans' faults, was declaring that the breach between them and the Jews—which had greatly widened since the defilement of the Court of the Priests twenty years before—must be speedily healed, and could be healed only by generosity. But in the Roman version the text has been amended to emphasize the Gentile Chrestians' dislike of the Pharisees and of the Jews generally. The occasion of the story is presented as a dispute between Jesus and a Pharisee, while in the story itself the nationality of the victim is not mentioned and the kindly God-fearing Israelite is no longer an Israelite but a Samaritan. Again, what a clumsy forgery! The amended story does not make literary sense. It is as though one were to substitute "Carthaginian" for "Citizen" in a Roman moral tale of how Senator, Knight and Citizen behaved in some social crisis; for Priest, Levite and Israelite are the three estates of Jewry, as the three estates of Rome are Senator, Knight and Citizen. Moreover, the context in which according to both versions Jesus spoke the parable was his quotation of the text: "Thou shalt love thy neighbour as thyself", to which the Sadducee replied: "But who is my neighbour?" The answer forced from him: "The man to whom the Israelite showed mercy", has been illogically changed in the Roman version to "The man who showed mercy to the Israelite".

On one or two recorded occasions Jesus did criticize individual Pharisees, but never the sect as a whole. His words were directed either against those who failed in their high moral pretensions, or against outsiders who falsely pretended to be Pharisees—especially certain Roman or Herodian agents who, taking advantage of his dialectical method of teaching, tried to entrap him into revolutionary statements.

Jesus belonged to the direct line of the famous teachers of ethics of whom Hillel the Pharisee was the most humane and enlightened, and for this reason refrained from committing his thoughts to paper. The Pharisees well understood the tyranny of the written word. By Jesus's time the Law of Moses, originally established for the government of a semi-barbarous nation of herdsmen and hill-farmers, resembled a petulant great-grandfather who tries to govern a family business from his sick-bed in the chimney-corner, unaware of the

287

changes that have taken place in the world since he was able to get about: his authority may not be questioned, yet his orders, since no longer relevant, must be reinterpreted in another sense, if the business is not to go bankrupt. When the old man says, for instance: "It is time for the women to grind their lapfuls of millet in the querns", this is taken to mean: "It is time to send the sacks of wheat to the water-mill."

Hillel and his fellow-Pharisees insisted on a very close observance of the Law in so far as it was still practicable and inoffensive to their enlightened sense of divine mercy. But their glosses on the Law were oral and thus easily discarded when lapse of years proved them inaccurate or misleading. They recommended the tithing not only of wheat and fruit and other staple products but of garden herbs as well; at the same time they softened the rigour of the Law wherever to obey the letter would be to dishonour the spirit. For example, the stoning of adulterers and adulteresses. The Pharisees' view was as follows: "Either women are in general responsible creatures and should take the same part in religion as the men; or else they are irresponsible and must be limited in their activities. It occasionally happens in small country synagogues that educated and pious women are elected as synagogue officials; but for the most part women show no aptitude for religious learning and are not encouraged to attempt it. In Deuteronomy the ordinance occurs: 'You shall teach these laws to your sons'; daughters are not specified. An uneducated woman must therefore not be held responsible for any failure in chastity, since the man who has lain with her is likely to know the Law better than she. Moses, indeed, assumed in women a sufficient knowledge of the Law to make unchastity punishable with Death, and issued his regulations accordingly, but women were more responsible in those days than they are now, because the wilderness offered them fewer temptations than the city or the village and they were privileged to hear Moses's own utterances. Should we then stone the adulterer and let the adulteress go free? No, this would be manifestly unjust, since it would put the life of the weak man at the mercy of the predatory woman; and even our Father Adam was not proof against a woman's wanton smiles. Let us therefore leave them both to repentance and God's mercy; for he created our Mother Eve and he alone understands the heart of an adulterous woman. Is it not written: 'Such is the way of an adulteress: she eats, she wipes her mouth, she says: "I have done no wickedness" '?"

The Pharisees' enlightened point of view is perhaps best exemplified in their attitude to the observance of the Sabbath. They were scrupulous to prohibit on the Sabbath day the performance of any work that might be done on a week day; yet if the Commandment, attributed to Moses, that a man should love his neighbour as himself, seemed to be invalidated by scruples of Sabbath-breaking—if, for example, a neighbour's house collapsed on a Sabbath and he was heard shrieking for help from under the ruins—why, then the work must be done, Sabbath or no Sabbath. Hillel's own life had been saved by the breach of a Sabbath: as a young man he had been found one Sabbath morning standing frozen in four feet of snow outside the window of an Academy lecture-hall where he had been listening to a debate, prevented by extreme poverty from paying the janitor the few coppers which he demanded as entrance fee.. The Doctors of the Law worked hard to restore him to life, saying: "This is a man for whom the Sabbath may well be broken!" Jesus similarly was a scrupulous keeper of the Law, but he is recorded to have told a man whom he saw breaking the Sabbath in order to perform some small service to his neighbour: "If you do not know what you are doing, you deserve a reprimand from the President of your synagogue; if you do know, you deserve his praise!"

Jesus was not only a king and a teacher of ethics: he was a prophet—a healer and miracle-worker in the line of Elijah and Elisha, Isaiah, Jeremiah, Ezekiel, Daniel, Hosea, Amos, Zechariah, Zephaniah, Micah, Enoch and the rest. Throughout his missionary tour of Galilee he carried a pastoral staff and wore a shepherd's "rough garment" or hair mantle, as habitually worn by these ancient prophets; and later required his disciples to do the same. Many of his prophetic utterances have been wilfully misunderstood by the Gentile Chrestians. The prophet, as the word implies, regarded himself as the mouthpiece of Jehovah: what he spoke under prophetic influence was not his own utterance, but Jehovah's. Such an utterance was always prefaced with: "Thus saith the Lord", or "The word of the Lord came to me, saying"; and to keep his mouth holy he was bound to abstain from wine—a source of false prophecy—except when a royal marriage gave him dispensation. When Jesus is reported to have said: "I am the Resurrection and the Life", or "I am the Way, the Truth and the Life", he must be understood as speaking in Jehovah's name and the prefatory words must be restored to the text. Any other interpretation is historically unthinkable. His usual preface was the twice-repeated Hebrew word *Amen*, which literally means "He was firm", and which he used in the sense of "Jehovah has firmly declared". The Gentile Chrestians, wishing to exalt Jesus into a God, translate the irksome *Amen* merely as "Verily" and often omit it altogether. They also attribute to him several well-known sayings of Hillel, Shammai, Simeon the Just and other celebrated Jewish moralists, by the simple trick of suppressing his humble acknowledgement to them, as for example: *"Have you not heard what Antigonus of Soko received from the lips of Simeon the Just? For Simeon used to say:* 'Be not as slaves who serve their master in hope of reward, but as slaves that serve without hope of reward; and let the fear of Heaven be upon you.'" Or: *"Have you not heard what the learned Hillel—his memory be blessed—told the scoffer who asked to be taught the whole Law while standing upon one foot?* 'Do not to your neighbour what you would not have him do to you! This is the whole Law; the rest is gloss.'" *"And the converse of his judgement is found in the Letter of Aristeas:* 'Do to others as you would be done by.'"

As a courteous king he suited his speech to every class of his subjects. To prophets, such as John the Baptist, he spoke as a poet; to Doctors of the Law he spoke in their own learned language; to merchants and tradesmen more familiarly; to the mass of the people who were not subtle enough to understand either deep poems or complex religious theory, he sang songs and told fables.

Some of his songs survive. Most of them contain simple advice to men and women not to allow social ambition or preoccupation with the routine of daily life to draw their minds away from contemplation of the Kingdom of God. For example:

> *Consider the ravens*
>   *That neither plough nor reap,*
> *Nor build them a store-house*
>   *Their stores wherein to keep:*
> *For God tends them well,*
>   *As a shepherd his sheep.*

> *Consider the wind-flowers*
>   *That neither sew nor spin,*
> *Yet Solomon's sister,*
>   *All glorious within,*
> *Won never such beauty*
>   *Of dress as they win.*

In the prose-translation offered in this Acts and Sayings of Jesus, "Solomon" is written for "Solomon's sister", I suppose because the Queen of Sheba admired Solomon's magnificence; but this emendation spoils the poetic balance between the ravens as the men and the flowers as the women. It also obscures the reference to the coronation psalm: "The King's daughter is all glorious within"; for the King here is Solomon's father David and his daughter is Solomon's "sister and spouse", the Shunemite of the Canticles. This version unaccountably omits the two explanatory verses of the song:

> *God remembers the ravens*
> *That lightened the distress*
> *Of Elijah the Tishbite*
> *In the wilderness,*
> *Though the rulers of Israel*
> *Denied him their mess.*

> *God remembers the wind-flowers*
> *That reddened all the sward*
> *When the pure blood of Abel*
> *Was spilt by Cain's sword—*
> *Every spring-time they greet him,*
> *Renewing their Lord.*

It is possible that Jesus's strange commendation of the unclean ravens conceals a reference to the well-known enmity between the raven and the owl; as we say in Greek: "The voice of the owl is one thing, and the raven's voice another." For the raven was the bird of Elijah the healer and poet, and though unclean was regarded as of lucky omen, whereas the owl was the bird of Lilith the First Eve whom Jesus was set on destroying.

Simpler even than this raven and lily song is one which begins:

> *Do not sigh, do not mourn,*
> *I will lighten your cares:*
> *For blessèd are the poor—*
> *God's kingdom is theirs.*
> *Blessèd are the merciful—*
> *Merciful is he.*
> *Blessèd are the pure—*
> *His face they shall see.*
> *Blessèd are the meek—*
> *His carpet is spread.*
> *Blessèd are the hungry—*
> *They shall be fed. . . .*

and another that concerns divine mercy:

> Ask, it shall be given.
> Seek, you shall find.
> Knock, the door shall open—
> God's heart is kind.

The song, *When Your Right Eye Offends You*, recommends meek acceptance of external oppression combined with proud resistance to internal oppression. And *Judge the Tree* lays down a standard of moral judgement:

> Judge the tree by the fruit,
> Judge not by the leaf. . . .

Jesus put some of his fables into rough ballad form, such as the one about the rich man and the beggar and how they fared in the other world; and the one beginning:

> The farmer trudges out to sow,
> The leathern seed-bag slung at his side.
> Along the merry furrows watch him go
> To scatter the good seed far and wide.

He is credited with having also composed poems of a quality to compare with those of Isaiah and Ezekiel; but none of these has survived.

He sometimes impressed a moral judgement on his disciples by the performance of a symbolical act—as, for example, at Cana when he attended the marriage of his nephew Palti and at a late hour the wine gave out and no more could be procured. The master of ceremonies, distressed and ashamed, came to him for advice. Jesus instructed the servants to fill up the wine-jars again with the lustral water which every pious Jew uses for cleansing his hands before and after meals, and to serve it with the same ceremony as if it were wine. They hesitated to obey until his mother, as the senior matron, insisted on their doing so. He then himself accepted the first bowlful of water, praised its delicious bouquet and colour and sipped it like a connoisseur. "Adam drank such wine as this in Eden", he said. The master of ceremonies followed his example and swore that never had he tasted such good wine. He meant that he approved Jesus's message: "Cleanliness, that is to say 'holiness before the Lord', is better than excessive drinking. For Adam in the days of his innocency knew purer joys than his descendant Noah, the inventor of wine; wine is good, but wine taken to excess led Noah to shamelessness and his son Ham into sin and slavery." 'However, according to my Ebionite informant, Jesus was saying even more than this: he was saying that Adam and Eve in the days of innocency abstained from carnal love—of which the emblem in the Canticles is wine—and that when they succumbed to it after the Fall the fruit of their union was Cain, the first murderer, who brought Death into the world. Only by a return to that love between man and woman from which the dangerous joys of carnality are banished can mankind return to Eden.

Jesus and the master of ceremonies played their dramatic parts with such gravity and verisimilitude that they persuaded a few of the drunken guests that they were, in fact, drinking wine; and Jesus is therefore credited by Gentile Chrestians, who abstain neither from wine nor from marriage, with a vulgar and purposeless miracle of the sort performed by Syrian jugglers at fairs! They have made a similar miracle out of another of his symbolic acts—the pretended feeding of a great number of his followers with five loaves of bread.

He performed this act by the Lake of Galilee one afternoon, after taking refuge in a boat from a crowd of people, estimated at some five thousand, who came rushing about him near Taricheae. He coasted slowly in the boat for several miles along the south-eastern shore until all but a thousand of them, growing hungry and weary, returned to the city. Then he disembarked, satisfied that those who remained were not idle sightseers but sincere seekers after truth. "Of five thousand, four thousand are gone, one thousand remain. What shall we do with them?"

Peter said: "Lord, the four thousand have returned to eat bread; let the others do the same."

"No. I will feed them; for the sake of the saying: 'Let your right hand repel, but your left invite.' "

"Two hundred drachmae would not buy bread for them even were a baker's shop suddenly to spring up in this deserted place."

"I will give them living bread."

The sequel is recorded in the Acts and Sayings of Jesus, but the original meaning of his performance seems to have been forgotten, because the description is confused and vague.

Jesus sat on a rock and ordered the people to sit down on the grass. "Five loaves will suffice," he said, "for six full companies. Afterwards I will feed the rest."

"Who among you has loaves?" bawled Peter, and presently a boy came forward; he had five loaves in one bag and a few broiled fish in another.

Jesus gave his disciples their instructions: "Quartermasters, take a basket each. You are to distribute the rations. Number me six companies of men and women, and let them sit down in a circle facing me, with a gap at the southern end. But first let everyone wash his hands in the Lake!"

When this was done, he began to preach about the living bread, the word of God, how it is good to feed upon, day after day, all the year round. He also reminded them how Elisha the prophet had satisfied the hunger of a hundred men with only twenty loaves, after pronouncing: "Thus saith the Lord, they shall all eat bread and have bread left over!" For Elisha's loaves were not common ones, but first-fruit loaves baked from grain of the first sheaf thrashed at Beth Shalishah, grain thankfully dedicated to God, living bread in which the spirit of the harvest was immanent, bread from the House of Bread. "Bring me the five loaves for sanctification!"

They brought him the loaves. Jesus sanctified them with the formula used by the priests in dedicating the first-fruit, then broke them in fragments which he distributed equally among the baskets. "Quartermasters," he said, "take up your stations, each on the right hand of a half-company!"

They obeyed.

"To each one a loaf!"

Then, starting from the gap, he moved sunwise round the circle, taking each basket in turn from the disciple who held it, dealing out a phantom loaf to everyone, and returning the basket again when he had done.

"Eat heartily!" cried Jesus. "Tastier and more strength-giving bread was never baked." He set them an example by tearing at a phantom crust with his teeth and munching with relish.

Merrily or gravely, everyone followed his example.

When he came to the gap he paused and called his disciples to him. They came running. He cried: "Here is bread remaining. Turn it out on the grass."

They did so, and he said: "Look, as much as would make five whole loaves. Call five more eaters to fill the gap!"

Five more men were called, and each of them received his phantom loaf. After this he sanctified the broiled fish and distributed them among all, as if it were a fish to everyone.

"Four thousand are gone, one thousand remain. Whoever has eyes to see, let him see!"

Having said this, he instructed everyone in the circle to yield his place to someone who had not yet fed. When the circle had been re-formed he preached again about the living bread. He told how Joseph, when he foresaw a seven years' famine, built seven great granaries in Egypt, one of which he filled in every year of plenty as insurance against a year of famine.

He continued: "Joseph's father Jacob and his eleven sons came down to Egypt to be fed, and Joseph appointed his brothers and his sons to deal out the bread to the people, each in turn doing duty for a week, and drawing in turn from each of the seven granaries." With that, he divided the heap of broken bread into seven small heaps and put them into seven baskets. "Here are the granaries," he said, and named each of his twelve disciples after a patriarch; but since one more person was needed to act as Benjamin, he called out of the circle the boy to whom the loaves and fishes belonged.

Then began the second distribution. Each pretended patriarch in turn came forward and distributed bread to seven men, to each man a loaf from a different basket. Peter, playing the part of Reuben, began the distribution, and when he and his companions had each dealt out bread exactly four times, they came to the gap from which the boy had been called.

Jesus said to the boy: "Return to your place in the circle, Benjamin. The five loaves in these baskets are yours by right, for it is written: 'Benjamin's portion was five times as much as theirs.' And the Psalmist also says: 'There is little Benjamin, their ruler.'" Then he cried in a loud voice: "Whoever has eyes to see, let him see. Four thousand are gone and one thousand remain. And another Joseph is at hand!"

When all members of the crowd had been fed, and had washed their hands, he blessed them, dismissed them and returned to his seat in the stern of the boat. The sail was hoisted, and as they drew away from land he asked his disciples: "How many loaves of bread did I divide among the crowd on the first occasion?"

"Five."

"And how many baskets were there?"

"Twelve."

"And how much bread was left over?"

"Enough for five more people."

"And on the second occasion?"

"The same number of loaves, but distributed in seven baskets. Five loaves were left over, which were all given to the same person."

"You have answered well. The first occasion concerned the four thousand that went away; the second, the remaining fifth thousand. Who understands my reckoning?"

Only Thaddaeus and Matthew could claim to understand it.

"Thaddeus, expound the four thousand who went away!"

"The four thousand years, of which you have taught us, that have elapsed since Adam's day."

"And the twelve baskets?"

"The twelve signs of the Zodiac and the twelve Egyptian months of thirty days apiece, of which you have also taught us."

"And the five loaves?"

"The five seventy-two-day seasons of which you have also taught us; which together make three hundred and sixty days of the Egyptian public year."

"And the five loaves left over?"

"The five days added to the public year, each a day of power."

"You have answered well. Matthew, expound the other riddle!"

"The thirteen overseers are the thirteen months; each a month of four weeks, as you have taught us. The year has three hundred and sixty-four days, as may be read in the book of the prophet Enoch. One merciful day is added, the day of the Chrestos, the Propitious Child. To him all the five powers yield to whom the five days were formerly sacred."

"Who is the Child?"

"The seed sown in good soil who, as you have also taught us, is reaped at the first-fruits and sanctified to God's use."

"And the thousand that remain?"

"The thousand years of the approaching Kingdom of God."

"You have answered well. Who will expound the fish?"

Peter said: "It is written: 'We remember the fish which we ate in Egypt.'"

Jesus said reproachfully: "Peter, Peter, bold in your errors!"

After a silence, Philip spoke: "Joshua was the son of Nun, which is to say Son of a Fish. You are Joshua, for Jesus is the Greek for Joshua; and the son of a fish is a fish like his father. Joshua means: 'Jehovah will save.' You, a fish, distributed Joshua among the hungry, meaning that God will save them if they listen to your words and obey the Law of Moses; for Moses was also a fish."

"How so?"

"He was drawn out of the water."

Jesus was pleased with Philip; and to this day the secret password among Chrestians is to draw a fish with one's toe in the dust or to form a fish's head with the fingers of the left hand.

According to my informant, however, this was not yet all. What Jesus had done was, in the manner of a poet, to convey a plain meaning and a difficult meaning simultaneously. The plain meaning was that the God of Israel would feed his people daily with the staples of life if they dedicated themselves to his service all the year round, feeding on the words which he had delivered to Moses and the Prophets. But the difficult meaning was this, that Moses followed the Egyptian calendar, which ran by thirty-day months, each divided up into three ten-day weeks, with five days over; but that neither in this system nor in the system which had been substituted for it during the Captivity—a year of twelve months regulated by the moon, and a period of eleven days for intercalation at regular intervals—was the sacred seven-day week an exact division of the month.

Among the many great deeds prophesied for the Messiah son of Joseph was the reform of the calendar. Jesus had not yet revealed himself as the Messiah, so that though his plan for its reform was now delivered he had been content to make the demonstration without publicly drawing the moral. By dividing the year into thirteen months, each of twenty-eight days—which was the system followed by the ancestors of the Jews before they entered Egypt—each month would have four weeks, and only one day be left over from the count, namely the day of the winter solstice, the day of Jesus's own birth, the day on which the sacred corn is sown; and then the last seven-day week would be enlarged into an ogdoad, or eight-day week. Eight is the traditional number of plenty, for which reason an eight-pointed cross was marked on the Temple shewbread. In the new calendar, instead of the five days left over, which in Egypt were sacred to Osiris, Horus, Set, Isis and Nephthys, only one would be left over, sacred to the Son of Man prophesied by Daniel. To him all the seasons of the year would pay tribute. For Benjamin means "Son of my Right Hand", and the Son of Man was to sit on the right hand of his Father, the Ancient of Days; and the right hand among the Jews also signifies the south, where the boy had his station in the circle of listeners.

That Jesus abstained from an explanation has misled the Gentile Chrestians into thinking that he meant: "I am the fulfilment of all prophecies which refer to Tammuz the Corn-god." For he was born on the birthday of Tammuz at Bethlehem, the "House of Bread", in the cave of Tammuz and was cradled in the harvest-basket of Tammuz. And they also hold that he had hinted at Cana: "I am the fulfilment of all prophecies which refer to the Vine-god, Noah or Dusares.

or Dionysus. I am from Nazareth, the 'House of Wine'." For, later, he told the disciples: "I am the Vine, you are the branches"; but on that occasion he was speaking of Jehovah, not of himself and prefaced the prophecy with a doubled *Amen*. Later still he gave them far more solid grounds for their misunderstanding, as will be shown in due course. So far have some Chrestians gone in this mystical cult of Jesus that they wear thumb-rings inscribed with the letters *Iota Eta Sigma*, the well-known initials of Dionysus as "Disposer of the Waters of Life"; for these are also the first three letters of Jesus's name when spelt out in Greek.

Jesus's concern with the coming Kingdom of God is revealed in a prophetic intuition which suddenly came to him in a boat on the Lake of Galilee. He advised Peter and Andrew, who were with him and had caught nothing all night, to shoot their nets in a certain place and count their catch. They did so, and the catch was one hundred and fifty-three fish. This is a story hardly worth recording —for foolish and stupid people are often granted more remarkable intuitions—unless it is understood that one hundred and fifty-three is a symbolical number, representing all the distinct languages of the known world. Jesus was saying: "When the Kingdom comes it will include men from every nation in the entire world."

CHAPTER TWENTY-TWO

THE BRIDEGROOM

MATTHEW son of Alpheus had been a customs official of Capernaum. Though he resigned his post when he answered Jesus's sudden call to discipleship, he was not the man to forget his former associates, and Jesus, who often resorted to his house before he sold it and settled his affairs, came through him to know most of the tax-gatherers of the district. Theirs was the most hated profession in all Palestine: they were classed with thieves and highwaymen not only by the common people but by the High Court itself. No money that they offered to the Temple or to religious charities might be accepted, because it was almost certainly acquired by fraud; nor might their evidence be accepted in any Jewish court of law, because of the judgement: "No tax-gatherer is capable of truth." In both of these respects the tax-gatherer was the male counterpart of the prostitute; and indeed fashionable prostitutes and tax-gatherers were often profitably related in business which included blackmail and brothel-keeping.

Taxation in Galilee was a source of general misery. Antipas the Tetrarch followed the example of his father King Herod by taxing land, cattle, fruit-trees, houses and every sort of marketable merchandise, besides imposing a poll-tax, a road-tax and a tax on exports and imports. His tetrarchy measured little more than fifty miles in length by thirty miles in breadth, yet he leased the farming of taxes to a ring of contractors for no less than two hundred gold talents [1] a year, and the ring subleased it profitably to smaller men, who employed paid collectors. The collectors relied on the police to support their demands and paid them a handsome commission on their takings, and the police employed spies to inform against evaders of taxation; and the spies prospered on blackmail. Thus a tax of nominally five per cent. of the national income was increased to ten, twelve and fifteen per cent. as contractors, sub-contractors and collectors rewarded themselves for shouldering this unpopular burden; and the cost of police protection brought it up to nearly twenty per cent. Thus, since the incidence of taxation is always heaviest on the poor man and highest on the rich, at least half the earnings of a manual labourer or small farmer were taken from him under one pretext or another; and the cost of living was higher even than at Naples, famous for its high prices.

Matthew was a sub-contractor, and, like every Israelite who had either adopted this profession voluntarily or inherited it from his father, was disabled by the odium it entailed from close observance of the Law; though a Levite by birth, he had become half-Greek in his ways. But he was a man of such sensibility and shrewdness, and so whole-hearted a convert to Jesus's teaching, that he soon outdistanced all the other disciples in his understanding of the finer points of the Law.

The synagogue elders of Capernaum were astonished to hear that Jesus was cultivating the friendship of the tax-gatherers. Two of them came as a deputation to him and begged him to stop the mouth of scandal by discontinuing his visits to Matthew's house. They had been fishermen, but were now living on the proceeds of a wholesale

---

[1] About £1,000,000 pre-war value.

fish-business in which they were partners and which their sons managed for them.

Jesus explained that he regarded tax-gatherers and prostitutes as sick people in need of a physician—a physician must not shrink from the loathsome diseases and injuries of his patients—or as lost sheep for whom a good shepherd must go in search, leaving the rest of his flock securely penned in their sheep-cote.

"But it is whispered of you in the porch of our synagogue: 'He visits a certain house either to take part in some impure Greek cult, or because he counts on the fraudulent contractors and thievish prostitutes who make this house their rendezvous for money to support him in idleness.'"

"Is that how they whisper in the porch? What else do they whisper?"

"That, aided by Matthew the tax-gatherer, you are leading your other disciples into the same way of wickedness."

Jesus smiled and ironically addressed his disciples: "Sons, keep well in with the fraudulent contractors and the thievish prostitutes, for perhaps when your own business fails they will persuade the prophet Enoch to admit you by a side door into the Kingdom of Heaven, where they have already reserved comfortable suites of rooms for all eternity. These children of darkness are more shrewd by far than those who live by the light of the Law."

They roared with laughter. Then he addressed the synagogue elders again, asking casually: "Did you hear the tale of the landowner of Tiberias and his fraudulent estate steward?"

"The rumour reached our kitchens, and our wives chattered, but since the steward was a Greek we stopped our ears against it."

"It is a tale worthy of your attention. The steward was called upon to show his accounts, and knowing well that he would be instantly dismissed when he did so, with no hope of finding another employer, decided to provide against poverty by further frauds. While he still had authority to speak in his master's name he made a round of all the creditors of the estate and reduced their debts by a quarter, or a half. You can well imagine the land-owner's delight when he discovered what had been done!"

"What is this unjust steward to us?"

"The stewards of the Lord's house of Capernaum not only mismanage his estate but discourage his creditors—the tax-gatherers and prostitutes and those whom misfortune has made unclean—from paying their full debts of love to him, and dare to do this in his name. You have read the prophecy in the Testament of Moses?"

"It is not in the Canon."

"Nevertheless listen: 'And in their time'—the time that is now—'destructive and impious men shall rule, declaring themselves righteous. They shall devour the goods of the poor, in the name of justice; they shall be complainers, deceivers, impious men, filled with sin and lawlessness from sunrise to sunset. "We shall have feasting and good cheer, eating and drinking," they shall say, "and esteem ourselves princes." They shall touch what is unclean and think what is unclean, yet they shall say: "Away, Sir, away—you will pollute me with your very shadow!" ' "

One of the elders cried out: "Have a care, Sir! Some of your disciples are members of our synagogue. You do ill to weaken our authority. If we have sinned, the sin must be laid at the door of Heaven, for no one can accuse us of breaking the Law that has been delivered to us by our fathers; and we are strictly enjoined to separate ourselves from the company of the unclean man and the sinner."

Jesus turned again to his disciples: "The elders of your synagogue sit in the seat of Moses and dispense the Law. This Law must be obeyed to the letter, and to the very fraction of a letter. Though they lay heavy obligations of ritual cleanliness on you—burdens which are nothing to them, because they are wealthy men with servants and Canaanite slaves and do not earn a living with their hands—do always as they tell you, even where the spirit of the Law has been plainly falsified by them. Far be it from me to weaken their authority. Do as they tell you, however absurd their legal fictions for evading a plain duty to God. Do as they tell you—but not as they do! For, in the words of the proverb: they strain from their broth the unclean gnat, yet swallow the unclean camel."

The elders, trained from childhood to accept reproof humbly and patiently, kept silence but could hardly contain their rage as Jesus continued: "The preacher, the Son of Sira says: 'Let none declare: "My sin comes from God." For why should God cause a man to do what he hates? Let him not say either: "God caused me to err." For what need has God of a sinner?' And I say: Amen, Amen: the Law, holy and righteous as it is, has been made a stumbling-block to the poor. You are the sinners, rich men, who have caused these poor children to despair of salvation by shunning them as unclean and refusing them admittance to the synagogue. It is your wealth that has led you into sin: for wealth begets leisure, and leisure begets an evil conscience, and an evil conscience begets over-scrupulousness in the Law, and over-scrupulousness in the Law begets presumption, and presumption dries up the fountains of the heart. Therefore when it is written in the Testament of Moses: 'They shall touch what is unclean', the meaning is: 'The idle rich man rides on the neck of the poor man and forces him to eat what is unclean; and thereby contaminates himself.' In the Day of Judgement you will be made to answer for your sins and it will go hard with you."

They asked him: "Do you dishonour the memory of the learned Hillel from whom we learned these 'absurd legal fictions', as you call them, these 'falsifications of the Law'?"

"Hillel was a carpenter who never ceased to labour with his hands and remained a poor man to the last. If any man now pleads poverty as an excuse for not studying the Law, it is asked of him: 'Are you poorer even than Hillel was?' He interpreted the Law in the spirit of love and laid no burden on the people that he would not himself undertake with joy. It is written that when Moses died all the men of Israel mourned for him; but at the death of Hillel, as at Aaron's death, not only men but women and children also mourned. Honouring his memory, I say: Sell your profitable business, merchants, distribute the proceeds to the poor, return to the boats and nets that you foolishly abandoned, and as you labour on the waters of the Lake remember again your duty towards your neighbour! For is it not written: 'Six days *shalt* thou labour'? And the learned Shammai, who received from Simeon son of Shetach, said: 'Love work, and hate lordship.' And others of the wise have said: 'A man should hire himself out to a stranger rather than sit idle; let him flay a carcase in the street to earn his bread rather than say: "I am a priest", or "I am a great and learned man".'"

"You are called Jesus the carpenter. Where then are your hammer, saw, chisel and mallet?"

"From a carpenter I have become a shepherd." He displayed his pastoral staff and mantle. "Let no man envy me my laborious new trade."

"And these idle disciples of yours?"

"Let no man envy them their laborious apprenticeship."

The elders took their leave of him without another word; and he received no more invitations to preach in any synagogue of Capernaum.

The reason for the suspicion that he accepted tainted money was that two Jewish sisters who frequented Matthew's house were financing his tour of preaching. One of them, Joanna, was the wife of Chuza, the estate-steward of Antipas; the other, Susanna, was married to a colleague of Matthew's, the collector of road-taxes for

Lower Galilee. Jesus gladly accepted their offer of assistance on an assurance that the money was drawn from their own dowries and therefore clean. Susanna also collected money from her women friends, being careful to accept none of doubtful origin. But the sum that they had to find was no small one. Though at this time the disciples seldom needed to buy food in the market, but on the contrary were often embarrassed by the lavish hospitality offered them by admirers of Jesus, one of them was rich and all had families to support, homes to keep up, and taxes to pay.

They used Peter and Andrew's boat for travelling together around the Lake, and fished between religious labours; but carefully as they lived, the sense that they were playing truant from their homes and trades haunted them, and was not dispelled by the sense of virtue that they won in abandoning their former sins. Jesus found that some of them were deriving what he regarded as illegitimate satisfaction from being the chosen disciples of a famous healer and teacher. He quoted Hillel's judgement to them: "A name made great is a name destroyed." Thereafter he performed cures rarely and in secret, and ceased to emphasize his preaching with mysterious symbolical acts.

As this novelty of his preaching wore off, this apparent failure of his powers was soon observed and commented upon disparagingly in the market-places: it was said that he had come to the Lake a few months before as a pale ascetic, but had now forfeited his curative powers through gluttony at the tables of his disreputable supporters. And though at first he had been welcomed as a prophet who laid light obligations on his listeners and did not insist on fatiguing ritual or cramping self-denial, critics now complained that this was no fiery John the Baptist, whose words scorched them to the marrow like the hot desert wind. Was this a time for soft words, a time for eating and drinking and good cheer? True, Jesus preached the coming of the Messiah as John did: but John's disciples fasted and abstained from earthly pleasures, knowing that the Messiah would come only when the truly penitent separated themselves from the mass of evil-doers and presented themselves as his holy bodyguard. Jesus's disciples, on the other hand, looked merry and prosperous and seemed oblivious of the sin and oppression which surrounded them.

When publicly challenged on this score, Jesus replied: "Do you not know that the bridegroom's companions are exempt from the obligation of fasting and even of prayer during the seven days of the wedding feast? Let them fast beforehand, let them fast afterwards, but this is a time to dance, sing and be glad. I preach the mercy of God to those who seek him, not his vengeance on those who oppose him."

His former friends of the Capernaum synagogue discovered that Judas of Kerioth, as Jesus's treasurer, went at regular intervals to draw money from the house of Antipas's estate-steward. They began to regard Jesus as a false prophet and a traitor to his country. Having originally sponsored him, they were now anxious to disavow him for their own credit. It stuck in their minds that he had compared himself to a bridegroom—why a bridegroom? They had a proverb: "The bridegroom is like a king." Was he hinting that he was a Great One? They sent two other elders to him as a deputation.

These asked: "You say that you are a bridegroom. In what sense do you mean it?"

He would say no more than that this was a marriage to which the best-bred people in the land had been invited—priests, land-owners, lawyers, elders of the synagogue—but many had made excuses and their seats had therefore been filled with tax-gatherers, prostitutes, beggars and the sick.

The elders then asked him to prove by some clear sign that he was a person of sufficient eminence to be judged superior to scandal.

He replied that he was no magician who caught the attention of the mob by vulgar miracles. To lust after signs and miracles was spiritual adultery. "Even King Solomon, for all the authority that he exercised over demons, gave no sign to the Queen of Sheba when she came to visit him except the moral wisdom which he imparted to her. Therefore you will be given no more than the sign that Jonah gave the people of Nineveh: namely, that he preached repentance to them. If you do not repent, you will be given the sign that they escaped the threatened destruction of their city." He added: "You propose, I hear, to rebuild the tomb of Nahum in marble and gilt bronze. Pious men, your ancestors killed Nahum. Were he alive now and prophesying against his oppressors as he prophesied against Nineveh, would you kill him yourselves? Or would you avoid the blood-guilt by betraying him to the Tetrarch?"

This answer decided the synagogue that he had become a public danger. They kept a jealous watch on him, hoping to catch him in some overt breach of the Law. Jesus warned his disciples that they must live without possibility of reproach, and must keep perpetual guard against sin. They had been charged with greed and unseemly merriment; let them not resent the charges. He uttered a judgement: "Love your neighbour when he forgives, but your enemy when he condemns; repay with gratitude those who hate your follies, pray for those who ill-treat you without provocation."

It was on this same occasion—they were eating broiled fish by the Lake-side—that Simon of Cana muttered a complaint that the salt had no taste to it, and that until the Romans had been driven out of the country it would grow more and more tasteless every year. This was fair comment, for the result of the salt-tax, which was farmed out with the other taxes, was that salt had not only become costly but was adulterated with chalk and earth; but Jesus reminded Simon that the Romans were permitted to oppress the Israelites only because they had failed in their duty towards God, and that the adulteration of the salt was an apt reminder of this. At Jerusalem no sacrifice was offered without salt: salt was sprinkled even on the incense. "Salt purifies, but when salt loses its saltiness, what else will salt it? Sons, keep your own salt pure, and one day I will take you to Jerusalem to salt the salt that you find there."

The first of these two sayings has been over-simplified by the Gentile Church. It now runs: "Love your enemies, do good to those who hate you, pray for those who ill-treat you", and becomes either a counsel of impossible perfection, or an incitement to godlessness where (as in Jesus's own case) a man acknowledges no enemies but the enemies of God. Another judgement of his which has been similarly misrecorded may be noticed here. It originally ran: "Amen, Amen: Whoever is not with me is against me, whoever is not against me is with me." The two delicately balanced halves of this antithesis have been considered contradictory by dull-witted editors, and a dispute has arisen as to which of them is authentic! Some quote only one half; some only the other. Yet the sense is plain. Jesus meant that between two active extremes of opinion there is a passive middle region; but passivity does not mean indifference. In other words: "The time has now come when everyone must decide whether he is on the side of good or evil; even to say that one is 'not against' as opposed to 'not with' is a clean indication of choice."

At last he was caught in what seemed to the Capernaum elders a clear breach of the Law: he healed on a Sabbath day a man with a paralysed arm. Now, the religious rule was perfectly clear. It was forbidden to do work of any sort on a Sabbath, the only exception being work necessary for the saving of life. The man's arm had been paralysed for many years and his life could not by any hyperbole be regarded as in danger. Why had Jesus not healed it on the Friday or waited until the Sunday? An ordinary physician was bound by

these rules, and though danger of death might be generously interpreted in the case of a wound, which might or might not prove fatal
if left undressed, he would no sooner set about curing a paralysed
arm on the Sabbath, by the accepted treatment of massage and blis-
tering, than he would hoe cabbages in his garden.

Jesus, when indignantly questioned on this point, asked: "Is it
lawful to save human life on the Sabbath day?"

They answered: "You know as well as we do that it is lawful."

"Is it even lawful on the Sabbath day to save the life of an ox or
an ass that has fallen into a gully or dry well and injured itself?"

"The door is left open. But what life did you save?"

"The life of the man's right arm," he said, "which was more to
him than any ox or ass; for without his use of it he could not fully
perform the duties enjoined on him by the Sabbath ordinances."

"But the arm, being only a part of the man, has no separate existence, though it is his right arm!"

"You know the proverb, not to let your right hand know what
your left hand does. This is to allow them separate souls; and justly.
For the right hand repels, but the left hand beckons; the left hand
holds the chisel, the right wields the hammer; the right hand guides
the pen, the left steadies the parchment. Come now, is it not said
by the Sages: 'A man may profane one Sabbath, that a man may
preserve many Sabbaths'? And does not our Father himself undertake cures on his holy day? Have you never known him to heal
thorn-scratch or headache between the eve of a Sabbath and its
close?"

Had this shrewd answer been uttered in a Jerusalem academy by a
famous Doctor of the Law it would doubtless have been applauded
and gratefully added to the Corpus of Comment; but Capernaum
was a small provincial town, far less liberal than Jerusalem. Now
the rumour began to fly about that Jesus had begun his ministry
shortly after a descent from Mount Tabor where he had been
initiated in the rites of the Demon Beelzebub, and that he performed
his miracles by invocation of this power. Beelzebub is one of the
"names of scorn" in which Jewish sacred literature abounds. By a
slight alteration of letters, a title of honour is converted into one of
dishonour. Thus the chieftain of Carmel whose widow King David
married has had his honourable name Laban "the white man",
changed to Nabál "the fool". And by a similar change the statue of
Olympian Zeus set up by Antiochus Epiphanes in the Temple of
Jerusalem is called not "The statue of the Lord of Heaven", but
"The Abomination of Desolation". So also Beelzebub, "The Lord

of Bluebottles", is a name of scorn for Baal Zebul, "The Lord of Zebulon", or Atabyrius, by whom Ahaziah King of Judah had once sought to be cured of the internal injuries he had sustained in a fall from an upper window.

Jesus derided the charge. "Baal Zebul, the Prince of the Demons," he said, "must have grown senile if he now empowers magicians to evict his subjects from their pleasant dwelling-houses!"

The Passover had come round and Jesus went up to Jerusalem with his disciples in the company of thousands of other Galilean pilgrims. On his arrival at the Temple he entered boldly, conscious of his legitimacy. He took his stand in the Court of Gentiles and expounded the text in the Psalms: "Blessed be the Lord, who dwells in Jerusalem", to a large audience, for the most part Galileans. This was an occasion of great importance in his ministry, since it was the first time that he had preached in Jerusalem. His thesis was novel and provocative: that God dwelt in the hearts of the people who came up for the East, rather than in the Temple itself. When the Temple had been profaned and destroyed, had Jehovah been houseless? Had he haunted the bare hill-top like a demon, or had he gone into exile with his people to comfort them? The Temple raised by Solomon was gone; the Temple raised by Zerubbabel had made way for another. Did Jehovah himself order the building of the present Temple, or was it built to satisfy the ambitions of King Herod— Herod who had desecrated Zerubbabel's Temple when he besieged and took it by storm, killing many priests and pious men in the action?

"Though in the narrowness of your understanding you desire a visible sanctuary to which you may turn when you address our God in prayer, what need have you of these splendid buildings? Destroy this Temple, and by God's grace I will build him as acceptable a dwelling-place in three days; for your servant is a carpenter. Israel was great when our God was worshipped as dwelling in an ark of acacia-wood; until at last that narrow house was made an idol, and was removed from the eyes of men by the prophet Jeremiah at the orders of our God himself. Yet this same Jeremiah prophesied in his Name: 'For your sake, Israel, I will remember the love you showed me in your youth in the Wilderness; for then Israel was holiness to his God and the first-fruit of his increase.'

"How say you, Men of Israel? Has not this mountain-top too become an idol? Its stones are stained with innocent blood, from the blood of Abel the first shepherd to the blood of Zacharias the son of

Barachias, wickedly shed in our fathers' day at the Altar of Incense. The prophets railed against Mount Tabor in Galilee when in ancient times idols were raised upon it; but now the idols are gone and the place is clean. On Mount Zion the idols remain. You have made grinning golden idols of these towers and gates."

This daring speech was well received by the Galileans, but rather because it flattered their provincial self-esteem than because they accepted Jesus's transcendental view of God; to the Judaeans it was impious and they showed their resentment by hissing and shooting out their tongues. The Captain of the Temple Watch came up with a small party of Levites, fearing a breach of the peace, but Jesus's staff and rough mantle earned him a prophet's privilege and no riot followed.

He did not eat the Passover lamb and restrained his disciples from doing so. The Essenes say: "To shed the blood of sacrifice is to murder Abel again." Their oral tradition is that Abel the shepherd offered, on that very hill-top, a sober sacrifice of sheep's milk and wild honey, and that Jehovah accepted it, while rejecting Cain's sacrifice of a plough-ox; and that Cain killed Abel in jealousy. Jesus had similar scruples, reinforced by the pronouncement against blood-sacrifices made by the prophet Amos. On the evening of the Passover he went out of the City to the suburb of Bethany to eat un-leavened bread and bitter herbs in the house of his brother-in-law Lazarus; and there he met his queen for the first time since their coronation.

Mary had been ill at ease all this while. Her brother Lazarus, whom she loved dearly, had frequently spoken to her in praise of sexless wedlock and assured her that only by practising it would man and wife avoid death and live to their promised thousand years in the Messianic Kingdom.

"Desire for progeny in marriage is an ancient error implanted in men and women by God's Adversary," he said. "He has persuaded them that by this means they are staving off the ultimate victory of Death over mankind. 'We shall die,' they say, 'but our children and grandchildren will live.' But the truth is that by performing the act of death they are yielding Death the victory. Abstain from the act of death, and what need is there for progeny? Jesus and you and I will live in Paradisal love together and never grow old."

"Yet I desire children. Why should I be denied children? Why should my children and I not share together in the Kingdom of which you speak?"

"Because those who do the act of death must taste of death. You are fortunate beyond all other brides that your husband by abstaining from the enjoyment of your body has devoted you to eternal life."

"Our sister Martha says: 'He is intent only on his own salvation, Mary, and cares little for your shame: you are returned to this house as if you had a secret deformity or a perverse nature.' "

"Those are malicious words and you should defend the honour of your husband against all malice. Your husband acts in pure love."

"Yet he has chosen twelve disciples, I am told, of whom all but two or three·are married men, and some are fathers. Does he preach the Kingdom of God to men already doomed?"

"When he comes to this house he will answer your question."

"Until he comes I will withhold my opinion."

As soon as Jesus entered the house, Mary came to him and washed his feet and sat silent with her eyes fixed on his face all the afternoon while he talked with Lazarus and his kinsmen. Jesus, after greeting her affectionately but with reserve, paid no further attention to her until Martha ran in complaining loudly that Mary was shirking her household duties.

"Let her be," said Jesus. "She has chosen the better part."

Later in the day, when Jesus and Mary were left alone for a while, she began to question him.

"My lord, some of your disciples are fathers. Are they therefore doomed to death?"

"Who am I to pronounce sentence of doom? Only our Father in Heaven judges."

"It is recorded that the prophet Enoch has avoided death. Yet he performed the act of death and begot a son, our long-lived ancestor Methuselah."

"It is prophesied that neither Enoch nor Elijah has avoided death for ever; both must presently return to earth and die and there await the general resurrection."

"Why have you cast me off, my lord, to go walking through Galilee? With your disciple John to-night you exchanged looks of love; from me you withhold your love. Am I not beautiful? Am I not yours?"

"There is beauty of the flesh and there is beauty of the spirit. The beauty of the flesh is ás the wind-flower's, which is swiftly cut down and withers, and is flung into the hay-loft or the furnace of a baker's oven. John's beauty is of the spirit—as King David cried to the corpse of his blood-brother Jonathan: 'Thy love for me was wonderful, surpassing the love of woman.' "

"I love you, and you only. As the Shunemite said to Solomon: 'Bind me like a phylactery on your arm, the satchel turned towards your heart. For jealousy is cruel as the grave, and burns like a fire of charcoal. Many waters cannot quench love, neither can the floods drown it. If any other man offered all his worldly goods for my love, I would reject them with scorn.'"

"Solomon puts these words into the Shunemite's mouth as an allegory of the love of the repentant soul for his God."

"Yet Solomon, though he may have spoken in allegories, did not deny himself the pleasures of love. Not content with seven hundred queenly wives, he also maintained three hundred concubines; and it is written that he surpassed all the kings of the earth in wisdom. You have said that God does not desire men to injure their excellent bodies by fasting. They fast awhile in order to eat again. Must a man injure his body by perpetual fasting from love? Love is an appetite as natural and excellent as food, else our God would assuredly never have given men means of satisfying it. My lord, I charge you to answer me, for I am a woman and you cannot conceal from me that your body longs to be joined in love with mine."

He did not answer.

"Do not be angry with your servant, but answer a fair question fairly, for she has the right to ask it."

He sighed, and looking away from her unveiled face said: "Jose the son of Jochanan of Jerusalem wisely ordered: 'Do not prolong converse with a woman'; and this is interpreted by the Sages as meaning: 'not even with your own wife.' Hence they have said: 'Each time a man disobeys the order, he does evil to himself, desists from the Law and at last inherits Hell.'"

"How so?" asked Mary. "Are women all evil? Why then did you marry me?"

"Women are not all evil, for our God created woman to be man's helpmeet. Yet it is well said: 'Man is to woman as reason is to the bodily senses, as upper to lower, as right to left, as the Divine to the human.'"

"Yet, my lord, what is reason when it is divorced from the bodily senses? Or can an upper storey stand without a lower to bear it up? Or can an ass stand on his two off-legs only? And what honour has our God on earth unless humankind worship him? Command your servant to come with you on your wanderings and she will obey."

Greatly troubled, he rose and left her.

It was at Bethany that Nicodemon son of Gorion came secretly to

Jesus, having paused to hear him preach in the Court of the Gentiles and been wonderfully drawn by his words. Nicodemon was one of the three richest men of Jerusalem, having the monopoly of conveying lustral water to the City in festival time; he was also a member of the Great Sanhedrin and an elder of the Temple Synagogue, to which all the synagogues throughout the world looked for guidance in doctrine and ritual—the biggest fish that had yet come into Jesus's net. Jesus welcomed him, but found that he was a timorous man and of more service to him as a hidden disciple than as an open one.

It was at Bethany, too, that Jesus revealed himself to the Free Essenes, at the house of their Overseer Simeon. He came knocking at the door and said to the porter: "Tell them that I am the man whom they have been expecting!"

"Your name?"

"Jeshuah son of Jose; not Esu son of Ose."

Presently an old Essene came out, and led him through the first door.

"If that is indeed your name, man, give us proof."

"Split the tree; I shall be found. Raise the stone; I shall be revealed."

"Which tree, Lord?"

"The heather-tree, but not that of Byblos."

"Which stone, great Lord?"

"The altar stone, but not that of Tyre."

The old man, trembling with excitement, drew him into the inner chamber, where his cross-examination was continued before a circle of adepts.

"Greatest of Lords, how is the tree split?"

He signed to them with his hands: "David cleaves it."

"Who dares raise the stone?"

He signed again: "Telmen dares, not Telamon, nor yet Ouri-Tal."

"Who will reveal you?"

"Caleb shall reveal me, not Calypso."

The signs that he made with his fingers were these:

DAVID DAVIZEI

TELMEN TOLMAEI

CALEB APOCALYPSEI

"Where did you learn to read the lintel of our mysteries?"

"It was given to me at Callirrhoë. I also visited the House of Spirals and dared the Dog."

"You returned safe from the House of Spirals?"

"I am the King, the son of the eldest son of the eldest son, and my mother was the daughter of the youngest daughter of the youngest daughter."

"Where were you crowned?"

"Where bulls once roared and holy mallow grows. Have I not the seven marks of royalty, and the eighth?" He bared his right shoulder and thrust out his left foot.

They bowed before him and asked: "Lord, Lord, when will you come riding into the City by the East Gate?"

"Not in this month of willows, but in the next, when I shall visit you. Yet I have come to end all mysteries, not to perpetuate them. Carry these words to the college-overseers of Callirrhoë and Engedi and Middin. Tell them also this: that when Herod died, word went about: 'The Lion is dead'; yet from his carcase honey will yet be taken."

"It is no news that the Lion of Edom is dead; let our Lord prophesy rather of the Eagles of Rome."

"It is written: 'Wherever the body is, there shall the eagles be gathered together'; but living men need fear no carrion birds."

CHAPTER TWENTY-THREE

THE KINGDOM OF GOD

JESUS asked his disciples: "Are you prepared to receive the baptism that I received at the hands of John?"

Peter answered: "John has already baptized my brother Andrew and myself, also Philip here, and Simon of Cana."

"He baptized many. But did he wash away your pride of manhood? Some men are born unmanned; some are unmanned in the slave-market; some, forewarned of the coming Day, as it were unman themselves for the sake of the Kingdom of God. For the Day will come like a thief when least expected, and then it shall be again as in the days of Noah: there was eating and drinking in the bridal hall, and soft embracing in the bridal chamber, when suddenly the rains fell, the waters rose, and all but Noah and his sons were swept away. Renounce delight in the flesh, Children, or you will never become citizens of this Kingdom. Whoever can receive this other baptism, let him receive it."

Peter was the first to cry out: "Lord, I am able," and the others said the same, though less readily.

Philip asked:·"If we are no longer permitted to company with our wives, what prevents us from divorcing them and returning them to their fathers' houses? For we are no longer the men who contracted for them in marriage, and divorce is licenced by the Law."

"Moses gave this licence to an evil generation doomed to die in the wilderness. The learned Shammai held it to be a permanent ordinance but pronounced: 'Adultery is the sole ground.' Then Hillel— his memory be blessed—pronounced: 'To those who hold that the licence is yet valid, adultery cannot remain the sole ground: the licence can be so stretched by the hard-hearted that a man may justify himself before the Court for divorcing his wife if she spoils his dinner or loses her beauty. Beware of accepting this licence: for if a wife serves a husband a graceless meal, or neglects her appearance, or commits adultery, she thereby accuses him of a failure in loving-kindness towards her. The graver her fault, the heavier the accusation. Let him be aware of his own sin and forgive her, as he would have our God forgive him, and think well before he divorces her.'"

"And what do you yourself say?"

"Hillel has the last word. Let those who love the Lord forgo the licence even where there is adultery. For once a man marries a wife they are become one flesh, joined by God and not to be parted. If he sins, he draws her with him into sin; if she sins, he is answerable for her sin as if it were his own. So Solomon says: 'A good wife is more precious than rubies.' And I say to you: only by refraining from carnal love are man and wife joined together in the love of God. For whoever sows to the flesh, from the flesh he shall reap corruption."

So from Jerusalem Jesus led his disciples southward to Ain-Rimmon, where word had come to him from John, and there in a stream that flowed through a pomegranate grove John baptized them all and anointed them prophets; they were now bound, as Jesus was, to abstain from wine and all other intoxicants. Jesus gave them his blessing and this simple order: "Children, love one another."

John afterwards asked: "By what road now, Lord?"

"Through the land plagued by unfertility to the land plagued by fertility; then, God willing, to the Mountain of the North."

"I will prepare the way."

"Do so, and let us meet on the Mountain."

"All shall hear my voice, from the dunghill beggar to the throned prince."

John thereupon left his own disciples under the charge of Simon of Gitta, the most zealous of them, and hurried off towards Galilee, shouting wild exhortations to every man and woman whom he met: "Repent, repent, for the King is coming!" On the third day he reached Sephoris, where Herod Antipas was in residence, and unceremoniously thrusting aside the sentries at the gate, burst into the palace, shook his staff at the major-domo and demanded an immediate audience with Antipas.

Antipas was dispensing justice in the Great Hall, his wife Herodias seated beside him, when John ran in. "I am John son of Zacharias, a prophet of the Lord!" His words echoed shrilly down the marble corridors.

The attendants reprimanded him. "Offer obeisance to the King, man!"—for within the walls of the palace they flattered Antipas with the title of King—"Prostrate yourself on the carpet!"

"A tetrarch is no king. My allegiance is to the King of Israel."

Antipas stared at John's gaunt frame, bloodshot eyes, red beard and matted hair, and at his camel-hair mantle so ragged and worn, it hardly held together. More puzzled than offended, he asked: "Is my father Herod returned from the dead that you should say this?"

"Your father was King of the Jews, never King of Israel. Come with me at once to pay homage to the King of Israel, and send for your brother Philip to do the same."

"Who is this King?"

"In your ear," said John. He leaped up the steps of the throne, bent down and whispered: "One who escaped the Thracian spearmen."

Antipas paled.

John twirled his staff and addressed him again in the hearing of all: "The word of the Lord: Put away this woman, Tetrarch, lest you die in miserable exile. Put her away, sinful Edomite, lest your name stink to the end of time!" For Antipas, thirty years before, had committed the same offence against the Levirate law as his brother Archelaus: at Alexandria on his return from Rome he had persuaded his cousin Herodias to divorce her husband, his half-brother Herod Philip, and marry him, though she already had a daughter by the marriage.

Herodias asked indignantly: "My lord, will you let this madman rave at his pleasure? He has insulted both me and yourself and the daughter of our marriage. You will be no prince but a son of sixty dogs if you do not instantly throw him into prison."

Antipas gulped and nodded, but feared to act. It was Herodias who detailed two guardsmen to lead John away to the palace prison; and ten more were needed before he was securely gyved and fettered.

Antipas visited him the same evening and, dismissing the attendants, said to him: "That you are fettered grieves me; but my wife is proud. Tell me the name of this new King, pray, and where he is to be found."

"Release me, and I will gladly lead you to him."

"To-morrow?"

"If to-night you put away your wife."

"Must I lose my wife first and then my throne?"

"Better even lose your life than your hope of salvation."

Antipas once more urged John to reveal the whereabouts of the King. "I will write a letter to my brother Philip, if you will." But John would only nod and say: "You will know in good time, you will know in good time."

Antipas threatened to put him to the torture, but John laughed in his face.

Jesus meanwhile was making a slow progress northward through a district of Judaea that had suffered severely during the troubled reign of Archelaus and not since recovered its former modest prosperity. The villages were ruinous and miserably poor, and though he might have been well received had he travelled alone, thirteen mouths discouraged hospitality. The harvest was not yet ripe and stocks of corn were almost exhausted. Besides, all but Jesus and Judas were Galileans: the people of Galilee were despised in Judaea for their uncouth accents, their keenness in bargaining, their ill-temper and their obstinacy. At each village that they entered the elders of the synagogue excused themselves from feeding them, on the ground that the laws of hospitality compelled them to feed the wayfarer, but not a troop of wayfarers, and directed Jesus with a polite blessing to the next village. One elder quoted the Preacher, the Son of Sira: "Give a portion to seven men, or even to eight; for you know not what evil may befall you", and said sincerely: "Were you only seven men, or eight, I should gladly obey this injunction." At Kirjath-Jearim, Jesus ordered his disciples to disperse in pairs and meet him again in three days' time at Lebona, on the Samaritan border.

Once or twice he preached by the way, but the people who listened were vacant-eyed and inattentive. He said to James and John, whom he had chosen to accompany him: "The vision that came to the prophet Ezekiel. Tell me: when in the Great Day of the Lord the letter *Tav* is marked in blood on the brows of the faithful to reserve them from the slaughter, how many will cry out: 'I am a Judaean from the hills which stand between Jerusalem and the plain'?"

James and John shook their heads gravely. Nevertheless, on that same day a poor man gave them a lapful of locust-beans for the love of God, and on the next day they had mouldy cheese and a little bread from a poor widow, and they did not lack for well-water.

At Lebona they found the other disciples already assembled, and all of them together helped a rich farmer to cut and carry his harvest, and were well rewarded. Thence they passed through Samaria, where the peasants grudged them even water, and hurried forward to reach Galilee before the oncoming Sabbath prevented further travel. They came to En-Gannim late in the afternoon before the Sabbath, but the hospitality of the place had been exhausted by Passover pilgrims; that night they nearly fainted for hunger.

The next morning they entered the cornfields of a large estate. Philip and James the Less who walked ahead of the rest began plucking the ripe corn as they passed through and rubbing it between their hands to husk it. The estate-steward, on his way to the synagogue with two of his neighbours, caught them in the act. Husking corn was regarded by the Sages as a sort of threshing and a desecration of the Sabbath, and the steward therefore warned Jesus that he intended to make an example of the two offenders. "To what township do these wretches belong?"

"These two hungry men are of Capernaum."

"Very well," said the steward; "the charge will be referred to the elders of Capernaum. I myself will accompany you and your disciples there as witness. With Samaritans or Greeks or beggars I should not trouble myself, for I can ill afford to lose two days' work at this season, but when two men clothed in garments of deception, and in company with eleven others, similarly clothed, thresh my master's corn on a Sabbath day, conscience will not permit me to condone the crime. If justice is done they will be well beaten and their staffs broken across the beadle's knee."

"We will come with you," said the neighbours. "We also witnessed the offence."

That evening the estate-steward fed Jesus and his disciples well, saying: "Until you are found guilty you are innocent. I would not have my master's house defamed by you as inhospitable. Eat, men, eat, until the tears flow!" But he was still stern in his resolution to bring them to justice.

At Capernaum the synagogue elders thanked the steward for showing public spirit in bringing the case before them, and agreed that it seemed a most serious one. But Jesus demanded that the charge of breaking the Sabbath should not be preferred against Philip and James until he had himself been charged with inciting them to break it.

His demand was granted, and presently Jesus stood as defendant in a court for the first time in his life. Yet it was soon clear who was, in fact, the judge and who were the accused.

Jesus admitted that the two disciples had done what was charged against them, but pleaded necessity and quoted a precedent: "Have you not read what King David did at Nob when he was starving? He demanded from Ahimelech the priest—Abiathar's father—the hallowed shew-bread laid up at the altar, and shared five loaves with his comrades."

"These men were not starving."

"Must a man die to prove that he is starving?"

"Nor are you King David."

"Nor did my disciples eat hallowed bread; they only exercised their ancient pluck-right. If our accusers from En-Gannim had invited us into their houses, as was their duty, and set food before us, these men would not have done what they did. It is the duty of every householder to feed the hungry traveller; if the Sabbath was broken, it was our accusers who broke it."

"Food was not wanting; for it was afterwards set before us in shame," Peter interposed. "But I know En-Gannim of old. On week-days they set an armed guard at the gate leading through the fields to deny pilgrims returning from the Passover the exercise of their pluck-right."

One of the judges said: "That is neither here nor there, Son of Jonah. That you might not eat corn on the day before the Sabbath, or on the day after, does not entitle you to break the Sabbath. You should have brought provisions with you!"

Jesus answered for Peter: "So Ahimelech might well have told

317

King David. But was man created for the Sabbath, or the Sabbath for man? Was it instituted as a day of refreshment and joy, or as a day of fasting and grief? And can a hungry man be joyful and refresh himself?"

The corn-factor whom Jesus had cured on his first visit to the synagogue sat among the judges. He said severely: "King David himself counselled us to put our trust in the Lord, testifying that he had never in all his life seen a righteous man forsaken or his children begging for bread. Those who keep the Law do not go hungry on the Sabbath."

"Do you say this in self-praise? Being one of the rich yourself, you shun the society of poor men because they do not keep the Law —though it is you yourselves who prevent them. Must a cattleman or labourer forfeit the blessing of God because, worked nearly to death, he is unable to pay all the ritual debts which you impose on him as necessary to salvation? Can he don and doff his praying robe thirty times a day to make long set prayers in unison with yours, and wash his hands a hundred times? You find delight in the Law, in voluntarily undertaking burdens never envisaged by Moses, and the Law is indeed for delight; but what is delight for you is misery for the poor. You say: 'This man is unclean; let him not enter into our clean congregation.'"

"We are warned by the Sages to guard the Law from infringement by setting a fence about it."

"The Sages have said: 'Set a fence about the Law and guard it well, but do not take up your station within the enclosure; he who does so cannot watch behind his back. Rather, take up your station outside and you will see all.' Yet you take up your station within the enclosure; you turn the fence into a high wall and the enclosure into a private demesne, from which the poor are barred."

"Would you have us consort with eaters of unclean food?"

"It is not only what goes into a man that defiles him, but also what goes out of him. Even clean food is turned into uncleanness when the body voids the noisome residue. Though you feed on the sweet food of the Law—as it is written: 'It was in my mouth as honey for sweetness'—you void it again in evil thoughts, pride and foolishness." With that Jesus pointed his finger at the corn-factor and spoke a parable of a demoniac who, when rid of the evil spirit that has driven him out into dangerous and filthy places, decides to return home; finds his house swept and cleansed and then, lonely for company, invokes seven other evil spirits to share it with him.

The aged President of the Synagogue asked: "Do you, a young

318

man, set yourself up in authority against us Doctors who have grown white-headed in the study of the Law?"

"Let the prophet Jeremiah answer for a young man who must be silent when the old speak folly: 'How say you: "We are wise and the Law of the Lord is with us"? For the false pen of the commentator leads you to falsehood.'"

This ended the case, and the judges, after a brief conference, publicly reprimanded Jesus and his disciples for their action at En-Gannim but imposed no other punishment. Privately, they sent a message to Jesus's elder brothers Jose, Judah and Simeon to the effect that, unless they could persuade him to return to his carpenter's bench at Nazareth, the Herodian police would be requested to place him under restraint as a lunatic.

Two days later the three brothers arrived in consternation at Capernaum, bringing Jesus's mother with them. They learned that Jesus was preaching at a tax-gatherer's house to a large crowd of his poorer and more disreputable followers. Jose, the eldest, sent a boy in with the message: "Your mother and brothers desire to see you outside at once."

Despite the Commandment, "Honour thy father and mother", Jesus did not break off his discourse and go out to greet Mary, as other pious Jews in his position would have done: it was clear to him that the peremptory message came from his brothers rather than from her.

He replied: "A prophet has no father, mother nor brothers, except his fellow-prophets. Moreover, Moses blessed the tribe of Levi in these words: 'They preserved the commandment of the Merciful One and kept their covenant with him, when each one of them denied his mother and father, and had no regard for his brothers and children.' Then let each one of you deny his father, his mother, his brothers and his children, if they would restrain him from serving God in love."

Jose reported this answer to the elders of the synagogue, and sighed: "Alas, what more can we do? Our brother has been impudent and shameless from his youth up. We wash our hands of him. Let him be handed over to the authorities, for it is written: 'Whoever curses his father or mother, let him die the death.' What our brother has said to his mother falls little short of cursing."

But Mary turned on Jose and asked: "Who cursed his mother? Not my loving son. Dare you say this, you who grudged him his rightful inheritance? Dare you say this of your brother Jesus who reconciled you to Judah and Simeon? Remember the matter of the broken harness and be silent for shame." She turned to the elders: "As for honouring his mother, what could a son do more than he has done? He made over to me his house and all his goods before he went to the Essenes of Callirrhoë. Nor did he disobey my order; for it was Jose's order, not mine. As the Lord lives, I have no complaint against him."

The elders shook their heads at her pityingly, and said: "Alas, the mothers of Israel, the mothers of Israel! Always ready to forswear themselves to save the lives of worthless sons." And whatever Mary might say to the contrary, it was generally agreed that Jesus had put her to public dishonour. When he left the tax-gatherer's house he was waylaid in the street and upbraided by a synagogue elder.

Jesus answered: "Peace, man! If I have offended my mother, bring her in witness against me and I will ask her forgiveness. But I know a man, and you know a man, who cried *Corban* and devoted an olive orchard to the Lord's uses. Was this done in love of the Lord? Or was it to spite his father who wished to buy the orchard from him at a price which he reckoned too low?"

The elder turned pale and trembled for shame.

Jesus was then informed in a letter signed by the presidents of the three Capernaum synagogues that by his love of uncleanness he had separated himself from the congregation, and that if he continued to preach in the town he would be reported to the Herodian police as a trouble-maker.

He retired to Chorazin, and there preached more urgently than ever the approach of the Kingdom of God. His conception of this Kingdom was a practical return to the Golden Age, or near it; and meanwhile he warned his disciples again and again not to think anxiously about food, clothing and money, which their God always provided for those that loved him. Let them rid themselves of all worldly encumbrances that might unfit them for the citizenship of the Kingdom; as a jeweller might sell the whole contents of his shop for the chance of buying a single exquisite pearl.

"Obey the Doctors of the Law," he said, "but do not think that they can draw you to the Kingdom merely by their scrupulous recensions of the Law."

"Who then can draw us to the Kingdom?" Judas asked.

"The birds, the fish, the snakes, the wild things. They never plot and scheme. One day of life to them is as a thousand. They glorify the Lord, as they are enjoined in Daniel's Song of the Three Children, where the worship of the holy and humble-hearted is compared with theirs. Therefore Daniel called his three companions 'Children': for the Kingdom of Heaven is for the childish-hearted and simple, the eaters of pulse, not for the worldly rich."

He enlarged on this by declaring that at Jerusalem the God of Israel was wrongfully worshipped as a proud and capricious despot; his Temple courts were of marble and gold, his servants were haughty, jealous and greedy, and as Hillel had said: "More servants, more thefts." The God of Israel was, in truth, the merciful father of countless sons and daughters, and his Kingdom could not come until the common people acknowledged him as their father and re-fused any longer to support the false pomp which money and the sword had created. This, Jesus explained, was not to counsel the abandonment of handicrafts or husbandry. Husbandry could not yet be relieved of the curse pronounced on Adam: "You shall eat bread in the sweat of your brow", but it could be relieved of the curse of money-making. Let each village be self-supporting and let the vil-lagers have in common all such things as ploughs, beasts, store-houses; but let every man sit under his own fig-tree and drink from his own well, give of his superfluity to those who asked for it and take no money in return. And the rich man? If he would not work with the rest, he must starve among the gold-bags of his useless treasury.

Thomas asked: "Can all this be accomplished easily?"

"I do not prophesy immediate peace; I prophesy war. The sword will be drawn in defence of the present way of the world. But how can the sword prevail if the common people remember their God? By massacre the lords of this earth will defeat their own end: they will set their own house on fire—would it were already alight! For as the prophet Malachi writes: 'The day of the Lord comes as a burn-ing oven and shall consume all the wicked.' The Pangs of the Messiah which are the prelude to the thousand years of peace must begin with these very wars and massacres."

Having thus prepared and educated his disciples in the doctrine of the Kingdom of Heaven, he sent them out in pairs: one of each pair to preach, the other to heal. They were to carry his message of repentance and hope to those who needed it most—the beggars, the needy, the sick, the sinners—but were to visit only Israelite towns and villages, and attempt nothing in places where they were given no welcome. The mission was to be undertaken without money, food, wallet or spare garments, and every day at dawn they were to kneel down and pray for the speedy coming of the Kingdom, for the for-giveness of their sins, and for bread sufficient for the oncoming day.

James the Less complained: "Alas, that we are not better instructed in the Law."

"Whoever has the will to obey the Law shall know it."

He gave them authority to heal the sick in these words: "Trust in the Lord: he will save." So saying, they were to anoint with oil the affected limbs or other parts of the body: using olive oil, which as anointed prophets they had themselves blessed. He advised them to combine the simplicity of doves with the cunning of serpents, but charged them strictly: "If anyone asks you by whose authority you do what you do, make no evasions. Do not cast down your eyes, shuffle with your feet, and mumble at last: 'Jesus of Nazareth sent us out', but answer boldly: 'We do these things by authority of the Lord God of Israel—blessed be his name—whose prophets we are.' For a good shepherd has pride in his King."

Jesus then visited Samaria alone, and is known to have attended a meeting of Samaritan priests on Mount Gerizim—he had convened the meeting on his passage through the province, just before the Passover, by a word of power spoken at the well of Sychar to their Dove-priestess—but no record survives of the transactions. Before he returned to Chorazin, where he had agreed to meet his disciples again, the grievous news reached him that John the Baptist was dead. Antipas had beheaded him at the request of Herodias and their daughter Salome.

Jesus mourned thirty days for John, and when his disciples met him at Chorazin he was emaciated and hollow-eyed. They themselves were in good heart and reported that the healing had been successful, the preaching had taken root. They brought crowds of converts with them, all eager to see the master of such disciples. With them, too, came the disciples of John, asking: "Are you the Great One whom our master prophesied, or should we look for another? We have heard marvellous accounts of your feats of healing: how the lame walk, the blind see, the lepers are cleansed, the deaf hear."

"Who sent you to me?"

"Simon of Gitta, John's deputy."

Jesus knew the man, the son of an apostate Zadokite who had been one of the Lady Livia's chief agents in Syria. Simon was zealous, eloquent and courageous, but interested in power rather than in virtue. He had adopted circumcision in order to marry into a High-Priestly family; but when his father was suddenly disgraced and lost all his money, he was in no position to implement the marriage contract, and the girl was married to someone else. Simon fell into a revengeful despair, and after various adventures in the service of an Arabian caravan-master became a disciple of John, from whom he hoped to learn the secret of prophetic power. Now that John was gone, he hoped to attach himself to Jesus, for whom John had obscurely expressed his veneration, and learn from him what John could not teach.

Peter drew Jesus aside and reported in indignation that Simon was using the healing formula which Jesus had given them; but he replied that nobody could claim a lien on these words, which were not a secret charm of the sort used by sorcerers. However, he did not trust Simon and sent back this message: "Tell him no more than this, that I preach the mercy of God to the poor, and that I shall be happy if he is not offended by me."

(Simon of Gitta later broke away from Judaism altogether, and took over from one Dosithens the leadership of a new syncretic cult based on that of Hercules-Melkarth and the Moon-goddess his mistress. He had twenty-eight disciples, arranged in four weeks; and the extra day and a half that compose a lunar month were represented by himself and a woman. The woman was Jezebel, a priestess of Hierapolis, whom he married and who was thereafter known to his followers as Selene the Moon, while he was known as Simon the Telchin, or "the Abiding One who stands, stood and shall stand", both titles making him appear an incarnation of the Sun-god. Simon claimed the power to control the weather, to bless or blast with his eye, to fly through the air on wings, to assume any shape he pleased. But none of John's disciples followed him, and his pretensions were far greater than his capacities.)

Two synagogue elders of Chorazin visited Jesus one night, forbade him ever again to preach in their city, and at the same time advised him to leave Galilee as he valued his life. They told him that Antipas, at the request of Chuza his estate-steward, was on the point of issuing a warrant for his arrest.

"From whom have you heard this?"

"From Joanna, Chuza's wife. She dared not send one of her own servants to you."

"Hating me as you do, why have you come with this warning?"

"We are Israelites and would never let a fellow-Israelite fall into the hands of Edom if we could save him by any means in our power."

"Yet you have forbidden me to preach in Chorazin; and this prohibition overlies a threat."

"Chorazin is not all Galilee."

Jesus thanked them ironically and said: "If that fox inquires after me in your hearing, tell him that I shall preach wherever it pleases me; that I have no fear of the demon which possesses him; and that we two shall meet one day in Jerusalem."

Yet it was not Jesus's custom, as he said, to throw pearls to the hogs; and he never returned to preach in any town or village that had once officially rejected him. He removed from Chorazin, and crossed the Jordan to New Bethsaida, or Julias, the capital city of Philip's Tetrarchy, which adjoins Old Bethsaida. There he preached for a while, but though he had forbidden the new converts to come after him, a great many of them disobeyed and raised such an enthusiastic clamour about him that he was requested by the local magistrates to leave the city. He symbolically shook the dust off his sandals after passing through the city gates, and declared that on the Day of Judgement it would be more tolerable for Sodom and Gomorrah, the Dead Sea cities which had been destroyed by fire from Heaven, than for New Bethsaida, Capernaum and Chorazin.

Undeterred by his rebuff, he called his disciples together and required each of them to choose out six of the new converts and send them out, two by two, on missionary journeys throughout the country. Having given this order, he went alone into Lower Trans-jordania to consult with his brother James the Ebionite.

When he returned and found that the disciples had performed their missions creditably he sent them down to Jerusalem to keep the Feast of Tabernacles, but told them not to expect him, since he might be prevented from coming. He reached Jerusalem on the last day of the Feast, the Day of Willows, when the Great Altar was decorated with willow boughs. Every evening of the seven it was the custom for a priest to go down to the Pool of Siloam, at the head of a festal procession, carrying a golden pitcher of the capacity of three logs. He filled it and brought it by torchlight up the hill to the sound of trumpets, then through the Water Gate of the Temple and into the Court of the Gentiles. There other priests received the pitcher from him, intoning the words of Isaiah: "You will draw water with joy from the wells of salvation", and all the people took up the refrain. Then, while the trumpets blew again and the Levites sang psalms, waved the thyrsus and danced around the Great Altar, the water from Siloam was poured over it simultaneously with a libation of the new wine. From the altar the water ran into a silver basin and disappeared down a pipe which communicated with the Kidron brook. The authority for this rite was the ancient tradition: "The Holy one, blessed be he, said: 'Pour out water before me at the Feast, that the rains of the year may be blessed to you.'" But on the evening of the Day of Willows the Levites danced not once but seven times around the Altar, to commemorate the seven days' encompassing of the walls of Jericho.

This Day of Willows was marked by an interruption: at the moment when the priest stooped at the Pool with his pitcher, a loud sweet voice broke the customary religious hush. "Amen, Amen: Ho, everyone that thirsts, come to the waters, whether he has money or none. Listen, and come to me! Hear, and you shall live!" Then every pious man found himself continuing in his mind the quotation from Isaiah: "And I shall make an everlasting compact with you—the sure mercies of a David. Behold, I have given him for a witness to the people, a leader and commander of the people."

In order not to mar the sanctity of the occasion no attempt was made to arrest Jesus, who was surrounded by a crowd of his Galilean followers, and when the procession had moved forward on its way towards the Water Gate, he was not to be found.

The incident was brought up at a meeting of the Great Sanhedrin on the following morning. It was not doubted that Jesus had uttered the cry, but nobody could positively swear to this, since it had been evening and he was not a tall man whose head could be distinguished above the crowd. Annas, the former High Priest, proposed that he should be summoned before the Court for a breach of the solemnities, not so much because he had given way to an ecstatic impulse, as because his quotation was a provocative one: a direct promise to the people of a revolutionary leader. "Himself, no doubt," said Annas dryly, and his colleagues laughed as he added: "A David who does not need to feign madness and let the spittle run down his beard."

Nicodemon warmly opposed the motion as inconsistent with the dignity of the Court. Even if it could be proved that Jesus, or any other person, had uttered the words, they could not be construed in a provocative sense. Isaiah was quoted at the reception of the water in the Court of the Gentiles; why should he not be quoted at the drawing of the water outside the Temple precincts?

Annas asked him jocosely: "What? Are you also a follower of this mad Galilean?"

Nicodemon's intervention was decisive, since he was the accepted authority on all questions concerned with libations and lustrations; but Annas had startled him by his question and he regretted that he had not spoken with a more careful show of disinterest.

Jesus returned with his disciples to the Lake of Galilee. He preached on the outskirts of Magdala, centre of the fish-curing industry, but did not enter the market-place or any synagogue. Because of the notoriety that he had acquired as a sponger on prostitutes and tax-gatherers, a Sabbath-breaker, and a man cast off by his family, only the dregs of the populace came to listen to him. His audiences were indeed now so thin that the police, though instructed to keep a watch on his movements, did not molest him in any way, and said to one another: "He seems an honest enough fellow. That the synagogue elders hate him is a clear proof of his friendship for Rome."

From Magdala he sailed with his disciples across the Lake to Old Bethsaida, where they hauled their boat ashore and went on foot along the Upper Jordan until they reached Mount Hermon, the immense mountain which marks the northern limit of the ancient Land of Israel. Here they visited the grotto of Baal-Gad, famous as the source of the River Jordan; it lies at the water-reddened base of a high limestone cliff crowned with the city of Caesarea Philippi. The grotto is sacred to the Lord of Gad, the goatish god of good fortune, whom the Greeks identify with Pan. Judas of Kerioth read a Greek inscription carved on the rock-face: "To Pan and the Nymphs." He asked Jesus: "Did John the Baptist ever inspect the source of the water in which he baptized us?"

"This water, which the Lord has blessed for our uses, would be clean though the jaws of a dead dog were its faucet; as, at the synagogue lectern, the Law of Moses still flows clean between the lips of a sinner."

They sat on the rocks idly tossing pebbles into the water. He suddenly asked them: "Who do the people say that I am?"

"Some say that the mantle of John the Baptist has fallen on you, as Elijah's fell on Elisha."

"Some say that you are Elisha; but others that Elisha is dead and that you must be Elijah."

"I have 'heard you named Enoch."

"And Isaiah."

"But who do you say that I am?"

Peter spoke in tones of conviction: "You are the Messiah, of whom our God spoke through the mouth of David: 'My Son, I have begotten you to-day.'"

Jesus prayed aloud: "Father in Heaven, if you have revealed the truth to this child, I thank you; if he has spoken foolishly, let him be forgiven. Anointed though I am, my destiny is known to you alone. With King David I cry: 'Keep me from the sin of presumption, lest it master me. Keep me undefiled and innocent from the great offence.'" He charged them all to silence in the matter.

He took Peter, James and John climbing up the southern slope of Mount Hermon, while the others went off to preach in the neighbouring villages. They started before dawn and by noon had reached a place near the summit where the wind blew cold and snow lay in drifts under the bright sun, dazzling their eyes. There he stood still, and his face became transfigured as he conversed aloud with two invisible persons, who gradually took on substantial form: a majestic white-bearded elder spirit, robed in light and wearing a golden mitre, and a red-bearded younger spirit, in pastoral dress and with a lamb under his arm. The disciples could understand only a part of what was said, because the voices came to them as if in a dream; but the spirits were clearly warning Jesus against going to Jerusalem.

The red-bearded spirit was saying: "Brother, that road does not lead to the gates of the Kingdom but is swallowed up in the marshes. Avoid it!"

And the white-bearded: "Beware of the fourth beast, my Son, lest it catch you on its horns and toss you into the bottomless abyss!"

"Should I shrink from my task?" Jesus asked. "Should I flee to the Wilderness as Elijah fled from Jezebel the harlot? Or temporize with evil as Moses did at Meribah when he humoured the rebels and struck the rock with his staff of kerm-oak?"

The red-bearded again: "Worse things even than my father suffered you will suffer! Be warned: the Female's snares are already laid."

And the white-bearded: "Abtalion's judgement: 'Wise men, guard your words; for if you are exiled to the place of corrupt waters—as clear streams flow into the accursed sea and are mingled with it—those who come after will drink of them and die, and the Name of Heaven will be profaned.'"

Jesus cried in a loud voice: "What Israelite except only Enoch the pure ever paid the uttermost farthing of his debt to our God? Yet I will pay mine. Only at Jerusalem can it be paid. A word of Hillel's —his memory be blessed—'if not now, when?'"

He was not to be deflected from his course. The dispute continued less and less intelligibly, until Peter broke the spell by babbling the first random words that entered his head. "Master, this is a pleasant place, but the wind is wild and houses are few. Give us leave to build three snow huts; one for you, one for Moses, one for Elijah."

Immediately the vision faded.

Judas, when Peter told him the story later, divined that the spirit whom he had mistaken for Elijah was John the Baptist, and that the spirit whom he had mistaken for Moses was Simon son of Boethus. He began to grow anxious on Jesus's behalf, because spirits of upright men appear only to the upright and do not deceive.

CHAPTER TWENTY-FOUR

THE DEBT

HE DID not make directly for Jerusalem, but first took the westward road to the province of Sidon, where he visited the scattered Jewish communities that lie just inside the border. At Sarepta a Phoenician widow, under whose fig-tree he was sheltering from the rain, implored him to heal her cataleptic daughter. He refused, on the ground that his duty was only to the Israelites, and asked: "Woman, what have I to do with you?"

"My fig-tree has given you shelter."

"For that I thank you, but bread from the children's table may not be thrown to the dogs."

The widow was importunate. "Do not grudge the dogs the fallen crumbs," she pleaded.

Then, remembering Elijah who, some seven hundred years before, had performed the miracle of the inexhaustible oil-cruse and flour-barrel for a Phoenician widow in that very town, he relented and cured the girl. She was the only foreigner for whom he ever relaxed his exclusive rule.

It must be understood that his capacity to perform cures was limited. As experienced physicians are aware, the act of healing by faith, even though performed in a divine name, is physically exhausting and when too often performed dulls the spirit. Once at the height of his popularity Jesus was jostled by a crowd outside the synagogue doors of Chorazin. Sensible of a sudden drain of power, he cried out: "Who touched me?" A woman confessed that she had touched the sacred fringe of his praying-robe in the hope of a cure; she suffered from a menstrual discharge which made her perpetually unclean. "Would you make a magician of me, thievish one?" he cried in indignation, then hastily spoke the words which would dedicate the cure to God.

As the winter drew on he left Sidon and made for Samaria by way of Galilee. In order to distract attention from himself he dispersed his disciples in twos and threes. As he and Peter passed through Capernaum, the synagogue treasurer whose duty it was to collect the Temple-tax stopped them and demanded payment of their arrears. The amount authorized in the Book of Deuteronomy was half a shekel, that is, two drachmae, for every adult Jew throughout the country; it was the one tax which nobody dared to evade, and which therefore cost nothing to collect. Although in Jesus's view the Temple priesthood grossly misused the enormous sums of money that the tax brought in, he did not refuse payment. But he was at the end of his resources, Joanna and Susanna having been forbidden by their husbands to continue their support of his mission. He told Peter: "Collect the shekel from the fish, while I wait here."

Peter thereupon borrowed a line, hook and bait from a friend and, going down to the Lake, swam out to a rock some distance off-shore. There he had extraordinary luck, soon landing a huge fish of the sort called *mouscos* that the surly fishmongers would bid against one another to buy. In the market he held out for four drachmae, got his price and brought a four-drachmae piece to the treasurer's house within the hour. He told the treasurer with mock gravity: "I baited my hook with prayer and let it down. Look what sort of a stone I found in the mouth of the first *mouscos* that I pulled up!" For this fish is alleged to open its mouth as a refuge for its fry when enemies are about, and close it with a stone chosen from the Lake-bottom.

But Peter's luck did not hold. He returned to the rock and caught nothing at all.

The disciples were beginning to be disheartened by the shifts to which they were reduced for obtaining food, and most of them had not eaten a good meal for weeks. Their clothes were stained and ragged and their sandals worn out. "Anyone might mistake us for the Gibeonites on their visit to Joshua," complained Philip, who had been something of a dandy in his day.

At Shunem Jesus comforted them with the promise that any man who abandoned home, family and trade for the love of the Lord would not go unrewarded in the Heavenly Kingdom. As they munched locust-beans in a fallow field he said: "It is written in the Apocalypse of Baruch: 'The day shall come when vines grow with ten thousand branches on each stock, and with ten thousand shoots on each branch, and with ten thousand clusters on each shoot, and with ten thousand grapes on each cluster, and when every grape when pressed yields five-and-twenty measures of wine. As soon as a citizen of that rich land reaches out his hand to a cluster, another cluster will cry out: "No, take me, I am juicier, and praise the Lord with me." ' "

"We shall not lack for wine, then," said John, "unless the jars give out."

"It shall be the same with the corn. Every grain planted shall grow into a plant of ten thousand ears, with each ear of ten thousand grains; and each grain, when milled, will yield ten pounds of fine white flour. The date-palms and fig-trees and quinces shall yield in the same prodigious manner."

"And will butter and honey be as plentiful?" Thaddaeus asked in his high voice. His real name was Lebbaeus, but he was nicknamed Thaddaeus ("Bosoms") because of his matronly figure. "My belly wearies of locust-beans and stale crusts."

"Isaiah prophesied butter and honey for the Messiah in the Kingdom; they shall be as plentiful as sour looks and harsh words are to-day."

"That is difficult to believe. How will the soil support such growth?"

"You will see."

Then he said: "When the Son of David is seated on his royal throne, twelve men shall be seated on twelve lesser thrones judging the twelve tribes. Whatever they have renounced to-day shall be restored to them a hundredfold."

Their eyes glistened with hope. "May those twelve kings prove to be your twelve disciples!"

"The thrones are not in my giving; and even the humblest citizen of the Kingdom must first drink the bitter cup, the Pangs of the Messiah. Dare you set it to your lips?"

"We dare," they said, not knowing to what they had committed themselves.

"Fear not, little flock," he said. "Our God will feed you."

At the Samaritan frontier he sent James and John ahead to Mount Gerizim, to the house of the Samaritan High Priest. They were to say: "The King and his followers are on their way to Jerusalem. Prepare to acclaim him!" But when they delivered the message, they were told: "Inform the King that his priests are not yet ready. On his return in triumph from Jerusalem they will welcome him as he deserves."

James and John brought the answer back to Jesus and cried in indignation: "Lord, give us leave to call down fire from Heaven to consume those wretches, as Elijah did with the captains of King Ahaziah."

He calmed them: "I have come not to destroy life, but to save it. They are weak men, but in time your faith will strengthen them. Since we may not go through Samaria, let us pass through the Pride of Jordan."

They crossed the Jordan and travelled southward through the forest-land on the further side where white poplars and mallows and tamarisks grow. The country people had heard of Jesus from his brother James the Ebionite and flocked out to see him; some brought their little children for him to bless. The disciples would have sent them away, for the sake of a proverb: "From two years forward the child is a hog, revelling in filth." Yet Jesus blessed them, saying that whoever was not as improvident and trustful as a little child should not participate in the Kingdom. Of the elder children he said: "These see clearly the divine Brightness of God, for the world has not yet clouded their eyes, and their voices turn away his wrath."

Among these elder children was myself, Agabus the Decapolitan, the son of a Syrian father and a Samaritan mother. When Jesus spoke these words, my heart cried: "It is true!" My world at that time was lit by a soft inexplicable radiance, which gave a sheen, or nap, to the commonest objects on which it shone, but which has never shone since I became a man. To me he gave no blessing, since I dared not pass myself off as a Jew; but I saluted him respectfully and he smiled at me in return. Since this was the first and last time that I saw Jesus, it is not unfitting that I should here record his appearance.

He was below the middle height and broad-shouldered, his eyes were deep-set and shining like beryls; his face pallid and much lined; his lips full and pouting; his teeth even; his forked beard well trimmed, red inclining to black like his hair; his hands broad; his fingers short. He limped and supported his weight either on an almond-wood staff carved with fruit and flowers, or on another carved with plain bands. When he sat down and laid the staffs on either side of him in the dust, what took my eye was the variety and beauty of his gestures; he spoke with his hands almost as much as with his lips.

My father pondered for a long while after Jesus had passed on to the next village, saying constantly: "Something in his face is familiar, and yet strange, but what? Where have I seen it before? Perhaps only in a dream, though I cannot think so. Does it seem a strange face to you, my dearest Antinoë? Strange, yet familiar?"

My mother answered: "To me it seems the face of one who converses familiarly with the gods, or with demons. Such grief and beauty I never saw before, except once. It shone in the face of the nobleman's son in the great house this side of Pella—Meleager was his name—a master of the lyre and a soothsayer, but an epileptic."

My father gave an impatient sweep of his hand. "That is not what I am asking, wife. It is someone whom I saw very long ago—" Then bewilderment clouded his face as at last he recalled the man. "It was King Herod himself!" he cried. "By all the gods, it was old Herod himself whom I saw in my own childhood, sixty years ago, before his hair turned white. Now, how in the world does this come about? Jesus of Nazareth resembles our old benefactor more closely than do any of his own sons!"

Jesus came to Jerusalem. He preached in the fruit-market and in the brazier-market and at the City gates with much the same success as had attended him during his first visit to Capernaum. The people recognized the authority in his voice, and his feats of healing confirmed it. Since his doctrine was considered sound in the Pharisaic sense, he was invited to preach at several of the poorer synagogues—there were two or three hundred of them in Jerusalem at this time—and the attendance was always large. But the Sadducee priesthood, mistrusting him because he preached the imminent approach of the Kingdom of God, kept him under constant observation, and were ready to arrest him on the slightest suspicion of revolutionary activity.

The Pharisees, who had succeeded the ancient prophets as the recognized guardians of public morality, had reached a tacit understanding with the Sadducees. Since the High Priest was a Roman nominee and, by virtue of his office, President of the Great Sanhedrin, they agreed that the suppression of revolutionary doctrine was solely his concern; in return, the Sadducees agreed that the suppression of heretical doctrine was solely the concern of the joint-Presidents of the Pharisaic High Court, who not only were the heads of the Jewish judicial system which dispensed the Mosaic Law but co-ordinated synagogue-worship throughout the world. The judges of the High Court had no direct dealings with the Roman Governor-

General and used the Great Sanhedrin as intermediaries; they were still represented in the Great Sanhedrin by a few members, such as Nicodemon son of Gorion and Joseph of Arimathea, but this was principally an insurance against Sadducee doctrine being misrepresented to the Romans as the doctrine of the people at large. Shammai's precept: "Love work, hate office and be not known as a friend of the Government" made quietists of the Pharisees. They had a proverb: "When arms clash in the street, retire to your chamber", and profoundly as they dissented from the Sadducees in religious theory, especially in the vexed doctrine of resurrection, they agreed with them at least in deprecating Messianic fervour as being always hottest among the idle, ignorant and impatient. A Sage, they said, should never be unprepared for the coming of the Messiah, but should shut his ears to wild cries of "Lo, here!" and "Lo, there!" When the hour came, and with it the Messiah, the celestial signs would be unmistakable.

The Presidents of the High Court sent their eloquent secretary, Joseph of Arimathea, to Caiaphas the High Priest to discuss Jesus's case with him. Joseph urged Caiaphas to leave Jesus alone: "He is a simple and, I think, pious man. He hopes to redeem from destruction Israelites who for various reasons are either not qualified to attend the synagogue or have been expelled for misbehaviour: criminals, tax-collectors, prostitutes and so on. To my mind, this is valuable work. Last year there was friction between him and the men of Capernaum and Chorazin, but you must be aware how narrow-minded and intolerant provincial elders can be. If I had been in their position, I should have given him a free hand and my blessing. Granted the difficulty of admitting penitents with a bad history into a respectable synagogue; yet his converts were numerous and a separate synagogue could doubtless have been built for them somewhere or other by public subscription—which would have been pleasing to Heaven and also a valuable contribution to political stability."

"No, no, friend Joseph: from what I hear of Jesus, I doubt whether your solution would have been acceptable to him. He attempts to force the unclean on the clean in a most offensive way, and my sympathies are wholly with the Capernaum authorities. Yet, in general, I incline to agree with you. If we leave him alone, the mob will tire of his rantings, and the synagogue elders when they find out what sort of company he keeps will soon close their doors to him. Inform your learned and pious Presidents with my compliments that I shall refrain from any disciplinary action against this miracle-monger until he forgets himself one day and bawls out some anti-Imperial nonsense of which I am forced to take cognisance By the way, do you not think that he has a touch of insanity? Does he perhaps believe himself to be the Messiah? I ask because of the cry with which he interrupted last year's solemnities on the Day of Willows."

"Prophets who continually preach the coming of the Kingdom in the name of our God are liable to become confused in their minds; it is a dangerous profession. John the Baptist behaved very strangely towards the end. Yet I cannot think that Jesus nurses any grandiose delusions; in general, these are betrayed by an affectation of military glory, with shouted orders, banners, trumpet music, and the like. I am grateful to you, Holy Father, for your obliging attitude."

"And I to your learned and pious Presidents for having sent you to see me."

Jesus's preoccupation with the outcasts of the synagogue has led many Gentile Chrestians to suppose that, in his view, the greater the sinner the more acceptable his repentance and therefore the greater the reward laid up for him in the Kingdom of God: that, in fact, a man who could present Enoch, the recorder of Heaven, with a roll of frightful crimes redeemed by a complete, if hasty, repentance would be awarded a higher seat in the Kingdom than the devout God-loving Pharisee who never swerved a hair's breadth from the Law. This is an absurd travesty of his teaching. He was set on converting the outcasts because they were outcasts, not because their sins recommended them to his esteem. In his view the Kingdom could not come until all Israel repented, and he had no fears for the salvation of the mass of synagogue-goers. "They have the Law and the Prophets; they need only listen with care and, when the Day of the Lord dawns, they will share in the general repentance. But the outcasts lack instruction in the divine will. Hillel's judgement —his memory be blessed—'The ignorant man sins with a clear conscience.' "

He is not recorded ever to have looked on a sinner with love, though on one occasion, it is said, he looked with love on a rich young man who had kept the Law in every respect since boyhood. This was the man to whom he said: "Only one thing remains: to sell all your goods and distribute them among the poor." As the young man went off, debating sadly whether he could take this advice without cutting himself off from his friends and doing an injustice to his many dependants, Jesus sighed and asked his disciples: "Have you ever seen a stranger to Jerusalem trying to haul a well-laden camel through the Needle-eye Archway? So it is with a rich man and the Kingdom of Heaven." To a synagogue elder who reproached him for wasting his spiritual labour on the dregs of the City he said: "You have a custom here at Jerusalem of making one convert to the faith every year from a new city or nation and of publicly rejoicing over him; that the world may know that the Law is offered freely to all men whatsoever who desire to serve the Lord. But will the Lord be pleased to see you scouring the deserts of Mauretania or the shores of the Caspian Sea to catch, circumcise and instruct next year's painted savage? Not while you neglect the masses of our fellow-Israelites who have the first claim on your love and zeal."

He spent the months of December and January at Jerusalem, secretly financed by Nicodemon, but never once visited the house of Lazarus, aware of Mary's hostility to him; and Lazarus, pained by this neglect, did not seek him out in the market-places. At the midwinter Feast of Dedication—the anniversary of the resanctifying of the Temple after its desecration by Antiochus Epiphanes—Nicodemon sent his son to ask Jesus privately: "If you are the Messiah, why do you not declare yourself? If not, who are you?"

Jesus answered: "Tell your father that I am a shepherd busied with the feeding of my flock. I have no concern with 'if's'; 'if's' are wolves that tear the flock of the hireling shepherd."

As the winter drew on, Caiaphas the High Priest was disturbed to learn from his spies that Jesus's influence was increasing rather than waning. A deputation from the Jewish Temple at Leontopolis was reported to have visited him early in February and afterwards to have returned in haste to Egypt. Caiaphas was disquieted by this report, though he could not make much sense of it, and without troubling to consult the Presidents of the High Court, summoned the Captain of the Temple and told him: "Let your Levites throw no stones at the miracle-worker from Nazareth; I have promised the High Court not to molest him."

The Captain understood exactly what was meant. He passed on the message to his Levite sergeants, who went to the Old Quarter and informed the faction leaders of the Jebusites: "Jesus of Nazareth is no longer under the High Priest's protection. If stones fly at the Fish Gate this evening and he is driven out of the City, none of our people will be there to make arrests. Nevertheless, let no murder be done."

Thus licensed, the Jebusite street-gangs assembled in force that evening at the Fish Gate, and as soon as Jesus appeared let fly at him with a volley of cobble-stones and rotten fish. He showed no sign of alarm and was not touched by the missiles, though he made no movement to avoid them. He contented himself with saying to his disciples: "When stones are cast at prophets, they remove; and every stone rebounds as a curse against the man who has cast it." He calmly led them out through the Fish Gate, and then down the road towards the Jordan.

For a time he made Beth Nimrah in Transjordania his centre, and went to preach in all the neighbouring villages; but about the middle of March the evil days of his life suddenly began, and he was forced to return across the Jordan.

A messenger had come to him from his Queen, Mary daughter of Cleopas: "Come to Bethany: my brother Lazarus is sick. You can cure him."

He sent the messenger back: "Tell the woman that I am not a physician. Are there no physicians in Bethany? Is there none in Jerusalem?"

The messenger returned three days later. "Come at once; my brother Lazarus is sick to death. You alone can cure him."

He sent the messenger back: "It is not I who performs cures. If your brother is sick to death, let him call upon the Lord's name; he will save."

He was resolved not to see Mary, suspecting that the summons was an excuse to bring him to her house. He confided to Judas of Kerioth: "The hand of the Female is in this."

"How so?"

"She strikes at a man through his loved ones."

"Who is the witch? Is it Mary the Hairdresser?"

"All women are daughters of the Female; and the Female is the mother of all witches."

On the next day another messenger arrived, wearing mourning garments. "Lazarus is dead," he reported.

"How can that be? There is a sleep that is as deep almost as death. Surely Lazarus is sleeping."

"He is dead," the messenger repeated. "His breath does not stir the dove's feather. Only the trumpet of Gabriel will ever wake him."

After a long and dreadful silence, Jesus said: "Children, let us return to Bethany."

"Bethany is close to Jerusalem," said Matthew. "The stones were a warning."

336

But Thomas: "Are you afraid, Matthew? I go with the Master though it were to my death."

Even so, Jesus made no haste to return, but spent the whole of that day in prayer and the next in preaching.

They came to Bethany towards evening of the third day: Jesus waited in an orchard about a mile from the town and sent Judas forward to fetch Lazarus's sister Martha to him. When she came he asked her calmly: "Is my brother Lazarus yet awakened from his sleep?"

Martha was very angry. "Why did you not come when you were summoned? Now it is too late. My brother is dead and buried these four days; by now his body is putrifying. O Jesus, Jesus, beware of my sister! She has a heavy accusation against you."

"Bring her to me."

Martha ran back to her home and there whispered in Mary's ear: "He has sent for you."

Mary excused herself to the mourners who filled the house: "Do not take it ill if I leave you and go alone to weep at his tomb."

She came with Martha to the orchard and, choking with grief and anger, told Jesus: "If you had come to Bethany, my brother would never have died."

He made no reply, but signed to his disciples to leave him for a while.

Mary continued: "You denied me your love, you denied me a child. You fed us all with golden hopes that the Kingdom of God would come quickly. Lazarus, you and I would enjoy it together in blessedness, if we followed your rule of chastity. Now he is dead; but you and I are still alive. You have no love in your heart, else you could never have refused me my dearest wish, which is the wish of every honourable woman in Israel. Yet you are known as a just man. If you are a just man, pay your debts. You have debts to God, and these you pay and are glad to pay; but you owe me a debt too, the debt of flesh and blood. Pay either with a new life or an old: either give me a child to end my shame, or give me back my brother. Why will you not restore him to life? For I am told that you know the Unspeakable Name."

Jesus heaved a deep sigh, but still kept silent. Then he fell on his knees in prayer. Presently he arose and most solemnly prophesied to Mary: "Thus saith the Lord: I am the resurrection and the life. He who believes in me shall not taste of death."

"Will you then give me back my brother Lazarus?"

"Not I, but our God, if he shows mercy."

"By utterance of the Name the dead may be restored to life; but what of the ransom? The prophet Elijah, when by his invocation of the Lord the widow's son was raised from the dead, paid the ransom with the lives of many soldiers from the army of King Ahaziah; and Elisha the prophet paid the ransom of the Shunemite's son with the life of Ben-Hadad, King of Syria, though indeed Ben-Hadad had treated him like a brother."

"Who instructed you in the secret tradition?"

"Have I misheard it? If not, who is the victim to be?"

"I have not come to take life."

"Yet the ransom must be paid."

After a long pause he answered: "Greater love has no man than this: that he lays down his life for a friend's. Come, Mary, show me where your brother is laid."

She led him to the tomb, which was not far off—a cypress-shaded cave hewn from the rock, its mouth at present stopped with a boulder; after the days of mourning were over, it would be sealed with masonry. The disciples followed, not knowing what he had in mind.

It was cold, the sun was low in the sky, and on the slope above the tomb three large pariah dogs sat on their haunches in an evil row, grumbling and snarling. Jesus wept. Among the Greeks the tradition is "a life for a life": King Admetus of Pherae was ransomed from Hades by his wife Alcestis, who offered to die on his behalf; from Aesculapius, who raised Glaucus of Ephyra from the dead, his own life was taken by Zeus at the demand of Hades. The same tradition obtains secretly among the Jews.

Jesus cried: "O Lord of Hosts, how long will you permit the Female to cut off your sons by her witchcrafts?" He groaned as though his heart would break.

By this time a small crowd had gathered, including friends of Lazarus. Not knowing the cause of his grief, they said to one another: "Alas, how he loved the dead man!"

He signed to the disciples to roll away the stone. They did so, and he went a little way into the tomb, knelt and prayed: "O Lord, be merciful to me on the Great Day; what I do, I do in your honour, laying down the full ransom. Only free the soul of my erring brother Lazarus from the dark place to which he has been enticed by witchcraft. For it is written: 'Sheol is naked before the Lord; she has no covering from him.'"

Then he stood up and spoke in a loud voice. "Lazarus son of Cleopas, I conjure you in the Name of your Creator, come forth from Sheol; come forth, in the Name of Jɪᴇᴠᴏᴀꜱ̄; come forth and live!"

He stepped back and stood with arms outstretched. Horror and dismay seized the disciples and the bystanders. They stood trembling, their eyes fixed on the square black mouth of the tomb.

For a while nothing happened. Then a white shape was seen moving uncertainly towards them through the darkness. A long-drawn-out shriek went up and the crowd scattered in all directions. Only Mary, Peter and Judas stood their ground.

Lazarus tottered slowly out of the mouth of the tomb, his jaw still bound with the napkin, his body still swathed in the myrrh-scented pall.

Jesus said to Mary: "Take your brother. The debt is paid." And to Peter and Judas: "Free him, clothe him, let him go in peace!"

Leaning heavily on his staff carved with flowers, he swung himself about; and limped away.

Ordering his disciples back to Beth Nimrah, he went by a circuitous route to Bozrah in Edom, where he remained for about a month, preaching to the proud and violent Edomites. Only Judas was with him, and only to him did he confide the story of what had passed between Mary and himself.

Judas said: "Master, our God is merciful. Your life may not be required of you; another's may serve."

"No man can read his purposes. Let his will be done."

"Who then will reign in the Kingdom, if not you?"

"It is not for me to ask. Only let the Lord raise me up at the Day of Judgement." Then sorrowfully he quoted these verses from the thirty-first chapter of the Book of Jeremiah:

How long will you continue in your ways, back-sliding daughter?
Behold, the Lord has shown a new thing here on earth: a woman shall hem a man about.

CHAPTER TWENTY-FIVE

THE BUTCHER'S CROOK

SIX days before the Passover he led his disciples through the famous ford across the Jordan, not far from Jericho, by which in ancient times Joshua had led the embattled Israelites into the Promised Land. On the further bank, by agreement, he met his brother James and a large company of Ebionite ascetics who greeted him with extraordinary tokens of respect, kissing his hands, his cheeks and the fringes of his robe. As they went off together to confer in a date grove near by, a blind beggar cried out to him from the wayside: "Son of David, have mercy on me! Have mercy on me, Son of David!"

"What mercy can I show you?"

"Lord, let me be restored to sight."

Jesus went over to the beggar, took him by the chin and gazed searchingly into his eyes; satisfied that the principle of sight was not destroyed, he prayed long and earnestly, and then plastered them over with clay mixed with his own spittle. "Go apart from the crowd, Son of Faith, kneel down by the river and repeat the *Hear, O Israel* three times; when you have done, strip off the plaster and wash your face in the flowing water."

The beggar obeyed, and presently shrill cries of joy were heard as he came hurrying back to give thanks to Jesus. His sight was already returning, though he could not yet distinguish men from trees, except by their movement. "No thanks to me; only to our God," said Jesus. By evening the beggar could see as clearly as he had ever done; yet he had been blind for twenty years.

The news of this cure spread among the crowds of pilgrims from Transjordania who streamed across the ford. They asked one another in wonder: "Who is this holy prophet who has healed the blind man of the ford? And is it true that the blind man addressed him as the Son of David?"

On the next morning Jesus reached the outskirts of Jerusalem. He sent James and John ahead to a cross-roads where they would find a young unbroken ass tied to a post outside an inn. They were to untie it and bring it to him. If anyone should challenge them, the password was: "The Master has need of it." Nobody challenged them and they led the ass back to Jesus. They found him seated under a palm-tree, wearing a new scarlet cloak and tunic which, unknown to them, Judas had brought back from Bozrah wrapped in a blanket. His head was wreathed with vine, in his right hand he held a flowering pomegranate branch. They threw up their hands in astonishment and shouted as joyfully almost as the blind beggar had done.

Jesus said nothing; there was no need. The long-awaited hour of manifestation was here at last, the triumphal hour foretold by the prophet Isaiah when he said:

> Who is this who comes from Edom, with dyed garments from Bozrah?

and by the prophet Zechariah when he said:

> *Shout aloud, daughter of Mount Zion,*
> *Shout, I say, Daughter of Jerusalem!*
> *Look, for your King comes riding in to you,*
> *Your righteous King whom God has saved for you.*
> *Meekly riding in upon an ass,*
> *Meekly riding in upon a young he-ass.*

They heaped their garments on the beast's back, as the men of Ramoth-Gilead had done hundreds of years before when they acclaimed Jehu king. Jesus mounted, and rode royally into the City through the Jericho Gate, the disciples singing at the top of their voices these verses from the psalm, *O Give Thanks to the Lord:*

> *Open to me the gates of righteousness. I will go through and praise the Lord,*
> *Through the gates of the Lord, by which the righteous shall enter.*
> *I will praise you, Lord, for you have heard me and you will save.*
> *The stone which the builders refused has become the quoin that bears up the roof.*
> *This is the Lord's doing and is marvellous in our eyes.*
> *Today is the Lord's own Day; we will rejoice and be glad in it.*
> *SAVE NOW, I beseech you, Lord; Lord, I beseech you, send prosperity.*
> *Blessed be he who comes in the name of the Lord.*

They threw down their mantles for him to ride over and danced ecstatically on either side of him. The younger and more riotous members of the crowd, catching the enthusiasm, strewed the road with palm branches that they were carrying into the City as fuel for the Passover ovens; they clashed drinking-cups together and, pouting out their lips, imitated the loud blare of trumpets.

It is untrue to say that the City was greatly stirred, as might well have happened if the wild ash-smeared Ebionites had kept to their engagement by acting as whifflers. But all of them, except only Jesus's brother James, had abandoned him at Jericho on the previous evening, deeply offended that instead of remaining in their austere company he had elected to spend the night at the house of Zacchaeus, who was the chief tax-gatherer of the district and a notorious enemy of the people. Nevertheless, the noise of the shouting and rough music brought many townsfolk running to their roofs and doors. "Who is that scarlet-clad nobleman on the white ass?" neighbour asked neighbour.

"It is Jesus of Nazareth, the prophet, whom not long ago the Jebusites drove out through the Fish Gate with stones and rotten fish. He is returning boldly in the guise of a Great One."

"He a Great One! Let him first prove it!"

"They say that at the ford yesterday he restored a blind man's sight."

"Does that make him a Great One? Then the fairs are full of Great Ones—travelling physicians who make old men young, who graft new noses on diseased faces, who banish warts and pimples with a pass of the hand."

"They say, too, that at Bethany about a month ago he revived a young Essene whom Mary the Hairdresser, a Kenite witch, had thrown into a trance as deep as death. Four days he had lain in the tomb, and his spirit had already descended to the lowest caverns of Sheol before this prophet called it back."

"They say; but they say many foolish and incredible things. Once a spirit has descended into Sheol it cannot return until the Last Day when Gabriel with his ram's horn sounds the Unspeakable Name."

"No, not unless the Name is spoken by a prophet beforehand."

"Did this Jesus then dare to speak it? The penalty is death by stoning!"

"Who knows for certain? The City is full of headless rumours. Nevertheless, it is agreed that Jesus differs from all other men."

"And all other men from one another. If he is a Great One, why is he so ill attended? What are a dozen madmen and a rabble of ill-mannered little boys?"

"HOSANNA!"—"SAVE NOW!"—the disciples were shouting. "SAVE NOW, I beseech you, Lord!" For "Save now" was the cry prescribed by the prophet Jeremiah for the Day of Trouble that had dawned at last. Jesus dismounted from his ass at the Eastern Gate of the Temple, where he cast down his wreath and branch, changed his scarlet garments for white ones, removed his shoes, and was soon swallowed up in the great throng of pilgrims that pressed into the Temple Courts. The cries of "HOSANNA!" were drowned in the universal clamour of rejoicing and the ringing psalm:

Oh, enter then his gates with praise,
Approach with joy his Courts unto!

Jesus remained all afternoon with his disciples in the Court of the Gentiles, leaning on his staff, observing and observed; but nobody acclaimed him, and he uttered no royal edict. In the evening he went quietly out to Bethany, to the house of Simeon the Lowly, used by the Free Essenes as their club-house, where he had promised to spend the night.

Here an ominous event occurred. As he sat eating with Simeon his host, a wild-eyed woman came to the door and knocked loudly three times. The porter asked what her business was.

"I wish to see Jesus of Nazareth."

"No women are admitted here."

"Then let Jesus of Nazareth come out to me."

"Who are you?"

"I am the Third Mary."

The porter went in to give the message to Jesus, but Mary the Hairdresser darted past him into the dining-hall, an alabaster jar of terebinth ointment in her hand. Gliding up to Jesus, she cracked the jar on the table edge and let the scented ointment stream over his head, beard and tunic. The whole house filled with the scent. Then she knelt weeping; tears wetted his feet, but she unbound her hair and wiped them with it. "Alas for Adam!" she sobbed. "Alas for Adam in his journey from ark to ark!"

Jesus, his face more pallid than ever, asked her: "Woman, whose gift is this?"

"The Second Mary's gift of peace."

"Gladly accepted even from your hands, and in defiance of your Mistress."

343

She rose and hurried out again.

The Essenes were outraged. They admit no women into their assemblies and also consider the use of ointments at banquets indecent. One of them asked: "Who was the woman? And why was this ointment wasted?"

They began reckoning the value of the ointment and how much money it would have fetched, if sold, as alms for the poor.

The disciples hotly defended Jesus. Judas said: "The poor are always at your gates. Why do you grudge this honour to one who has renounced all worldly possessions? Were you serious in your solicitude for the poor you would do as he has done. To be a proud Sadducee is one thing, to be a humble Ebionite is another; each has his reward. But to be a Free Essene is to dally on the bridge 'over the waters of destruction."

Jesus then said: "That was Mary the Hairdresser. She came to anoint me for burial. Let her deed not be forgotten, for she came as a peacemaker. Love was her ruin, leading her into witchcraft by the road of jealousy."

When they heard Mary's name, the Essenes rose hastily and went out to purify themselves, crying in astonishment to one another: "We have been wonderfully deceived! How can this madman be the Holy One whom John the Baptist and the venerable Watchman of Horeb promised us?"

Deserted except by his disciples, Jesus sat brooding at the table. Galilee had rejected him. The hill country of Judaea had not made him welcome, nor had Transjordania. The Samaritans, the Edomites, the Jews of Leontopolis had temporized with him. Jerusalem had rejected him with the right hand of the Jebusites and the left hand of the Levites. The Female had plotted against his life. The Ebionites had deserted him, and now the Essenes. Yet still he was King of Israel, the last of an ancient line, a King though unacclaimed, and still he trusted in the goodness of Jehovah and in the truthfulness of the prophets. Though he were fated to tread the path of Adam, he would tread it with a difference.

Presently he began to recite the beautiful though dark poem of Isaiah:

Who has believed our report? And to whom is the arm of the Lord revealed?
For he shall grow up before him as a tender plant, and as a root out of a dry ground: he has no form nor comeliness; and

when we shall see him, there is no beauty that we should desire him.

He is despised and rejected of men; a man of sorrows, and acquainted with grief: and we hid as it were our faces from him; he was despised, and we esteemed him not.

Surely he has borne our griefs, and carried our sorrows: yet we did esteem him stricken, smitten of God, and afflicted.

But he was tormented for our transgressions, he was bruised for our iniquities: the chastisement of our peace was upon him; and with his scourgings we are healed.

All we like sheep have gone astray; we have turned everyone to his own way; and the Lord has made the iniquity of us all to meet him.

He was oppressed, and he was afflicted, yet he opened not his mouth: he was brought as a lamb to the slaughter, and as a sheep before the shearers is dumb, so he opened not his mouth.

He was taken away by distress and judgement: and who shall declare his generation? For he was cut off out of the land of the living: for the transgression of my people was the stroke laid upon him.

And he made his grave with the wicked, and with the rich in his death; because he had done no violence, neither was any deceit in his mouth.

Yet it pleased the Lord to bruise him; he has put him to grief: when his soul shall make an offering for sin, he shall see his seed, he shall prolong his days, and the pleasure of the Lord shall prosper in his hand.

He shall see of the travail of his soul, and shall be satisfied: by his knowledge shall my righteous servant justify many; for he shall bear their iniquities.

Therefore will I divide him a portion with the great, and he shall divide the spoil with the strong; because he has poured out his soul unto death: and he was numbered with the sinners; and he bare the sin of many, and made intercession for the sinners.

When he had done, he gazed around him at the disconsolate faces of his twelve disciples, drew a deep breath and fell silent again. None of them dared move; even to have shifted an elbow would have seemed an offence against him, so deep and lamentable was his grief. Then they were aware that his breast was heaving and his face working; he seemed to increase in size and majesty, and they knew that he was about to prophesy.

They waited in a daze, until suddenly the words burst from his mouth with frightful force. "Amen, Amen: I will not feed the flock!" he roared, and seizing his stout pastoral staff, the one carved with flowers, he exerted all his strength and snapped it in two across his right knee.

They stared aghast.

"Amen, Amen: My sons, why do what is unprofitable? Why offend the clean for the sake of the unclean? Leave the ewe struggling in the thorn thicket, leave the lost lamb bleating in the marsh; leave the broken limb unbound; leave all; forget your duty to me! Return to the fold, become masters of the fold, pipe merrily there, dance, sing, and eat the flesh with the fat!"

Peter picked up the pieces of almond-wood and gazed ruefully at them, as a child might gaze at a broken toy, piecing them together. For answer, Jesus took up his other staff, the one carved with bands, and broke that also, flinging the pieces out of the open window.

"What will you do now for a staff, Lord?" Peter asked reproachfully.

"Tomorrow morning go early to the slaughterhouse and fetch me back a butcher's crook and a length of butcher's cord."

Then the prophetic spirit left him. He sank back into his seat and began to laugh softly at them. He seemed altogether changed in person and manner, jovial now and light-hearted. They were frightened at the change, but smiled timidly back at him.

He clapped Peter on the shoulder, and said: "Be of good courage, Peter! The End is not yet!" Eyeing the newly filled cups of wine which the Essenes had abandoned, he asked: "Comrades, what hinders us from drinking and making merry to-night? I will grant you a dispensation from your vows if you will drink with me like honest men." He seized the nearest cup, which he emptied at a draught, and clattering it on the table, began singing the verses of a merry Galilean marriage song. The disciples, now drinking too, clapped their hands in time to the music and joined in the chorus. Then some of them began to dance on the table, cracking their fingers, while Thaddaeus and Simon of Cana shouted obscene jests unrebuked. Jesus said: "The tear of grief, the tear of rage, the tear of merriment—ah, but the tear of merriment was ever the best! Cease awhile from prophecy, Children, and laugh at the follies of this world."

A great load was lifted from their hearts. They no longer needed

346

to pretend to themselves that they were more pious men at heart than they were. They had been loyal to Jesus through good times and bad, but now that he had resolved the doubt which had been torturing them for months, and for entertaining which they had secretly reproached themselves as traitors to him, they loved him more than ever before. No, the End was not yet! Israel was as yet unprepared for salvation. They might relax the taut strings of the heart.

Only Judas abstained from wine, on a plea of sickness, and by midnight was the only disciple who could still stand upright on his feet. He reassured himself: "It cannot be; I know the Master well. He is not one to yield, as he seems to have yielded, to a sudden despondency. He is a King, he is true-born, he is of those who endure to the very end. He is playing a part, that is all. He is playing a part to try us. To-morrow he will make everything clear."

Yet the next morning Jesus was still in the same strange mood. He reminded Peter of his commission at the slaughterhouse and drank unmixed wine, which he pressed on the other disciples. Judas remembered the words of Isaiah: "Woe to those who rise up in the morning to follow strong drink!" When Peter returned with the crook and cord, all went outside into the garden. Jesus said to Judas: "I am hungry. Climb up into this fig-tree and fetch me a handful of figs."

"There is none on it."

"What, none?"

"No, Master, it is not the season."

Jesus flew into a passion and, stretching out his fingers, solemnly invoked the Worm that had gnawed at the roots of Jonah's gourd to destroy the fig-tree in the same manner. Its tender leaves began to wilt before their eyes, and by the next day it was dead.

Judas said: "Master, your parable of the wise farmer and the fig-tree—the tree which is an emblem of Israel. He refrained from felling it though it had not fruited for three years; yet you are destroying this tree without even waiting to see what it will yield in the fig-season!"

Jesus laughed scornfully. "What? Do you not see my new staff, splashed with the blood of the flock? Come with me, children of the slaughterhouse! Let us perform a great deed to-day, an honourable deed, a deed to fire the hearts of simple pilgrims. Let us cleanse the Outer Courts of the Temple, beginning at the Basilica of King Herod." He led them off towards the Temple. Wine made

347

their hearts bold and their feet unsteady. They stopped to drink again at an inn near the City gates.

Judas said nothing, but wondered to himself: "What is this? If the Temple is an idol, what need to cleanse it? Especially the outer parts? The other day he spoke a parable of a man who carefully cleansed the outside of a covered dish without lifting the lid to disclose the unclean food inside; and he spoke it against the Temple priesthood."

The strict Pharisaic rule against entering the Temple Mount with money or merchandise, or even with shoes on one's feet, was scorned by the Levite priesthood, who considered that only the Sanctuary and the Inner Courts were holy in any true sense; that nobody need tread with much awe in the Court of Israel or the Court of Women, and that the Court of the Gentiles was no holier than any other part of the Old City of Jerusalem. As for the Basilica built by Herod to the south of the Court of the Gentiles, they regarded it as a mere lobby and allowed stalls to be set up there for pilgrims who found it inconvenient to climb up the Mount of Olives to buy pigeons, doves, lambs and other beasts of sacrifice in the regular market under the cedars there. This trade in livestock brought another with it: that of money-changing. A great inconvenience of the Roman occupation was that the Romans reserved the sole right to mint gold and silver, and that because of the Commandment against the worship of false gods, the head of the Emperor on the more recent coins, with the inscription: *"Tiberius Caesar Augustus, High Priest, Son of the God Augustus"*, prevented them from being carried into the Temple. Thus any Jew who came to the Basilica to buy a dove or pigeon and had only unclean money with him must change it first into clean at the money-changers'. Certain types of foreign money were tolerated as clean, and Herod's copper coins stamped with Jewish emblems were still current.

On his arrival at the Basilica, Jesus took up his station just inside the gate, clapped his hands for silence and instructed the disciples to do the same. An inquisitive crowd gathered. Then, pitching his voice high and clear, he recited part of a prophecy from the Book of Jeremiah as follows:

The word of our God came to Jeremiah: "Stand in the Gate of the Temple and there proclaim these things which I put into your mouth. Say: Listen to the words of the God of Israel, the Lord of Hosts, all you Jews who enter by these gates to worship him. He says: Amend your ways and your deeds and I will establish you securely in this city. Do not deceive yourselves in lying repetitions: 'The Temple of the Lord, the Temple of the Lord, all is well with the Temple of the Lord, all will be well with the Temple of the Lord!' Has this house which is called by my name become a robber's den in your eyes?"

And he also says: "I have observed and seen all. But go to my former shrine at Shiloh in Ephraim, which was once called by my name, and see what I have done 'to it to punish the wickedness of my people Israel."

And he also says: "Because you have done all this"—and I myself delivered his words to you at cock-crow, I called to you and you neither answered nor listened—"because you have done all this I will do a thing to this Temple which is now called by my name, and in which you trust, and to the city and land which I gave to your fathers and to yourselves: I will do the very same thing that I did to Shiloh and cast you out of sight as I cast out your kinsmen the Ephraimites."

And he says: "Offer no prayers for this people, no prayers and no supplications, no supplications and no intercessions. For I will shut my ears to them."

This passage he recited three times, and his disciples stood about him and compelled the people to listen; the crowd increased and the market-stalls were deserted of customers. Then he said: "The Jews of Jeremiah's day would not listen, or repent, but the words of the Lord were proved true, for the Temple was destroyed. On the ninth day of the month Ab it was destroyed by fire. But the people repented by the waters of Babylon, and the Temple rose again, and is now rebuilt more gloriously than ever; yet the ancient abominations are revived. Men of Israel, our God is dishonoured in his own house! Whose is the sin? The Sons of Levi are the sinners. They take too much upon themselves, reserving holiness for their own tribe at the expense of all other Israelites. Is it not written in the fifteenth Psalm that no man shall dwell on this Holy Hill who traffics in money? And is not this place where we stand a part of the Holy Hill? Yet the Sons of Levi care nothing for its desecration so long only as their own enclosure remains inviolate. They shut their eyes to wickedness, and say: 'We know nothing,' though porters with profane burdens make the outer Courts a short-cut between one quarter of the City and another. How long is this to be borne? Look about you at these great buildings! Unless you amend your ways there will presently not be left one stone on another, but all will be cast down." So saying, he took his length of butcher's cord and plaited it into a scourge as they watched. When he had done, he cried: "Who is on my side, who? With this plaited cord I will purge these Courts of their filth!"

All the disciples, except Judas alone, shouted: "Lord, we are with you!" The crowd took up the cry exultantly: "We are with you!" and Jesus advanced to the traders and money-changers. "Go, go, be off I say, lest this plaited cord leave its mark on you for the rest of your days!"

Some of the traders began at once to fold up their trestle tables, and gathering their goods together made off; they knew the proverb: "A pilgrim crowd is a dangerous crowd." But the president of the Money-changers' Guild came boldly forward and thrust a paper at Jesus, crying: "Read this, Sir, if you can read! It is a receipt from the Treasurer of the Temple, son-in-law to the High Priest himself, a receipt for a thousand shekels in lawful money which our guild pays four times a year for the privilege of changing money at this gate. Do you set yourself above the authority of the Temple Treasurer?"

Jesus answered: "Do you not set the God of Israel above the authority both of the Treasurer and of the High Priest? Beware this plaited cord!"

Then he began to overturn the tables of the money-changers and the money slid down to the pavement in heaps; gold, silver and copper together. The money-changers threw themselves on the heaps in despair, clawing the coins together, snatching them from under the feet of the mob and screaming like women in travail. As for the doves and pigeons, the disciples opened the coops in which they were caged and released them in fluttering flocks, and the lambs ran hither and thither bleating. The confusion was increased by a number of wild young fellows in the crowd, who scrambled for loose coins or stray birds with shouts of laughter. Though no one was shameless enough to rob the trembling money-changers of any large sum, their president afterwards complained that, in all, his guild was the poorer by a month's earnings.

Jesus continued into the Temple itself and purged the Courts of all forbidden traffic, as far as the barrier beyond which only a Levite might pass. Several hundreds of people supported him, and his word was taken up: "Is this Temple become a robbers' den?" For the Galileans who formed the greater part of the crowd had long resented not only the presence of the money-changers and sellers of livestock in the Basilica, but the extortionate prices with which they offset the high fees demanded by the Temple Treasurer.

The High Priest, when news of the rioting first reached him, took it calmly enough. "Passover pilgrims are hot-blooded men," he told his son-in-law the Treasurer, "and the traders of the Basilica have perhaps overreached themselves and suffered justly for their greed. Indeed, the so-called purge that has been made of the outer Temple Courts does great credit to the religious feelings of the populace, though little to their intelligence. No serious injuries are reported, and now that they have had their fling the grandeur and vastness of the Temple and the dignified demeanour of our Tribe may be counted upon to restrain them from any further act of ruffianism. No, I have no intention of disciplining them with clubs. If I summoned the Watch they would run mad, and out would come their hidden daggers. In the end we should be obliged to call in the Romans, and then the fat would be in the fire."

The Treasurer said: "But, Holy Father, what of the traders? Are they to resume their employment to-morrow?"

"It were better not."

"That would be a great loss to them and to the Temple revenue: and honest pilgrims wishing to change money or buy birds would be greatly vexed."

"And the traders would learn to be content with smaller profits; and pilgrims who are short of breath would soon realize the inconvenience of an over-scrupulous conscience when they had to retrace their steps and climb the Mount of Olives as far as the Booths of Hino to buy their offerings. No, I shall give the order that all trading must cease until the Feast is over."

"But what action are you taking against this Jesus of Nazareth? He engineered the whole affair."

"Jesus of Nazareth? I had no idea that it was he! According to my report it was an Edomite from Bozrah. So he did not take the hint at the Fish Gate, the obstinate fellow?"

"No; and strange stories are current about him. The strangest and most persistent is that he restored a dead man to life at Bethany a few weeks ago, by use of the Name!"

"Since the dead are, by definition, incapable of living again, and since, in any case, nobody but a High Priest can know the Name— even the version treasured by the High Court is not the true one —I hardly think that we need trouble ourselves with nonsense of this sort. What else have you heard?"

"Yesterday he rode through the City dressed in scarlet with a branch in his hand, and a rabble of little boys shouting behind him."

"Indeed? Why was I not informed? The affair, then, is more serious than I had supposed. Now that his insanity has taken a violent form we must act as quickly as possible. We should have arrested him at the Tabernacles; Nicodemon son of Gorion officiously prevented us, you may remember."

"By the way, Holy Father, someone of importance—I forget who— told me at the time that this Jesus is the same man who some twenty years ago was warned to keep out of the Temple until he could clear himself of the suspicion of bastardy."

The High Priest's son, the Chief Archivist, said: "Yes, it was I. I heard the story and it interested me, so I turned up the records. They go far to prove the charge. Unfortunately, however, the file is incomplete—the marriage contract of his mother is no longer there. Without it we cannot accuse Jesus of trespass, for his supposed father, the only relevant witness, has been dead for several years, I find."

"He is a dangerous man," said the Treasurer, "dangerous, reckless, and more than usually gifted. I shall be in suspense for the rest of the Feast unless we can place him under restraint. I fear that the rebuff that he was given as a boy set him brooding on imagined wrongs, and, like many an impoverished country Pharisee, he has come to identify his own sufferings with those of the people at large. Holy Father, may I convey your order for his arrest at once to the Captain of the Temple?"

"Arrest him in the Temple?" cried Caiaphas. "Son, would you make matters a thousand times worse? Wait until dark, wait until he goes off for the night to his lodgings. As that wind-bag Joseph of Arimathea never tires of telling the Sanhedrin, we must do our good deeds by stealth."

"With your permission," said the Chief Archivist, "I will send a person of importance to confront him in the Temple to-morrow and ask him a few questions: questions that will make a fool of him; questions that he cannot answer without falling into trouble either with the Romans or with his own supporters—questions, therefore, that he will not attempt to answer. We will not need to arrest him if the affair goes as I hope it will."

"I will leave it to you, my Son. Why not ask the questions yourself?"

CHAPTER TWENTY-SIX

THE SWORD

THAT evening Jesus returned with his disciples to Bethany. He went to the house of Lazarus, but the porter would not admit him. Lazarus sent Martha out to explain that, by a general resolution of the Free Essenes, none of them was permitted to converse with him again, as being in league with a witch and having himself used witchcraft. Nevertheless, to show that he was not ungrateful to the man in whose debt he stood beyond hope of payment, he would put his house at Jesus's free disposal, and remove elsewhere with his two sisters. Jesus accepted the offer without comment, spent the night cheerfully there with his disciples and returned to the Temple on the following day.

By this time news of what he had done at the Basilica had run through the City like fire through dry grass. There was a sharp division of opinion. The Sadducees condemned the action as a wanton interference with legitimate trade. The leading Pharisees agreed with them in deploring the use of violence on the Temple Hill: for though the traders had been at fault, it was an inexcusable presumption to chastise sins of sacrilege which could be confidently left to the vengeance of Jehovah. But crowds of Zealots and Anavim—injudicious, easily stirred to religious zeal in festival time and careless of consequences—praised Jesus to the sky for his piety and daring. If anyone asked: "But surely this is the same Jesus who was expelled from Capernaum and Chorazin by the elders of the synagogue?" the answer came pat: "It was done in jealousy. They could find no fault in him, except that he was not too proud to preach to poor men like ourselves."

Tales of the remarkable cures that he had performed lost nothing in the telling: the cure of one vitiliginous leper became the cure of ten true lepers, and he was credited with having revived three or four dead persons in different parts of the country, including another Shunemite boy, his mother's only child, like the one whom the prophet Elisha had raised from the dead. It was also asserted that he had the power of suddenly disappearing, and reappearing on the same day at a place fifty miles off, and of walking dry-shod over water. Many were stirred by huge hopes. Had the Messiah come at last, with Elijah in the guise of John the Baptist as his forerunner? Already certain of the required signs had been fulfilled: Jesus had entered the City in the manner prescribed by the prophet Zechariah, wearing the dyed garments prescribed by Isaiah, and had called Israel to repentance in no uncertain voice.

From a flight of marble steps on the shady side of the Court of the Gentiles he preached to a crowd of some five thousand men and women who listened to him with rapt attention. This time he did not prophesy in his usual manner, of the Pangs of the Messiah, the dangerous times, the times of national affliction, wars and rumours of wars, nation rising against nation and kingdom against kingdom, earthquakes, famines and disasters such as had never been since the Creation. Instead, he eloquently recalled the glorious feats of King David and his thirty-seven chosen companions in their war of liberation against the Philistines, and in their wars of conquests against the Moabites and Syrians. Companions worthy of their leader: Adino the Esnite who killed eight hundred men in a single battle, and Shammah the Hararite who fought the Battle of the Lentil Patch against six companies of Philistines and left them all dead on the field; and Benaiah of Kabzeel who set a pitfall for mountain lions in the snow and when one fell into it, leaped down and strangled it with his bare hands. Surely that heroic breed was not yet extinct in Israel?

He made these ancient tales live again by the power of his voice and gestures. "Swell with martial pride, pacific heart! Strut proudly, meek foot! For it was here at Jerusalem that King David elected to reign, and his free-hearted companions worshipped on this very hill!" He also told of the splendid reign of David's son Solomon, whose navies sailed over all the seas of the world and in whose army twelve thousand horsemen served, and fourteen hundred chariot-men—Solomon King of Israel, who acknowledged no overlord, the wisest king and the most favoured of God who had ever reigned in Israel. Solemnly he recited the prayer that Solomon had uttered on that same hill at the dedication of the First Temple, publicly holding Jehovah to the promise, sworn to his father David, that there should never fail a prince of the royal line to sit on the throne of Israel. "Whoever has ears to hear, let him hear."

Trumpet music sounded, and twenty venerable white-robed priests filed out from the Inner Court and made for the stairs from which

Jesus was preaching. Side by side in the middle of the procession paced the Chief Archivist and the Captain of the Temple, wearing their ceremonial cloaks. In deep reverence the crowd made way for them.

The Chief Archivist courteously saluted Jesus, who acknowledged the salute with equal courtesy.

"You, Sir, are Jesus of Nazareth?"

"I am so called."

"You are an Israelite?"

"I am."

"Were you not warned twenty years ago, by men who had assisted in the building of the most sacred part of this Temple, never again to enter its gates until you could disprove an accusation of bastardy which a Doctor of the Law had laid against you?"

"I am true born; I am a native of Bethlehem."

"You mean, I suppose, the obscure Galilean hamlet—Bethlehem of Zebulon?"

"I mean Bethlehem of Judah, which the prophets have celebrated without obscurity."

"How are we to know that you are no bastard but true born? What persons of repute have so accepted you?"

"The Essenes of Callirrhoë, when I entered their strict community shortly after the Romans usurped the government of our country."

"Whom can you call as witness to this?"

"Simeon and Hosea, Free Essenes of Bethany, both men of honour. They were my fellow-postulants."

The Chief Archivist was taken aback. He had expected Jesus to shuffle, stammer, contradict himself and cut a poor figure in the eyes of his followers. He shifted his ground of attack. "We will question Simeon and Hosea at our leisure," he said, frowning. "Meanwhile, be good enough to tell us this: by whose authority did you incite your followers to drive from the Basilica of King Herod the authorized vendors of sacrificial beasts and birds, and the changers of unclean money?"

"You have now asked me four or five questions, all of which I have answered. Be good enough to answer one in return. You have heard of John the Baptist—John of Ain-Rimmon—my kinsman, whom Herod Antipas the Tetrarch of Galilee lately beheaded in the Fortress of Machaerus and of whose baptism my disciples and I partook when he anointed us prophets. Was John a true prophet of the Lord, or was he an impostor?"

The Chief Archivist found himself caught in a dilemma. He

knew that the Galileans, the Transjordanians and the hillmen of the South had reverenced John as a great prophet: to declare him an impostor was to approve of his execution by the hated Antipas and so bring the whole priesthood into disrepute. Yet to acknowledge him as an inspired prophet was to confirm Jesus's own authority; everywhere it was now said: "The mantle of John has fallen upon his kinsman Jesus."

He turned for support to the Captain of the Temple, but the Captain of the Temple could not prompt him. Finally he answered: "Prophet or impostor, how can I tell?"

"Then how can I answer your question, which hinges upon mine?"

The crowd applauded Jesus, clapping their hands for delight, and the disciples beamed proudly—all but Judas of Kerioth, who was once again astonished and grieved. Why had Jesus broken the principle which he had strictly laid down for them? When asked by whose authority he had acted, why had he mentioned John? Why had he not answered boldly that Jehovah was his authority? And worse: why had he, hitherto a quietist and a prophet of peace, stood up to incite the Zealots and Anavim to passionate thoughts of military glory?

Jesus lifted a hand for silence and told the priests a parable. "A land-owner planted a vineyard, hedged it securely about, hewed a wine-vat from the rock, and then, being suddenly called abroad, let it out to tenants. After three years, as the agreement was, he sent an agent to collect the rent, but the tenants beat him and sent him away empty-handed. Another went to them and they wounded him in the head, and a third they nearly killed. When the land-owner heard this news, he was very angry. He sent his own son, whom he loved dearly, to collect the rent that was due and demand reparation for the injuries to his servants; for the tenants would surely respect him. But they said to one another: 'Here comes the heir, let us kill him and the vineyard will be ours. The owner is far away; we are safe from his vengeance.' Smooth-spoken son of the High Priest—you who smiled to hear that John, the prophet of the Lord, had been sacrificed to the adulteress of Sepphoris—confess, did you not plot murder last night against a Son of David born at Bethlehem of Judah?"

The Chief Archivist stood speechless, his mouth agape. "Come, let us leave this madman to his raving," said the Captain of the Temple, plucking him by the sleeve.

As they turned and left Jesus in possession of the field, he sent this

356

arrow after them: "You spoke of my rejection by the builders of this Temple. Have you not read the psalm in which King David says: 'You have thrust cruelly at me, but the Lord saved me from falling'? And again: 'Open to me the gates of righteousness; I will go through and praise the Lord. The stone which the builders refused has become the quoin that bears up the roof'?"

The crowd swelled still further, and he resumed his preaching.

Herod Antipas, who had arrived in Jerusalem for the Passover, was alarmed. His servants told him that Jesus was inciting the pilgrim crowds against Herodias and himself as the murderers of John the Baptist. What was he to do? He had no jurisdiction in Judaea, and was on equally bad terms with the Great Sanhedrin, the High Court and Pontius Pilate the Roman Governor-General, whom he had recently offended by refusing to support him when, in defiance of the Law, he introduced into the City a set of votive shields inscribed with the Emperor's name. But it was not for nothing that Jesus had styled him a fox. He knew a question that Jesus could hardly answer without embarrassment, and he knew the right man to ask it—his bitter-mouthed estate-steward Chuza.

Chuza was not afraid to accept the charge. He went at once to the Court of the Gentiles, thrust his way through the crowd with knees and elbows, and emerging close to where Jesus stood, interrupted his discourse with the reiterated cry: "A question! A question!"

The disciples tried to silence him, but he persisted: "A question! A question!"

"Ask on, importunate one," said Jesus at last.

"Does the Law permit us to pay the poll-tax to Caesar?"

When Chuza asked this question the crowd, tense with emotion, believed that it was pre-arranged: Jesus, who had so far spoken only of the glories of the past, was about to commit himself to an open defiance of the Romans. "Ah," they sighed expectantly.

He asked in pretended innocence: "The poll-tax? In what coin is a Jew called upon to pay Caesar? Have you a coin to show me?"

Chuza produced from the corner of his kerchief a new silver denarius. Jesus examined it for a long time, turning it over and over in his hands. At last he asked: "Pray, tell me: who is this mournful-looking man in the laurel-wreath?"

A tremendous laugh went up and it was some time before Chuza's answer could be heard: "It is Tiberius Caesar Augustus, Emperor of the Romans."

Jesus cast the coin from him with repulsion. "Dare you bring this thing into the Temple?" he shouted indignantly.

Chuza met anger with anger. Picking up the fallen coin and carefully knotting it into his kerchief again, he shouted loudly: "The fault is yours; I had counted on changing it at the Basilica, but you drove away the money-changers. And now that you have seen and handled it, answer my question without prevarication."

"Do not pay God what is Caesar's, nor Caesar what is God's."

The meaning of this statement has often been argued, though in the context in which it was spoken it conveyed only one sense: "Jehovah is your sole sovereign; and in paying your debt of life to him you must bring him nothing tainted with the Gentile curse." It followed that all taxation, except the Temple-tax authorized in Deuteronomy, was illegal, and that if the Jews were to keep their lives untainted, they must expel the Romans from their shores. But since Jesus had not committed himself to an answer which would have justified the Captain of the Temple in arresting him, Chuza, never at a loss, took advantage of its ambiguity. He answered boldly: "Chuza thanks you—Chuza, estate-steward to Herod Antipas the Tetrarch. I am glad to know that you approve of paying Caesar what is Caesar's. My wife Joanna, greatly against my wishes, has been financing your ministry; infatuated, I doubt not, by your cheap eloquence. Yet I am glad to know that whatever your morals may be—for my wife confesses that three or four well-known prostitutes are of your party—you are at least a loyal supporter of Rome. If I thought otherwise, I should take a stick to her and beat this nonsense out of her." Then he bawled: "Make way there!" and forced his way out again.

Chuza succeeded where the Chief Archivist had failed, for a crowd is always impressed by a bold, angry man whose wits are sharpened by a private grievance. Jesus's audience broke up into a number of hotly disputing groups, and when he attempted to speak again he was greeted with such a hubbub of questions and counter-questions that he disdained to answer. With a curt, contemptuous signal of dismissal he stepped from the stair, and limped, chin high, down the lane that opened for him, and then out of the Court by the nearest gate, his disciples following behind.

An hour or so later he was back again, unrecognized because of the richly embroidered cloak that he now wore. With impassive face and resolute bearing he threaded his way through the crowd, making for the Chamber of the Hearth, where by ancient tradition a fire was kept burning for the Messiah and his cushioned throne stood behind a low barrier of gilt railings. Peter and Andrew were already standing outside, amicably teasing the Levite sentry at the entrance. Jesus greeted Peter and Andrew and then said gently: "Make way, porter! I would be seated on my throne."

The sentry smiled at what he thought was another jest. "Man, are you mad? If you go in there and seat yourself on the throne, fire from Heaven will scorch you up. It is the seat of the Anointed One!"

"Who is the Anointed One?"

"Are you a fool, or do you take me for one? He is the Son of David, who will lead the armies of Israel against their oppressors. Only he may sit on that throne!"

"Then why do you bar my path?"

"Are you then the Son of David?"

"King David himself says in the psalm: 'The God of Israel said to my Lord'—meaning the Messiah—' "sit at my right hand until I make a footstool of your foes".' How can the Son of David be the Messiah? Does a father address his son as 'my Lord'?"

While the sentry's slow mind was puzzling over the question, Jesus slipped past into the Chamber. The sentry grasped his truncheon and ran after him; but Andrew tripped him up, Peter disarmed him, and between them they gagged his mouth with a kerchief. They were alone in the Chamber. Jesus stepped over the barrier and solemnly seated himself on the throne of the Messiah. He said to Peter and Andrew: "Remove the gag!" and to the Levite: "Go in peace, man! Tell the Captain of the Temple that you have seen the Son of David seated on the Throne of David." The Levite stumbled off in anguish of mind.

Presently Jesus descended from the throne, to saunter out of the Chamber and then out of the Temple again, still unrecognized. Levites with truncheons rushed wildly about in search of him, and the tremendous news ran through the crowd: "Jesus of Nazareth has dared to sit in the Messiah's seat, yet no harm has overtaken him!"

That same morning Jesus had told his disciples: "I have a great longing to eat the Passover in the manner of my fathers. Why should we deny ourselves flesh-food and eat only fish and unleavened bread? Let us eat both the flesh and the fat." Judas was sent with a private request to Nicodemon son of Gorion for a room in which to eat the meal.

This was the Thursday of the week and, as it happened that year, the Passover fell on a Saturday; therefore, according to a ruling of

Shammai's the disciples could not roast the Paschal lamb on the Friday evening, because the prescribed moment for the roasting is sunset, and the Sabbath day begins at the previous sunset, and work is forbidden on the Sabbath, and roasting is work. Shammai's solution was to celebrate the Feast on the Thursday night and the Galileans had adopted it, with Levite permission, though the Judaeans followed a ruling of Hillel's, by which the Passover was held superior to the Sabbath, so that the meal might legitimately be eaten on the Friday evening.

Judas went to Nicodemon's son, who agreed on his father's behalf to provide an upper room, also the lamb, the wine and all that was necessary; only let Jesus be discreet, allow nobody to know to whom he was indebted for the entertainment, and conceal his identity from the inmates of the house.

"Where will this room be?"

"I cannot tell you yet, but an hour before sunset one of my watermen will be watching in the Street of Coopers, at the end nearest the Temple, and he will take you to the place."

"I thank you on behalf of my Master. But, my lord, if I should wish to speak to your father urgently—for I fear that my Master will put himself into great danger before the day is out—how can I do this without bringing trouble to your house?"

"Knock at the little door next the stables, to the right of the entrance gate. Say that you have come for the copying work. I will arrange for a confidential clerk to admit you."

So now when Jesus left the Temple, which was thronged with Galileans carrying lambs for sacrificial slaughter by the Levite butchers, he sent Peter and John ahead to the Street of Coopers, where the waterman was looking out for them. They were led to a house in a side street and asked the porter there: "The guest-room for our Master to eat the Passover with us?" The porter conducted them to a large upper room where they found everything prepared down to the smallest detail: lustral water, basins and towels laid out; the table set for thirteen; a batch of Passover bread ready for the oven; the wine decanted into flagons; the endives cleaned and shredded; the ingredients for the sweet sauce carefully measured; a fine fat lamb already skinned and gutted, and with its sacred shoulder removed for Levite eating, suspended from a hook. Nicodemon's son had even been thoughtful enough to supply the thirteen wayfaring staffs, cut from a hedge, which the company must have with them during the meal, in memory of their ancestors' hasty flight from Egypt.

360

Peter went out on the balcony which served as kitchen, lighted the fire, fanned it into a blaze, and at the exact moment of nightfall, when the trumpets sounded from the Temple Hill, took the lamb, impaled it on the traditional spit of pomegranate-wood and began to roast it. This spit is another evident relic of the Canaanite cult of Rimmon the Pomegranate-god which, as has already been mentioned, was swallowed up about the time of King Saul by the cult of Jehovah; the lamb must once have been dedicated to Rimmon and may well have superseded a child victim, a surrogate of the god himself, though of this no tradition remains among the Jews. Similarly, the wayfaring staffs seem to be relics of those carried in ancient times by the celebrants of Rimmon when they performed the *Pesach*, a hobbling dance in invocation of their god, from which the festival derives its Hebrew name. Those who have taken part in the Dionysian Mysteries will understand precisely what I mean, though pious Jews would be horrified to think that there was even the least connexion between the cult of Dionysus and that of Jehovah; for the explanation of the Festival in terms of the story of the exodus from Egypt under Moses is universally accepted by them.

What Jesus had said about longing to eat flesh-food had sounded doubly strange in Judas's ears: he was breaking not only a private rule that he had kept since his youth, but a principle publicly laid down by Hillel, that the Passover lamb must not be eaten gluttonously as if it were ordinary flesh, but must be regarded as the symbol of a common participation of all Jews in the mercies of Jehovah. In theory the lamb might not be eaten by fewer persons than ten or by more than twenty, but this rule was observed only in strict Sadducee households. The obligation to hospitality among the Pharisaic synagogue-goers was such that throughout Jerusalem house-doors stood open for all to enter who could find room at table, and the lamb of a single household might well be shared among two or three hundred persons. The official ruling was: "To partake of the Passover you shall eat a piece of the victim no smaller than an olive," which explains the proverb: "Though the Passover be but an olive, let the *Hallel* (the hymn of praise) split the roof."

The Temple priesthood would doubtless have opposed this ruling, which curtailed their dues, if they had been able to cope with the work of slaughtering enough lambs to feed the army of pilgrims who came up to eat the Passover: but to provide a victim for every twenty persons in a crowd of at least two or three hundred thousand was manifestly impossible in the course of a single evening. The Levite butchers began work in the exact middle of the afternoon and

361

worked with extraordinary dexterity and speed, while the priests formed an endless chain between the slaughtering-blocks and the altar, passing from hand to hand small silver tumblers each containing a few drops of a victim's blood, and passing them back again as soon as the contents had been poured on the altar. Hour after hour they kept up the action, like automatons worked by a swinging pendulum, and when the evening trumpet blast ended their labours were like men who wake up exhausted after prolonged nightmare. That Jesus ate this Passover with his disciples in private and with doors shut, and with a whole victim provided for the consumption of only thirteen men, is therefore worthy of remark, even when the need for secrecy is granted.

John, who had been assisting Peter, went back to the end of the street to find Jesus and the rest of the party. Before long they were all sitting down together, staff in hand, shoes on feet, to eat the Passover according to the ancient custom: the whole lamb with no bones broken, the bitter endives, the sweet sauce, the unleavened bread of affliction. Jesus, as head of the household, said the prescribed Grace: "Blessed be Thou, the Eternal, our God, the King of the World, who hast sanctified us by Thy commands and hath ordained that we eat the Passover."

The meal began with the First Cup, which he blessed, adding: "This is the last wine which I shall drink before the Kingdom is established!" The disciples cheered boisterously; the smell of the roast meat after more than a year's abstinence excited them wonderfully, as the treadmill ass kicks up his heels and brays on being turned loose into a green meadow. Only Judas caught the undertone of grief in his master's words, and only he noticed that Jesus ate the meat with concealed loathing; in sympathy, his own spirit plunged into black despair. *Praise ye the Lord* he could not sing, and he longed for the Second Cup to warm his chilled inwards.

John, as the youngest member of the household, asked Jesus the prescribed questions, and when *Israel out of Egypt* had been uproariously chanted through, Jesus took a cake of Passover bread—round, tough, thin as paper, and hot from the side of the clay oven—tore it in pieces and distributed it. He said: "So would my enemies use me. Yet eat of it, eat of my mangled body, for I was born in the House of Bread." Then he reached for the flagon and poured out the Second Cup, saying: "So would my enemies use me. Yet drink of it, drink of my living blood, for I was reared in the House of Wine."

All the disciples, except Judas, heedlessly ate and drank what he

362

gave them; but Judas asked himself in horror: "What is this? Are we to eat abominable food at our God's own Feast, as the Greeks eat the body and drink the blood of their god in the Mysteries?" He set the cup to his lips and accepted the bread, but neither ate nor drank.

"Lord," said Peter, "you did not end your story of the tenants and the vineyard. Dared they kill the owner's son?"

"He was killed and his body was thrown over the wall."

All at once they were suddenly aware of his sorrow. Conversation flagged and died away at his end of the table, though at the other end Thaddaeus and Simon of Cana continued to argue in loud voices as to which of them would be given the more responsible appointment in the promised Kingdom. Suddenly they found themselves shouting at each other in a hushed room, and broke off in embarrassment. All eyes were now fixed expectantly upon Jesus. He waited for a good while longer, slowly running his finger round the rim of the wine-cup, and at last broke the silence: "One of you twelve shall kill me!"

There was a general gasp. Every man's cheek burned with the flush of accused innocence, and they gazed incredulously at one another.

"One of you shall kill me, one of you who dips his hand into this dish; as it is written in the psalm: 'My familiar friend, in whom I trusted, who has eaten bread with me, has lifted up his heel against me.'"

The disciples asked: "Is it I? Is it I?"

He stared back at them with unseeing eyes, and muttered darkly: "At a goodly price you have valued me!"

At these words Judas's heart gave a sudden leap; a fierce beam shone through his head and he understood everything.

This account of the Passover supper must be interrupted by a more ancient story without which it is wholly unintelligible; it may be found, somewhat obscurely told, in the long poem which forms the last chapters of the Book of Zechariah. The author of the poem, who lived in the age of the Seleucids, is to be distinguished from the author of the earlier chapters, who lived shortly after the Babylonian Captivity. In the prologue he relates how, suddenly obeying a prophetic call, he bound himself to the service of Jehovah by a vow, exchanged his urban dress for a rough pastoral garment—the traditional dress of Jehovah's prophets—and carved himself two pastoral staffs which he called *Grace* and *Concord*. Armed with these staffs, he went out to feed the flock: that is to say, he preached repentance to the people in the style of his predecessors, prophesying Jehovah's mercy if they turned to him, and his hot displeasure if they would not. From the earliest times the prophets had been loyal assistants of the priesthood: while the priests calmly and deftly performed the Temple sacrifices and attended to their other ritual obligations, the prophets ran up and down the country passionately exhorting the people to moral virtue. But not even Zechariah's fellow-prophets had remained faithful to the pure worship of Jehovah: the Seleucid overlords of the Jews had so popularized the rites of the Olympian Gods and of the Queen of Heaven that it had become almost extinct. Zechariah found himself alone and preaching to deaf ears.

He grew exasperated, and cried out in the market-place: "I will not feed this flock! Thus says the Lord: 'Let the sick beasts die, and let those that are caught in the thicket perish and, for all I care, let the remainder devour one another.'" Displaying his staff of *Grace,* he publicly snapped it in two and went up to the Temple to vow himself as a Temple Slave, never again to tread the profane streets of the City. He told the priests at the Treasury: "I have come to devote myself to God. At what price do you value me?"

They answered scornfully: "For a man in the prime of life who gives himself to our God, the price is fixed by the Law at fifty shekels of the Sanctuary weight; and for a woman at thirty. However, according to the eighth verse of the twenty-seventh chapter of Leviticus we are permitted to reduce the price paid to inferior persons. Come now, worthless shepherd, we value you at thirty shekels; for indeed you have chattered as idly as a woman."

They weighed him out thirty shekels of the Sanctuary weight (heavier than the contemporary Phoenician shekel) and handed them to him, saying: "Go now to the High Priest and register your vow."

Zechariah was enraged. "At a goodly price you have valued me!" As he stood undecided, with the thirty shekels in one hand and his remaining staff in the other, there in the Temple itself he saw a Gibeonite potter, whose trade was to make drinking-vessels, dabbling clay with his bare feet; for the Gibeonites, though an unclean Canaanite guild, were at that time employed as Temple craftsmen. His rage seethed over. He threw the thirty shekels at the potter's feet for him to tread into the clay—a symbolic act admirably expressive of his feelings—and ran in fury out of the Temple, still a free man, and still a prophet.

On reaching the market-place, he summoned the people with a shout and then broke his other staff, called *Concord,* crying out as he did so: "For Judah and the rest of Israel I proclaim discord in the name of the Lord!"

At this point the prologue ends and the poem proper begins. In a vision Zechariah sees himself playing a terrible part under divine orders: impersonating the Worthless Shepherd who neither goes in search of lost lambs, nor feeds the sick beast that cannot stand on its legs to graze, nor rescues the beast caught in a thicket—the Worthless Shepherd who neglects all his duties and (like the Temple Levite) feeds sumptuously and complacently on roast flesh—eats "both the flesh and the fat." A frightful paradox: he sees himself preaching falsely in God's name, and in pure love of God taking all the people's sins upon himself.

Then occur the lines—I quote the original text, confused in the Greek version:

> Woe to my worthless shepherd, who has forsaken the flock. His right arm shall utterly wither and his right eye be utterly dimmed. Sword, awake against this shepherd, though he is my friend! Smite the shepherd and the sheep shall be scattered! But for those that are humble-hearted my chastisement shall be a loving one.

He sees himself preaching falsely in the very Courts of the Temple, trying to stir the people to shame, until at last his own father and mother cry out: "You have spoken lies in the name of Jehovah—you shall not live!" and thrust him through.

This act breaks the spell of evil. The people are suddenly moved to repentance, and Jehovah proves merciful. A fountain of Grace gushes up in Jerusalem for the removal of sin and uncleanness. The idols are thrown down, and all the false prophets who have taken part in the worship of the Queen of Heaven, of Tammuz, Dionysus and Zeus, are hounded from the City. Zechariah sees them taking refuge in the suburban villages, and there pretending to be simple cattle-men, explaining the wounds which they have dealt themselves in their Orgies as inflicted in a brawl in a friend's house. Meanwhile, "they shall look upon him whom they pierced": the people of Jerusalem gaze down upon the corpse of the dead man and understand him at last: he has saved them from destruction by his provocative falsehoods. They mourn him as bitterly as if he were an only son.

Thereupon the Day of the Lord dawns frightfully. All the nations of the world march against Jerusalem, the City is taken, the houses rifled, the women ravished and half the population carried off into captivity. But the Son of God suddenly manifests himself; and his feet bestride the Mount of Olives, which splits in two. The faithful ones, preserved from slaughter, take refuge in his shadow. That day the sky is darkened into a twilight, but at evening it clears again and living waters—a metaphor interpreted by the Pharisees as meaning "divine doctrine"—flow out from the City eastward to the Dead Sea and westward to the Mediterranean Sea. Two-thirds of the nation have perished; but the remaining part is refined, as gold and silver are refined in the fire. Jehovah says: "It is my people," and they: "It is our God."

With Jerusalem saved by this miracle, Jehovah strikes all the City's oppressors with a plague. They fight one another furiously and myriads perish, but at last strife ceases for very exhaustion, and the plague is stayed. Their poor remnants are converted and every year go up to Jerusalem to keep the Feast of Tabernacles. The plague has also stricken the horses and mules that wore brass moon-amulets in honour of the Queen of Heaven, and every one of these is dead. All is now clean and holy throughout the City: Canaanite potters are no longer found in the Temple, and the horses and mules display Jehovah's name on the bells that jingle from their collars, bells as holy as those sewn on the High Priest's robes.

Thus the poem ends; but Zechariah never dared to translate this vision into action, and it had therefore become a prophecy awaiting fulfilment.

"Jesus intends to fulfil it!" Judas cried to himself. "He is now impersonating the Worthless Shepherd, the false prophet who neglects his pastoral duties to go out in the name of Jehovah to mislead the people in the very Courts of the Temple." And he recalled the words of Amos:

"I raised up your sons to be prophets and Nazirites, but you gave them wine to drink and commanded them not to prophesy. I am weighed down under your iniquities as a cart under a load of sheaves. Therefore the swift of foot shall lose their swiftness, the strong shall not increase his strength, nor shall the powerful one deliver himself. And in that day he who is strongest-hearted of the mighty ones shall flee away naked," says the Lord.

All that had puzzled and grieved him was now explained at last: the

366

revelry that Jesus had led in the club-house; his cursing of the fig-tree; his forcible purging of the Temple; his refusal to acknowledge the authority of Jehovah; his abandonment of a sincere message announcing the imminent Kingdom of God in favour of a false message announcing a revival of the blood-thirsty Davidic monarchy; and now this idolatrous eucharist! Clearly, he had resolved upon self-destruction, upon becoming the scape-goat that should bear away the sins of the whole people. He had combined in himself Zechariah's prophecy of the Shepherd and Isaiah's prophecy of the Suffering Servant—the Marred Man, the Man of Sorrows who would go to his death as a willing sacrifice and be numbered among the sinners. To be numbered among the sinners is to commit sin, and the Man of Sorrows must sin grievously in order to take the iniquity of all the people upon him: it was the very consciousness of grievous sin that would make him a Man of Sorrows.

But how could Jesus's mother and father thrust him through? Then Judas remembered what Jesus had said in the tax-gatherer's house at Capernaum: "A prophet has no father, mother or brothers, except his fellow-prophets." Was he then inciting his own disciples to turn against him and destroy him as a false prophet, so that when the people of Jerusalem looked on his pierced body they would understand at last, and repent, and thus precipitate the Pangs of the Messiah?

Judas sat dazed, weeping with his head between his hands. He tried to persuade himself that he was mistaken, but the next words which Jesus spoke made all plain beyond possibility of doubt. He called down the table to the disciples at the further end: "Children, when I sent you out two and two without staff, wallet or shoes, did you want for anything?"

"Never, Lord."

"Those days are gone. Now you can no longer count on the Lord's protection. Let every man take a staff, wallet and a purse too, if he has one. And if there is no money in it, let him sell his pastoral mantle and *buy a sword.*" He turned, looked Judas full in the face and said in a low voice: "For it is written: 'He was numbered among the sinners'; and through me let the End be brought about!"

Peter came over to John, who was reclining next to Jesus, and whispered in his ear: "I can bear this no longer. Dear brother, ask who is the traitor who is to kill him." For neither Peter nor any other disciple but Judas alone understood that Jesus was issuing an order, not levelling an accusation.

John leaned his head affectionately on Jesus's breast and quietly passed on the question. For answer, Jesus dipped a piece of bread in sweet sauce and pointedly handed it to Judas, saying as he did so: "What must be done, do quickly!"

Judas rose at once and went out, pale with terror. His instructions were clear: he was to buy a sword with which to kill his master. How could he obey? How could he take the life of the man he loved best? And why had Jesus chosen him as the assassin? Why not young John, his favourite? Or James, the strong-hearted? Or Peter, who had first named him the Messiah? Or that obedient twin Thomas? Was it because he was the only one who had realized that the new doctrine was false, the only one who had abstained from wine in the club-house and from violence in the Temple, the only one who had refused the idolatrous eucharist, and thus the only one who had remained faithful to his mission? Yet in the poem Zechariah's father and mother had been deceived, taking him for a false prophet and running him through in indignation; whereas he himself had not been deceived, but was convinced in his heart that despite all appearances Jesus was still faithful to his God. Knowing him for what he was, how could he run him through? "Thou shalt do no murder!" To kill Jesus except in righteous indignation would be plain murder: and murder he could not commit.

Stumbling blindly through the moonlit streets he found himself wandering in the direction of Nicodemon's house. He broke into a run; he ran like a mountain hare.

When he reached the house, he knocked at the little door and said, gasping: "I am the copyist." At once he was taken before Nicodemon—plump, pink-faced, short-bearded, affable, near-sighted—who was checking accounts in his study.

Nicodemon jumped from his chair, and asked in anxiety: "Is all well? You have been running. They have not followed you to this house?"

Judas shook his head sorrowfully, unable to speak, and refused the wine that he was offered. At last he found his voice and said in broken tones: "It is this. He has appointed me his executioner. Yet I cannot kill my dearest friend; I cannot kill the man whom John anointed: rather, I would take my own life, as the armour-bearer did on Mount Gilboa when ordered by King Saul to run him through."

Nicodemon asked, in horror and amazement: "Is he then suddenly determined on death? What evil spirit has overtaken him?"

Judas briefly described the events of the past two days, while Nicodemon stared and listened, shaking his head in commiseration and making clucking noises with his tongue. He had a quick brain and

Judas had only to mention Zechariah's poem for him to understand everything. Before the story was finished Nicodemon's mind was already made up, and the words came gushing out as soon as it was his turn to speak. "Be comforted, true-hearted Judas; I know the secret of your Master's birth, which was communicated to me by Simon son of Boethus. And I also understand your covert reference to King Saul's armour-bearer, for the secret of Jesus's coronation was communicated to me by Nicanor the Essene. It is indeed because I know these secrets that I have supported him these many months. No, I will not let you do what he is inciting you to do: for I cannot approve the new course which he is steering, like a navigator who wilfully piles his heavily freighted vessel on the rocks. This is to force the Lord's hand, to hasten the Hour before the due time. We have a tradition: 'The Messiah will not come except to a generation either wholly guilty or wholly guiltless', and that time is not yet, for to-day in Jerusalem great goodness and great evil are near neighbours. Moreover, we are taught in the Academy that the hastening of the Hour is displeasing to the Lord. The Salvation of Israel, we learn, is to be compared to four things: to the Harvest, to the Vintage, to the Gathering of Spices and to Childbirth. To the Harvest: because if the field is harvested before its time, even the straw is not good, but if in due time, the straw and grain are alike good. So the prophet Joel says: 'Put in the sickle, for the harvest is ripe.' To the Vintage: because when a vineyard is stripped before its time, even the vinegar is not good, but if in due time, the grapes and wine are alike good. So the prophet Isaiah says: 'Sing unto her, a vineyard of red wine.' To the Gathering of Spices: because if spices are gathered when green and tender—"

Judas broke in: "O my lord Nicodemon, forgive me, but there is no time to lose! When he understands that I cannot bring myself to destroy him, he will persuade one of my comrades to take my place."

Nicodemon reluctantly left his argument unfinished. He agreed: "No, no, we must act at once. He is the one hope of Israel, as Israel is of the world. We must not let him die. He has despaired too soon and so fallen into error; but error that springs from the love of the Lord is easily repaired. I undertake to save him, and more than this, I undertake to bring about at one stroke all that we most dearly desire. Trust me, man of Kerioth, and I will act; but I need your assistance, for what I do must be done with subtlety."

"What is my part to be?"

"Only this: you must go to the High Priest at once and offer him your help in arresting your master. You had better ask for payment, or else the subterfuge may be suspected. Once he is safely in custody, all will be well. But I will not yet reveal my plan to you, lest it miscarry."

Judas eyed him doubtfully, but at last yielded to his persuasions. He knew Nicodemon to be honest, pious and loyal—perhaps the best of all God-fearing Pharisees in Jerusalem.

Nicodemon's plan was based on his observation that Jesus had never preached against Rome—had never, except in his impersonation of the Worthless Shepherd, countenanced any sort of revolutionary activity. "After all," he argued to himself, "what need is there for conflict between Rome and Israel? In ancient days Israel was subject to Egypt and to Assyria and to Persia, and even the prophets approved of this, so long as the tribute paid to foreign kings in return for their military protection did not conflict with the obligations owed to Jehovah. Look what grand commendation Cyrus of Persia gained from the prophet Isaiah! Now, why may Jesus not show friendship to the Romans, and peacefully put forward his claim to the throne of Herod, at the same time entering upon the Sacred Kingship of the whole Jewish race? The Emperor will be surprised at first at this revival of a claim so long dormant, but he is a reasonable man and will at once see the advantage of having a person of Jesus's quality at the head of Jewish affairs: a Roman citizen, a quietist, a man of extraordinary personal power and Herod's heir by the Will deposited with the Vestals."

His plan was, that when Judas had saved Jesus from the swords of his disciples by helping Caiaphas to arrest him, Nicodemon would approach Pilate, with whom he was on fairly good terms, and inform him that Caiaphas had arrested a Roman citizen, none other than the secret heir to the Herodian throne. Pilate, after asking for proof, for which he would be referred to Jesus himself, would ask: "What sort of a man is he?" and Nicodemon would then praise Jesus in the most glowing terms. He would say: "Your Excellency, he is the one man who can solve all the outstanding problems of Jewish government for you Romans by guaranteeing peace throughout the land and vastly increased revenues, with no further need of an expensive army of occupation."

Then he would explain that Jesus's self-imposed task during the past two years had been to strengthen the Pharisee party by the inclusion of the lower orders of Jewish society, with the object of bringing the whole nation, except the Temple priesthood, under the religious control of the central synagogue. That at the same time he had preached the simplification of Temple ritual and the abolition of blood-sacrifice: if Jesus had his way, the twenty thousand priests and Levites whose support was so burdensome to the Province would be reduced to a few score—the able-bodied Levites could be drafted as police to replace the Roman soldiers. Moreover, such ancient local shrines as Shiloh, Tabor and Ain-Kadesh would be re-dedicated, so that the inconvenience of the immense pilgrim traffic to Jerusalem at the three great Feasts would be abated, and even the Samaritan question would be solved; with Jews and Samaritans reconciled under a Sacred King whom both acknowledged. The whole country would be contented (for the Jews love a monarchy), and the Imperial tax, in the form of a free donation, would be paid as cheerfully as the Temple-tax, without need of tax-farmers and a corrupt police. Beggary and banditry would be no more. The dispossession of Antipas and Philip from their tetrarchies, and the unification of the whole country into a single state, would end the costly absurdity of frontiers and petty courts. The Romans would, of course, be given full facilities for the passage of troops through the country to their necessary garrisons across the Jordan.

Pilate would surely see the cogency of this argument, and in any case the ultimate decision did not rest with him. He would be obliged to remove Jesus from the custody of the High Priest, who had no right to try a Roman citizen, and then to make a full report to the Emperor Tiberius.

Nicodemon was in high spirits and, strangely enough, never once paused to consider whether Jesus would accept the part assigned to him.

CHAPTER TWENTY-SEVEN

THIRTY SILVER SHEKELS

JESUS meanwhile anxiously awaited Judas's return. Why did he delay? Had he been unable to find anyone who would sell him a sword? Though the civil population was forbidden to carry swords, they were come by easily enough in the Galilean quarter. Or had some accident happened to him? Or had his righteous indignation been smothered by a scruple against bloodshed, so that he had shirked his task and run off? If he did not soon return, a more resolute disciple must strike the blow.

He spoke with greater plainness: "It is written that the Worthless Shepherd shall be smitten and his sheep scattered. Children, in a little while you will see me no more."

Still they did not understand. Peter asked: "Where are you going, Master? Let me go with you."

"You cannot follow where I am going."

"I will follow you wherever you go, and do whatever you command, even if I must die for it."

Jesus looked about him, and said: "Before this night is out you will all be offended to be called my disciples. You will all be ashamed of your visions and of your prophetic mantles. When you are questioned, you will answer: 'We are countrymen, we know no trade but cattle-driving.'"

Peter protested: "Lord, I will never be offended—everyone else, but not I!"

"Before the second cock-crow you will have thrice denied me!"

"I will never deny you."

Jesus sighed as he quoted Isaiah:

> *He has blinded their eyes,*
> *He has hardened their hearts,*
> *That they should not see with their eyes,*
> *Nor understand with their hearts,*
> *And be converted, that I should heal them.*

The Paschal lamb had been eaten, every morsel of it, and all the bread. The Third and Fourth Cups had been drained and they had sung their last hymn: *O give thanks unto the Lord, for he is good.* John had blown up the fire again and burned the bones of the lamb; the finger-bowl had gone round, and they had washed their hands and wiped them on the napkins. It was time to leave. Then Jesus rose, took off all his garments except his breech-cloth, tied a large towel round his middle, poured water into a basin and, as if he were a bath-attendant, began washing the disciples' feet and wiping them dry with the towel. They were surprised, and asked: "Master, what is the meaning of this jest? Have you become our servant?"

"Every man is servant to some other man; the king is servant to his people; and all are servants of Heaven. As for me, I am the Servant in whom the iniquity of all Israel meets."

"You a sinner? There's a riddle for us!"

"You will solve it in good time."

At first Peter refused to allow Jesus to wash his feet, but Jesus threatened that, unless he submitted, he would cast him off; then Peter cried: "Not my feet only, but my hands and head as well!"

"Being baptized by John, you need no further lustration except for your feet: they must be well cleansed, because of the mire into which God's Adversary has led them, before they stand in a holy place to-night."

"What place is that?"

"The Mount of Olives, upon which the Son of Man is destined to alight from Heaven."

They left the house, and as they went down the street Jesus asked them: "Which of you has obeyed me?"

Peter answered proudly: "I have obeyed you: while the others were making ready, I bought two swords from the people of the house. I understand at last on whom I am to use it."

"Not too soon, God-fearing son of Jonah! Keep one sword, entrust the other to John. Two will suffice for the execution of the Lord's vengeance. Alas, is it not written: 'As for our iniquities, we know them: transgression and lies against the Lord, the preaching of oppression and revolt, concealing and uttering falsehood from the heart'?"

They left the City by the East Gate, descended into the Kidron valley and crossed the brook by a foot-bridge; then they climbed the Mount of Olives, taking a path which led them to the high-walled olive orchard called Gethsemane, "the oil-press", which Nicodemon had offered Jesus as a refuge if he were in trouble. They met nobody on their way, found the orchard without difficulty, unlocked the gate with the key that Judas had fetched two days before, and entered. The olive-trees were very old and fantastically gnarled: four or five were recorded to have been planted in the year that King Solomon dedicated his Temple. Countrymen say: "Buy an ox, buy an ass, they are your servants while they live; but buy an olive-tree, and you are its servant while you live." There was an oil-mill in the orchard, a furnace for making brazier-charcoal of the crushed stones, and a hut with rough bunks used by the harvesters in the season.

Jesus led them to the hut, which stood in the furthest corner from the gate, and pushed open the door. "Peter, James and John must remain with me; they are the strongest-hearted among you all. The

373

others may wait here until they are summoned; and if they are weary, let them sleep awhile."

As he walked away with the three chosen disciples, James asked him: "Where is Judas? Why is he not with us?"

"I fear he has turned traitor and flinched from his task."

Peter cried: "All may prove traitors to their tasks, but not I. I will boldly use my sword on the wretch who has disgraced us all, and in sight of all Jerusalem, though I die for it."

"I too will strike without fear," said John, "for though I loved him, I always loved another better. And is it not my duty to hate the enemies of our God?"

Jesus asked eagerly: "When did you first suspect the truth?"

"When you made merry in the club-house."

"It is well. Come back with me towards the gate, and watch over me until morning, while I make my peace with the Father whom I have offended. Are your swords sharp?"

"As a priest's sacrificial knife."

"Do not let me out of your sight. As you love me, keep a jealous watch; and when the blow is to be struck, strike home!"

The irony of this dialogue at cross-purposes—recorded in the Ebionite tradition—could hardly have been improved by the most skilful Attic writer of tragedies.

Jesus left the three disciples under a hollow tree and retired to a spot about a stone's cast away, where he knelt down and prayed. They could hear his vehement words: "Father, sweet Father, to whom alone all things are possible, I beseech you to take this bitter cup from my lips. Yet not what I will, but what you will."

Worn out after their long day, and drowsy with the wine and the roast meat, they wrapped themselves in their mantles and fell asleep. Half an hour later their mantles were twitched away from them and they awoke. Jesus was standing over them, holding the two swords in his hand: "See how easily I could have robbed you of your weapons. Watch again, and pray that you do not succumb to temptation and so fail in your duty. Pray for me too, that I am not tempted to rise and flee away from you to Galilee."

He handed them back their swords and they started shamefacedly to their knees, while he went off to resume his prayers. Presently they fell asleep again, and he roused them a second time. "Peter, could you not keep watch for a single hour?"

"Lord, my spirit is willing but the flesh is weak."

Once more Jesus prayed, and once more the three disciples fell asleep. Then came a sudden clamour of voices and sounds of the orchard gate being battered down. He saw the twinkling of torches and then a crowd of white figures hurrying through the olive-trees towards him. Hobbling back to the sleeping men, he shook James violently by the shoulder and said: "Quick, rise up! Warn your comrades in the hut that enemies are here. Tell them to scatter and run for their lives."

James grunted and snored, but would not wake. Jesus cried bitterly: "Snore on, then, and finish your sleep! It is now too late to rise."

But Peter and John had been roused by a sudden sense of danger. They dragged James to his feet and pummelled him into wakefulness as a strong company of Levite halberdiers came running up. At their head were Judas and a Levite officer.

Judas muttered to the officer: "Arrest the man whom I kiss." He went up to Jesus and kissed him, and as he did so whispered reassuringly: "All is well. Trust Nicodemon." Then he shouted over his shoulder: "This is your man! This is Jesus of Nazareth."

Jesus asked: "Judas, do you kiss the man whom you betray?" And then: "Am I a bandit that these Sons of Levi come against me with weapons in their hands? I preached daily in the Temple—why did they not take me then?"

"Stand back, men!" the officer ordered. "You are not to use your weapons unless he resists arrest."

Jesus shouted in a tremendous voice: "Woe to my Worthless Shepherd who has forsaken the flock! His right arm shall utterly wither and his right eye be utterly dimmed. Sword, awake against this shepherd, though he is my friend! Smite the shepherd, and the sheep shall be scattered!" He let fall his butcher's crook, which he had carried with him all this while and, flinging out his arms, awaited the blow.

While John stood irresolute, Peter grasped his sword and rushed forward with a shout. "Save him, save him!" cried Judas. But it was at Judas himself, not at Jesus, that Peter lunged.

A Levite darted in to ward off the blow with his halberd, while Judas flung himself sideways and scrambled behind a tree. Peter then aimed a swinging blow at the Levite, but the sword glanced off his helmet, merely gashing his ear. Other halberdiers hurried to the rescue and, finding himself one against fifty, Peter took to his heels and, being swift of foot, escaped over the orchard wall. John tossed his sword away and followed Peter's example.

James was nearly caught. Someone snatched at his tunic, but he struggled violently; it tore in two and he broke away naked, with a sword-cut on his shoulder. Thus the prophecy of Amos was fulfilled.

Judas returned to where Jesus was standing in sorrowful resignation. He stooped down, picked up the fallen crook and asked: "Master, have you further need of this?"

"It is your spoil. Keep it."

The disciples in the hut meanwhile made good their escape. Andrew had started up from sleep at the noise of shouting and quickly roused the rest; they had all stolen away unobserved under cover of the hut, helping one another over the orchard wall. Thomas reassured them: "We need not fear for the Master. If he could elude arrest by daylight and in open country at Nazareth, surely he can do so again here by moonlight and among the olive-trees."

But Jesus made no attempt to escape. He was led out of the orchard towards the house of the former High Priest Annas, where the High Priest Caiaphas, son-in-law to Annas, was staying for the Feast. It was the largest and most luxurious house on the Mount of Olives and stood only a few hundred paces away from Gethsemane.

Peter followed behind at a safe distance. The night was quiet and he expected at any moment to see a company of bright angels swooping down from Heaven to the rescue. Was it not on the Mount of Olives that Ezekiel had once beheld the Chariot and the Glory of the Lord, and was it not there that the Messiah would stand in the Great Day? "I am glad that I submitted to the foot-washing," he said to himself. "I am prepared for anything."

But nothing notable happened; only the noise of howling dogs across the Kidron grew louder and steadier. At Passover the full moon and the maddening presence of many lambs always disturbed the City dogs, and to-night the smell of roasted lamb ascended from a thousand fires in the Galilean quarter. Yet the dogs were denied even the bones to crack.

Jesus was brought into the house of Annas, and Peter, standing in the shadow of the wall, his sword still clutched in his hand, heard the Levite officer making his report to the Captain of the Temple. The Captain answered: "Good! Good! But how did the armed bandits manage to get away? You should have surrounded the place first." The officer mumbled his excuses, which the Captain cut short with: "Send the informant along to the Treasurer and see that he is given the blood-money. One hundred and twenty drachmae was the agreed sum." (For Judas, asked to name a price, had remembered Zechariah and demanded thirty Sanctuary shekels, which were worth four drachmae apiece. "It is too much," they had protested. "Not so," Judas had insisted, "it is the value of a Canaanite slave as established by the Law; and I am selling you a free Israelite.")

Peter listened in incredulous horror. How in the world could Judas, his comrade Judas, whom he had regarded as the most generous and scrupulous of the Twelve, have ever brought himself to sell his Master for a paltry sum of silver? God's Adversary must surely have entered into him.

At first cock-crow, the false alarm of dawn, Peter stole into the hall, his sword concealed under his mantle. He looked around in the hope of finding Judas, whom he was determined to kill; but Judas was not there. Warming himself at the fire, he noticed for the first time that his fingers were bleeding—he had cut them on his sword while climbing into an olive-tree before leaping from an upper branch over the orchard wall.

A cook asked him: "How did you wound your hand?"

"In the house of some friends of mine, in a rough-and-tumble."

"Who are you, eh?"

"I am a cattle-man. I never had any other trade. I have just driven a prime herd of beef down from the north."

Then a maid-servant said: "I know you, big lout! I saw you the other day at the Basilica during the riot. You are one of the Nazareth gang, a follower of that Jesus."

"I am nothing of the sort."

"I could swear to it. I can tell by your *iod's* and *ain's* that you are a Galilean."

"Forty crates full of plump harlots! Upon my soul, I never set eyes on this Jesus."

"But you are the man who let all the doves fly away! I would know you anywhere."

"May the Adversary father a litter of devilkins on your fubsy body, witch! I arrived in Jerusalem only twelve hours ago."

"Then what are you doing out here, on the Mount of Olives, at this hour of night?"

"I have already told you. I have been eating the Passover with friends near the Booths of Hino. It ended in a brawl."

"But what are you doing here?"

"What do you think? I am warming my hands. In Galilee, if a man sees an open door and a fire inside, he enters and warms his hands, and the people bring him wine and a bit of bread and fish. Here, it seems, he gets nothing but insults. Come up to Galilee one day, daughter of sixty camels, and we will teach you manners!"

So he passed it off, and stayed there cursing and swearing to himself for nearly an hour, before he swaggered out into the street again. Then the cocks began to crow in earnest, and he wept bitterly to hear them.

Meanwhile Jesus was taken for examination to the Court-room, which might have been the very same room in which Zacharias had been examined some thirty-three years previously, for the furniture and hangings were the same; but it was a very thin Sanhedrin that had been summoned to hear the case. Nicodemon had not been notified, nor Joseph of Arimathea, nor any of those who might have been counted upon to show favour or leniency. All those present were Sadducees of the ruling families, who were guided in all their actions by one over-riding principle: the need of close collaboration with the Romans. It had been impressed on the Sanhedrin by Pilate, and by his predecessor in office, that the Temple-cult continued only on sufferance, and that any renewal of disorder in the Province would be the signal for its immediate suppression. No act of violence performed in the name of religion that might prejudice cordial relations with Rome must be overlooked or left unpunished.

The Sadducee leader was old Annas, who had been High Priest for nine years beginning with the year in which Archelaus the Ethnarch was deposed, and without consulting whom Caiaphas, who had now held the office for eleven years, took no important decision. Annas had five sons; one had been High Priest in the interim between Annas's term of office and that of Caiaphas, and the other four were all destined to become High Priests in after years.

It was the constant complaint of these seven gifted men, who formed the junta which controlled the Sanhedrin, that the greatest enemies of peace between the Romans and Jews were the members of the High Court, whose lack of political common sense was a national disgrace. The Pharisaic High Court, they declared, never made the smallest pretence of studying Roman sensibilities and judged every breach of the peace strictly by Mosaic standards, as though the Romans did not exist at all; moreover, because of the absurd leniency of the Court's procedure, it was well-nigh impossible to secure a conviction in it, even of notorious mischief-makers. They therefore made it their business to review every case of political importance before it could be heard by the High Court, and if there seemed the least likelihood that the Governor-General would be offended by an acquittal, to turn it over to him for settlement, with a summary of evidence and a provisional verdict for his guidance.

"This Court is declared open," said Caiaphas. His real name was

Joseph, but he was popularly nicknamed Caiaphas, "the diviner", because of his well-developed faculty of intuition; Pilate called him "the perfect valet", because of his obsequiousness to his masters, his haughtiness to his inferiors, his adroitness, his correctness and his fundamental falsity.

"I must preface my remarks with a sincere expression of thanks to the members of this honourable Court who have answered a most unseasonable summons to try the case of Jesus of Nazareth. I had feared that the considerable distance of this house from the City might prevent our securing the necessary quorum. The need for an emergency meeting will be apparent to you all as the case proceeds. We could not, with safety, have arrested the prisoner by daylight yesterday because of his strong hold on the Galilean pilgrim crowds; yet it was imperative not to allow him to remain at liberty during Passover Eve. An incident sufficient to justify armed Roman intervention would be ruinous to the nation; I need not enlarge on this. Our agents scoured the Galilean quarter where he was reported to be eating the early Passover, but without success, and the information that led to his eventual arrest close to this house did not reach us until about an hour after midnight. My request for your attendance went out as soon as the prisoner was reported to be safely in our hands.

"The case has unusual features. The Court may be surprised to learn that the prisoner, Jesus of Nazareth, though a Galilean fanatic, has hitherto enjoyed the reputation of a quietist, and that his dossier, which has lately reached me from our police agents in Galilee, is marked 'Friend of the Government'. It appears that he has criticized certain of the pietistic local Pharisees in a sense that deserves our praise, and has even attempted to reconcile the country people of Galilee to the customs-men and tax-gatherers. According to trustworthy reports, he is on intimate terms with many of the most influential tax-gatherers in the country, including Zacchaeus of Jericho. Yet some evil spirit seems to enter into him whenever he comes up here to keep a Feast. Not content with brawling at the Pool of Siloam during this year's Tabernacles, he now fancies himself to be a Great One of sorts. On the eleventh of this month Nisan he rode into Jerusalem on an ass in pseudo-regal style, and to-day after passionately expatiating to the pilgrim mob on the glories of the Davidic Kingdom, is alleged to have forced his way into the Chamber of the Hearth and to have seated himself for a while on the throne of the Messiah. Unfortunately, the Levite sentry is the only witness to this insane act, and since no member of the general public can yet be found to swear that he saw the prisoner either enter the Chamber or emerge from it, and since no disorder was caused, the Levite's evidence must, I admit, be treated with reserve. It is possible, however, that before we come to this charge we shall be able to secure confirmatory evidence, perhaps from the informant who assisted us to procure the arrest.

"There remains the well-established incident at the Basilica on the previous morning, which we discussed at our last meeting. I confess that I took a less serious view of it than subsequent events have warranted; and it is greatly to be regretted that my son the Chief Archivist and the Captain of the Temple were yesterday unable to check his impertinence in the Court of the Gentiles. However, we now hold him under close arrest and, I trust, will have no difficulty in sentencing him to the maximum penalty of lashes for a scandalous breach of the peace; and if my venerable father Annas or any others of the elders of Israel consider that we should press for a capital charge, I should be the last to challenge the view."

An elder rose, to ask whether any life had been lost at the Basilica.

"No loss of life has been reported, but Phaleron, the head of the Money-changers' Guild, is suffering from severe shock; and the case has been aggravated to-night by the brutal attack made by one of the prisoner's disciples on the informant who helped us to make the arrest. A Levite halberdier intervened and, for his pains, had an ear sliced nearly off with a sword. In the confusion the rascal managed to escape."

"Was the prisoner himself armed?"

"No arms were found on him."

"Well, let us examine him at once," said querulous old Annas. "Passover Eve is always a tiring day and I wish to resume my interrupted sleep as early as possible."

"March the prisoner in," said Caiaphas, and presently Jesus appeared, escorted by an unarmed warder, and was led to the witness-stand.

"You are Jesus of Nazareth?"

"Of Bethlehem."

"Do you mean the Galilean Bethlehem?"

"I mean Bethlehem of Ephráth."

"I believe that to be correct," the Chief Archivist interposed hastily, "and after all the point is immaterial."

The clerk of the Court read out the first charge: "Jesus of Nazareth, you are accused of a breach of the peace, committed about noon on the twelfth day of the present month Nisan, in that you

380

incited certain persons to riot in the Basilica of King Herod, wrecking the tables of the money-changers, and releasing the doves, pigeons and lambs of the livestock-dealers. You are further accused of the use of insulting language and of wielding a plaited cord and therewith striking Phaleron the money-changer on the head, causing him grievous bodily harm."

Caiaphas asked: "Do you plead guilty or not guilty?"

"I have seen the *Mezuzah* on the door-post of this Chamber."

Caiaphas flushed angrily at this reminder that, though he was High Priest, the Court that he had convened had no authority in the eyes of any pious Jew.

He repeated: "Guilty or not guilty?"

Jesus made no reply.

"It is clear that he is a Galilean, not a Judaean. Galilean criminals always take refuge in dumb insolence."

Three witnesses to the events in the Basilica were called, and the Court found Jesus guilty of incitement to destroy property but, by a small majority, not guilty of incitement to murder.

The next charge was that of influencing a certain person unknown to do grievous bodily harm to Malluch, a halberdier in the High Priest's service, while the said Malluch was assisting the officer charged with making the arrest. Though Jesus put in no plea, the charge failed. Malluch, with a bandaged head, himself testified that the prisoner's behaviour had been correct. He added: "If it please Your Holiness, this man Jesus appeared greatly disturbed by the incident. He touched my ear where the sword had sliced it, muttering some words which I did not catch."

"With what object, do you suppose, Malluch?"

"He wished to heal the wound, Holy Father."

"Indeed! And with what success?"

"The pain ceased, Holy Father. The ear is in a fair way to heal, the surgeon tells me; he says that I must have remarkably quick-healing flesh."

Caiaphas said to Annas: "Venerable Father, with your consent I propose to leave to the last the most serious charge against the prisoner, that of seating himself on the Messiah's throne in the Chamber of the Hearth."

"It is well."

The next charge was that of using language calculated to foment popular disorder in the Temple Courts. Various witnesses were called, but the first three or four could charge him with nothing more serious than having glorified the reigns of King David and

King Solomon in somewhat extravagant terms, and having encouraged his hearers to be worthy sons of their fathers. One of them quoted Jesus's injunction against paying God what was Caesar's, or Caesar what was God's; but Annas and Caiaphas reluctantly agreed that, whatever rebellious intention might underlie the words, in themselves they were unexceptionable.

Then a witness testified that Jesus had said in the Court of the Gentiles during the previous Passover season: "Destroy this Temple, and in three days by magic I will build another as grand and beautiful."

At this Judas, who had been called as a witness and was waiting at the back of the Court, volunteered to go on the witness-stand, and gave the correct version: "Destroy this Temple, and by God's grace I will build him as acceptable a dwelling-place in three days; for your servant is a carpenter. Israel was great when our God was worshipped as dwelling in an ark of acacia-wood." This disposed of Jesus's alleged claim to magical powers, and though the saying incensed the Sadducees beyond expression, Caiaphas was obliged to admit that the charge was not proved, because of a conflict of evidence. He was passing to the last charge, when a door-keeper entered with an urgent message for him. "The personal aide-de-camp to His Excellency the Governor-General desires an audience with Your Holiness."

The aide entered with a clatter, grinned amicably, and gave the Court a perfunctory salute. He was a foppish, effeminate, very young man named Lucius Aemilius Lepidus, who was chiefly distinguished by being the great-grandson of the Emperor Augustus. In a loud, drawling, drunken voice he delivered his message: "The compliments of His Excellency the Governor-General of Judaea. He understands that one Jesus of Nazareth has been arrested by order of this Court and is now under examination. He wishes it to be understood that he has a strong personal interest in the case and that no action must be taken without reference to himself."

Caiaphas was startled. He asked Lepidus how the Governor-General had received such early intelligence of the arrest, which had taken place hardly two hours before. Lepidus laughed, and replied confidentially: "Between you and me, High Priest, it was someone whom you did not see fit to invite to your club-meeting, and I gather that he suspects you of trying to put out of the way a good friend of the Emperor's. No names, mind, and the Governor-General only dropped me a gentle hint; but, by my Divine Great-Grandfather, you may take it from me that you must mind where you tread to-night. I may look somewhat of a fool, but my guess is as good as the next man's. Old Pilate would hardly have pulled me out of bed at this godless hour to send me down here to you fellows unless he meant what he said, now would he? Especially as he knew that I was not sleeping alone. I mean, in fact, that there must be something in this case that interests him, somehow or other: money probably, or perhaps a woman, or else you have arrested one of his best secret agents, or—well, you never know with the Governor-General."

Caiaphas replied with dignity: "His Excellency may rest assured that neither on this or any other occasion will he have cause to question either our justice, our discretion or our loyalty."

"I hope you are right," said Lepidus. "Is that poor fellow over there the prisoner?"

"He is the prisoner."

"A fine-looking man, but a little frightening, eh?—he reminds me of the stories that my pedagogue used to tell me about the magicians in Egypt: they would wave their sticks at you in a sort of slow pattern—like this, watch!—and hypnotize you, and when you awoke you would find yourself in the crocodile pool! But before I send you all off to sleep, I simply must get back to bed myself, or I shall get into trouble with—well, with someone. Good night, and remember the Governor-General's message."

They bowed; he waved his hand, blew a kiss, grinned and clattered out again.

"Nicodemon!" said Caiaphas. "It will be Nicodemon. I—" Then he stopped short, realizing that the Court had not been cleared, and ordered the clerk to read out the last charge.

"You are accused of an act of sacrilege, committed towards evening of the thirteenth day of Nisan, in that you did insolently and impiously seat yourself, in disregard of the warning of the Temple sentry there on duty, upon the throne reserved by tradition for the Blessed One, the Messiah Son of David."

"Do you plead guilty or not guilty?"

Jesus did not reply.

The sentry was called as first witness, and reported the incident veraciously enough, except that he doubled the number of his assailants.

Judas, called as a second witness, deposed that he had not been in Jesus's company at the time that the alleged incident took place; and all efforts on the part of the Court to make him alter his statement were unsuccessful.

Caiaphas looked round the Court and shot out his lip at Jesus.

He hoped to repair the lack of any second evidence by startling him into a confession. He said, with ironical courtesy: "Perhaps since you were good enough earlier in this trial to confess to your identity, you will now do us the favour of answering this question too. Are you by any chance the Blessed One, the Messiah Son of David?"

Jesus answered: "You will know who I am—may it be before this very day is over—when you see the Son of Man coming with the clouds of Heaven and seated on the right hand of Power. This holy mountain shall bear the imprint of his foot."

Caiaphas rose and tore the blasphemy-seams of his robe. He cried: "Need we call more witnesses? We have heard blasphemy pronounced in open court!"

The Court then retired to a lobby to discuss procedure. One of the elders said: "In normal circumstances, I should advise the transfer of this case to the High Court. They are empowered to inflict the death-penalty for blasphemy; whereas thirty-nine strokes are the most that can be inflicted by the Sanhedrin in punishment of the only charge that has been proved against this man. As the Holy Father has himself pointed out, we cannot allege any violence or incitement to disorder either in the prisoner's historical review of the departed glories of Israel, or in the action which he is alleged to have taken in the Chamber of the Hearth. The only objection to this course is that it would be extremely difficult to persuade the High Court to convict him."

Caiaphas took up the point. "My learned friend is right. It can hardly have escaped him that, by a ridiculous High Court ruling, blasphemy is not a capital offence unless accompanied by the Name of God. Technically, since the prisoner used the word 'Power' as a synonym for the Name and did not positively claim to be the Blessed One, the Messiah, he is guilty only of a misdemeanour which the High Court cannot punish by more than these same thirty-nine strokes. It is a most provoking situation. Has anyone any advice to offer?"

Annas said: "There is nothing for it but to refer the case to the Governor-General. I do not know how seriously we should take the suggestion made by the Governor-General's puppy that the prisoner is a secret agent of Rome. No use of provocative agents, as distinguished from spies, has been reported in Judaea since old Herod's days; but Pilate is not too nice to employ them, and if the man really is a provocative agent, we must be all the more zealous in bringing him to justice. It will be enough to produce the evidence of the riot and the evidence of the prisoner's Messianic claim—evidence which, though unfortunately not good in Mosaic Law, will be good enough to satisfy the Governor-General. I move that we should also mention the prisoner's reply to the last question, which to anyone but a devious-minded Pharisee is plain blasphemy and deserving of death; and that we should ask the Governor-General's permission to have him stoned to death outside the City as an act of popular justice. His Excellency will doubtless accede to our wishes, the prisoner being a proved trouble-maker, and I will let him know privately, through his Oriental Secretary, that we are setting aside certain Pharisaic legal rulings in the interests of peace and the original Law. The stoning had best be unofficially entrusted to the Fish Gate factions; they gave him his warning on the last occasion that he made trouble in the City. One last word: unless we adopt this course at once, we will be unable to despatch the business before to-morrow evening, when not only the Passover but the Sabbath begins. I need hardly remind you that a death-sentence cannot at the best of times be pronounced in the High Court on the same day as the trial, and that no Jewish Court has power to detain a prisoner in custody during Feast days on which it is not in session. But Roman justice is conveniently short and swift."

Annas's motion was approved with only three dissentients, none of them members of his own family. The court returned to the Council Chamber, and Caiaphas announced: "This Court orders the case to be referred with a summary of evidence to the Governor-General of Judaea. Witnesses are required to hold themselves in readiness to proceed to the Residency when summoned. The Court must be regarded as still in session until that event. Warder: remove the prisoner to the anteroom."

CHAPTER   TWENTY-EIGHT

THIRTY GOLD TALENTS

FOILED in his attempt to kill Judas, Peter hurried back to the City. He went at once to the Galilean quarter, where he knocked up the local headquarters of the Zealot party—the militant nationalists—and announced the arrest of Jesus. Holding a naked sword in his hand, he urged all brave men present to follow him in an assault on Annas's house: Jesus must be rescued, and Judas the traitor hacked in pieces, for the honour of Galilee. He convinced the Zealot leaders that Jesus had dropped his mask of meekness and taken up the sword at last for the liberation of all Israel. Word was passed round to hostels and club-rooms frequented by party-members, and soon twenty men, emboldened by Passover drinking, came in with arms concealed under their mantles and swore either to set Jesus free or die in the endeavour.

Peter led them out into the street, but though he impressed on them the need for caution they were soon cheering, yelling, uttering threats of vengeance and waving weapons above their heads. Someone broke into the well-known ballad against the grandees of the High-Priestly families; and all chanted it lustily through the narrow, empty streets:

> *A curse on the House of Boethus,*
> *   On their truncheons a curse!*
> *A curse on the House of Annas,*
> *   On their whispers a curse!*
>
> *A curse on the House of Cantheras,*
> *   A curse on their pens!*
> *A curse on the House of Phiabi,*
> *   A curse on their fists!*
>
> *A curse on the High Priests*
> *   And their Treasurer sons!*
> *A curse on their sons-in-law,*
> *   The Temple grandees!*
> *A curse on their Levite servants,*
> *   The proud halberdiers!*

A Roman patrol of a sergeant and eight men met them unexpectedly at a street corner. There was a clash and a short, furious skirmish. The Zealots, despite their numbers, were no match for well-armoured Roman veterans. Though one soldier fell, mortally wounded in the throat, five Zealots were cut down before the remainder took flight, leaving three prisoners in Roman hands; namely Peter, whose swiftness of foot had deserted him, and two drunken Upper Galileans named Dysmas and Gestas. These three were marched off at once to the guard-room at the Roman barracks, flogged and knocked about by the guards and, after a brief trial, in which they were advised to plead guilty unless they cared to be put to the torture, sentenced by the Commanding Officer to crucifixion. Peter, not wishing to be called in evidence against Jesus, withheld his true name: he described himself in Court as Barabbas, "my father's son", which was taken to be a surname.

Soon after dawn Jesus was fetched under Levite guard to the Residency, which was the Palace of Herod under a new name; Pilate used part of it as his Headquarters when he brought troops three times a year from Caesarea to forestall trouble at the great Feasts. Caiaphas and the five sons of Annas followed at some little distance, at the head of a large company of their retainers, and sent in a message to Pilate, requesting an immediate audience.

Pilate, formerly a colonel in the Praetorian Guard, owed his Governorship to his friendship with the notorious Sejanus, now the Emperor Tiberius's right-hand man. He was humorous, bold, greedy and entirely unprincipled. Philo, in an extant letter to the Emperor Caligula, further describes him as inflexible, merciless and obstinate; but malicious humour was his chief characteristic, and his greatest delight lay in upsetting the dignity of the shrewd, witty, but humourless grandees of the Great Sanhedrin. He sent out a message: "The Governor-General will be charmed if the High Priest will join him and the Lady Barbata at their private breakfast table." Warm kitchen smells drifted down the corridor.

Caiaphas replied with a slight shudder: "My thanks to your master: pray inform him that by a vexatious old tradition we Jews are forbidden to partake of his desirable breakfast dishes. My colleagues and I will wait on the porch of the inner court until he is at leisure to see us."

It pleased Pilate to keep Caiaphas waiting on the porch for half an hour while he breakfasted comfortably with his wife. Then he sauntered out, napkin in hand, wiping his lips.

He greeted Caiaphas affably enough: "You are up early, Your Holiness; I presume that you have come to discuss the Jesus affair before I try my morning's cases?"

"We have handed the prisoner over to Your Excellency's guard."

"What is the charge against him?"

"Leading a riot in the Basilica of Herod, with damage to property and danger to life."

"No one killed? Then what is all the commotion about? Surely this is not a case for the Praetorian Court?"

"It is aggravated by sedition and blasphemy. Your prisoner has set himself up as the Messiah, the Sacred King, and has blasphemed

387

the Name of our God, for which the penalty prescribed by Moses is death by stoning. We have come for your permission to have him handed over to popular justice at the Fish Gate."

"As a simple Roman I cannot understand your paradox. How can a man claim to be the Sacred King and at the same time blaspheme the very God by whose favour, presumably, he intends to reign? And your esteemed colleague Nicodemon son of Gorion assures me that the man is a loyal friend to the Romans, which seems equally inconsistent with his claim to the Sacred Kingship. You cannot consider the prisoner mad, or you would not have troubled either yourselves or me with the case: you would have beaten him well and let him go. In any case, I cannot grant your plea for popular justice, which would set a dangerous precedent. Why not give him an official execution if he is guilty of a capital crime, as you allege?"

Caiaphas began an explanation, which Pilate cut short: "—Really, Your Holiness, it is of no consequence. I shall examine the prisoner myself. Nicodemon assures me that he speaks Greek fluently, so I need not ask you for an interpreter—or misinterpreter."

"Shall I send the witnesses in?"

"Do not trouble. I hardly think that I shall press the petty matter of the rioting in the Basilica, where—so I understand from my Oriental Secretary—the money-changers and livestock-dealers have no right to trade. By the way, see that their contracts are cancelled without delay. I will tolerate no provocation to the religious scruples of the Galilean pilgrims. Upon my word, you are much to blame for allowing your Treasurer to turn your Sacred Hill into a common market-place. As for the blasphemy, surely that is a matter for the High Court to settle, not for you or me?"

Humming a tune, he went into the Judgement Hall, the very place where Antipater had been judged by his father Herod, and gave instructions for Jesus to be brought before him.

"Unshackle him," he ordered, when a sergeant and two files of soldiers escorted Jesus into his presence. "Now bring him a comfortable chair, and send someone in with Cyprian wine and some cakes. Then clear the Hall and keep everyone well away from the doors. I intend to examine this prisoner in private."

The sergeant showed no surprise and did what he was told. On his return to the guard-room he said: "That smart High Priest has blundered badly this time. I will take you on at ten drachmae to three that he has arrested one of our own secret agents; and now the Samnite is treating the fellow to wine and getting the story from him. At least, that is how it looks."

"Yes, that is right, I think. Did you see how he let the Sanhedrin gang cool their heels on the porch while he finished his bacon and devilled kidneys? I had to laugh, though the High Priest kept his temper pretty well, I must say."

Pilate asked Jesus kindly: "You drink no wine?"

"I have a Nazirite vow."

"I see. I will not press you to break it. How fortunate that you speak Greek. By the way, you ought to go to a good surgeon with that leg of yours, unless the injury is an old one. Hippocrates in his treatise on dislocations gives precise directions for setting the head of the femur back into its socket. If you leave things to Nature, who is a notorious bungler, a false joint forms and you will suffer agonies from sciatica in your old age. My household surgeon will see to it for you, if you care to put yourself in his charge; he is skilful enough. The operation may be painful, but in the long run is worth the pain. However, we can discuss the matter at our leisure. Meanwhile, I wish to ask you a routine question or two, which perhaps you will not mind answering. I will confine myself to questions of identity."

"Say on."

"Your name is Jesus?"

"It is."

"You were born at Bethlehem—Bethlehem of Ephrath in Judaea?"

"I was."

"And you are reckoned of the House of David?"

"I am."

"Tell me, are you the Jesus whose name appears on this paper? It is a sheet from the Quirinus census of twenty-two years ago; I have just had it extracted from the file."

"I am that man."

"I had hoped so. According to this entry you were born at Bethlehem three months or so before King Herod's death. By the way, Jesus of Bethlehem"—here he wheeled suddenly round in his chair —"*Are you the King of the Jews?*"

"Do you ask me this of yourself, or did someone put it into your mouth?"

Pilate brushed aside the question with pretended candour. "Do you think that I am a Jew, trying to trap you into a statement which can be twisted into a criminal charge? I am a Roman magistrate, and I am asking you a straightforward Roman question, a simple question of identity. Are you the rightful heir to the Herodian throne by the legal marriage of your two parents?"

Jesus answered reluctantly: "I am." He added: "But my Kingdom is not of this world."

"I understand you perfectly. The Crown has been in demise since your infancy and you waive your claim because you have neither money nor influence to press it. Nevertheless, you are conscious of your royalty; you have therefore amused yourself with a modest progress on ass-back through the streets of this City and a brief, if somewhat furtive, occupation of the Davidic throne in the Chamber of the Hearth."

Jesus did not reply.

"In fact, you claim the spiritual sovereignty while forgoing the temporal. But, my friend, what in the world prevents you from enjoying both? You must be aware that, unless a king is invested with temporal power, his spiritual power cannot possibly become effective. Nicodemon son of Gorion, who is a staunch supporter of yours, has talked the matter over with me, and I have assured him that if you trust your affairs entirely to my management, the chief problems of your unhappy nation can be settled to the satisfaction of everyone. Under the last valid Will of your grandfather, which the late Emperor approved and deposited with the Vestals, you come next in the succession to your uncle Philip the Boethian; but since he has long ago signed away his claims, you have an irrefutable title to the entire dominions of your grandfather and to the dignity of King. My suggestion is this: I will draw up a memorial to the Emperor with a sworn statement of your claim, emphasizing your loyalty to him and mentioning your outspoken condemnation both of the costly farce of Temple ritual and of the self-righteous disdain in which the Pharisees hold police officers, tax-gatherers and other Government servants. I will suggest that you should be given a free hand in spiritual matters, as well as the title of Allied King, on condition that you engage yourself to break down the misunderstandings between your country and ours; to decentralize worship; to foster commerce and agriculture; and generally to bring Judaea into line with other civilized members of the Imperial community. The Emperor, who is taking a holiday from public business at Capri, will not, of course, see the memorial. It will be dealt with by my friend and patron Lucius Aelius Sejanus, who implicitly trusts my judgement in Palestinian affairs. But come, Sir, you are not listening! Are you unwell?"

"My Kingdom is not of this world."

390

"So you have already informed me. Does this mean that you will not accept my proposal? Your father was a King. For what other reason than to reign do you suppose that you were born into this world?"

"To bear witness to the Truth."

Pilate cried scornfully: "What is truth? Every so-called truth has its antithetical truth, equally valid in logic. The salt of life is humour: the realization that, in the long run—praise* to the Gods!—nothing really matters. Do you never relax from your monomania of holiness?"

Jesus was silent.

"Come, Sir, I am not a man to be trifled with. You must realize that I have the power of life and death in this Province—that I can even crucify you, if it pleases me."

Jesus was silent.

Pilate recovered quickly from his pique, and chuckled at the fantastic humour of the situation. "Upon my word, I cannot make you out. You seem to be *chrestos* rather than *christos!*" (He meant: "simpleton rather than anointed king".) "Well, think it over while I go out for another chat with my Prefect Valet."

He went out to the porch and said off-handedly to Caiaphas: "I find no fault in your prisoner."

"No fault in that seditious wretch? Why, he has stirred up the whole land from Galilee to Edom!"

Pilate smiled engagingly: "I thank Your Holiness for the suggestion. He may well be wanted by Herod Antipas of Galilee—whose subject he is—for political offences committed in the Tetrarchy; I will inquire about this at once from Antipas, who arrived here this morning to keep the Feast. He has never quite forgiven me for not asking his permission before I crucified that batch of Galileans who tore down my new Bethlehem aqueduct. If this fellow Jesus has already got into trouble there, we shall be saved a deal of embarrassment. Have the goodness to wait here a little longer, unless you prefer to enter my unclean apartments and listen to a little gentle music."

Caiaphas had known Pilate long enough and been humiliated by him often enough to be frightened by his jocose manner. He must have hit on a new and profitable scheme, in which Jesus somehow figured, for blackmailing the Sanhedrin; but precisely what the scheme was remained obscure.

Pilate went into the Judgement Hall again. "Come now, King Jesus, you cannot be the simpleton that you pretend to be. I am ready to overlook your highly discourteous silence and to give you one more chance to secure glory for yourself and your posterity and to inaugurate a new Golden Age for your distressed subjects. I am prepared to put your claim before Aelius Sejanus, first securing the endorsement of my immediate superior, the Governor-General of Syria. I need not conceal from you that I make this offer largely because of my dislike of the tubby Tetrarch and of those Sanhedrin rats on the porch; and of course I expect you to remember me generously once you have come to power. I realize that the news of your good fortune must come as something of a shock after the poverty of your early life and your recent fugitive existence. But compose yourself, pray, and try to behave more like a King and less like a peasant. Your scoundrel of a grandfather would weep tears of shame if he could get leave of absence from Hades and look in on us this morning. Here is my right hand, offered in sincere friendship. Do you accept it?"

Jesus sighed deeply, smiled at Pilate and gave a hardly perceptible shake of his head.

Pilate rose briskly. "Very well, then. If you refuse, you refuse; and Heaven help you! If you will not be King Jesus of Judaea, you are still plain Jesus of Nazareth, a subject by domicile of your paternal uncle Herod Antipas, to whom I shall send you for trial. I sincerely hope that he treats you as unhandsomely as he treated your maternal cousin John of Ain-Rimmon."

He clapped his hands and shouted. The sergeant ran in. "Jucundus, bring me pen, ink, parchment. And march this Galilean half-wit back to the guard-room."

Jesus was led out, and Pilate sat down to write a letter.

To His Excellency Prince Herod Antipas, Tetrarch of Galilee, from Q. Pontius Pilatus, the Governor-General of Judaea—Greeting.

I am sending you herewith an interesting personage. I may disclose to you in confidence that he is reported to be the rightful heir to your father Herod's dominions under the terms of his last valid Will. Be good enough to examine his claims, which have satisfied my cursory examination. As a child he escaped the Bethlehem Massacre which your brothers Archelaus and Philip the Tetrarch carried out at your father's order, and has since resided partly in Egypt, as you will gather from his Alexandrian idiom, and partly in your own Tetrarchy. Because I must assume him to be a Roman citizen until the contrary is proved,

392

pray act on the same assumption and refrain from putting him to the torture. You will be as strongly impressed as I was by the characteristically Herodian cast of his features. I shall not, of course, report on the case to the Emperor, or mention it to a living soul, until I have heard your private view; I should be loth to spoil the friendly relations that exist between our two governments by submitting to Rome a claim which would have the effect of dislodging you from your comfortable Lake-side quarters.

Farewell.

"I think," muttered Pilate, smiling in self-congratulation as he sealed the letter, "I think, clever man, that this letter will net you anything up to thirty talents, which will come in handy these penurious days. . But you must not forget to buy your wife the most beautiful necklace in Jerusalem. After that dream of hers, which nearly spoilt your breakfast, she will take it hard if the man is strung up. Your own fault, for confiding Nicodemon's story to her last night when you went back to bed and found her awake. You talk too much, clever man. It is your greatest weakness."

He ordered Jesus to be taken to Antipas, who by long-standing agreement used the West wing of the Residency as his headquarters during the Feasts.

Antipas and Herodias were ill at ease when Jesus was led into their private sitting-room by a staff subaltern, but both did their best to conceal it. Antipas dismissed the subaltern, and offered Jesus a chair and wine.

Jesus declined both. "I have a vow," he said.

"I am not offended," Antipas replied. "But I regret your vow. Wine is a useful mediator in business affairs, and my friend the Governor-General has sent you here, if I have read his letter intelligently, on a business errand. Assuming that you are what you profess to be, and that the Governor-General is not playing with me in his jocose way—assuming, that is to say, that your identity can be proved before a Senatorial Court—the question naturally arises . . ."

Herodias broke in with crude directness: "What is your price, man?"

Jesus was silent.

"My half-brother Herod Philip in somewhat similar circumstances accepted an annuity, which I am still obliged to pay him, in return for a document waiving his rights to our father's estate. Archelaus the Ethnarch, my brother Philip, Salome our aunt and I, agreed to give him the interest on a sum of thirty talents, banked at Alexandria . . ."

Herodias interrupted again. "Nonsense, it was only twenty-five!"

"You are right, my dear—I remember now that it was only twenty-five talents, of which Archelaus and I each contributed nine, my brother Philip five more, and Salome the remainder. Silver talents, not gold ones, of course. Now he draws only the interest of my nine and Philip's five, for Salome made the Lady Livia her sole heiress, and Archelaus forfeited his estate to the Emperor as a punishment for bungling the affairs of his Ethnarchy. Still, the interest on fourteen silver talents at three per cent. is a very comfortable sum, and he enjoys it without any of the cares and troubles of kingship. Do not misunderstand me: I cannot offer you anything approaching the same amount, my revenues being what they now are. Philip might be persuaded to disburse a few talents more; his affairs continue to be in good order. But I must warn you: Pilate will not be so accommodating as either of us. You should have come straight to me instead of interesting him in your claim. He will demand at least half your annuity, if not more, as his cut of the cheese. However, that is your business, not mine. Shall we say the interest on three talents? I will guarantee to extract three more from my brother Philip."

Jesus made an impatient movement.

"Not enough? Well, what about four? You can live very comfortably on the interest of four talents at Alexandria."

Jesus turned away.

"I wish you would do me the courtesy of answering. I know that you are an artisan unused to Court life, but surely you have a tongue in your head?"

Gradually Antipas raised his bid to ten talents, and then looked despairingly at Herodias. Her eyes were blazing. She clapped her hands for the major-domo: "Philemon, fetch that moth-eaten old scarlet cloak of His Royal Highness from the chest by the armoury door and get hold of a papyrus-reed and a pair of theatrical buskins. Dress this impudent fellow up as a King, with the reed in his hand, the buskins on his feet, and a copper pan on his head, and send him back to the Governor-General with the compliments of His Royal Highness."

To Jesus she said: "Very well, then, be a King, and to the ravens with you!"

Antipas was frightened. As soon as Jesus had been led away, with the Palace guard playing him down the colonnades to discordant music, he hurried along to Pilate, who had meanwhile rapidly disposed of two criminal cases and several petitions, and was signing documents in his study. He begged him to pay no attention whatever to Herodias's jest. "Put him out of the way, Your Excellency, and you shall have ten talents."

"Forgive my unmannerly smile."

"Fifteen."

"Try again."

"Twenty!"

"Twenty gold talents? Not good enough. Nor would twenty-five tip the pan."

"Twenty-five! My Herodias would never forgive me if I paid you that."

"Nor would my Barbata forgive me if I accepted it."

Antipas groaned. "My last word is thirty."

"Thirty? Not so bad. Very well, you could easily afford more, but I will not haggle: your friendship is worth far more to me than mere money."

"I will pay you when I see his crucified corpse."

"But you will write me out a bond for half the sum at once."

"How am I to know that the fellow is not an impostor?"

"That will be for my friend Aelius Sejanus to decide, if you cannot."

Antipas held out his right hand. "You are a hard man, Your Excellency."

"But appreciative of your generosity, my dear Prince, which cancels any slight resentment that I may have been harbouring against you since you supported the High Court in that affair of the votive shields. Do you know, I would almost have given half to-day's earnings to have been present when you and the Princess Herodias were screaming away like melon-sellers at your dumb country cousin. It must have been perfect Atellan comedy."

"I sincerely hope that the jest will not one day recoil on Your Excellency's head."

"My one regret is that your irreligious brother the Tetrarch Philip has not come up for the Feast, and that we are obliged to hurry this business through so indecently fast that you lose your chance of recouping from him his due share of these thirty talents. By Hercules, I think it is very hard on you."

"Or do you rather regret, Excellency, that you cannot squeeze a second thirty talents out of him?"

Pilate guffawed. "How well we understand each other! Yes, I must confess that the disgusting affluence of his cities—Hippos, Pella, Gerasa and the rest—is a constant source of irritation to me. But you are a good loser, my dear Prince, and if henceforth we can work together, we may yet be able to pluck out a few of his gaudy feathers and line our nests with them."

The High Priest was still standing outside the breakfast-room at the Residency. Pilate went out again to apologize for having kept him and his associates waiting so long, and on a day of such importance in the Jewish sacred calendar.

"Your lame King," he said, grinning, "causes me a deal of anxiety. I see no justification for executing him. His attitude is correct and my friend Nicodemon son of Gorion has asked me as a personal favour to release him. What do you say? Why not be charitable and forgive him his blasphemy? You know that this is the day on which the Emperor has authorized me to perform an annual act of clemency, the granting of a free pardon to one Jewish criminal—in theory, any criminal without exception. The choice is supposed to be made by a popular show of hands, but your servants will serve the purpose of a crowd."

He beckoned the Levites, and asked: "Shall I pardon your King? Or would you prefer me to pardon Simon Barabbas, the leader of a gang of Galilean Zealots who killed one of my men in the early hours of this morning?"

"Barabbas!" the grandees cried in unison, and "Barabbas, Barabbas!" echoed the Levite servants.

"What, crucify your true-born King? Why should I do anything so barbarous?"

"You will be an enemy of the Emperor's if you do not," cried Caiaphas. "This man is planning a religious revolution which, if we do not check it, will be the prelude to a nationalistic revolt. I do not doubt that the Zealot parade was organized as a demonstration against his arrest."

"Indeed, is it as serious as that? Why in the world did you not tell me so at once? Well—I do not know—perhaps I shall let you have your way after all. But if so, you must accept the entire responsibility. I 'wash my hands of the matter', to borrow a Hebrew metaphor. You may kill him or you may let him go, just as you please; but if he is to die, it must be by a regular crucifixion, with no nonsense about 'popular justice'."

"Will a beheading not suffice? Crucifixion carries a curse with it, and we do not wish to antagonize the Galileans unnecessarily. His closest adherents are all Galileans."

"Your Holiness underrates the care and piety with which I have studied the Mosaic Law. First you ask my permission to have your prisoner stoned for blasphemy, well aware that the body of a'man so stoned must be afterwards hanged on a tree to make it accursed, and now you inconsistently suggest that the curse should be forgone."

The High Priest explained: "Our custom of hanging corpses has long fallen into desuetude, and the last stoning for blasphemy took place more than thirty years ago."

"Indeed, I was under the impression that your Laws were still observed in all their primitive starkness; you have destroyed a favourite illusion of mine and I hardly know what to believe now. I feel like the simple satyr in Aesop's fable, who saw the countryman blow hot to warm his hands and cold to cool his porridge. At all events, in this case, if the punishment is to have the necessary deterrent effect, it must be crucifixion."

"We cannot refuse the responsibility," answered Caiaphas, though with evident reluctance. "He is a dangerous criminal, and we are content that his blood should be on our heads."

Pilate called for a basin, and publicly washed his hands in a solemn caricature of the Jewish ceremony by which City elders absolve themselves from guilt when an unexplained murder occurs in their district. He told Caiaphas: "If you decide to crucify your King, I will lend you a crucifixion party. That is as much as I can undertake to do."

"But the statement of crime? An execution is illegal without a statement of crime, and I have no authority to write one, especially as crucifixion is not a Jewish practice. You must at least write us out the statement; so much authority you are bound to accept."

"Very well. Wait only a little longer, and you shall have one written out for you; and, while we are about it, two more for the pair of Zealots who were sentenced with Barabbas this morning—which reminds me that I have yet to sign their death warrants. They can all three be tied up in a row."

The grandees waited, fuming with impatience, and presently the statements were ready, inscribed in Latin on short pieces of board with Greek and Hebrew translations underneath. The two prepared for Dysmas and Gestas read:

LATROCINIUM: QUOD PROVINCIAM PERTURBAVERUNT.
Banditry: to wit, disturbing the peace of the Province.

But Jesus's statement of crime surprised and alarmed the grandees. It was not, as they had expected:

MAJESTAS: QUOD SE REGEM JUDAEORUM FINXIT ESSE.
High Treason: to wit, pretending to be King of the Jews.

but:

HIC EST JESUS NAZARAEUS, REX JUDAEORUM.
This is Jesus the Nazirite, the King of the Jews.

Caiaphas begged Pilate to alter the wording, but he obstinately refused. "What I have written, I have written. You have undertaken full responsibility for crucifying your King. If you change your minds at the last moment, let me know, and I confess that I shall not be sorry. I have come to pity and even to admire the man. Well, before I say good-bye, I must remind you that I grant favours to provincials neither often nor cheaply, and that this morning you have wasted with this petty criminal case nearly two hours of valuable time which were not my own to waste. I had promised to hurry through my legal business and take the Lady Barbata for a drive into the country, and now, I fear, it is already too late. The only adequate apology that you could make would be to club together and present her with the most beautiful necklace to be found in Jerusalem. Emeralds are her favourite gems, but she turns up her nose at the yellowish sort, and they must be cut and set by an experienced Alexandrian lapidary."

"We will not forget, Your Excellency."

Joseph of Arimathea learned from his servants that Jesus had been arrested and handed over to the Romans. He went at once to Gamaliel the grandson of Hillel, who had recently been elected a joint-President of the High Court. They hurried together to the Residency in the hope of saving Jesus's life, and met Caiaphas as he was leaving the building.

Caiaphas expressed surprise that they should be interested in the case: Jesus, he said, was not only a seditious rascal, but a rank blasphemer.

"Holy Father," Joseph asked, "is the charge against him one of sedition or of blasphemy?"

"What is that to you?"

"I am a member of the Sanhedrin and will be a party to no injustice. If the charge is sedition, let the Romans see to it; if blasphemy, let the High Court see to it."

398

"The prisoner spoke a fearful blasphemy in the hearing of the whole House of Annas."

Gamaliel protested severely: "Unless an alleged blasphemy is instantly avenged by Heaven, it is nothing until the High Court shall have pronounced it blasphemy. Had the Sanhedrin been moved by sudden indignation to pick up stones and administer rough justice in the manner of the barbarous Samaritans, they would have dishonoured the High Court and themselves, but to hand an alleged blasphemer over to the Romans for crucifixion is to dishonour the Holy One of Israel himself, blessed be he!"

"Not so loud. My men are listening."

"Let all Jerusalem listen!"

"Learned men, I beg you to step aside and keep silent while I explain to you the case."

He drew them behind a pillar of the cloister, and said urgently: "The Governor-General is playing with us. He knows as well as we do that this Jesus is a rebel who has publicly claimed to be the Blessed One, the Messiah Son of David. Unless we show our loyalty to the Emperor by disposing of the prisoner before the Feast, he will use this as a whip to our backs; he has even challenged us to dismiss the case, doubtless in the hope that the prisoner will then raise an easily smothered revolt among the Zealots. He seeks an excuse to intervene in our affairs and put an end not only to the pilgrim traffic from Galilee and Transjordania, but to Temple worship altogether. If he attempts any such thing, it will mean a general uprising and the total extinction of our liberties. Better that one man should die than that the whole nation should perish. I beg you to leave well alone."

"To hand over an innocent man to the Romans for crucifixion on Passover Eve is to invite the avenging wrath of our God!"

"Had you listened to his blasphemies, you would quake to hear him pronounced innocent."

"Since when has the House of Annas become the High Court?"

Caiaphas signified that the conversation was at an end, and strode off angrily.

Gamaliel was a worthy successor of his grandfather Hillel. He told Joseph of Arimathea: "Hurry, brother, to the houses of all your ten colleagues"—the Pharisee representatives in the Sanhedrin—"and urge them to accompany you to the Governor-General with a plea for mercy. You must tell him that the High Priest convened an irregular Court last night in his father-in-law's house, and that the decision taken there is against the principles of the majority of Sanhedrin members. I myself will seek out my joint-President and one or two of my most eloquent colleagues: I will persuade them to overcome their scruples against traffic with the Romans, and together we will go before Pilate. To save an innocent life I would swallow much filth, and they the same."

Gamaliel and Joseph went off in different directions, but by the time that they had assembled their delegations at the gate of the Residency, Pilate and the Lady Barbata had already driven out of the City in a fast gig, followed by several others containing members of the Staff and their wives, to celebrate their good fortune in a luxurious dinner-party by the Pools of Bethlehem. The major-domo told the delegates that his master was not expected to return before nightfall, and referred them to Pilate's deputy, the commander of the regiment quartered at Caesarea.

At this distressing news, Gamaliel and his joint-President united the two delegations into one party which went up to the House of Hewn Stone to intercede with Jehovah. After a general confession of their weakness and sinfulness, and the singing of penitential psalms, they knelt down and prayed with great fervour—that the All-Merciful should spare the life of an innocent man, who was to be given over to the Curse; and that, if his life might not be spared, the Curse at least should not fall upon him.

When they had done, Gamaliel said: "Brothers, we have offered intercessions to the All-Merciful in company. Now let us offer intercessions in our homes, apart from one another: let us mourn bitterly with all our households until the moment of nightfall, when a double obligation to rejoice will fall upon us: the Sabbath and the Passover. It may be that our God will be gracious, observing the loving sincerity of our hearts, and for our sakes acquit Israel of the name of harlot; for only harlots sell their children into slavery, and only harlots despise the name of love."

His suggestion was accepted by the whole assembly. The Doctors of the Law returned to their homes, where they mourned and made intercession all day long—to the distress of their families and guests, who were obliged to do the same; and rose to rejoice only when night fell. Thus (so the Ebionites claim) another article of Zechariah's prophecy was fulfilled, the great mourning in Jerusalem for the murdered prophet:

> And the land shall mourn, every family apart: the family of the House of David apart, and their wives apart; the family of the House of Nathan apart, and their wives apart.

400

The family of the House of Levi apart, and their wives apart; the family of the House of Simeon apart, and their wives apart.

All the families that remain, every family apart, and their wives apart.

Judas, who had waited all morning in company with the other witnesses outside the Residency, his mind torn between hope and terror, understood at last that Nicodemon's scheme had miscarried and that Jesus had been condemned to the cross. When finally the witnesses in the case were dismissed, he ran along to the Temple and, bursting into the office of the Chief Treasurer, flung the thirty shekels on the broad desk.

"This is the price of innocent blood," he cried.

The Chief Treasurer's deputy answered coldly: "What is that to us? The money is yours. If you have sinned, you must make your peace with the All-Merciful as best you may."

"At a goodly price have you valued your prophet! Cast this accursed silver to the potter, that the prophecy may be fulfilled!"

He ran out again and compelled Nicodemon's son, whom he met on the Bridge, to go with him outside the City. There in a paddock Judas abased himself before his God, and cried aloud: "O God of Israel, have mercy on a wretch who has sinned through presumption and cowardice and by his gross folly has betrayed your Anointed One to worse than death. Let it now be again as in the days of our Father Abraham, when his son Isaac went obediently to the place of sacrifice, carrying a burden on his shoulder, as your Anointed One goes now; but your heart was turned to mercy and you accepted a ram's life in exchange. Just Lord, accept now my life in exchange for my Master's, and more than my life: let me die accursed, so only that he may escape the Curse. For it is written: 'A curse of God is on that which is hanged on a tree.' Spare his life, and let the soul of one who loved him too well perish for ever!"

Then Judas kissed his weeping companion, saying: "Son of Nicodemon, now is the time for you to expiate your father's fault by acting as my hangman, for I would not seem ungrateful to the All-Merciful by taking my own life. And if you refuse me this charge, then I will assuredly make you the victim. It is a life for a life."

Nicodemon's son, seeing no help for it, took Judas's girdle, tied it in a noose and hanged him, out of public sight, on a crooked thorn-tree which grew near by in a hollow.

The silver was now doubly tainted, and the Chief Treasurer could not on any pretext enter it as a contribution to the Temple Funds. He therefore "cast it to the potter", by buying with it the very field where Judas was found hanging; this happened to be called The Potter's Field because one end of it was strewn with broken pots from a near-by kiln. Its name was changed to Aceldama, "the Field of Blood", its walls were broken down and it was let go to waste.

Let me offer no moral judgement in the case of Judas; it is enough to re-tell the story as I heard it. An Alexandrian sect of Chrestians, called the Cainites, glorify Judas on the ground that if he had not arranged for Jesus's arrest there would have been "no Crucifixion and no triumph over death"; but the Ebionites reject this view as mischievous. They say: "Judas, as a disciple under vows, was bound to obey his master's orders, knowing them securely based on the Law and the Prophets. In the passage that Jesus quoted from the Blessing of Moses, the Levites are praised for their resolution in using the sword against their idolatrous kinsmen. Had Judas obeyed these orders, instead of pitying himself for having been chosen to carry them out and then presumptuously going behind his master's back in a foolish attempt to save his life, all would have been well: the Kingdom of God, for which he had been taught to pray daily, would have come infallibly, just as Zechariah had prophesied. But whether Judas's fault, which was cowardice rooted in intelligence, was graver than Peter's, which was pugnacity rooted in unintelligence, and whether he made full amends for it by his death, that let our God decide, who ordained that Peter too should die accursed on a cross. All that we know is that between them these two postponed the Great Day."

CHAPTER TWENTY-NINE

THE POWER OF THE DOG

ANCIENTLY, it seems, in every country around the Mediterranean Sea, crucifixion was a fate reserved for the annual Sacred King: crucifixion within a circle of undressed stones upon a terebinth-tree, a kerm-oak, a royal oak, a pistachio-pine or a pomegranate, according to varying tribal custom. The practice is said to persist in North Britain and the wilder parts of Gaul: the King's companions bind him with osiers to an oak that has been lopped to the shape of a T; he is then decked with the green branches, crowned with whitethorn, flogged and ill-treated in a manner shameful to record, and finally roasted alive; while his companions dressed in bull-hides dance around the pyre. But his soul escapes upwards in the form of an eagle—as did the soul of Hercules from his pyre on Mount Oeta—and becomes immortal, while the bull-men feast eucharistically on his remains. In Greece crucifixion survives in a partial and playful sense: the annual pelting of the so-called Green Zeus at Olympia. But closer parallels to the Gallic practice are to be found in Asia Minor, Syria and Palestine, especially the great Syrian tree-sacrifice at Hierapolis and its Phrygian counterpart which the Emperor Claudius introduced into Rome about twenty years after the events here recorded. In every case the Sacred King is regarded as a sacrifice made on behalf of the tribe to its Goddess Mother.

Among the Israelites the King was still annually crucified at Hebron, Shiloh, Tabor and elsewhere in the time of the Judges; and the *Tav*-cross which is T-shaped, was tattooed as a royal caste-mark on the brows of the clansmen from whose ranks the Sacred King was chosen. As a caste-mark it is still to be seen among Kenite tribesmen of Judaea and Galilee and appears in Hebrew sacred literature in two contradictory senses: in Genesis as the brand of Cain the murderer—the eponymous ancestor of the Kenites—and in Ezekiel as the divine mark set on the brows of all just men as a sign to distinguish them from sinners in the day of Jehovah's vengeance.

With the first Israelite dynasty, that of Saul, çannibalism was abolished and the custom begun of prolonging the King's reign for a term of years and meanwhile sacrificing a *dod,* or yearly surrogate. This practice survived until the reign of Good King Josiah, though latterly, except in times· of drought or other national disaster, a yearling ram was used as a *dod* instead of a man, and the anomaly justified by the myth of Abraham and Isaac. Josiah abolished crucifixion by inserting an article in his recension of the Law—the Book called Deuteronomy—to the effect that whatever was crucified was not blessed, but accursed. Once this altered principle, fathered on Moses, had been accepted as of divine inspiration, it was used as a means of discouraging crime: the body of a man who had been stoned for blasphemy or other horrid wickedness was hanged up after death on a *Tav*-shaped cross to make it accursed, and denied decent burial.

Among other nations the Sacred King was likewise excused crucifixion, on condition that he found a *dod;* at first the victim was his son or maternal nephew, whom he invested with the temporary insignia of royalty—this explains the legend of Zeus's sacrifice of Dionysus—but presently more distant kinsmen were accepted and, later still, royal prisoners taken in battle; and when in times of peace royal prisoners were hard to come by, prisoners of lesser rank were crucified, and in the end even criminals might serve. Crucifixion then became merely a punishment for crime, and so it is to-day; yet elements of the traditional ritual persist long after its sacred origin has been forgotten, and among the Romans these include the laming of the victim while he is hanging on the cross—since the Sacred King was originally lame, the substitute must also be lamed. It is difficult to discover how much of the Roman ritual is of native origin and how much is Canaanite; for the early Romans used an X-shaped cross, but during the war against Hannibal the present T-shaped one was borrowed from the Carthaginians, who are Canaanites by origin. At all events, it is a remarkable paradox that crucifixion, which in Palestine had once been a magical means of procuring immortality, was now regarded by the Jews as a felonious punishment involving the extinction of their souls, and was therefore used by the Romans as a means of terrorizing political malcontents; and that Jesus as a Sacred King in the antique style, despite his defiance of the Queen of Heaven and all her works, despite his extraordinary efforts to avoid the destiny entailed upon him by his birth and marriage—or, you may well say, in consequence of these very efforts—was about to be immortalized in the antique style.

Still dressed in his regal finery, he was taken to Herod's citadel, the Tower of Phasael, which was now the Roman barracks. There he was stripped naked and underwent the preliminary scourging which is an inseparable part of crucifixion. The captain on duty laid on unmercifully with his supple vine-rod until weariness obliged him to desist. Then he handed Jesus over, bruised and bleeding, to the common soldiers, who dressed him up again and tried to make him play "Guess who struck you", and the cruel May Day game of "King and Courtiers", for which they plaited him a diadem of thorny acacia; but he provided them with poor sport and after half an hour or so they let him go and settled down to dice.

There was a deep poetic irony in their choice of diadem, for at Ain-Kadesh a divine voice had spoken to Moses from an acacia-bush; and it was from acacia-timber that the ark of Noah, the ark of Moses, the ark of Armenian Xisuthrus and the ark of Egyptian Osiris were all built. Throughout the Near East the tree is sacred to the many-named Divine Mother of the many-named Divine Son; its flowers are white and pure, its thorns sharp, and its wood impervious to corruptive waters.

The provost-captain detailed to command the crucifixion party was a humane man. He told the soldiers: "Your orders are to mock and ridicule the prisoners on their way out of the City. This is merely a precaution against trouble; however great a prisoner's popularity, the laughter-loving City crowd will always refrain from attempting a rescue if his plight is absurd enough. However, though you may play whatever fantastic tricks you please on the two Zealots, from all accounts the cripple is a harmless enough fellow, and if you knock him about any more, by the Body of Bacchus I will so knock you about when we get back to barracks that you will wish yourselves in the Navy. And once we are well out in the open country, see that you keep your mouths shut and preserve good march discipline."

He paraded them in column outside the barracks, where a large subdued crowd gathered, consisting mostly of women; then sent a sergeant's party to draw three crosses from the provost stores and bring them back in a transport cart. Meanwhile Dysmas and Gestas were fetched from the cells and placed with Jesus at the head of the column. Both of them had been shockingly ill-used: Dysmas had lost several teeth and Gestas the sight of an eye.

The captain hung the statements of crime about the necks of the three prisoners and gave them their cross-beams to carry. The cross-beam is a six-foot baulk of timber which fits horizontally into a socket of the heavy upright, close to the top; the upright is carried to the place of crucifixion in a cart, but by ancient custom the criminal must shoulder his own cross-beam. Jesus recognized the wood: it was terebinth, which no Galilean carpenter would work, since it was held to be unlucky, just as black poplar-wood is in Italy because of its connexion with the Death-goddess.

The order to march was shouted. The procession moved off, and passed without incident through the near-by Joppa Gate. Jesus was walking with a staff, but needed both hands to balance the cross-beam on his shoulder and could not keep the pace. When a sergeant tried to hurry him he was thrown off his balance and fell heavily; the soldiers roared with laughter. The flogging had left him short of breath, and he had difficulty in rising. After a second fall the captain intervened and, stopping a sturdy pilgrim who was about to enter the City, compelled him to carry the cross-beam for Jesus.

This Libyan Jew, who had heard Jesus preach at Capernaum in

the previous year, made a virtue of necessity. He cried out to the people: "Men of Jerusalem, gladly I shoulder the burden of this true prophet. May it wipe out the reproach that Nahum spoke against my native land. For when he prophesied against Nineveh as a well-favoured harlot and queen of witchcrafts, he said: 'The Land of Put and the Libyans were thy helpers.' Though Put be my mother and the Libyans my brothers, I am no wretch:. I will not praise a newer Nineveh that gives her prophets to be crucified by the filthy unbeliever." The captain, knowing no Aramaic, let this go by.

The procession skirted the City walls and turned north-eastward along a level road towards the Grotto of Jeremiah, which lies about three-quarters of a mile away. The day was sultry, the road thick with dust. A contingent of the Passover Eve crowd of pilgrims, known as the Lazy Ones because the main body always arrived two or three days before, marched in from the north; they were singing for joy at the sight of the walls and towers of Jerusalem, but the psalm died on their lips as the ill-omened procession approached. All stood still, averting their faces while it trudged silently by.

When the Grotto and the tall, spreading Palm of Jeremiah came into clear view, a sudden wailing of women arose from the rear. The news of Jesus's arrest had spread rapidly through the City, and though few of his male supporters dared join the procession, Joanna and Susanna were there, and Mary, Jesus's mother, leaning on the arm of Shelom the midwife; and Mary his queen, with her sister Martha, and their grandmother Mary wife of Cleopas; and Mary the Hairdresser, with a party of Rechabite women.

Jesus turned and said, panting for breath: "Weep for yourselves, not for me. The Day of Wrath is at hand when she will be considered blessed who has borne and suckled no children to perish under the wrath of Heaven; when with one voice the Daughters of Jerusalem will cry to the hills to fall and bury them. For if the green tree is stripped, what will be done to the dry?"

The proverb refers to the religious awe in which certain ancient trees—usually palms and terebinths—are held in Palestine, as being those under which patriarchs or prophets once rested. Though from all other trees branches are torn for firewood, the people fear to touch them. They grow tall and green, even in the desert beside well-frequented tracks, while other trees are stripped and dry. Jesus meant: "If even prophets are crucified, what fate is in store for the common people?"

Beyond the Grotto rose the small skull-shaped hill called Golgotha, where in ancient times sentences of stoning were carried out and where the Romans now crucified political prisoners on a platform at the summit. It overlooked the main road into Jerusalem from the north and derived its name "Skull Hill" not from its configuration only, but from the legend that when King David had moved his capital from Hebron to Jerusalem he took Adam's skull from the cave of Machpelah and buried it at Golgotha as a charm to protect the City. This legend must not be lightly dismissed, for the head of King Eurystheus, task-master to Hercules, was buried in a pass near Athens to protect Attica from invasion; and several other ancient instances of the same custom occur in Greek and Latin history. Jesus had prophesied truly when he told Thomas that his journey would end where Adam's had ended.

At the Grotto the captain gave the order to halt, while two old women came forward: they belonged to the pious Guild of Frankincense, licensed by the Pharisaic High Court, and their self-imposed task was to provide a grain of frankincense for every condemned Jewish felon to swallow as an anaesthetic. Dysmas and Gestas gratefully accepted the gift, but Jesus said: "Burn it, rather, as a sweet sacrifice to the Lord. For this Son of Adam must endure to the end."

At Golgotha he was stripped of his clothes, and the soldiers seized them as perquisites, though in Jewish Law they were the property of his next-of-kin. The sergeant-executioner slit open the seams of the robe and allotted a length of the material to each of his four assistants, but lots were cast for the seamless undergarment bequeathed him by Simon son of Boethus.

They fixed the uprights into the cement sockets prepared to receive them, then made each prisoner in turn lie down on his back close to his upright. The cross-beam was thrust under his head, his outstretched arms were fastened to it with osiers and his hands secured to the wood with a long copper nail hammered through each palm to prevent him from struggling free. Then with ropes and a pulley he was hauled to the top of the upright until the cross-beam engaged in the slot cut for it, after which the two pieces of timber were bolted together. In each upright, about three feet below the cross-piece, were a row of peg-holes, into the most convenient of which the peg which helped to support his weight was thrust under the crutch. His legs were bound fast to the upright with osiers, and his feet secured to the sides with two more nails driven through the flesh behind the sacred tendon—which some call "the tendon of Achilles" because Achilles, the son of the sea-goddess Thetis, was mortally wounded by an arrow in the same sacred spot. The statement of crime was fastened to the top of the upright, protruding over the victim's head.

Jesus was given the central place, with Dysmas hanging on his right and Gestas on his left. As he was hauled up to the cross he uttered a last prayer: but not for himself. It was borne upon him at last that his sacrifice had been in vain and that he had incurred Jehovah's inexorable wrath. The sins that he had committed in his impersonation of the Worthless Shepherd were proved to have been sins of presumption, and by leading his disciples into the same error he had earned his own prophetic reproach: "Whoever deceives the childish-hearted deserves to be thrown into the corruptive sea, a millstone about his neck." His prayer was for them alone: "Father in Heaven, forgive them! Theirs is the sin of ignorance."

He recognized his mother in the crowd and his disciple John, no longer wearing his prophetic mantle, standing close to her; pitying her desolate look, he commended her to John's care.

As the sun rose high in the sky, his pain grew so great that his whole body was shaken with spasms; yet he choked back every cry. The flies were black upon the broken flesh of his back and sides; sweat poured from his face. Gestas shouted and raved, cursing Jesus as the cause of his ruin, for the frankincense had not taken effect on him; but Dysmas, oblivious of his approaching death, said drowsily to Jesus: "My Lord, remember me in your Kingdom. Give me office in your new Kingdom."

Jesus comforted him, concealing the bitter irony of his words: "When to-night I enter the Other Kingdom, you will be at my right hand."

Frightened, heavy-hearted and utterly bewildered, most of the other disciples had by now struggled out to Golgotha; but not James, Peter or Andrew. James could not come because of his wound, which had festered. Peter had been beaten by the Romans until he was senseless, and thrown out naked into the street; Andrew found him there and carried him off to his lodgings, but he did not recover his senses until nightfall.

Mary the Hairdresser came up to Shelom and said: "You brought this Son of Adam into the light of day, Sister; but it is my task to return him to the darkness."

"Who are you, woman?" Shelom asked.

"I will confide a secret to you. The Fourth Beast, the Beast of the southern quarter of the circle in which he sat on Horeb, was the Bull of Haste. His fault was this: that he tried to force the hour of doom by declaring war upon the Female. But the Female abides and cannot be hastened."

Shelom looked despairingly at Jesus. His calm fortified her, and she answered as if with his mouth: "Peace, woman! Is it not written of the Kingdom of God: 'I, the Lord, will hasten it in his time'?"

About noon, when the soldiers had begun to prepare their dinner, a hot wind blew from the east and the sky darkened. It was not the wholesome darkness that heralds rain with the distant growl of thunder and flicker of lightning, but a smoky darkness such as terrifies those who live in the neighbourhood of active volcanoes; and as the cloud spread across the sky as far as the western horizon, blotting out the sun, the earth began to heave sickeningly and a distant rumble and crash was heard as an enormous piece of masonry fell from the Temple into the valley below. A scream of terror went up and many of the women fell on their knees and gazed upwards, believing that the Day of Wrath had come at last. But the Son of Man did not manifest himself and no company of angels rode to the rescue.

The captain reassured his men: "The darkness is caused by desert sand, carried high up into the air by a whirlwind in Elam. To-morrow the whole City will be powdered with it. There is nothing to fear."

Jesus felt the royal virtue slipping away from him, leaving his body common flesh and his heart drained of courage. He cried hoarsely: "My God, my God, why have you deserted me?"

The executioners thought that he was complaining of thirst. With obscene laughter they offered him a sponge soaked in myrrh-wine to suck, sticking it on the point of a javelin.

He declined to drink. "The end has come," he muttered, his lips continuing to move, though almost soundlessly. Those who watched felt their lips moving with his through the verses of that terrible psalm: the ancient Lament of the Crucified Man.

My God, my God, why have you forsaken me? I roar to you like the child who is far from help, crying unceasingly day and night; but you do not hear me.

Holy One, secure in the praises of Israel, my fathers trusted in you and you delivered them: they cried to you and were not lost.

But I am a naked worm, a man no longer, reproached and despised by all. The onlookers laugh me to scorn, shooting out their lips and shaking their heads.

They say: "He trusted in his God to deliver him; O, let him be delivered by the God in whom he delighted."

But you are he that took me from my mother's womb and taught me hope while I lay on her breast.

You are my God from the day of my birth. Be not far from me, for great trouble is upon me and I have no helpers.

Many bulls ring me in, the wild oxen of Basan, wide-mouthed, roaring like lions.

My life drips away like water, my bones are out of joint, my heart melts like wax and drops into my bowels.

I am as dry as a pot in the kiln, my tongue cleaves to my jaws. You have brought me to the dust of death.

Evil bull-men ring me in, they have pierced my hands and feet; my naked frame is exposed to their stare.

They part my robes among them and cast lots for my shift.

But be not far from me, Lord, in whom is my strength. Hasten to help me: deliver my life from the blade, my dear life from the Power of the Dog.

Save me from the Lion's mouth, from the horns of the wild oxen; for you have heard me.

I will declare your name to my brothers, I will praise you to the crowd gathered about me.

Crying: "Praise God, all you who fear him; fear and glorify him, all you sons of Jacob. For he has not despised or contemned the plight of this afflicted one, who calls upon him and is heard."

But the Kenites knew the Lament in its elder version: "Eve, Eve, why have you forsaken me?"; the last four stanzas holding the Mother of All Living to her ancient covenant, charging her not to let Azazel triumph for ever, nor to deny Adam his meed of immortality.

At the ninth hour Jesus uttered a frightful cry as a last spasm shook him. His features twisted awry, his eyes stood staring, his mouth fell open, his heaving breast was still.

"He died remarkably quickly," said the captain. "I am glad of that; he was a brave man, though a dog of a Jew. I have known them hang for five days or more, but for that, of course, they have to thank the man who flogs them. If he lays on hard enough, he saves them pain in the long run."

Slowly the sky cleared, and the sun shone brightly again though the tremors continued at intervals. Towards evening Pilate's Oriental Secretary rode out to remind the captain that in Mosaic Law accursed bodies might not remain hanging beyond sunset, and that on the Eve of Passover it would be as well not to offend native susceptibilities. Jesus and the two other victims should be despatched at once. The captain gave the order: "Lame the two who are still alive and then run them through. You need not lame the other; he is already a cripple. But give him a jab to make sure that he is dead."

They broke the right legs of the Zealots with blows from a stone-mason's hammer, and then despatched them with javelin-thrusts under the ribs. A soldier also aimed a half-hearted upward thrust at Jesus, driving the javelin-point under his ribs from the right-hand side. This would have torn open the lung, had it not been pressed inward by a watery effusion, in the part called the pleural cavity, caused by the scourging; when the soldier disengaged his javelin, out came a discharge of water mixed with a little blood.

Then the bodies were taken down, piled on a cart with the crosses and tackle and taken back to the mortuary in the Tower of Phasael.

Jesus was dead. In the official Jewish view he had died at the moment of being hauled up to the cross; for he thereby ceased to be a member of the congregation of Israel and became "a naked worm, a man no longer". In the general view of the crowd he had died after uttering his cry at the ninth hour—the precise time when the Levite butchers began their slaughtering for the Passover. In the official Roman view he had died under the javelin-thrust: because of the blood, which does not flow from a wound when life is already extinct. He was then certified as dead by the captain and accepted as dead by Antipas, who later came to the mortuary to identify the body. But in the view of the twelve Kenite notables who had assisted at his coronation and who stood in the forefront of the crowd during the crucifixion, he had died when his royal virtue left him and he said: "The end has come"—that is to say, the Sacred King who had been born at the descent of the Dove died then.

Mary the mother of Jesus was the last to leave Golgotha. On her way home she found the Kenites waiting for her by the roadside. With a reverent salute they said: "Permit us to inter the body of our King."

"Ask this of the daughter of Jose Cleopas."

"She has given us her permission, but we need yours also."

"How can you touch what is accursed, noble children of Rahab?"

"Ours is the elder Law; with us crucifixion sanctifies."

"Where will you inter him?"

"In the sepulchre of the First Adam."

"Will you go to the Romans and demand the body?"

"We have no right to do so. The request must come from you as his mother—for his queen fears to reveal herself—and nobody must know on whose account you make it."

"I will do gladly what you would have me do, because of the friendship that your fathers showed me long ago when I was in danger of death."

She went to the house of Joseph of Arimathea and at midnight, when the Passover meal was over, made herself known to him. She asked him to beg her son's body from Pilate.

He commiserated with her, but said: "Alas, woman, while he was alive I did all that lay in my power to save him. Now that he is dead, I can do no more; for though he was an innocent man, yet his body is accursed and I cannot bury him. Were I to go before Pilate with this request he would refuse it scornfully; but perhaps a mother's tears might move him to pity."

"Would Pilate grant an audience to a poor woman like myself? He will listen only to persons of rank or wealth. But I have found men of another nation who are ready to carry my son away to a place where his interment is permitted, and if it is true that you were not among those who consented to his death, prove your piety by this service. I am a widow, and he was my only child."

Mary persisted, and he reluctantly undertook to do as she asked.

When Joseph visited the Residency the next morning, Pilate was highly amused at his request. "Why in the world do you want this gruesome relic, if you are not allowed to touch it, or give it decent burial? Or had I better not ask?"

Joseph winced, but had his answer ready. "Your Excellency must be aware that the Syrian witch-cult has of late taken firm root in Jerusalem. If your soldiers are permitted to sell the body to an unauthorized person, the nose, fingers and other extremities will be put to magical uses, but especially the fingers; for the fingers of a crucified man are held to be of great virtue. Grant me the body, and I will dispose of it."

Pilate laughed loudly: "Oh, Joseph, Joseph! Confess, you are something of a wizard yourself and covet the extremities of this lame wonder-worker. How much are you prepared to offer? You can have the body for five hundred drachmae; that, I believe, is the usual price. You must pay the money to the provost-captain who supervised the execution: the bodies are his perquisite. Here, let me write you an order. No, I will charge you nothing; I am in a generous mood this morning."

Joseph of Arimathea thanked Pilate and went off with the order to the Tower of Phasael, where he found the three bodies still lying on the stone floor where they had been flung. The provost-captain would accept no money, and when Joseph explained that he could not have the body removed that day because work was forbidden on the Sabbath, undertook for a hundred drachmae to have it wrapped in a linen pall and laid on the slab in a new tomb which Joseph had bought for his own eventual use near the Grotto of Jeremiah. He also undertook for another hundred drachmae to set a sergeant's guard over the tomb and keep the body there until the following morning, when Joseph would be able to dispose of it.

When Nicodemon heard what had been arranged, he sent Joseph a costly parcel of myrrh and aloes with the message: "For the interment of a certain innocent man."

CHAPTER THIRTY

THE FAREWELL

THE guards, though chosen for their age and experience, did not relish the task assigned them by the provost-captain, of watching over a crucified magician's body when witches and tomb-robbers might be about. Night drew on, and their uneasiness increased hour by hour as one of them, a native of Larissa, told them a number of horrific tales of Thessalian magic. He concluded the budget with: "And these are not lies or hearsay, comrades, for my young step-mother was a witch herself, as I have told you, a true daughter of Pan, and I myself stirred her cauldron when I was a child." They dared not sleep and kept close to the camp fire, a few paces away from the tomb, plying the wine-cup.

Presently they were aware of vague figures prowling in the distance. They shouted a challenge, but no reply came.

"They are here, my lads," muttered the sergeant, fumbling for his phallic amulet of Indian coral.

"How much longer until the dawn?" they asked one another.

"At Larissa they seldom appear in their own shapes," said the Thessalian, "but by use of unguents assume the disguise of weasel or cat, and can slip through any chink. To sever the extremities they use neither knives nor razors; only their teeth will serve, and they file them for the purpose. Watch carefully for small creeping things. Fling a lighted brand at anything that moves."

"Hist!" the sergeant interrupted. "Did you hear that?"

"What was it? What?"

"A groaning noise from inside the tomb."

They held their breath in an agony of suspense, but heard nothing.

At first cock-crow the earth began to quake again. There were distant crashes and they felt as though they were on a raft tossed by a heavy swell.

"Look out there, look out!" someone yelled. The large boulder with which they had stopped the mouth of the tomb dislodged and came rolling down an incline, straight towards them. They flung themselves to safety, shouting for terror, and it crashed through the camp fire, scattering the brands and overturning their wine-jar. This was too much even for these veterans. They fled, and did not stop running until they reached the Joppa Gate.

The figures which they had seen in the distance were Mary the mother of Jesus, Mary his queen, Mary the Hairdresser, John, Peter and three Kenite chieftains, who had not trusted the Romans to guard the tomb and were taking turns to watch from a safe distance. When the camp fire was suddenly extinguished and the soldiers rushed past them, bawling unintelligibly, all but Mary the Hairdresser caught the contagion of fear.

They looked wildly at one another. "What happened? Did anyone see?"

John, who had been lying concealed behind a thorn-bush close to the Romans, came back trembling to report: "The boulder came rushing out and scattered the sticks of the camp fire."

Mary the Hairdresser said: "This is the time of most danger. Who will come with me to mend the fire and keep watch beside it until dawn?"

The Kenites excused themselves. "There is no need. The moon gives sufficient light. It is best not to meddle with such things by moonlight."

"Are you afraid because the boulder rolled away?"

"Do stones move of themselves?"

She walked resolutely to the camp fire, heaped the sticks together, and knelt down to blow up the flames. Then she rose and went towards the tomb. The flickering light from the fire illuminated the interior dimly. At the foot of the slab upon which she had expected to see the body stood a squat white figure. She shrieked: "O! O! Look where it stands! Look!"

"What is there?" Peter shouted back.

"A headless spirit at the foot of the slab. The corpse is gone."

Peter started up and ran towards her. But he was stiff from his scourging, and John, who went with him, reached the tomb first. He peered in and, by the light of a flaming brand which he had snatched from the fire, saw that the spirit was only a pile of grave-clothes.

He said to Peter as he hobbled up: "The Romans have tricked us! Someone has broken into the tomb and left only the grave-clothes."

Peter entered without hesitation. What surprised him was that the robbers had neatly folded the linen pall and draped it over the end of the slab, with the head-napkin laid close beside it.

The rest of the company then came up, and each in turn ventured into the tomb. No one knew what to do, but since the guards had left their arms and cloaks and cooking utensils behind, they decided to await their return.

The guards reappeared at the first light of dawn, and a loud altercation immediately began between the sergeant and Peter, each accusing the other of grave-robbing. Peter produced Pilate's order for the possession of the body and threatened to make trouble with the provost-captain.

The sergeant laughed derisively: "Why, Simon Barabbas, what a glutton you are for blows!"

The Kenites intervened and peace was presently restored. After a great deal of argument it was established that nobody present could have spirited away the body, that its disappearance was due to supernatural causes, and that nothing could be done.

It was now broad daylight and everyone returned to the City except Mary the queen, who remained weeping by the tomb.

A man tightly wrapped in a cloak and wearing no shoes emerged from the Grotto garden. He stopped beside her and asked her why she was weeping.

"The body of one whom I loved has been stolen. Are you the caretaker of the Grotto? Can you tell me where to look for it?"

"Mary!" he said.

She stared incredulously. It was Jesus.

"Lord, have you then conquered Death?" She would have clasped his knees, but he stepped back.

"Do not touch one who has hung upon a cross. Leave me now, beloved. Go back to the City and tell my disciples that I am alive."

In a daze she hurried to where they had agreed to meet—the room that Nicodemon had provided for their use throughout the Feast—and burst in upon them. "He is alive! Jesus is alive! Peter, I have seen him; he is wearing your cloak. I recognized the patch in the shoulder." For Peter had left his cloak behind him when Mary the Hairdresser had screamed for help and forgotten to recover it.

John said reprovingly: "Woman, you are out of your senses. We have been already deceived once in the matter of a spirit that proved to be only a pile of grave-clothes."

"I assure you that I have seen him."

They would not believe her and angrily told her to be gone.

She went away, and not long afterwards Jesus himself silently entered the room. They nearly died of fear. He stood half-smiling with one hand on the latch, looking like a child who comes down-stairs at midnight into a room when his parents are entertaining guests, and does not know what welcome to expect.

Peter stared at him, opening and shutting his mouth, unable to speak; Thaddaeus fainted away.

Thomas was the first to recover his voice: "If you are Jesus, allow me to touch you, to make sure that you are no demon."

"Look at my hands. Look at my feet. But do not touch what is accursed."

"If you are accursed, let me be accursed with you. I am called your twin." He gently touched the injured palms.

Jesus told them: "Children, I have come to say farewell. In a little while you shall see me for the last time, and again in a little while you shall see me more clearly than heretofore."

Philip asked: "Where are you going, Lord?"

"There are many apartments in our Father's house." Then he turned to Peter: "Simon son of Jonah, do you love me still?"

He gasped: "Yes, Lord, I love you."

"Then feed my lambs—but do you love me truly, son of Jonah?"

"Lord, you know that I love you."

"Then feed my sheep—but, Simon, are you sure that you still love me?"

"Lord, you know everything. You know that I love you with all my heart."

"Then feed the lambs and sheep which I led astray."

"And the Kingdom of God? Is it at hand, after all?"

"On Passover Eve I learned this: that the Kingdom is **not to be** taken by violence."

"But may we expect to live out our thousand years?"

"While you are still young you clothe and gird yourself; your feet go wherever your eye directs. But one day old age will overtake you, with feebleness and blindness; others will clothe and gird you, you will walk gropingly, and at last a Power will come to conduct you to a hated place. Yet is it not written: 'Though I make my bed in Sheol, behold thou, Lord, art there also'? Come now, follow me!"

Peter, still confused with fear, asked: "Is John to come too?"

"What is it to you whether he comes or not?"

He glided noiselessly downstairs. Peter stumbled after, and then all the others without exception. They followed him through the dark narrow streets, and out through the East Gate, and down the steep hill into the Kidron valley, and over the foot-bridge up into the Mount of Olives. It seemed to them that the slower or faster they walked, the slower or faster also he walked, so that they never either caught up with him or lost sight of him. The strangest part of this experience, when they looked back upon it afterwards, was that he no longer seemed to be lame.

They passed Gethsemane and climbed still higher. Near the summit three women stood side by side on a knoll: Mary the mother of Jesus, Mary his queen, and a very tall woman whose face was veiled. These three beckoned to him as if with a single hand, and he went towards them, smiling. But before he reached them, a sudden mist enveloped the mountain and, when it cleared, Jesus and the three women were gone.

The disciples never saw any of them again, though Jesus appeared frequently to them in dreams and occasionally in daylight visions. Once, after their return to Galilee, they had so plain a view of him at the Lakeside, broiling a trout on the red embers of a wood fire, that they could almost hear and smell the sizzling of the fish.

Here the story of Jesus seemingly ends, but the Ebionite bishop declared to me: "No, it is not ended. Jesus by his defeat of death remains alive, an earth-bound Power, excused incarceration in Sheol but not yet risen to Heaven. He is a Power of Good, who persuades men to repentance and love whereas all other earth-bound Powers (except only Elijah) are evil, and persuade men to sin and death. In those days neither piety nor iniquity was universal in Israel; therefore the Kingdom could not be established, but established it will be in the end, when the Female is conquered, and then he will reign his thousand years and all the world will obey him. For he will be crowned once more, but this time his queen will be worthy of his virtues: a woman not carnal, nor arrayed in splendour as formerly, but modestly clothed in fine white linen. Seven lamps of wisdom shall burn perpetually before his throne and the four beasts of Horeb shall crouch as guardians about it, singing praise to him without cease. And the corruptive Sea shall be no more. Until that day Israel must remain a peculiar nation, though scattered and persecuted, and at Jerusalem the twelve tribes shall be reunited at last."

HISTORICAL COMMENTARY

MY FIRST clue to a new solution of the Nativity problem came from the *Acts of the Apostles,* chapter xiii., in which Sergius Paulus the Roman Procurator of Cyprus is recorded to have been "amazed" by Paul and Barnabas when they told him about Jesus. I could see no good reason for questioning the general truth of this story, despite Hilgenfeld's plausible suggestion that in the original version Barnabas's wicked opponent Bar-Jesus, alias Elymas the Sorcerer, was really Paul. And I knew that it took a great deal to amaze one of Claudius's hard-headed Governor-Generals, whose guiding juridical principle was *title:* for example, they would have classed the followers of a man who had falsely claimed to be King of the Jews with the abettors of one found in possession of stolen Government property. Paulus is unlikely to have been in the least interested in religious or ethical theory, and there is no suggestion in the *Acts* that he was baptized into the Christian faith. These considerations made me ponder on Pilate's extraordinary favour in granting Jesus a private interview, usually reserved for Roman citizens, and on the unconventional *titulus* which was fixed to the Cross at his orders. The logical development of these interrelated problems, in the light of certain passages in the *Gospel to the Egyptians* and the *Protoevangelium,* was so startling that for a while I did not know what to make of it. I confided it in outline to Sir Ronald Storrs, Classical scholar and Orientalist, who also happens to have been a successor in office to both Sergius Paulus and Pontius Pilate. It was his generous encouragement—though he did not commit himself to accepting my hypothesis—that started me working on the book. However, who Jesus was by birth is of much less interest to-day than what he did and said; and I hope that critical attention will be focussed rather on my later chapters—especially on those dealing with his attempted fulfilment of the Deutero-Zechariah's prophecy, which I believe to be the only valid explanation of the extraordinary events which immediately preceded his arrest.

A detailed commentary written to justify the unorthodox views contained in this book would be two or three times as long as the book itself, and would take years to complete; I beg to be excused the task. Take, for example, the incident in Chapter Six of the terrifying apparition which appeared in the Sanctuary to Zacharias the Priest. It would not be enough to quote Epiphanius on the lost Gnostic Gospel *The Descent of Mary* ("in which are horrible and deadly things") as my authority for a story which nobody has hitherto taken seriously and which is usually connected with Tacitus's ill-informed account of a secret Levite ass-cult. Nor would it help to quote Apion, who is my sole authority for the story of Zabidus the Edomite and the golden ass-mask of Dora, because nobody has questioned Josephus's good faith in rejecting it as unhistorical, despite his dishonest denial that any such place as Dora existed in Edom. My acceptance of both unlikely stories depends on a view of Herod's Messianic obsession and his attempt at reviving the ancient onager-cult of Set-Typhon, which could be justified only by adducing an impressive set of authorities and commenting on them at length. Then there is Dr. M. R. James, who holds that the Zacharias story in *The Descent of Mary* is a libel connected with early *graffiti* of a crucified ass; whereas I take these to be not caricatures but pious Judaeo-Christian identifications of Jesus with the Messiah Son of David, whose symbol in Rabbinical literature was the ass, as that of the Messiah Son of Joseph was the ox. This contention would involve me in another long critical argument.

Or take the Unspeakable Name, which according to the Jewish tradition of the *Tol'doth Yeshu* was illegitimately employed by Jesus for raising Lazarus. My arrangement of the letters is based on original research which begins with an account of the origin of the alphabet given by the mythographer Hyginus (*Fable* 277) and ends with various guesses at the Name made by Clement of Alexandria, Origen, Philo Byblius and others. I take both the Name and cult of Jehovah to be of non-Semitic origin, but could not prove this credibly in less than a hundred pages. So, refraining even from a bibliography, which would be more impressive than helpful, I undertake to my readers that every important element in my story is based on some tradition, however tenuous, and that I have taken more than ordinary pains to verify my historical background. These researches have taken me into uncomfortably remote fields. For example, the mystical meanings here given to the Golden Calf and the Seven Pillars of Wisdom are deduced largely from the remnants of Gnostic, ultimately Essene, secret lore preserved in Calder's *Hearings of the Scholars* and other miscellanies of ancient Irish poetic doctrine, and in the thirteenth-century Welsh *Llyfr Coch o Hergest*;

and they yield their full sense only in the light of Babylonian astrology, Talmudic speculation, the liturgy of the Ethiopian Church, the homilies of Clement of Alexandria, the religious essays of Plutarch, and recent studies of Bronze Age archaeology.

I write without any wish to offend orthodox Catholics, who can afford to disregard my story as irrelevant to their faith; for Catholicism is an incontrovertibly logical system of thought, once it is granted that many of the events mentioned in the Gospels transcend human understanding and must therefore be taken on faith. Though I reject this premiss, it will be clear at least that I respect Jesus as having been more uncompromising, more consistent, and more loyal to his God than even most Christians allow.

To write a historical novel by the analeptic method—the intuitive recovery of forgotten events by a deliberate suspension of time—one must train oneself to think wholly in contemporary terms. This is most easily done by impersonating the supposed author of the story, who has much the same function as the carefully costumed figure placed in the foreground of an architectural drawing to correct misapprehensions about its size, date and geographical position. I have chosen to be the mouthpiece of old Agabus the Decapolitan, who wrote in the year A.D. 93, rather than of some closer contemporary of Jesus, because the divergences of the Synoptic tradition from what appears to be the true story call for explanatory comment on Church policy after the Fall of Jerusalem.

Perhaps the greatest hindrance to a reasonable view of Jesus is not the loss of a large part of his secret history but the influence of the late and propagandist *Gospel according to John*. Though it embodies valuable fragments of a genuine tradition not found in the Synoptic Gospels, the critical reservations that have to be made in reading it are proved by the metaphysical prologue, which makes no sense whatever in the original context; by the author's wilful ignorance of Jewish affairs; and by the Alexandrian Greek rhetoric unfairly ascribed to a sage and poet who never wasted a word.

My solution to the problem of Jesus's nativity implies a rejection of the mystical Virgin Birth doctrine and will therefore offend many otherwise irreligious Christians, even though the doctrine cannot be traced earlier than the second century A.D. and cannot be reconciled either with *Romans* i. 3, *Hebrews* vii. 14 or *Galatians* iv. 4—documents which are earlier in date than any of the Canonical Gospels. Its value as a means of asserting the divinity of Jesus and glorifying him equally with heathen gods was first remarked upon by Justin Martyr in his philosophical *Apology for the Christians* (A.D. 139);

and its value in exculpating the earlier Christians from any suspicion of trying to revive the Davidic dynasty is clear from the persecutions of the House of David under the Emperors Trajan and Domitian. But the Christians were not wilful liars, and the bold theory of Jesus's miraculous birth could never have been advanced had there not already been a mystery connected with his parentage: it must have seemed the only way of harmonizing the apparently contradictory traditions that Joseph was not Jesus's father though contracted in marriage to Mary (*Matthew* i. 18-19) and that Jesus was "born under the Law"—that is, legitimately—"that he might redeem those who were under the Law" (*Galatians* iv. 5).

No store should be set by the earliest extant text of *Matthew* i. 16, discovered only recently, according to which "Joseph begat Jesus". I take it for an Ebionite interpolation designed to champion Jesus's legitimacy against enemies of Christianity who, like the Roman Celsus, falsely described him as the bastard son of a Greek soldier. The Ebionites' difficulty was that if Mary had already been contracted in marriage to Joseph when he found her pregnant, this would in Jewish Law (*Deuteronomy* xxii. 13-21) have bastardized her child even if the marriage had not been consummated and she had in the interval secretly married someone else. But the solution is infelicitous as contradicting the credible account of Joseph's embarrassment given two verses later in the canonical text and as making nonsense of the story of the interview with Pilate. On the other hand, the Virgin Birth doctrine, now that no one believes the God Hermes to be the Word of Zeus, and Hercules and Dionysus to be his sons, no longer has the same force in religious polemics as it had in Justin's day; and since the prevailing view in Protestant countries is that Jesus was, beyond everything, a moral exemplar, the suggestion that he was not a man in the ordinary sense of the word, and not therefore subject to human error, may be said to discourage imitation of his virtues. True, many saints have held the doctrine serenely, and it can be argued on their behalf that if Jesus is regarded as a mere man his authority is greatly diminished; but to the mass of people nowadays the choice is between a Jesus born in the ordinary course of nature and one as mythical as Perseus or Prometheus.

The long dialogue in Chapter Nineteen, between Jesus and Mary, may puzzle readers who do not know their Bible or Bible origins well. I am here suggesting a new theory of the composition of the early historical books: that to the parts not already existing in, say, the ninth century B.C. in the form of ballads or prose-epics were added anecdotes based on deliberate misinterpretation of an ancient set of ritual icons, captured by the Hebrews when they seized Hebron from the "Children of Heth", whoever these people may have been. A similar technique of misinterpretation—let us call it iconotropy—was adopted in ancient Greece as a means of confirming the Olympian religious myths at the expense of the Minoan ones which they superseded. For example, the story of the unnatural union of Pasiphaë ("She who shines for all") and the bull, the issue of which was the monstrous Minotaur, seems to be based on an icon of the sacred marriage between Minos, the King of Cnossus (pictured with a bull's head), and the representative of the Moon-goddess, in the course of which a live bull was sacrificed. The story of the rape of Europa ("Broadface") by Zeus disguised as a bull belongs to a companion icon—an example of which has been found in a pre-Hellenic burial near Midea—showing the same Goddess riding on a bull. Again, the story of Oedipus ("Club-foot") and the Sphinx who committed suicide when he guessed her riddle seems to be based on an icon of the Lame King (Hephaestus) adoring the Triple Goddess of Thebes after having killed his predecessor Laertes. The riddle, "four legs at dawn, two legs at noon and three legs at sunset", suggests an attached cartoon showing a child, a youth and an old man with a staff—the meaning of which is that the Triple Goddess is man's sovereign from the cradle to the grave.

In iconotropy the icons are not defaced or altered, but merely interpreted in a sense hostile to the original cult. The reverse process, of reinterpreting Olympian or Jahvistic patriarchal myths in terms of the mother-right myths which they have displaced, leads to unexpected results. The unpleasant story of the seduction of Lot by his two daughters, which reflects Israelite hostility to Moab and Ammon—tribes reputedly born of these incestuous unions—becomes harmless when restored to its original iconic form: it is the well-known scene in which Isis and Nephthys mourn at the bier of the ithyphallic recumbent Osiris, in an arbour festooned with grapes, each with a son crouched at her feet. The story of Lot and the Sodomites suggests the same ancient icon from which Herodotus derived his iconotropic account of the sacking of the Temple of the Love-goddess Astarte at Ascalon by the Scythians. He records that "upon these Scythians and upon all their posterity the Goddess visited a fatal punishment: they were afflicted with the female disease"—that is to say with homosexuality. But the icon probably represents a legitimate Dog-priest orgy, against a background of swirling sacrificial smoke. It was to suppress sodomitic orgies at

Jerusalem that good King Josiah of Judah (637–608 B.C.)—or Hilkiah, or Shaphan, or whoever the reformer was—inserted into *Deuteronomy* xxii. a prohibition against the wearing of women's clothes by men. The pillar of salt into which Lot's wife was turned is presumably represented in the icon by a white obelisk, the familiar altar of Astarte; and Lot's daughter who was abused by the mob is presumably a sacred prostitute of the sort that made Josiah forbid the bringing into the house of the Lord of "the hire of a whore". "The price of a dog", which goes with this prohibition in the same text (*Deuteronomy* xxiii. 18), evidently means the hire of a Dog-priest or Sodomite: both fees were devoted to Temple funds in related Syrian cults.

It should be noted that many of the historic assumptions made by characters in this story are not necessarily valid: for example, the theory of millennia and phoenix-ages propounded by Simon son of Boethus, or Manetho's view of the founding of Jerusalem by the expelled Hyksos kings, or the general ascription of the Canticles to King Solomon. All that matters is the influence on events exercised by these assumptions; I have hesitated to credit Agabus with archaeological knowledge sufficient to correct them.

I must express deep gratitude to my friend and neighbour Joshua Podro, who has helped me from the start with critical comment from the Hebrew-Aramaic side of the story, and to my niece Sally Graves, who has done the same from the Graeco-Roman side. I could have made no headway without either of them. Also to Dr. George Simon for his illuminating physiological comments on the Passion narrative.

R. G.

GALMPTON-BRIXHAM,
S. DEVON.

THE END.